新制多益 NEW TOEIC 聽力 Listening 滿分奪金演練

1000題練出黃金應試力

作者 PAGODA Academy 譯者 蘇裕承／關亭薇

嚴選完整10回精華全真考題，一次掌握多益聽力必考題型和常見陷阱。

收錄多國口音，有效提升臨場聽覺反應力。

附錄音文稿和試題中譯，幫助釐清考點，累積奪金硬實力 ！

MP3

目錄

何謂多益？

TOEIC 為 Test of English for International Communication 的縮寫，針對英語非母語人士所設計，測驗其在日常生活或國際業務上所具備的英語應用能力。

該測驗的評量重點在於「與他人溝通的能力」(communication ability)，著重英語的運用與其功能層面，測驗「運用英語的能力」，而非單純針對「英語知識」出題。

1979 年美國 ETS（Educational Testing Service）研發出 TOEIC，而後在全世界 160 個國家中獲得超過 14,000 個機構採用，作為升遷、外派、人才招募之依據，全球每年超過 700 萬人次報考。

›› 多益測驗題型

<table>
<tr><th></th><th>Part</th><th colspan="2">測驗題型</th><th>題數</th><th>時間</th><th>分數</th></tr>
<tr><td rowspan="4">聽力
Listening
Comprehension</td><td>1</td><td colspan="2">照片描述</td><td>6</td><td rowspan="4">45 分鐘</td><td rowspan="4">495 分</td></tr>
<tr><td>2</td><td colspan="2">應答問題</td><td>25</td></tr>
<tr><td>3</td><td colspan="2">簡短對話</td><td>39</td></tr>
<tr><td>4</td><td colspan="2">簡短獨白</td><td>30</td></tr>
<tr><td rowspan="4">閱讀
Reading
Comprehension</td><td>5</td><td colspan="2">句子填空</td><td>30</td><td rowspan="4">75 分鐘</td><td rowspan="4">495 分</td></tr>
<tr><td>6</td><td colspan="2">段落填空</td><td>16</td></tr>
<tr><td rowspan="2">7</td><td rowspan="2">閱測</td><td>單篇閱讀</td><td>29</td></tr>
<tr><td>多篇閱讀</td><td>25</td></tr>
<tr><td>總計</td><td></td><td colspan="2"></td><td>200</td><td>約 150 分鐘 ✷</td><td>990 分</td></tr>
</table>

✷ 含基本資料及問卷填寫

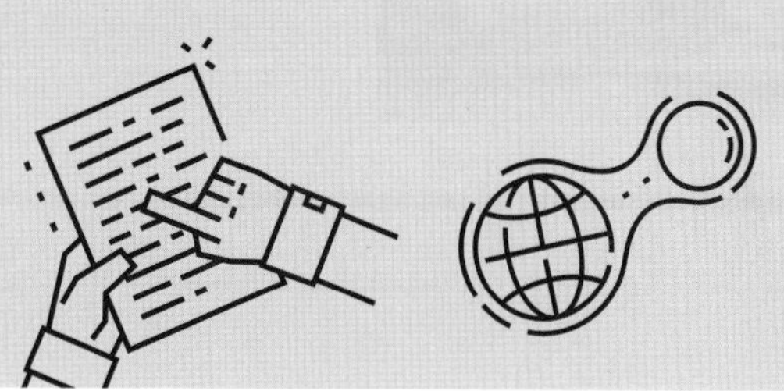

多益各大題簡介

PART 1 PHOTOGRAPHS 照片描述

Part 1 考生須根據照片呈現的畫面選出正確描述。錄音會播放四句簡短描述，這四句選項並不會印在試題本上，因此請仔細聆聽，並從中選出最正確描述照片的句子作為答案。

題數	**6 題（第 1 至第 6 題）**
指示（Direction）播放時間	約 1 分 30 秒
播放題目的時間	約 20 秒
下一題播放前的空檔	約 5 秒
考題類型	• 單人獨照 • 雙人、多人照片 • 事物與背景照

>> 試題本上呈現的考題形式

>> 聽力測驗播放的錄音內容

Number 1. Look at the picture marked number 1 in your test book.

(A) They're writing on a board.

(B) They're taking a file from a shelf.

(C) They're working at a desk.

(D) They're listening to a presentation.

答案 (C)

PART 2 QUESTION-RESPONSE 應答問題

Part 2 考生須根據題目句選出適當的回答。錄音會依序播放題目句以及三句回應句，題目句和三句選項僅會播放一次。題目句與回應句皆不會印在試題本上，請直接選出最適合用來回應題目句的回答作為答案。

題數	25 題（第 7 至第 31 題）
指示（Direction）播放時間	約 25 秒
播放題目的時間	約 15 秒
下一題播放前的空檔	約 5 秒
考題類型	• WH- 開頭的問句（Who/When/Where/What/Which/How/Why） • 否定疑問句／附加問句 • 直述句／選擇疑問句 • 表示建議或要求的問句 • Be 動詞開頭的問句 • 助動詞 Do 開頭的問句／間接問句

>> 試題本上呈現的考題形式

>> 聽力測驗播放的錄音內容

Number 1. How was the English test you took today?

(A) I took the bus home.

(B) I thought it was too difficult.

(C) I have two classes today.

答案 (B)

PART 3 SHORT CONVERSATIONS 簡短對話

Part 3 考生須聆聽短篇對話並回答內容相關問題。首先錄音會播放一段簡短對話，接著播放相關問題。題目與四個選項皆會印在試題本上，請於聽完題目後，從四個選項中選出最適當的答案。

題數	13 個題組共 39 題（第 32 至第 70 題）
指示（Direction）播放時間	約 30 秒
播放題目的時間	約 30-40 秒
下一題播放前的空檔	約 8 秒
對話類型	職場生活、日常生活、公共場合與服務機構等 ➡ 三人會話、增加對話一來一往的次數 ➡ 新增生活上實際用到的對話（口語用法）
考題類型	• 與整篇對話相關的提問：詢問主旨、目的、人物、地點 • 相關細節題：詢問理由、方法、找出關鍵字相關內容 • 詢問建議與要求 • 詢問下一步的行動 • 掌握說話者意圖題 • 推測、推論題 • 圖表整合題

>> 試題本上呈現的考題形式

32. What is the conversation mainly about?
    (A) Changes in business policies
    (B) Sales of a company's products
    (C) Expanding into a new market
    (D) Recruiting temporary employees

33. Why does the woman say, "There you go"?
    (A) She is happy to attend a meeting.
    (B) She is frustrated with a coworker.
    (C) She is offering encouragement.
    (D) She is handing over something.

34. What do the men imply about the company?
    (A) It has launched new merchandise.
    (B) It is planning to relocate soon.
    (C) It has clients in several countries.
    (D) It is having financial difficulties.

>> 聽力測驗播放的錄音內容

Questions 32-34 refer to the following conversation with three speakers.

A: How have you two been doing with your sales lately?

B: Um, not too bad. My clients have been ordering about the same amount of promotional merchandise as before.

C: I haven't been doing so well. But I do have a meeting with a potential new client tomorrow.

B: There you go. I'm sure things will turn around for you.

A: Yeah, I hope it works out.

B: It's probably just temporary due to the recession.

C: Maybe, but I heard that the company may downsize to try to save money.

A: Actually, I heard that, too.

答案 32. (B) 33. (C) 34. (D)

PART 4 SHORT TALKS 簡短獨白

Part 4 要聆聽短篇獨白並回答相關問題。首先錄音會播放一段簡短獨白，接著播放相關問題。問題題目與四個選項皆印在試題本上，請於聽完題目後，從四個選項中選出最適當的答案。

題數	**10 篇獨白共 30 題（第 71 至第 100 題）**
指示（Direction）播放時間	約 30 秒
播放題目的時間	約 30-40 秒
下一題播放前的空檔	約 8 秒
獨白類型	通話內容、語音留言、公告、簡介、人物介紹、廣告、廣播、報導等 ➡ 獨白中包含發音上的省略、多餘的贅字、不完整的句子、新增生活用語（口語用法）
考題類型	• 與整篇對話相關的提問：詢問主旨、目的、人物、地點 • 相關細節題：詢問疑難問題、理由、方法、找出關鍵字相關內容 • 詢問建議與要求 • 詢問下一步的行動 • 掌握說話者意圖題 • 圖表整合題

>> 試題本上呈現的考題形式

71. Where most likely is the speaker?
(A) At a trade fair
(B) At a corporate banquet
(C) At a business seminar
(D) At an anniversary celebration

72. What are the listeners asked to do?
(A) Pick up programs for employees
(B) Arrive early for a presentation
(C) Turn off their mobile phones
(D) Carry their personal belongings

73. Why does the schedule have to be changed?
(A) A speaker has to leave early.
(B) A piece of equipment is not working.
(C) Lunch is not ready.
(D) Some speakers have not yet arrived.

>> 聽力測驗播放的錄音內容

Questions 71-73 refer to the following talk.

I'd like to welcome all of you to today's employee training and development seminar for business owners. I'll briefly go over a few details before we get started. There will be a 15 minute break for coffee and snacks halfway through the program. This will be a good opportunity for you to mingle. If you need to leave the room during a talk, make sure to keep your wallet, phone, and …ah… any other valuable personal items with you. Also, please note that there will be a change in the order of the program. Um… Mr. Roland has to leave earlier than originally scheduled, so the last two speakers will be switched.

答案 71. (C) 72. (D) 73. (A)

學習計畫表

雙週計畫表

DAY 1	DAY 2	DAY 3	DAY 4	DAY 5
TEST 01 設定時間作答 計算分數並參閱錄音稿及中譯 複習錄音檔解題 背誦考題的陌生單字	**TEST 02** 設定時間作答 計算分數並參閱錄音稿及中譯 複習錄音檔解題 背誦考題的陌生單字	**TEST 03** 設定時間作答 計算分數並參閱錄音稿及中譯 複習錄音檔解題 背誦考題的陌生單字	**TEST 04** 設定時間作答 計算分數並參閱錄音稿及中譯 複習錄音檔解題 背誦考題的陌生單字	**TEST 05** 設定時間作答 計算分數並參閱錄音稿及中譯 複習錄音檔解題 背誦考題的陌生單字

DAY 6	DAY 7	DAY 8	DAY 9	DAY 10
TEST 06 設定時間作答 計算分數並參閱錄音稿及中譯 複習錄音檔解題 背誦考題的陌生單字	**TEST 07** 設定時間作答 計算分數並參閱錄音稿及中譯 複習錄音檔解題 背誦考題的陌生單字	**TEST 08** 設定時間作答 計算分數並參閱錄音稿及中譯 複習錄音檔解題 背誦考題的陌生單字	**TEST 09** 設定時間作答 計算分數並參閱錄音稿及中譯 複習錄音檔解題 背誦考題的陌生單字	**TEST 10** 設定時間作答 計算分數並參閱錄音稿及中譯 複習錄音檔解題 背誦考題的陌生單字

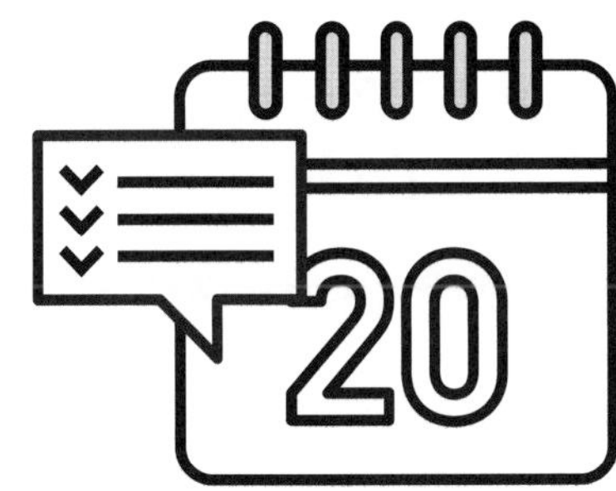

四週計畫表

DAY 1	DAY 2	DAY 3	DAY 4	DAY 5
TEST 01 設定時間作答 計算分數並參閱錄音稿及中譯	TEST 01 複習錄音檔解題 複習考題的陌生單字	**TEST 02** 設定時間作答 計算分數並參閱錄音稿及中譯	TEST 02 複習錄音檔解題 複習考題的陌生單字	**TEST 03** 設定時間作答 計算分數並參閱錄音稿及中譯

DAY 6	DAY 7	DAY 8	DAY 9	DAY 10
TEST 03 複習錄音檔解題 複習考題的陌生單字	**TEST 04** 設定時間作答 計算分數並參閱錄音稿及中譯	TEST 04 複習錄音檔解題 複習考題的陌生單字	**TEST 05** 設定時間作答 計算分數並參閱錄音稿及中譯	TEST 05 複習錄音檔解題 複習考題的陌生單字

DAY 11	DAY 12	DAY 13	DAY 14	DAY 15
TEST 06 設定時間作答 計算分數並參閱錄音稿及中譯	TEST 06 複習錄音檔解題 複習考題的陌生單字	**TEST 07** 設定時間作答 計算分數並參閱錄音稿及中譯	TEST 07 複習錄音檔解題 複習考題的陌生單字	**TEST 08** 設定時間作答 計算分數並參閱錄音稿及中譯

DAY 16	DAY 17	DAY 18	DAY 19	DAY 20
TEST 08 複習錄音檔解題 複習考題的陌生單字	**TEST09** 設定時間作答 計算分數並參閱錄音稿及中譯	TEST 09 複習錄音檔解題 複習考題的陌生單字	**TEST 10** 設定時間作答 計算分數並參閱錄音稿及中譯	TEST 10 複習錄音檔解題 複習考題的陌生單字

各國口音差異簡介

(01)

美國腔 vs 英國腔

多益聽力測驗中，除了美國腔之外，還會出現英國、澳洲、加拿大等英語圈國家的口音。而在台灣的學習者大多較常接觸美式發音，因此建議在此一併熟悉其他國家的口音，以期能避免因聽不懂口音而感到慌亂的窘境。

加拿大腔與美國腔相似；澳洲腔則與英國腔相似。為方便讀者學習，本書僅分成美國腔與英國腔兩大類別進行說明。

子音上常見的差異

1.「r」的發音差異

美國：一定會保留捲舌音。
英國：僅在置於單字字首時發音。若置於字尾或子音前方時皆會省略捲舌音。

>> 字尾為「r」的例子

	美國腔	英國腔		美國腔	英國腔
car	[kɑr]	[kɑ]	**wear**	[wɛr]	[wɛr]
her	[hɝ]	[hɜ]	**where**	[(h)wɛr]	[wɛr]
door	[dor]	[dɔ]	**there**	[ðɛr]	[ðɛr]
pour	[por]	[pɔ]	**here**	[hɪr]	[hɪə]
mayor	[ˋmeɚ]	[ˋmɛr]	**year**	[jɪr]	[jɪə]
sure	[ʃur]	[ʃɔ]	**repair**	[rɪˋpɛr]	[rɪˋpɛr]
later	[letɚ]	[letə]	**chair**	[tʃɛr]	[tʃɛr]
author	[ˋɔθɚ] ✸本處所列為標準音標，實際發音請參照錄音檔。	[ˋɔθə]	**fair**	[fɛr]	[fɛr]
cashier	[kæˋʃɪr]	[kæˋʃɪə]	**hair**	[hɛr]	[hɛr]

>> 置於子音前方「r+ 子音」的例子

	美國腔	英國腔		美國腔	英國腔
airport	[ˋɛrˏport]	[ˋɛrˏpɔt]	**short**	[ʃɔrt]	[ʃɔt]
award	[əˋwɔrd]	[əˋwɔd]	**turn**	[tɝn]	[tɜn]
board	[bord]	[bɔd]	**alert**	[əˋlɝt]	[əˋlɜt]
cart	[kɑrt]	[kɑt]	**first**	[fɝst]	[fɜst]
circle	[ˋsɝkl]	[ˋsɜkḷ]	**order**	[ˋɔrdɚ]	[ˋɔdə]
concert	[ˋkɑnsɚt]	[ˋkɑnsət] ❶	**purse**	[pɝs]	[pɜs]

❶ 此處英式發音的 [ɑ] 音近 [o]，詳見 p. 13「『o』的發音差異」

2.「t」的發音差異

美國：置於母音之間時，[t] 的發音介於 [d] 和 [r] 之間，類似輕微捲舌音。
英國：置於母音之間時，直接發 [t] 的音。

	美國腔	英國腔		美國腔	英國腔
bottom	[ˋbɑtəm]	[ˋbɑtəm] ❶	**computer**	[kəmˋpjutɚ]	[kəmˋpjutə]
better	[ˋbɛtɚ]	[ˋbɛtə]	**item**	[ˋaɪtəm]	[ˋaɪtəm]
chatting	[ˋtʃætɪŋ]	[ˋtʃætɪŋ]	**later**	[letɚ]	[letə]
getting	[ˋgɛtɪŋ]	[ˋgɛtɪŋ]	**meeting**	[ˋmitɪŋ]	[ˋmitɪŋ]
letter	[ˋlɛtɚ]	[ˋlɛtə]	**notice**	[ˋnotɪs]	[ˋnotɪs] ❷
little	[lɪtl̩]	[lɪtl̩]	**patio**	[ˋpɑtɪˏo] ✱本處所列為標準音標，實際發音請參照錄音檔。	[ˋpætɪˏo] ❷
matter	[ˋmætɚ]	[ˋmætə]	**water**	[ˋwɔtɚ] ✱本處所列為標準音標，實際發音請參照錄音檔。	[ˋwɔtə]
potted	[ˋpɑtɪd]	[ˋpɑtɪd] ❶	**waiter**	[ˋwetɚ]	[ˋwetə]
setting	[ˋsɛtɪŋ]	[ˋsɛtɪŋ]	**cater**	[ˋketɚ]	[ˋketə]
sitting	[ˋsɪtɪŋ]	[ˋsɪtɪŋ]	**competitor**	[kəmˋpɛtətɚ]	[kəmˋpɛtɪtə]
putting	[ˋpʊtɪŋ]	[ˋpʊtɪŋ]	**data**	[ˋdetə]	[ˋdetə]

❶ 此處英式發音的 [ɑ] 音近 [o]，詳見 p. 13「『o』的發音差異」。
❷ 此處英式發音的 [o] 和美式發音略有不同，請聆聽錄音檔參照。

3.「nt」置於母音之間的發音差異

美國：[t] 不發音。
英國：直接發 [t] 的音。

	美國腔	英國腔		美國腔	英國腔
Internet	[ˋɪntɚˏnɛt]	[ˋɪntəˏnɛt]	**twenty**	[ˋtwɛntɪ]	[ˋtwɛntɪ]
interview	[ˋɪntɚˏvju]	[ˋɪntəˏvju]	**advantage**	[ədˋvæntɪdʒ]	[ədˋvɑntɪdʒ]
entertainment	[ˏɛntɚˋtenmənt]	[ˏɛntəˋtenmənt]	**identification**	[aɪˏdɛntəfəˋkeʃən]	[aɪˏdɛntɪfɪˋkeʃən]
international	[ˏɪntɚˋnæʃənl̩]	[ˏɪntəˋnæʃənl̩]	**representative**	[ˏrɛprɪˋzɛntətɪv]	[ˏrɛprɪˋzɛntətɪv]

4.「t . . . n」的發音差異

美國：出現 [t] 時不發音，而是稍稍停頓一秒後，由鼻腔發出近似 [n] 的鼻音。
英國：保留 [t] 的音，且會特別強調其發音。

	美國腔	英國腔		美國腔	英國腔
button	[ˋbʌtn̩]	[ˋbʌtn̩]	**mountain**	[ˋmaʊntn̩]	[ˋmaʊntɪn]
carton	[ˋkɑrtən]	[ˋkɑtən]	**written**	[ˋrɪtn̩]	[ˋrɪtn̩]
important	[ɪmˋpɔrtn̩t]	[ɪmˋpɔtn̩t]	**certainly**	[ˋsɝtənlɪ]	[ˋsɜtənlɪ] ❶

❶ 此處英式發音的 [ɜ] 和美式發音不同，詳見 p. 10「『r』的發音差異」。

5.「rt」的發音差異

美國：省略 [t] 的音。
英國：省略 [r] 的音，但特別強調 [t] 的音。

	美國腔	英國腔		美國腔	英國腔
party	[ˋpɑrtɪ]	[ˋpɑtɪ]	**reporter**	[rɪˋportɚ]	[rɪˋpɔtə]
quarter	[ˋkwɔrtɚ]	[ˋkwɔtə]	**property**	[ˋprɑpɚtɪ]	[ˋprɑpətɪ] ❶

❶ 此處英式發音的 [ɑ] 音近 [o]，詳見 p. 13「『o』的發音差異」。

母音上常見的差異

1.「a」的發音差異

美國：發音一般為 [æ]。
英國：發音一般為 [ɑ]。

	美國腔	英國腔		美國腔	英國腔
can't	[kænt]	[kɑnt]	**pass**	[pæs]	[pɑs]
grant	[grænt]	[grɑnt]	**path**	[pæθ]	[pɑθ]
plant	[plænt]	[plɑnt]	**vase**	[ves]	[vɑz]
chance	[tʃæns]	[tʃɑns]	**draft**	[dræft]	[drɑft]
advance	[ədˋvæns]	[ədˋvɑns]	**after**	[ˋæftɚ]	[ˋɑftə]
answer	[ˋænsɚ]	[ˋɑnsə]	**ask**	[æsk]	[ɑsk]
sample	[ˋsæmpl̩]	[sɑmpl̩]	**task**	[tæsk]	[tɑsk]
class	[klæs]	[klɑs]	**behalf**	[bɪˋhæf]	[bɪˋhɑf]
grass	[græs]	[grɑs]	**rather**	[ˋræðɚ]	[ˋrɑðə]
glass	[glæs]	[glɑs]			

2. 「o」的發音差異

美國：發音為 [ɑ]。
英國：發音會偏向 [o]。

	美國腔	英國腔		美國腔	英國腔
stop	[stɑp]	[stɑp]	**bottle**	[ˋbɑtḷ]	[ˋbɑtḷ]
stock	[stɑk]	[stɑk]	**model**	[ˋmɑdḷ]	[ˋmɑdḷ]
shop	[ʃɑp]	[ʃɑp]	**dollar**	[ˋdɑlɚ]	[ˋdɑlə]
got	[gɑt]	[gɑt]	**copy**	[ˋkɑpɪ]	[ˋkɑpɪ]
hot	[hɑt]	[hɑt]	**possible**	[ˋpɑsəbḷ]	[ˋpɑsəbḷ]
not	[ˋnɑt]	[ˋnɑt]	**topic**	[ˋtɑpɪk]	[ˋtɑpɪk]
parking lot	[pɑrkɪŋ lɑt]	[pɑkɪŋ lɑt]	**doctor**	[ˋdɑktɚ]	[ˋdɑktə]
knob	[nɑb]	[nɑb]	**borrow**	[ˋbɑro]	[ˋbɑro] ❶
job	[dʒɑb]	[dʒɑb]	**document**	[ˋdɑkjəmənt]	[ˋdɑkjəmənt]
box	[bɑks]	[bɑks]			

❶ 此處英式發音的 [o] 和美式發音略有不同，請聆聽錄音檔參照。

3. 「i」的發音差異

英國腔有時會將「i」發成 [aɪ]。

	美國腔	英國腔		美國腔	英國腔
direct	[dəˋrɛkt]	[daɪˋrɛkt]	**mobile**	[ˋmobḷ]	[ˋmobaɪl] ❶
either	[ˋiðɚ]	[ˋaɪðə]	**organization**	[ˏɔrgənəˋzeʃən]	[ˏɔgənaɪˋzeʃən]

❶ 此處英式發音的 [o] 和美式發音略有不同，請聆聽錄音檔參照。

4. 「ary」與「ory」的發音差異

英國腔有時會省略「ary」和「ory」當中的「a」和「o」的音，僅發 [rɪ] 的音。

	美國腔	英國腔		美國腔	英國腔
laboratory	[ˋlæbrəˏtorɪ]	[ləˋbɑrətrɪ] ❶	**secretary**	[ˋsɛkrəˏtɛri]	[ˋsɛkrətrɪ]

❶ 此處英式發音的 [ɑ] 音近 [o]，詳見本頁「『o』的發音差異」。

其他發音差異

	美國腔	英國腔		美國腔	英國腔
advertisement	[ˏædvɚˋtaɪzmənt]	[ədˋvɜtɪsmənt] ❶	**garage**	[gəˋrɑʒ]	[ˋgærɪdʒ]
fragile	[ˋfrædʒəl]	[ˋfrædʒaɪl]	**often**	[ˋɔf(t)ən]	[ˋɑfən] ❷
however	[haʊˋɛvɚ]	[haʊˋɛvə]	**schedule**	[ˋskɛdʒul]	[ˋʃɛdʒul]

❶ 此處英式發音的 [ɜ] 和美式發音不同，詳見 p. 10「『r』的發音差異」。

❷ 此處英式發音的 [ɑ] 音近 [o]，詳見 p. 13「『o』的發音差異」。

連音差異

	美國腔	英國腔		美國腔	英國腔
a lot of	[ə lɑt ʌv]	[ə lɑt əv] ❶	**not at all**	[nɑt æt ɔl]	[nɑt æt ɔl] ❶
get in	[gɛt ɪn]	[gɛt ɪn]	**out of stock**	[aʊt ʌv stɑk]	[aʊt əv stɑk] ❶
in front of	[ɪn frʌnt ʌv]	[ɪn frʌnt əv]	**pick it up**	[pɪk ɪt ʌp]	[pɪk ɪt ʌp]
it is	[ɪt ɪz]	[ɪt ɪz]	**put on**	[pʊt ɑn]	[pʊt ɑn] ❶
look it up	[lʊk ɪt ʌp]	[lʊk ɪt ʌp]	**talk about it**	[tɔk əˋbaʊt ɪt]	[tɔk əˋbaʊt ɪt]

❶ 此處英式發音的 [ɑ] 音近 [o]，詳見見 p. 13「『o』的發音差異」。

口音聽力訓練

請聆聽下方句子並完成填空。錄音將會播放美國腔與英國腔各一遍。

1. The __________ will be held next week. 就業博覽會將於下週舉行。
2. She's the ________________ a best-selling book. 她是一本暢銷書的作者。
3. The ______________________________________. 市長赴外地出差。
4. ___________________________ network technicians?
   難道我們不能多僱用幾個網路技術員嗎？
5. We need to advertise ________________________________. 我們需要宣傳新系列的運動鞋。
6. She is ______________________ into glasses. 她把水倒進玻璃杯裡。
7. You ______________________________________ last fall.
   我們公司去年秋天出遊時由您提供餐點。
8. ______________________________ for me. 對我來說，六點以後比較好。
9. Some _____________________ have been placed in a waiting area. 有幾棵盆栽擺在等候區。
10. ___________________________ are the same. 很多品項是一樣的。
11. Please sign on the _____________________________. 請在最後一頁的底部簽名。
12. Do you know of a __________________ in this area? 你有認識這個領域／地區不錯的醫生嗎？
13. ___________________. 一點也不。
14. _________________________________ posted on the Web site.
    我在網站上看到貴公司的招聘廣告。
15. Why don't you ____________________________ and speak to him?
    你何不打給你的醫生和他談談？
16. What's __________________________ to the bank? 到銀行最快的路要怎麼走？
17. _______________________ if she's available. 我再問她有沒有空。
18. I'm so happy to see that ____________________ are here today.
    今天我很高興看到你們全體舞者都在這裡。
19. ________________________ hold some flowers. 玻璃花瓶裡插著幾朵花。
20. ________________________ travel in the morning or in the evening?
    你比較喜歡在早上還是晚上出遊？
21. The shipment is __________________. 出貨進度落後了。
22. _______________ is fine with me. 哪個我都可以。
23. _____________________. 我也沒做過。
24. Why wasn't ____________________________ printed in the magazine?
    為什麼雜誌上沒印我們的廣告？
25. Can you get me ______________________________________?
    你能跟我說怎麼去實驗室嗎？

答案

1. job fair 2. author of 3. mayor is out of town 4. Can't we hire more 5. our new line of sports footwear 6. pouring water 7. catered our company outing 8. After six is better 9. potted plant 10. A lot of the items 11. bottom of the last page 12. good doctor 13. Not at all 14. I saw your job ad 15. call your doctor 16. the fastest way 17. I'll ask her 18. all you dancers 19. A glass vase 20. Would you rather 21. behind schedule 22. Either one 23. Neither have I 24. our advertisement 25. directions to the laboratory

ACTUAL TEST

ACTUAL TEST

LISTENING TEST 03

In the Listening test, you will be asked to demonstrate how well you understand spoken English. The entire Listening test will last approximately 45 minutes. There are four parts, and directions are given for each part. You must mark your answers on the separate answer sheet. Do not write your answers in your test book.

PART 1

Directions: For each question in this part, you will hear four statements about a picture in your test book. When you hear the statements, you must select the one statement that best describes what you see in the picture. Then find the number of the question on your answer sheet and mark your answer. The statements will not be printed in your test book and will be spoken only one time.

Example

Statement (B), "A man is pointing at a document," is the best description of the picture, so you should select answer (B) and mark it on your answer sheet.

1.

2.

GO ON TO THE NEXT PAGE

3.

4.

5.

6.

GO ON TO THE NEXT PAGE

PART 2 04

Directions: You will hear a question or statement and three responses spoken in English. They will not be printed in your test book and will be spoken only one time. Select the best response to the question or statement and mark the letter (A), (B), or (C) on your answer sheet.

7. Mark your answer on your answer sheet.

8. Mark your answer on your answer sheet.

9. Mark your answer on your answer sheet.

10. Mark your answer on your answer sheet.

11. Mark your answer on your answer sheet.

12. Mark your answer on your answer sheet.

13. Mark your answer on your answer sheet.

14. Mark your answer on your answer sheet.

15. Mark your answer on your answer sheet.

16. Mark your answer on your answer sheet.

17. Mark your answer on your answer sheet.

18. Mark your answer on your answer sheet.

19. Mark your answer on your answer sheet.

20. Mark your answer on your answer sheet.

21. Mark your answer on your answer sheet.

22. Mark your answer on your answer sheet.

23. Mark your answer on your answer sheet.

24. Mark your answer on your answer sheet.

25. Mark your answer on your answer sheet.

26. Mark your answer on your answer sheet.

27. Mark your answer on your answer sheet.

28. Mark your answer on your answer sheet.

29. Mark your answer on your answer sheet.

30. Mark your answer on your answer sheet.

31. Mark your answer on your answer sheet.

PART 3 

Directions: You will hear some conversations between two or more people. You will be asked to answer three questions about what the speakers say in each conversation. Select the best response to each question and mark the letter (A), (B), (C), or (D) on your answer sheet. The conversations will not be printed in your test book and will be spoken only one time.

32. Where do the speakers most likely work?
(A) At a publishing company
(B) At a bank
(C) At a concert hall
(D) At a café

33. What does the man say he dislikes doing?
(A) Contacting performers
(B) Ordering supplies
(C) Rearranging furniture
(D) Reviewing contracts

34. What does the woman say she will print out right now?
(A) A discount voucher
(B) A magazine article
(C) A sales report
(D) A guest list

---

35. What product is being discussed?
(A) A software program
(B) A piece of jewelry
(C) A laptop
(D) A bag

36. What does the man like about a product?
(A) It is attractive.
(B) It comes in many sizes.
(C) It is durable.
(D) It can be customized.

37. What does Valerie agree to do?
(A) Provide a Web address
(B) Track a delivery
(C) Contact a store
(D) Complete a form

38. Who most likely is the woman?
(A) A flight attendant
(B) A music teacher
(C) A tour operator
(D) A hotel clerk

39. What is the man concerned about?
(A) The safe transport of instruments
(B) The size of a room
(C) An additional luggage fee
(D) A travel connection

40. What does the woman suggest?
(A) Speaking with a security officer
(B) Calling the vendor directly
(C) Revising a travel itinerary
(D) Purchasing extra tickets

---

41. What does the woman say she needs?
(A) A ride to work
(B) Directions to a car repair shop
(C) An office floor plan
(D) A product serial number

42. What does the man imply when he says, "Actually, I just got to work a few minutes ago"?
(A) He had to deal with heavy traffic.
(B) He would like to reassure the woman.
(C) He will be late for a meeting.
(D) He is unable to assist the woman.

43. What does the woman decide to do?
(A) Talk to another coworker
(B) Request a vacation day
(C) Call a client
(D) Ask for a deadline extension

GO ON TO THE NEXT PAGE →

44. Why is the woman at Mr. Winfield's office?
(A) To register for a seminar
(B) To interview for a job
(C) To sell a product
(D) To plan for a trip

45. Why is Mr. Winfield unable to meet with the woman?
(A) He is working from home.
(B) He is with a client.
(C) He is still out of town.
(D) He is training employees.

46. What will the man probably do next?
(A) Contact Mr. Winfield's assistant
(B) Postpone an appointment
(C) Give Mr. Winfield's number to the woman
(D) Make changes to an event schedule

---

47. Where does the woman work?
(A) At an electronics store
(B) At a medical clinic
(C) At a post office
(D) At a construction company

48. Why is the woman calling?
(A) To locate a shipment
(B) To refill a prescription
(C) To request details about a property
(D) To provide updated information about an order

49. Why is Mr. Alvez out of the office?
(A) He is feeling ill.
(B) He is working at a different location.
(C) He is on vacation.
(D) He is having lunch at a restaurant.

50. What career is the man interested in?
(A) Flight dispatcher
(B) Customs agent
(C) Aircraft mechanic
(D) Commercial pilot

51. What does the man say he will do?
(A) Obtain a loan
(B) Look at a handbook
(C) Compare different schools
(D) Submit some documents

52. According to the woman, what should the man ask about?
(A) Job placement
(B) Facility size
(C) Experience requirements
(D) Course length

---

53. What are the speakers talking about?
(A) An annual meal
(B) A movie premiere
(C) A product launch
(D) A play audition

54. How do the speakers know Ms. Romo?
(A) She gave a tour.
(B) She made a presentation.
(C) She provided some equipment.
(D) She planned a charity event.

55. What does the man say he will do?
(A) He will change some menu items.
(B) He will revise a guest list.
(C) He will book a room.
(D) He will arrange some transportation.

56. What are the speakers mainly discussing?
(A) A city election
(B) A town hall meeting
(C) A budget proposal
(D) A landscaping project

57. What does the man imply when he says, "Wow, I didn't expect that"?
(A) He is unhappy about a change.
(B) He is surprised by a request.
(C) He is pleased by some news.
(D) He is worried about some costs.

58. What will the man receive soon?
(A) An electronic bill
(B) A schedule update
(C) An agreement form
(D) A product catalog

---

59. What does the woman say is a problem?
(A) Several employees have been arriving late at work.
(B) There has been an increase in workload.
(C) A piece of equipment is not working properly.
(D) Some items have been damaged during transit.

60. How does the man propose solving the problem?
(A) By offering better incentives
(B) By purchasing additional machines
(C) By revising an inspection process
(D) By hiring more workers

61. What does the man request that the woman do?
(A) Put together some data
(B) Set up a meeting
(C) Update a Web site
(D) Reschedule some deliveries

Tour Schedule

Time	Spots Available
1:00 P.M.	2
2:00 P.M.	4
4:00 P.M.	3
6:00 P.M.	0

62. What do the speakers plan to tour?
(A) An old plant
(B) A historic library
(C) An art gallery
(D) A local restaurant

63. What does the man remind the woman about?
(A) Registering for a class
(B) Storing her personal belongings
(C) Participating in a demonstration
(D) Having dinner with colleagues

64. Look at the graphic. For what time will the speakers make reservations?
(A) 1:00 P.M.
(B) 2:00 P.M.
(C) 4:00 P.M.
(D) 6:00 P.M.

GO ON TO THE NEXT PAGE

Name: Chris Walker
Account: 510-11-1211

Description	Amount
Bally Grocery (5/9)	$32.00
XD Gas (5/9)	$25.00
Rick's Hardware (5/9)	$7.25
Foreign transaction fee (5/9)	$3.50

65. Where does the woman probably work?
(A) At a credit card company
(B) At a supermarket
(C) At a job recruiting agency
(D) At a hardware store

66. Look at the graphic. What amount will be removed?
(A) $32.00
(B) $25.00
(C) $7.25
(D) $3.50

67. Why does the woman ask the man to wait?
(A) To explain a new process
(B) To have him talk to her manager
(C) To verify some contact information
(D) To receive some feedback

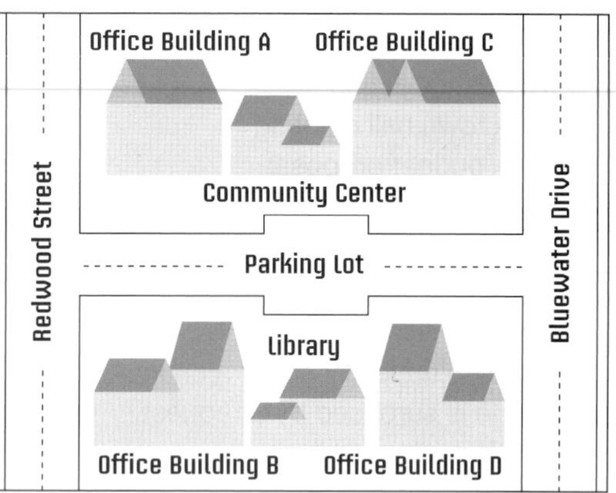

68. What are the speakers mainly discussing?
(A) A business opening
(B) A job interview
(C) A renovation project
(D) A moving plan

69. Look at the graphic. In which office building is Nertech, Inc. located?
(A) Office Building A
(B) Office Building B
(C) Office Building C
(D) Office Building D

70. What does the man tell the woman about parking?
(A) A parking space has been reserved for her.
(B) A parking permit must be displayed.
(C) She will need to pay cash for a parking space.
(D) She should park in a guest spot.

PART 4  

Directions: You will hear some talks given by a single speaker. You will be asked to answer three questions about what the speaker says in each talk. Select the best response to each question and mark the letter (A), (B), (C), or (D) on your answer sheet. The talks will not be printed in your test book and will be spoken only one time.

71. What is the announcement about?
(A) A music concert
(B) A radio show
(C) A sports tournament
(D) A lunch picnic

72. What caused the date of an event to be changed?
(A) The weather
(B) Registration issues
(C) Missing equipment
(D) Some construction

73. Why are listeners told to visit a Web site?
(A) To obtain directions
(B) To view a calendar
(C) To buy tickets
(D) To register a team

---

74. What is the destination of the flight?
(A) New York
(B) Miami
(C) Rio de Janeiro
(D) Barcelona

75. What have some people inquired about?
(A) Storing their luggage
(B) Moving to another seat
(C) Ordering duty-free items
(D) Using mobile phone devices

76. Why are passengers instructed to notify a flight attendant?
(A) To get a magazine
(B) To request a special meal
(C) To obtain a headset
(D) To fill out a customs form

77. What is the purpose of the talk?
(A) To request feedback from residents
(B) To introduce a new procedure
(C) To announce a training session
(D) To discuss staff changes

78. What will the coordinator do?
(A) Reschedule work hours
(B) Invite more guests
(C) Set up another meeting
(D) Review residents' records

79. What advantage does the speaker mention?
(A) Improved work environment
(B) Faster delivery
(C) Reduced food waste
(D) Lower prices

---

80. What is the speaker calling about?
(A) Reassigning a project
(B) Changing a schedule
(C) Preparing a presentation
(D) Moving into a new office

81. Why does the speaker say, "you're right next to the staff lounge"?
(A) To refuse a coworker's request
(B) To ask for extra supplies
(C) To suggest renovating a lounge
(D) To point out that an area is undesirable

82. What does the speaker say will take place on Friday?
(A) The opening of a new store
(B) The installation of some equipment
(C) A training workshop
(D) A management meeting

GO ON TO THE NEXT PAGE

83. What is the purpose of the speech?

(A) To describe a new project
(B) To introduce an award recipient
(C) To demonstrate a process
(D) To honor a retiring employee

84. What industry does Maggie Olmstead most likely work in?

(A) Construction
(B) Software
(C) Medical
(D) Travel

85. According to the speaker, what does Ms. Olmstead plan to do?

(A) Hire additional employees
(B) Update a logo
(C) Launch an advertising campaign
(D) Relocate her business

---

86. What business is being advertised?

(A) An electronics store
(B) An equipment rental shop
(C) A conference center
(D) A shipping company

87. What new service is available this year?

(A) 24-hour photocopying
(B) Online reservation
(C) Wireless Internet
(D) Express delivery

88. How can listeners get a discount?

(A) By mentioning an advertisement
(B) By referring a friend
(C) By printing out a voucher
(D) By booking one month in advance

89. What does the speaker mean when he says, "You're all aware of last quarter's sales performance"?

(A) The listeners will not review a report.
(B) Some data should not have been released.
(C) The listeners know that a product has not sold well.
(D) Some sales figures are incorrect.

90. What does Raymond's report indicate?

(A) A competitor's product is more affordable.
(B) A competitor's advertising campaign is better.
(C) Consumers cannot tell the difference between some products.
(D) Consumers have complained about the features of an item.

91. What are listeners asked to do next?

(A) Submit an invoice
(B) Contact some clients
(C) Test some devices
(D) Look over a document

---

92. Who most likely is the speaker?

(A) A manager
(B) A researcher
(C) A chef
(D) A waiter

93. According to the speaker, what is the business known for?

(A) High-quality food
(B) Cheap prices
(C) Helpful staff
(D) Fast service

94. What does the speaker mean when she says, "I know you can do it"?

(A) She wishes employees will stay later.
(B) She hopes customers will give feedback.
(C) She thinks new dishes can be created.
(D) She believes staff can work faster.

Health Inspection	
Name of Store: The Boxton	**Officer:** Marcus Graham
Health Checklist: ☑ Sanitation ☑ Waste Disposal ☑ Employee Hygiene	**Notes:** Failure of inspection: Freezer

95. Where does the speaker work?

(A) At a flower shop
(B) At an appliance store
(C) At a catering business
(D) At a delivery company

96. Look at the graphic. Which section of the report does the speaker ask about?

(A) Name of Store
(B) Officer
(C) Health Checklist
(D) Notes

97. What does the speaker say she is concerned about?

(A) Fulfilling an order
(B) Losing merchandise
(C) Hiring more workers
(D) Paying a penalty

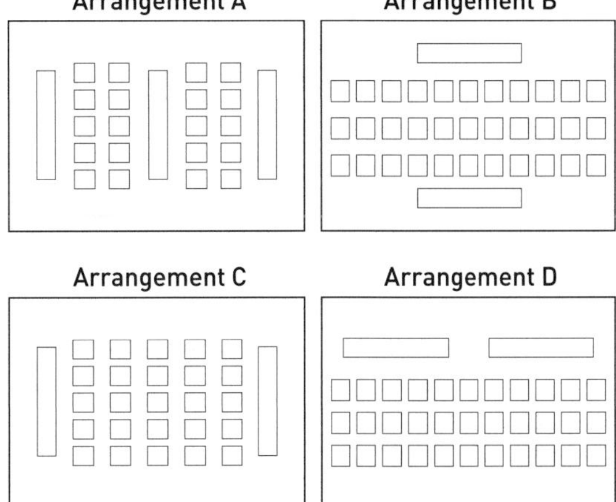

98. What kind of event is being discussed?

(A) A medical conference
(B) A movie premiere
(C) An anniversary celebration
(D) An investors' meeting

99. Why is the speaker anticipating attendance to be high?

(A) Many volunteers were recruited.
(B) The venue is in a convenient location.
(C) Some experts will be giving talks.
(D) Some prizes will be distributed.

100. Look at the graphic. Which arrangement will be used in the Malone Auditorium?

(A) Arrangement A
(B) Arrangement B
(C) Arrangement C
(D) Arrangement D

This is the end of the Listening test.

ACTUAL TEST 02

LISTENING TEST 07

In the Listening test, you will be asked to demonstrate how well you understand spoken English. The entire Listening test will last approximately 45 minutes. There are four parts, and directions are given for each part. You must mark your answers on the separate answer sheet. Do not write your answers in your test book.

PART 1

Directions: For each question in this part, you will hear four statements about a picture in your test book. When you hear the statements, you must select the one statement that best describes what you see in the picture. Then find the number of the question on your answer sheet and mark your answer. The statements will not be printed in your test book and will be spoken only one time.

Example

Statement (B), "A man is pointing at a document," is the best description of the picture, so you should select answer (B) and mark it on your answer sheet.

1.

2.

GO ON TO THE NEXT PAGE

3.

4.

5.

6.

GO ON TO THE NEXT PAGE

PART 2 08

Directions: You will hear a question or statement and three responses spoken in English. They will not be printed in your test book and will be spoken only one time. Select the best response to the question or statement and mark the letter (A), (B), or (C) on your answer sheet.

7. Mark your answer on your answer sheet.

8. Mark your answer on your answer sheet.

9. Mark your answer on your answer sheet.

10. Mark your answer on your answer sheet.

11. Mark your answer on your answer sheet.

12. Mark your answer on your answer sheet.

13. Mark your answer on your answer sheet.

14. Mark your answer on your answer sheet.

15. Mark your answer on your answer sheet.

16. Mark your answer on your answer sheet.

17. Mark your answer on your answer sheet.

18. Mark your answer on your answer sheet.

19. Mark your answer on your answer sheet.

20. Mark your answer on your answer sheet.

21. Mark your answer on your answer sheet.

22. Mark your answer on your answer sheet.

23. Mark your answer on your answer sheet.

24. Mark your answer on your answer sheet.

25. Mark your answer on your answer sheet.

26. Mark your answer on your answer sheet.

27. Mark your answer on your answer sheet.

28. Mark your answer on your answer sheet.

29. Mark your answer on your answer sheet.

30. Mark your answer on your answer sheet.

31. Mark your answer on your answer sheet.

PART 3 (09)

Directions: You will hear some conversations between two or more people. You will be asked to answer three questions about what the speakers say in each conversation. Select the best response to each question and mark the letter (A), (B), (C), or (D) on your answer sheet. The conversations will not be printed in your test book and will be spoken only one time.

32. What has been written about the company?
(A) It received an award.
(B) It is growing quickly.
(C) It will relocate soon.
(D) It has launched a new product.

33. According to the speakers, what will the article help to do?
(A) Increase job applications
(B) Lower operating costs
(C) Improve staff training
(D) Attract international customers

34. What will the man do next?
(A) Revise a schedule
(B) Post a job opening
(C) Send an email
(D) Update a Web site

---

35. What problem has the woman identified?
(A) Some documents are out of date.
(B) Some files have been misplaced.
(C) A software program is not working properly.
(D) Two seminars have been double-booked.

36. What does the woman say about employees who were certified last year?
(A) They must contact their managers.
(B) They may work at another plant.
(C) They will train new staff members.
(D) They need to attend a review session.

37. What does the man ask the woman to do?
(A) Lead a training workshop
(B) Complete a registration form
(C) Provide names of employees
(D) Send out invitations

38. What is the conversation mainly about?
(A) Visiting a friend
(B) Reporting on an event
(C) Attending university
(D) Shopping for clothes

39. What does the man say he wants to do before he travels?
(A) Take some courses
(B) Call a hotel
(C) Book a tour
(D) Research some designers

40. What does the woman offer to do?
(A) Show some product catalogs
(B) Check a schedule
(C) Find some contact information
(D) Make a reservation

---

41. Why is the man calling?
(A) To purchase a train ticket
(B) To request a ride
(C) To discuss a car repair service
(D) To inquire about a charge

42. According to the woman, what has recently changed?
(A) Hiring requirements
(B) A company policy
(C) Business hours
(D) An office location

43. What does the woman agree to do?
(A) Revise an agreement
(B) Contact a manager
(C) Cancel an appointment
(D) Remove a fee

GO ON TO THE NEXT PAGE

44. What does the woman offer to do?

(A) Reschedule an appointment
(B) Transport some boxes
(C) Track a delivery
(D) Call another department

45. According to the woman, what happened last week?

(A) A shipment was damaged.
(B) A storage room was cleaned.
(C) A door would not open.
(D) An elevator broke down.

46. Why does the man say, "the control system had to be reconfigured"?

(A) To give a reason for a delay
(B) To request new equipment
(C) To point out an inefficient process
(D) To apologize for a costly service

---

47. What product are the speakers discussing?

(A) Stationery
(B) Cosmetics
(C) Computers
(D) Beverages

48. What does Chris recommend?

(A) Offering discounts
(B) Recruiting more workers
(C) Updating a Website
(D) Adjusting a budget

49. What does the woman propose?

(A) Expanding store space
(B) Delaying a decision
(C) Extending business hours
(D) Distributing a questionnaire

50. Who most likely is the woman?

(A) An HR manager
(B) A corporate intern
(C) A financial analyst
(D) A marketing director

51. What does the man ask the woman for?

(A) Some samples of a design
(B) Some details about a company
(C) Some feedback on an experience
(D) Some funding for a project

52. What will the woman receive?

(A) An increased budget
(B) A compensation package
(C) A pay raise
(D) A work schedule

---

53. What kind of product is being discussed?

(A) A laptop computer
(B) A mobile phone
(C) A home appliance
(D) A digital camera

54. What feature of the product is the woman particularly proud about?

(A) Its speed
(B) Its durability
(C) Its color
(D) Its weight

55. Why does the woman say, "I'm watching a play that evening"?

(A) To praise a performance
(B) To turn down an invitation
(C) To reschedule a meeting
(D) To ask for a recommendation

56. What kind of event is being organized?

(A) A business convention
(B) A product launch
(C) A graduation ceremony
(D) An anniversary celebration

57. What does the woman inquire about?

(A) Food preferences
(B) Accommodations
(C) Parking
(D) Fitness facilities

58. What does the resort provide for free?

(A) Transportation
(B) Breakfast
(C) Wireless Internet
(D) Travel guides

---

59. According to the woman, what caused some shipments to be late?

(A) Some workers were not available.
(B) Some documents could not be located.
(C) There was an issue with an online system.
(D) A delivery van experienced engine trouble.

60. What step does the woman suggest adding to a procedure?

(A) Distributing a survey
(B) Making phone calls
(C) Reviewing an inventory list
(D) Performing daily inspections

61. What do the speakers agree to do tomorrow morning?

(A) Contact some job candidates
(B) Visit a new facility
(C) Provide an update
(D) Book some plane tickets

Dental Work Type	Code #
Teeth whitening	T30
Gum surgery	G55
Root canal surgery	R01
Tooth extraction	T86

62. What is the woman having a problem with?

(A) Making an invoice
(B) Locating a package
(C) Performing a surgery
(D) Calling a patient

63. Look at the graphic. Which code should the woman use?

(A) T30
(B) G55
(C) R01
(D) T86

64. What does the man say will happen next week?

(A) A doctor will go on vacation.
(B) Some important clients will visit.
(C) Some staff members will attend a workshop.
(D) A chart will be accessible electronically.

GO ON TO THE NEXT PAGE

STANDARD SHIPPING RATES
(For orders under 5kg)

Domestic Zone	U.S., Canada	$3
Overseas Zone A	Central and South America	$5
Overseas Zone B	Europe, Asia, Africa	$7
Overseas Zone C	Australia, South Pacific	$9

65. Who most likely is the man?
(A) A customer service associate
(B) A delivery driver
(C) A fashion designer
(D) A Web site developer

66. Look at the graphic. What rate will the woman pay for shipping?
(A) $3
(B) $5
(C) $7
(D) $9

67. What will the woman most likely do next?
(A) Update a contact number
(B) Choose some product features
(C) Confirm a delivery address
(D) Provide some payment information

Product Name	LluviaWear
Country of Origin	Dominican Republic
Color	Black
Material	Nylon
Cleaning Instructions	Dry clean only

68. What does the man say they will have to do?
(A) Increase inventory
(B) Find a new storage facility
(C) Create an ad campaign
(D) Print a clothing catalog

69. What does the woman recommend?
(A) Taking pictures of a product
(B) Updating a Web site
(C) Calling some clients
(D) Talking to another department

70. Look at the graphic. Which part of the tag will need to be changed?
(A) Country of Origin
(B) Color
(C) Material
(D) Cleaning Instructions

PART 4 (10)

Directions: You will hear some talks given by a single speaker. You will be asked to answer three questions about what the speaker says in each talk. Select the best response to each question and mark the letter (A), (B), (C), or (D) on your answer sheet. The talks will not be printed in your test book and will be spoken only one time.

71. Where does the speaker most likely work?
(A) At a newspaper company
(B) At a furniture store
(C) At a conference center
(D) At a real estate office

72. What is the purpose of the call?
(A) To address a delivery error
(B) To review a defective product
(C) To resolve a scheduling conflict
(D) To acknowledge an incorrect charge

73. What will the speaker email the listener?
(A) A discount coupon
(B) A sample item
(C) A new invoice
(D) A refund form

---

74. Which is mentioned about the restaurant?
(A) It received positive reviews.
(B) Its head chef received an award.
(C) Its menu will change.
(D) It has been open for over 10 years.

75. What does the restaurant specialize in?
(A) Seafood
(B) Pizza
(C) Vegetable dishes
(D) Pastries

76. What will customers receive if they mention the advertisement?
(A) A T-shirt
(B) A discount coupon
(C) A cook book
(D) A free dessert

77. What event is being held?
(A) A job fair
(B) A sales conference
(C) A fundraising dinner
(D) A retirement party

78. Which is Travis Kim's most outstanding achievement?
(A) He developed a training program.
(B) He created a best-selling product.
(C) He expanded a client base.
(D) He founded a charity organization.

79. What does the speaker ask Travis Kim to do?
(A) Make a donation
(B) Accept a gift
(C) Give a speech
(D) Watch a presentation

---

80. What is the broadcast mainly about?
(A) A traffic report
(B) City council nominees
(C) A new shopping center
(D) Upcoming local events

81. What are the listeners encouraged to do by Friday morning?
(A) Donate some items
(B) Fill out a survey
(C) Enter an art contest
(D) Sign up for volunteer work

82. What does the speaker suggest when she says, "we may be looking at some heavy rain on those days"?
(A) Listeners should avoid going outside.
(B) Listeners should not use a certain road.
(C) The weather can affect a schedule.
(D) A weather report was wrong.

GO ON TO THE NEXT PAGE

83. According to the speaker, what is special about the café?

(A) It operates a farm.
(B) It has a remodeled kitchen.
(C) It provides a cooking course.
(D) It employs an Indian chef.

84. Who is Marco?

(A) A food critic
(B) A university professor
(C) An interior designer
(D) A business owner

85. Why does the speaker say, "All my friends come here to eat this"?

(A) She recommends a menu item.
(B) She knows that a restaurant is popular.
(C) She would like to try a new dish.
(D) She knows how to prepare a dish.

89. Where does the speaker most likely work?

(A) At an advertising agency
(B) At a publishing company
(C) At a bookstore
(D) At a library

90. What does the speaker mean when she says, "we were very surprised"?

(A) Some documents are missing.
(B) A positive review was given.
(C) Some complaints were made.
(D) An employee is resigning.

91. What will employees be required to do in the future?

(A) Meet monthly sales goals
(B) Request days off in advance
(C) Submit original receipts
(D) Fill out an authorization form

---

86. What is the main topic of the talk?

(A) Changes to a production schedule
(B) Instructions for repairing machines
(C) Software for teaching work skills
(D) Consequences of a recent merger

87. What does the speaker recommend doing?

(A) Comparing service costs
(B) Extending staff contracts
(C) Talking to a manager after a meeting
(D) Beginning a program with new recruits

88. According to the speaker, what can the company expect to see?

(A) Increased productivity
(B) Higher employee morale
(C) Improved sales
(D) Better customer relations

92. What does the speaker mention about himself?

(A) He is a scientist.
(B) He grew up in the region.
(C) He started a new job recently.
(D) He has received an award.

93. According to the speaker, why will the group make several stops?

(A) To take some breaks
(B) To study animal behavior
(C) To learn about different plants
(D) To perform some experiments

94. According to the speaker, what can the listeners do on a Web site?

(A) Read some articles
(B) Download pictures
(C) Sign up for a membership
(D) Complete a questionnaire

Arca Department Store Directory

4F	Clothing & Accessories
3F	Electronics & Appliances
2F	Office Supplies & Furniture
1F	Sporting Goods & Customer Support

95. Look at the graphic. Where is the sale being held at?

(A) The 1st Floor
(B) The 2nd Floor
(C) The 3rd Floor
(D) The 4th Floor

96. According to the speaker, how can shoppers locate sale items?

(A) By checking for a special label
(B) By looking at a product catalog
(C) By speaking to a worker
(D) By going on a store Web site

97. Why are listeners encouraged to visit the customer support center?

(A) To sign up for a membership card
(B) To exchange an item
(C) To schedule a delivery
(D) To purchase a gift certificate

98. Which department is the speaker calling?

(A) Technology
(B) Personnel
(C) Finance
(D) Security

99. Look at the graphic. What information does the speaker say is incorrect?

(A) 839287
(B) Analyst
(C) Miller
(D) 555-3824

100. What does the speaker request the listener to do?

(A) Return a call
(B) Check a database
(C) Make a reservation
(D) Submit a document

This is the end of the Listening test.

ACTUAL TEST 03

LISTENING TEST

In the Listening test, you will be asked to demonstrate how well you understand spoken English. The entire Listening test will last approximately 45 minutes. There are four parts, and directions are given for each part. You must mark your answers on the separate answer sheet. Do not write your answers in your test book.

PART 1

Directions: For each question in this part, you will hear four statements about a picture in your test book. When you hear the statements, you must select the one statement that best describes what you see in the picture. Then find the number of the question on your answer sheet and mark your answer. The statements will not be printed in your test book and will be spoken only one time.

Example

Sample Answer

Ⓐ ● Ⓒ Ⓓ

Statement (B), "A man is pointing at a document," is the best description of the picture, so you should select answer (B) and mark it on your answer sheet.

1.

2.

GO ON TO THE NEXT PAGE

3.

4.

5.

6.

GO ON TO THE NEXT PAGE

PART 2 12

Directions: You will hear a question or statement and three responses spoken in English. They will not be printed in your test book and will be spoken only one time. Select the best response to the question or statement and mark the letter (A), (B), or (C) on your answer sheet.

7. Mark your answer on your answer sheet.

8. Mark your answer on your answer sheet.

9. Mark your answer on your answer sheet.

10. Mark your answer on your answer sheet.

11. Mark your answer on your answer sheet.

12. Mark your answer on your answer sheet.

13. Mark your answer on your answer sheet.

14. Mark your answer on your answer sheet.

15. Mark your answer on your answer sheet.

16. Mark your answer on your answer sheet.

17. Mark your answer on your answer sheet.

18. Mark your answer on your answer sheet.

19. Mark your answer on your answer sheet.

20. Mark your answer on your answer sheet.

21. Mark your answer on your answer sheet.

22. Mark your answer on your answer sheet.

23. Mark your answer on your answer sheet.

24. Mark your answer on your answer sheet.

25. Mark your answer on your answer sheet.

26. Mark your answer on your answer sheet.

27. Mark your answer on your answer sheet.

28. Mark your answer on your answer sheet.

29. Mark your answer on your answer sheet.

30. Mark your answer on your answer sheet.

31. Mark your answer on your answer sheet.

PART 3 13

Directions: You will hear some conversations between two or more people. You will be asked to answer three questions about what the speakers say in each conversation. Select the best response to each question and mark the letter (A), (B), (C), or (D) on your answer sheet. The conversations will not be printed in your test book and will be spoken only one time.

32. What are the speakers mainly discussing?
(A) Local grocery stores
(B) Public libraries
(C) Auto repair shops
(D) Neighborhood restaurants

33. Why does the woman say she likes the man's suggestion?
(A) The workers are friendly.
(B) The location is convenient.
(C) The business closes late.
(D) The food is healthy.

34. What does the man say is available this week?
(A) A price discount
(B) Free parking
(C) A sample product
(D) Cooking courses

---

35. What would the woman like to do?
(A) Reserve a tour
(B) Check a city map
(C) Book a flight
(D) Review an event calendar

36. What is the woman asked to select?
(A) Menu items
(B) A payment method
(C) A departure time
(D) Entertainment options

37. What does the man recommend doing?
(A) Bringing some cash
(B) Printing out a voucher
(C) Checking a Web site
(D) Wearing warm clothing

38. What are the women trying to do?
(A) Post some signs
(B) Reserve a meeting room
(C) Order a new computer
(D) Get ready for a training session

39. Who is the man?
(A) A delivery driver
(B) A store owner
(C) A facility manager
(D) A software developer

40. What does the man advise the women to do?
(A) Relocate to another room
(B) Update a system
(C) Provide some feedback
(D) Read a user guide

---

41. What are the speakers discussing?
(A) Repairing some furniture
(B) Renovating some bathrooms
(C) Recycling some clothes
(D) Replacing some flooring

42. What is the man concerned about?
(A) A price
(B) Some noise
(C) An odor
(D) Some designs

43. What does the woman say she will do?
(A) Change a date
(B) Provide an estimate
(C) Inspect an apartment
(D) Employ a contractor

GO ON TO THE NEXT PAGE →

44. Where do the speakers most likely work?
(A) At a library
(B) At an electronics store
(C) At a hospital
(D) At a financial firm

45. What did Ms. Shah recommend?
(A) Purchasing a magazine subscription
(B) Watching a video demonstration
(C) Holding personal meetings with staff
(D) Enrolling in some online courses

46. What does the man say he will do?
(A) Review a presentation
(B) Try out a product
(C) Research some pricing information
(D) Print out an article

---

47. Where are the speakers?
(A) At a training workshop
(B) At a fashion show
(C) At a department meeting
(D) At a company luncheon

48. What project are the women working on?
(A) A budget proposal
(B) A catalog redesign
(C) A marketing campaign
(D) An instructional video

49. What does the man say he was responsible for?
(A) Looking over customer feedback
(B) Hiring new staff members
(C) Organizing a volunteer program
(D) Revising some news articles

50. According to the man, what will happen on Friday?
(A) A business will reopen.
(B) A newspaper will be published.
(C) A workshop will begin.
(D) A staff member will be interviewed.

51. What does the woman request?
(A) Directions to an office
(B) Permission to bring a colleague
(C) A sample of a product
(D) A tour of a facility

52. What does the man say he will prepare?
(A) Some badges
(B) Some pictures
(C) Some snacks
(D) Some documents

---

53. What does the man request the woman do?
(A) Mail some invitations
(B) Review some charts
(C) Reserve a booth
(D) Postpone an event

54. What does the man plan to do today?
(A) Register for a workshop
(B) Meet with a client
(C) Purchase a ticket
(D) Contact a catering company

55. Why does the man say, "I haven't been here long, and it's a big presentation"?
(A) He wants to get feedback from the woman on a proposal.
(B) He is providing an excuse for why he has postponed an event.
(C) He would like to thank the woman for helping him with a project.
(D) He is concerned about performing a task by himself.

56. Who most likely is the woman?

(A) A receptionist
(B) A reporter
(C) A salesperson
(D) An actress

57. According to the man, what change is expected?

(A) More colors will be used in clothing designs.
(B) Production costs will significantly increase.
(C) Consumers will spend less money in the future.
(D) Merchandise will only be sold online.

58. What does the woman want to do?

(A) Visit a store
(B) Take photographs
(C) Meet the company CEO
(D) Take a tour

---

59. What did a client dislike about the stairway lights?

(A) Their shape
(B) Their cost
(C) Their brightness
(D) Their color

60. Why does the woman say, "according to the contract, we need to finish everything by this week"?

(A) She believes some contract terms should be changed.
(B) She is concerned about meeting a deadline.
(C) She is surprised at the progress of a landscaping project.
(D) She will repair some broken equipment this week.

61. What does the man say he will do?

(A) Go to a work site
(B) Revise a document
(C) Place an order
(D) Contact a customer

Possible Event Locations	
Venue	**Guest Capacity**
Ocean Grill	200 guests
Bistro 324	150 guests
The Vine	125 guests
Olive Grove	100 guests

62. What information about the party did the man receive this morning?

(A) The finalized date
(B) The amount of budgeted funds
(C) The number of attendees
(D) The directions to the event

63. Look at the graphic. Which venue will the speakers most likely choose?

(A) Ocean Grill
(B) Bistro 324
(C) The Vine
(D) Olive Grove

64. What does the woman say she will take care of?

(A) A security deposit
(B) Entertainment
(C) Menu items
(D) Transportation

GO ON TO THE NEXT PAGE

Invoice (#483740) Customer Name: Raymond Posner	
Description	**Price**
9"x12" Oil Painting	$380
12"x16" Watercolor Painting	$560
20"x24" Acrylic Painting	$720
30"x40" Landscape Painting	$910

65. What does the man say he will do with the restored paintings?

(A) Sell them at an auction
(B) Use them as office decorations
(C) Display them at a museum
(D) Give them as gifts to coworkers

66. Look at the graphic. Which amount will be taken off of the invoice?

(A) $380
(B) $560
(C) $720
(D) $910

67. What does the woman say her assistant will do?

(A) Print out some forms
(B) Give the man a tour of a store
(C) Carry some items to a vehicle
(D) Process a payment

Boston to Chicago		
Train	**Departure**	**Arrival**
Train 1024	12:50 P.M.	9:50 A.M.
Train 116	3:15 P.M.	12:10 P.M.
Train 894	5:30 P.M.	3:40 P.M.
Train 3479	7:25 P.M.	5:45 P.M.

68. Why does the woman apologize?

(A) A payment was not processed.
(B) A ticket is not available online.
(C) A train has been overbooked.
(D) A schedule is incorrect.

69. Look at the graphic. What train will the man most likely take?

(A) Train 1024
(B) Train 116
(C) Train 894
(D) Train 3479

70. What does the man say he will do in Chicago?

(A) Attend a seminar
(B) Tour a factory
(C) Watch a performance
(D) Meet a client

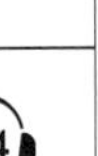

PART 4 14

Directions: You will hear some talks given by a single speaker. You will be asked to answer three questions about what the speaker says in each talk. Select the best response to each question and mark the letter (A), (B), (C), or (D) on your answer sheet. The talks will not be printed in your test book and will be spoken only one time.

71. Who most likely are the listeners?
(A) Sales associates
(B) Product designers
(C) Computer specialists
(D) Human resources employees

72. According to the speaker, what is the next step of the project?
(A) To develop training materials
(B) To create a prototype
(C) To determine a cost
(D) To obtain some feedback

73. What does the speaker ask for help with?
(A) Reviewing some documents
(B) Interviewing job candidates
(C) Contacting other departments
(D) Selecting some instruments

---

74. Where does the speaker work?
(A) At a uniform retailer
(B) At a taxi company
(C) At a car dealership
(D) At a post office

75. What does the speaker mean when he says, "some of our drivers are out sick at the moment"?
(A) A shipment will not arrive on time.
(B) A company will hire more employees.
(C) Some staff will be working extra shifts.
(D) Some automobiles are available for use.

76. What does the speaker offer?
(A) A future discount
(B) A product catalog
(C) A complimentary item
(D) A full refund

77. What does the business produce?
(A) Car tires
(B) Mobile phones
(C) Airplane engines
(D) Laptop computers

78. According to the speaker, what will the business do in August?
(A) Raise its workers' wages
(B) Launch a new product line
(C) Create additional parking spaces
(D) Open a new manufacturing plant

79. What does the mayor expect will happen in Willington?
(A) A recycling program will begin.
(B) New traffic laws will be enforced.
(C) More public transportation will be provided.
(D) Employment opportunities will increase.

---

80. What is being advertised?
(A) Residential real estate
(B) Heating maintenance
(C) Appliance recycling
(D) A technology institute

81. Why are listeners asked to call?
(A) To sign up for a class
(B) To set up an inspection
(C) To arrange transportation
(D) To receive a brochure

82. What will happen at the end of the month?
(A) A special offer will expire.
(B) A report will be published.
(C) Payments will be due.
(D) Construction will begin.

GO ON TO THE NEXT PAGE

83. Where is the talk taking place?

(A) In a factory
(B) In a laboratory
(C) In a supermarket
(D) In a bakery

84. What are listeners given?

(A) A location map
(B) A discount coupon
(C) Product samples
(D) Some ingredients

85. What does the speaker remind the listeners to do?

(A) Wear safety equipment
(B) Use a back entrance
(C) Return their passes
(D) Fill out a security form

86. What does the speaker remind listeners to do by the end of the day?

(A) Submit a task report
(B) Make a reservation
(C) Pick up a visitor's pass
(D) Nominate an employee

87. What good news does the speaker mention?

(A) Workers will receive cash incentives.
(B) Production has gone up.
(C) A product launch was successful.
(D) A shipment arrived on time.

88. Why does the speaker say, "we've been hosting visitors from Japan for several days"?

(A) To introduce a guest speaker
(B) To begin a tour of a facility
(C) To review details of a business trip
(D) To give a reason for a delay

89. What is the purpose of the talk?

(A) To ask for financial contributions
(B) To share information about a program
(C) To explain a job application process
(D) To announce a new exhibit

90. What requirement does the speaker mention?

(A) Holding local events
(B) Providing weekly feedback
(C) Submitting work samples
(D) Visiting different cities

91. Who is invited to speak next?

(A) School teachers
(B) Museum directors
(C) Famous artists
(D) Professional athletes

92. Why is the speaker postponing today's meeting?

(A) A manager was busy.
(B) A room was not available.
(C) Some designs were not completed.
(D) His travel arrangements were changed.

93. According to the speaker, what was the listener's report about?

(A) Suggestions for being more environmentally friendly
(B) Results of a recent customer survey
(C) Plans to cut back on operating costs
(D) Strategies to attract new customers

94. What does the speaker imply when he says, "Let's discuss this in more detail"?

(A) He is planning to research some new suppliers.
(B) He believes a proposal may cause problems.
(C) He would like review a contract more carefully.
(D) He wants to extend a project deadline.

Service	Fee
Late payment	$20
Line reconnection	$40
In-home service	$60
Early cancelation	$80

95. Where does the speaker most likely work?
(A) At a book publisher
(B) At a fitness center
(C) At a telephone provider
(D) At a landscaping company

96. Look at the graphic. How much will Ms. Preston pay?
(A) $20
(B) $40
(C) $60
(D) $80

97. What is Ms. Preston encouraged to do on the Web site?
(A) Provide feedback
(B) Renew her membership
(C) Download a contract
(D) Register for a mailing list

Innomax Convention Schedule		
Time	**Event**	**Speaker**
13:00	Best Sport Cars	Jeremy Fong
14:00	Latest Navigation Systems	Kelly Brown
15:00	Improving Fuel Efficiency	Sherman Bernstein
16:00	Designing Your Vehicle	Emily Lithmore
17:00	Reception	Innomax President

98. What is the purpose of the call?
(A) To offer a job
(B) To check on an order
(C) To request product samples
(D) To make a reservation

99. Look at the graphic. Who is the speaker calling?
(A) Jeremy Fong
(B) Kelly Brown
(C) Sherman Bernstein
(D) Emily Lithmore

100. What does the speaker ask the listener to do?
(A) Provide pricing information
(B) Visit a Web site
(C) Review a convention schedule
(D) Send a registration payment

This is the end of the Listening test.

ACTUAL TEST 04

LISTENING TEST 15

In the Listening test, you will be asked to demonstrate how well you understand spoken English. The entire Listening test will last approximately 45 minutes. There are four parts, and directions are given for each part. You must mark your answers on the separate answer sheet. Do not write your answers in your test book.

PART 1

Directions: For each question in this part, you will hear four statements about a picture in your test book. When you hear the statements, you must select the one statement that best describes what you see in the picture. Then find the number of the question on your answer sheet and mark your answer. The statements will not be printed in your test book and will be spoken only one time.

Example

Sample Answer

Ⓐ ● Ⓒ Ⓓ

Statement (B), "A man is pointing at a document," is the best description of the picture, so you should select answer (B) and mark it on your answer sheet.

1.

2.

GO ON TO THE NEXT PAGE

3.

4.

5.

6.

GO ON TO THE NEXT PAGE

PART 2 16

Directions: You will hear a question or statement and three responses spoken in English. They will not be printed in your test book and will be spoken only one time. Select the best response to the question or statement and mark the letter (A), (B), or (C) on your answer sheet.

7. Mark your answer on your answer sheet.

8. Mark your answer on your answer sheet.

9. Mark your answer on your answer sheet.

10. Mark your answer on your answer sheet.

11. Mark your answer on your answer sheet.

12. Mark your answer on your answer sheet.

13. Mark your answer on your answer sheet.

14. Mark your answer on your answer sheet.

15. Mark your answer on your answer sheet.

16. Mark your answer on your answer sheet.

17. Mark your answer on your answer sheet.

18. Mark your answer on your answer sheet.

19. Mark your answer on your answer sheet.

20. Mark your answer on your answer sheet.

21. Mark your answer on your answer sheet.

22. Mark your answer on your answer sheet.

23. Mark your answer on your answer sheet.

24. Mark your answer on your answer sheet.

25. Mark your answer on your answer sheet.

26. Mark your answer on your answer sheet.

27. Mark your answer on your answer sheet.

28. Mark your answer on your answer sheet.

29. Mark your answer on your answer sheet.

30. Mark your answer on your answer sheet.

31. Mark your answer on your answer sheet.

PART 3 17 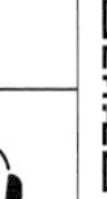

Directions: You will hear some conversations between two or more people. You will be asked to answer three questions about what the speakers say in each conversation. Select the best response to each question and mark the letter (A), (B), (C), or (D) on your answer sheet. The conversations will not be printed in your test book and will be spoken only one time.

32. Where does the conversation most likely take place?
(A) In a shopping mall
(B) In a train station
(C) In a fitness center
(D) In a coffee shop

33. What does the woman ask the man to do?
(A) Respond to a survey
(B) Try out a product
(C) Provide contact information
(D) Come back later

34. What does the man suggest?
(A) Extending business hours
(B) Improving exercise facilities
(C) Offering more discounts
(D) Increasing dining options

---

35. What is the woman's occupation?
(A) Floral designer
(B) Car repairperson
(C) Landscape professional
(D) Construction worker

36. What is the woman's problem?
(A) Her vehicle is not starting.
(B) She cannot make it to her next appointment.
(C) Her coworker is not available.
(D) She doesn't have enough supplies.

37. What does the man recommend doing?
(A) Reading a manual
(B) Extending a project deadline
(C) Taking a detour
(D) Checking a traffic report

38. What type of product is being discussed?
(A) Office furniture
(B) Clothing
(C) Electronics
(D) Home appliances

39. What does the woman imply when she says, "It looks like only three boxes are left"?
(A) She is too busy to check inventory.
(B) She wants a worker to organize some shelves.
(C) Some boxes need to be moved.
(D) An item is very popular.

40. What will the woman do next?
(A) Contact a Sales Department
(B) Hang up some signs
(C) Clean some shelves
(D) Place a new order

---

41. Where most likely are the speakers?
(A) At a manufacturing plant
(B) At a post office
(C) At a hotel
(D) At a retailer

42. What does the man say will happen tomorrow?
(A) A shipment will be delivered.
(B) A seminar will be held.
(C) An inspection will be conducted.
(D) An advertisement will be posted.

43. What will the woman probably do next?
(A) Organize a storage room
(B) Order some food
(C) Send out some invitations
(D) Show a customer some merchandise

GO ON TO THE NEXT PAGE →

44. What is the main topic of the conversation?
(A) Chocolate
(B) Pastries
(C) Vegetables
(D) Fruit

45. What is the man's problem?
(A) A computer is malfunctioning.
(B) A credit card payment was not approved.
(C) A box is too heavy to carry.
(D) A shipment is missing some items.

46. What does the woman say she will give the man?
(A) A discount voucher
(B) A postage stamp
(C) Complimentary merchandise
(D) Cash reimbursement

---

47. Who most likely is the man?
(A) A professional photographer
(B) A corporate event organizer
(C) A customer service associate
(D) A computer technician

48. What does the woman inquire about?
(A) Repairing a camera
(B) Arranging a photo session
(C) Purchasing a warranty
(D) Applying an Internet discount

49. According to the man, what should the woman do?
(A) Visit a store
(B) Send a photograph
(C) Download a manual
(D) Contact a manufacturer

50. What is the conversation mainly about?
(A) Relocating a business
(B) Hiring better workers
(C) Reviewing features of a new product
(D) Expanding a section of a store

51. What is the woman asked to do?
(A) Place an online ad
(B) Contact a supplier
(C) Submit a sales report
(D) Download a catalog

52. What will the man probably do next?
(A) Take inventory
(B) Compare some costs
(C) Visit another branch
(D) Put up some posters

---

53. What is the man working on?
(A) A user guide
(B) A software program
(C) A market survey
(D) An event schedule

54. What does the man mean when he says, "You'll need to ask someone in the IT Department about that"?
(A) He is unable to give an answer.
(B) A project requires additional team members.
(C) The department made a specific request.
(D) He has to attend a meeting soon.

55. What is the woman worried about?
(A) Training new employees
(B) Attracting many customers
(C) Exceeding a budget
(D) Meeting a deadline

56. What is the woman inquiring about?

(A) Flight arrival times
(B) Payment methods
(C) Extra baggage allowances
(D) Seat upgrades

57. What does the woman say she needs to do in Rome?

(A) Visit a local bank
(B) Rent a car
(C) Catch a connecting flight
(D) Prepare for a talk

58. What does the man recommend?

(A) Using a credit card
(B) Taking an alternate route
(C) Rescheduling a meeting
(D) Speaking to a supervisor

59. Why will the man meet with Ms. Gomez?

(A) To receive marketing advice
(B) To interview her
(C) To sign a contract
(D) To show her some products

60. What does the man agree to do?

(A) Reschedule an appointment
(B) Make a donation
(C) Complete a visitor form
(D) Purchase a magazine subscription

61. Why does Ms. Gomez apologize?

(A) A meeting will not start on time.
(B) She does not know the man's phone number.
(C) She lost some documents.
(D) An article contains inaccurate information.

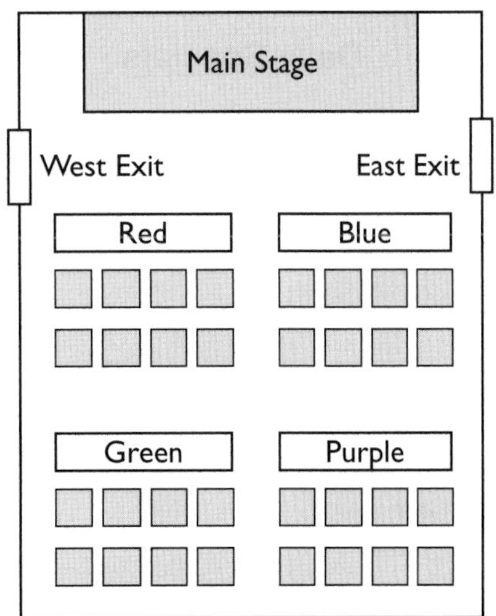

62. What kind of event are the speakers planning to attend?

(A) A product demonstration
(B) A dance show
(C) A movie premiere
(D) A business conference

63. Look at the graphic. Where will the speakers most likely sit?

(A) The red section
(B) The blue section
(C) The green section
(D) The purple section

64. What does the woman recommend?

(A) Calling different vendors
(B) Inviting more coworkers
(C) Using a public transit service
(D) Viewing an online map

GO ON TO THE NEXT PAGE

Daily Specials

1. Mini burgers................................$9.75
2. Steak nachos..............................$10.50
3. Sausage platter $11.25
4. Cobb salad $7.50

65. What most likely is the woman's job?

(A) Delivery driver
(B) Chef
(C) Server
(D) Restaurant manager

66. According to the man, why will a list be updated?

(A) Some ingredients are not available.
(B) A package will not come in today.
(C) A chef prepared the wrong item.
(D) Many complaints were filed.

67. Look at the graphic. How much will the new special cost?

(A) $9.75
(B) $10.50
(C) $11.25
(D) $7.50

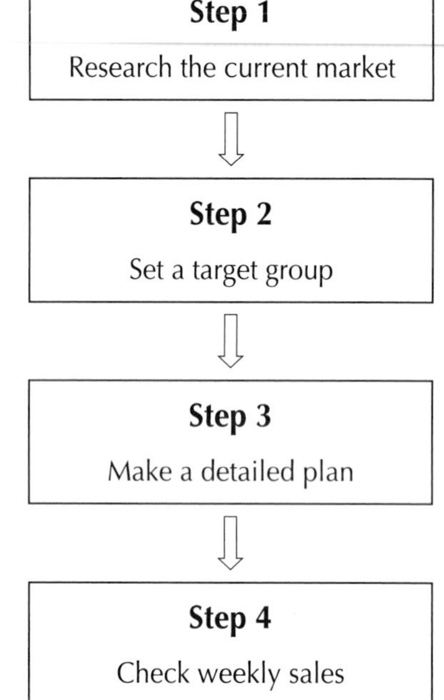

68. What type of business does the woman operate?

(A) An online clothing store
(B) A travel agency
(C) A digital marketing firm
(D) A computer shop

69. What does the woman hope to do in the future?

(A) Become a fashion designer
(B) Earn an advanced degree
(C) Increase her customer base
(D) Move to another country

70. Look at the graphic. What step would the woman like to discuss?

(A) Step 1
(B) Step 2
(C) Step 3
(D) Step 4

PART 4 (18)

Directions: You will hear some talks given by a single speaker. You will be asked to answer three questions about what the speaker says in each talk. Select the best response to each question and mark the letter (A), (B), (C), or (D) on your answer sheet. The talks will not be printed in your test book and will be spoken only one time.

71. What type of business is being advertised?
(A) An art studio
(B) A grocery store
(C) A software company
(D) An exercise club

72. What will the listeners be able to do beginning in October?
(A) Participate in a competition
(B) Receive a consultation
(C) Access a database
(D) Purchase a new product

73. Why does the speaker invite the listeners to visit a Web site?
(A) To download a program
(B) To view some testimonials
(C) To read a manual
(D) To get some directions

74. Why does the speaker thank the listeners?
(A) For organizing a seminar
(B) For working overtime
(C) For conducting an interview
(D) For teaching a course

75. What will happen later this month?
(A) An athletic competition will take place.
(B) Some remodeling will be finished.
(C) A book fair will be held
(D) Some rooms will be booked.

76. What does the speaker mean when he says, "there's plenty of room"?
(A) Everybody will be able to attend an event.
(B) Accommodations are available at a hotel.
(C) A number of staff could be hired.
(D) Space is available to add a product to an exhibit.

77. For whom is Mr. Greenwald's advice intended?
(A) Web designers
(B) Event organizers
(C) Film producers
(D) Department heads

78. According to Mr. Greenwald, what is a good way to improve productivity?
(A) Offering better incentives
(B) Setting reasonable deadlines
(C) Taking regular breaks
(D) Reducing meeting times

79. What are the listeners encouraged to do?
(A) Watch some videos
(B) Read an article
(C) Download an application
(D) Call a radio station

80. Why is the speaker calling?
(A) To apologize for a mistake
(B) To explain a policy
(C) To reschedule a meeting
(D) To set up a delivery

81. What does the speaker say happened last week?
(A) A facility was closed for repairs.
(B) New products were launched.
(C) Some data were recorded incorrectly.
(D) Some employees were not available.

82. What will the company provide to the listener?
(A) Express shipping
(B) Complimentary shuttle service
(C) A seat upgrade
(D) A free meal

GO ON TO THE NEXT PAGE

83. Who is the speaker?

(A) A delivery person
(B) A product designer
(C) A store receptionist
(D) A plant manager

84. What does the company sell?

(A) Consumer electronics
(B) Automotive parts
(C) Office furniture
(D) Garden equipment

85. What does the speaker imply when he says, "I've only seen houses"?

(A) He believes an error was made.
(B) He is worried about a new housing rule.
(C) A construction permit cannot be provided.
(D) Some funds cannot be acquired.

---

86. What department does the speaker work in?

(A) Marketing
(B) Finance
(C) Administration
(D) Sales

87. What is the topic of the workshop?

(A) Creating detailed financial plans
(B) Presenting business proposals
(C) Reducing work-related stress
(D) Setting up client meetings

88. What will the listeners do next?

(A) Find a partner
(B) Complete a questionnaire
(C) Watch a video
(D) Discuss a contract

89. What is the message mainly about?

(A) Signing up for a cooking contest
(B) Updating some files
(C) Revising an itinerary
(D) Organizing a celebration

90. What does the speaker imply when she says, "I still can't believe what happened"?

(A) She is unhappy with the results of a competition.
(B) She misunderstood some instructions.
(C) She is surprised by a decision.
(D) She wants to avoid making a mistake again.

91. What is the speaker going to do after work?

(A) Visit a dining establishment
(B) Attend a performance
(C) Shop at a store
(D) Depart for a conference

---

92. Why is the speaker qualified to host the program?

(A) He has received many broadcasting awards.
(B) He has extensive work experience.
(C) He has studied business at a famous university.
(D) He has published many financial books.

93. Why does the speaker say, "having a booth at an expo isn't cheap"?

(A) To suggest paying in installments
(B) To agree with a professional's advice
(C) To refuse a request
(D) To acknowledge a common concern

94. What will the speaker most likely do next?

(A) Call some listeners
(B) Announce contest winners
(C) Sign up for a conference
(D) Give some detailed advice

Thursday	Friday	Saturday	Sunday
Rain	Cloudy	Sunny	Partly Cloudy

95. What event is being described?

(A) A charity function
(B) An art contest
(C) A sports competition
(D) A book fair

96. According to the speaker, what can the listeners find on a Web site?

(A) A weather report
(B) A list of participants
(C) A schedule of events
(D) A park map

97. Look at the graphic. On which day will the event be held?

(A) Thursday
(B) Friday
(C) Saturday
(D) Sunday

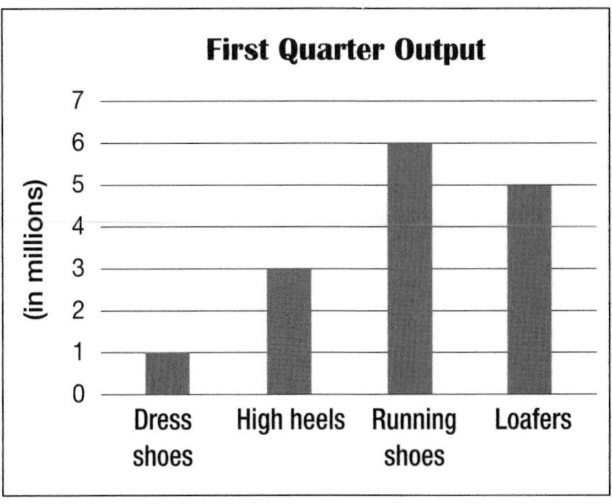

98. Who most likely are the listeners?

(A) Factory workers
(B) Sales associates
(C) Fashion designers
(D) Financial planners

99. Look at the graphic. Which category is the speaker concerned about?

(A) Dress shoes
(B) High heels
(C) Running shoes
(D) Loafers

100. What has the company decided to do?

(A) Purchase some equipment
(B) Delay a schedule
(C) Revise a safety policy
(D) Recruit more employees

This is the end of the Listening test.

ACTUAL TEST

LISTENING TEST 19

In the Listening test, you will be asked to demonstrate how well you understand spoken English. The entire Listening test will last approximately 45 minutes. There are four parts, and directions are given for each part. You must mark your answers on the separate answer sheet. Do not write your answers in your test book.

PART 1

Directions: For each question in this part, you will hear four statements about a picture in your test book. When you hear the statements, you must select the one statement that best describes what you see in the picture. Then find the number of the question on your answer sheet and mark your answer. The statements will not be printed in your test book and will be spoken only one time.

Example

Sample Answer

Ⓐ ● Ⓒ Ⓓ

Statement (B), "A man is pointing at a document," is the best description of the picture, so you should select answer (B) and mark it on your answer sheet.

1.

2.

GO ON TO THE NEXT PAGE

3.

4.

5.

6.

ACTUAL TEST 05

GO ON TO THE NEXT PAGE

PART 2 (20)

Directions: You will hear a question or statement and three responses spoken in English. They will not be printed in your test book and will be spoken only one time. Select the best response to the question or statement and mark the letter (A), (B), or (C) on your answer sheet.

7. Mark your answer on your answer sheet.

8. Mark your answer on your answer sheet.

9. Mark your answer on your answer sheet.

10. Mark your answer on your answer sheet.

11. Mark your answer on your answer sheet.

12. Mark your answer on your answer sheet.

13. Mark your answer on your answer sheet.

14. Mark your answer on your answer sheet.

15. Mark your answer on your answer sheet.

16. Mark your answer on your answer sheet.

17. Mark your answer on your answer sheet.

18. Mark your answer on your answer sheet.

19. Mark your answer on your answer sheet.

20. Mark your answer on your answer sheet.

21. Mark your answer on your answer sheet.

22. Mark your answer on your answer sheet.

23. Mark your answer on your answer sheet.

24. Mark your answer on your answer sheet.

25. Mark your answer on your answer sheet.

26. Mark your answer on your answer sheet.

27. Mark your answer on your answer sheet.

28. Mark your answer on your answer sheet.

29. Mark your answer on your answer sheet.

30. Mark your answer on your answer sheet.

31. Mark your answer on your answer sheet.

PART 3 (21)

Directions: You will hear some conversations between two or more people. You will be asked to answer three questions about what the speakers say in each conversation. Select the best response to each question and mark the letter (A), (B), (C), or (D) on your answer sheet. The conversations will not be printed in your test book and will be spoken only one time.

32. What is the main topic of the conversation?
(A) Renovating a cafeteria
(B) Reviewing research findings
(C) Designing some furniture
(D) Finding an event venue

33. What will happen during the first week of February?
(A) A budget proposal will be presented.
(B) A business will extend its office hours.
(C) A new CEO will be appointed.
(D) A company gathering will take place.

34. What will the woman most likely send in the afternoon?
(A) A blueprint
(B) Some pictures
(C) An invoice
(D) Some equipment

---

35. What is the main topic of the conversation?
(A) The recipes of a renowned chef
(B) Extending a store's business hours
(C) The availability of a special dish
(D) How to best advertise a restaurant

36. What does the man say will happen soon?
(A) A delivery will be made.
(B) A group of customers will arrive.
(C) Some new employees will be hired.
(D) Some products will become available.

37. What does the woman ask the man?
(A) How many customers are waiting
(B) Where a chef learned to cook
(C) What time he will be leaving
(D) If she should update the menu offerings

38. Who most likely are the women?
(A) Corporate lawyers
(B) New workers
(C) Fitness trainers
(D) Construction managers

39. What does the man say about the leisure facilities?
(A) The sauna is being renovated.
(B) They close early on the weekends.
(C) The membership fee has recently increased.
(D) They require a company ID to enter.

40. What will the women do after lunch?
(A) Participate in another building tour
(B) Meet some department members
(C) Listen to a speech
(D) Complete a questionnaire

---

41. Why is the man calling?
(A) To recommend a new office
(B) To request assistance with a computer
(C) To report a leak
(D) To reserve a meeting room

42. What does the woman say she will do?
(A) Revise a client list
(B) Send an employee to help
(C) Install an accounting program
(D) Call a utility company

43. What does the man say he will be doing at 3 o'clock?
(A) Meeting with a client
(B) Examining some documents
(C) Interviewing job applicants
(D) Leaving for a business trip

GO ON TO THE NEXT PAGE →

44. What industry do the speakers most likely work in?

(A) Food service
(B) Architecture
(C) Fine arts
(D) Packaging

45. What does the man mean when he says, "It's supposed to be delivered around 6 P.M."?

(A) He may not be available for a task.
(B) He will have to place a new order.
(C) He plans to request a refund.
(D) He is not satisfied with a service.

46. What does the man say about Corinna?

(A) She will enroll in a training workshop.
(B) She drives her car to the office.
(C) She is more experienced than him.
(D) She is interested in working more hours.

---

47. What is the woman preparing for?

(A) A business trip to Seoul
(B) An engineering seminar
(C) A corporate merger
(D) A meeting with investors

48. What is the woman calling about?

(A) A travel itinerary
(B) Translation services
(C) A conference room
(D) Contract details

49. What does the man offer to do?

(A) Make a reservation
(B) Send an email
(C) Refer a colleague
(D) Explain a schedule

50. What are the speakers discussing?

(A) An inventory check
(B) A finance presentation
(C) A business merger
(D) A television advertisement

51. What does the man say he is missing?

(A) A video file
(B) A signature
(C) A desk key
(D) An account password

52. What does the man ask the woman to do after lunch?

(A) Attend a committee meeting
(B) Submit an investment proposal
(C) Check a computer
(D) Review a contract

---

53. What will the woman do next week?

(A) Submit a research paper
(B) Give a guest lecture
(C) Publish a book
(D) Take an exam

54. What did Drew do in the morning?

(A) He edited a document.
(B) He met with a professor.
(C) He purchased office supplies.
(D) He delivered a package.

55. What does Drew ask the woman to do?

(A) Complete a form
(B) Come back later
(C) Present identification
(D) Visit another office

56. Who most likely are the speakers?
(A) Hotel workers
(B) Broadcasting executives
(C) Travel agents
(D) Restaurant employees

57. What does the man imply when he says, "but winter's nearly over"?
(A) The woman needs to finish an assignment quickly.
(B) A marketing campaign will be released too late.
(C) Some data in a sales report must be revised.
(D) He would like to take his vacation at a later time.

58. What will the woman do next?
(A) Speak with a supervisor
(B) Distribute a questionnaire
(C) Contact some businesses
(D) Print out additional flyers

---

59. Who most likely is the woman?
(A) A corporate accountant
(B) A delivery driver
(C) A sales representative
(D) A plant manager

60. What feature of the Pro-X Gauge does the man mention?
(A) It tracks packages.
(B) It monitors pressure levels.
(C) It records daily finances.
(D) It calculates shipping rates.

61. Why does the woman say she will call back tomorrow?
(A) She has to review a financial plan.
(B) She is late for a meeting.
(C) She requires her supervisor's authorization.
(D) She would like to check out other models.

Monthly Report	
Equipment Expenses	$9,000
Packaging Materials	$8,000
Property Rent	$6,000
Utilities (gas and electricity)	$1,000

62. What kind of product does the company most likely make?
(A) Office furniture
(B) Cleaning supplies
(C) Clothing
(D) Electronics

63. What does the woman point out about the report?
(A) Some monthly objectives were achieved.
(B) Some figures were incorrect.
(C) Some expenditures have gone up.
(D) Some sections are blank.

64. Look at the graphic. Which amount does the woman say might change?
(A) $9,000
(B) $8,000
(C) $6,000
(D) $1,000

GO ON TO THE NEXT PAGE

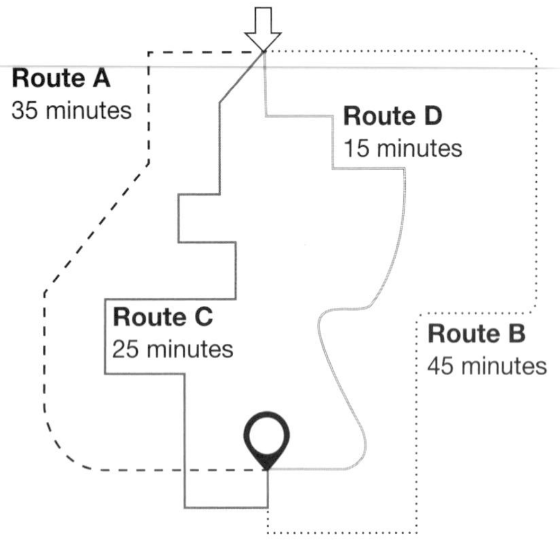

65. Why is the man driving the woman to work?
(A) Her public transit pass expired.
(B) She does not own a car.
(C) She recently moved to a new city.
(D) Her vehicle is being repaired.

66. What event does the man say is being held today?
(A) A retirement banquet
(B) A cycling competition
(C) An art exhibition
(D) A film festival

67. Look at the graphic. What route will the man probably take?
(A) Route A
(B) Route B
(C) Route C
(D) Route D

To	Raya Shah
From	Brian McFadder

Plant Location	Completion Date
Newcrest	July 31
Westmark	September 26
Callington	October 27
Plateforth	November 30

68. What did the speakers just attend?
(A) An employee meeting
(B) A factory tour
(C) A career fair
(D) A product demonstration

69. Look at the graphic. What date has to be changed?
(A) July 31
(B) September 26
(C) October 27
(D) November 30

70. What is causing a delay in construction?
(A) Some equipment is not working.
(B) Some materials have not been delivered.
(C) A building permit has been denied.
(D) An area has had inclement weather.

PART 4 (22)

Directions: You will hear some talks given by a single speaker. You will be asked to answer three questions about what the speaker says in each talk. Select the best response to each question and mark the letter (A), (B), (C), or (D) on your answer sheet. The talks will not be printed in your test book and will be spoken only one time.

71. According to the speaker, what event was postponed?
(A) A film festival
(B) A bicycle race
(C) A dance performance
(D) A cooking competition

72. Why was the event postponed?
(A) An application was rejected.
(B) A guest could not make it.
(C) Some funds were not secured.
(D) Some repair work needs to be done.

73. What will the listeners hear next?
(A) A new song
(B) A celebrity interview
(C) A traffic report
(D) A business advertisement

---

74. What happened in the afternoon?
(A) An old structure was sold.
(B) A movie premiere was held.
(C) A new product was released.
(D) An anniversary party took place.

75. According to the speaker, why was Wight and Company chosen?
(A) It knows how to do challenging renovations.
(B) It owns multiple shopping complexes.
(C) It will offer jobs to local residents.
(D) It has previously worked on government projects.

76. What do city council members hope to do?
(A) Increase revenue
(B) Hire better building designers
(C) Expand public transportation
(D) Construct more parks

77. What is the subject of the convention?
(A) Finance
(B) Agriculture
(C) Healthcare
(D) Travel

78. What does the speaker mean when she says, "I hope everyone brought plenty of business cards"?
(A) Identification cards are required for registration.
(B) Event organizers will be holding a raffle.
(C) There will be many networking opportunities.
(D) Some guests do not have name tags.

79. What does the speaker say is difficult?
(A) Preparing a presentation
(B) Managing a facility
(C) Securing a venue
(D) Quitting a role

---

80. What is the purpose of the message?
(A) To make changes to an order
(B) To request additional workers
(C) To inquire about office vacancies
(D) To explain details about a delivery

81. What does the speaker want the listener to do?
(A) Contact a factory supervisor
(B) Send a package to an office
(C) Review a company policy
(D) Allow access to a building

82. What does the speaker say he will be doing this morning?
(A) Training an employee
(B) Cleaning his apartment
(C) Working in his office
(D) Visiting a client

GO ON TO THE NEXT PAGE

83. What problem is being addressed?

(A) Inclement weather
(B) Passenger delays
(C) Technical difficulties
(D) Missing bags

84. What are listeners asked to do?

(A) Prepare to present documents
(B) Go to a different gate of the airport
(C) Complete a special request form
(D) Request a refund for a ticket

85. According to the speaker, what will attendants be doing?

(A) Checking departure times
(B) Issuing new tickets
(C) Offering shuttle service
(D) Distributing luggage tags

---

86. Why does the speaker say, "There was an unexpected turn of events"?

(A) Some equipment is not working.
(B) Some instruments are missing.
(C) A musician is arriving late.
(D) The venue is being renovated.

87. According to the speaker, what can be purchased in the lobby?

(A) Snacks and drinks
(B) Performance tickets
(C) An orchestra's recordings
(D) Signed posters of musicians

88. What is being advertised at the auditorium?

(A) Music lessons
(B) Upcoming performances
(C) Guided tours
(D) Famous restaurants

89. Where do the listeners most likely work?

(A) At an electronics manufacturer
(B) At a courier company
(C) At a security firm
(D) At a grocery store

90. Why does the speaker say, "All of this information is coming from our customers"?

(A) To emphasize the importance of a process
(B) To express her disagreement with an opinion
(C) To recognize the listeners' efforts
(D) To ensure listeners report to their supervisors

91. According to the speaker, what will a new manager start doing?

(A) Working on the weekends
(B) Visiting different branches
(C) Conducting inspections
(D) Purchasing replacement parts

---

92. What is the announcement mainly about?

(A) A revised safety policy
(B) A new office manager
(C) A conversion to an electronic database
(D) A directory of local health clinics

93. What is mentioned as an advantage of the change?

(A) There will be more free space.
(B) Information will be protected.
(C) There will be fewer accidents.
(D) Productivity will be increased.

94. What has the office manager been asked to do?

(A) Arrange for medical checkups
(B) Send patient records
(C) Contact a document-disposal company
(D) Create an employee evaluation form

Informational Sessions	
Monday	Advanced Computer Skills Course
Tuesday	Best Accounting Software Programs
Wednesday	Popular Social Networking Sites
Thursday	Effective Employee Motivation Techniques

95. Which department does the speaker most likely work in?

(A) Information Technology
(B) Marketing
(C) Accounting
(D) Human Resources

96. Look at the graphic. When are the listeners encouraged to attend a session?

(A) Monday
(B) Tuesday
(C) Wednesday
(D) Thursday

97. What will participants receive at every session?

(A) A free meal
(B) A certificate
(C) A bonus
(D) A survey form

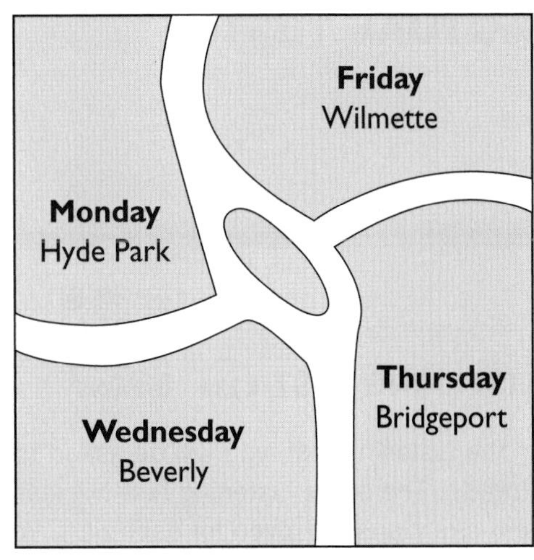

98. Where does the speaker most likely work?

(A) At a vehicle rental agency
(B) At a dental clinic
(C) At a recycling company
(D) At a public transportation service

99. Look at the graphic. Which neighborhood will be affected by a schedule change?

(A) Hyde Park
(B) Beverly
(C) Bridgeport
(D) Wilmette

100. What does the speaker hope to purchase?

(A) New machinery
(B) Packaging boxes
(C) A larger warehouse
(D) More advertising space

This is the end of the Listening test.

ACTUAL TEST 06

LISTENING TEST 23

In the Listening test, you will be asked to demonstrate how well you understand spoken English. The entire Listening test will last approximately 45 minutes. There are four parts, and directions are given for each part. You must mark your answers on the separate answer sheet. Do not write your answers in your test book.

PART 1

Directions: For each question in this part, you will hear four statements about a picture in your test book. When you hear the statements, you must select the one statement that best describes what you see in the picture. Then find the number of the question on your answer sheet and mark your answer. The statements will not be printed in your test book and will be spoken only one time.

Example

Sample Answer

Ⓐ ● Ⓒ Ⓓ

Statement (B), "A man is pointing at a document," is the best description of the picture, so you should select answer (B) and mark it on your answer sheet.

1.

2.

GO ON TO THE NEXT PAGE

3.

4.

5.

6.

GO ON TO THE NEXT PAGE

PART 2 (24) 

Directions: You will hear a question or statement and three responses spoken in English. They will not be printed in your test book and will be spoken only one time. Select the best response to the question or statement and mark the letter (A), (B), or (C) on your answer sheet.

7. Mark your answer on your answer sheet.

8. Mark your answer on your answer sheet.

9. Mark your answer on your answer sheet.

10. Mark your answer on your answer sheet.

11. Mark your answer on your answer sheet.

12. Mark your answer on your answer sheet.

13. Mark your answer on your answer sheet.

14. Mark your answer on your answer sheet.

15. Mark your answer on your answer sheet.

16. Mark your answer on your answer sheet.

17. Mark your answer on your answer sheet.

18. Mark your answer on your answer sheet.

19. Mark your answer on your answer sheet.

20. Mark your answer on your answer sheet.

21. Mark your answer on your answer sheet.

22. Mark your answer on your answer sheet.

23. Mark your answer on your answer sheet.

24. Mark your answer on your answer sheet.

25. Mark your answer on your answer sheet.

26. Mark your answer on your answer sheet.

27. Mark your answer on your answer sheet.

28. Mark your answer on your answer sheet.

29. Mark your answer on your answer sheet.

30. Mark your answer on your answer sheet.

31. Mark your answer on your answer sheet.

PART 3 (25)

Directions: You will hear some conversations between two or more people. You will be asked to answer three questions about what the speakers say in each conversation. Select the best response to each question and mark the letter (A), (B), (C), or (D) on your answer sheet. The conversations will not be printed in your test book and will be spoken only one time.

32. Where does the conversation probably take place?
(A) At a health clinic
(B) At a hotel
(C) At a restaurant
(D) At a law firm

33. Why does the man apologize?
(A) An invoice is incorrect.
(B) Some data was not saved.
(C) There are no more parking spaces.
(D) A product is defective.

34. What does the man encourage the woman to pick up?
(A) A parking permit
(B) A magazine
(C) Some forms
(D) Some refreshments

---

35. What does the man mention about the Telco Complex?
(A) It offers cheap rental rates.
(B) It is in a quiet neighborhood.
(C) It offers a free parking space.
(D) It is conveniently located.

36. What does the woman say she has done?
(A) She has purchased a vehicle.
(B) She has scheduled a meeting.
(C) She has quit her current job.
(D) She has contacted a relocation firm.

37. What does the man invite the woman to?
(A) A store opening
(B) A cooking contest
(C) A building tour
(D) A lunch gathering

38. Why did the man call the meeting?
(A) To discuss a budget report
(B) To give a new employee orientation
(C) To come up with some solutions
(D) To go over a revised policy

39. What will probably change at the business?
(A) A brochure
(B) A Web site
(C) Some operating hours
(D) Some devices

40. What will the man do next?
(A) Submit a payment
(B) Make an appointment
(C) Review some applications
(D) Install some equipment

---

41. What most likely is the woman's profession?
(A) Journalist
(B) Interior designer
(C) Software technician
(D) Realtor

42. Why does the woman say, "The work here will take me all day"?
(A) To turn down a request
(B) To approve a plan
(C) To volunteer for an assignment
(D) To ask for an extension

43. What does the man say he will do?
(A) Go to an office
(B) Purchase more supplies
(C) Check a colleague's schedule
(D) Contact a client

GO ON TO THE NEXT PAGE →

44. What did the woman recently do?
(A) Registered at a fitness center
(B) Exchanged a defective product
(C) Taught a business course
(D) Canceled enrollment in a class

45. What has caused a delay?
(A) A name was missing.
(B) A system malfunctioned.
(C) A form was incomplete.
(D) A payment was not made.

46. What does the man suggest?
(A) Signing up for another class
(B) Reading a manual
(C) Checking a Web site
(D) Coming back at a later time

---

47. What was the topic of the woman's lecture?
(A) Web site designs
(B) Vacation spots
(C) Self-publishing
(D) Popular books

48. What problem did the man have during the lecture?
(A) He had trouble finding a seat.
(B) He did not understand some material.
(C) He could not ask any questions.
(D) He was not able to write down some information.

49. What does the woman say she will send to attendees?
(A) Links to some Web sites
(B) A survey form
(C) A list of future events
(D) A copy of some slides

50. What kind of business does the woman work at?
(A) A utility company
(B) An appliance manufacturer
(C) An auto shop
(D) A catering business

51. What does the woman say the business is known for?
(A) Its affordable pricing
(B) Its helpful employees
(C) Its wide collection
(D) Its durable products

52. What problem does the man mention?
(A) Some merchandise is damaged.
(B) An item is missing.
(C) An extra fee has been charged.
(D) Some boxes are too heavy to transport.

---

53. Where does the woman probably work?
(A) At a party decoration shop
(B) At a packaging plant
(C) At a café
(D) At a hotel

54. Why does the man say, "Gallagher's Tavern's cheapest bottle is $25"?
(A) To correct a mistake
(B) To compliment a service
(C) To recommend an item
(D) To request a discount

55. How does the woman offer to assist the man?
(A) By refunding his purchase
(B) By letting him sample a product
(C) By reserving some merchandise
(D) By talking to a supervisor

56. What is the man asking for?

(A) Some job descriptions
(B) An increase in his salary
(C) More funds for a project
(D) Some time off from work

57. What is the woman concerned about?

(A) Achieving a sales target
(B) Impressing an important client
(C) Meeting a project deadline
(D) Recruiting skilled employees

58. What does the man say he can do?

(A) Accept additional assignments
(B) Train more staff members
(C) Post a vacation schedule
(D) Contact the human resources manager

---

59. What industry do the speakers most likely work in?

(A) Jewelry
(B) Healthcare
(C) Journalism
(D) Marketing

60. What is the problem?

(A) Some descriptions are inaccurate.
(B) An image is missing.
(C) A design is not good.
(D) Some materials were damaged.

61. What does the woman promise to do by the end of today?

(A) Install a program
(B) Create a new draft
(C) Send an invoice
(D) Call a business

Winter Suits Manufacturer: Groenlandia Ltd.	p. 3
Sweater Vests Manufacturer: La Lluvia	p. 6
Padded Jackets Manufacturer: Allons Co.	p. 9
Long Coats Manufacturer: Cara Norte	p. 11

62. What most likely is the man's job?

(A) Computer programmer
(B) Fashion designer
(C) Sales representative
(D) Personal trainer

63. Look at the graphic. Which manufacturer does the woman say she likes?

(A) Groenlandia Ltd.
(B) La Lluvia
(C) Allons Co.
(D) Cara Norte

64. What does the man offer to do?

(A) Provide a coupon
(B) Print a catalog
(C) Call a different branch
(D) Search a system

GO ON TO THE NEXT PAGE

Custom USB Flash Drives	
1 GB Memory	$5.25
2 GB Memory	$5.75
4 GB Memory	$6.00
8 GB Memory	$6.50

65. What does the woman plan to do with the flash drives?
(A) Display them at a shop
(B) Send them to her friends
(C) Sell them to some clients
(D) Give them to event guests

66. Look at the graphic. Which memory capacity does the woman decide to choose?
(A) 1 GB
(B) 2 GB
(C) 4 GB
(D) 8 GB

67. What does the man suggest?
(A) Calling another store
(B) Selecting a different product
(C) Adjusting the quantity of an order
(D) Revising a budget

Arriving From	Time	Status
Dalian	2:30 P.M.	Arrived
Tianjin	2:55 P.M.	Arrived
Fukuoka	3:25 P.M.	On schedule
Vladivostok	3:40 P.M.	Delayed

68. Look at the graphic. Which city is Michelle Funakoshi traveling from?
(A) Dalian
(B) Tianjin
(C) Fukuoka
(D) Vladivostok

69. According to the woman, why should the speakers leave soon?
(A) A highway is inaccessible.
(B) Tickets must be bought in advance.
(C) A store will be closing within the hour.
(D) The port is undergoing construction.

70. What does the man suggest doing while they wait?
(A) Going over a presentation
(B) Touring a facility
(C) Checking a map
(D) Getting a beverage

PART 4 (26)

Directions: You will hear some talks given by a single speaker. You will be asked to answer three questions about what the speaker says in each talk. Select the best response to each question and mark the letter (A), (B), (C), or (D) on your answer sheet. The talks will not be printed in your test book and will be spoken only one time.

71. Why is the speaker contacting the listener?
(A) To arrange a transportation service
(B) To check a client's schedule
(C) To postpone an appointment
(D) To discuss a job advertisement

72. What is the speaker doing tomorrow afternoon?
(A) Filming a commercial
(B) Going on a business trip
(C) Holding a training session for new employees
(D) Sharing information about some projects

73. What does the speaker recommend that the listener do?
(A) Contact a business
(B) Book a larger conference room
(C) Speak to another coworker
(D) Register for a marketing class

---

74. What industry does Mr. Sawada work in?
(A) Information Technology
(B) Healthcare
(C) Engineering
(D) Finance

75. What main accomplishment is Mr. Sawada recognized for?
(A) Making financial donations
(B) Improving work conditions
(C) Revising a national curriculum
(D) Developing a computer program

76. According to the speaker, what will Mr. Sawada do next?
(A) Provide a demonstration
(B) Tour a building
(C) Present an award
(D) Attend a book signing

77. What does the speaker imply when he says, "there seems to be a lot of construction on the highway"?
(A) He is going to take public transportation.
(B) He wants to change a project location.
(C) He will arrive late to a meeting.
(D) He is unable to hear the listener's message.

78. What will the speaker send to the listener?
(A) A list of participants
(B) A proposal
(C) An invoice
(D) Directions to an office

79. What does the speaker want Jeanell to do?
(A) Prepare a report
(B) Contact a client
(C) Conduct some training
(D) Transfer some money

---

80. What product is being advertised?
(A) A software program
(B) A video recorder
(C) A mobile phone
(D) A laptop computer

81. What does the speaker say is special about the product?
(A) It has an extended warranty.
(B) It supports any language.
(C) It includes instructional material.
(D) It can be custom-made.

82. Why should listeners visit a Web site?
(A) To order a product
(B) To sign up for a lesson
(C) To download a user guide
(D) To read customer testimonials

GO ON TO THE NEXT PAGE →

83. Who most likely are the listeners?

(A) Job recruiters
(B) Event coordinators
(C) Financial advisors
(D) Local reporters

84. What does the speaker imply when she says, "the application deadline is at the end of the month"?

(A) She is planning to extend a deadline.
(B) She does not want the listeners to worry.
(C) Some guidelines need to be revised.
(D) Some fees have not been received.

85. Why should the listeners talk to the speaker after the meeting?

(A) To borrow some materials
(B) To submit a payment
(C) To join a project group
(D) To decide on some menu items

---

86. Where most likely is the talk being given?

(A) At a training session
(B) At a company dinner
(C) At a job fair
(D) At a sales meeting

87. What does the speaker say is broken?

(A) A phone
(B) A speaker
(C) A camera
(D) A projector

88. What will the listeners do next?

(A) Give a presentation
(B) Obtain identification badges
(C) Report to their managers
(D) Enter some data

89. What does the man imply when he says, "Who can say how long that will take"?

(A) He wants the exact completion date of a project.
(B) He is requesting suggestions from the listeners.
(C) He would like staff members to work more hours.
(D) He does not know when a merger will be finalized.

90. What is the subject of the meeting?

(A) Expanding a product line
(B) Opening a new store
(C) Increasing profits
(D) Finding a different supplier

91. What does the man say he will make some time to do?

(A) Visit various branches
(B) Conduct individual meetings
(C) Revise some legal documents
(D) Contact a Dos Mundos employee

---

92. What was recently authorized?

(A) The construction of some residential buildings
(B) The opening of a community library
(C) The extension of some subway lines
(D) The restoration of a historic museum

93. According to the speaker, what is an advantage of a location?

(A) The area is quiet.
(B) A fitness facility is nearby.
(C) There are many parking spaces.
(D) The scenery is beautiful.

94. Why are listeners encouraged to visit a Web site?

(A) To sign up for a membership
(B) To watch a video
(C) To fill out a survey
(D) To download some files

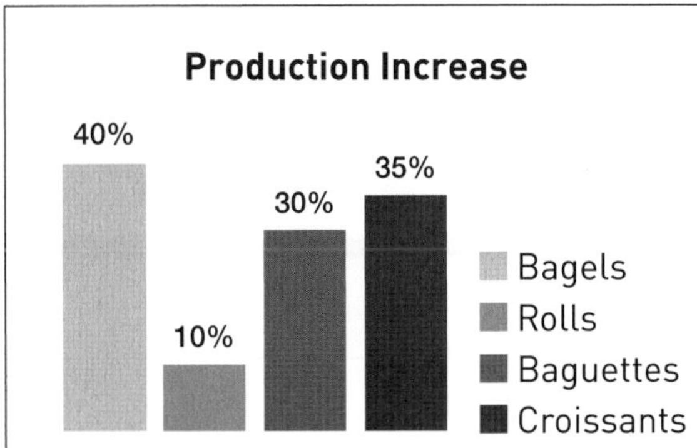

Nutrition Facts

Serving size - 1 Bar

Calories 180

Sodium - 210mg

Fiber - 8g

Sugar - 25g

Potassium - 150mg

95. Who is the message for?

(A) A bakery manager
(B) A warehouse supervisor
(C) A machinery salesperson
(D) A food importer

96. Look at the graphic. Which product's production does the speaker mention?

(A) Bagels
(B) Rolls
(C) Baguettes
(D) Croissants

97. What will happen at the end of the month?

(A) Building renovation will start.
(B) New products will be offered.
(C) A special offer will expire.
(D) A demonstration will be given.

98. What is the main purpose of the meeting?

(A) To introduce a new employee
(B) To discuss the sales of a product
(C) To announce the building of a new plant
(D) To describe a manufacturing process

99. What type of business is Fresh and Good?

(A) A grocery store
(B) A restaurant
(C) A local farm
(D) A food manufacturer

100. Look at the graphic. Which of the ingredients does the speaker say needs to be reduced?

(A) Sodium
(B) Fiber
(C) Sugar
(D) Potassium

This is the end of the Listening test.

ACTUAL TEST 07

LISTENING TEST 27

In the Listening test, you will be asked to demonstrate how well you understand spoken English. The entire Listening test will last approximately 45 minutes. There are four parts, and directions are given for each part. You must mark your answers on the separate answer sheet. Do not write your answers in your test book.

PART 1

Directions: For each question in this part, you will hear four statements about a picture in your test book. When you hear the statements, you must select the one statement that best describes what you see in the picture. Then find the number of the question on your answer sheet and mark your answer. The statements will not be printed in your test book and will be spoken only one time.

Example

Sample Answer

Ⓐ ● Ⓒ Ⓓ

Statement (B), "A man is pointing at a document," is the best description of the picture, so you should select answer (B) and mark it on your answer sheet.

1.

2.

GO ON TO THE NEXT PAGE

3.

4.

5.

ACTUAL TEST 07

6.

GO ON TO THE NEXT PAGE

PART 2 28

Directions: You will hear a question or statement and three responses spoken in English. They will not be printed in your test book and will be spoken only one time. Select the best response to the question or statement and mark the letter (A), (B), or (C) on your answer sheet.

7. Mark your answer on your answer sheet.

8. Mark your answer on your answer sheet.

9. Mark your answer on your answer sheet.

10. Mark your answer on your answer sheet.

11. Mark your answer on your answer sheet.

12. Mark your answer on your answer sheet.

13. Mark your answer on your answer sheet.

14. Mark your answer on your answer sheet.

15. Mark your answer on your answer sheet.

16. Mark your answer on your answer sheet.

17. Mark your answer on your answer sheet.

18. Mark your answer on your answer sheet.

19. Mark your answer on your answer sheet.

20. Mark your answer on your answer sheet.

21. Mark your answer on your answer sheet.

22. Mark your answer on your answer sheet.

23. Mark your answer on your answer sheet.

24. Mark your answer on your answer sheet.

25. Mark your answer on your answer sheet.

26. Mark your answer on your answer sheet.

27. Mark your answer on your answer sheet.

28. Mark your answer on your answer sheet.

29. Mark your answer on your answer sheet.

30. Mark your answer on your answer sheet.

31. Mark your answer on your answer sheet.

PART 3 (29)

Directions: You will hear some conversations between two or more people. You will be asked to answer three questions about what the speakers say in each conversation. Select the best response to each question and mark the letter (A), (B), (C), or (D) on your answer sheet. The conversations will not be printed in your test book and will be spoken only one time.

32. What would the man like to do tomorrow?
(A) Leave the office early
(B) Speak to a client
(C) Work from home
(D) Make a presentation

33. What is the woman concerned about?
(A) Losing customers
(B) Submitting work late
(C) Holding a conference
(D) Finding some paperwork

34. What does the woman say will happen next week?
(A) A business will open.
(B) A proposal will be given.
(C) A machine will be installed.
(D) A new employee will be hired.

---

35. What most likely is the woman's job?
(A) Travel agent
(B) Bus driver
(C) Telephone operator
(D) Hotel clerk

36. What does the man ask the woman to do?
(A) Direct him to a tour company
(B) Make a lunch reservation for him
(C) Take a message for him
(D) Move him to a larger room

37. What does the woman offer to do?
(A) Arrange transportation
(B) Ask for directions
(C) Purchase a ticket
(D) Inquire about a schedule

38. What would the woman like the man to do?
(A) Give a demonstration
(B) Revise some designs
(C) Fix some machines
(D) Visit an office

39. Why is the woman unavailable on Friday?
(A) She will be meeting her parents.
(B) She will be on a business trip.
(C) She will be getting a medical check-up.
(D) She will be leaving on vacation.

40. What does the man remind the woman to do?
(A) Print out a map
(B) Review an invoice
(C) Arrive before a certain time
(D) Talk to a store manager

---

41. What does the woman say will happen today?
(A) Kitchen appliances will be installed.
(B) A corporate event will take place.
(C) Repair work will begin.
(D) A plant inspection will be performed.

42. What is the woman worried about?
(A) Losing customers
(B) Spending more money
(C) Delayed shipments
(D) Power outages

43. What does the man offer to do?
(A) Contact some customers
(B) Work additional hours
(C) Order some supplies
(D) Display a sign

GO ON TO THE NEXT PAGE

44. What is the main topic of the conversation?
(A) Arranging travel accommodations
(B) Changing an event coordinator
(C) Planning a musical performance
(D) Selecting a better venue

45. What does Donna instruct the man to do?
(A) Meet with some clients
(B) Conduct some research
(C) Monitor a budget
(D) Review a floor plan

46. What does Donna say she looks forward to?
(A) Going on international business trips
(B) Managing a new team
(C) Working on a promotional campaign
(D) Receiving an award

---

47. Who most likely is the man?
(A) An insurance agent
(B) A receptionist
(C) A cleaning worker
(D) A technician

48. Why did the woman visit the office?
(A) To make a delivery
(B) To complete an application
(C) To submit a payment
(D) To visit a colleague

49. What does the man mean when he says, "Ms. Dorsett has just stepped out for lunch"?
(A) He will order some lunch.
(B) Ms. Dorsett is unavailable.
(C) Ms. Dorsett forgot about an appointment.
(D) A meeting must be postponed.

50. Why does the man apologize to the woman?
(A) He did not respond to a telephone message.
(B) He is not able to complete a project on time.
(C) He will be late for a meeting.
(D) He submitted the wrong document.

51. What must be ready by Tuesday?
(A) An employee questionnaire
(B) An expense report
(C) A client presentation
(D) A flight itinerary

52. What does the woman request that the man do?
(A) Pick up a customer
(B) Collaborate with a colleague
(C) Reserve a meeting room
(D) Hire a consultant

---

53. What did the man recently do?
(A) He returned from his vacation.
(B) He moved to a new city.
(C) He purchased swimming gear.
(D) He started working at a new company.

54. What does the woman mean when she says, "I think that should be OK"?
(A) A membership fee will be discounted.
(B) A schedule can be adjusted.
(C) The man can pay by credit card.
(D) The man will be able to upgrade his service.

55. What will the man probably do next?
(A) Email the woman a file
(B) Sign up for some classes
(C) Provide some information
(D) Look around a facility

56. What upcoming event are the speakers talking about?
(A) A business trip
(B) A retirement celebration
(C) A holiday party
(D) A board meeting

57. What problem occurred last year?
(A) Some documents were lost.
(B) Some equipment was damaged.
(C) A reservation was lost.
(D) A budget was exceeded.

58. What does Michael say he will do?
(A) Make a deposit
(B) Conduct some research
(C) Contact a manager
(D) Review some itineraries

---

59. What change does the woman suggest?
(A) Renovating a Web site
(B) Ordering from another company
(C) Hiring additional workers
(D) Lowering some prices

60. What does the man mean when he says, "that doesn't really apply to us"?
(A) A service fee cannot be waived.
(B) An item cannot be shipped.
(C) A coupon cannot be used.
(D) A policy cannot be changed.

61. What might staff be asked to do?
(A) Fill out forms in advance
(B) Purchase less than usual
(C) Make deliveries
(D) Train employees

Train Timetable

	Hemsforth	Bertiz	Faverton	Poly
XB10 Train	2:20 P.M.	2:50 P.M.		3:40 P.M.
XB20 Train	2:50 P.M.	3:05 P.M.	3:20 P.M.	

62. What is the woman's problem?
(A) An express train has just departed.
(B) A train is experiencing mechanical issues.
(C) She brought an expired train ticket.
(D) She boarded the wrong train.

63. Look at the graphic. At which station should the woman transfer?
(A) Hemsforth
(B) Bertiz
(C) Faverton
(D) Poly

64. Why is the woman in a hurry?
(A) She will be speaking at a conference.
(B) She is going to watch a performance.
(C) She needs to get on a train.
(D) She is interviewing for a job.

GO ON TO THE NEXT PAGE

	Name	Award
1	**Stacey Roberts**	Investment Management
2	**Brian Lee**	Global Pension
3	**Richard Kim**	Corporate Finance
4	**Jamie Brown**	Real Estate

65. Who is the man?

(A) An event planner
(B) An executive officer
(C) An awards presenter
(D) A job applicant

66. What is mentioned about the Reinheim Consulting Group?

(A) It is located overseas.
(B) It offers group sessions.
(C) It has a position open.
(D) It specializes in advertising.

67. Look at the graphic. Who most likely will the man talk to next?

(A) Stacey Roberts
(B) Brian Lee
(C) Richard Kim
(D) Jamie Brown

Discount Coupon

Order for 100 business cards → $5 OFF
Order for 200 business cards → $10 OFF
Order for 300 business cards → $15 OFF
Order for 400 business cards → $20 OFF

68. Why is the man calling?

(A) To reschedule a delivery
(B) To increase an order
(C) To apply for a membership card
(D) To inquire about an invoice

69. Where does the woman probably work?

(A) At a printing company
(B) At a flower shop
(C) At a bookstore
(D) At a bank

70. Look at the graphic. What discount will the man most likely receive?

(A) $5
(B) $10
(C) $15
(D) $20

PART 4 30

Directions: You will hear some talks given by a single speaker. You will be asked to answer three questions about what the speaker says in each talk. Select the best response to each question and mark the letter (A), (B), (C), or (D) on your answer sheet. The talks will not be printed in your test book and will be spoken only one time.

71. According to the speaker, what is scheduled for the afternoon?
(A) A store opening
(B) A road closure
(C) A sports event
(D) A musical performance

72. What does the speaker suggest for the people traveling to the city center?
(A) Sharing cars
(B) Allowing extra time
(C) Taking a detour
(D) Bringing an umbrella

73. Who is Michael Robinson?
(A) A news reporter
(B) A rock musician
(C) A financial expert
(D) A city official

74. Why does the speaker thank the listener?
(A) For attending a convention
(B) For opening up a business
(C) For submitting a payment
(D) For preparing a presentation

75. What does the speaker imply when he says, "I'm driving to the convention center now"?
(A) He does not know where to park.
(B) He cannot make it to a meeting on time.
(C) He is unable to take care of an issue.
(D) He needs to take an alternate route.

76. According to the speaker, what will happen in the afternoon?
(A) An order will be placed.
(B) A sale will start.
(C) Some devices will be installed.
(D) Some documents will be mailed.

77. What is the speaker discussing?
(A) Hiring a head chef
(B) Relocating a corporate office
(C) Changing a menu
(D) Renovating a diner

78. What does the speaker say Harold will help do?
(A) Train some kitchen workers
(B) Create some healthy recipes
(C) Manage a new restaurant location
(D) Find a different food supplier

79. According to the speaker, what is the purpose of the change?
(A) To retain current personnel
(B) To lower business expenses
(C) To improve employee morale
(D) To bring in more customers

80. What problem is the speaker addressing?
(A) Some project deadlines will not be met.
(B) A contract has not been finalized.
(C) Some time-recording information is out of date.
(D) A client account has been terminated.

81. What are listeners instructed to do?
(A) Correct their timesheets
(B) Meet their clients
(C) Remove current software
(D) Use new passwords

82. Why should listeners contact Perry Kay?
(A) To resolve customer complaints
(B) To update contact information
(C) To request a code
(D) To submit a proposal

GO ON TO THE NEXT PAGE →

83. Where is the introduction taking place?

(A) At a fundraising banquet
(B) At a professional conference
(C) At a training seminar
(D) At an awards ceremony

84. Who is Charlene Young?

(A) A human resources manager
(B) A chief executive officer
(C) An environmental engineer
(D) An event organizer

85. What does the speaker mean when she says, "compliments of Barry's Corner"?

(A) Beverages were supplied by a business.
(B) A company has received positive feedback.
(C) Food was catered by a restaurant.
(D) A demonstration was given by an organization.

---

86. What has the company recently done?

(A) Bought new equipment
(B) Received customer feedback
(C) Recruited more employees
(D) Updated a computer system

87. What does the speaker say was surprising?

(A) Complaints about a product
(B) Costs of delivery
(C) Forecasts of sales
(D) Advancements in technology

88. What does the speaker ask Brian to do?

(A) Complete a questionnaire
(B) Lead a group
(C) Try out a product
(D) Visit a store

89. What is being advertised?

(A) A digital camera
(B) A fitness watch
(C) A computer
(D) A television

90. What does the speaker emphasize about the product?

(A) It is colorful.
(B) It is affordable.
(C) It is lightweight.
(D) It is durable.

91. Why should the listeners visit a Web site?

(A) To check out user reviews
(B) To reserve an item
(C) To find a store location
(D) To obtain a discount voucher

---

92. What industry is the speaker reporting on?

(A) Hospitality
(B) Construction
(C) Finance
(D) Agriculture

93. According to the speaker, what benefit will the project provide to the public?

(A) Access to cheaper products
(B) Better financing options
(C) More job openings
(D) Improvement of public health

94. What does the speaker imply when she says, "this is an enormous task"?

(A) A budget should be adjusted.
(B) More workers should be hired.
(C) Extra time may be needed.
(D) A larger venue may be required.

Sushi Heaven
Private parties welcome! Book a banquet hall for 5 hours! 20% discount for groups of 20 or more! Offer valid at all Sushi Heaven locations until October 21.

95. Why is the event being held?

(A) To reward some employees
(B) To mark a company's anniversary
(C) To welcome new staff
(D) To celebrate an office relocation

96. Look at the graphic. Why is the speaker unable to use the coupon for the event?

(A) The coupon does not apply to large groups.
(B) The coupon will expire before the event takes place.
(C) The event will run longer than anticipated.
(D) The event will be held on the weekend.

97. What does the speaker want the listener to do?

(A) Decide on a venue
(B) Provide a meal preference
(C) Make a deposit
(D) Create a list

Bus 909 Timetable	
Union Drive	12:10 P.M.
Market Lane	12:25 P.M.
Oakwood Avenue	12:40 P.M.
Orchard Road	12:55 P.M.

98. Who most likely is the speaker?

(A) A career advisor
(B) A construction manager
(C) A public transportation official
(D) A real estate agent

99. What does the speaker remind the listener to do?

(A) Sign a document
(B) Retrieve an item
(C) Review a reservation
(D) Make a deposit

100. Look at the graphic. When would the listener board the bus?

(A) 12:10 P.M.
(B) 12:25 P.M.
(C) 12:40 P.M.
(D) 12:55 P.M.

This is the end of the Listening test.

ACTUAL TEST 08

LISTING TEST 31

In the Listening test, you will be asked to demonstrate how well you understand spoken English. The entire Listening test will last approximately 45 minutes. There are four parts, and directions are given for each part. You must mark your answers on the separate answer sheet. Do not write your answers in your test book.

PART 1

Directions: For each question in this part, you will hear four statements about a picture in your test book. When you hear the statements, you must select the one statement that best describes what you see in the picture. Then find the number of the question on your answer sheet and mark your answer. The statements will not be printed in your test book and will be spoken only one time.

Example

Statement (B), "A man is pointing at a document," is the best description of the picture, so you should select answer (B) and mark it on your answer sheet.

1.

2.

GO ON TO THE NEXT PAGE

3.

4.

5.

6.

GO ON TO THE NEXT PAGE

PART 2 (32)

Directions: You will hear a question or statement and three responses spoken in English. They will not be printed in your test book and will be spoken only one time. Select the best response to the question or statement and mark the letter (A), (B), or (C) on your answer sheet.

7. Mark your answer on your answer sheet.

8. Mark your answer on your answer sheet.

9. Mark your answer on your answer sheet.

10. Mark your answer on your answer sheet.

11. Mark your answer on your answer sheet.

12. Mark your answer on your answer sheet.

13. Mark your answer on your answer sheet.

14. Mark your answer on your answer sheet.

15. Mark your answer on your answer sheet.

16. Mark your answer on your answer sheet.

17. Mark your answer on your answer sheet.

18. Mark your answer on your answer sheet.

19. Mark your answer on your answer sheet.

20. Mark your answer on your answer sheet.

21. Mark your answer on your answer sheet.

22. Mark your answer on your answer sheet.

23. Mark your answer on your answer sheet.

24. Mark your answer on your answer sheet.

25. Mark your answer on your answer sheet.

26. Mark your answer on your answer sheet.

27. Mark your answer on your answer sheet.

28. Mark your answer on your answer sheet.

29. Mark your answer on your answer sheet.

30. Mark your answer on your answer sheet.

31. Mark your answer on your answer sheet.

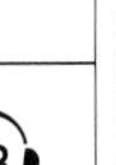

PART 3 (33)

Directions: You will hear some conversations between two or more people. You will be asked to answer three questions about what the speakers say in each conversation. Select the best response to each question and mark the letter (A), (B), (C), or (D) on your answer sheet. The conversations will not be printed in your test book and will be spoken only one time.

32. What kind of business do the speakers most likely work for?
(A) A public library
(B) An architecture firm
(C) A printing shop
(D) A history museum

33. What problem is being discussed?
(A) Some supplies are running low.
(B) Some paperwork is missing.
(C) Some glass is dirty.
(D) Some expenses are too high.

34. What will the woman probably do next?
(A) Install some equipment
(B) Contact some businesses
(C) Review a budget
(D) Make a deposit

---

35. Why is the man calling?
(A) To inquire about a bill
(B) To report a gas leak
(C) To open an account
(D) To cancel a service

36. Why is the woman unable to help the man?
(A) He lost his password.
(B) He called the wrong department.
(C) The company's office is not open.
(D) A Web site is down.

37. What will the man probably do next?
(A) Visit a Web site
(B) Provide a confirmation number
(C) Call another company
(D) Complete an application

38. What does the man say has caused a problem?
(A) Some damaged machines
(B) Inclement weather
(C) Heavy traffic
(D) An old booking system

39. What is the woman planning to do tomorrow?
(A) Get a medical check-up
(B) Attend a seminar
(C) Fix a computer
(D) Visit a factory

40. Why does the man say, "there's a train that leaves at 8 o'clock"?
(A) To recommend an alternative choice
(B) To provide a seat upgrade
(C) To offer an explanation for a delay
(D) To point out an error

---

41. Where is the man calling from?
(A) An apartment management office
(B) A hotel front desk
(C) A furniture store
(D) A construction company

42. What problem are the speakers discussing?
(A) A water leak
(B) A reservation error
(C) Some missing orders
(D) Some defective cables

43. What does the woman request?
(A) An exchange for a product
(B) A discount on a service
(C) A list of replacement parts
(D) An inspection for damage

GO ON TO THE NEXT PAGE →

44. What does the man want to purchase?

(A) Gym equipment
(B) Office supplies
(C) Advertising space
(D) Promotional clothing

45. How can the man receive a discount?

(A) By subscribing to a magazine
(B) By placing a large order
(C) By signing up for a membership
(D) By paying in cash

46. What does the woman tell the man to do?

(A) Visit another location
(B) Speak to a supervisor
(C) Go to a Web site
(D) Check out a sample

---

47. What is the company's plan?

(A) To increase energy efficiency
(B) To reduce travel expenses
(C) To open an overseas branch
(D) To elect new board members

48. What is the woman considering?

(A) Submitting a proposal
(B) Contacting an organizer
(C) Joining a committee
(D) Performing a survey

49. Why is the man unable to attend the meeting?

(A) He is picking up a client.
(B) He is giving a presentation.
(C) He is training an employee.
(D) He is going on a vacation.

50. What type of event are the speakers discussing?

(A) A music festival
(B) A gallery opening
(C) A business seminar
(D) A company party

51. What does the woman ask the man to do?

(A) Transport some equipment
(B) Reserve a reception hall
(C) Set up some tables
(D) Contact a band

52. What does the man say he has to do Sunday morning?

(A) Practice a musical instrument
(B) Attend a sporting event
(C) Work extra hours
(D) Get his car repaired

---

53. Who most likely are Mr. Anderson and Ms. Walsh?

(A) Real estate agents
(B) Business owners
(C) Construction workers
(D) City officials

54. What are Mr. Anderson and Ms. Walsh concerned about?

(A) Paying for major renovations
(B) Attracting more clients
(C) The size of an office space
(D) The date of a move

55. What is mentioned about the landlord?

(A) He will meet the speakers tomorrow.
(B) He will negotiate a price.
(C) He is currently on a business trip.
(D) He is relocating overseas.

56. What industry do the speakers most likely work in?

(A) Clothing manufacturing
(B) Event organizing
(C) Equipment sales
(D) Food production

57. What problem are the speakers discussing?

(A) A customer complaint was received.
(B) The quality of a product is poor.
(C) Some tools have not been cleaned.
(D) More workers are needed.

58. What does the man suggest?

(A) Lowering prices
(B) Informing a manager
(C) Discarding some materials
(D) Replacing a machine

---

59. Who is visiting the company?

(A) A property manager
(B) A local journalist
(C) A government employee
(D) An overseas client

60. Why does the man say, "I'm leading a workshop all day on Friday"?

(A) He is unable to take on a task.
(B) He would like some help with an event.
(C) He would like an updated guest list.
(D) He is concerned about giving a presentation.

61. According to the woman, what does the company hope to do by the end of the year?

(A) Transfer some workers
(B) Launch a product line
(C) Build another facility
(D) Appoint a new CEO

Mallie's Place

Dessert Deals for May

Strawberry Pie – 10% OFF
Vanilla Ice Cream – 20% OFF
Chocolate Cake – 30% OFF
Banana Pudding – 40% OFF

62. What information does the woman share with the man?

(A) A product will be launched early.
(B) A managers' meeting will be held.
(C) A contract will be awarded soon.
(D) A colleague will be transferred.

63. Look at the graphic. Which discount will the speakers most likely receive?

(A) 10%
(B) 20%
(C) 30%
(D) 40%

64. What does the man offer to do?

(A) Update a calendar
(B) Contact a different café
(C) Make a reservation
(D) Rent a vehicle

GO ON TO THE NEXT PAGE

65. What does the woman say is the target market for Max Energy Bar?
(A) Food experts
(B) Traveling workers
(C) Fitness enthusiasts
(D) Senior citizens

66. Look at the graphic. What will be displayed at the top of the bar wrapper after a change?
(A) The firm's logo
(B) The product's name
(C) The energy meter
(D) The price

67. What is scheduled for next week?
(A) An industry convention
(B) A store opening
(C) A client visit
(D) A sales event

HEALTH AWARENESS WEEK

Only open to LCO Employees
Free Admission!

Mon	Tue	Wed	Thu	Fri
Medical Consultations	Nutrition Seminar	Cooking Class	Farm Visit	Well-being Lunch

68. What does the woman say is new about the Health Awareness Week this year?
(A) A contest will be held.
(B) A movie will be shown to staff.
(C) Presents will be provided to staff.
(D) Celebrities will be signing autographs.

69. Look at the graphic. Which event will the woman probably attend?
(A) The medical consultations
(B) The nutrition seminar
(C) The cooking class
(D) The farm visit

70. What does the man ask the woman to do?
(A) Contact some department managers
(B) Review an order form
(C) Complete a questionnaire
(D) Distribute some materials

PART 4 

Directions: You will hear some talks given by a single speaker. You will be asked to answer three questions about what the speaker says in each talk. Select the best response to each question and mark the letter (A), (B), (C), or (D) on your answer sheet. The talks will not be printed in your test book and will be spoken only one time.

71. Who is the intended audience for the talk?
(A) Sales staff members
(B) Delivery drivers
(C) Factory employees
(D) Security guards

72. What is mentioned as an advantage of the new machines?
(A) They work faster.
(B) They seldom malfunction.
(C) They are reasonably priced.
(D) They are energy-efficient.

73. What is the speaker about to do?
(A) Give a demonstration
(B) Place an order
(C) Attend a meeting
(D) Call a supplier

---

74. Which department in Culliver Hills recorded the message?
(A) Health
(B) Transportation
(C) Parks and Recreation
(D) Planning and Development

75. According to the message, why is a procedure taking longer to complete?
(A) More applications are being received.
(B) A community center is being renovated.
(C) There has been a shortage of workers.
(D) There has been inclement weather.

76. What does the speaker ask the listeners to do?
(A) Meet with a city official
(B) Submit a payment
(C) Present a photo ID
(D) Include a detailed description

77. What does the speaker imply when she says, "you won't be late for any of your appointments"?
(A) Appointments must be canceled in advance.
(B) Some members have complained.
(C) Workers should come to work on time.
(D) A meeting will be short.

78. What does the speaker say happened on Monday?
(A) An expert examined a business.
(B) A fitness center closed early.
(C) A promotional event was held.
(D) A new policy was announced.

79. According to the speaker, what will the listeners practice?
(A) Building customer relationships
(B) Selling some products
(C) Cooking healthy meals
(D) Installing exercise machines

---

80. What type of business do the listeners work for?
(A) A post office
(B) A stationery store
(C) A printing center
(D) A health clinic

81. According to the speaker, what is being changed?
(A) How work schedules are created
(B) How payments are processed
(C) How information is recorded
(D) How facilities are inspected

82. What will the listeners do next?
(A) Fill out some forms
(B) Use some devices
(C) Watch a demonstration
(D) Read a user guide

GO ON TO THE NEXT PAGE →

83. What type of event is taking place?

(A) A business opening
(B) A product launch
(C) A marketing presentation
(D) A retirement party

84. Why was the event delayed?

(A) Some devices were not working.
(B) A speaker arrived late.
(C) A facility was being cleaned.
(D) Some bad weather was approaching.

85. What does the speaker imply when she says, "I have extras here in the front"?

(A) Some listeners should pick up a document.
(B) Complimentary beverages are available.
(C) Tickets will be given away.
(D) Attendees should return some merchandise.

---

86. What is the purpose of the announcement?

(A) To describe a new printer
(B) To outline safety regulations
(C) To announce an upcoming inspection
(D) To share some sales figures

87. What benefit does the speaker mention?

(A) Less maintenance work
(B) Increased sales
(C) Reduced damage to the environment
(D) Greater morale among employees

88. According to the speaker, why have two training sessions been scheduled?

(A) To ensure sufficient practice time
(B) To accommodate all employees
(C) To meet a project deadline
(D) To comply with company policy

89. Why does the speaker apologize?

(A) A machine is not working.
(B) A presentation was canceled.
(C) A program was inaccurate.
(D) A registration procedure was confusing.

90. Who most likely is Mr. Griffin?

(A) An event organizer
(B) A financial advisor
(C) A building manager
(D) A newspaper journalist

91. What will Mr. Griffin discuss?

(A) Team management tips
(B) Public speaking skills
(C) Marketing trends
(D) Careful planning

---

92. Where do the listeners work?

(A) At a software company
(B) At a graphic design studio
(C) At a construction firm
(D) At a travel agency

93. According to the speaker, how can the listeners save money?

(A) By selecting an affordable distributor
(B) By hiring a foreign business partner
(C) By using fuel-efficient vehicles
(D) By holding online meetings

94. What does the speaker imply when she says, "Did everybody turn on their laptops"?

(A) She will update a system.
(B) She will demonstrate a product.
(C) Her laptop is not working.
(D) Her password is incorrect.

Dress Shirt Styling	
Color: 6 choices	**Fabric: 3 choices**
Blue Indigo Red Yellow Green Purple	Polyester Cotton Flannel
Collar: 4 choices	**Sleeves: 2 choices**
Classic Mandarin Spread Pinned	Long Short

95. What is the speaker mainly discussing?

(A) Customer comments
(B) A delivery method
(C) A marketing strategy
(D) Sales figures

96. Look at the graphic. Which option quantity will increase in February?

(A) 6
(B) 3
(C) 4
(D) 2

97. What is the speaker concerned about?

(A) A Web site needs to be updated.
(B) Some employees have wrong information.
(C) Some items are getting damaged.
(D) A rival has launched a similar product.

Customer order: BSA

Order Item	Total number
Hamburgers	20
Chicken soup	24
Bottled water	20
Forks and spoons	24

98. What kind of event is being held?

(A) A business conference
(B) An awards ceremony
(C) A graduation party
(D) A cooking demonstration

99. Look at the graphic. Which item on the order form will be removed?

(A) Hamburgers
(B) Chicken soup
(C) Bottled water
(D) Forks and spoons

100. What does the speaker ask the listener to do?

(A) Pick up a package
(B) Make a payment
(C) Update an invoice
(D) Give a speech

This is the end of the Listening test.

ACTUAL TEST 09

LISTENING TEST 35

In the Listening test, you will be asked to demonstrate how well you understand spoken English. The entire Listening test will last approximately 45 minutes. There are four parts, and directions are given for each part. You must mark your answers on the separate answer sheet. Do not write your answers in your test book.

PART 1

Directions: For each question in this part, you will hear four statements about a picture in your test book. When you hear the statements, you must select the one statement that best describes what you see in the picture. Then find the number of the question on your answer sheet and mark your answer. The statements will not be printed in your test book and will be spoken only one time.

Example

Sample Answer

Ⓐ ● Ⓒ Ⓓ

Statement (B), "A man is pointing at a document," is the best description of the picture, so you should select answer (B) and mark it on your answer sheet.

1.

2.

ACTUAL TEST 09

GO ON TO THE NEXT PAGE

3.

4.

5.

6.

ACTUAL TEST 09

GO ON TO THE NEXT PAGE

PART 2 36

Directions: You will hear a question or statement and three responses spoken in English. They will not be printed in your test book and will be spoken only one time. Select the best response to the question or statement and mark the letter (A), (B), or (C) on your answer sheet.

7. Mark your answer on your answer sheet.

8. Mark your answer on your answer sheet.

9. Mark your answer on your answer sheet.

10. Mark your answer on your answer sheet.

11. Mark your answer on your answer sheet.

12. Mark your answer on your answer sheet.

13. Mark your answer on your answer sheet.

14. Mark your answer on your answer sheet.

15. Mark your answer on your answer sheet.

16. Mark your answer on your answer sheet.

17. Mark your answer on your answer sheet.

18. Mark your answer on your answer sheet.

19. Mark your answer on your answer sheet.

20. Mark your answer on your answer sheet.

21. Mark your answer on your answer sheet.

22. Mark your answer on your answer sheet.

23. Mark your answer on your answer sheet.

24. Mark your answer on your answer sheet.

25. Mark your answer on your answer sheet.

26. Mark your answer on your answer sheet.

27. Mark your answer on your answer sheet.

28. Mark your answer on your answer sheet.

29. Mark your answer on your answer sheet.

30. Mark your answer on your answer sheet.

31. Mark your answer on your answer sheet.

PART 3 (37)

Directions: You will hear some conversations between two or more people. You will be asked to answer three questions about what the speakers say in each conversation. Select the best response to each question and mark the letter (A), (B), (C), or (D) on your answer sheet. The conversations will not be printed in your test book and will be spoken only one time.

32. What does the man want to do at the art gallery?
(A) Register for a class
(B) Display a painting
(C) Meet an artist
(D) Volunteer for an event

33. What problem does the woman mention?
(A) A board is broken.
(B) A document is missing.
(C) A curator is not available.
(D) A room is not big enough.

34. What does the woman offer to do for the man?
(A) Refund a payment
(B) Order materials from a store
(C) Post a schedule
(D) Add his name to a list

---

35. What does the woman want to do?
(A) Use a computer
(B) Claim a package
(C) Book a room
(D) See a friend

36. Why most likely is the woman's name missing from the list?
(A) Her name was spelled incorrectly.
(B) Her subscription was canceled.
(C) She is a past employee.
(D) She is a new resident.

37. What does the man ask for?
(A) A contract
(B) An account number
(C) A photo identification
(D) A mailing address

38. What would the man like to purchase?
(A) Bathroom supplies
(B) Patio furniture
(C) A carpet
(D) A beverage machine

39. What does the woman suggest the man do?
(A) Select a different model
(B) Come back later
(C) Check some measurements
(D) Sign up for a payment plan

40. What does the man ask the woman about?
(A) The operation hours of a business
(B) The location of a store
(C) The length of an application process
(D) The details of a warranty

---

41. Where are the speakers?
(A) At an athletic competition
(B) At a technology convention
(C) At a music festival
(D) At a gallery opening

42. What is the man's problem?
(A) He missed an important event.
(B) He brought an expired credit card.
(C) He is unable to reach a manager.
(D) He misplaced a badge.

43. What does the manager ask the man to do?
(A) Submit an extra fee
(B) Refer to a map
(C) Sign some paperwork
(D) Return at another time

GO ON TO THE NEXT PAGE →

44. What does the man require assistance with?

(A) Finding a language course
(B) Scheduling a business trip
(C) Preparing for a presentation
(D) Submitting a job application

45. Why is Yuriko Sugimoto unable to help immediately?

(A) She is working on another project.
(B) She is away on vacation.
(C) She has not received training.
(D) She is meeting a client.

46. What does the man want to know about Yuriko Sugimoto?

(A) The contact information of her references
(B) The arrival time of her flight
(C) Her hourly fee
(D) Details about her work experience

---

47. What does the woman say she is unsure about?

(A) Whether a message was received
(B) Whether a facility is available
(C) The arrangements for a meeting
(D) The length of a project

48. Why does the man apologize?

(A) He sent the woman incorrect information.
(B) He missed an important meeting.
(C) He did not contact the woman yesterday.
(D) He will not be able to meet a deadline.

49. What does the woman want to have for a meeting?

(A) A list of attendees
(B) A budget estimate
(C) A blueprint of a building
(D) An updated agenda

50. Why did Mr. Collins miss his consultation?

(A) He forgot to check a schedule.
(B) He woke up too late.
(C) He experienced some traffic.
(D) He had to finish an assignment.

51. What is mentioned about Ms. Feinstein?

(A) She went on vacation.
(B) She is a well-known lawyer.
(C) She will retire soon.
(D) She received a prize.

52. What will Mr. Workman do next?

(A) Review an agreement
(B) Fax some papers
(C) Give a tour
(D) Call some clients

---

53. Why is Mr. Hemsley calling?

(A) To arrange a recording session
(B) To ask for a document
(C) To reschedule an appointment
(D) To report an issue

54. What does Mr. Hemsley mean when he says, "we'll be conducting an interview here in 10 minutes"?

(A) He will be temporarily unavailable.
(B) He requires assistance immediately.
(C) He is going to leave the office soon.
(D) He wants to reserve a conference room.

55. What does Mr. Hemsley say is unique about the interview?

(A) It will include a meeting with the CEO.
(B) It will be a group interview.
(C) It will include a luncheon.
(D) It will be done remotely.

56. What most likely is the man's job?
(A) Instructor
(B) Lawyer
(C) Architect
(D) Realtor

57. Why does the man want an office on the top floor?
(A) It is reasonably priced.
(B) It is quiet.
(C) It has the most space.
(D) It has a good view.

58. What benefit is mentioned?
(A) An office has been expanded recently.
(B) A complex has its own dining area.
(C) An office is fully furnished.
(D) A complex is in a convenient location.

---

59. Where is the conversation most likely taking place?
(A) At a factory
(B) At a restaurant
(C) At a clothing store
(D) At an advertising agency

60. What does Giselle imply when she says, "I'm meeting with them in our office in 20 minutes"?
(A) She has to print some documents.
(B) She is unable to participate in an event.
(C) She needs a larger meeting room.
(D) She will have an answer soon.

61. What may happen due to a delay?
(A) Some overtime could be required.
(B) Some training sessions could be held.
(C) A deadline could be extended.
(D) A new supplier could be hired.

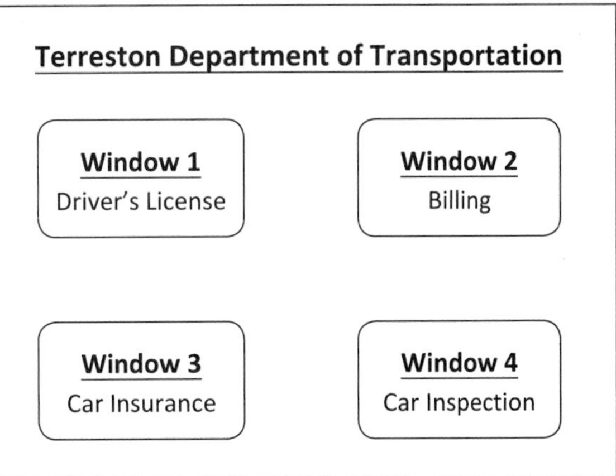

62. What is the woman surprised about?
(A) A wait time
(B) A sign-up fee
(C) Results of a car inspection
(D) The speed of a service

63. According to the woman, what will she do during the last week of May?
(A) Order some parts
(B) Enroll in a class
(C) Rent a vehicle
(D) Go on a business trip

64. Look at the graphic. Which window will the woman most likely go to next?
(A) Window 1
(B) Window 2
(C) Window 3
(D) Window 4

GO ON TO THE NEXT PAGE

65. Why does the man say he is moving to Cerksville?

(A) He is opening his own store.
(B) He is being transferred to another office.
(C) He would like a more convenient commute.
(D) He wants to live closer to his family.

66. Look at the graphic. Which apartment is the man most interested in?

(A) Apartment A
(B) Apartment B
(C) Apartment C
(D) Apartment D

67. What will the speakers probably do next?

(A) Look over a rental contract
(B) Discuss parking options
(C) Set up an appointment
(D) Edit some blueprints

www.employnet.com

Open positions

· Brand Manager	Some in-state travel
· Marketing Manager	Overseas business trips
· Advertising Director	Work at headquarters
· Publicity Director	Visit local regions

68. What does the woman like about her current job?

(A) The hours are flexible.
(B) Her boss is kind.
(C) It offers a good salary.
(D) It is in a convenient location.

69. Look at the graphic. Which position will the woman probably apply for?

(A) Brand Manager
(B) Marketing Manager
(C) Advertising Director
(D) Publicity Director

70. What does the man say he will do soon?

(A) Go on a trip
(B) Relocate to another team
(C) Accept a promotion
(D) Start his own company

PART 4 (38)

Directions: You will hear some talks given by a single speaker. You will be asked to answer three questions about what the speaker says in each talk. Select the best response to each question and mark the letter (A), (B), (C), or (D) on your answer sheet. The talks will not be printed in your test book and will be spoken only one time.

71. What does the speaker say is available to staff?
(A) A fitness program
(B) A company loan
(C) A volunteer opportunity
(D) A medical checkup

72. According to the speaker, what will employees receive for their participation?
(A) Complimentary parking
(B) Extra vacation days
(C) A cash bonus
(D) Free refreshments

73. What must employees do to register?
(A) Submit a form
(B) Contact a business
(C) Attend a workshop
(D) Pay a fee

---

74. What kind of team does the speaker coach?
(A) Baseball
(B) Soccer
(C) Hockey
(D) Golf

75. What does the speaker mention about her players?
(A) Many of them live far away.
(B) Most of them work late.
(C) They are going to participate in a tournament.
(D) They need to practice more often.

76. Why does the speaker say, "Your team has the field from 6 to 7"?
(A) To request a switch
(B) To extend a game time
(C) To praise a team member
(D) To verify an appointment

77. What is the purpose of the announcement?
(A) To describe a new menu
(B) To explain a parking policy
(C) To promote a volunteer opportunity
(D) To introduce a keynote speaker

78. What will happen on May 12?
(A) Some equipment will be installed.
(B) Some gardening work will be done.
(C) An art exhibition will be held.
(D) A parking area will be closed.

79. What does the speaker say will be distributed?
(A) A book
(B) A tool
(C) Some food
(D) Some plants

---

80. What is the report mainly about?
(A) A town festival
(B) A community fundraiser
(C) An art exhibition
(D) A renovation project

81. What does the speaker say is available on a Web site?
(A) Job descriptions
(B) A price chart
(C) A list of events
(D) Traffic updates

82. Why does the speaker say, "there are a few subway lines"?
(A) The subway system is complex.
(B) He takes the subway to the office daily.
(C) Visitors should ride the subway to an event.
(D) Additional subway lines must be built.

GO ON TO THE NEXT PAGE

83. What industry does the speaker most likely work in?

(A) Automobile
(B) Publishing
(C) Sports
(D) Advertising

84. What would the speaker like the listeners to do at today's meeting?

(A) Watch a video
(B) Test some products
(C) Discuss some ideas
(D) Sign a document

85. What will the speaker do next?

(A) Take a group picture
(B) Provide details about some vehicles
(C) Meet some new staff members
(D) Print out a catalog

---

86. What is the purpose of the speech?

(A) To announce an award recipient
(B) To honor a retiring employee
(C) To explain organizational changes
(D) To promote a marketing campaign

87. What does the speaker say he appreciates about Randy Milton?

(A) His leadership ability
(B) His technical knowledge
(C) His design skills
(D) His financial expertise

88. What does the speaker say about the company?

(A) It will have a new headquarters.
(B) It was featured in a magazine.
(C) It is well-known throughout the country.
(D) It plans on hiring more workers.

89. Who are the listeners?

(A) Property managers
(B) Interior designers
(C) Company executives
(D) Mechanical engineers

90. Why is the speaker discussing a change?

(A) A budget is being reduced.
(B) A work area is too noisy.
(C) A department is understaffed.
(D) A manager is retiring.

91. Why does the speaker say, "We can't afford for Engineering to lose focus"?

(A) To approve a revised process
(B) To criticize another team
(C) To justify the reason for a proposal
(D) To complain about a new product

---

92. What is the speaker mainly discussing?

(A) A corporate policy
(B) A visiting client
(C) An annual budget
(D) An evaluation process

93. What are the listeners encouraged to do?

(A) Participate in a survey
(B) Join a social gathering
(C) Take some time off
(D) Visit some clients

94. What will the speaker do after the meeting?

(A) Distribute a brochure
(B) Order some tickets
(C) Interview some candidates
(D) Send out a survey

	Suggested Items to Repair
1	Damaged passenger seat
2	Worn out tires
3	Broken glove compartment
4	Loose rearview mirror

95. What does the speaker mention about Mecho Auto?

(A) It offers a pick-up service.
(B) It has extended its operating hours.
(C) It will undergo renovations.
(D) It is moving to another location.

96. According to the speaker, what did Ms. Menks do yesterday?

(A) Provided an email address
(B) Approved a request
(C) Made a payment
(D) Ordered additional supplies

97. Look at the graphic. Which item number can Ms. Menks receive a discount on?

(A) 1
(B) 2
(C) 3
(D) 4

Hooper's Supermarket	Memorial Park	Police Station
Central Road		
Jorgensen's Donuts	Lionel's Coffee	Moon's Gym

98. What most likely is the speaker's job?

(A) Hair stylist
(B) Supermarket manager
(C) Coffee shop owner
(D) Real estate agent

99. Look at the graphic. Which location is the speaker describing?

(A) Hooper's Supermarket
(B) Lionel's Coffee
(C) Jorgensen's Donuts
(D) Moon's Gym

100. What plan does the speaker recommend changing?

(A) A building design
(B) A budget
(C) An advertisement
(D) A project timetable

This is the end of the Listening test.

ACTUAL TEST 10

LISTENING TEST 39

In the Listening test, you will be asked to demonstrate how well you understand spoken English. The entire Listening test will last approximately 45 minutes. There are four parts, and directions are given for each part. You must mark your answers on the separate answer sheet. Do not write your answers in your test book.

PART 1

Directions: For each question in this part, you will hear four statements about a picture in your test book. When you hear the statements, you must select the one statement that best describes what you see in the picture. Then find the number of the question on your answer sheet and mark your answer. The statements will not be printed in your test book and will be spoken only one time.

Example

Sample Answer

Statement (B), "A man is pointing at a document," is the best description of the picture, so you should select answer (B) and mark it on your answer sheet.

1.

2.

GO ON TO THE NEXT PAGE

3.

4.

5.

6.

GO ON TO THE NEXT PAGE

PART 2 (40)

Directions: You will hear a question or statement and three responses spoken in English. They will not be printed in your test book and will be spoken only one time. Select the best response to the question or statement and mark the letter (A), (B), or (C) on your answer sheet.

7. Mark your answer on your answer sheet.
8. Mark your answer on your answer sheet.
9. Mark your answer on your answer sheet.
10. Mark your answer on your answer sheet.
11. Mark your answer on your answer sheet.
12. Mark your answer on your answer sheet.
13. Mark your answer on your answer sheet.
14. Mark your answer on your answer sheet.
15. Mark your answer on your answer sheet.
16. Mark your answer on your answer sheet.
17. Mark your answer on your answer sheet.
18. Mark your answer on your answer sheet.
19. Mark your answer on your answer sheet.
20. Mark your answer on your answer sheet.
21. Mark your answer on your answer sheet.
22. Mark your answer on your answer sheet.
23. Mark your answer on your answer sheet.
24. Mark your answer on your answer sheet.
25. Mark your answer on your answer sheet.
26. Mark your answer on your answer sheet.
27. Mark your answer on your answer sheet.
28. Mark your answer on your answer sheet.
29. Mark your answer on your answer sheet.
30. Mark your answer on your answer sheet.
31. Mark your answer on your answer sheet.

PART 3 (41)

Directions: You will hear some conversations between two or more people. You will be asked to answer three questions about what the speakers say in each conversation. Select the best response to each question and mark the letter (A), (B), (C), or (D) on your answer sheet. The conversations will not be printed in your test book and will be spoken only one time.

32. What does the woman need help with?
(A) Organizing a workshop
(B) Using a computer program
(C) Making a presentation
(D) Finding a report

33. Why is the man unable to help?
(A) He is leaving work soon.
(B) He lost some documents.
(C) He missed a training session.
(D) He has to meet a client.

34. What will the speakers probably do next?
(A) Speak with a coworker
(B) Complete a project
(C) Prepare some forms
(D) Send out some emails

35. Where are the speakers?
(A) At a car rental business
(B) At a travel agency
(C) At a public library
(D) At an electronics repair shop

36. What will the man do next week?
(A) Attend an autograph signing session
(B) Participate in a tour
(C) Renew a membership contract
(D) Depart for a business trip

37. Why does Tammy talk to Ms. Chin?
(A) To refer her to a service
(B) To get approval for a purchase
(C) To inquire about a rule
(D) To check on the status of a delivery

38. What event are the speakers discussing?
(A) A guided tour
(B) A luncheon
(C) A training session
(D) A client meeting

39. What problem does the man mention?
(A) Some items are unavailable.
(B) There are not enough seats.
(C) Reservations have not been made.
(D) More staff is needed.

40. What does the woman decide to do?
(A) Send an email
(B) Postpone a gathering
(C) Use a company facility
(D) Hire a new employee

41. What does the woman say she has heard about?
(A) The renovation of a building
(B) The acquisition of a company
(C) The construction of a new facility
(D) The launch of a new product

42. What benefit is expected?
(A) Lower rental rates
(B) More employment opportunities
(C) Increased tourism
(D) Clearer company guidelines

43. What does the man suggest the woman do?
(A) Tell her son to call him directly
(B) Forward a résumé
(C) Visit a company's Web site
(D) Speak with a manager

GO ON TO THE NEXT PAGE

44. What special feature does the woman request for the card holders?

(A) Water-resistant material
(B) A company logo
(C) Specific colors
(D) An extra-large size

45. What does the man say she must do?

(A) Order from a Web site
(B) Make a deposit
(C) Provide a sample
(D) Speak to a craftsperson

46. What does the man say about discounts?

(A) They must be approved by a supervisor.
(B) They require a membership card.
(C) They are not available for customized items.
(D) They are only offered for online orders.

---

47. What type of business does the woman want to work for?

(A) A translation firm
(B) A law firm
(C) A marketing agency
(D) A publishing agency

48. What job requirement is mentioned?

(A) A degree in business
(B) Knowledge of a specific product
(C) Event organizing skills
(D) International experience

49. What does the man ask the woman to do?

(A) Prepare a presentation
(B) Fill out a questionnaire
(C) Return at a later time
(D) Submit a reference letter

50. Where does the man work?

(A) At a law firm
(B) At a printing center
(C) At a recycling plant
(D) At an advertising agency

51. What would the man like to do?

(A) Register for a training session
(B) Purchase new equipment
(C) Store some merchandise
(D) Get rid of old electronics

52. What will Kathy probably do next week?

(A) Deliver a package
(B) Give the man a tour
(C) Participate in a workshop
(D) Visit the man's office

---

53. Where will the speakers be on November 21?

(A) At a job fair
(B) At a store opening
(C) At a technology conference
(D) At an anniversary celebration

54. What does the man mean when he says, "That's a good idea"?

(A) The location of an event should be changed.
(B) The start date of an internship should be moved.
(C) The length of a training session should be shortened.
(D) The order of speakers should be switched.

55. What will the man probably do next?

(A) Talk to an HR employee
(B) Make a reservation
(C) Prepare a contract
(D) Look for a piece of equipment

56. What does the man want to do?

(A) Buy some furniture
(B) Return some supplies
(C) Replace a broken item
(D) Organize a warehouse

57. What does the woman say about some merchandise?

(A) A color is not in stock.
(B) A size is not available.
(C) The prices have been reduced.
(D) The products are handmade.

58. What does the woman caution the man about?

(A) Complicated installation procedures
(B) Costly shipping charges
(C) An easily damaged item
(D) A long waiting period

---

59. What is the woman calling about?

(A) A damaged phone
(B) A pool service
(C) A travel itinerary
(D) A promotional deal

60. What does the woman imply when she says, "I've tried that"?

(A) She spoke with a technician earlier.
(B) She is pleased with some results.
(C) A coupon code was applied.
(D) An idea was not effective.

61. What does the woman decide to do?

(A) Place another order
(B) Visit a business
(C) Talk to the man's supervisor
(D) Cancel a trip

Order Form	
Menu Item	**Quantity**
Cheeseburger	5
Fruit Bowl	7
Shrimp Pasta	9
Chicken Sandwich	15
Beverages	36

62. Look at the graphic. Which quantity on the order form must be revised?

(A) 5
(B) 7
(C) 9
(D) 15

63. Who most likely is Mr. Burke?

(A) A custodian
(B) A researcher
(C) A chef
(D) A musician

64. What will the woman probably do next?

(A) Mail a package
(B) Forward a file
(C) Contact a store
(D) Update a schedule

GO ON TO THE NEXT PAGE

GALAXY WAY
MOVIE THEATER

VOUCHER

$7 OFF FILMS ON MON-THU
$5 OFF FILMS ON FRIDAY
$3 OFF FILMS ON WEEKENDS

23872983472
(EXPIRES 4/5)

65. What does the man mention about *Marvelous Fiction*?
   (A) Its actors are all famous.
   (B) It is sold out for the weekend.
   (C) Its first screening is on Friday.
   (D) It has received positive reviews.

66. Look at the graphic. Which discount did the woman receive?
   (A) $3
   (B) $5
   (C) $7
   (D) $9

67. What does the man recommend?
   (A) Bringing a receipt
   (B) Checking out a restaurant
   (C) Arriving early to a theater
   (D) Using a credit card

Warranty Restrictions

The following are not covered under warranty:

1. Products owned for more than one year
2. Products damaged by an accident
3. Products that get lost
4. Products with parts from different manufacturers

68. What kind of product is being discussed?
   (A) A phone
   (B) A television
   (C) A computer
   (D) A watch

69. Look at the graphic. Which restriction does the man refer to?
   (A) Restriction 1
   (B) Restriction 2
   (C) Restriction 3
   (D) Restriction 4

70. What does the woman say she will do?
   (A) Check a user guide
   (B) Speak to a manager
   (C) Test some other items
   (D) Compare some costs

PART 4 42

Directions: You will hear some talks given by a single speaker. You will be asked to answer three questions about what the speaker says in each talk. Select the best response to each question and mark the letter (A), (B), (C), or (D) on your answer sheet. The talks will not be printed in your test book and will be spoken only one time.

71. What is the speaker giving instructions about?
(A) Updating a system
(B) Completing some documents
(C) Entering some work hours
(D) Ordering office supplies

72. According to the speaker, what could happen if a deadline is missed?
(A) A delivery could be delayed.
(B) A vacation request could be denied.
(C) A payment could be postponed.
(D) A budget proposal could be rejected.

73. What does the speaker say he can do?
(A) Address some inquiries
(B) Contact a department
(C) Check some equipment
(D) Provide a tour

---

74. What is the focus of the workshop?
(A) Management skills
(B) Investment tips
(C) Advertising solutions
(D) Sales strategies

75. What are the listeners encouraged to do at home?
(A) Design a cover letter
(B) View a video
(C) Make a daily schedule
(D) Write a review

76. Why does the speaker say, "Francine has more than 25 years of experience"?
(A) To recommend Francine's services
(B) To announce Francine's promotion
(C) To discuss Francine's retirement
(D) To support Francine's decision

77. What is the broadcast about?
(A) A public holiday
(B) A new stadium
(C) Results of a sports competition
(D) Improvements to public transportation

78. According to the speaker, why has a change been made?
(A) To promote local shops
(B) To attract more tourists
(C) To respond to complaints
(D) To comply with new laws

79. What does the speaker encourage listeners to do?
(A) Buy tickets in advance
(B) Consult a map
(C) Volunteer at an event
(D) Vote in an election

---

80. What is the topic of the talk?
(A) An industry convention
(B) An advertising proposal
(C) A worksite regulation
(D) A revised brochure

81. What are the listeners asked to do?
(A) Examine some paperwork
(B) Work additional hours
(C) Clean an area
(D) Distribute some beverages

82. What will the speaker do next?
(A) Review a schedule
(B) Conduct an interview
(C) Test some products
(D) Meet some clients

GO ON TO THE NEXT PAGE

83. Where does the speaker most likely work?

(A) At a bookstore
(B) At a laboratory
(C) At a museum
(D) At a café

84. Why does the speaker say, "talk to Heather"?

(A) To check the availability of an item
(B) To check the number of visitors
(C) To check the choices on a menu
(D) To check the payment of an invoice

85. What will the listeners do next?

(A) Fill out a form
(B) Go to lunch
(C) Tour an office building
(D) Watch a demonstration

---

86. What type of event is taking place?

(A) A retirement dinner
(B) A community fundraiser
(C) A business opening
(D) An awards ceremony

87. What will Arnold Vans be in charge of?

(A) Renovating a public property
(B) Designing new products
(C) Managing a branch office
(D) Improving marketing strategies

88. What are the attendees asked to do at the end of the evening?

(A) Take a group picture
(B) Register for membership
(C) Submit comments
(D) Pick up a gift

89. Where does the speaker most likely work?

(A) At a bank
(B) At a factory
(C) At a software developer
(D) At a telephone service provider

90. What does the speaker mean when she says, "but we're still getting a lot of calls"?

(A) More employees are required.
(B) Complaints are still being received.
(C) A marketing strategy was successful.
(D) Some orders have not been fulfilled.

91. What will the listeners probably do next?

(A) Review a file
(B) Sign a contract
(C) Contact some clients
(D) Upgrade a program

---

92. What product is the speaker discussing?

(A) A finance software program
(B) An assembly machine
(C) A storage container
(D) An inventory barcode scanner

93. What does the speaker say the product will help avoid?

(A) Having incorrect data
(B) Causing product defects
(C) Experiencing system failures
(D) Losing important documents

94. What will the speaker do next?

(A) Distribute some brochures
(B) Print a document
(C) Answer some questions
(D) Give a tutorial

Rita Matsumoto's Friday Appointments

10:00 A.M.	Management meeting
11:00 A.M.	Budget review
12:00 P.M.	Client consultation
1:00 P.M.	HR presentation

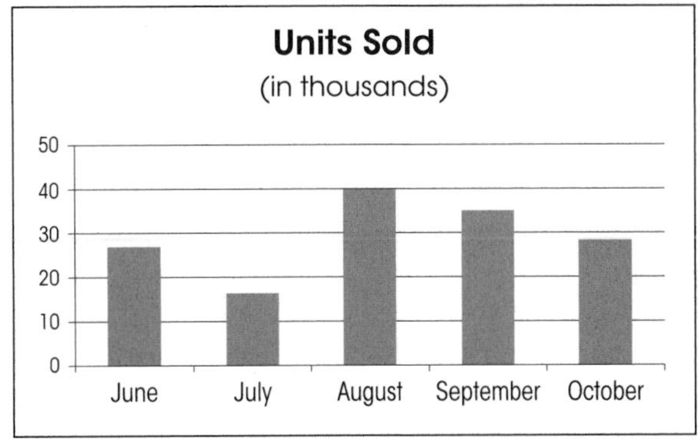

95. What does the speaker want to talk about?
(A) A production deadline
(B) A new TV series
(C) A job opening in Osaka
(D) A construction proposal

96. Look at the graphic. Which of the speaker's appointments was postponed?
(A) Management meeting
(B) Budget review
(C) Client consultation
(D) HR presentation

97. What does the speaker ask the listener to send?
(A) An application form
(B) A travel itinerary
(C) A guest list
(D) A price estimate

98. Where does the speaker most likely work?
(A) At a sporting goods store
(B) At an electronics maker
(C) At an accounting firm
(D) At a broadcasting station

99. According to the speaker, what caused a decrease in sales?
(A) A consumer gave a poor rating.
(B) A manufacturer raised its prices.
(C) A factory closed down.
(D) A competitor released a new product.

100. Look at the graphic. When did the company discount a product?
(A) In June
(B) In July
(C) In August
(D) In September

This is the end of the Listening test.

AUDIO SCRIPT & TRANSLATION

ACTUAL TEST ①

PART 1 P. 18-21

03

1. **(A) She's cycling through a park.**
   (B) She's securing a bicycle to a post.
   (C) She's leaning against a tree.
   (D) She's walking down a road.

2. (A) The men are installing electrical wiring.
   (B) The men are working on a roof.
   (C) The men are repairing a window.
   (D) The men are laying tiles on the floor.

3. **(A) They are sitting at opposite workstations.**
   (B) They are adjusting a computer monitor.
   (C) One of the people is cleaning a desk.
   (D) One of the people is pulling open a file drawer.

4. (A) The woman is waiting at a counter.
   (B) The woman is putting groceries into a bag.
   (C) The woman is lifting a basket.
   (D) The woman is studying an item.

5. **(A) Potted plants have been placed on a desk.**
   (B) A laptop is covered with some papers.
   (C) Some cabinets are filled with books.
   (D) Some magazines have been scattered on a desk.

6. (A) A woman is storing her camera in a carrying case.
   (B) A woman is taking a picture out of the frame.
   (C) Some structures are casting shadows on the ground.
   (D) Photographic equipment has been set up by a fence.

1. **(A) 她騎著腳踏車穿越公園。**
   (B) 她正在把腳踏車固定到桿子上。
   (C) 她倚著樹。
   (D) 她走在路上。

2. (A) 男人們正在裝設電線。
   (B) 男人們正在屋頂工作。
   (C) 男人們正在修理窗戶。
   (D) 男人們正在地板上鋪設地磚。

3. **(A) 他們坐在面對面的工作區。**
   (B) 他們在調整一台電腦螢幕。
   (C) 其中一人正在清桌子。
   (D) 其中一人拉開檔案櫃的抽屜。

4. (A) 女子正在收銀台前等候。
   (B) 女子把食品雜貨放進袋裡。
   (C) 女子提起籃子。
   (D) 女子仔細看著商品

5. **(A) 盆栽擺在桌上。**
   (B) 筆記型電腦上堆放著幾張紙。
   (C) 有些櫃子裡塞滿了書。
   (D) 桌上散落幾本雜誌。

6. (A) 女子把相機放入相機包。
   (B) 女子正從相框取下照片。
   (C) 幾棟建築的陰影落在地面上。
   (D) 圍欄邊架起了攝影設備。

PART 2 P. 22

04

7. Who arranges the store's display shelves?
   (A) Tanner usually does that.
   (B) Those items are on sale.
   (C) Some new furniture.

7. 這家店的貨架由誰整理？
   (A) 通常是坦納負責做。
   (B) 那些商品正在特價中。
   (C) 一些新家具。

8. How long is your presentation on leadership?
(A) At 3 o'clock.
(B) Just for the managers.
(C) About 15 minutes.

9. When can we get started on the new product design?
(A) Right after this meeting.
(B) With the product development team.
(C) Due to its smaller size.

10. Is there a printer in this room?
(A) The ink cartridges in the supply cabinet.
(B) There are no empty rooms on this floor.
(C) Actually, it needs to be repaired.

11. Easter Café is closing, right?
(A) Turn left at the next street.
(B) Yes, they didn't get enough customers.
(C) I'd like a coffee with cream, please.

12. How much should we charge for the new sweater?
(A) I'll talk to the manager.
(B) Do you have it in blue?
(C) The fall clothing line.

13. Which laptop belongs to you?
(A) No, I put it on top of the table.
(B) The black one with an orange sticker.
(C) Is the battery charged?

14. Could you put the extra computers in the storage room?
(A) Yes, but after I send this email.
(B) We don't need any more office equipment.
(C) Thank you for your input.

15. Didn't you sell your bike recently?
(A) The new trail in the park.
(B) That's a nice model.
(C) No, I still have it.

16. Where can I adjust the volume of this speaker?
(A) There are buttons on the left side.
(B) It has the best sound quality.
(C) We've made an adjustment to the process.

8. 你關於領導力的簡報有多長？
(A) 在三點。
(B) 只給主管們。
(C) 約 15 分鐘。

9. 我們何時可以開始設計新產品？
(A) 這場會議開完後馬上開始。
(B) 與產品開發團隊合作。
(C) 因為它的尺寸較小。

10. 這間有印表機嗎？
(A) 在辦公用品櫃裡的墨水匣。
(B) 這層樓沒空房。
(C) 其實它需要修理了。

11. 伊斯特咖啡廳要結束營業了嗎？
(A) 下一條街左轉。
(B) 對，他們客人不夠多。
(C) 我要一杯咖啡加鮮乳油／奶精，麻煩了。

12. 這件新毛衣我們要賣多少錢？
(A) 我再和主管談。
(B) 你們有藍色的嗎？
(C) 秋裝系列。

13. 哪台筆電是你的呢？
(A) 不是，我把它放在桌上。
(B) 黑色貼有橙色貼紙的那台。
(C) 電池有充電嗎？

14. 能請您把多的電腦放到倉庫嗎？
(A) 好，但等我送出這封電郵。
(B) 我們不需要更多辦公設備。
(C) 感謝您的付出。

15. 你最近不是才把腳踏車賣掉了？
(A) 公園裡新的小路。
(B) 這型號很好。
(C) 不，我還留著。

16. 我在哪裡可以調整這台喇叭音量？
(A) 左側有按鈕。
(B) 它的音質最好。
(C) 我們調整了流程。

17. Would you prefer to go to the Japanese or Chinese restaurant for lunch?
(A) I'd rather get Chinese.
(B) A table for six.
(C) No, my friend referred me.

17. 您午餐偏好去吃日本料理，還是吃中式餐廳？
(A) 我比較想吃中式。
(B) 一張六人桌。
(C) 不，朋友介紹我的。

18. Did you set the timeline for the renovation project?
(A) The recent renovation of the Belleview Complex.
(B) A new construction manager.
(C) Yes, I just sent you an email about it.

18. 整修作業的日程你訂好了嗎？
(A) 美景綜合大樓最近的整修。
(B) 一位新的工程經理。
(C) 有，我剛寄了相關電子郵件給你。

19. Why don't I get you a drink while you wait for your interview?
(A) That'd be great, thanks.
(B) I'll call the waiter.
(C) I brought my résumé.

19. 你等候面試時我給你拿杯喝的吧？
(A) 可以的話就太好了，謝謝。
(B) 我會叫服務生。
(C) 我帶了我的履歷。

20. The company sports festival was postponed, wasn't it?
(A) Yes, at the stadium.
(B) The team wearing blue.
(C) Where did you hear that?

20. 公司運動會延後了，對吧？
(A) 對，在體育館。
(B) 穿藍色的那隊。
(C) 你從哪裡聽說的？

21. Shouldn't you get your mobile phone repaired?
(A) A wireless Internet service provider.
(B) I'm waiting for the new model to come out.
(C) You'll be contacted by email soon.

21. 你的手機不是該修了嗎？
(A) 無線網路服務供應業者。
(B) 我正等新機上市。
(C) 很快就會用電子郵件通知你。

22. Why is the department hiring?
(A) The application is on the Web site.
(B) At the end of the month.
(C) We've acquired more clients recently.

22. 部門為何在徵人？
(A) 徵才表格在網站上。
(B) 在月底。
(C) 近來我們客戶增加了。

23. Could I borrow a pen for the meeting?
(A) I took notes for you.
(B) No, I couldn't attend.
(C) It's almost out of ink.

23. 我可以借支筆開會嗎？
(A) 我幫你做了筆記。
(B) 不，我不能參加。
(C) 這支幾乎沒水了。

24. I sent you the contract, didn't I?
(A) Standard terms and conditions.
(B) The Internet is not working.
(C) The conference room next door.

24. 我把合約寄給你了，對嗎？
(A) 標準合約條款。
(B) 現在網路斷了。
(C) 隔壁的會議室。

25. Our recycling bin is full again.
(A) I'll empty it out today.
(B) I ride my bicycle to work.
(C) Thanks, but I'm still full.

25. 我們的回收桶又滿了。
(A) 我今天會把它清空。
(B) 我騎腳踏車上班。
(C) 謝謝，但我還很飽。

26. Do you know which room the IT Department office is at?
(A) It's on my desk.
(B) Don't forget to turn off your computer.
(C) I just started working here.

26. 你知道資訊技術辦公室在哪間嗎？
(A) 在我桌上。
(B) 別忘記關電腦。
(C) 我剛來這裡工作。

27. Don't we need more volunteers to finish handing out the flyers?
(A) Jonah is checking the list right now.
(B) I took the direct flight back home.
(C) We recently hired a new engineer.

27. 我們不需要更多志工來把傳單發完嗎？
(A) 喬納現在正在確認名單。
(B) 我搭直飛班機回家。
(C) 我們最近僱了新的工程師。

28. When will Ms. Egert leave for Japan?
(A) Four hours from Tokyo.
(B) She's at the airport right now.
(C) The moving company is here.

28. 埃格特女士什麼時候出發去日本？
(A) 離東京四小時路程。
(B) 她現在就在機場。
(C) 搬家公司到了。

29. There's an opening for the shipping director position.
(A) Yes, I live quite close.
(B) The shipment arrived today.
(C) How do I apply?

29. 貨運主任的職位有開缺。
(A) 對，我住得很近。
(B) 貨今天到了。
(C) 我該如何應徵？

30. Who will be leading the workshop session on project management?
(A) Here's the program.
(B) It will start right after the break.
(C) About communication.

30. 專案管理的研習課程由誰主導進行？
(A) 課程（的資料）在這裡。
(B) 休息後馬上開始。
(C) 和溝通有關。

31. Let's find a cheap supplier, so we can minimize our costs.
(A) We have a lot in stock.
(B) Try maximizing the window on the screen.
(C) The Purchasing Department is looking into it.

31. 讓我們找個便宜的供應商，這樣就能把成本降到最低。
(A) 我們有很多庫存。
(B) 試著把螢幕視窗放到最大。
(C) 採購部門正在研究這件事。

PART 3 P. 23–26

Questions 32-34 refer to the following conversation.

32–34 會話

W：**I think it was the right move to have bands perform at our coffee shop on Saturday nights.** 32 Our sales have really increased over the last few weeks.

女：我覺得在每週六晚上找樂隊到我們咖啡店表演，是對的作法。32 最近幾個星期，銷售額真的成長了。

M：Yeah. **Although I don't really enjoy rearranging the chairs and tables frequently** 33 to create space for the performances, it's still worth it.

W：Right, and we're attracting a lot of attention. **Have you read the online article in *Galveton Entertainment Magazine*?** 34 It has a list of our town's top 10 live entertainment venues. And we're number four on the list.

M：Oh, I didn't know that. **I think we should put the article in a frame and hang it where customers can see it.** 34

W：**I'll print it out right now.** 34

男：對啊。**雖然我不是很喜歡一直搬動桌椅，** 33 就為了挪出表演空間，但還是很值得。

女：對啊，而且我們現在吸引到很多關注。**你有讀《加爾維敦娛樂雜誌》的網路文章嗎？** 34 它有一份我們鎮上十大現場表演場地的名單，我們排在第四位呢。

男：哦，這我不知道。**我想我們應該把文章裱框，再掛到客人看得到的地方。** 34

女：**我現在就去印出來。** 34

32. Where do the speakers most likely work?
(A) At a publishing company
(B) At a bank
(C) At a concert hall
(D) At a café

32. 說話者最有可能在哪裡工作？
(A) 在出版社
(B) 在銀行
(C) 在音樂廳
(D) 在咖啡廳

33. What does the man say he dislikes doing?
(A) Contacting performers
(B) Ordering supplies
(C) Rearranging furniture
(D) Reviewing contracts

33. 男子說他不喜歡做何事？
(A) 聯絡表演者
(B) 訂購用品
(C) 重新擺放家具
(D) 審查合約

34. What does the woman say she will print out right now?
(A) A discount voucher
(B) A magazine article
(C) A sales report
(D) A guest list

34. 女子說她現在要印什麼？
(A) 折價券
(B) 雜誌文章
(C) 銷售報告
(D) 來賓名單

Questions 35-37 refer to the following conversation with three speakers.

35–37 三人會話

W1：**I have to get a new briefcase.** 35 One of the locks broke on my old one. Can either of you recommend a brand?

M：Why don't you check out Luxmore Accessories? **I purchased a Luxmore leather bag, and it's really nice—a lot more stylish than most other brands I've seen.** 36

W2：Yeah, and they're also offering a special deal on their Web site. If you order a Luxmore briefcase, you will receive a small traveling pouch free of charge.

女 1：**我得買個新的公事包。** 35 我舊包有一顆鎖壞了。你們兩位誰能推薦一個品牌嗎？

男：那妳要不要看看麗仕摩爾飾界？**我買了麗仕摩爾的皮包，真的很不錯——比我看過的多數品牌來得時尚多了。** 36

女 2：對啊，他們網站上還提供特別優惠呢。如果妳訂購一只麗仕摩爾公事包，還將免費獲得一個小旅行袋。

W1：Oh really? **Can you give me the link to their home page, Valerie?** 37
W2：**Sure.** 37

女 1 ：哦，真的嗎？**瓦萊麗，妳可以給我他們官網首頁的連結嗎？** 37
女 2 ：**當然可以。** 37

35. What product is being discussed?
(A) A software program
(B) A piece of jewelry
(C) A laptop
(D) A bag

35. 他們在討論什麼產品？
(A) 軟體程式
(B) 珠寶
(C) 筆電
(D) 包包

36. What does the man like about a product?
(A) It is attractive.
(B) It comes in many sizes.
(C) It is durable.
(D) It can be customized.

36. 關於產品，男子有何中意之處？
(A) 外表漂亮。
(B) 有各種尺寸。
(C) 耐用。
(D) 可客製化。

37. What does Valerie agree to do?
(A) Provide a Web address
(B) Track a delivery
(C) Contact a store
(D) Complete a form

37. 瓦萊麗同意做什麼？
(A) 提供網址
(B) 追蹤貨運
(C) 聯絡商店
(D) 填寫表格

Questions 38-40 refer to the following conversation.

38–40 會話

M：Hi, my name is Patrick Simms, the director of the Meadow Philharmonic Orchestra. We'll be traveling abroad next June to begin our concert series in Europe. And **my colleagues highly recommended you for the tour arrangements you made for other orchestras.** 38
W：Thank you. I'd be happy to assist you. **I have over 10 years of experience in the tourism industry,** 38 and prior to that, I was actually a professional violinist, so I understand what you need.
M：That's good to hear. **I'm a bit worried about our instruments, though. They're very expensive, and I want to make sure that they're not damaged during travel.** 39
W：Well, most of your instruments should be fine as carry-on luggage, but larger instruments take up much more space, so **you'll probably need to buy additional tickets** 40 for them. It might be costly, but it's the best way to transport those instruments.

男：您好，我是草原交響樂團的團長，名叫派翠克・西姆斯。我們明年六月將出國，在歐洲展開系列音樂會。而**您為其他交響樂團安排的巡迴演出很成功，我同事極力推薦可以找您。** 38
女：謝謝，很高興能協助您。**我在旅遊業有十多年的經驗，** 38 在這之前，我其實是位專業的小提琴家，所以我知道您的需求。
男：聽您這樣說我就放心了。**不過我還是有點擔心我們的樂器，它們非常貴，我想確保它們在旅途中不會受損。** 39
女：嗯，您大部分的樂器作為隨身行李沒問題，但較大的樂器會佔更大空間，因此**您可能需要為其再買幾張機票。** 40 這可能會很貴，卻是運送樂器最好的方式。

38. Who most likely is the woman?
(A) A flight attendant
(B) A music teacher
(C) A tour operator
(D) A hotel clerk

39. What is the man concerned about?
(A) The safe transport of instruments
(B) The size of a room
(C) An additional luggage fee
(D) A travel connection

40. What does the woman suggest?
(A) Speaking with a security officer
(B) Calling the vendor directly
(C) Revising a travel itinerary
(D) Purchasing extra tickets

38. 女子的工作最可能是？
(A) 空服員
(B) 音樂教師
(C) 旅遊業者
(D) 飯店員工

39. 男子擔心什麼？
(A) 樂器的安全運送
(B) 房間的大小
(C) 行李的額外費用
(D) 旅行的轉乘路線

40. 女子建議了什麼？
(A) 和維安人員談話
(B) 直接致電供應商
(C) 更改旅遊行程
(D) 加購機票

Questions 41-43 refer to the following conversation.

M：Hey, Celia.
W：Hi, Robert. I'm so glad you picked up. **I wanted to see if you could give me a ride to the office today.** 41 42
M：**Actually, I just got to work a few minutes ago.** I had to come in earlier than usual this morning to get ready for our product demonstration. Can you still make it in time for the demo?
W：Hmm . . . I don't know. My car won't start.
M：Oh, I hope it's nothing serious. Well, I would pick you up, but the representatives from JRA, Inc. are arriving soon. **Why don't you ask Lisa? She's coming in later today, and I believe she lives near you.** 43
W：**All right, I'll do that now.** 43 Let's hope I can make it to the demo.

41–43 會話

男：嘿，西莉亞。
女：嗨，羅伯特，很開心你接了電話。**我想知道你今天能不能載開車我去辦公室。** 41 42
男：**其實，我幾分鐘前就已經去上班了。**我今天早上得比平時更早到，好把我們產品展示會準備好。妳還能趕上展示會嗎？
女：嗯……我不知道。我的車無法發動。
男：喔，我希望這不嚴重。嗯，我很想去接妳，但是 JRA 企業的代表很快就要到了。**妳何不問問麗莎呢？她今天稍晚會進辦公室，我想她住在妳家附近。** 43
女：**好吧，我馬上問她。** 43 希望我能趕上展示會。

41. What does the woman say she needs?
(A) A ride to work
(B) Directions to a car repair shop
(C) An office floor plan
(D) A product serial number

41. 女子說她需要什麼？
(A) 開車接送上班
(B) 去汽車維修行的路線
(C) 辦公室平面圖
(D) 產品序號

42. What does the man imply when he says, "Actually, I just got to work a few minutes ago"?
(A) He had to deal with heavy traffic.
(B) He would like to reassure the woman.
(C) He will be late for a meeting.
(D) He is unable to assist the woman.

42. 男子說：「其實，我幾分鐘前就已經去上班了」，其暗示為何？
(A) 他得應付塞車。
(B) 他想讓女子放心。
(C) 他開會會遲到。
(D) 他無法幫女子。

43. What does the woman decide to do?
(A) Talk to another coworker
(B) Request a vacation day
(C) Call a client
(D) Ask for a deadline extension

43. 女子決定做什麼？
(A) 與另一個同事商量
(B) 申請休假一天
(C) 致電一位客戶
(D) 要求延長期限

Questions 44-46 refer to the following conversation.

W：Hi, my name is Suzanne Rouse. **I'm here to see Mr. Winfield for a job interview.** 44 It's for a sales position. Could you please let him know that I'm here?
M：Oh, I'm afraid **his flight home was canceled last night. So unfortunately, he won't be back here until late tonight.** 45 Would it be OK if I rescheduled your interview for tomorrow morning?
W：Actually, I'm busy all day tomorrow so that won't work for me.
M：Well, **Mr. Winfield's assistant sometimes handles his interviews for him when he's away. Why don't I give her a call and see if she's available now?** 46

44–46 會話

女：您好，我叫蘇珊・魯斯。**我來這裡是要找溫菲爾德先生面試工作，** 44 應徵的是業務的職位。能請您告訴他我到了嗎？
男：哦，恐怕沒辦法，**他的回程班機昨晚取消了。所以非常遺憾，他要到今天深夜才會回來。** 45 如果我把您的面試改排到明天早上，這樣可以嗎？
女：我其實明天一整天都很忙，所以沒辦法呢。
男：那麼，**溫菲爾德先生不在時，他的助理有時會替他處理面試。那我打電話給她，看她現在有沒有空好了？** 46

44. Why is the woman at Mr. Winfield's office?
(A) To register for a seminar
(B) To interview for a job
(C) To sell a product
(D) To plan for a trip

44. 女子為什麼會在溫菲爾德先生的辦公室？
(A) 要報名參加研討會
(B) 要面試工作
(C) 要銷售產品
(D) 要規劃旅程

45. Why is Mr. Winfield unable to meet with the woman?
(A) He is working from home.
(B) He is with a client.
(C) He is still out of town.
(D) He is training employees.

45. 為什麼溫菲爾德先生不能見女子？
(A) 他現在在家上班。
(B) 他正在陪客戶。
(C) 他仍在外地出差。
(D) 他正在培訓員工。

46. What will the man probably do next?
(A) Contact Mr. Winfield's assistant
(B) Postpone an appointment
(C) Give Mr. Winfield's number to the woman
(D) Make changes to an event schedule

46. 男子接下來可能會做什麼？
(A) 聯絡溫菲爾德先生的助理
(B) 延後面試時間
(C) 把溫菲爾德先生的電話號碼給女子
(D) 更改活動行程

Questions 47-49 refer to the following conversation.

47–49 會話

W：Hello, **my name is Kimberly Hughes, a sales representative at Millennium Electronics.** 47 I wanted to talk to Mr. Alvez about the tablet PC he ordered last week. May I speak to him, please?
M：I'm sorry, but he's not in the office at the moment. Would you like to leave a message?
W：Yes. **Could you tell him that his computer is here? I told him that it wouldn't arrive at our store until next week, but we received an early shipment this morning.** 48
M：OK. **He's supervising a construction site right now,** 49 but I'll make sure he gets the message when he comes back.

女：您好，**我叫金柏莉・休斯，我是千禧電子的業務代表。** 47 我想和阿爾維茲先生談談他上週訂購的個人平板電腦。請問我方便和他說話嗎？
男：抱歉，他目前不在辦公室。您方便留個訊息嗎？
女：好的。**可以請您轉告他，他的電腦已經到達店裡了嗎？我之前跟他說，貨要下週才會抵達本店，但我們今天早上提前收到貨了。** 48
男：好的。**他現在正在工地監工，** 49 但我保證他回來後會收到留言的。

47. Where does the woman work?
(A) At an electronics store
(B) At a medical clinic
(C) At a post office
(D) At a construction company

47. 女子在哪裡工作？
(A) 在電子用品店
(B) 在醫療診所
(C) 在郵局
(D) 在建設公司

48. Why is the woman calling?
(A) To locate a shipment
(B) To refill a prescription
(C) To request details about a property
(D) To provide updated information about an order

48. 女子為何打電話？
(A) 為確認貨物地點
(B) 為按處方箋配藥
(C) 為要求房地產的詳情
(D) 為提供訂單的最新消息

49. Why is Mr. Alvez out of the office?
(A) He is feeling ill.
(B) He is working at a different location.
(C) He is on vacation.
(D) He is having lunch at a restaurant.

49. 阿爾維茲先生為何不在辦公室？
(A) 他不舒服。
(B) 他正在其他地方工作。
(C) 他正在休假。
(D) 他正在餐廳吃午餐。

Questions 50-52 refer to the following conversation.

M： Hi, **I want to take the professional pilot training program** 50 at your school, but there isn't any information about the enrollment fee on your Web site.

W： That's because it varies depending on what each student's experience level is and what their needs are. But it's normally between 25 and 40 thousand dollars. The total cost includes renting a plane, fueling it, and paying the instructor.

M： I guess that makes sense, but I had no idea it was that expensive. I think **I'd better look into other commercial flight schools and compare the fees.** 50 51 Is there anything in particular I should be aware of when checking out different programs?

W： Well, the fees are about the same at most flight schools, but you should be aware that **not every school guarantees job placement** 52 like we do. I'm sure you'll agree that's probably the most important thing. **So be sure to ask about their placement services.** 52

50. What career is the man interested in?
(A) Flight dispatcher
(B) Customs agent
(C) Aircraft mechanic
(D) Commercial pilot

51. What does the man say he will do?
(A) Obtain a loan
(B) Look at a handbook
(C) Compare different schools
(D) Submit some documents

52. According to the woman, what should the man ask about?
(A) Job placement
(B) Facility size
(C) Experience requirements
(D) Course length

50–52 會話

男： 您好，**我想參加**貴校的**專業飛行員培訓課程**，50 但你們網站上沒有任何有關學費的資訊。

女： 那是因為費用會根據每位學生的經驗和需求而有所不同。不過通常介於 2 萬 5 千到 4 萬美元之間。總額包括租用飛機、加油和支付給教官的費用。

男： 我想這還蠻有道理的，但我沒想到會那麼貴。我想**我還是再研究一下其他商用飛行學校，比較一下費用好了。** 50 51 我參考不同的課程時，有什麼特別需要注意的地方嗎？

女： 嗯，大多數飛行學校的學費都差不多，但您需要留意，**並非所有學校都**像我們一樣**保證就業安置**，52 我確信您會同意這或許是最重要的事，**所以請務必詢問他們的就業安置服務。** 52

50. 男子對什麼職業感興趣？
(A) 飛行簽派員
(B) 海關人員
(C) 航空器維修人員
(D) 商用機師

51. 男子說他會做什麼？
(A) 取得貸款
(B) 查看手冊
(C) 比較不同的學校
(D) 提出一些文件

52. 據女子說法，男子應詢問什麼？
(A) 就業安置
(B) 設施規模
(C) 經驗要求
(D) 課程長度

Questions 53-55 refer to the following conversation with three speakers.

W1：Clark, Lois, I'm glad I ran into you both. **It looks like preparations are going well for next week's yearly reception party** 53 for our theater's donors.

M：Yes. **Arrangements for the dinner have been finalized.** 53 Do you need us to do anything else?

W1：**I just got off the phone with one of our donors, Mary Romo.** 54

W2：**If I recall, she was responsible for getting us the new sound system, right?** 54

W1：**Yeah.** 54 Anyway, she initially told me that she would be going on vacation this week, but it got canceled at the last minute. So now, she is saying she would like to attend.

M：All right. **I'll put her name on the attendance sheet right now.** 55

53–55 三人會話

女 1：克拉克、露意絲，很高興遇到你們倆。**看來下週**為劇院捐款人舉辦的**年度招待會的籌備進展得很順利。** 53

男：是啊。**晚餐的籌備工作已經落定。** 53 還需要我們做些什麼嗎？

女 1：**我剛和其中的一位捐款人瑪麗・羅莫講完電話。** 54

女 2：**如果我沒記錯，她捐了新的音響系統給我們，對吧？** 54

女 1：**對。** 54 總之，她原本跟我說這週要去度假，但行前臨時被取消了。所以現在她說她想參加。

男：好。**我馬上把她的名字加到與會名單上。** 55

53. What are the speakers talking about?
   (A) An annual meal
   (B) A movie premiere
   (C) A product launch
   (D) A play audition

54. How do the speakers know Ms. Romo?
   (A) She gave a tour.
   (B) She made a presentation.
   (C) She provided some equipment.
   (D) She planned a charity event.

55. What does the man say he will do?
   (A) He will change some menu items.
   (B) He will revise a guest list.
   (C) He will book a room.
   (D) He will arrange some transportation.

53. 說話者的話題為何？
   (A) 年度餐會
   (B) 電影首映
   (C) 產品發表會
   (D) 戲劇試鏡

54. 說話者怎麼認識羅莫女士的？
   (A) 她帶過導覽。
   (B) 她做過簡報。
   (C) 她提供過一些設備。
   (D) 她籌劃過慈善活動。

55. 男子說他會做什麼？
   (A) 他會更改部分菜色品項。
   (B) 他將修改賓客名單。
   (C) 他會預約一間房間。
   (D) 他將安排部分交通方式。

Questions 56-58 refer to the following conversation.

W：Hello, Mr. Shubert.

M：Good morning, Ms. Bolton. **The City Council wanted to know how far along you are with the landscaping work on the Town Hall Garden.** 56 Is everything going smoothly?

56–58 會話

女：您好，舒伯特先生。

男：早，波頓女士。**市議會想知道您現在市政廳花園的景觀美化工程進展得如何。** 56 一切順利嗎？

W：Yes, **we're actually a bit ahead of schedule, so it should be done by August.** 57

M：**Wow, I didn't expect that**. 57 Now, we don't have to worry about making the deadline.

W：Yes. I'm happy about it as well. Residents probably can visit the garden earlier than anticipated.

M：Hmm . . . I still need to check with the local nursery. They are providing all of the plants and flowers, so **it really depends on their delivery schedule. They promised to give me an update by the end of the week.** 58

女：是，**事實上我們比原訂進度快了點，所以八月前應就會完成了。** 57

男：**哇，出乎我意料之外。** 57 這樣我們就不用擔心趕不上期限。

女：是，對此我也很高興。民眾可能可以比預期的更早來參觀花園。

男：嗯……我還得和當地苗圃業者確認。植物和花卉都由他們提供，所以**其實還得看他們的交貨進度。他們承諾會在週末之前給我後續消息。** 58

56. What are the speakers mainly discussing?
(A) A city election
(B) A town hall meeting
(C) A budget proposal
(D) A landscaping project

57. What does the man imply when he says, "Wow, I didn't expect that"?
(A) He is unhappy about a change.
(B) He is surprised by a request.
(C) He is pleased by some news.
(D) He is worried about some costs.

58. What will the man receive soon?
(A) An electronic bill
(B) A schedule update
(C) An agreement form
(D) A product catalog

56. 說話者主要討論何事？
(A) 市級選舉
(B) 市政廳會議
(C) 預算提案
(D) 景觀美化工程

57. 男子說：「哇，出乎我意料之外」，言下之意為何？
(A) 某項異動讓他不滿意。
(B) 某項請求讓他驚訝。
(C) 某些消息讓他高興。
(D) 某些開銷讓他擔心。

58. 男子很快將會收到什麼？
(A) 電子帳單
(B) 時程的進度更新
(C) 同意書
(D) 產品型錄

Questions 59-61 refer to the following conversation.

W：Hi, Larry. We need to talk about all the extra orders that have been coming in for the Manufacturing Department recently.

M：**Ah, I heard you were getting a lot more orders. Is it an issue?** 59

W：**Yeah, the volume of orders we need to fulfill has increased dramatically,** 59 and my crew can't keep the same levels of quality control if we try to speed up production.

M：Hmm, OK. We can't install more equipment right now, but **I may be able to get authorization to add more employees to our assembly lines.** 60

59–61 會話

女：嗨，賴瑞。我們需要討論一下生產部近期所有新增的訂單。

男：**啊，我聽說你們多接到很多訂單。這會有問題嗎？** 59

女：**是，我們必須完成的訂單數量大幅增加，** 59 而如果試著提昇生產速度，我們同仁將無法維持相同水準的品質管理。

男：嗯，好。我們現在無法加裝設備，但**我也許能得到授權，在我們的產線上增加員工。** 60

W: Oh, that would be great. Is there anything you need from me?

M: **If I could get you to create a chart comparing the number of orders now to last quarter's, that'd help me out a lot.** 61

女：哦，這樣就太好了。你需要我幫什麼忙嗎？

男：**如果我能請妳做個圖表，比較目前和上一季度的訂單數量，將能幫我不少忙。** 61

59. What does the woman say is a problem?
(A) Several employees have been arriving late at work.
(B) There has been an increase in workload.
(C) A piece of equipment is not working properly.
(D) Some items have been damaged during transit.

60. How does the man propose solving the problem?
(A) By offering better incentives
(B) By purchasing additional machines
(C) By revising an inspection process
(D) By hiring more workers

61. What does the man request that the woman do?
(A) Put together some data
(B) Set up a meeting
(C) Update a Web site
(D) Reschedule some deliveries

59. 女子說出了什麼問題？
(A) 多名員工上班遲到。
(B) 工作量增加。
(C) 一項設備失靈。
(D) 一些產品在運送時受損。

60. 男子提議如何解決問題？
(A) 提供更好的獎勵措施
(B) 買進額外的機器
(C) 修改檢驗流程
(D) 僱用更多員工

61. 男子請女子做什麼？
(A) 統整一些數據
(B) 安排會議
(C) 更新網站
(D) 重新安排交貨

Questions 62-64 refer to the following conversation and schedule.

M: It's great that we have the afternoon off from this training workshop. **I heard from one of our instructors that we should take a tour of the Chateau Archives. It's the oldest library in this region.** 62

W: **Yeah, I can't wait to see it.** 62

M: Same here. **But let's not forget that we agreed to be back at the hotel tonight to eat dinner with our other team members.** 63

W: Right, of course. OK, let's read more about the tours on Chateau Archives' Web site on my laptop. **All right, it shows that there are still three spots left at this time.** 64

M: That's perfect. I'll call them now and reserve our places.

62–64 會話和行程表

男：太好了，我們這次培訓研習的下午有空檔。**我們一位講師跟我說，我們應該參加「行宮檔案館」的導覽行程。那是本地最古老的圖書館。** 62

女：**好啊，我等不及去參觀了。** 62

男：我也是。**但別忘了我們約好今晚要回飯店，和其他團隊成員共進晚餐。** 63

女：對哦，當然。好，我們現在就用我的筆電查閱行宮檔案館的網站，了解更多導覽的相關資訊。**沒問題，上面顯示目前還有三個名額。** 64

男：真是完美。我現在就打電話預約名額。

Tour Schedule

Time	Spots Available
1:00 P.M.	2
2:00 P.M.	4
4:00 P.M. 64	**3**
6:00 P.M.	0

導覽行程表

時間	空缺名額
下午 1:00	2
下午 2:00	4
下午 4:00 64	**3**
下午 6:00	0

62. What do the speakers plan to tour?
(A) An old plant
(B) A historic library
(C) An art gallery
(D) A local restaurant

62. 說話者打算去哪裡參觀？
(A) 舊工廠
(B) 歷史悠久的圖書館
(C) 美術館
(D) 當地餐廳

63. What does the man remind the woman about?
(A) Registering for a class
(B) Storing her personal belongings
(C) Participating in a demonstration
(D) Having dinner with colleagues

63. 男子提醒女子有關什麼的事？
(A) 註冊某課程
(B) 寄放個人物品
(C) 參加展示會
(D) 與同事共進晚餐

64. Look at the graphic. For what time will the speakers make reservations?
(A) 1:00 P.M.
(B) 2:00 P.M.
(C) 4:00 P.M.
(D) 6:00 P.M.

64. 請參照圖表作答。說話者將會預約幾點的行程？
(A) 下午 1:00
(B) 下午 2:00
(C) 下午 4:00
(D) 下午 6:00

Questions 65-67 refer to the following conversation and bill.

W：**Thank you for calling Westfield Credit Card Services.** 65 How may I help you?
M：Hi, there. My name is Chris Walker, and I've got a question about my monthly account statement. **I noticed on May 9, I was charged a foreign transaction fee, but I never made an overseas purchase.** 66
W：OK, let's have a look. Ah, we had a system error that day, and it must have affected your account. I'll take out that charge right away.
M：Thank you.
W：Now, Mr. Walker, we take all of our customer concerns very seriously. **If you don't mind, would you remain on the line for a few minutes to take a brief survey about your experience today?** 67

65–67 會話和帳單

女：**感謝您來電西田信用卡服務。** 65 請問需要什麼協助呢？
男：您好。我叫克里斯・沃克，我對我的月結帳單有疑問。**我注意到 5 月 9 日我被扣了一筆國外交易費，但我從來沒使用海外購物。** 66
女：了解，我們來看一下。噢，那天我們系統出錯，想必影響到您的帳戶。我馬上取消該筆扣款。
男：謝謝。
女：那麼沃克先生，我們對於客戶的需求相當重視。**如果您不介意，可否請您先不要掛斷電話，針對您今天的經驗，用幾分鐘的時間回覆一份簡短的問卷調查？** 67

Name: Chris Walker	
Account: 510-11-1211	
Description	**Amount**
Bally Grocery (5/9)	$32.00
XD Gas (5/9)	$25.00
Rick's Hardware (5/9)	$7.25
Foreign transaction fee (5/9)	**$3.50** 66

65. Where does the woman probably work?
(A) At a credit card company
(B) At a supermarket
(C) At a job recruiting agency
(D) At a hardware store

66. Look at the graphic. What amount will be removed?
(A) $32.00
(B) $25.00
(C) $7.25
(D) $3.50

67. Why does the woman ask the man to wait?
(A) To explain a new process
(B) To have him talk to her manager
(C) To verify some contact information
(D) To receive some feedback

Questions 68-70 refer to the following conversation and office park map.

M：Hello, Ms. Crowlie. It's Martin Sanchez from Nertech, Inc. **After careful review of your job application, we have decided to call you in for an interview.** 68 Does next Wednesday at 10 A.M. work for you?

W：I'm so glad to hear back from you. Just a minute, I'll check my schedule. Yes, that time should be fine.

M：Great. Now, Nertech is on the west side of town. **Our office building is located on Redwood Street, right by the community center.** 69

W：All right. And **can I just park anywhere in the lot, or do I have to get a pass?** 70

M：**As long as you're in a spot that's marked "guest", you won't have a problem.** 70

姓名：克里斯•沃克	
帳戶：510-11-1211	
細項	**金額**
百利雜貨店（5/9）	32.00 美元
XD 加油站（5/9）	25.00 美元
里克五金行（5/9）	7.25 美元
海外交易費（5/9）	**3.50 美元** 66

65. 女子可能在哪裡工作？
(A) 在信用卡公司
(B) 在超市
(C) 在人力仲介公司
(D) 在五金行

66. 請根據圖表作答。哪筆款項將刪除？
(A) 32.00 美元
(B) 25.00 美元
(C) 7.25 美元
(D) 3.50 美元

67. 女子為何請男子稍候？
(A) 為了解釋新流程
(B) 為了讓他和她的主管通話
(C) 為了驗證他的一些聯絡資訊
(D) 為了聽取一些回饋意見

68–70 會話和產業園區地圖

男：您好，克勞利女士。我是奈爾科技的馬丁•桑切茲。**我們仔細審過您的求職表後，決定通知您過來進行面試。** 68 下週三上午十點您方便嗎？

女：我很高興收到您的答覆。請您稍等，讓我確認一下我的行程。可以，那個時段沒問題。

男：很好。那麼奈爾科技位於城鎮的西側。**我們的辦公大樓位於紅杉街，就在社區活動中心旁。** 69

女：好的。另外，**請問我是否可以將車停在停車場的任何位置，還是要取得通行證呢？** 70

男：**您只要使用標有「訪客」的空車位就沒問題了。** 70

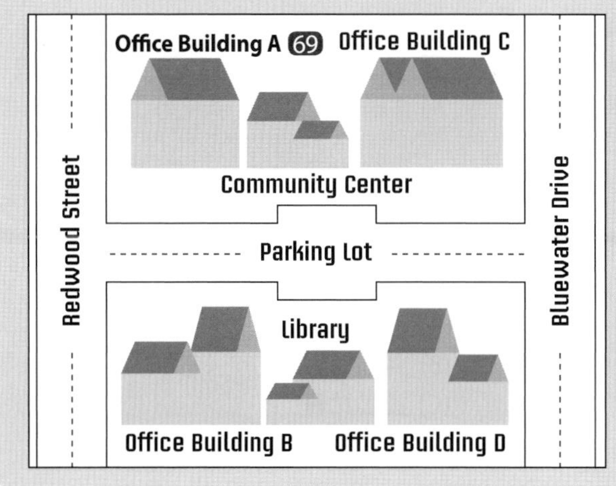

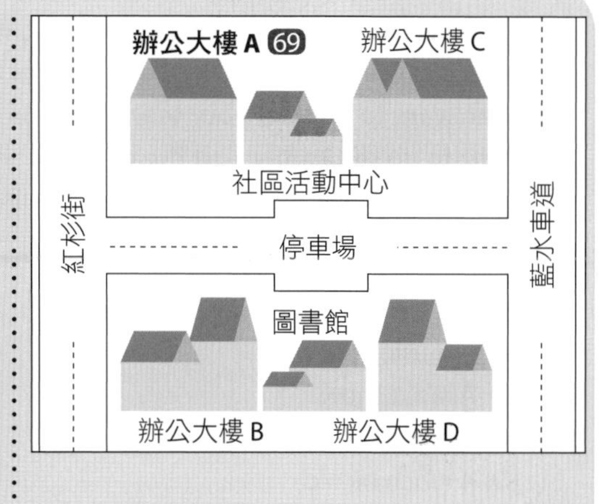

68. What are the speakers mainly discussing?
(A) A business opening
(B) A job interview
(C) A renovation project
(D) A moving plan

69. Look at the graphic. In which office building is Nertech, Inc. located?
(A) Office Building A
(B) Office Building B
(C) Office Building C
(D) Office Building D

70. What does the man tell the woman about parking?
(A) A parking space has been reserved for her.
(B) A parking permit must be displayed.
(C) She will need to pay cash for a parking space.
(D) She should park in a guest spot.

68. 說話者主要在討論什麼？
(A) 公司開業
(B) 求職面試
(C) 整修案
(D) 搬遷計畫

69. 請根據圖表作答。奈爾科技位於哪個辦公大樓？
(A) 辦公大樓 A
(B) 辦公大樓 B
(C) 辦公大樓 C
(D) 辦公大樓 D

70. 關於停車，男子對女子說了什麼？
(A) 停車位已為她預留。
(B) 須出示停車許可證。
(C) 她須支付現金才能使用停車位。
(D) 她應把車停在訪客車位。

PART 4 P. 27–29

06

Questions 71-73 refer to the following broadcast.

W： This is K-wave Radio with your local news. **Oceanside City officials announced that this year's annual charity soccer tournament has been postponed.** 71 It was originally scheduled to be held tomorrow afternoon, but **due to**

71–73 廣播

女： 這是 K 頻廣播，為您播送地方新聞。**海濱市官員宣布，今年的年度公益足球聯賽已經延期。** 71 它原定明天下午舉行，但**由於天氣預報指出屆時將有雷雨，因此改為下週舉**

thunderstorms in the weather forecast, it has been rescheduled for next week. 72 **For those who want to register your team, there is still time to do so. Simply visit the city Web site,** 73 and click on the tournament registration link.

行。 72 **若有人想要替隊伍報名參賽，目前仍有時間。只需前往市政府官網，** 73 並點擊賽事報名連結即可。

71. What is the announcement about?
(A) A music concert
(B) A radio show
(C) A sports tournament
(D) A lunch picnic

72. What caused the date of an event to be changed?
(A) The weather
(B) Registration issues
(C) Missing equipment
(D) Some construction

73. Why are listeners told to visit a Web site?
(A) To obtain directions
(B) To view a calendar
(C) To buy tickets
(D) To register a team

71. 廣播內容和什麼有關？
(A) 音樂會
(B) 廣播節目
(C) 運動比賽
(D) 午間野餐

72. 活動日期變更的原因為何？
(A) 天氣
(B) 報名問題
(C) 設備遺失
(D) 一些工程

73. 為什麼要請聽眾前往網站？
(A) 以得知交通路線
(B) 以查看日程
(C) 以購買門票
(D) 以替隊伍報名

Questions 74-76 refer to the following announcement.

M： Good morning, ladies and gentlemen. On behalf of Captain Gonzalo and the rest of the flight crew, we welcome you aboard **Flight 927, flying directly from Miami to Barcelona.** 74 There are some vacant seats on today's flight, and **several passengers have inquired about changing their seats.** 75 You are free to do so, but we ask that you wait until the fasten seat belt sign has been turned off. Also, **please let one of the flight attendants know if you require a headset** 76 for the in-flight movie. Meanwhile, make yourself comfortable, and have a look at our brochures and magazines which are located in the pocket of the seat in front of you. We are scheduled to arrive in Barcelona at 12 P.M. local time.

74–76 宣布

男： 各位女士先生，早安。我們謹代表貢薩洛機長和全體機組人員，歡迎各位搭乘 **927 號航班，本班機將從邁阿密直飛巴塞隆納。** 74 本日班機尚有幾個空位，且**有多位乘客詢問換位的問題。** 75 各位貴賓可以自由換位，但我們請您等到安全帶指示燈熄滅以後再行動。另外，**如您需要耳機，請告知我們的空服員，** 76 以便您觀賞機上電影。 同時也請您不用拘束，可翻閱在您前方座位掛袋內的手冊和雜誌。我們預計將在當地時間中午 12 點抵達巴塞隆納。

74. What is the destination of the flight?
(A) New York
(B) Miami
(C) Rio de Janeiro
(D) Barcelona

74. 該班機的目的地為何？
(A) 紐約
(B) 邁阿密
(C) 里約熱內盧
(D) 巴塞隆納

75. What have some people inquired about?
(A) Storing their luggage
(B) Moving to another seat
(C) Ordering duty-free items
(D) Using mobile phone devices

75. 有些人詢問了什麼事？
(A) 放置行李
(B) 移到其他座位
(C) 訂購免稅品
(D) 使用手機設備

76. Why are passengers instructed to notify a flight attendant?
(A) To get a magazine
(B) To request a special meal
(C) To obtain a headset
(D) To fill out a customs form

76. 乘客受指示要通知空服員，是為了什麼事？
(A) 為了取得一本雜誌
(B) 為了要求特別餐點
(C) 為了取用耳機
(D) 為了填寫海關申報表

Questions 77-79 refer to the following excerpt from a meeting.

77–79 會議摘錄

M：**I've asked all the food service staff to gather this morning to explain a change in the way we are going to serve meals** 77 to our residents at Fairview Nursing Home. **The facility will now be using a system whereby residents can phone in their meal orders and have the food delivered to their rooms. To ensure that residents' dietary restrictions are adhered to, the food service coordinator on duty will check the database** 78 before any meal is prepared. **The system, which has already been successfully implemented in local hospitals, has many advantages, the most significant of which is that far less food is wasted.** 79

男：**我在今早已請全體餐飲服務的同仁集合，以便說明我們**對於美景安養院的院民**供餐方式的異動。** 77 **該院現在將使用一套新系統，使院民可以透過電話訂餐，讓餐點送到房間。為了確實遵守院民的飲食限制，值班的餐飲服務負責人將**在每道餐點備餐前，**先核對資料庫。** 78 **這套系統已在當地多間醫院成功實施，具備多項優點，其中最重要的是大幅減少食物浪費。** 79

77. What is the purpose of the talk?
(A) To request feedback from residents
(B) To introduce a new procedure
(C) To announce a training session
(D) To discuss staff changes

77. 這段談話的目的為何？
(A) 為了徵詢院民意見
(B) 為了引進新流程
(C) 為了宣布培訓課程
(D) 為了討論人事異動

78. What will the coordinator do?
(A) Reschedule work hours
(B) Invite more guests
(C) Set up another meeting
(D) Review residents' records

78. 負責人將做什麼？
(A) 重新安排上班時間
(B) 邀請更多賓客
(C) 安排另一場會議
(D) 檢查院民的紀錄

79. What advantage does the speaker mention?
(A) Improved work environment
(B) Faster delivery
(C) Reduced food waste
(D) Lower prices

79. 說話者提及哪項優勢？
(A) 改善工作環境
(B) 送餐更快
(C) 減少食物浪費
(D) 價格較低

Questions 80-82 refer to the following telephone message.

80–82 語音留言

W：Ms. Johanson, this is Sally. **I'm calling to let you know that due to your recent promotion, you will be moving from your cubicle into a manager's office on the 3rd floor.** 80 **I know you're happy with where you're sitting right now, but you're right next to the staff lounge. It's a lot quieter on the 3rd floor.** 81 Also, as we often have management meetings on the 3rd floor, it would be convenient for you to be here. I'll send someone down to help you pack up tomorrow morning. **On Friday, the IT Department will set up a new computer and printer for you at your new workspace.** 82

女：約翰遜女士，我是莎莉。**我打電話是想通知您，由於您最近升遷，您將從原來的隔間座位移到三樓的經理辦公室。** 80 **我了解您很滿意現在的座位，但您就坐在員工休息室旁邊。三樓會安靜很多。** 81 此外，因為我們經常在三樓舉行主管會議，在這邊對您比較方便。我會派人明天早上下去幫您收拾物品。**週五時，資訊技術部門會在您的新辦公室安裝新的電腦和印表機。** 82

80. What is the speaker calling about?
(A) Reassigning a project
(B) Changing a schedule
(C) Preparing a presentation
(D) Moving into a new office

80. 說話者打電話是要聯絡什麼事？
(A) 重新指派專案
(B) 更改行程表
(C) 準備簡報
(D) 搬入新辦公室

81. Why does the speaker say, "you're right next to the staff lounge"?
(A) To refuse a coworker's request
(B) To ask for extra supplies
(C) To suggest renovating a lounge
(D) To point out that an area is undesirable

81. 說話者說：「您就坐在員工休息室旁邊」，其意思為何？
(A) 以拒絕同仁的要求
(B) 以要求額外的用品
(C) 以建議整修休息室
(D) 以指出不理想的區域

82. What does the speaker say will take place on Friday?
(A) The opening of a new store
(B) The installation of some equipment
(C) A training workshop
(D) A management meeting

82. 說話者提到週五會發生什麼事？
(A) 新店開張
(B) 安裝一些設備
(C) 培訓研習
(D) 主管會議

06

Questions 83-85 refer to the following speech.

W: Hello, everyone, and **welcome to tonight's celebration of BH Industries' Entrepreneur of the Year Awards Show. It is my honor to recognize Maggie Olmstead of Olmstead, Inc.** 83 **Maggie's company first entered the spotlight for its anti-virus program, Mag-O, which has received great reviews from users everywhere.** 84 Olmstead is now working on another application that compresses files to save space on all mobile devices. If it is anything like Mag-O, it will surely sell well. With Olmstead, Inc. looking to grow and expand, **Maggie has plans to move her company's offices to Nickel Hills at the start of next year.** 85 Now, let's all give a big welcome to Maggie Olmstead.

83–85 演講

女：各位好，**歡迎來到今晚 BH 產業年度企業家的頒獎典禮。我很榮幸表揚奧姆斯特德企業的瑪姬•奧姆斯特德。** 83 **瑪姬的公司首度大受矚目的原因，就是推出防毒程式 Mag-O，該程式已獲得各地用戶的好評。** 84 奧姆斯特德公司目前正在開發另一款應用程式，能為各種行動裝置壓縮檔案以節省空間。它如果能和 Mag-O 並駕齊驅，肯定也會銷售長紅。有鑑於奧姆斯特德公司可望成長擴張，**瑪姬計劃明年初將其公司的辦公室搬到鎳之丘。** 85 現在，讓我們熱烈歡迎瑪姬•奧姆斯特德。

83. What is the purpose of the speech?
(A) To describe a new project
(B) To introduce an award recipient
(C) To demonstrate a process
(D) To honor a retiring employee

83. 這段演講的目的為何？
(A) 以講解一個新專案
(B) 以介紹獲獎者
(C) 以展示流程
(D) 以表揚退休員工

84. What industry does Maggie Olmstead most likely work in?
(A) Construction
(B) Software
(C) Medical
(D) Travel

84. 瑪姬•奧姆斯特德最有可能在哪個產業工作？
(A) 營建
(B) 軟體
(C) 醫藥
(D) 旅遊

85. According to the speaker, what does Ms. Olmstead plan to do?
(A) Hire additional employees
(B) Update a logo
(C) Launch an advertising campaign
(D) Relocate her business

85. 據説話者説法，奧姆斯特德女士打算做什麼？
(A) 增聘員工
(B) 更新公司標誌
(C) 開始廣告活動
(D) 搬遷公司

Questions 86-88 refer to the following advertisement.

M: **If you want to use the best business meeting facilities in the city, then Lloyd Conference Center has everything you need.** 86 We have a wide range of small and large meeting rooms,

86–88 廣告

男：**若您想使用本市最好的商務會議設施，那麼勞埃德會議中心就為您提供了一切所需。** 86 我們備有各種不同大小的會議室，以及最先進的電

and state-of-the-art electronic equipment. And **starting this year, our copying services are available 24 hours a day.** 87 For detailed information about our services and rates, call 555-3578. **Tell us about this ad when you make your next reservation, and you will receive 15 percent off** 88 our regular rates.

子設備。且**今年開始，我們更提供 24 小時複印服務。** 87 想知道更多我們服務和費用的詳細資訊，請來電 555-3578。**您於下次預約時，請告訴我們聽過這則廣告，就可獲得**我們原價**折 15%的優惠。** 88

86. What business is being advertised?
(A) An electronics store
(B) An equipment rental shop
(C) A conference center
(D) A shipping company

86. 哪種公司正在打廣告？
(A) 電子用品店
(B) 設備出租店
(C) 會議中心
(D) 航運公司

87. What new service is available this year?
(A) 24-hour photocopying
(B) Online reservation
(C) Wireless Internet
(D) Express delivery

87. 今年有哪項新服務可用？
(A) 24 小時複印
(B) 線上預約
(C) 無線網路
(D) 快遞

88. How can listeners get a discount?
(A) By mentioning an advertisement
(B) By referring a friend
(C) By printing out a voucher
(D) By booking one month in advance

88. 聽眾如何取得折扣？
(A) 提及廣告
(B) 介紹朋友
(C) 印出優惠券
(D) 提前一個月預約

Questions 89-91 refer to the following excerpt from a meeting.

89–91 會議摘錄

M：Now, **the next thing we need to discuss is the ScanMaster 3000, our hand-held scanning device. You're all aware of last quarter's sales performance. We have to work on getting more customers to purchase it.** 89 **Raymond has done some research, and according to his report, the main issue is that consumers see no difference between the ScanMaster 3000 and our largest competitor's product, which looks almost exactly the same.** 90 There are five unique features we need to make clear in all our advertisements, so buyers can make the distinction. **I'll go over them one by one, but first, let's take a few minutes to review this data chart.** 91

男：那麼，**接下來要討論的是我們的手持型掃描機「掃描大師 3000」。你們都知道上一季的銷售表現。我們須努力吸引更多顧客購買該產品。** 89 **雷蒙有做了研究，根據他的報告，主要問題是消費者看不出掃描大師 3000 和我們最大競爭對手的產品有何區別，兩者看起來幾乎一樣。** 90 我們的產品有五大特色，須在廣告裡講清楚，以便買家能夠做出區別。**我將逐一仔細介紹，但首先，讓我們花幾分鐘看一下數據圖表。** 91

89. What does the speaker mean when he says, "You're all aware of last quarter's sales performance"?
(A) The listeners will not review a report.
(B) Some data should not have been released.
(C) The listeners know that a product has not sold well.
(D) Some sales figures are incorrect.

89. 說話者說：「你們都知道上一季的銷售表現」，其意思為何？
(A) 聽眾將不會看報告。
(B) 有些數據不應公開。
(C) 聽眾知道有個產品賣得不好。
(D) 有些銷售數據有誤。

90. What does Raymond's report indicate?
(A) A competitor's product is more affordable.
(B) A competitor's advertising campaign is better.
(C) Consumers cannot tell the difference between some products.
(D) Consumers have complained about the features of an item.

90. 雷蒙的報告指出什麼？
(A) 競爭對手的產品價格更親民。
(B) 競爭對手的廣告活動更好。
(C) 消費者分辨不出某些產品之間的差異。
(D) 消費者抱怨產品的特色。

91. What are listeners asked to do next?
(A) Submit an invoice
(B) Contact some clients
(C) Test some devices
(D) Look over a document

91. 聽眾被要求接下來要做什麼？
(A) 提交一張帳單
(B) 聯絡一些客戶
(C) 測試一些裝置
(D) 檢視一份資料

Questions 92-94 refer to the following excerpt from a meeting.

92–94 會議摘要

W：Good afternoon, everyone. **Before your shifts start tonight, I'd just like to say a couple of things.** 92 **As always, we received a lot of positive feedback last month on the quality of the dishes.** 93 However, we did not get such positive feedback on the speed of service. Some customers complained that they had to wait up to 40 minutes for their meals, especially between courses. **As we cater to a lot of business customers, particularly at lunchtime, we need to ensure that meals are prepared and served quickly. All waiting staff, please make sure that orders are immediately sent to the kitchen. And kitchen staff, make every effort to get orders cooked as fast as possible.** 94 **I know you can do it.** Thanks.

女：大家午安。**在你們今晚輪班開始前，我有一些事想說。** 92 **一如以往，我們上個月收到很多關於餐點品質的正面回饋。** 93 但我們在服務速度方面，卻沒有收到這樣的好評。有些客人抱怨，他們等餐需要 40 分鐘之久，特別是在兩道餐點之間。**因為我們服務的客人很多是上班族，尤其在午餐時段，我們得確保餐點能儘快備齊上桌。全體服務員，務必將點單即時送到廚房。廚房工作人員，盡最大的努力儘快把餐點做好。** 94 **我知道你們辦得到。** 謝謝。

92. Who most likely is the speaker?
(A) A manager
(B) A researcher
(C) A chef
(D) A waiter

92. 說話者最有可能是誰？
(A) 經理
(B) 研究員
(C) 廚師
(D) 服務生

93. According to the speaker, what is the business known for?

(A) High-quality food
(B) Cheap prices
(C) Helpful staff
(D) Fast service

94. What does the speaker mean when she says, "I know you can do it"?

(A) She wishes employees will stay later.
(B) She hopes customers will give feedback.
(C) She thinks new dishes can be created.
(D) She believes staff can work faster.

Questions 95-97 refer to the following telephone message and inspection report.

W： Good afternoon. **It's Becky Hamlin from The Boxton—the caterer on Pearl Street.** 95 You conducted a health inspection at our business this morning, and I have a question regarding the report. The top section looks fine, **but at the bottom, we were not given any details as to why we didn't pass the inspection. I would like to know the reason why our freezer's condition was unacceptable,** 96 so we can get it repaired right away. **I'm worried because we need to complete a large order for a party in a few days, and we have to get ready for it soon.** 97

Health Inspection	
Name of Store: The Boxton	**Officer:** Marcus Graham
Health Checklist: ☑ Sanitation ☑ Waste Disposal ☑ Employee Hygiene	**Notes:** 96 **Failure of inspection: Freezer**

95. Where does the speaker work?

(A) At a flower shop
(B) At an appliance store
(C) At a catering business
(D) At a delivery company

93. 據說話者說法，該店家以什麼聞名？

(A) 優質餐點
(B) 低價
(C) 樂於助人的員工
(D) 服務快速

94. 說話者說：「我知道你們辦得到」，其意思為何？

(A) 她想要員工待晚一點。
(B) 她希望客人給回饋意見。
(C) 她認為可以發想新菜色。
(D) 她相信員工可以加快作業。

95–97 語音留言和檢查報告

女：午安。**我是貝姬‧哈姆林，任職於珍珠街上的外燴業者波克斯頓。** 95 您今天早上到我們店裡執行衛生檢查，而我對報告有個疑問。前面的部分看起來還不錯，**但最後關於為何我們未通過檢查，卻沒有提供任何細節。我想了解我們冷凍庫的狀況未獲准通過的原因，** 96 以便我們能夠立即把它修好。**我會擔心是因為我們需要在幾天後完成一個宴會的大訂單，我們得儘快準備。** 97

衛生檢查	
店家名稱： 波克斯頓餐飲	**稽查人員：** 馬可斯‧葛蘭姆
衛生檢查項目： ☑ 環境衛生 ☑ 廢棄物處理 ☑ 員工衛生	**備註：** 96 **未通過檢查：冷凍庫**

95. 說話者在哪裡工作？

(A) 在花店
(B) 在電器行
(C) 在外燴業者
(D) 在快遞公司

96. Look at the graphic. Which section of the report does the speaker ask about?
(A) Name of Store
(B) Officer
(C) Health Checklist
(D) Notes

97. What does the speaker say she is concerned about?
(A) Fulfilling an order
(B) Losing merchandise
(C) Hiring more workers
(D) Paying a penalty

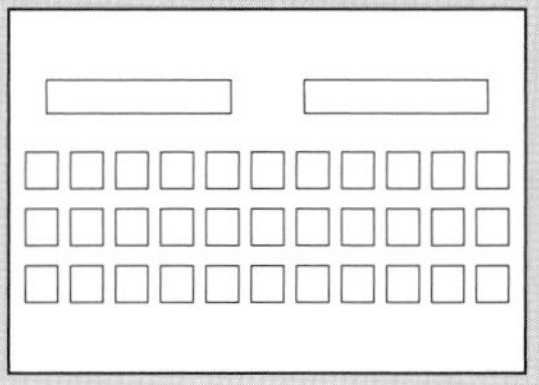

96. 請根據圖表作答。說話者詢問的是報告的哪個部分？
(A) 店家名稱
(B) 稽查人員
(C) 衛生檢查項目
(D) 備註

97. 說話者說她在擔心什麼事？
(A) 完成訂單
(B) 遺失商品
(C) 增聘員工
(D) 繳納罰款

Questions 98-100 refer to the following excerpt from a meeting and diagrams.

M：**Welcome to our first planning session for this year's Public Health Conference.** 98 **This conference will feature presentations by some world-renowned experts in the public health industry. As a result, all advance tickets have sold out, and we are anticipating that a lot more people will sign up for the event in the upcoming weeks.** 99 Sanjiv Singh, the dean of GSU's School of Public Health, will be our main speaker. He'll be presenting in Malone Auditorium. **He wants us to arrange the room so that he is in front of as many people as possible, rather than having people on all sides of him. We'll put two tables in front of him, and then set up chairs in rows.** 100 Who can take care of setting that up?

Arrangement A

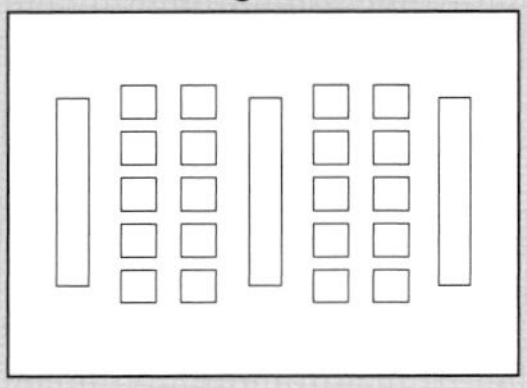

Arrangement B

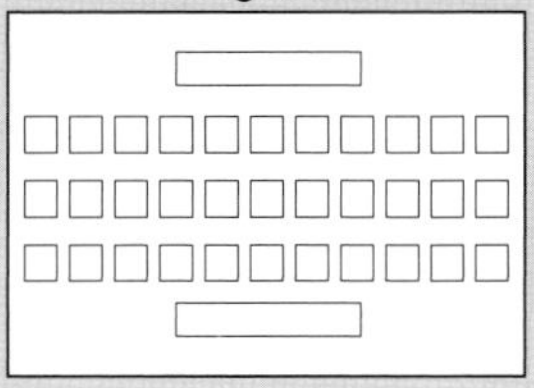

Arrangement C

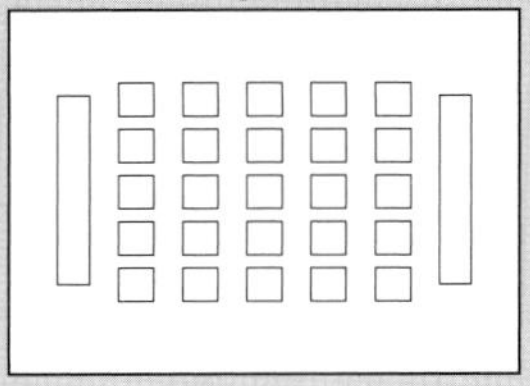

Arrangement D

98–100 會議摘錄和圖示

男：**歡迎參加今年公共衛生會議的第一場籌備會。** 98 **這次會議將有幾位全球著名的公衛產業專家發表演講。因此，預售票已經銷售一空，我們預計未來幾週還會有多很多人報名參加。** 99 GSU 公共衛生學院院長桑吉夫．辛格會擔任主講者，他將在馬龍禮堂進行演講。**他想要我們安排場地，以便他站的地方能面向越多人越好，而不是讓他被人群包圍。我們會在他的前方擺兩張桌子，然後再把椅子排列成幾排。** 100 有誰可以負責這項布置？

布置 A

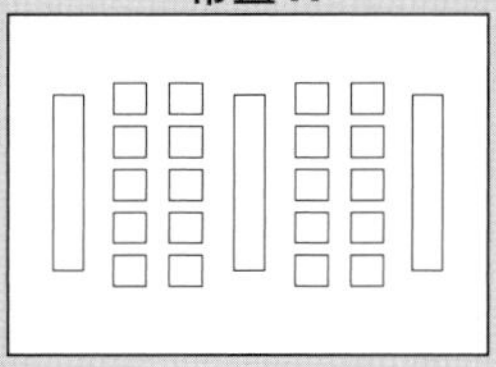

布置 B

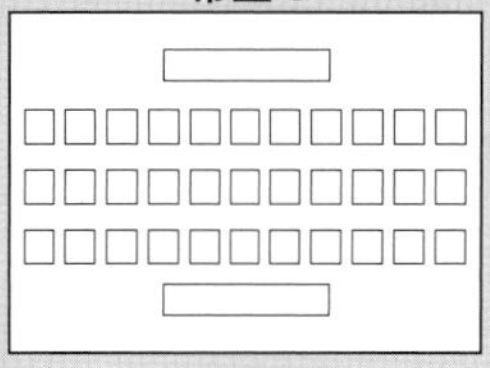

布置 C

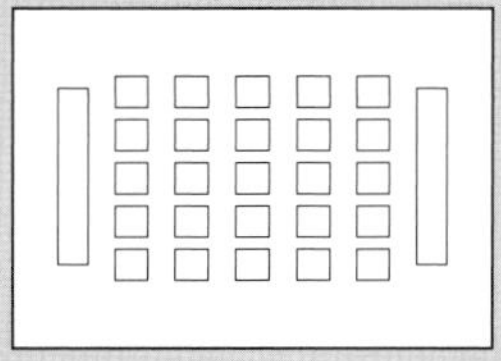

布置 D

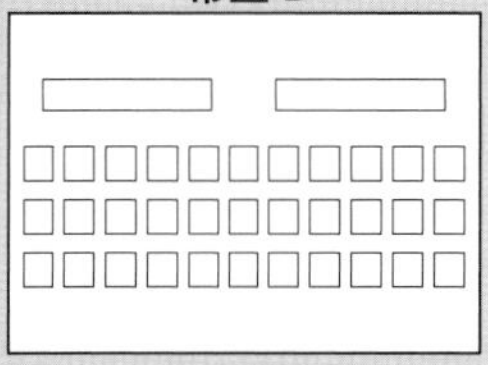

98. What kind of event is being discussed?

(A) A medical conference

(B) A movie premiere

(C) An anniversary celebration

(D) An investors' meeting

99. Why is the speaker anticipating attendance to be high?

(A) Many volunteers were recruited.

(B) The venue is in a convenient location.

(C) Some experts will be giving talks.

(D) Some prizes will be distributed.

100. Look at the graphic. Which arrangement will be used in the Malone Auditorium?

(A) Arrangement A

(B) Arrangement B

(C) Arrangement C

(D) Arrangement D

98. 在討論的是哪一種活動？

(A) 醫學會議

(B) 電影首映

(C) 週年慶活動

(D) 投資者會議

99. 為什麼說話者預期出席人數很多？

(A) 招募了很多志工。

(B) 場館位置交通方便。

(C) 幾位專家將發表演講。

(D) 將頒發數個獎項。

100. 請根據圖表作答。馬龍禮堂將採用哪種布置？

(A) 布置 A

(B) 布置 B

(C) 布置 C

(D) 布置 D

ACTUAL TEST 2

PART 1 P. 30-33

1. (A) A woman is cutting grass.
   (B) A trash bin is being emptied.
   (C) A man is sweeping the floor.
   (D) A chair is being adjusted.

2. (A) The man is pouring a drink into a glass.
   (B) One of the people is wearing glasses.
   (C) The women are holding their forks.
   (D) The people are waiting to be seated.

3. (A) They are watering flowers in the garden.
   (B) They are strolling through a walkway.
   (C) A trolley has been filled with items.
   (D) Potted plants have been loaded onto a truck.

4. (A) A flight attendant is checking tickets.
   (B) A fence is being installed outside a building.
   (C) Boxes are being pushed along the runway.
   (D) People are walking toward an entrance.

5. (A) She is unpacking a package.
   (B) She is wheeling a baggage cart.
   (C) An airline employee is loading some luggage.
   (D) A suitcase is being removed from an overhead compartment.

6. (A) A worker is pulling up a blind over a glass door.
   (B) Some desks are positioned one in front of the other.
   (C) Some chairs are stacked in a storeroom.
   (D) Light fixtures are being hung over a meeting table.

1. (A) 女子正在割草。
   (B) 有人正在清空垃圾桶。
   (C) 男子正在掃地。
   (D) 有人在調整椅子。

2. (A) 男子把飲料倒進玻璃杯。
   (B) 其中一人戴著眼鏡。
   (C) 女子們拿著叉子。
   (D) 人們正在等著入座。

3. (A) 他們正在澆花園裡的花。
   (B) 他們正漫步在人行道上。
   (C) 推車裝滿了物品。
   (D) 盆栽被放到卡車上。

4. (A) 空服員正在檢查機票。
   (B) 建築外正在裝設圍欄。
   (C) 有人沿著跑道推動箱子。
   (D) 人們正朝入口走去。

5. (A) 她正在開包裹。
   (B) 她推著行李推車。
   (C) 航空公司職員正在裝載行李。
   (D) 有人正從座位上方置物櫃拿下行李箱。

6. (A) 工人拉起玻璃門的百葉窗。
   (B) 幾張桌子前後排列著。
   (C) 庫房堆了幾把椅子。
   (D) 會議桌上方懸掛著幾盞燈具。

PART 2 P. 34

7. Does this subway go to City Hall?
   (A) No, it doesn't.
   (B) I saw it on the bus.
   (C) The station was crowded.

7. 這條地鐵是去市政廳的嗎？
   (A) 不，不是。
   (B) 我在公車上看到了。
   (C) 車站很擁擠。

8. Where did you purchase these concert tickets?
(A) At the box office.
(B) Last weekend.
(C) Some instruments.

9. How was the annual trade exposition?
(A) I traded it in for a new one.
(B) Not as good as last year's.
(C) Yes, at the same location.

10. Who's responsible for ordering the office supplies?
(A) It's a big responsibility.
(B) That's not my order.
(C) That would be Ms. Kroll.

11. When will the yearly sales figures be available?
(A) Yes, the data is still available.
(B) Sometime tomorrow.
(C) A monthly subscription.

12. Which branch did you send the package to?
(A) I paid for it this morning.
(B) The express option.
(C) The Remington office in New York.

13. Would you like some assistance preparing your proposal?
(A) Yes, he did.
(B) It does occasionally.
(C) I just emailed it to our manager.

14. How far away is your office from your home?
(A) I can walk there.
(B) OK. I'll give you a ride.
(C) On the 5th floor.

15. Why is Grover Avenue blocked off this morning?
(A) For the bike race.
(B) At the next street.
(C) In three hours.

16. Have the discount coupons for August been printed yet?
(A) Twice a month.
(B) I appreciate the update.
(C) Robert in Marketing should know.

8. 這幾張演唱會門票你在哪裡買的？
(A) 在售票處。
(B) 上個週末。
(C) 一些樂器。

9. 這次的年度貿易展如何？
(A) 我拿它換成新的。
(B) 不像去年的那麼好。
(C) 對，在同一個地點。

10. 辦公用品是由誰負責訂購的？
(A) 這責任重大。
(B) 那不是我的訂單。
(C) 應是克羅爾女士。

11. 什麼時候可以取得年度銷售數據？
(A) 是，那筆資料還能取得。
(B) 明天以內。
(C) 每月訂閱。

12. 你把該件包裹寄到哪個分部？
(A) 我今天早上付了它的錢。
(B) 快遞選項。
(C) 紐約的雷明登辦公室。

13. 你準備提案時需要一點協助嗎？
(A) 是，他做了。
(B) 偶爾會這樣。
(C) 我剛把它用電子郵件寄給我們經理了。

14. 辦公室離你家多遠？
(A) 我走路可以到。
(B) 好，我會順路載你一程。
(C) 在五樓。

15. 為什麼格羅弗大道今天早上封閉？
(A) 為了辦自行車競賽。
(B) 在下一條街上。
(C) 三小時後。

16. 八月份的折價券印好了嗎？
(A) 每個月兩次。
(B) 我很感謝這項更新資訊。
(C) 行銷部的羅伯特應該知道。

17. Where do I apply to participate in the art competition?
(A) For a museum exhibit.
(B) At the main booth.
(C) A trophy will be awarded.

18. Why don't we recycle our used plastic bottles?
(A) Oh, she already did?
(B) OK, I'll tell the others to do the same.
(C) Our new packaging process.

19. Aren't we supposed to submit the budget report to Mr. Rogers' assistant?
(A) A financial advisor.
(B) I was asked to email it directly to him.
(C) No, the train is late.

20. I heard that Barbara will be transferring to the Huntington branch.
(A) The new branch manager.
(B) No. I'll transfer the money now.
(C) Yes, they're short on staff.

21. Are you going to hold the training workshop at our office or do it online?
(A) Most likely early next week.
(B) There isn't a meeting room big enough here.
(C) What did you think about the presentation on international markets?

22. Could you prepare an agenda for tomorrow's conference call?
(A) I'll have it ready by lunchtime.
(B) A call from the company president.
(C) We'll need to repair the projector.

23. How many planners should I bring to the new staff orientation?
(A) Let me review the list.
(B) Yes, I've seen them.
(C) A charitable organization.

24. Do you have any seats available for this show?
(A) His best performance yet.
(B) No, that's an old seating chart.
(C) All of the tickets are sold out.

17. 我要在哪裡申請參加美術比賽？
(A) 用於博物館展覽。
(B) 在主展位。
(C) 將頒發獎杯。

18. 我們為何不回收使用我們用過的塑料瓶？
(A) 哦，她已經做了嗎？
(B) 好，我會通知其他人也照做。
(C) 我們新的包裝流程。

19. 我們不是應該把預算報告交給羅傑斯先生的助理嗎？
(A) 理財顧問。
(B) 我受指示用電郵直接寄給他。
(C) 不，火車誤點了。

20. 我聽說芭芭拉將轉調到杭亭頓分公司。
(A) 新的分公司經理。
(B) 不。我現在就把錢轉過去。
(C) 對，他們人手短缺。

21. 你打算在我們辦公室舉行培訓研習，還是在線上舉辦？
(A) 最有可能在下週的前幾天。
(B) 這裡的會議室都不夠大。
(C) 你覺得國際市場主題的簡報如何？

22. 能請你準備明天電話會議的議程嗎？
(A) 我會在午餐時間前準備好。
(B) 公司總裁打來的電話。
(C) 我們得修好投影機。

23. 我應該帶幾位規劃人員去參加新進員工說明會？
(A) 讓我確認一下名單。
(B) 有，我看過他們。
(C) 一個慈善團體。

24. 這場表演還有座位嗎？
(A) 他至今的最佳表現。
(B) 不，那是舊的座位表。
(C) 票全都賣光了。

25. You've visited Italy before, haven't you?
(A) I went there just last year.
(B) I've tried that pasta before.
(C) Many historic sites and monuments.

26. Who should I talk to about getting a new ID issued?
(A) I'll take you to my supervisor.
(B) Would you like to discuss this issue?
(C) No. I don't have an ID card.

27. Shouldn't we interview additional applicants?
(A) Yes, it's a beautiful view.
(B) I think we met enough.
(C) Through an online application.

28. How frequently does Ms. Chung want to hold the professional development seminars?
(A) The lecture at 6 o'clock.
(B) It will be in seminar room B.
(C) What did she do last year?

29. We'll most likely have to work extra hours this month, right?
(A) I attended the workshop last month.
(B) It took almost two hours to get to work.
(C) Actually, the project has been put on hold.

30. Should we repair this printer or just buy a new one?
(A) I don't think it can be fixed.
(B) The paper is in the supply closet.
(C) An online store.

31. I think it's too early to enter the theater.
(A) You're right. The movie was great.
(B) I see some people going in now.
(C) Two general admission tickets, please.

25. 你有去過義大利，不是嗎？
(A) 我去年才去過。
(B) 我吃過那種義大利麵。
(C) 許多歷史古蹟和遺址。

26. 我需要領新的識別證，應該跟誰說呢？
(A) 我帶你去找我的主管。
(B) 你想討論這個問題嗎？
(C) 不，我沒有識別證。

27. 我們不是應該再面試其他應徵者嗎？
(A) 對啊，風景很美。
(B) 我覺得我們面試的人夠多了。
(C) 透過網路申請。

28. 鍾女士想要多久舉辦一次職業發展研討會？
(A) 六點的課程。
(B) 它將在 B 研討室舉行。
(C) 她去年的做法是什麼？

29. 我們這個月很可能得加班，對嗎？
(A) 我上個月參加了研習。
(B) 上班路程近兩小時。
(C) 其實該專案暫緩了。

30. 我們要修理這台印表機，還是買台新的就好？
(A) 我不認為它修得好。
(B) 紙放在用品儲藏室裡。
(C) 網路商店。

31. 我覺得現在進電影院太早了。
(A) 你說得對。這部電影很好看。
(B) 我看到有些人正在入場。
(C) 兩張普通票，麻煩了。

PART 3 P. 35–38

Questions 32-34 refer to the following conversation.

M: Hi, Alison. **Have you seen this week's *Business World Net Magazine*? There is an online article that says we're the fastest growing mobile phone company in the country.** 32

32–34 會話

男：嗨，艾莉森。**妳有看這週的《商界網路雜誌》嗎？上面有一篇網路文章說我們是國內成長最快的手機公司。** 32

W：Yes, I just read it. In fact, **it would be great if you could post a link on our Web site that directs people to the article.** 34 **That kind of media coverage will definitely help our campaign to recruit new employees.** 33

M：**It will certainly attract more prospective job applicants to our company.** 33 **I'll go to my computer right now and add the link.** 34

女：有，我剛看完。其實**你可以在我們網站張貼連結，引導大家過去看文章，應該會很不錯。** 34 **這類媒體報導絕對會有助於我們招募新人的活動。** 33

男：**這一定會幫公司吸引更多潛在的求職者上門。** 33 **我馬上去用我的電腦把連結加上去。** 34

32. What has been written about the company?
(A) It received an award.
(B) It is growing quickly.
(C) It will relocate soon.
(D) It has launched a new product.

33. According to the speakers, what will the article help to do?
(A) Increase job applications
(B) Lower operating costs
(C) Improve staff training
(D) Attract international customers

34. What will the man do next?
(A) Revise a schedule
(B) Post a job opening
(C) Send an email
(D) Update a Web site

32. 關於公司，文章中寫到什麼？
(A) 它得獎了。
(B) 它正在快速成長。
(C) 它即將搬遷。
(D) 它近期推出新產品。

33. 據説話者説法，該篇文章能幫助到何事？
(A) 增加應徵件數
(B) 降低營運成本
(C) 改善員工訓練
(D) 吸引國際客戶

34. 男子接下來會做什麼？
(A) 修改行程
(B) 公告職缺
(C) 寄電子郵件
(D) 更新網站

Questions 35-37 refer to the following conversation.

W：Mr. Mason, I just went over our plant's health and safety records, and **it looks like some of our employees' safety certificates have been expired.** 35

M：Really? I thought we had a training session a few months ago, and all of our workers were certified. And aren't the certificates good for one year?

W：Yes, they are, but that session was only for our new employees. Now, **we need to do another session for those who were certified last year. But all they need to do is attend a short refresher session** 36 for their recertification.

M：I see. **Could you send me a list of the employees who need to get recertified?** 37 Then we can organize a session for them.

35-37 會話

女：梅森先生，我剛檢查完我們工廠的衛生及安全紀錄，而**看來我們有些員工的安全證書過期了。** 35

男：真的嗎？幾個月前才辦過培訓課程，我以為全體員工都拿到證書了。證書效期不是一年嗎？

女：對，是一年，但那次的課程只針對新進員工。現在**我們需要為去年拿到證書的同仁再辦一次課程。但他們只需要參加簡短的進修複習講習** 36 即可換發新證書。

男：了解。**妳可以把需要重新換證的員工名單寄給我嗎？** 37 然後我們就可以為他們安排講習。

35. What problem has the woman identified?
(A) Some documents are out of date.
(B) Some files have been misplaced.
(C) A software program is not working properly.
(D) Two seminars have been double-booked.

36. What does the woman say about employees who were certified last year?
(A) They must contact their managers.
(B) They may work at another plant.
(C) They will train new staff members.
(D) They need to attend a review session.

37. What does the man ask the woman to do?
(A) Lead a training workshop
(B) Complete a registration form
(C) Provide names of employees
(D) Send out invitations

35. 女子發現了什麼問題？
(A) 有些文件過期了。
(B) 有些檔案放錯了。
(C) 軟體程式無法正常運作。
(D) 兩場研討會的場地被重複預訂了。

36. 關於去年拿到證書的員工，女子說了什麼？
(A) 他們必須聯絡其主管。
(B) 他們可以到別間工廠工作。
(C) 他們將訓練新進員工。
(D) 他們須參加複習課程。

37. 男子請女子做什麼？
(A) 帶領培訓研習
(B) 填寫報名表
(C) 提供數名員工姓名
(D) 送出邀請函

Questions 38-40 refer to the following conversation.

M：Hi, Donna. **The company is sending me to Prague in two weeks to cover a fashion show at the Moda Exhibition Center. They want me to write a special article about it** 38 for our magazine. Weren't you there recently?
W：Yes, and a close friend of mine is one of the designers whose clothing line will be displayed at the event. **Would you like to get in touch with him?** 40
M：Yes. **It'd be great to get as much information as I can about the designers that will be featured before attending the show.** 39
W：OK, **I have his business card in my office. Let me go get it for you.** 40

38-40 會話

男：嗨，唐娜。**公司兩週後會派我去布拉格，報導在時尚展覽館的時裝秀。他們要我針對活動寫篇特稿** 38 登在我們的雜誌上。妳最近不是才去過那裡嗎？
女：對，而且我有個好朋友是設計師，他的系列服裝也會在那場活動展出。**你想跟他聯絡看看嗎？** 40
男：想，**我如果能在參加那場秀之前，掌握愈多參展設計師的資訊愈好。** 39
女：好，**我辦公室裡有他的名片。讓我去拿來給你。** 40

38. What is the conversation mainly about?
(A) Visiting a friend
(B) Reporting on an event
(C) Attending university
(D) Shopping for clothes

38. 對話的主旨為何？
(A) 拜訪朋友
(B) 報導活動
(C) 上大學
(D) 買衣服

39. What does the man say he wants to do before he travels?
(A) Take some courses
(B) Call a hotel
(C) Book a tour
(D) Research some designers

40. What does the woman offer to do?
(A) Show some product catalogs
(B) Check a schedule
(C) Find some contact information
(D) Make a reservation

Questions 41-43 refer to the following conversation.

W：You've reached Rally Rental Cars. How may I assist you?
M：Hello, I returned a rental car at your Bixby location two days ago, and a representative dropped me off at the nearest train station. **I'm looking at the bill right now, and I was wondering why there's an extra fee for the drop-off service.** 41 This is the first time I've had to pay for it.
W：Ah, **due to the increase in gas prices this year, our agency had no choice but to add a fee for that service.** 42
M：Oh, I wasn't aware of that ...
W：I apologize that you weren't told about this earlier. **I'll remove the fee this time,** 43 but starting next time, we'll have to charge for the service.

41. Why is the man calling?
(A) To purchase a train ticket
(B) To request a ride
(C) To discuss a car repair service
(D) To inquire about a charge

42. According to the woman, what has recently changed?
(A) Hiring requirements
(B) A company policy
(C) Business hours
(D) An office location

39. 男子說出發前想做什麼？
(A) 參加課程
(B) 致電給飯店
(C) 預約觀光行程
(D) 調查設計師的資訊

40. 女子提議幫忙做什麼事？
(A) 展示產品型錄
(B) 確認行程
(C) 找出某項聯絡資訊
(D) 預約

41-43 會話

女：這裡是勁力租車。需要什麼協助呢？
男：您好，我兩天前在貴公司的比克斯比站點歸還租車，然後一名員工載我到最近的火車站。**現在我看到帳單了，我想知道為什麼多了一筆載客服務費。** 41 這是我第一次得付這筆帳。
女：啊，**由於今年油價上漲，本公司別無選擇，只好加收這項服務費。** 42
男：哦，我不知道這一點……
女：很抱歉未事先告知您。**這次我會扣除該筆費用，** 43 但下次開始，我們將會收取這項服務的費用。

41. 男子為何來電？
(A) 要購買火車票
(B) 要提出搭車需求
(C) 要討論汽車維修服務
(D) 要詢問某項收費

42. 據女子說法，最近有何異動？
(A) 徵才需求
(B) 公司政策
(C) 營業時間
(D) 辦公地點

43. What does the woman agree to do?
(A) Revise an agreement
(B) Contact a manager
(C) Cancel an appointment
(D) Remove a fee

43. 女子同意做什麼？
(A) 修改合約
(B) 聯絡經理
(C) 取消預約
(D) 刪除一筆費用

Questions 44-46 refer to the following conversation.

W：Hey, Ron. **Would you like me to help you carry those boxes up to our storage room?** 44 There are quite a lot.
M：I would appreciate that very much! **The elevator isn't working right now, so we'll need to take the stairs.** 45
W：**But it stopped working last week.** 45 **Why hasn't Maintenance fixed it yet?** 46
M：Well, I heard that **the control system had to be reconfigured.** 46
W：That makes sense. Well, it's a good thing the storage room is just on the third floor, so we won't need to carry these too far.
M：Yeah. Thanks again for helping me with these boxes. It would have taken a long time if I had to do it myself.

44-46 會話

女：嘿，榮恩，**你想要我幫你一起把那些箱子搬到樓上倉庫嗎？** 44 還真不少。
男：感激不盡！**目前電梯故障，所以我們得走樓梯。** 45
女：**但它上星期就壞了。** 45 **維修部怎麼還沒修好？** 46
男：這個嘛，我聽說是**控制系統需要重新配置。** 46
女：那算有道理。嗯，還好倉庫只在三樓，所以我們不用搬得太遠。
男：對啊。再次謝謝妳幫忙搬這些箱子。要是只有我來搬會花很多時間。

44. What does the woman offer to do?
(A) Reschedule an appointment
(B) Transport some boxes
(C) Track a delivery
(D) Call another department

44. 女子提議幫忙做什麼？
(A) 重新安排會面時間
(B) 搬運一些箱子
(C) 追蹤貨運
(D) 致電其他部門

45. According to the woman, what happened last week?
(A) A shipment was damaged.
(B) A storage room was cleaned.
(C) A door would not open.
(D) An elevator broke down.

45. 據女子説法，上週發生了什麼事？
(A) 貨物受損。
(B) 清理倉庫。
(C) 門打不開。
(D) 電梯故障。

46. Why does the man say, "the control system had to be reconfigured"?
(A) To give a reason for a delay
(B) To request new equipment
(C) To point out an inefficient process
(D) To apologize for a costly service

46. 為何男子要説：「控制系統需要重新配置」？
(A) 說明耽擱的原因
(B) 要求新設備
(C) 指出流程沒效率
(D) 為昂貴服務道歉

Questions 47-49 refer to the following conversation with three speakers.

W : Thank you both for meeting me today. **How well did our cosmetics sell this month? 47**

M1 : Um . . . Sales have increased by 4 percent, but I don't think our spring promotional event attracted as many customers as we had hoped.

W : Hmm . . . That's a bit worrisome. Chris, what do you think is the reason for these disappointing sales figures?

M2 : We probably didn't sell as many cosmetics because **we have a smaller marketing budget this time. I think we should request that our budget be increased. 48**

W : Well, **why don't we wait a few more weeks? If we're still not drawing in many customers, we'll look into requesting more funds. But for now, I'd like to wait on this decision. 49**

47-49 三人會話

女 ：感謝兩位今天和我開會。**這個月我們的化妝品賣得如何？47**

男 1：嗯……銷售成長了 4%，但我覺得我們春季促銷活動吸引到的顧客人數未達我們的期望。

女 ：嗯……那有點讓人擔心。克里斯，你覺得業績數字差強人意的原因是什麼？

男 2：我們化妝品沒賣出那麼多，可能是因為**這次我們的行銷預算比較少。我認為我們應該要求增加預算。48**

女 ：嗯，**我們何不再等幾個禮拜？要是接下來還是無法吸引到很多顧客，我們就考慮要求更多預算。但現階段，我想等一陣子再決定。49**

47. What product are the speakers discussing?
(A) Stationery
(B) Cosmetics
(C) Computers
(D) Beverages

48. What does Chris recommend?
(A) Offering discounts
(B) Recruiting more workers
(C) Updating a Web site
(D) Adjusting a budget

49. What does the woman propose?
(A) Expanding store space
(B) Delaying a decision
(C) Extending business hours
(D) Distributing a questionnaire

47. 說話者正在討論什麼產品？
(A) 文具
(B) 化妝品
(C) 電腦
(D) 飲料

48. 克里斯建議了什麼？
(A) 提供折扣
(B) 招募更多人力
(C) 更新網站
(D) 調整預算

49. 女子有何提議？
(A) 擴大門市空間
(B) 延後一項決定
(C) 延長營業時間
(D) 發放一份問卷

Questions 50-52 refer to the following conversation.

M : Good morning, Angela. **It's been a few months since you've been with us. I was wondering how your internship has been so far. 50 51**

W : It's been a lot of fun, and I've learned a lot about marketing strategies. Coming up with campaign ideas is challenging, but I enjoy doing it.

50-52 會話

男：安琪拉早。**妳加入我們團隊已經過幾個月了。我想了解妳到目前為止實習狀況怎麼樣。50 51**

女：真的很有趣，我在行銷策略方面學到很多。廣告活動的發想很有挑戰性，但我做得很開心。

M: That's great. I know you still have a few months left in your internship, but since your work has been so outstanding, **we're going to increase your hourly rate by 10 percent** 52 starting next month.

W: I'm thrilled to hear that. Thank you so much!

男：太好了。我知道妳的實習期間還有幾個月，但因為妳工作表現非常出色，**我們將**從下個月起**把妳的時薪提高 10%**。52

女：很高興聽到這個消息。非常感謝！

50. Who most likely is the woman?

(A) An HR manager

(B) A corporate intern

(C) A financial analyst

(D) A marketing director

50. 女子最有可能是什麼人？

(A) 人力資源經理

(B) 企業實習生

(C) 財務分析師

(D) 行銷總監

51. What does the man ask the woman for?

(A) Some samples of a design

(B) Some details about a company

(C) Some feedback on an experience

(D) Some funding for a project

51. 男子詢問女子什麼事？

(A) 一些設計的樣本

(B) 公司的某些詳情

(C) 經驗的一些意見回饋

(D) 專案的一些資金

52. What will the woman receive?

(A) An increased budget

(B) A compensation package

(C) A pay raise

(D) A work schedule

52. 女子會得到什麼？

(A) 增加過的預算

(B) 薪酬待遇

(C) 加薪

(D) 工作時間表

Questions 53-55 refer to the following conversation.

M: Lettie, **we're excited to have you over here at our Tokyo branch next week. We're looking forward to seeing the updated design of our RV400 laptop.** 53

W: Me, too. **I'm especially pleased about the one feature of the laptop.** 54

M: Oh, which one?

W: **This is the lightest model we've ever produced. It only weighs 1 kilogram!** 54

M: Wow, that's amazing! I'm eager to find out more about the other features during your talk. And if you're free, **several of us from the office will be going out to dinner that night.** 55

W: Hmm . . . **I'm watching a play that evening.**

M: Ah, I see. I'll see you next week then!

53-55 會話

男：萊蒂，**我們很開心妳下星期將會加入我們這裡的東京分部。我們很期待看到 RV400 筆記型電腦的更新版設計**。53

女：我也是。**我特別中意這款筆電的其中一項特色**。54

男：哦，哪項特色？

女：**這個機型是我們歷來產品中最輕的，只有一公斤重！** 54

男：哇，太厲害了！我迫不急待想聽妳說明，來了解其他特色。另外妳有空的話，**我們辦公室幾名同仁那天晚上會一起去吃晚餐**。55

女：嗯……**我當晚有場劇要看。**

男：哦，了解。那下週見！

53. What kind of product is being discussed?
(A) A laptop computer
(B) A mobile phone
(C) A home appliance
(D) A digital camera

54. What feature of the product is the woman particularly proud about?
(A) Its speed
(B) Its durability
(C) Its color
(D) Its weight

55. Why does the woman say, "I'm watching a play that evening"?
(A) To praise a performance
(B) To turn down an invitation
(C) To reschedule a meeting
(D) To ask for a recommendation

53. 他們討論的是哪種產品？
(A) 筆電
(B) 手機
(C) 家電
(D) 數位相機

54. 產品的哪項特色讓女子特別驕傲？
(A) 速度
(B) 耐用度
(C) 顏色
(D) 重量

55. 為何女子說：「我當晚有場劇要看」？
(A) 以稱讚演出
(B) 以拒絕邀請
(C) 以重排會議時間
(D) 以要求推薦

09

Questions 56-58 refer to the following conversation with three speakers.

M1: Welcome to Cadalisk Resort. I'm in charge of event planning, and this is my assistant, Roy. Are you interested in holding an event at one of our facilities?

W: Yes. I represent Lepton Manufacturing. **We're organizing a company anniversary party** 56 for November—around 150 people will be attending.

M2: OK. I think the Sapphire Hall would be the perfect venue for your event. Many companies have used it for their anniversary celebrations in the past.

W: Great. Also, about 50 guests will be visiting from other cities. **Will there be enough vacant rooms for all of them?** 57

M1: I think so. Let me see what's available and what group discounts we offer.

M2: Oh, and **we provide complimentary bus rides back and forth to the airport.** 58

56-58 三人會話

男 1：歡迎來到卡達利斯克度假村。我負責活動規劃，這位是我助理羅伊。您有意在我們的設施舉辦活動嗎？

女：對。我代表輕子工業。**我們正在籌備 11 月的公司週年慶宴會，**56 到時會有約 150 人出席。

男 2：好的。我想這場活動最完美的場地會是藍寶石廳。很多公司之前都選用該場地來舉辦週年慶祝活動。

女：很好。另外，大約會有 50 位賓客從其他城市來訪。**到時能有足夠的空房給他們所有人嗎？**57

男 1：我想會有的。讓我看看哪些房間方便使用，以及我們能提供哪些團體折扣。

男 2：哦，還有**我們免費提供往返機場的接駁巴士。**58

56. What kind of event is being organized?
(A) A business convention
(B) A product launch
(C) A graduation ceremony
(D) An anniversary celebration

57. What does the woman inquire about?
(A) Food preferences
(B) Accommodations
(C) Parking
(D) Fitness facilities

58. What does the resort provide for free?
(A) Transportation
(B) Breakfast
(C) Wireless Internet
(D) Travel guides

Questions 59-61 refer to the following conversation.

M：Iris, I need to talk to you about last week's shipments of our computers. **Apparently, 11 orders weren't delivered on time.** 59

W：**Yes, we experienced a problem with our online ordering system.** 59 Some of the confirmation emails that were sent to customers included incorrect delivery times.

M：Has the issue been resolved?

W：Yes. But you know, **I think we should add one more step to our process to ensure that customers receive the most up-to-date information regarding their orders. How about if we have our drivers give every customer a call before they deliver a package?** 60

M：That's a good idea! **We'll update our drivers on this change tomorrow morning during our meeting.** 61

W：**All right.** 61

59. According to the woman, what caused some shipments to be late?
(A) Some workers were not available.
(B) Some documents could not be located.
(C) There was an issue with an online system.
(D) A delivery van experienced engine trouble.

56. 正在籌備哪一種活動？
(A) 商務會展
(B) 產品發布會
(C) 畢業典禮
(D) 週年慶祝會

57. 女子詢問哪方面的事宜？
(A) 飲食喜好
(B) 住宿
(C) 停車
(D) 健身設施

58. 度假村免費提供什麼？
(A) 交通方式
(B) 早餐
(C) 無線網路
(D) 旅行指南

59-61 會話

男：艾莉絲，我需要和妳討論上週我們電腦的發貨狀況。**很明顯，有 11 筆訂單沒有按時交貨。** 59

女：**是的，我們的網路訂購系統出了問題。** 59 部分寄給客戶的確認信裡，寫入了錯誤的交貨時間。

男：問題解決了嗎？

女：解決了。但你知道，**我認為我們應該在我們的流程增加一個步驟，以確保客戶得到訂單的最新資訊。我們要不要請司機在每次送貨前，都先打電話給客戶？** 60

男：這主意不錯！**我們明早開會時，再和司機更新這項異動。** 61

女：**好的。** 61

59. 據女子說法，部分交貨延遲的原因為何？
(A) 有些員工沒空。
(B) 有些文件找不到。
(C) 網路系統有狀況。
(D) 貨車引擎發生問題。

60. What step does the woman suggest adding to a procedure?
(A) Distributing a survey
(B) Making phone calls
(C) Reviewing an inventory list
(D) Performing daily inspections

61. What do the speakers agree to do tomorrow morning?
(A) Contact some job candidates
(B) Visit a new facility
(C) Provide an update
(D) Book some plane tickets

60. 女子建議在流程中增加什麼步驟？
(A) 發放問卷
(B) 撥打電話
(C) 重新檢查庫存清單
(D) 執行每日檢查

61. 說話者同意明早要做什麼？
(A) 聯絡幾名應徵者
(B) 參觀新設施
(C) 提供更新說明
(D) 預訂幾張機票

Questions 62-64 refer to the following conversation and table.

W：Hey, Liam. **I'm preparing an invoice for Dr. Park's patient this morning, but whenever I enter this code, an error message pops up.** 62
M：Ah, the invoice codes were updated a few days ago. You're probably looking at the old chart.
W：Oh, where can I get the new one?
M：I have one on my desk. What kind of procedure was it?
W：**Gum surgery.** 63
M：**OK. This is the code you have to use.** 63
W：Thank you. Can I make a copy of that chart?
M：Of course. **But they're going to be inputting all of the codes into our invoice program next week, so we won't have to use paper charts anymore.** 64

Dental Work Type	Code #
Teeth whitening	T30
Gum surgery	**G55** 63
Root canal surgery	R01
Tooth extraction	T86

62-64 會話和表格

女：嘿，連恩。**我今天早上在幫帕克醫生的病患開立帳單，但每次輸入這個代碼都會跳出錯誤訊息。** 62
男：啊，帳單代碼幾天前有更新。妳可能看到舊表單了。
女：喔，我要在哪取得新表單？
男：我的桌上有一張。是哪種療程？
女：**牙齦手術。** 63
男：**好的。這就是妳要使用的代碼。** 63
女：謝謝。我可以複印這張表嗎？
男：當然可以。**但下星期他們就會把這些代碼全部輸入我們的帳單程式，所以之後就不須用到紙本表格了。** 64

牙科治療類型	代碼 #
牙齒美白	T30
牙齦手術	**G55** 63
根管治療	R01
拔牙	T86

62. What is the woman having a problem with?
(A) Making an invoice
(B) Locating a package
(C) Performing a surgery
(D) Calling a patient

62. 女子做什麼事遇到問題？
(A) 開立帳單
(B) 確認包裹位置
(C) 執行手術
(D) 致電病患

63. Look at the graphic. Which code should the woman use?
(A) T30
(B) G55
(C) R01
(D) T86

64. What does the man say will happen next week?
(A) A doctor will go on vacation.
(B) Some important clients will visit.
(C) Some staff members will attend a workshop.
(D) A chart will be accessible electronically.

63. 請看圖表作答。女子應使用哪個代碼？
(A) T30
(B) G55
(C) R01
(D) T86

64. 男子說下週會發生何事？
(A) 有醫師將休假。
(B) 有些重要的客戶將來訪。
(C) 有些同仁將參加研習。
(D) 表單將有電子版。

Questions 65-67 refer to the following conversation and chart.

M：Thank you for calling Mon Chapeau Fashions.
W：Yes, hi. **I'm browsing through the catalog on your Web site, and I'm hoping to order several hats.** 65 **But it's for a friend who is living in South America at the moment. Do you ship there?** 66
M：Hold on, let me check . . . **Yes, we do. It's in our Overseas Zone A.** 66
W：Ah, good. I want five black cowboy hats and three Russian fur caps, please.
M：OK. I've entered your order and added the fee for shipping to that destination.
W：Thank you. **I'll give you my credit card number.** 67

STANDARD SHIPPING RATES
(For orders under 5kg)

Domestic Zone	U.S., Canada	$3
Overseas Zone A 66	**Central and South America**	**$5** 66
Overseas Zone B	Europe, Asia, Africa	$7
Overseas Zone C	Australia, South Pacific	$9

65-67 會話和表格

男：這裡是法式我帽時尚，感謝您的來電。
女：是，您好。**我目前正在瀏覽你們網站的型錄，想訂購幾頂帽子。** 65 **但我是想買給正住在南美洲的朋友。你們有送貨到那裡嗎？** 66
男：請先別掛斷，讓我確認一下……**有的，我們會送。它在我們的海外地區 A。** 66
女：噢，那就好。我想要五頂黑色牛仔帽和三頂俄羅斯毛帽，麻煩了。
男：好的。我已輸入好您的訂單，並加上寄送到該目的地的運費。
女：謝謝。**我再給您我的信用卡號碼。** 67

標準運費
（五公斤以下訂單適用）

國內地區	美國、加拿大	3 美元
海外地區 A 66	**中南美洲**	**5 美元** 66
海外地區 B	歐、亞、非洲	7 美元
海外地區 C	澳洲、南太平洋	9 美元

65. Who most likely is the man?
(A) A customer service associate
(B) A delivery driver
(C) A fashion designer
(D) A Web site developer

65. 男子最有可能的職業為何？
(A) 客服人員
(B) 貨運司機
(C) 時裝設計師
(D) 網站開發人員

66. Look at the graphic. What rate will the woman pay for shipping?
(A) $3
(B) $5
(C) $7
(D) $9

67. What will the woman most likely do next?
(A) Update a contact number
(B) Choose some product features
(C) Confirm a delivery address
(D) Provide some payment information

66. 請看圖表作答。女子要付多少運費？
(A) 3 美元
(B) 5 美元
(C) 7 美元
(D) 9 美元

67. 女子接下來最有可能做什麼？
(A) 更新聯絡電話
(B) 選擇產品功能
(C) 確認收貨地址
(D) 提供付款資訊

Questions 68-70 refer to the following conversation and tag template.

M： Bunmi, we've gotten a lot of calls about that new collection of men's jackets we're launching this fall. I think we're going to have a lot of orders, **so we should increase inventory** 68 so that they don't sell out.

W： **OK, why don't we call the Manufacturing Department and let them know we'd like to double production?** 69

M： Yes, I'll talk to them right now.

W： Good. I'm getting the tags for those jackets ready now. Here's the template I'm going to use for those.

M： Oh, let's see. Hmm . . . **The jackets are made of nylon, so I don't think they need to be dry-cleaned.** 70

W： Ah, you're right. **I'll change that part right now.** 70

Product Name	LluviaWear
Country of Origin	Dominican Republic
Color	Black
Material	Nylon
Cleaning Instructions	Dry clean only

68-70 會話和洗標樣板

男： 邦米，我們今年秋天推出的新款男用夾克系列已獲得大量來電詢問。我想我們會接到很多筆訂單，**所以需要增加存貨量，** 68 以免供不應求。

女： **好，我們何不打給製造部門，告知他們我們想要加倍產量？** 69

男： 好，我馬上就會跟他們說。

女： 好的。我正在準備那些夾克要用的標籤。這是我打算用於那款商品的樣板。

男： 喔，我看一下。嗯……**夾克是尼龍製的，所以我想不需要乾洗。** 70

女： 啊，你說的對。**我馬上修改這個部分。** 70

產品名稱	LluviaWear
生產國	多明尼加共和國
顏色	黑
材質	尼龍
洗滌說明	限乾洗

68. What does the man say they will have to do?
(A) Increase inventory
(B) Find a new storage facility
(C) Create an ad campaign
(D) Print a clothing catalog

68. 男子說他們應該怎麼做？
(A) 增加存貨量
(B) 找到新的庫存設施
(C) 建立廣告活動
(D) 列印服裝型錄

69. What does the woman recommend?
(A) Taking pictures of a product
(B) Updating a Web site
(C) Calling some clients
(D) Talking to another department

69. 女子提議什麼？
(A) 幫產品拍照
(B) 更新網站
(C) 致電幾名客戶
(D) 和其他部門談話

70. Look at the graphic. Which part of the tag will need to be changed?
(A) Country of Origin
(B) Color
(C) Material
(D) Cleaning Instructions

70. 請看圖表作答。洗標的哪個部分需要修改？
(A) 生產國
(B) 顏色
(C) 材質
(D) 洗滌說明

PART 4 P. 39-41

10

Questions 71-73 refer to the following telephone message.

71-73 語音留言

W： Hi, **this is Jessica Finch calling from Finch Home Furnishings.** 71 I actually went over our billing records, and . . . It looks like you were right. **We did charge you extra for the kitchen chairs you recently ordered.** 72 I made a mistake. I've resolved this issue, and you've been fully refunded for the additional charge. Also, **I will email you a coupon, which is good for a 30 percent discount** 73 on your next purchase. Please do not hesitate to contact me if you have further questions. Once again, I apologize for the error.

女： 您好，**我是芬奇家具的潔西卡·芬奇。** 71 我確實重新查過帳務紀錄了，而……看來您是對的。**我們先前確有超收您最近訂購的餐廳座椅的貨款。** 72 這是我的疏失。我已解決這項問題，並已向您全額退還超收費用。此外，**我也會用電子郵件寄送30%的折價券給您，** 73 供您下次消費時使用。如有其他疑問請不吝和我聯絡。我再次為這次疏失向您致歉。

71. Where does the speaker most likely work?
(A) At a newspaper company
(B) At a furniture store
(C) At a conference center
(D) At a real estate office

71. 說話者最有可能在哪裡上班？
(A) 在報社
(B) 在家具行
(C) 在會議中心
(D) 在房仲公司

72. What is the purpose of the call?
(A) To address a delivery error
(B) To review a defective product
(C) To resolve a scheduling conflict
(D) To acknowledge an incorrect charge

72. 這通電話的目的為何？
(A) 為了處理誤送問題
(B) 為了檢查瑕疵品
(C) 為了解決行程衝突
(D) 為了承認收費錯誤

73. What will the speaker email the listener?
(A) A discount coupon
(B) A sample item
(C) A new invoice
(D) A refund form

73. 說話者將用電子郵件寄給聽者什麼？
(A) 折價券
(B) 樣品
(C) 新的帳單
(D) 退款單

09 10

Questions 74-76 refer to the following radio advertisement.

74-76 廣播廣告

M：Join us this weekend in celebrating the grand opening of Jerome's Oceanside Restaurant in Gulliver Bay. **You'll be able to experience the same excellent service and mouthwatering dishes as our Jarome's downtown restaurant, a local favorite for over a decade.** 74 **Our specialty dishes are made from the freshest fish** 75 caught in the bay. Whether you are hosting a company dinner or eating out with close friends, Jarome's Oceanside Restaurant is the perfect place. **Tell us that you heard this ad, and we will give you any one of our desserts at no extra cost.** 76

男：傑若姆海濱餐廳盛大開幕，就在格列佛海灣，這個週末請來和我們一起慶祝。**您將體驗到本店一貫的優質服務和令人垂涎的美食，就像置身十多年來深受當地人熱愛的傑若姆市中心餐廳。** 74 **本店招牌料理是**採用在灣區捕撈的**最新鮮魚獲。** 75 無論是舉辦公司晚宴或和親密好友外出用餐，傑若姆海濱餐廳都是最佳地點。**只要告知我們您聽過這則廣告，我們將免費招待您一道任選甜點。** 76

74. Which is mentioned about the restaurant?
(A) It received positive reviews.
(B) Its head chef received an award.
(C) Its menu will change.
(D) It has been open for over 10 years.

74. 廣告中提及餐廳什麼事？
(A) 接獲正面評論。
(B) 主廚得獎。
(C) 菜單將更改。
(D) 開業超過十年。

75. What does the restaurant specialize in?
(A) Seafood
(B) Pizza
(C) Vegetable dishes
(D) Pastries

75. 餐廳專精什麼料理？
(A) 海鮮
(B) 披薩
(C) 蔬食
(D) 糕點

76. What will customers receive if they mention the advertisement?
(A) A T-shirt
(B) A discount coupon
(C) A cook book
(D) A free dessert

76. 顧客提及廣告後會得到什麼？
(A) T 恤
(B) 折價券
(C) 食譜
(D) 免費甜點

Questions 77-79 refer to the following speech.

W：**It's nice to see that so many people have come here tonight to help celebrate Travis Kim's last day with our company before his retirement.** 77 Over the years, **my client numbers have increased considerably thanks to my friend's hard work and dedication. He has secured the most number of business contracts in the history of the firm, which has been his most outstanding achievement** 78 at Primeau Company. We thank you, Travis. At this time, **we'd like to ask you to come up to the stage so that we can present you with a special engraved watch.** 79 Now, let's give Travis a big, warm welcome.

77. What event is being held?
(A) A job fair
(B) A sales conference
(C) A fundraising dinner
(D) A retirement party

78. Which is Travis Kim's most outstanding achievement?
(A) He developed a training program.
(B) He created a best-selling product.
(C) He expanded a client base.
(D) He founded a charity organization.

79. What does the speaker ask Travis Kim to do?
(A) Make a donation
(B) Accept a gift
(C) Give a speech
(D) Watch a presentation

77-79 演講

女：**很高興看到今晚這麼多人前來一同慶祝崔維斯・金退休前在本公司服務的最後一天。** 77 多年以來，**多虧了我這位朋友認真工作和奉獻，我的客戶人數得到了大幅成長。他拿下了這間公司有史以來最多的商業合約，這即是他**在普里莫公司任職期間**最傑出的成就。** 78 我們大家都很感謝你，崔維斯。此刻，**我們想請你移步上台，好讓大家為你獻上一只特製的鐫刻手錶。** 79 現在請各位熱烈歡迎崔維斯。

77. 正在舉行什麼活動？
(A) 就業博覽會
(B) 業務會議
(C) 募款晚宴
(D) 退休慶祝會

78. 崔維斯・金最傑出的成就為何？
(A) 他制定了教育訓練課程。
(B) 他打造了最暢銷的產品。
(C) 他擴大了客群。
(D) 他創辦了慈善機構。

79. 說話者請崔維斯・金做什麼？
(A) 捐款
(B) 接收禮物
(C) 發表演講
(D) 觀看簡報

Questions 80-82 refer to the following broadcast.

M：All right, **it's time for the Avocado Valley weekly events update.** 80 This Saturday, the AV Youth Arts Club will be holding their yearly art sale fundraiser, and they could use all of our help. **If you have any paintings or other art objects that you'd like to donate to the cause, please bring them to the community center by Friday morning.** 81 **Also scheduled for this weekend is Avocado Valley's yearly outdoor film festival,**

80-82 廣播

男：好的，**以下請聽酪梨谷每週最新活動訊息。** 80 這星期六，酪梨谷青年藝術社將舉行年度藝術品義賣募款活動，需要我們大家的幫忙。**如果你有任何畫作或其他藝術品想捐給這場活動，請在週五早上帶到社區活動中心。** 81 **同樣在這個週末，酪梨谷年度露天電影節預定於南湖公園舉行。但請再留意官網的最新**

which will be held at South Lake Park. But check our Web site for updates, 82 **because we may be looking at some heavy rain on those days.** To find out more, let's hear from Dave Contreras in our Weather Department . . .

資訊，82 **因為那幾天我們可能會遇上大雨。**欲知更多消息，請聽我們氣象部門的戴夫・康崔拉斯以下報導……

10

80. What is the broadcast mainly about?
(A) A traffic report
(B) City council nominees
(C) A new shopping center
(D) Upcoming local events

80. 廣播的主旨為何？
(A) 交通報導
(B) 市議會提名人選
(C) 新購物中心
(D) 即將登場的當地活動

81. What are the listeners encouraged to do by Friday morning?
(A) Donate some items
(B) Fill out a survey
(C) Enter an art contest
(D) Sign up for volunteer work

81. 聽眾受邀在週五早上做什麼？
(A) 捐贈物品
(B) 填寫問卷
(C) 參加美術比賽
(D) 報名當志工

82. What does the speaker suggest when he says, "we may be looking at some heavy rain on those days"?
(A) Listeners should avoid going outside.
(B) Listeners should not use a certain road.
(C) The weather can affect a schedule.
(D) A weather report was wrong.

82. 說話者說：「那幾天我們可能會遇上大雨」，其意思為何？
(A) 聽眾應避免外出。
(B) 聽眾不該使用特定道路。
(C) 天氣可能影響排程。
(D) 氣象預報錯誤。

Questions 83-85 refer to the following talk.

W：Hello, I am Camila, and I'll be your server today. **It looks like it's your first time at our café, so let me tell you a little bit about us. All of the fruits used in our dishes are grown organically at our very own farm.** 83 **Marco, the owner of this restaurant,** 84 is dedicated to serving fresh and chemical-free meals. **Now, this evening's special is a great Indian dish. It's a delicious chicken curry salad with fresh mangoes and apples.** 85 **All my friends come here to eat this.** Now, can I get you anything to drink while you look at the menu?

83-85 談話

女：您好，我是卡蜜拉，今天將為您服務。**您好像是第一次來到我們的咖啡廳，所以請容我為您介紹一下我們這家店。本店餐點使用的水果全都是我們的自家農場有機種植。** 83 **本店老闆馬可** 84 致力提供新鮮且無化學添加的餐點。**至於今晚特餐，是一道很棒的印度料理：美味咖哩雞肉沙拉佐新鮮芒果和蘋果。**85 **我朋友來店都是為了嘗這一味。**那麼，您看菜單的時候，需要先喝點什麼嗎？

83. According to the speaker, what is special about the café?
(A) It operates a farm.
(B) It has a remodeled kitchen.
(C) It provides a cooking course.
(D) It employs an Indian chef.

83. 根據說話者，這家咖啡館有何特色？
(A) 有經營農場。
(B) 備有整修過的廚房。
(C) 提供烹飪課。
(D) 僱用印度廚師。

84. Who is Marco?
(A) A food critic
(B) A university professor
(C) An interior designer
(D) A business owner

85. Why does the speaker say, "All my friends come here to eat this"?
(A) She recommends a menu item.
(B) She knows that a restaurant is popular.
(C) She would like to try a new dish.
(D) She knows how to prepare a dish.

84. 馬可是誰？
(A) 美食評論家
(B) 大學教授
(C) 室內設計師
(D) 老闆

85. 說話者為什麼說：「我朋友來店都是為了嘗這一味」？
(A) 她推薦菜單上的某道餐點。
(B) 她知道某家餐廳很受歡迎。
(C) 她想試新菜。
(D) 她知道怎麼準備某道料理。

Questions 86-88 refer to the following talk.

M： Thank you for attending this year's first managers' meeting. When we met last time, **Gloria requested that the company purchase a computer program made specifically for training textile machine workers.** 86 I met with several software developers to look at their products, and the one I think would be the most useful for our company is from the Witro Tech Company. They emphasized how quickly the program prepares workers to do their jobs. **They also guaranteed a significant increase in work efficiency and productivity.** 88 So **I propose that we start using this program with the four new workers** 87 who will be joining us next week.

86-88 談話

男： 感謝各位參加今年首場主管會議。我們上次開會時，**格羅莉亞請公司購買一套電腦程式，專門用來培訓紡織機械作業員。** 86 我和幾家軟體開發業者見面、了解各家產品後，我認為其中對本公司最有幫助的是維緯科技公司的產品。他們強調該程式如何快速地幫助工人做好上工的準備。**他們也保證能顯著提升工作效率和產能。** 88 所以**我建議本公司從**下週新進的**四名新人開始啟用這套軟體。** 87

86. What is the main topic of the talk?
(A) Changes to a production schedule
(B) Instructions for repairing machines
(C) Software for teaching work skills
(D) Consequences of a recent merger

87. What does the speaker recommend doing?
(A) Comparing service costs
(B) Extending staff contracts
(C) Talking to a manager after a meeting
(D) Beginning a program with new recruits

88. According to the speaker, what can the company expect to see?
(A) Increased productivity
(B) Higher employee morale
(C) Improved sales
(D) Better customer relations

86. 談話主題為何？
(A) 生產時程異動
(B) 機器維修指示
(C) 教導工作技能的軟體
(D) 最近合併案的結果

87. 說話者建議做什麼？
(A) 比較服務費用
(B) 展延員工合約
(C) 會後和主管談談
(D) 讓新進員工啟用軟體

88. 據說話者說法，公司可以預期什麼成效？
(A) 產能提高
(B) 員工士氣提振
(C) 業績改善
(D) 客戶關係好轉

Questions 89-91 refer to the following excerpt from a meeting.

W： I called everyone to this meeting to talk about . . . um . . . a serious problem. As you all know, **Durham Publishers** 89 prides itself on publishing top-selling books and maintaining an excellent reputation. So **we were very surprised when we found out that four manuscripts of unpublished works have disappeared.** 90 To prevent similar occurrences from happening, **you will now be required to complete a form asking for authorization** 91 when you take out manuscripts from the office. This will help us keep track of the documents. If there are any questions or concerns regarding this matter, please talk to your department manager.

89. Where does the speaker most likely work?
(A) At an advertising agency
(B) At a publishing company
(C) At a bookstore
(D) At a library

90. What does the speaker mean when she says, "we were very surprised"?
(A) Some documents are missing.
(B) A positive review was given.
(C) Some complaints were made.
(D) An employee is resigning.

91. What will employees be required to do in the future?
(A) Meet monthly sales goals
(B) Request days off in advance
(C) Submit original receipts
(D) Fill out an authorization form

Questions 92-94 refer to the following tour information.

M： Welcome to Flatiron National Park. My name is Liam, and I'll be your tour guide today. **I was raised in Flatiron, so I'm very familiar with the region.** 92 The path we're taking today has some steep areas, so you'll have to pay extra attention while walking. And just so you know—

89-91 會議摘錄

女： 我召集大家開會是要討論……嗯……一項很嚴重的問題。如各位所知，**杜然出版社** 89 引以為傲的就是出版暢銷書並維持卓越的商譽。因此，**當我們發現有四份未出版作品的原稿遺失一事，我們深感詫異。** 90 為防止類似事件再重演，**爾後各位都須填表申請授權，** 91 才能將原稿帶離辦公室。這會有助我們追蹤文件的下落。如果對此有任何疑問或疑慮，請洽詢所屬部門經理。

89. 說話者最有可能在哪裡工作？
(A) 在廣告公司
(B) 在出版社
(C) 在書店
(D) 在圖書館

90. 說話者說：「我們深感詫異」，所指為何？
(A) 部分文件遺失。
(B) 被給予正面評價。
(C) 一些投訴被提出。
(D) 有名員工正要辭職。

91. 員工被要求未來要做什麼？
(A) 達成每月業績目標
(B) 提前請假
(C) 繳交收據正本
(D) 填寫授權表

92-94 導覽資訊

男： 歡迎蒞臨熨斗國家公園，我叫連恩，今天擔任各位的嚮導。**我就在熨斗地區長大，所以算是人親土親。** 92 今天我們要走的路程有些地方比較陡峭，因此各位行走時要格外小心。這邊也先告訴大家，**我們**

we're going to stop several times throughout the walk, so you will have the opportunity to sit down and rest. 93 Also, **a photographer will be accompanying us today to take some pictures of the tour. They will be made available for download on the park's Web site tomorrow.** 94 If you have any questions during the hike, please let me know.

一路上會停留幾次，讓大家有機會能坐下來休息。93 另外，**今天會有一位攝影師跟大家同行，替這趟旅途拍照留影。照片明天就能在公園的網站下載。** 94 本次健行期間如您有任何疑問，請再告訴我。

92. What does the speaker mention about himself?
(A) He is a scientist.
(B) He grew up in the region.
(C) He started a new job recently.
(D) He has received an award.

92. 關於自己，說話者提到什麼？
(A) 他是科學家。
(B) 他在當地長大。
(C) 他最近開始新工作。
(D) 他得了獎。

93. According to the speaker, why will the group make several stops?
(A) To take some breaks
(B) To study animal behavior
(C) To learn about different plants
(D) To perform some experiments

93. 據說話者說法，為什麼該團體會停留數次？
(A) 以做幾次休息
(B) 以研究動物行為
(C) 以認識不同種類的植物
(D) 以做些實驗

94. According to the speaker, what can the listeners do on a Web site?
(A) Read some articles
(B) Download pictures
(C) Sign up for a membership
(D) Complete a questionnaire

94. 據說話者說法，聽者可在網站上做什麼？
(A) 閱覽文章
(B) 下載照片
(C) 註冊會員
(D) 填寫問卷

Questions 95-97 refer to the following announcement and directory.

95-97 廣播通知和指引

M： Attention, Arca Department Store shoppers. For this week only, **we are selling select laptops and desktop computers at 40 percent off.** 95 **You can identify which items are on sale by looking for a small yellow sticker attached to the price tag of the laptop or computer.** 96 Remember this deal only applies to products with a yellow sticker. Also, **if you're an Arca Loyalty Club member, you can earn twice the number of points when making purchases at our store. Not a member? You can register for a card at our customer support center** 97 on the first floor.

男： 阿爾卡百貨的顧客請注意。僅在本週期間內，**我們將以六折販賣指定的筆記型電腦和桌上型電腦。**95 **特賣筆電或桌機的價格標籤上貼有黃色小貼紙，您可以藉此辨別出特賣中的商品。** 96 請注意，本次優惠僅適用貼有黃色貼紙的品項。此外，**若您是阿爾卡常客俱樂部會員，凡在店內購物即可獲得雙倍積分。還沒加入會員嗎？您可以到我們一樓的客服中心辦卡。** 97

	Arca Department Store Directory
4F	Clothing & Accessories
3F	**Electronics & Appliances** 95
2F	Office Supplies & Furniture
1F	Sporting Goods & Customer Support

	阿爾卡百貨公司樓層指南
4 樓	服飾及配件
3 樓	**電子用品及家電** 95
2 樓	辦公用品及家具
1 樓	運動用品及客服

10

95. Look at the graphic. Where is the sale being held?
(A) The 1st Floor
(B) The 2nd Floor
(C) The 3rd Floor
(D) The 4th Floor

96. According to the speaker, how can shoppers locate sale items?
(A) By checking for a special label
(B) By looking at a product catalog
(C) By speaking to a worker
(D) By going on a store Web site

97. Why are listeners encouraged to visit the customer support center?
(A) To sign up for a membership card
(B) To exchange an item
(C) To schedule a delivery
(D) To purchase a gift certificate

95. 請看圖表作答。特賣在哪裡舉辦？
(A) 一樓
(B) 二樓
(C) 三樓
(D) 四樓

96. 據說話者說法，購物者要如何認出特賣商品？
(A) 藉由檢查特殊標籤
(B) 藉由查看產品型錄
(C) 藉由詢問員工
(D) 藉由瀏覽店家網站

97. 為什麼要請聽者前往客服中心？
(A) 以申辦會員卡
(B) 以換貨
(C) 以安排出貨時間
(D) 以購買禮券

Questions 98-100 refer to the following telephone message and identification card.

W：Hello, **this is Wendy Parker leaving a message for Eric Mendes, the Personnel Manager.** 98 I was in your office earlier today to pick up my new company ID card and business cards. **I just got back to my office and noticed that the job title on my card is wrong.** 99 Aside from that, everything is fine. **If you could, please call me back at 555-3824** 100 when you get this message, I'd appreciate it. Thank you.

98-100 語音留言和識別證

女：您好，**我是溫蒂．帕克，要留言給人事經理艾瑞克．門德斯。** 98 我今天稍早去您的辦公室領取新的員工識別證和名片，**現在剛回到我的辦公室，發現到識別證上的職稱有誤。** 99 除此之外，一切都正確。**若您方便，**聽到留言後**請回撥 555-3824 給我，** 100 在此致謝。謝謝您。

98. Which department is the speaker calling?
(A) Technology
(B) Personnel
(C) Finance
(D) Security

99. Look at the graphic. What information does the speaker say is incorrect?
(A) 839287
(B) Analyst
(C) Miller
(D) 555-3824

100. What does the speaker request the listener to do?
(A) Return a call
(B) Check a database
(C) Make a reservation
(D) Submit a document

姓名：溫蒂·帕克
識別號碼：839287
職稱：分析師 99

部門：財務部
辦公大樓：米勒
聯絡方式：555-3824

98. 說話者打電話給哪個部門？
(A) 技術
(B) 人事
(C) 財務
(D) 保全

99. 請看圖作答。說話者說哪項資訊有誤？
(A) 839287
(B) 分析師
(C) 米勒
(D) 555-3824

100. 說話者請聽者做什麼？
(A) 回電
(B) 查看資料庫
(C) 預約
(D) 繳交文件

ACTUAL TEST 3

PART 1 P. 42–45

1. (A) He's cutting up some ingredients.
   (B) He's turning on a blender.
   (C) He's hanging up some utensils.
   (D) He's looking in a drawer.

2. **(A) A woman is approaching an archway.**
   (B) A woman is grasping a handrail.
   (C) A staircase leads up to a hillside.
   (D) Fountains are casting a shadow.

3. (A) A fence runs along the edge of the yard.
   (B) A railing separates some steps.
   (C) A man is repairing a sidewalk.
   (D) Lampposts line both sides of a staircase.

4. **(A) A picture is positioned above a bed.**
   (B) A rug has been laid near a door.
   (C) A ceiling fan has been taken down.
   (D) A nightstand is being repositioned in a corner.

5. (A) Some people are organizing items on a desk.
   (B) Some people are stacking folders in a corner.
   (C) One of the women is closing a cabinet.
   (D) One of the women is distributing papers.

6. **(A) Some tables have been arranged in a row.**
   (B) Some furniture is being assembled outside.
   (C) Some customers are ordering a meal.
   (D) Some people are taking their seats.

1. (A) 他正在切食材。
   (B) 他正在開啟食物攪拌機。
   (C) 他正在掛廚房用具。
   (D) 他正在查看抽屜。

2. **(A) 女子正在走近拱門。**
   (B) 女子握著扶手。
   (C) 階梯向上通往山坡。
   (D) 噴泉投射出陰影。

3. (A) 院子邊緣有一道圍欄。
   (B) 欄杆把階梯隔開。
   (C) 男子正在維修人行道。
   (D) 路燈排列在階梯兩側。

4. **(A) 畫作擺在床鋪上方。**
   (B) 地毯鋪在門邊。
   (C) 吊扇已被卸下。
   (D) 床頭櫃正被移至角落。

5. (A) 一些人正在整理桌面的物品。
   (B) 一些人正在角落推放檔案夾。
   (C) 其中一名女子在把櫥櫃關上。
   (D) 其中一名女子正在分發文件。

6. **(A) 幾張桌子排成一排。**
   (B) 有人正在戶外組裝家具。
   (C) 幾名客人正在點餐。
   (D) 幾個人正在入座。

PART 2 P. 46

7. When did you begin your job as a medical assistant?
   (A) At the medical center.
   (B) That's right.
   (C) Just last year.

7. 你何時開始醫務助理的工作？
   (A) 在醫學中心。
   (B) 沒錯。
   (C) 就在去年。

8. Who's in charge of the Browley marketing campaign?
(A) No, I can't tell.
(B) It's Mr. Gordon.
(C) The commercial is finished.

9. Did you contact the caterer for the anniversary dinner yet?
(A) I'm not responsible for the catering.
(B) For over 45 years.
(C) He made a reservation at the restaurant.

10. Where should I leave this spare set of keys?
(A) On top of the front desk.
(B) Please close the door.
(C) Sure, you can.

11. Can I get you something to drink while you wait?
(A) I couldn't find it.
(B) No, I'm fine, thanks.
(C) Check the final weight.

12. Haven't you kept in touch with the architectural firm?
(A) I'm waiting for a response.
(B) No, don't touch the glass.
(C) The new building design.

13. Jeff has been promoted to operations manager, hasn't he?
(A) It's operating fine.
(B) Just enter the promotional code.
(C) I think it was Norah.

14. I have an appointment at 3 P.M. today.
(A) You should go now then.
(B) No, I can't.
(C) We will appoint a new CEO.

15. Don't you need to give another presentation tomorrow?
(A) No, this was the last one for the week.
(B) That was a great demonstration.
(C) I thought the presenter was too quiet.

16. How much is the seminar registration fee?
(A) It should say on the flyer.
(B) About an hour more.
(C) I'd rather register online.

8. 誰負責布羅利的行銷活動？
(A) 不，我看不出來。
(B) 是戈登先生。
(C) 廣告已經做好。

9. 你有聯絡外燴業者準備週年慶晚宴了嗎？
(A) 餐飲不是我負責的。
(B) 超過 45 年了。
(C) 他在一家餐廳訂位了。

10. 這組多餘的鑰匙我該放哪裡？
(A) 在櫃檯上。
(B) 請關門。
(C) 當然，你可以。

11. 您等待時，要不要喝點什麼？
(A) 我找不到。
(B) 不用，我這樣就好，謝謝。
(C) 確認最後的重量。

12. 你沒有和建築公司保持聯絡嗎？
(A) 我還在等答覆。
(B) 不，請勿觸摸玻璃（杯）。
(C) 新的建築設計。

13. 傑夫已獲提拔為營運經理，對嗎？
(A) 正常運作中。
(B) 只要輸入優惠碼即可。
(C) 我想是諾拉才對。

14. 我今天下午三點與人有約。
(A) 那你現在該出發了。
(B) 不，我不能。
(C) 我們將任命新的執行長。

15. 你明天不是還須做另一場報告嗎？
(A) 不，這是本週最後一場。
(B) 這次的展示會很棒。
(C) 我覺得講者的聲音太小。

16. 研討會的報名費是多少？
(A) 傳單上應該有寫。
(B) 大約再一個小時。
(C) 我寧願用網路報名。

17. Would you care for some tea?
(A) In the beverage section.
(B) They were very caring.
(C) Sure, that'd be great.

18. Was there a problem with the subway last night?
(A) I see. I'll just drive.
(B) Get off at the next station.
(C) Yes, I had to take a taxi.

19. The research states that our numbers have dropped this year.
(A) I'll take another look at the report.
(B) Here's my account number.
(C) He searched online.

20. Where can I purchase a desk fan?
(A) You can use mine.
(B) He's at his desk.
(C) The purchase was just approved.

21. Should I buy the sports equipment at the shop or from the Web site?
(A) It was an amazing game.
(B) Some new soccer gear.
(C) Please get it from the shop.

22. How do I log in to the company system using my smartphone?
(A) Install the mobile app.
(B) On the cabinet, right next to the wall phone.
(C) The company workshop is next week.

23. I need to assemble some furniture in the conference room.
(A) How long will that take?
(B) A brand-new couch.
(C) Today on the news.

24. What restaurant do you recommend for the company dinner?
(A) Someone with a lot of experience.
(B) I can't remember its name.
(C) The food was delicious.

25. Didn't you buy some extra ink cartridges?
(A) They haven't arrived yet.
(B) By next month.
(C) Put them in the cart.

17. 您想來點茶嗎？
(A) 在飲料區裡。
(B) 他們很會照顧人。
(C) 當然，太好了。

18. 昨晚地鐵有出問題嗎？
(A) 了解。我開車就好。
(B) 下一站下車。
(C) 對啊，我只好搭計程車。

19. 研究指出，今年我們的數值下降了。
(A) 我會再查看這份報告。
(B) 這是我的帳號。
(C) 他用網路搜尋。

20. 我可以在哪裡買桌上型風扇？
(A) 你可以用我的。
(B) 他在位子上。
(C) 採購剛剛核准。

21. 我應該去門市買運動器材，還是該網購？
(A) 這場比賽很精采。
(B) 新的足球用具。
(C) 請到門市買。

22. 我要怎麼用智慧型手機登入公司系統？
(A) 安裝手機應用程式。
(B) 在櫃子上，就在壁掛電話旁。
(C) 公司研習在下週舉行。

23. 我得要在會議室組裝一些家具。
(A) 會花多久時間？
(B) 全新的沙發。
(C) 今天的新聞裡。

24. 公司晚上聚餐你推薦去哪家餐廳？
(A) 經驗豐富的人。
(B) 我不記得那家叫什麼名字了。
(C) 食物很美味。

25. 你不是有多買一些墨水匣嗎？
(A) 它們還沒到貨。
(B) 下個月之前。
(C) 把它們放進購物車。

26. Can you sign for my package on Friday?
(A) I'll be working at another location.
(B) Let's hang this sign up.
(C) The delivery service.

26. 你週五能幫我簽收包裹嗎？
(A) 我那天會在別的地方工作。
(B) 讓我們把這個牌子掛起來。
(C) 送貨服務。

27. It's difficult to say when the exact completion date of the construction project will be.
(A) Exactly two months ago.
(B) That's true. I'll ask for more details.
(C) It was an easy question.

27. 建案確切完工日期很難說得準。
(A) 正好在兩個月前。
(B) 確實。我會再詢問詳情。
(C) 這問題很簡單。

28. Do you want to walk around the park more or take a break?
(A) The parking lot around the corner.
(B) I can take it for you.
(C) Actually, I'm a little tired.

28. 你想多在公園走走，還是要休息？
(A) 轉角附近的停車場。
(B) 我可以拿給你。
(C) 其實我有點累。

29. The sunglass advertisement is nearly done, isn't it?
(A) The agency is making additional changes.
(B) Behind the department store.
(C) The monthly reviews.

29. 太陽眼鏡的廣告快做好了，不是嗎？
(A) 廣告公司正在做額外的修改。
(B) 在百貨公司後方。
(C) 每月回顧。

30. I'm not sure how to connect this printer to the network.
(A) One for each person.
(B) I'll show you.
(C) At the online store.

30. 我不確定怎麼把這台印表機連上線。
(A) 一人一台。
(B) 我操作給你看。
(C) 在網路商店裡。

31. Why was the team dinner moved to next Monday?
(A) I can reschedule it to tomorrow.
(B) I moved to Seoul last weekend.
(C) Yes, I'll be there.

31. 為什麼團隊聚餐移到下週一了？
(A) 我可以改排到明天。
(B) 我上個週末搬到首爾。
(C) 對，我會去。

PART 3 P. 47–50

13

Questions 32-34 refer to the following conversation.

W： Hey, Troy! **I just found out that the Chinese restaurant near the local library closed last week.** 32 I really liked their food.

M： That's unfortunate. **But a new Chinese restaurant just opened on Sanhee Lane** 32 yesterday. It's only 10 minutes from here. Why don't you check it out?

32-34 會話

女： 嘿，崔伊！**我剛發現社區圖書館附近的中式餐廳上週就收起來了。** 32 我真的很喜歡他們的餐點。

男： 好可惜喔。**但是，昨天尚熙巷剛新開了一家中式餐廳，** 32 離這裡只有十分鐘路程，妳何不去看看？

W：Oh. That sounds great. Sanhee Lane is close to my home, so I wouldn't have to take my car. I can just walk there. 33 Trying to find parking around here is always a hassle.

M：Right. And they have a promotion where **you can receive a 15 percent discount if you go there this week.** 34

女：哦，聽起來還不錯。我家離尚熙巷很近，所以我不用開車，用走的就可以到。 33 這附近想要找停車位總讓人不勝其煩。

男：對啊。而且他們現在還有優惠活動，**妳如果這星期去吃，還能獲得15%的折扣。** 34

32. What are the speakers mainly discussing?

(A) Local grocery stores
(B) Public libraries
(C) Auto repair shops
(D) Neighborhood restaurants

32. 說話者主要在討論什麼？

(A) 當地雜貨店
(B) 公共圖書館
(C) 汽車維修廠
(D) 附近餐廳

33. Why does the woman say she likes the man's suggestion?

(A) The workers are friendly.
(B) The location is convenient.
(C) The business closes late.
(D) The food is healthy.

33. 女子為何說她喜歡男子的提議？

(A) 工作人員很友善。
(B) 地點方便。
(C) 商家很晚關門。
(D) 餐點很健康。

34. What does the man say is available this week?

(A) A price discount
(B) Free parking
(C) A sample product
(D) Cooking courses

34. 男子說本週可以獲得什麼？

(A) 價格折扣
(B) 免費停車
(C) 試吃樣品
(D) 烹飪課程

Questions 35-37 refer to the following conversation.

35-37 會話

W：I want to reserve two spots for tomorrow's All Day City Tour. 35

M：Of course. We still have some spots left. Just so you know, this tour will make stops at six local attractions and finish at Marley's Bistro.

W：Sounds great! My cousin is here on vacation. She'll definitely enjoy it.

M：That's good. **Also, you'll have to place your restaurant order in advance. You can choose between two options: the fish special or the creamy garlic pasta.** 36

W：We'll both get the fish.

M：OK, these are your tickets. Also, the weather forecast says that it's going to be a little windy tomorrow. **You should probably wear some warm clothes.** 37 You wouldn't want to catch a cold.

女：我想預約明天的市區一日遊行程，我們有兩位。 35

男：沒問題，我們還有剩幾個名額。向您說明一下，本行程會遊歷六個當地景點，最後在馬利餐酒館解散。

女：聽起來很棒！我表姐來這裡度假，一定可以帶她玩得很盡興。

男：太好了。**另外，您須提前向餐廳訂餐。您可以從以下兩個選項中任選：鮮魚特餐或奶油蒜味義大利麵。** 36

女：兩位都點鮮魚。

男：好的，這邊是您的票。另外，天氣預報說明天風會有點大，**您也許應該穿些保暖衣物。** 37 您不會想要感冒的。

13

35. What would the woman like to do?
(A) Reserve a tour
(B) Check a city map
(C) Book a flight
(D) Review an event calendar

36. What is the woman asked to select?
(A) Menu items
(B) A payment method
(C) A departure time
(D) Entertainment options

37. What does the man recommend doing?
(A) Bringing some cash
(B) Printing out a voucher
(C) Checking a Web site
(D) Wearing warm clothing

35. 女子想做什麼？
(A) 預訂行程
(B) 查閱市區地圖
(C) 預訂航班
(D) 查看活動行事曆

36. 女子被要求選擇什麼？
(A) 菜單品項
(B) 付款方式
(C) 出發時間
(D) 娛樂活動

37. 男子提出什麼建議？
(A) 帶點現金
(B) 印出優惠卷
(C) 查看網站
(D) 穿著保暖衣物

Questions 38-40 refer to the following conversation with three speakers.

W1：Hey, Ciara. **I've printed out all the documents for the training seminar. Are you almost done setting up the room?** 38
W2：My slides aren't displaying on the projector screen. **Could you get in touch with the maintenance supervisor?** 39 He'll know what to do.
W1：Of course. **I'm calling him now. Hello, Jack?** 39 Ciara and I are in meeting room B. We're unable to connect the computer to the projector.
M ：Ah, **the cables in that room haven't been working properly. You'll have to go to another one.** 40
W1：Hmm, there isn't any other place available right now.
M ：Well, actually, the conference in meeting room C was postponed. I'll go there right now to check if everything is working.

38-40 三人會話

女 1：嘿，夏拉，**我印好培訓研討會要用的所有文件了。會議室妳都布置得差不多了吧？** 38
女 2：我的投影片沒辦法顯示在投影幕上。**能請妳幫我聯絡維修組長嗎？** 39 他會知道該怎麼處理。
女 1：沒問題。**我現在就打給他。喂，傑克嗎？** 39 夏拉和我正在 B 會議室。我們的電腦連不上投影機。
男 ：噢，**那間的線路運作不太正常。你們得去另外一間。** 40
女 1：嗯，現在沒有其他間可以用。
男 ：喔，其實 C 會議室的會議延後了。我現在就去那裡檢查一切是否正常。

38. What are the women trying to do?
(A) Post some signs
(B) Reserve a meeting room
(C) Order a new computer
(D) Get ready for a training session

38. 女子們想做什麼？
(A) 張貼標誌
(B) 預借會議室
(C) 訂購新電腦
(D) 準備培訓課程

39. Who is the man?
(A) A delivery driver
(B) A store owner
(C) A facility manager
(D) A software developer

40. What does the man advise the women to do?
(A) Relocate to another room
(B) Update a system
(C) Provide some feedback
(D) Read a user guide

Questions 41-43 refer to the following conversation.

M：Hello, **I received a notice today, and it said some repairs have been scheduled for my apartment** 41 on Thursday, the 15th.
W：Yes, that's right. **The owner of the building has arranged to put in new kitchen floor tiles in all apartments.** 41
M：Hmm, **I was planning on finishing up a report at home on that day, and I'm afraid I won't be able to concentrate with all the noise from the work.** 42
W：OK. The times are flexible, so **I'll reschedule you for Tuesday, the 20th then.** 43

41. What are the speakers discussing?
(A) Repairing some furniture
(B) Renovating some bathrooms
(C) Recycling some clothes
(D) Replacing some flooring

42. What is the man concerned about?
(A) A price
(B) Some noise
(C) An odor
(D) Some designs

43. What does the woman say she will do?
(A) Change a date
(B) Provide an estimate
(C) Inspect an apartment
(D) Employ a contractor

39. 男子的身分為何？
(A) 貨運司機
(B) 商店老闆
(C) 設備主管
(D) 軟體開發員

40. 男子建議女子們做什麼？
(A) 換到另一間
(B) 更新系統
(C) 提供意見回饋
(D) 閱讀使用說明

41-43 會話

男：您好，**我今天收到通知，裡面提到我的公寓套房預計** 15 號週四**會進行一些維修。** 41
女：對，沒錯。**房東安排在所有套房鋪設新的廚房地磚。** 41
男：嗯，**我那天本來打算在家把一份報告趕完，而現在很擔心施工的噪音會讓我無法專注。** 42
女：了解。時間可以彈性調整，所以那**我幫您把日期改到 20 號週二。** 43

41. 說話者正在討論什麼？
(A) 修理家具
(B) 整修浴廁
(C) 回收衣服
(D) 更換地板

42. 男子擔心什麼？
(A) 價格
(B) 噪音
(C) 氣味
(D) 設計

43. 女子說她會做什麼？
(A) 更改日期
(B) 提供估算
(C) 檢查公寓
(D) 僱用包商

TEST 3
PART 3
13

Questions 44-46 refer to the following conversation.

44-46 會話

W：Good to see you, Earl. Did you enjoy the medical conference?
M：I did, and I picked up some useful information.
W：Oh, like what?
M：Well, one of the presenters, **Riya Shah, suggested that doctors such as ourselves** 44 **take online courses** 45 to keep up with the latest trends in medical science and technology.
W：Ah, that's a good idea. It's difficult for us to make time to attend classes in person.
M：Yeah. Oh, and also, there is a mobile app we can download. It was developed by the Seneca Medical Society.
W：I see. Isn't that expensive?
M：I'm not sure. **I'll look into how much it costs** 46 and let you know by tomorrow.

女：厄爾，很高興看到你。你喜歡這次的醫學會議嗎？
男：我喜歡，而且我聽到一些有用的資訊。
女：哦，像是什麼？
男：嗯，其中一位講者**瑞亞・沙阿建議我們醫生** 44 **可以參加線上課程** 45，以便掌握醫學科技的最新動態。
女：啊，這辦法很好。我們很難抽出時間去上實體課程。
男：對啊。喔還有，我們可以去下載一款手機應用程式，那是由塞內卡醫學會開發的。
女：了解。那不會很貴嗎？
男：我不確定。**我會查一下要多少錢，** 46 明天再告訴妳。

44. Where do the speakers most likely work?
(A) At a library
(B) At an electronics store
(C) At a hospital
(D) At a financial firm

44. 說話者最有可能在哪裡工作？
(A) 在圖書館
(B) 在電子用品店
(C) 在醫院
(D) 在金融企業

45. What did Ms. Shah recommend?
(A) Purchasing a magazine subscription
(B) Watching a video demonstration
(C) Holding personal meetings with staff
(D) Enrolling in some online courses

45. 沙阿女士建議了什麼？
(A) 付費訂閱雜誌
(B) 觀看影片展示
(C) 和員工個別開會
(D) 報名參加線上課程

46. What does the man say he will do?
(A) Review a presentation
(B) Try out a product
(C) Research some pricing information
(D) Print out an article

46. 男子說他會做什麼？
(A) 再檢查簡報
(B) 測試產品
(C) 調查價格資訊
(D) 印出文章

Questions 47-49 refer to the following conversation with three speakers.

47-49 三人會話

M ：**Hi, Leslie. Hi, Donna. It's nice seeing you two at this company luncheon.** 47
W1：Ah, it's been a while, Matt. The last time I saw you was at the training workshop in April. It's been a busy month.

男 ：**嗨，萊斯利。嗨，唐娜。很高興在公司的午餐會見到兩位。** 47
女 1：啊，麥特，好久不見。我上次見到你是在四月的培訓研習。這個月好忙。

M ：Yeah, **I know that your department is revising the fall clothing catalog.** 48

W2：“Revising” isn’t the word I’d use. **We’re actually recreating the whole thing.** 48 The new one will be much simpler.

M ：Oh, that’s good. **I was in charge of reviewing customer feedback last quarter.** 49 Many customers who participated in the questionnaire said that our catalog was too confusing to read.

男 ：是啊，**我知道妳的部門正在修訂秋裝型錄。** 48

女 2：我不會把這叫作「修訂」。**我們實際上是把整個型錄重做。** 48 新的型錄會更簡單明瞭。

男 ：哦，太好了。**上一季我負責檢討客戶的回饋意見。** 49 很多參與問卷調查的客戶都說我們的型錄太過雜亂難讀。

47. Where are the speakers?
(A) At a training workshop
(B) At a fashion show
(C) At a department meeting
(D) At a company luncheon

47. 說話者人在哪裡？
(A) 在培訓研習
(B) 在時裝秀
(C) 在部門會議
(D) 在公司午餐會

48. What project are the women working on?
(A) A budget proposal
(B) A catalog redesign
(C) A marketing campaign
(D) An instructional video

48. 女子們正在從事什麼專案？
(A) 預算提案
(B) 重新設計型錄
(C) 行銷活動
(D) 教學影片

49. What does the man say he was responsible for?
(A) Looking over customer feedback
(B) Hiring new staff members
(C) Organizing a volunteer program
(D) Revising some news articles

49. 男子說他之前負責什麼？
(A) 檢視客戶意見
(B) 招聘新員工
(C) 籌備志工計畫
(D) 修改新聞報導

Questions 50-52 refer to the following conversation.

M：Hello, **I’m calling from Jonathan Lim’s office regarding Mr. Lim’s interview with your newspaper on Friday.** 50 Do we need to arrange anything else before you arrive?

W：Actually, there is one request. I’d like to put some pictures of Mr. Lim in our article. So **would it be OK if I brought our photographer to the interview?** 51

M：Sure. **Just give me your photographer’s name so that I can make ID badges for both of you.** 52 I’ll leave the badges at the front desk in the main lobby of the building.

50-52 會話

男：您好，**我是強納森．林辦公室的人員，來電是想討論關於貴報週五與林先生的採訪一事。** 50 有任何其他事項需要我們在您抵達前安排嗎？

女：我其實有個請求。我想在文章中放幾張林先生的照片。因此**想請問我可以帶我們的攝影師去採訪嗎？** 51

男：當然可以。**告知我攝影師的姓名即可，方便我能為兩位製作識別證。** 52 我會將識別證放在本棟大樓大廳的接待處。

50. According to the man, what will happen on Friday?
(A) A business will reopen.
(B) A newspaper will be published.
(C) A workshop will begin.
(D) A staff member will be interviewed.

50. 據男子說法，週五有何安排？
(A) 商家將重新開張。
(B) 報紙將出刊。
(C) 研習將展開。
(D) 有員工將受訪。

51. What does the woman request?
(A) Directions to an office
(B) Permission to bring a colleague
(C) A sample of a product
(D) A tour of a facility

51. 女子有什麼請求？
(A) 到辦公室的路線
(B) 帶同事同行的許可
(C) 產品樣品
(D) 設施參訪

52. What does the man say he will prepare?
(A) Some badges
(B) Some pictures
(C) Some snacks
(D) Some documents

52. 男子說他會準備什麼？
(A) 一些證件
(B) 幾張照片
(C) 一些零食
(D) 幾份文件

Questions 53-55 refer to the following conversation.

53-55 會話

M：Hi, George. **Do you have some time to check out the charts in my slides? 53**
W：I went through them this morning. They were very detailed. Great job!
M：Thanks! **I think I'm all set for the convention now. I'll purchase my train ticket today. 54** Would you like me to purchase yours as well?
W：Um, actually, the deadline for the Routaber project was moved up, so I don't think I can attend the convention. **You'll probably have to present on your own. 55**
M：Hmm . . . **I haven't been here long, and it's a big presentation.**
W：It's OK. No one knows that material better than you.

男：嗨，喬治。**妳有時間檢查我投影片上的圖表嗎？53**
女：我今早看過了，鉅細靡遺，做得很好！
男：謝謝！**我想我現在準備好參加會展了，今天就會買火車票。54** 要我也幫妳一起買嗎？
女：嗯，其實因為路特博專案的結案期限提前，所以我想無法參加這場會展了。**你可能要單獨去發表簡報。55**
男：唔……**我進公司還沒多久，這又是場重要的簡報。**
女：沒問題的。最懂這份資料的人非你莫屬。

53. What does the man request the woman do?
(A) Mail some invitations
(B) Review some charts
(C) Reserve a booth
(D) Postpone an event

53. 男子請女子做什麼事？
(A) 寄出邀請函
(B) 檢查圖表
(C) 預約展位
(D) 延後活動

54. What does the man plan to do today?
(A) Register for a workshop
(B) Meet with a client
(C) Purchase a ticket
(D) Contact a catering company

55. Why does the man say, "I haven't been here long, and it's a big presentation"?
(A) He wants to get feedback from the woman on a proposal.
(B) He is providing an excuse for why he has postponed an event.
(C) He would like to thank the woman for helping him with a project.
(D) He is concerned about performing a task by himself.

54. 男子今天打算做什麼？
(A) 報名參加研習
(B) 會見客戶
(C) 買票
(D) 聯絡外燴業者

55. 為何男子說：「我進公司還沒多久，這又是場重要的簡報」？
(A) 他想聽女子對提案的回饋意見。
(B) 他在提出活動延後的理由。
(C) 他想感謝女子協助他的專案。
(D) 他擔心要獨自進行任務。

TEST 3
PART 3
13

Questions 56-58 refer to the following conversation.

W：Mr. Johnson, thank you for meeting me today. **I am planning to write a newspaper article** 56 on popular trends in men's casual wear. As head designer of ALBATA Fashion, could you give me a preview of the upcoming clothing line for the fall?
M：Yes, I would love to. Using different colors is the most popular fashion trend right now in men's casual wear. **We are currently redesigning all our standard casual jackets to have a wider variety of colors.** 57 We anticipate that this will be popular among men between the ages of 20 and 30.
W：How interesting! I see you've got some samples of your new jackets from the showroom. **Would it be OK if I took some photographs** 58 for the article I'm going to write?

56-58 會話

女：強森先生，謝謝您今天和我見面。**我打算在報上寫篇報導** 56 來探討男性休閒服飾的流行趨勢。您身為洋銀時尚的首席設計師，能否預先透露即將在秋季推出的系列服裝？
男：可以，我很樂意。時下男士休閒服飾最流行的時尚趨勢就是使用多樣配色。**我們正在翻新旗下所有基本款休閒夾克的設計，要讓用色更多樣。** 57 我們預計這將在 20 到 30 歲的男性客群間造成風潮。
女：很有趣！我看您從展場帶來了幾件新款夾克的樣品。**方便讓我拍幾張照片** 58 供我執筆的文章使用嗎？

56. Who most likely is the woman?
(A) A receptionist
(B) A reporter
(C) A salesperson
(D) An actress

56. 女子最有可能的職業為何？
(A) 接待員
(B) 記者
(C) 銷售員
(D) 女演員

57. According to the man, what change is expected?
(A) More colors will be used in clothing designs.
(B) Production costs will significantly increase.
(C) Consumers will spend less money in the future.
(D) Merchandise will only be sold online.

58. What does the woman want to do?
(A) Visit a store
(B) Take photographs
(C) Meet the company CEO
(D) Take a tour

Questions 59-61 refer to the following conversation.

M：Hey, Mindy. I just got off the phone with Mr. Callahan. He visited the job site earlier today to check on the landscaping work, and **he was pleased with everything but the stairway lights. He said he would like round ones instead of the square ones.** 59
W：Hmm . . . But those are the lights he selected at our store.
M：I know, but he didn't think they looked good, so he wants different ones. **I was going to order them, but the earliest we'd receive them would be next Thursday.** 60
W：Well, **according to the contract, we need to finish everything by this week.**
M：Right. OK, **I'll send him a text message right now** 61 to see if he's fine with next week.

59. What did a client dislike about the stairway lights?
(A) Their shape
(B) Their cost
(C) Their brightness
(D) Their color

60. Why does the woman say, "according to the contract, we need to finish everything by this week"?
(A) She believes some contract terms should be changed.
(B) She is concerned about meeting a deadline.
(C) She is surprised at the progress of a landscaping project.
(D) She will repair some broken equipment this week.

57. 據男子說法，預期會有哪項變動？
(A) 服裝設計將使用更多色彩。
(B) 生產成本將顯著增加。
(C) 消費者未來將減少花費。
(D) 產品將只在網路販售。

58. 女子想做什麼？
(A) 造訪商店
(B) 拍幾張照
(C) 會見公司執行長
(D) 遊覽一下

59-61 會話

男：嘿，敏迪。我剛和卡拉漢先生通完電話。他今天稍早到施工地點視察景觀美化工程，而**他一切都滿意，只是對階梯照明有意見。他說不想要採用方型的燈款，要改用圓形的。** 59
女：嗯……但那一款燈是他之前到我們店裡自己選的。
男：我知道，但他覺得不太好看，所以現在他想要別款。**我才正要下單採買，但我們最快也要下週四才能收到貨。** 60
女：呃，**根據合約，我們本週以內就得完工。**
男：是的。那好，**我馬上就傳訊息問他，** 61 看他能不能通融到下週。

59. 客戶對階梯照明哪個地方不滿意？
(A) 形狀
(B) 費用
(C) 亮度
(D) 顏色

60. 為何女子說：「根據合約，我們本週以內就得完工」？
(A) 她認為部分合約條款應修改。
(B) 她擔心趕不上期限。
(C) 她對景觀美化案的進展感到驚訝。
(D) 她將在這週維修一些損壞的設備。

61. What does the man say he will do?
(A) Go to a work site
(B) Revise a document
(C) Place an order
(D) Contact a customer

61. 男子說他會做什麼？
(A) 去工地
(B) 修改文件
(C) 下訂單
(D) 聯絡客戶

Questions 62-64 refer to the following conversation and table.

M：Rachel, I'm glad we're nearly done organizing the company's year-end party. **Ms. Anderson also sent me the confirmed budget for the expenditures this morning,** 62 so we can start finalizing everything.
W：Sounds good. All right, now, we need to select the venue for the party. Here are some places we could choose.
M：Hmm, I was at Bistro 324 last week, and it has a nice atmosphere. **But we're probably going to have more than 150 guests attending the party, so it'll be good to have a venue with a lot of space. Let's book the largest one.** 63
W：**You're right.** 63 OK, once you set the exact date, **I'll call our agency and arrange for the live music show at the party.** 64

Possible Event Locations	
Venue	**Guest Capacity**
Ocean Grill 64	**200 guests**
Bistro 324	150 guests
The Vine	125 guests
Olive Grove	100 guests

62-64 會話和表格

男：瑞秋，太好了，公司尾牙的籌備工作已近尾聲。**安德森女士今早也已經寄給我確認的支出預算，**62 所以我們可以開始把各項事情敲定。
女：太棒了。好，現在我們得選出宴會地點。這裡有一些我們可以選擇的地方。
男：嗯，我上週去過「324 餐酒館」，那裡氣氛很好。**但這次宴會可能會有超過 150 位賓客出席，所以最好還是找個場地很寬敞的地點。我們就訂最大間的吧。**63
女：**你說的對。**63 好，等你確定好日期後，**我再打給我們的承辦業者，安排宴會上的現場音樂表演。**64

活動場地提案	
場地	**可容納人數**
大洋燒烤 64	**200 位賓客**
324 餐酒館	150 位賓客
葡萄藤	125 位賓客
橄欖園	100 位賓客

62. What information about the party did the man receive this morning?
(A) The finalized date
(B) The amount of budgeted funds
(C) The number of attendees
(D) The directions to the event

62. 男子今早收到哪項聚會相關的資訊？
(A) 確定日期
(B) 預算金額
(C) 出席人數
(D) 活動場地的路線

63. Look at the graphic. Which venue will the speakers most likely choose?
(A) Ocean Grill
(B) Bistro 324
(C) The Vine
(D) Olive Grove

63. 請據圖表作答。說話者最有可能會選擇哪個場地？
(A) 大洋燒烤
(B) 324 餐酒館
(C) 葡萄藤
(D) 橄欖園

64. What does the woman say she will take care of?
(A) A security deposit
(B) Entertainment
(C) Menu items
(D) Transportation

64. 女子說她會負責什麼？
(A) 保證金
(B) 娛樂
(C) 菜單品項
(D) 交通

Questions 65-67 refer to the following conversation and invoice.

W：Good afternoon, Mr. Posner. **Did you come to pick up the paintings you wanted restored?** 65
M：Yes. I appreciate you completing the work so quickly. **We're planning on auctioning them off at a fundraiser** 65 next week.
W：Ah, I see. I wish you the best of luck with that. Let me give you your invoice.
M：Thank you. Um . . . **Something is not right. I asked for three paintings to be restored, not four. I shouldn't be charged for this 20-by-24-inch painting.** 66
W：Hmm . . . Yes, you're right. **I'll remove that right now** 66 and give you a new invoice. **In the meantime, my assistant will take your paintings out to your van.** 67
M：Oh, I'd appreciate that. Thank you.

Invoice (#483740) Customer Name: Raymond Posner	
Description	**Price**
9"x12" Oil Painting	$380
12"x16" Watercolor Painting	$560
20"x24" Acrylic Painting	**$720** 66
30"x40" Landscape Painting	$910

65-67 會話和帳單

女：波斯納先生午安。**您是不是過來拿您要求修復的畫作了？** 65
男：對。感謝您辦事如此俐落。**我們計劃在下週的籌款活動上拍賣這些畫作。** 65
女：喔，了解，那麼祝您好運。這邊是您的帳單。
男：謝謝。嗯……**有點不太對。我要求修復的畫是三幅，不是四幅。這筆 20 X 24 英寸畫作的費用不應該跟我收。** 66
女：嗯……是，您說的對。**我馬上刪除這筆費用，** 66 再開新的帳單給您。**同時，我的助理會把畫作搬上您的廂型車。** 67
男：喔，太感謝了。謝謝。

帳單明細（#483740） 顧客姓名：雷蒙・波斯納	
項目描述	**價錢**
9 X 12 英寸 油畫	380 美元
12 X 16 英寸 水彩畫	560 美元
20 X 24 英寸 壓克力顏料畫	**720 美元** 66
30 X 40 英寸 風景畫	910 美元

65. What does the man say he will do with the restored paintings?
(A) Sell them at an auction
(B) Use them as office decorations
(C) Display them at a museum
(D) Give them as gifts to coworkers

65. 男子說他將把修復後的圖畫作何運用？
(A) 在拍賣中出售
(B) 用為辦公室裝飾
(C) 在博物館展示
(D) 送給同事當禮物

66. Look at the graphic. Which amount will be taken off of the invoice?
(A) $380
(B) $560
(C) $720
(D) $910

67. What does the woman say her assistant will do?
(A) Print out some forms
(B) Give the man a tour of a store
(C) Carry some items to a vehicle
(D) Process a payment

Questions 68-70 refer to the following conversation and schedule.

W：Speedline Railways, how can I assist you today?
M：Hello, I have to get from Boston to Chicago tomorrow. **I'm trying to purchase a train ticket through your Web site, but I keep getting an error message.** 68
W：**I'm sorry for the inconvenience.** 68 All tickets bought less than one day before departure must be ordered over the phone. I can help you with that now. When would you like to leave?
M：**Any departure time is fine, if it gets me to Chicago before noon the following day.** 69 **I'm enrolled in a seminar on that day.** 70

Boston to Chicago		
Train	Departure	Arrival
Train 1024 69	**12:50 P.M.**	**9:50 A.M.**
Train 116	3:15 P.M.	12:10 P.M.
Train 894	5:30 P.M.	3:40 P.M.
Train 3479	7:25 P.M.	5:45 P.M.

68. Why does the woman apologize?
(A) A payment was not processed.
(B) A ticket is not available online.
(C) A train has been overbooked.
(D) A schedule is incorrect.

66. 請據圖表作答。帳單中將會扣除哪筆金額？
(A) 380 美元
(B) 560 美元
(C) 720 美元
(D) 910 美元

67. 女子說她的助理會做什麼？
(A) 印出一些表格
(B) 帶男子參訪商店
(C) 把一些物品搬上車
(D) 處理付款

68-70 會話和行程表

女：這裡是高速鐵路，今天需要什麼協助嗎？
男：您好，我明天要從波士頓坐到芝加哥。**我正試著在你們官網上買車票，但是一直跳出錯誤訊息。** 68
女：**抱歉造成您的不便。** 68 欲購買一天以內發車的車次，都須經由電話訂票。我現在就能幫您訂票，請問您要何時出發？
男：**不限發車時間，只要隔天中午前能載我抵達芝加哥就好。** 69 **我當天有報名參加一場研討會。** 70

波士頓到芝加哥		
車次	出發時間	抵達時間
列車 1024 69	**下午 12:50**	**上午 9:50**
列車 116	下午 3:15	下午 12:10
列車 894	下午 5:30	下午 3:40
列車 3479	下午 7:25	下午 5:45

68. 女子為什麼道歉？
(A) 付款尚未處理。
(B) 無法線上購票。
(C) 列車座位超賣。
(D) 時刻表不正確。

69. Look at the graphic. What train will the man most likely take?
(A) Train 1024
(B) Train 116
(C) Train 894
(D) Train 3479

70. What does the man say he will do in Chicago?
(A) Attend a seminar
(B) Tour a factory
(C) Watch a performance
(D) Meet a client

69. 請據圖表作答。男子最有可能會搭乘哪班列車？
(A) 列車 1024
(B) 列車 116
(C) 列車 894
(D) 列車 3479

70. 男子說他將在芝加哥做什麼？
(A) 參加研討會
(B) 參訪工廠
(C) 欣賞表演
(D) 與客戶見面

PART 4 P. 51-53

14

Questions 71-73 refer to the following excerpt from a meeting.

M： I'd like to say a special thanks to the design team for your amazing work on the RK990 smartphone's user interface. **You all did a wonderful job in designing the product,** 71 and **we're now ready to move on to the next step of our project. We will present the interface to several groups of people who have never seen it to find out what they think.** 72 So **we need a person to call other departments and ask if anyone would like to participate in the upcoming product tests. Do we have a volunteer?** 73

71-73 會議摘錄

男：我想針對 RK990 智慧型手機的使用者介面，特別感謝設計團隊的精彩表現。**你們全員在設計產品上做得非常出色，** 71 而**我們現在也準備好進入專案的下個階段。我們要把這款介面展示給幾組從未看過本產品的人，來了解他們的想法。** 72 所以**我們需要有人去打電話給其他部門，徵詢有意參加接下來產品測試的人。各位有誰自願嗎？** 73

71. Who most likely are the listeners?
(A) Sales associates
(B) Product designers
(C) Computer specialists
(D) Human resources employees

72. According to the speaker, what is the next step of the project?
(A) To develop training materials
(B) To create a prototype
(C) To determine a cost
(D) To obtain some feedback

71. 聽者最有可能的職業為何？
(A) 銷售助理
(B) 產品設計師
(C) 電腦專員
(D) 人力資源人員

72. 據說話者說法，專案下一步為何？
(A) 開發訓練教材
(B) 製作產品原型
(C) 決定費用
(D) 獲取意見回饋

14

73. What does the speaker ask for help with?
(A) Reviewing some documents
(B) Interviewing job candidates
(C) Contacting other departments
(D) Selecting some instruments

73. 說話者要求哪方面的協助？
(A) 審查文件
(B) 面試應徵者
(C) 聯絡其他部門
(D) 選擇儀器

Questions 74-76 refer to the following telephone message.

74-76 語音留言

W：Hi, **I'm calling from Jack's Uniform Boutique.** 74 We have some information regarding your order. The shirts have been altered as requested. **According to the memo on your order form, you asked for them to be shipped by the end of the week. Unfortunately, some of our drivers are out sick at the moment. Also, we're still waiting on the pants that you wanted.** 75 **To make up for this delay,** 75 **we'll take 20 percent off on your next order.** 76

女：您好，**這裡是傑克家制服專賣店。** 74 我們想跟您告知訂單相關資訊。襯衫已按要求修改。**根據您訂單上的附註，您要求在週末前送貨。但很遺憾，我們有幾名司機目前因病告假。此外，我們還在等您要的長褲備齊。** 75 **為補償本次延誤，** 75 **我們會給您的下一筆訂單提供 20%的折扣。** 76

74. Where does the speaker work?
(A) At a uniform retailer
(B) At a taxi company
(C) At a car dealership
(D) At a post office

74. 說話者在哪裡上班？
(A) 在制服零售店
(B) 在計程車行
(C) 在汽車經銷商
(D) 在郵局

75. What does the speaker mean when she says, "some of our drivers are out sick at the moment"?
(A) A shipment will not arrive on time.
(B) A company will hire more employees.
(C) Some staff will be working extra shifts.
(D) Some automobiles are available for use.

75. 說話者說：「我們有幾名司機目前因病告假」，其意思為何？
(A) 貨物無法準時送達。
(B) 公司將增聘員工。
(C) 部分員工將增加輪班。
(D) 幾台汽車可供使用。

76. What does the speaker offer?
(A) A future discount
(B) A product catalog
(C) A complimentary item
(D) A full refund

76. 說話者提供什麼？
(A) 未來享折扣
(B) 產品型錄
(C) 贈品
(D) 全額退款

Questions 77-79 refer to the following broadcast.

77-79 廣播

M：In business news, **Fairways, the country's leading manufacturer of commercial aircraft engines,** 77 has been contracted as the supplier of engines for the newly developed Bering

男：焦點轉到財經新聞。**我國商用飛機引擎製造巨頭「順飛」** 77 已經簽約，成為新研發的一款白令 X20 機型的引擎供應商。為了滿足所需的

X20 airplane. In order to meet the required production numbers of the engines, **Fairways has decided to open an additional factory at the start of August. The new manufacturing plant will be built in the town of Willington.** 78 During a press conference this afternoon, **the mayor of Willington expressed his excitement about the construction of the facility, emphasizing that it will create an estimated 400 new skilled jobs in the community.** 79

引擎產量，**順飛已決定在八月初另外開設新的工廠，該製造廠將設在威靈頓鎮。** 78 今天下午的記者會上，**威靈頓鎮鎮長對廠房建設表示振奮不已，強調此舉估計將為當地新增 400 個專業技術職缺。** 79

77. What does the business produce?
(A) Car tires
(B) Mobile phones
(C) Airplane engines
(D) Laptop computers

78. According to the speaker, what will the business do in August?
(A) Raise its workers' wages
(B) Launch a new product line
(C) Create additional parking spaces
(D) Open a new manufacturing plant

79. What does the mayor expect will happen in Willington?
(A) A recycling program will begin.
(B) New traffic laws will be enforced.
(C) More public transportation will be provided.
(D) Employment opportunities will increase.

77. 該公司生產什麼？
(A) 汽車輪胎
(B) 手機
(C) 飛機引擎
(D) 筆電

78. 據說話者說法，該公司將在八月做什麼？
(A) 提高員工工資
(B) 發表新系列產品
(C) 增設停車位
(D) 開設新製造工廠

79. 鎮長預期威靈頓鎮上將發生何事？
(A) 回收計畫將開始。
(B) 新的交通法規將實施。
(C) 公共運輸將擴大提供。
(D) 就業機會將增加。

Questions 80-82 refer to the following advertisement.

W：**Every year, homeowners waste thousands of dollars using central heating systems that need maintenance. To make sure your system is working properly, call Cen-Tech Repair Services at 555-8162 and arrange for a free energy efficiency checkup.** 80 81 Our central heating expert will visit your home to inspect your system and explain in detail what needs to be done. And **until the end of the month, take advantage of our 25 percent discount** 82 on any parts you order from us. Don't hesitate—contact us today!

80-82 廣告

女：**每年，屋主都得為了使用需要維修的中央暖氣系統而使荷包失血數千美元。要確認府上的系統運作正常，請來電 555-8162 央科技維修服務公司，安排免費的能源效率測試。** 80 81 本公司的中央暖氣專家將到府檢查系統，並詳細說明需要改善的地方。而且**截至本月底前**，凡向我們訂購任何零組件，**全面享 25%的折扣。** 82 別猶豫，立即聯絡我們！

80. What is being advertised?
(A) Residential real estate
(B) Heating maintenance
(C) Appliance recycling
(D) A technology institute

81. Why are listeners asked to call?
(A) To sign up for a class
(B) To set up an inspection
(C) To arrange transportation
(D) To receive a brochure

82. What will happen at the end of the month?
(A) A special offer will expire.
(B) A report will be published.
(C) Payments will be due.
(D) Construction will begin.

80. 廣告主打什麼？
(A) 住宅房地產
(B) 暖氣維修
(C) 家電回收
(D) 科技研究所

81. 聽者為何被要求打電話？
(A) 以報名參加課程
(B) 以安排檢查
(C) 以安排交通
(D) 以收到手冊

82. 本月底將會發生何事？
(A) 特價將截止。
(B) 報告將發布。
(C) 繳款期限將至。
(D) 施工將開始。

TEST 3
PART 4
14

Questions 83-85 refer to the following talk.

W：**Now, we've reached the last part of our tour, the packaging area, which is also the final step for Heaven Cookies.** 83 After the cookies have been baked and cooled, they arrive here where they're put in sealed bags and sent to retail stores across the country. Over here, **we've got a small bag of our most popular cookies for each of you.** 84 While you're enjoying your delicious gift, feel free to look around the area and take pictures. And **don't forget to return your visitors' pass** 85 to the security desk **when exiting the factory.** 83

83-85 談話

女：**現在我們導覽的最後一站帶大家來到包裝區，這裡也是天堂餅乾的最後一道程序。** 83 餅乾經烘烤、冷卻後，會來到這裡裝進密封袋裡，然後送往全國各地的零售商店。在此，**我們要送各位每人一小袋我們最受歡迎的餅乾。** 84 各位一邊享用美味的餅乾的同時，也歡迎在四週走走看看並拍照。而**您離開工廠時，** 83 **也別忘了將訪客證交還**到保全櫃台。85

83. Where is the talk taking place?
(A) In a factory
(B) In a laboratory
(C) In a supermarket
(D) In a bakery

84. What are listeners given?
(A) A location map
(B) A discount coupon
(C) Product samples
(D) Some ingredients

83. 這段談話在哪裡發生？
(A) 在工廠
(B) 在實驗室
(C) 在超市
(D) 在麵包店

84. 聽者會收到什麼？
(A) 位置圖
(B) 折價券
(C) 試吃產品
(D) 一些食材

85. What does the speaker remind the listeners to do?
(A) Wear safety equipment
(B) Use a back entrance
(C) Return their passes
(D) Fill out a security form

85. 說話者提醒聽者做什麼？
(A) 穿戴安全裝備
(B) 使用後門
(C) 返還通行證
(D) 填寫安全表格

Questions 86-88 refer to the following excerpt from a meeting.

M：Hello, everybody. Thanks for joining our production meeting. **Before we start, though, just a reminder to finish up your task reports and hand those in to your supervisor by the end of the day today.** 86 **OK, first, I have some good news to share with you all. There has been a significant increase in our manufacturing output compared to last year, and that's thanks to the excellent work all of you have been doing.** 87 **Now, I was originally going to have everyone's work schedules for next month prepared for today's meeting, but as you know, we've been hosting visitors from Japan for several days. You should have your schedule by tomorrow morning.** 88

86-88 會議摘錄

男：大家好。感謝各位參加我們今天的生產會議。**不過在開始前，先提醒各位今天下班之前須完成工作報告並交給所屬主管。** 86 **那麼首先，我有一些好消息要和大家分享。和去年相比，我們的產量有顯著提升，而這要歸功於各位一向的優秀表現。** 87 **再來，我本來打算在今天會議就備妥大家下個月的班表，但各位都知道，我們這幾天接待了從日本來的賓客。班表應會在明早提供給大家。** 88

86. What does the speaker remind listeners to do by the end of the day?
(A) Submit a task report
(B) Make a reservation
(C) Pick up a visitor's pass
(D) Nominate an employee

86. 說話者提醒聽者下班前要做什麼？
(A) 提交工作報告
(B) 預約
(C) 領取訪客證
(D) 提名員工

87. What good news does the speaker mention?
(A) Workers will receive cash incentives.
(B) Production has gone up.
(C) A product launch was successful.
(D) A shipment arrived on time.

87. 說話者提到什麼好消息？
(A) 員工將獲得獎勵金。
(B) 產量有所提升。
(C) 產品發布會很成功。
(D) 貨物準時到達。

88. Why does the speaker say, "we've been hosting visitors from Japan for several days"?
(A) To introduce a guest speaker
(B) To begin a tour of a facility
(C) To review details of a business trip
(D) To give a reason for a delay

88. 說話者為何說：「我們這幾天接待了從日本來的賓客」？
(A) 以介紹客座講者
(B) 以開始工廠導覽
(C) 以檢查出差細節
(D) 以表明延誤原因

Questions 89-91 refer to the following talk.

W：**Thank you for attending today's introduction to the Hartman Arts Program. My name is Whitney Brown, and I'm the lead coordinator.** 89 As you're aware, this program assists hopeful artists in achieving their dreams by providing financial assistance. **In exchange, we require members to commit some of their time by holding events, such as extracurricular activities at schools, in their local area.** 90 **I've asked two former participants who became famous artists with the help of this program to join us tonight.** 91 They'll be talking to you about their experiences in the industry, and how the program has helped launch their careers.

89. What is the purpose of the talk?
(A) To ask for financial contributions
(B) To share information about a program
(C) To explain a job application process
(D) To announce a new exhibit

90. What requirement does the speaker mention?
(A) Holding local events
(B) Providing weekly feedback
(C) Submitting work samples
(D) Visiting different cities

91. Who is invited to speak next?
(A) School teachers
(B) Museum directors
(C) Famous artists
(D) Professional athletes

89-91 談話

女：**感謝你們今天蒞臨哈特曼藝術計畫的說明會。我叫惠特尼．布朗，我擔任總召集人。** 89 如各位所知，這項計畫旨在透過提供財務支援，幫助有潛力的藝術家實現夢想。**為求互惠，我們會要求成員在他們所在的社區，抽點時間舉辦活動，例如到學校帶領課外活動等。** 90 **我今晚已請來兩位參與過計畫的成員，透過這項計畫的協助，他們現在已成為著名藝術家。** 91 他們將和各位分享他們的從業經驗，以及這項計畫如何幫助他們開啟職業生涯。

89. 談話的主旨為何？
(A) 請求財務資助
(B) 分享計畫的相關資訊
(C) 解釋求職程序
(D) 宣布新辦展覽

90. 說話者提到哪些要求？
(A) 舉行在地活動
(B) 提供每週心得
(C) 繳交作品的樣品
(D) 造訪不同城市

91. 接下來是誰受邀發言？
(A) 學校老師
(B) 博物館館長
(C) 著名藝術家
(D) 職業運動員

14

Questions 92-94 refer to the following telephone message.

M：Heather, this is Rich. **I'm calling because I need to postpone our meeting later. My train back to Tokyo has been delayed, so I won't be able to make it into the office in time.** 92 **I was, however, able to look over the research proposal you created for expanding our client base.** 93 You noted that some design changes

92-94 語音留言

男：希瑟，我是里奇。**我打給妳是因為我得要把我們的會議延後。我回東京的火車誤點了，因此我無法及時趕回辦公室。** 92 **不過，我還是看了一下妳為擴大客戶群所寫的研究提案。** 93 妳提到我們的公司標誌設計需要一些修改，但它會依然可以辨

would be required to our logo, but it would still be recognizable. **It's a good idea, but I'm afraid it will confuse our current customers. Let's discuss this in more detail.** 94

識。**這個想法很好，但我擔心會讓現有顧客感到困惑。這方面我們要再更詳細討論。** 94

92. Why is the speaker postponing today's meeting?
(A) A manager was busy.
(B) A room was not available.
(C) Some designs were not completed.
(D) His travel arrangements were changed.

92. 說話者為何延後今天的會議？
(A) 有位經理很忙。
(B) 有會議室無法使用。
(C) 有些設計還未完成。
(D) 他的行程安排有變。

93. According to the speaker, what was the listener's report about?
(A) Suggestions for being more environmentally friendly
(B) Results of a recent customer survey
(C) Plans to cut back on operating costs
(D) Strategies to attract new customers

93. 據說話者說法，聽者的報告和什麼有關？
(A) 更能達成環保的建議
(B) 近期客戶調查的結果
(C) 削減營運成本的計畫
(D) 吸引新客戶的策略

94. What does the speaker imply when he says, "Let's discuss this in more detail"?
(A) He is planning to research some new suppliers.
(B) He believes a proposal may cause problems.
(C) He would like review a contract more carefully.
(D) He wants to extend a project deadline.

94. 說話者說：「這方面我們要再更詳細討論」，言下之意為何？
(A) 他打算調查幾個新的供應商。
(B) 他認為某個提議可能會引發問題。
(C) 他想更仔細審查合約。
(D) 他想延長專案期限。

Questions 95-97 refer to the following telephone message and list.

95-97 語音留言和清單

M：Hello. This message is for Rachel Preston. **This is Robert calling from Risbon Telephone. We are sorry to hear that you are discontinuing your service with us.** 95 Before we terminate your service, you should review the list of fees on the contract you signed. **Since you are terminating early, you will be subject to a penalty fee.** 96 **We also ask that you visit our Web site and fill out a survey** 97 to let us know if there is anything we can do to improve our service. Thank you.

男：您好。這是給瑞秋．普瑞斯頓的留言。**我是瑞斯本電信的羅伯特。我們很遺憾得知您將終止我們的服務。** 95 在我們終止服務前，須勞您查看您所簽訂合約的費用表。**因您提前終止，您將須負擔違約金。** 96 **我們也請您至我們的網站填寫調查表** 97 好讓我們了解我們的服務有什麼可以改進的地方。謝謝您。

Service	Fee
Late payment	$20
Line reconnection	$40
In-home service	$60
Early cancelation	**$80** 96

服務	費用
費用遲繳	20 美元
重新接線	40 美元
到府服務	60 美元
提前解約	**80 美元** 96

95. Where does the speaker most likely work?
(A) At a book publisher
(B) At a fitness center
(C) At a telephone provider
(D) At a landscaping company

95. 說話者最有可能在哪裡工作？
(A) 在書籍出版社
(B) 在健身房
(C) 在電信業者
(D) 在景觀美化公司

96. Look at the graphic. How much will Ms. Preston pay?
(A) $20
(B) $40
(C) $60
(D) $80

96. 請據圖表作答。普瑞斯頓女士將支付多少錢？
(A) 20 美元
(B) 40 美元
(C) 60 美元
(D) 80 美元

97. What is Ms. Preston encouraged to do on the Web site?
(A) Provide feedback
(B) Renew her membership
(C) Download a contract
(D) Register for a mailing list

97. 普瑞斯頓女士被鼓勵到網站做什麼？
(A) 提供回饋意見
(B) 延續會員資格
(C) 下載合約
(D) 申請加入郵寄名單

Questions 98-100 refer to the following telephone message and conference schedule.

W：Hello, it's Boram Lee from TRD Motors. We spoke briefly at the Innomax Convention three weeks ago. I listened to your informative talk, and we discussed TRD's upcoming vehicle line for a moment afterwards. **I'm contacting you because I want to hire you** 98 **to advise us on how to make our cars more fuel efficient. I know that this is your area of specialty, so I'd really like you to join us for this project.** 99 **Would you mind sending a chart of your consulting fees to me here at blee@trdmotors.com?** 100 Thank you.

98-100 語音留言和會議日程

女：您好，我是 TRD 汽車的李寶藍。我們三週前在創新極致展上有簡短聊過。我聽了您富含新知的演講，之後我們討論了一會 TRD 即將推出的車款。**我現在聯繫您是想聘請您** 98 **來指點我們如何讓我們的車款更省油。我知道這個領域是您的專長，所以我真的希望您能參與我們這次的專案。** 99 **能麻煩您將您的諮詢費用表寄至 blee@trdmotors.com 給我嗎？** 100 謝謝您。

TEST 3 PART 4

14

Innomax Convention Schedule		
Time	**Event**	**Speaker**
13:00	Best Sport Cars	Jeremy Fong
14:00	Latest Navigation Systems	Kelly Brown
15:00	**Improving Fuel Efficiency**	**Sherman Bernstein** 99
16:00	Designing Your Vehicle	Emily Lithmore
17:00	Reception	Innomax President

創新極致展日程表		
時間	活動主題	講者
13:00	最佳跑車	傑瑞米・馮
14:00	最新導航系統	凱莉・布朗
15:00	**提升燃油效率**	**謝爾曼・伯恩斯坦** 99
16:00	專屬汽車設計	艾蜜莉・李斯摩爾
17:00	招待會	創新極致總裁

98. What is the purpose of the call?
(A) To offer a job
(B) To check on an order
(C) To request product samples
(D) To make a reservation

99. Look at the graphic. Who is the speaker calling?
(A) Jeremy Fong
(B) Kelly Brown
(C) Sherman Bernstein
(D) Emily Lithmore

100. What does the speaker ask the listener to do?
(A) Provide pricing information
(B) Visit a Web site
(C) Review a convention schedule
(D) Send a registration payment

98. 這通電話的目的為何？
(A) 以提供工作
(B) 以確認訂單
(C) 以索取樣品
(D) 以進行預約

99. 請據圖表作答。說話者致電給誰？
(A) 傑瑞米・馮
(B) 凱莉・布朗
(C) 謝爾曼・伯恩斯坦
(D) 艾蜜莉・李斯摩爾

100. 說話者要求聽者做什麼？
(A) 提供價格資訊
(B) 瀏覽網站
(C) 查看會展日程表
(D) 寄送報名費

ACTUAL TEST 4

15

PART 1 P. 54–57

1. (A) A man's making a photocopy.
   (B) A man's turning on some lights.
   (C) A woman's putting on eye glasses.
   (D) A woman's typing on a laptop computer.

2. (A) She is stirring liquid in a container.
   (B) She is picking up a paint can.
   (C) She is standing in front of a fence.
   (D) She is looking at her reflection in a mirror.

3. (A) The man is getting into a vehicle.
   (B) The man is operating a forklift.
   (C) The man is moving some cartons on a cart.
   (D) The man is cleaning the floor of a warehouse.

4. (A) A pavilion is being built in the park.
   (B) A picnic area is empty.
   (C) The trees have lost most of their leaves.
   (D) There is a water hose on the path.

5. (A) A bicycle is being secured to a pole.
   (B) Some people are resting on the bench.
   (C) Some people are walking side by side.
   (D) Trees are being cut in a park.

6. (A) A sculpture is being cleaned.
   (B) A line of shops stretches along a shoreline.
   (C) Some vendors have closed their awnings.
   (D) Stalls have been erected outdoors.

1. (A) 男子正在影印。
   (B) 男子正在打開幾盞燈。
   (C) 女子正在戴眼鏡。
   (D) 女子在筆電上打字。

2. (A) 她正在攪拌容器裡的液體。
   (B) 她正在把油漆罐提起來。
   (C) 她正站在柵欄前。
   (D) 她正看著鏡中自己的倒影。

3. (A) 男子正在上車。
   (B) 男子正在操作推高機。
   (C) 男子正在移動拖車上的幾個紙箱。
   (D) 男子正在清潔倉庫地板。

4. (A) 公園裡有涼亭在興建中。
   (B) 野餐區空無一人。
   (C) 樹木的葉子大多掉光了。
   (D) 步道上有條水管。

5. (A) 腳踏車正被固定在桿子上。
   (B) 有些人正在長椅上休息。
   (C) 有些人正在並肩行走。
   (D) 公園裡正在砍樹。

6. (A) 雕塑正在清洗中。
   (B) 岸邊有一排商店。
   (C) 幾家攤販收起了棚子。
   (D) 攤位架設在戶外。

16

PART 2 P. 58

7. When are you interviewing the applicant?
   (A) For the HR Department.
   (B) It's been canceled.
   (C) Because there is a job opening.

7. 你何時會面試應徵者？
   (A) 為了人力資源部門。
   (B) 已經取消了。
   (C) 因為有個職位開缺。

8. Which express train did you book?
(A) The Web site is bookmarked.
(B) The one that leaves at 5.
(C) It received great reviews.

9. Would you like to try the chef's special pasta?
(A) I'll just get a salad.
(B) A table for four, please.
(C) Can you try calling again?

10. How old is the downtown theater?
(A) Twenty movies every day.
(B) It was built 70 years ago.
(C) My birthday was last week.

11. Do you think we should use a new marketing technique?
(A) I haven't been to that market.
(B) I used to shop there.
(C) What did you have in mind?

12. Where is the electronics trade show being held?
(A) No problem. I'm an engineer.
(B) In late June.
(C) I heard it's in Seoul.

13. There's a package for you in the lobby.
(A) Thanks, I've been expecting it.
(B) Did you finish packing yet?
(C) Multiple box sizes.

14. Who played the doctor in that film you saw?
(A) But I am friends with the producer.
(B) A new actress, Chun Hua.
(C) She's feeling better now.

15. The lease on our office can be extended, right?
(A) Have you checked with the building owner?
(B) Call extension number 473.
(C) I've been working here for a long time.

16. Do I need to set up four or five computers for the new employees?
(A) Only four people were hired.
(B) I am not available for training.
(C) Several new desks.

8. 你訂的是哪一班直達車？
(A) 該網站已加入書籤。
(B) 五點出發的那班。
(C) 它獲得很好評價。

9. 您想試試主廚特製義大利麵嗎？
(A) 我只要一份沙拉。
(B) 一桌四位，麻煩了。
(C) 您能再打一次電話嗎？

10. 市中心劇院有多久的歷史？
(A) 每天 20 部電影。
(B) 它建於 70 年前。
(C) 我上禮拜生日。

11. 你覺得我們應該用新的行銷技巧嗎？
(A) 我還沒去過那個市場。
(B) 我以前常去那裡購物。
(C) 你有什麼想法嗎？

12. 電子貿易展在哪裡舉行？
(A) 沒問題。我是工程師。
(B) 在六月下旬。
(C) 我聽說是在首爾。

13. 大廳裡有給你的包裹。
(A) 謝謝，我正在等它來。
(B) 你行李都收拾好了嗎？
(C) 多種尺寸的盒子。

14. 你看的那部電影裡是誰飾演醫師？
(A) 但我和製片人是朋友。
(B) 一名新人女演員，春華。
(C) 她現在感覺好多了。

15. 我們辦公室的租約可以延長，對嗎？
(A) 你和本棟的屋主確認過了嗎？
(B) 請撥分機 473。
(C) 我在這裡工作很久了。

16. 我需要幫新進員工安裝四台或五台電腦？
(A) 只有四人錄取。
(B) 我沒時間參加培訓。
(C) 幾張新桌子。

17. How much does it cost to repair the keyboard on a laptop?
(A) An extra pair of keys.
(B) Around 20 minutes.
(C) It depends on the model.

18. Make sure you turn off the heater before you leave the office.
(A) No, it's at my desk.
(B) Over 30 degrees.
(C) Of course. I always do.

19. Why is the front entrance of the building locked today?
(A) They're installing a security system.
(B) Probably not until tomorrow morning.
(C) It's not my locker.

20. This smartphone comes with a set of earphones, doesn't it?
(A) No, they're sold separately.
(B) It sounds clear to me.
(C) I will come alone.

21. Haven't you already signed up for the conference?
(A) A conference call at 3 P.M.
(B) The sign on the window.
(C) I'm going to do it after lunch.

22. Are the clients going to visit our new manufacturing plant?
(A) A new safety manual.
(B) It's still under construction.
(C) I've never visited it.

23. This is the newest model of the smartphone, isn't it?
(A) No, that one came out last year.
(B) It comes with an extended warranty.
(C) Would you like to buy a case?

24. Hasn't the budget proposal been approved yet?
(A) We just emailed it.
(B) The annual expenses.
(C) That's what I proposed.

17. 筆電鍵盤的維修需要多少錢？
(A) 一對備用鑰匙。
(B) 約 20 分鐘。
(C) 取決於型號。

18. 你離開辦公室前務必關閉暖氣。
(A) 不，是在我桌上。
(B) 超過 30 度。
(C) 當然。我一向如此。

19. 為什麼今天大樓的前門鎖住了？
(A) 他們正在安裝保全系統。
(B) 可能要等到明天早上。
(C) 這不是我的置物櫃。

20. 這支智慧型手機是搭配一副耳機販售的，不是嗎？
(A) 不，它們是分開販售的。
(B) 我聽得很清楚。
(C) 我會自己一個人去。

21. 你還沒報名參加會議嗎？
(A) 下午三點的電話會議。
(B) 窗戶上的牌子。
(C) 我午餐後會去報名。

22. 客戶要來參訪我們新的製造工廠嗎？
(A) 新的安全手冊。
(B) 它還在建設中。
(C) 我從未去過那裡。

23. 這是最新款的智慧型手機，不是嗎？
(A) 不，那台是去年推出的。
(B) 它有附延長保固。
(C) 您想買手機殼嗎？

24. 預算案還沒批准通過嗎？
(A) 我們剛才用電子郵件寄出。
(B) 年度開銷。
(C) 那就是我之前提議的。

25. We need to purchase a file cabinet to store these documents.
(A) Which drawer are they in?
(B) I prefer a hard copy.
(C) Order it with the company credit card.

25. 我們須買個檔案櫃來存放這些文件。
(A) 它們放在哪個抽屜裡？
(B) 我比較偏好紙本。
(C) 用公司信用卡訂貨吧。

26. Can you email me the contract for the construction project?
(A) The new office building downtown.
(B) A world-famous architect.
(C) I sent it this morning.

26. 你能用電子郵件寄給我建案的合約嗎？
(A) 市中心的新辦公大樓。
(B) 舉世聞名的建築師。
(C) 我今早寄了。

27. Do you want Jane or Su-Young to attend the client lunch meeting today?
(A) You're not going?
(B) The product launch was successful.
(C) They arrived last night.

27. 你想讓簡恩還是素妍參加今天的客戶午餐會議？
(A) 你不去嗎？
(B) 產品發布會很成功。
(C) 他們昨晚到。

28. How will you present your research results?
(A) With a slideshow.
(B) Yes, a slight increase.
(C) A famous researcher.

28. 你會如何呈現你的研究結果？
(A) 用投影片。
(B) 是，略有增加。
(C) 著名研究員。

29. Do you have time to look over my report?
(A) We all had a good time.
(B) I have a lot of work to do.
(C) Around 30 pages.

29. 你有時間檢閱我的報告嗎？
(A) 我們都度過了美好時光。
(B) 我有很多工作要做。
(C) 約 30 頁。

30. Where in the break room are the paper cups?
(A) I'll be careful with it.
(B) Did we purchase more?
(C) Sure. Let's get some coffee.

30. 紙杯放在休息室的哪裡？
(A) 我會小心使用。
(B) 我們有多買嗎？
(C) 好。來喝點咖啡吧。

31. Are you having problems connecting to the Internet, too?
(A) It's connected to the computer.
(B) Two new Web designers.
(C) Someone from IT will be here soon.

31. 你的網路連線目前也有問題嗎？
(A) 它已連上電腦。
(B) 兩名新進的網頁設計師。
(C) 資訊技術部的人就快到了。

PART 3 P. 59-62

Questions 32-34 refer to the following conversation.

W: Excuse me, sir. **I'm an employee of the company that currently manages this shopping mall,** 32 and **we're conducting a brief customer survey. Do you have a moment to answer some questions?** 33

32-34 會話

女：先生，不好意思。**我是這家購物中心目前的管理公司員工，** 32 **而我們正在進行簡短的客戶問卷調查。您有空回答幾個問題嗎？** 33

M: OK, I guess I can spare a few minutes. Does this have anything to do with the recent announcement about renovating the mall?

W: Yes, it does. So what do you think needs to be improved or added as far as facilities are concerned?

M: Well, **it would be better if there were a wider selection of restaurants.** 34 My office is nearby, so if there were more dining options to choose from, I'd probably come here more often for lunch and even shop a little.

男：好，花個幾分鐘我想無妨。這和最近購物中心宣布整修有關嗎？

女：是的，沒錯。那您覺得設施方面有需要改善或增加的部分嗎？

男：嗯，**如果可以擴增餐廳種類的話會更好。** 34 我的辦公室在附近，所以若能有更多用餐選項，我可能會更常前來吃午餐，甚至稍微消費。

32. Where does the conversation most likely take place?

(A) In a shopping mall
(B) In a train station
(C) In a fitness center
(D) In a coffee shop

32. 對話最有可能發生在何處？

(A) 在購物中心
(B) 在火車站
(C) 在健身房
(D) 在咖啡廳

33. What does the woman ask the man to do?

(A) Respond to a survey
(B) Try out a product
(C) Provide contact information
(D) Come back later

33. 女子要求男子做什麼？

(A) 回答問卷調查
(B) 試用產品
(C) 提供聯絡資訊
(D) 稍後再來

34. What does the man suggest?

(A) Extending business hours
(B) Improving exercise facilities
(C) Offering more discounts
(D) Increasing dining options

34. 男子有何建議？

(A) 延長營業時間
(B) 改善運動設施
(C) 提供更多折扣
(D) 增加餐飲選擇

Questions 35-37 refer to the following conversation.

35-37 會話

M: Hi, Leslie. **How's the landscaping work going so far?** 35

W: It's going well, Mr. Huntley. **I'm almost done planting the flowers around your house,** 35 but there's a slight problem.

M: What's wrong?

W: **I don't have enough fertilizer for the flowers in the back yard.** 36 I was about to drive to Panetta's on Johnston Avenue to get some more.

M: I was just around that area, and **there was heavy traffic on Johnston Avenue. You might want to take Walnut Lane instead.** 37

W: I'll do that. Thank you.

男：嗨，萊斯利。**景觀美化工程目前進行得如何？** 35

女：很順利，亨特利先生。**我已經幾乎完成貴府周圍的植花作業，** 35 但是有個小問題。

男：怎麼了嗎？

女：**我沒有足夠的肥料可供後院的花使用。** 36 我正打算開車到約翰斯頓大道的帕內塔花行補貨。

男：我剛才到過那附近，而**約翰斯頓大道上塞得很兇。妳改走核桃街可能比較好。** 37

女：就這麼辦。謝謝您。

35. What is the woman's occupation?
(A) Floral designer
(B) Car repairperson
(C) Landscape professional
(D) Construction worker

36. What is the woman's problem?
(A) Her vehicle is not starting.
(B) She cannot make it to her next appointment.
(C) Her coworker is not available.
(D) She doesn't have enough supplies.

37. What does the man recommend doing?
(A) Reading a manual
(B) Extending a project deadline
(C) Taking a detour
(D) Checking a traffic report

35. 女子的職業為何？
(A) 花卉設計師
(B) 汽車維修員
(C) 專業景觀人員
(D) 建築工人

36. 女子遇到的問題為何？
(A) 她的汽車無法啟動。
(B) 她到不了下個約定行程。
(C) 她的同事沒空。
(D) 她沒有足夠的用品。

37. 男子建議做什麼？
(A) 閱讀手冊
(B) 展延專案期限
(C) 繞道而行
(D) 查看交通報導

Questions 38-40 refer to the following conversation.

W：**Jerry, our summer computer sale is really attracting a lot of customers.** 38 We've only been open a few hours, but look at how busy we are.
M：I know. **I think displaying RDK's laptops out in front was the right move.** 38 39 **Have you seen the shelves?** 39
W：**I have. It looks like only three boxes are left.**
M：Yeah. RDK is a relatively new company, so I hadn't expected this. I think we should consider entering a partnership with them.
W：I agree. **Why don't I call their Sales Department and discuss their other product lines?** 40 This would be a good opportunity to improve our market share.

38-40 會話

女：**傑瑞，我們的夏季電腦促銷活動真是讓客人趨之若鶩。** 38 我們才剛開門營業幾個小時，但看看現在我們有多忙。
男：我知道。**我認為將 RDK 的筆電擺到前排展示是對的做法。** 38 39 **妳看過貨架了嗎？** 39
女：**我看了。看來只剩下三箱了。**
男：對啊。RDK 算相對新創的公司，所以這真讓我始料未及。我認為我們應考慮和該公司成為合作夥伴。
女：我同意。**何不讓我打電話給他們的銷售部門，討論一下他們其他的系列產品呢？** 40 這會是我們增加市占率的大好機會。

38. What type of product is being discussed?
(A) Office furniture
(B) Clothing
(C) Electronics
(D) Home appliances

39. What does the woman imply when she says, "It looks like only three boxes are left"?
(A) She is too busy to check inventory.
(B) She wants a worker to organize some shelves.
(C) Some boxes need to be moved.
(D) An item is very popular.

38. 正在討論哪種產品？
(A) 辦公家具
(B) 衣服
(C) 電子用品
(D) 家電

39. 女子說：「看來只剩下三箱了」，其意思為何？
(A) 她忙到沒時間檢查庫存。
(B) 她想要找名員工整理貨架。
(C) 有些箱子須搬動。
(D) 有項產品非常受歡迎。

40. What will the woman do next?

(A) Contact a Sales Department
(B) Hang up some signs
(C) Clean some shelves
(D) Place a new order

Questions 41-43 refer to the following conversation.

W： Tyler, do you mind helping me find some printers? **It seems like a lot of the merchandise in our stockroom was rearranged** (41) while I was on vacation last week, so I'm not sure where to look.

M： No problem. **We're expecting a large shipment of brand-new printers tomorrow morning** (42) **in preparation for our store's summer sale.** (41) That's why we moved so many things around. What exactly are you looking for?

W： **There's a customer in the showroom who wants to compare the G series and X series models. If you could point out where they are, I'll grab a cart and take them out to him.** (43)

41. Where most likely are the speakers?

(A) At a manufacturing plant
(B) At a post office
(C) At a hotel
(D) At a retailer

42. What does the man say will happen tomorrow?

(A) A shipment will be delivered.
(B) A seminar will be held.
(C) An inspection will be conducted.
(D) An advertisement will be posted.

43. What will the woman probably do next?

(A) Organize a storage room
(B) Order some food
(C) Send out some invitations
(D) Show a customer some merchandise

40. 女子接下來會做什麼？

(A) 聯絡銷售部門
(B) 掛上一些標示
(C) 清理一些貨架
(D) 下新的訂單

41-43 會話

女：泰勒，能麻煩你幫我找幾台印表機嗎？我上週休假期間，**我們倉庫很多商品的位置好像重整過了，**(41) 所以我不確定要到哪裡去找。

男：沒問題。**我們為了準備店裡的夏季特賣，**(41) **正等著一大批全新印表機明天早上到貨。**(42) 所以我們才會調動很多東西的位置。確切來說妳在找什麼呢？

女：**展場裡有一位顧客想要比較 G 系列和 X 系列的機型。如果你可以告訴我放置地點，我就會去找台推車把它們拿給客人看。**(43)

41. 說話者最有可能身在何處？

(A) 在製造廠
(B) 在郵局
(C) 在飯店
(D) 在零售店

42. 男子說明天會發生什麼？

(A) 一批貨物會送到。
(B) 將舉行研討會。
(C) 將執行稽察。
(D) 將發布廣告。

43. 女子接下來可能會做什麼？

(A) 整理倉庫
(B) 點餐
(C) 送出邀請函
(D) 向客人展示商品

Questions 44-46 refer to the following conversation.

44-46 會話

M：Hello, it's George Muntz calling from Muntz's Dessert Shop. **I wanted to talk about my recent order of apples.** 44

W：Of course. How can I help you?

M：Well, **my order arrived today, and I received only three boxes of apples. I was supposed to get five.** 45

W：All right. I'll pull up your information on my computer right now. Ah, it looks like there was an error. I apologize.

M：Do you know when I can expect to receive the rest of the boxes?

W：Hmm . . . I'll ship them out via expedited delivery, so they should arrive at your business by 3 P.M. tomorrow.

M：OK, I appreciate that.

W：Also, to make up for the mistake, **I'll send you a complimentary box of fresh oranges.** 46

男：您好，我是孟茲甜點店的喬治．孟茲。**我最近有訂蘋果，想跟您做洽詢。** 44

女：沒問題。有什麼我能協助您的嗎？

男：嗯，**我的訂單今天到貨，但我只收到三箱蘋果。我應該要拿到五箱才對。** 45

女：好的，我現在幫您在這邊電腦上查詢您的資訊。啊，看來有地方弄錯了，非常抱歉。

男：您知道我預計何時能收到剩下的幾箱嗎？

女：嗯……我會用快遞把貨寄出，應該明天下午三點前會送到貴店。

男：好的，謝謝。

女：另外，為彌補失誤，**我會免費寄送給您一箱新鮮的柳橙。** 46

44. What is the main topic of the conversation?
(A) Chocolate
(B) Pastries
(C) Vegetables
(D) Fruit

44. 對話的主題為何？
(A) 巧克力
(B) 糕點
(C) 蔬菜
(D) 水果

45. What is the man's problem?
(A) A computer is malfunctioning.
(B) A credit card payment was not approved.
(C) A box is too heavy to carry.
(D) A shipment is missing some items.

45. 男子遇到的問題為何？
(A) 電腦正出現故障。
(B) 信用卡付款未受核准。
(C) 箱子太重無法搬運。
(D) 貨物少了幾件。

46. What does the woman say she will give the man?
(A) A discount voucher
(B) A postage stamp
(C) Complimentary merchandise
(D) Cash reimbursement

46. 女子說會給男子何物？
(A) 折價券
(B) 郵票
(C) 免費商品
(D) 現金退款

Questions 47-49 refer to the following conversation.

47-49 會話

W：Hello, **I'm trying to order a camera on your Web site,** 47 **and I have a coupon for 25 percent off. The problem is, it doesn't say whether it can be used for online purchases.** 48

女：您好，**我正要在你們的網站上訂一台相機，** 47 **然後我有一張 25% 的折價券。問題是，它上面沒有寫能不能適用網路購物。** 48

M：Hmm . . . There should be a 13-digit code on it. Just enter it when you're asked to during the online checkout process.

W：I don't see a code anywhere, but according to the expiration date, the coupon should still be valid.

M：It must be an old one if it doesn't have an online code. **I'm afraid the only way to get a discount with that coupon is to come to our store.** 49

男：嗯……上面應該會有一組 13 位數的代碼。請您在進行線上結帳程序時，依指示輸入即可。

女：我在上面找不到代碼，但根據有效期限，這張優惠券應該還是有效。

男：如果上面沒有線上代碼，想必就是舊款優惠券。**那麼很抱歉，該優惠券必須來店使用才能享有折扣。** 49

47. Who most likely is the man?
(A) A professional photographer
(B) A corporate event organizer
(C) A customer service associate
(D) A computer technician

47. 男子最有可能的職業是？
(A) 專業攝影師
(B) 企業活動企劃人員
(C) 客服人員
(D) 電腦技術員

48. What does the woman inquire about?
(A) Repairing a camera
(B) Arranging a photo session
(C) Purchasing a warranty
(D) Applying an Internet discount

48. 女子詢問什麼事？
(A) 修理相機
(B) 安排拍照時間
(C) 購買保固
(D) 使用網路折扣

49. According to the man, what should the woman do?
(A) Visit a store
(B) Send a photograph
(C) Download a manual
(D) Contact a manufacturer

49. 據男子說法，女子應該怎麼辦？
(A) 前往商店
(B) 寄送照片
(C) 下載手冊
(D) 聯絡製造商

Questions 50-52 refer to the following conversation.

50-52 會話

W：James, **how are we doing with the expansion of our store's produce section?** 50

M：It's going well. But **we have to let our food supplier know that we need to place additional orders for broccoli and tomatoes. Can you get in touch with them?** 51

W：Yeah, I'll give them a call after lunch.

M：I appreciate that. Oh, by the way, I made some posters to inform our shoppers of our upcoming sale. **I'll put them up by our store's entrances right now.** 52

W：Great! Sounds like everything is progressing smoothly.

女：詹姆斯，**我們擴大店內蔬果區的事辦得怎麼樣了？** 50

男：進展順利。但**我們要告訴我們的食品供應商，說本店需要訂購更多青花菜和番茄。妳可以聯絡他們嗎？** 51

女：可以，午餐後我會打電話給他們。

男：謝謝。喔，順道一提，我做了幾張海報來告知客人本店即將舉辦特賣。**我現在就把海報張貼到我們店的出入口。** 52

女：太好了！聽起來一切進展順利。

TEST 4
PART 3
17

50. What is the conversation mainly about?
(A) Relocating a business
(B) Hiring better workers
(C) Reviewing features of a new product
(D) Expanding a section of a store

51. What is the woman asked to do?
(A) Place an online ad
(B) Contact a supplier
(C) Submit a sales report
(D) Download a catalog

52. What will the man probably do next?
(A) Take inventory
(B) Compare some costs
(C) Visit another branch
(D) Put up some posters

50. 對話主旨為何？
(A) 店家搬遷
(B) 僱用更好的員工
(C) 檢查新產品功能
(D) 擴大店內一處專區

51. 女子被要求做什麼？
(A) 設置網路廣告
(B) 聯絡供應商
(C) 繳交銷售報告
(D) 下載型錄

52. 男子接下來可能會做什麼？
(A) 盤點存貨
(B) 比較成本
(C) 造訪其他分店
(D) 張貼海報

Questions 53-55 refer to the following conversation.

W：**Gerard, I know you've been busy lately with the photo editing program for smart devices. How is that coming along?** 53

M：**Not too bad.** 53 The product development division and I have been trying to ensure that the program is released without any problems. But there seems to be an issue when it tries to save an edited image.

W：Hmm, I see. **Do you know when the program will be completed?** 54

M：**You'll need to ask someone in the IT Department about that.** I'm sure it'll be resolved soon.

W：OK. I'll get in touch with them. **I'm concerned since we're supposed to launch the product at the beginning of next month, and we have to conduct market testing before then.** 55

53-55 會話

女：**杰拉德，我知道你最近忙著做那款智慧型裝置用的照片編輯程式。進行得怎麼樣？** 53

男：**還不錯。** 53 產品開發部門和我一直努力確保程式上架能毫無差池。只不過圖片編輯後要存檔時，似乎還有問題。

女：嗯，了解。**你知道程式什麼時候會完成嗎？** 54

男：**這妳就要問資訊技術部門的人了。** 我確信這個問題很快就能解決。

女：好。我會和他們聯繫。**我會擔心是因為我們下個月月初就應該要讓產品上架，而在這之前我們還得進行市場測試。** 55

53. What is the man working on?
(A) A user guide
(B) A software program
(C) A market survey
(D) An event schedule

53. 男子正忙著做什麼？
(A) 使用說明書
(B) 軟體程式
(C) 市場調查
(D) 活動日程表

54. What does the man mean when he says, "You'll need to ask someone in the IT Department about that"?
(A) He is unable to give an answer.
(B) A project requires additional team members.
(C) The department made a specific request.
(D) He has to attend a meeting soon.

55. What is the woman worried about?
(A) Training new employees
(B) Attracting many customers
(C) Exceeding a budget
(D) Meeting a deadline

Questions 56-58 refer to the following conversation.

W：Hello, I want to book a flight to Rome for April 15. **Are there any direct flights that arrive in Rome in the early afternoon?** 56
M：Well, we have one that lands in Rome at 3:45 P.M.
W：Hmm, that's too tight. Do you have anything earlier? **I need enough time to prepare some materials for my 5 P.M. presentation.** 57
M：In that case, **your only option is to book a connecting flight through London. If that's OK with you, we have a flight that can get you to Rome earlier.** 58

56. What is the woman inquiring about?
(A) Flight arrival times
(B) Payment methods
(C) Extra baggage allowances
(D) Seat upgrades

57. What does the woman say she needs to do in Rome?
(A) Visit a local bank
(B) Rent a car
(C) Catch a connecting flight
(D) Prepare for a talk

59. What does the man recommend?
(A) Using a credit card
(B) Taking an alternate route
(C) Rescheduling a meeting
(D) Speaking to a supervisor

54. 男子說：「這妳就要問資訊技術部門的人了」，其意思為何？
(A) 他無法給出答案。
(B) 專案需要增加團隊成員。
(C) 部門提出了特定的要求。
(D) 他不久後要去開會。

55. 女子掛心著什麼？
(A) 訓練新進員工
(B) 吸引許多客戶
(C) 超出預算
(D) 如期完成

56-58 會話

女：您好，我想訂 4 月 15 號飛往羅馬的班機。**那天下午有早一點飛到羅馬的直飛航班嗎？** 56
男：嗯，我們有一班是下午 3 點 45 分抵達羅馬。
女：唔，那太趕了。你們還有更早的嗎？**我下午五點有場演講，需要留充足時間準備資料。** 57
男：那樣的話，**您就只能選須在倫敦轉機的航班。如果您可以接受，我們有一班飛機能讓您早點到羅馬。** 58

56. 女子詢問什麼事？
(A) 班機抵達時間
(B) 付款方式
(C) 超額行李限額
(D) 座艙升級

57. 女子說她須在羅馬做什麼？
(A) 到當地銀行
(B) 租車
(C) 轉乘飛機
(D) 準備演講

58. 男子有何建議？
(A) 用信用卡
(B) 改搭替代路線
(C) 更改會議時間
(D) 和主管談

TEST 4
PART 3
17

Questions 59-61 refer to the following conversation with three speakers.

M : Good afternoon. I'm Henry Yoon, a journalist for **the *Marketing Digest*. I'm here to interview Ms. Gomez. My appointment with her is at 2.** 59

W1 : Ah, yes, Mr. Yoon. I'll notify her right away. **While you wait, could you fill out this form? We keep a record of all our visitors.** 60

M : **Of course.** 60

W1 : Ms. Gomez will be with you shortly. Oh, here she is. **Ms. Gomez, Henry Yoon is here for your 2 o'clock appointment.** 61

W2 : Hello, Mr. Yoon. **I'm sorry, but I'm afraid I need you to wait just a little longer.** 61 I have to make a quick phone call, but I'll be right with you.

59-61 三人會話

男 ：午安。我是《行銷文摘》的記者尹亨利。**我來採訪戈麥茲女士。我和她約在兩點。** 59

女 1：噢，好的，尹先生。我現在通知她。**您等待時，能請您填寫這份表格嗎？我們需要記錄每一位訪客。** 60

男：**當然好。** 60

女 1：戈麥茲女士很快就會來見您了。喔，她到了。**戈麥茲女士，尹亨利到了，你們兩點有約。** 61

女 2：尹先生您好。**我很抱歉，但恐怕我得請您再稍等片刻。** 61 我需要打通簡短的電話，但我很快就會回來。

59. Why will the man meet with Ms. Gomez?
(A) To receive marketing advice
(B) To interview her
(C) To sign a contract
(D) To show her some products

59. 男子為何要見戈麥茲女士？
(A) 以獲取行銷建議
(B) 以採訪她
(C) 以簽合約
(D) 以向她展示產品

60. What does the man agree to do?
(A) Reschedule an appointment
(B) Make a donation
(C) Complete a visitor form
(D) Purchase a magazine subscription

60. 男子同意做什麼？
(A) 更改約訪時間
(B) 捐款
(C) 填寫訪客表格
(D) 付費訂閱雜誌

61. Why does Ms. Gomez apologize?
(A) A meeting will not start on time.
(B) She does not know the man's phone number.
(C) She lost some documents.
(D) An article contains inaccurate information.

61. 戈麥茲女士為何道歉？
(A) 訪談不會準時開始。
(B) 她不知道男子的電話號碼。
(C) 她遺失了一些文件。
(D) 報導內含不精確的資訊。

Questions 62-64 refer to the following conversation and chart.

W : Hello, Franklin. **I'm just about to purchase seats for the dance performance.** 62 Where would you like to sit?

M : Well, I usually like seats in the front row. That way, I'm able to see the performance better.

62-64 會話和圖表

女：哈囉，富蘭克林。**我正要買舞蹈表演的座位。** 62 你想坐在哪裡？

男：嗯，我通常喜歡前排的位置。這樣表演會得看比較清楚。

女：我也是。**前排靠左、西出口旁邊的座位怎麼樣？** 63

W：Me too. **How about these seats in the front row, to the left, near the west exit?** 63

M：**Looks good to me.** 63 Do you want to carpool after work?

W：Hmm . . . There's going to be a lot of traffic around that time. **We should probably take the subway.** 64

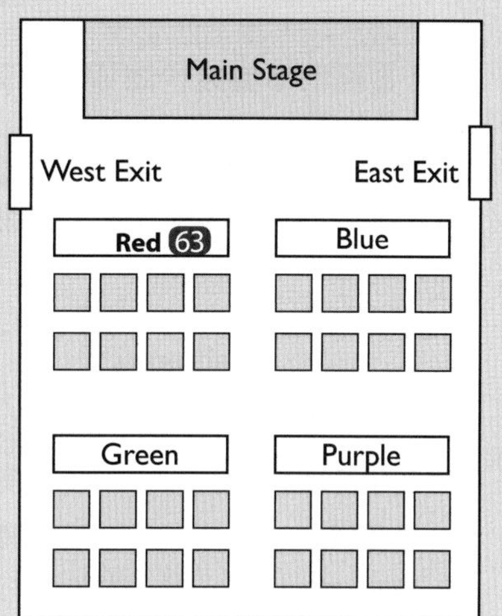

男：**我覺得不錯。** 63 下班後妳要不要一起共乘汽車前往？

女：嗯……那段時間車流量會很大。**我們也許應該搭地鐵。** 64

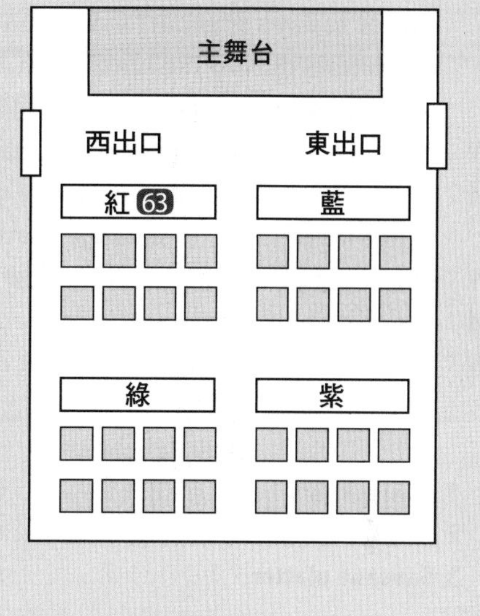

62. What kind of event are the speakers planning to attend?

(A) A product demonstration

(B) A dance show

(C) A movie premiere

(D) A business conference

62. 說話者打算參加哪項活動？

(A) 產品展示會

(B) 舞蹈表演

(C) 電影首映

(D) 商務會議

63. Look at the graphic. Where will the speakers most likely sit?

(A) The red section

(B) The blue section

(C) The green section

(D) The purple section

63. 請據圖表作答。說話者最有可能將坐在哪裡？

(A) 紅區

(B) 藍區

(C) 綠區

(D) 紫區

64. What does the woman recommend?

(A) Calling different vendors

(B) Inviting more coworkers

(C) Using a public transit service

(D) Viewing an online map

64. 女子建議做什麼？

(A) 打電話給不同廠商

(B) 邀約更多同事

(C) 使用公共運輸服務

(D) 查看網路地圖

Questions 65-67 refer to the following conversation and menu.

M: Hey, Sharon. Before you begin serving our customers today, can you please update the list for today's specials? 65 We had so many customers during the lunch rush, and now, we don't have any more sausages. 66

W: Of course. What change should I make?

M: Our head chef will prepare some chicken wings instead of the sausage platter. 67

W: OK. Is the price still the same? 67

M: Yes, it'll be the same as the sausages. 67

W: All right. I'll make the change right now.

Daily Specials	
1. Mini burgers	$9.75
2. Steak nachos	$10.50
3. **Sausage platter**	**$11.25** 67
4. Cobb salad	$7.50

65. What most likely is the woman's job?

(A) Delivery driver

(B) Chef

(C) Server

(D) Restaurant manager

66. According to the man, why will a list be updated?

(A) Some ingredients are not available.

(B) A package will not come in today.

(C) A chef prepared the wrong item.

(D) Many complaints were filed.

67. Look at the graphic. How much will the new special cost?

(A) $9.75

(B) $10.50

(C) $11.25

(D) $7.50

65-67 會話和菜單

男：嘿，雪倫。妳今天開始接待客人以前，能請妳更新今日特餐的菜單嗎？65 午餐尖峰時段的客人太多，於是現在店裡的香腸全都賣光了。66

女：當然好。我該怎麼改？

男：主廚會準備幾份雞翅，用來代替香腸拼盤。67

女：好的。價格維持一樣嗎？67

男：對，和香腸特餐的價格相同。67

女：好的。我馬上修改。

每日特餐	
1. 迷你漢堡	9.75 美元
2. 玉米脆片炒牛排	10.50 美元
3. **香腸拼盤**	**11.25 美元** 67
4. 科布沙拉	7.50 美元

65. 女子的職業最有可能為何？

(A) 貨運司機

(B) 廚師

(C) 服務生

(D) 餐廳經理

66. 據男子說法，為何將更新菜單？

(A) 有些食材用完了。

(B) 包裹今天不會到。

(C) 廚師備錯餐品。

(D) 遭到許多客訴。

67. 請據圖表作答。新款特餐價格為何？

(A) 9.75 美元

(B) 10.50 美元

(C) 11.25 美元

(D) 7.50 美元

Questions 68-70 refer to the following conversation and flow chart.

M：Good morning, Ms. Ludwitz. Welcome to Glamist Marketing Solutions. Let's start off by talking a little about your business.

W：Yes, of course. **I operate a small online store that sells vintage clothing.** 68

M：I see. Have you visited our Web site and checked out the marketing planning chart?

W：Yes, and it was pretty useful. **I aim to reach out to customers in other regions of the country in the next three years.** 69

M：That's good to hear. So where should we start?

W：Hmm . . . **I'm still in the process of creating a detailed plan to attract my target group. I actually came in today to go over this step with you.** 70

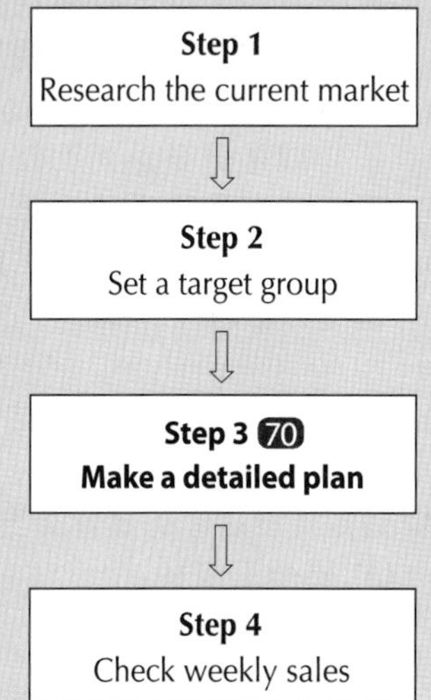

68-70 會話和流程圖

男：早安，魯德維茲女士。歡迎來到富魅行銷分析公司。我們首先簡單討論一下您的事業狀況。

女：當然好。**我目前經營一家小型網路商店、販賣古著服飾。** 68

男：了解。您有到我們的網站看過行銷規劃圖嗎？

女：有的，非常受用。**我的目標是在未來三年內要觸及來自國內其他地區的顧客。** 69

男：聽起來很棒。那我們該從哪裡開始？

女：嗯……**為了吸引到目標客群，我還在制定詳細的計畫當中。其實我今天過來就是想和您商討這個步驟。** 70

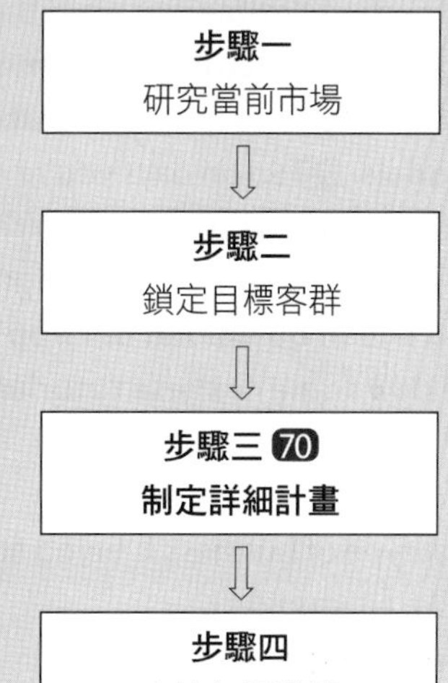

68. What type of business does the woman operate?
(A) An online clothing store
(B) A travel agency
(C) A digital marketing firm
(D) A computer shop

69. What does the woman hope to do in the future?
(A) Become a fashion designer
(B) Earn an advanced degree
(C) Increase her customer base
(D) Move to another country

68. 女子經營哪種商店？
(A) 服飾網拍店
(B) 旅行社
(C) 數位行銷公司
(D) 電腦店

69. 女子希望未來能做什麼？
(A) 成為時裝設計師
(B) 取得高等學位
(C) 增加她的客戶群
(D) 搬到另一個國家

70. Look at the graphic. What step would the woman like to discuss?
(A) Step 1
(B) Step 2
(C) Step 3
(D) Step 4

70. 請據圖表作答。女子想討論哪一個步驟？
(A) 步驟一
(B) 步驟二
(C) 步驟三
(D) 步驟四

PART 4 P. 63–65

Questions 71-73 refer to the following advertisement.

71-73 廣告

M：Ready to relieve stress and get healthy? **Core Yoga Fitness has just opened multiple studios in your town.** 71 Our qualified instructors will help you meet all your fitness goals, including strengthening your muscles, losing weight, and getting flexible. But wait–there's more! **Beginning in October, your membership will allow you to use our database of online tutorials.** 72 So on days you're out of town for work or just too busy to get to class, you can still keep up your workout program. **Go on our Web site to download our app so that can you preview some of these tutorials.** 73

男：準備好紓壓顧健康了嗎？**核心瑜珈健身中心已剛在您的市鎮上全新開設許多間健身房。** 71 我們的合格指導員將幫您實現所有健身目標，包括增強肌力、減重和加強柔軟度等。先別走開，好康在後頭！**十月起，您加入會員即可使用我們的線上課程資料庫。** 72 因此，在您外出工作或是分身乏術而無法到課的日子，健身課程都不中斷。**請到我們的網站下載應用程式，您就能預覽部分體驗課程。** 73

71. What type of business is being advertised?
(A) An art studio
(B) A grocery store
(C) A software company
(D) An exercise club

71. 這是什麼店家的宣傳廣告？
(A) 藝術工作室
(B) 雜貨店
(C) 軟體公司
(D) 運動會館

72. What will the listeners be able to do beginning in October?
(A) Participate in a competition
(B) Receive a consultation
(C) Access a database
(D) Purchase a new product

72. 十月起，聽者能做什麼？
(A) 參加比賽
(B) 獲得諮詢
(C) 使用資料庫
(D) 購買新產品

73. Why does the speaker invite the listeners to visit a Web site?
(A) To download a program
(B) To view some testimonials
(C) To read a manual
(D) To get some directions

73. 說話者為何鼓勵聽者訪問網站？
(A) 以下載一款程式
(B) 以查看評論
(C) 以閱讀手冊
(D) 以取得指示

Questions 74-76 refer to the following excerpt from a meeting.

W： The first thing **I want to do is thank all of you for all the extra hours you've devoted** 74 to making sure our new textbook series would be ready to publish. **The result of all that hard work is that now we'll be able to present the series at the book fair scheduled for later this month in New York.** 75 **It'll be presented along with all of our existing series, but that's fine. We've got a display case on the ground floor, and there's plenty of room.** 76

74. Why does the speaker thank the listeners?
(A) For organizing a seminar
(B) For working overtime
(C) For conducting an interview
(D) For teaching a course

75. What will happen later this month?
(A) An athletic competition will take place.
(B) Some remodeling will be finished.
(C) A book fair will be held.
(D) Some rooms will be booked.

76. What does the speaker mean when she says, "there's plenty of room"?
(A) Everybody will be able to attend an event.
(B) Accommodations are available at a hotel.
(C) A number of staff could be hired.
(D) Space is available to add a product to an exhibit.

74-76 會議摘錄

女：首先**我想做的是感謝大家付出額外的時間，**74 確保我們新系列教科書能夠做好出版準備。**多虧各位兢兢業業，如今我們將能在定於本月下旬的紐約書展上展出這系列叢書。**75 **該套書將和我們現有的全部叢書同場展出，但不會有問題的。我們在一樓會有個展示架，而且空間十分足夠。**76

74. 說話者為何感謝聽者？
(A) 因為籌辦研討會
(B) 因為加班
(C) 因為進行採訪
(D) 因為教課

75. 這個月下旬會發生什麼？
(A) 將舉行體育比賽。
(B) 將完成整修。
(C) 將舉辦書展。
(D) 將預訂飯店房間。

76. 說話者說：「空間十分足夠」，其意思為何？
(A) 人人都能參加該活動。
(B) 飯店有空房可入住。
(C) 將僱用許多員工。
(D) 展場有空間可增加展品。

Questions 77-79 refer to the following broadcast.

M： Thanks for tuning into *You and Your Business* on QMOE Radio. We have a special guest today, Martin Greenwald, founder of Productivity Squared Consulting. **His company teaches department leaders how to train their employees to be more productive.** 77 **He believes that having an efficient scheduling system is a great way to improve workplace productivity. On today's show, he'll reveal how reducing meeting times can lead to**

77-79 廣播

男：感謝您收聽 QMOE 電台《您和您的事業》節目。今天我們的特別嘉賓請到產能平方諮詢公司的創辦人馬丁．格林華德。**他的公司旨在教導部門主管如何培訓員工提高生產率。**77 **他認為提高職場產能的一個良策，就是有效率的排班系統。今天的節目裡，他將揭示如何透過減少開會次數，能達到事半功倍之效。**78 但很遺憾，我們只能和他簡

getting more work done. (78) Unfortunately, we'll only be able to talk to him for a short period, **so I recommend you all to check out his video seminars on our Web site.** (79)

短聊一下，**所以我建議大家到我們的網站上收看他的教學影片。**(79)

77. For whom is Mr. Greenwald's advice intended?
(A) Web designers
(B) Event organizers
(C) Film producers
(D) Department heads

77. 格林華德先生為誰提供建議？
(A) 網頁設計師
(B) 活動企劃人員
(C) 電影製片
(D) 部門主管

78. According to Mr. Greenwald, what is a good way to improve productivity?
(A) Offering better incentives
(B) Setting reasonable deadlines
(C) Taking regular breaks
(D) Reducing meeting times

78. 據格林華德先生所說，提高生產力的良方為何？
(A) 提供更好的誘因
(B) 設定合理的期限
(C) 定期休息
(D) 減少開會次數

79. What are the listeners encouraged to do?
(A) Watch some videos
(B) Read an article
(C) Download an application
(D) Call a radio station

79. 聽者被鼓勵做什麼？
(A) 觀看幾部影片
(B) 讀篇文章
(C) 下載應用程式
(D) 致電給電台

Questions 80-82 refer to the following telephone message.

80-82 語音留言

W：Mr. Brown, I'm calling from Alcon Airlines. **I'd like to apologize on behalf of our company for the confusion we have caused as a result of our mistake with your reservation.** (80) I discovered that **when your booking was being made last week, the wrong flight code was entered into our system.** (81) We have corrected this, and **we'd like to compensate you for our mistake by offering you a complimentary in-flight meal.** (82) Should you have any questions, do not hesitate to call our customer service hotline.

女：布朗先生您好，這裡是愛爾康航空來電。**我謹代表本公司，為我們在處理您的訂票時發生的錯誤、造成您的困擾一事致上歉意。**(80) 我發現**您上週訂票時，我們系統裡輸入了錯誤的航班代碼。**(81) 我們已對此修正，**且為了彌補我們的疏失，本公司將贈送您一份機上餐點。**(82) 如您有任何疑問，請不吝撥打我們的客服專線。

80. Why is the speaker calling?
(A) To apologize for a mistake
(B) To explain a policy
(C) To reschedule a meeting
(D) To set up a delivery

80. 說話者為何打電話？
(A) 為了為錯誤致歉
(B) 為了解釋一項政策
(C) 為了更改會議時間
(D) 為了安排送貨

81. What does the speaker say happened last week?
(A) A facility was closed for repairs.
(B) New products were launched.
(C) Some data were recorded incorrectly.
(D) Some employees were not available.

82. What will the company provide to the listener?
(A) Express shipping
(B) Complimentary shuttle service
(C) A seat upgrade
(D) A free meal

Questions 83-85 refer to the following telephone message.

M：**Hi, this is Keith. I'm one of your delivery drivers.** 83 **I have some new office furniture that I'm supposed to drop off at our shop in Memphis,** 84 but I'm having trouble finding it. **The shop is supposed to be at 61 Iris Way. I've been driving down this street for a few minutes now,** 85 **and I've only seen houses.** I'll take care of my other orders first, **but when you get this message, can you find out the correct address and call me back as soon as possible?** 85 Thanks.

83. Who is the speaker?
(A) A delivery person
(B) A product designer
(C) A store receptionist
(D) A plant manager

84. What does the company sell?
(A) Consumer electronics
(B) Automotive parts
(C) Office furniture
(D) Garden equipment

85. What does the speaker imply when he says, "I've only seen houses"?
(A) He believes an error was made.
(B) He is worried about a new housing rule.
(C) A construction permit cannot be provided.
(D) Some funds cannot be acquired.

81. 説話者説上週發生了什麼事？
(A) 設施關閉維修。
(B) 新產品上市。
(C) 資料記錄有誤。
(D) 幾名員工不在。

82. 公司將提供聽者什麼？
(A) 快遞運送
(B) 免費接駁服務
(C) 座艙升級
(D) 免費餐點

83-85 語音留言

男：**您好，我是基思，是您的其中一名送貨司機。** 83 **我載著幾張新的辦公家具，要到我們在孟菲斯的店面卸貨，** 84 但我現在找不到路。**店面應該是在鳶尾路 61 號。我已經沿著這條路開了幾分鐘，** 85 **而我只有看到住家。**我會先處理其他訂單，**但您聽到留言後，是否能請您儘快查出正確地址並回電給我？** 85 謝謝。

83. 説話者是誰？
(A) 貨運人員
(B) 產品設計師
(C) 商店接待員
(D) 工廠經理

84. 這家公司販售什麼？
(A) 消費性電子產品
(B) 汽車零件
(C) 辦公家具
(D) 園藝設備

85. 説話者説：「我只有看到住家」，言下之意為何？
(A) 他認為出了錯。
(B) 新的住宅規定讓他擔心。
(C) 無法發放施工許可證。。
(D) 無法取得部分資金。

Questions 86-88 refer to the following excerpt from a workshop.

86-88 研習摘錄

M：**I would like to thank you for attending the Sales Department's yearly training workshop.** 86 It's no secret that with the continuous traveling, negotiating, and catering to clients, **you are bound to get really stressed. In today's session, we'll talk about some relaxation techniques to relieve some pressure during work.** 87 Studies have shown that meditation reduces tension and can ease health concerns. By spending some quiet time alone, you will be able to clear your mind and calm down. **Now, I will play a video for you showing some common meditation techniques to help you get started.** 88

男：我想在此感謝大家蒞臨業務部門的**年度培訓研習。** 86 各位心照不宣的是，經常出差、談判和討好客戶**必定讓你們備感壓力。在今天的課程中，我們將探討幾個紓解工作壓力的放鬆技巧。** 87 研究顯示，冥想可以消除緊張並緩和健康問題。透過抽空安靜獨處，你將可以清除心中雜念並恢復平靜。**為了幫助各位入門，我現在會放一段影片，給大家看幾個常見的冥想技巧。** 88

86. What department does the speaker work in?
(A) Marketing
(B) Finance
(C) Administration
(D) Sales

86. 說話者在哪個部門工作？
(A) 行銷
(B) 財務
(C) 行政
(D) 業務

87. What is the topic of the workshop?
(A) Creating detailed financial plans
(B) Presenting business proposals
(C) Reducing work-related stress
(D) Setting up client meetings

87. 研習的主題為何？
(A) 制定詳細財務計畫
(B) 發表商業提案
(C) 減少工作相關壓力
(D) 安排與客戶開會

88. What will the listeners do next?
(A) Find a partner
(B) Complete a questionnaire
(C) Watch a video
(D) Discuss a contract

88. 聽者接下來會做什麼？
(A) 尋找夥伴
(B) 填寫問卷
(C) 觀看影片
(D) 討論合約

Questions 89-91 refer to the following telephone message.

89-91 語音留言

W: Hi, Kristy, how are you? It's Madison. **I wanted to talk about how we're going to celebrate Lance's retirement. If we want to have a surprise party, we'll need to get together to plan out the details,** 89 such as where it should be held. **More importantly, we need to keep this a secret from Lance, unlike the party we**

女：嗨，克里斯蒂，妳好嗎？我是麥迪遜。**我想討論我們要怎麼慶祝蘭斯的退休。如果要辦驚喜派對，我們就得一起把細節安排好，** 89 像是要在哪裡舉辦。**更重要的是，我們不可以讓蘭斯知情，不能重演去年我們為經理舉辦的派對。** 90 <u>我還</u>

had for our manager last year. 90 I still can't believe what happened. Anyway, I'm meeting a friend at the restaurant that just opened on Larimer Street after work. 91 I heard the food is good and that it's big enough to accommodate large groups. If the place is nice, I'll see if I can make a reservation. Call me when you get this message.

是難以置信會出這種事。總之，我下班後要去拉里默街上新開的餐廳和我朋友見面。 91 我聽說那裡餐點好吃，而且空間夠容納大型聚會。如果那間還不錯，我就看看能否預約。收到留言再回電給我。

89. What is the message mainly about?
(A) Signing up for a cooking contest
(B) Updating some files
(C) Revising an itinerary
(D) Organizing a celebration

89. 留言主旨為何？
(A) 報名烹飪比賽
(B) 更新文件
(C) 修改行程
(D) 舉辦慶祝活動

90. What does the speaker imply when she says, "I still can't believe what happened"?
(A) She is unhappy with the results of a competition.
(B) She misunderstood some instructions.
(C) She is surprised by a decision.
(D) She wants to avoid making a mistake again.

90. 說話者說：「我還是難以置信會出這種事」，指的是什麼？
(A) 她對比賽結果不滿。
(B) 她誤解了幾條說明。
(C) 有項決定讓她驚訝。
(D) 她想避免重蹈覆轍。

91. What is the speaker going to do after work?
(A) Visit a dining establishment
(B) Attend a performance
(C) Shop at a store
(D) Depart for a conference

91. 說話者下班後要做什麼？
(A) 前往用餐場所
(B) 去看表演
(C) 在商店購物
(D) 出發去開會

Questions 92-94 refer to the following broadcast.

92-94 廣播

M：**Good morning, and welcome to my program, *Business in a Flash*. I'm Michael Alvarez, and I've been running my store for over 15 years.** 92 I'm going to share with you some fast, effective tips for promoting your business. Today, we'll be looking at expos. **Now, having a booth at an expo isn't cheap, but expos are great for meeting many new buyers for your products in one location.** 93 Also, they're an excellent networking opportunity and a good way to see what your competitors are doing. Coming up, **I will suggest four ways to ensure that your expo booth gets a lot of attention.** 94

男：**早安，歡迎收聽我的節目《秒懂經商》。我是麥可．阿爾瓦雷茲，我自己開店已超過 15 年。** 92 我將會與你們分享一些快速、有效推廣生意的訣竅。今天我們來談談展覽會。**對，設攤參展並不便宜，但展覽會非常有助於讓你的產品就地接觸到許多新買家。** 93 另外，那也是建立人脈的絕佳機會，更是了解同行競爭者現況的好方法。稍後，**我將建議四種方法，來確保您的攤位可以吸引到許多人的注意。** 94

92. Why is the speaker qualified to host the program?
(A) He has received many broadcasting awards.
(B) He has extensive work experience.
(C) He has studied business at a famous university.
(D) He has published many financial books.

92. 說話者何以勝任主持這個節目？
(A) 他得過許多廣播獎項。
(B) 他有豐富的實務經驗。
(C) 他在知名大學修讀商學。
(D) 他出版了許多財經書籍。

93. Why does the speaker say, "having a booth at an expo isn't cheap"?
(A) To suggest paying in installments
(B) To agree with a professional's advice
(C) To refuse a request
(D) To acknowledge a common concern

93. 說話者為何說：「設攤參展並不便宜」？
(A) 以建議分期付款
(B) 以同意專業人士的建議
(C) 以拒絕請求
(D) 以承認常見的疑慮

94. What will the speaker most likely do next?
(A) Call some listeners
(B) Announce contest winners
(C) Sign up for a conference
(D) Give some detailed advice

94. 說話者接下來最有可能會做什麼？
(A) 致電幾名聽眾
(B) 宣布比賽贏家
(C) 報名參加會議
(D) 提出詳細建議

Questions 95-97 refer to the following news report and weather forecast.

W：**In other news, the always entertaining Greenwich Community Softball Tournament is upon us.** 95 This year, the event will be held at Caster Park. Contestants from a variety of local businesses and organizations will play a series of games. Winners will receive gift certificates for local businesses in the neighborhood. This day is filled with excitement and fun for the whole family. **To see a list of the teams that are taking part this year, visit the city's Web site. 96 On the day of the event, the weather forecast predicts a sunny day.** 97 There won't be a cloud in the sky, so don't forget to pack your sunglasses!

Thursday	Friday	**Saturday 97**	Sunday
Rain	Cloudy	**Sunny**	Partly Cloudy

95-97 新聞報導和天氣預報

女：**接下來的新聞帶您關心：一向歡樂的格林威治社區壘球錦標賽即將到來。**95 今年活動辦在卡斯特公園。各類在地店家、團體派出的選手將展開一系列比賽。獲勝隊伍將獲頒可於社區內在地店家使用的禮券。當天活動刺激好玩，能讓您闔家開心。**想查看今年度參賽隊伍名單，請上市政府網站。96 氣象預報指出，活動當天是晴朗的好天氣。**97 當天可望萬里無雲，所以別忘了帶上您的太陽眼鏡！

週四	週五	**週六 97**	週日
雨天	陰天	**晴天**	多雲時晴

95. What event is being described?
(A) A charity function
(B) An art contest
(C) A sports competition
(D) A book fair

95. 正在提及哪項活動？
(A) 慈善聚會
(B) 美術比賽
(C) 體育競賽
(D) 書展

96. According to the speaker, what can the listeners find on a Web site?
(A) A weather report
(B) A list of participants
(C) A schedule of events
(D) A park map

96. 據説話者説法，聽者可在網站上找到什麼？
(A) 天氣預報
(B) 參賽者名單
(C) 活動時程
(D) 公園地圖

97. Look at the graphic. On which day will the event be held?
(A) Thursday
(B) Friday
(C) Saturday
(D) Sunday

97. 請據圖表作答。活動將於哪一天舉行？
(A) 週四
(B) 週五
(C) 週六
(D) 週日

Questions 98-100 refer to the following excerpt from a meeting and chart.

W：**Let's finish today's production meeting by looking at our first quarter output numbers.** 98 As you know, the company just started selling dress shoes, so we don't have a lot of orders yet. This is no surprise. **But this output of 6 million is a bit troublesome. This is our most popular product line, and the sales team thinks that they could sell a lot more if we could just keep up with the growing demand.** 99 **So to resolve this issue, we have decided to buy more machines for the assembly lines to increase production.** 98 100

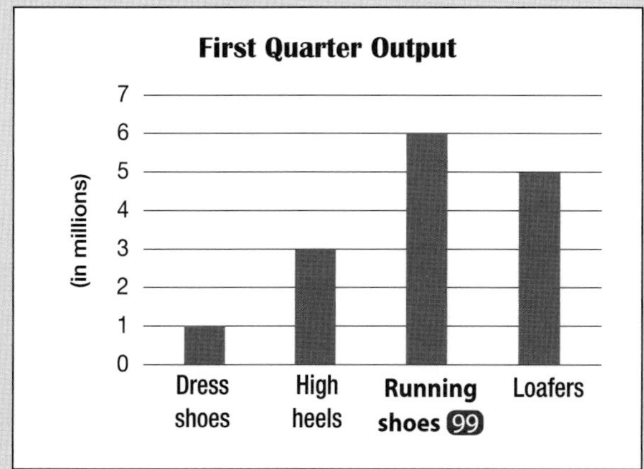

98-100 會議摘錄和圖表

女：**今天的生產會議結束前，我們來看一下第一季度的產量數據。** 98 誠如各位所知，公司才剛開始賣皮鞋，所以訂單還不多。這不教人意外。**但這產量600萬的部分就有點棘手了。這是我們最受歡迎的系列產品，而且銷售團隊認為，如果我們能夠跟上成長中的需求，他們就可以賣出更多。** 99 **所以為了解決這個問題，我們已決定為生產線添購機器來增加產量。** 98 100

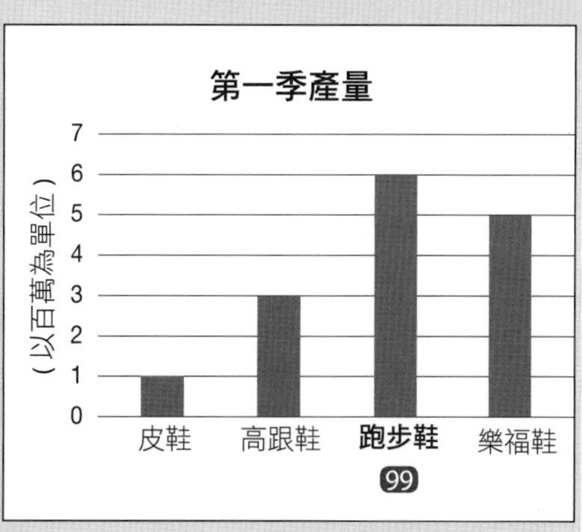

98. Who most likely are the listeners?

(A) Factory workers

(B) Sales associates

(C) Fashion designers

(D) Financial planners

99. Look at the graphic. Which category is the speaker concerned about?

(A) Dress shoes

(B) High heels

(C) Running shoes

(D) Loafers

100. What has the company decided to do?

(A) Purchase some equipment

(B) Delay a schedule

(C) Revise a safety policy

(D) Recruit more employees

98. 聽者最有可能是誰？

(A) 工廠工人

(B) 銷售助理

(C) 時裝設計師

(D) 理財規劃師

99. 請據圖表作答。說話者擔心的是哪一個類別？

(A) 皮鞋

(B) 高跟鞋

(C) 跑步鞋

(D) 樂福鞋

100. 公司決定做什麼？

(A) 購置設備

(B) 延後時程

(C) 修改安全守則

(D) 增聘員工

ACTUAL TEST 5

PART 1 P. 66–69

1. (A) Utensils have been piled up in the sink.
(B) Dishes are being wiped on the counter.
(C) A tray is being put into an oven.
(D) A pot is being lifted from the stove.

2. (A) Some people are cutting trees.
(B) Some seats are being set up outdoors.
(C) A performer is entertaining an audience.
(D) A musician is walking onto a stage.

3. **(A) A cyclist is viewing a town from a distance.**
(B) A tourist is taking a picture of the landscape.
(C) A man is seated on the grass.
(D) A man is setting his backpack on a ledge.

4. (A) A worker is washing the windows.
(B) Some plants are hanging next to each other.
(C) The roof of a home is being repaired.
(D) Some flowers are being watered in a garden.

5. (A) A carpet is being rolled up.
(B) A picnic table is being assembled.
(C) Cushions have been placed on sofas.
(D) Some chairs have been stacked on top of each other.

6. (A) One of the people is strolling past the bench.
(B) One of the people is leaning on a lamppost.
(C) They are facing away from each other.
(D) They are entering a hallway.

1. (A) 廚房用具堆放在水槽內。
(B) 盤子放在流理台上擦拭。
(C) 烤盤正要被放入烤箱。
(D) 鍋子正從爐上被提起。

2. (A) 幾個人正在伐木。
(B) 幾個座位正在戶外設置。
(C) 表演者在娛樂觀眾。
(D) 音樂家正步上舞台。

3. **(A) 自行車騎士遙望著村莊。**
(B) 遊客正在拍風景照。
(C) 男子正坐在草地上。
(D) 男子正把背包放到突岩上。

4. (A) 工人正在清洗窗戶。
(B) 幾盆植物並排掛著。
(C) 房屋的屋頂正在維修中。
(D) 花園裡正在灑水澆花。

5. (A) 地毯被捲起來。
(B) 野餐桌正在組裝中。
(C) 靠墊放在沙發上。
(D) 幾張椅子上下堆疊在一起。

6. (A) 其中一人漫步走過長椅。
(B) 其中一人倚著燈柱。
(C) 他們彼此別過頭去。
(D) 他們正走進門廳。

PART 2 P. 70

7. When did you purchase your computer?
(A) The shop across the street.
(B) I still use the monitor.
(C) Four years ago, when it first released.

7. 你什麼時候買電腦的？
(A) 在對街的店。
(B) 我還在用那台螢幕。
(C) 四年前，它剛推出的時候。

8. Do you know where Conference Hall C is?
(A) The keynote speaker.
(B) There's a map over there.
(C) A conference call on line 3.

9. That was quite a long concert, wasn't it?
(A) The venue is really small.
(B) I don't know where it is.
(C) Yes. It was over three hours.

10. Where can I find the information desk?
(A) In three days.
(B) On the other side of the building.
(C) I'm OK, thanks.

11. Who's going to manage the sales team?
(A) I managed to finish the report.
(B) Yes, he works in sales.
(C) Probably Mary Jensen.

12. How was the client lunch?
(A) An Italian restaurant.
(B) That's correct. At 1 P.M.
(C) He agreed to sign a contract.

13. You've shopped at Burlington Mall before, right?
(A) Is that the one on Rocker Avenue?
(B) No, it's on the left.
(C) I work the night shift.

14. Wasn't yesterday the deadline for this report?
(A) No, a decline in production.
(B) It took us longer than expected.
(C) The reporter won an award.

15. Whose turn is it to order lunch?
(A) The salmon sounds good.
(B) In the break room.
(C) I ordered yesterday.

16. Where will the corporate workshop be next month?
(A) In May I guess.
(B) No, I haven't been there.
(C) It will be determined later.

17. Let's talk about the office relocation this afternoon.
(A) Does she work in this office?
(B) For my vacation to Europe.
(C) Why don't we do it now?

8. 你知道 C 會議廳在哪嗎？
(A) 主題演講者。
(B) 那邊有張地圖。
(C) 第三線的電話會議。

9. 那場音樂會蠻久的，不是嗎？
(A) 場地真的很小。
(B) 我不知道在哪裡。
(C) 對。超過三個小時。

10. 我在哪裡可以找到詢問檯？
(A) 三天後。
(B) 在大樓的另一側。
(C) 我不要緊，謝謝。

11. 業務團隊將由誰管理？
(A) 我好不容易完成了報告。
(B) 對，他在業務部工作。
(C) 可能是瑪麗．詹森。

12. 客戶午餐會還好嗎？
(A) 一家義大利餐廳。
(B) 沒錯。在下午一點。
(C) 他同意簽約了。

13. 你在伯靈頓商場過買東西，是嗎？
(A) 是在搖滾客大道的那間嗎？
(B) 不，是在左邊。
(C) 我值夜班。

14. 這份報告的截止日不是昨天嗎？
(A) 不，產量減少。
(B) 比我們預期的更費時。
(C) 這名記者得獎了。

15. 輪到誰訂午餐？
(A) 鮭魚聽起來不錯。
(B) 在休息室。
(C) 昨天是我訂的。

16. 下個月的公司研習會在哪裡舉行？
(A) 我想是五月。
(B) 不，我沒去過那裡。
(C) 之後才會決定。

17. 我們今天下午來討論辦公室搬遷事宜吧。
(A) 她在這間辦公室工作嗎？
(B) 為了我去歐洲度假。
(C) 我們何不現在討論呢？

18. Why are there balloons out in the lobby today?
(A) The newspaper on the table.
(B) Because Ms. Webber is retiring today.
(C) I'll see who's here.

19. How are we supposed to set up our display booth in time?
(A) In room 501.
(B) The newest kitchen appliances.
(C) Maggie said she'd help.

20. Have you taken the employee development program yet?
(A) I didn't know I had to.
(B) An employee appreciation dinner.
(C) Sure. I can take her there.

21. Why don't we expand the products we carry at our store?
(A) Extend the business hours.
(B) I think that's a good idea.
(C) Put them in the storage room.

22. What type of laptop do you have?
(A) Are you planning to get one?
(B) At a computer store.
(C) I have some time to help you.

23. Wouldn't you rather get some food during your lunch break?
(A) I have a project to finish today.
(B) It's quite delicious.
(C) A table for four, please.

24. You sent the clients the invoice, didn't you?
(A) She has a great voice.
(B) Haven't they made the payment yet?
(C) A fast delivery service.

25. How soon can you get started on the building design?
(A) She's a new graphic designer.
(B) Try the rear entrance.
(C) I'll begin this afternoon.

18. 為什麼今天外面大廳裡有氣球？
(A) 桌上的報紙。
(B) 因為韋伯女士今天將退休。
(C) 我會看看誰在這裡。

19. 我們如何能來得及設置好展位？
(A) 在 501 室。
(B) 最新的廚房家電。
(C) 瑪姬說她會幫忙。

20. 你上過員工發展課程了沒有？
(A) 我不知道我得要去上。
(B) 員工感謝晚宴。
(C) 當然。我可以帶她去那裡。

21. 我們何不擴充我們店裡販賣的品項呢？
(A) 延長營業時間。
(B) 我想這個主意不錯。
(C) 把它們放進倉庫。

22. 你的筆電是哪一款？
(A) 你打算買一台嗎？
(B) 在電腦店。
(C) 我有點時間能幫你。

23. 你午休時不想要吃點東西嗎？
(A) 我今天有個專案得做完。
(B) 很好吃。
(C) 一桌四位，麻煩了。

24. 你有把請款明細寄給客戶們了，沒錯吧？
(A) 她的聲音很好聽。
(B) 他們還沒有付款嗎？
(C) 快速到貨服務。

25. 你多快可以開始著手建築設計？
(A) 她是新手平面設計師。
(B) 試著走後方入口。
(C) 我今天下午會開始。

26. Did you bring your current résumé with you for this interview?

(A) It's in my bag.

(B) She's a qualified candidate.

(C) Previous job experience.

27. The last day to book a reservation is on Wednesday.

(A) That's a nice hotel.

(B) No, I haven't read it yet.

(C) How do you know that?

28. Your train to Moscow has a dining car, doesn't it?

(A) Yes, and the food is good.

(B) The airport is nearby.

(C) It's easy to find parking.

29. Are you planning to buy the car you checked out yesterday?

(A) No, I can't pick you up.

(B) It's too pricey.

(C) Our check-in time is 2 P.M.

30. Would you like wireless Internet for your flight today?

(A) A window seat, please.

(B) Is it free of charge?

(C) It departs in two hours.

31. Should I print out the meeting agenda or email it to everyone?

(A) Everyone will bring their laptops.

(B) The first page of the report.

(C) In Conference Room B.

26. 您有帶您現在的履歷來面試嗎？

(A) 在我的包包裡。

(B) 她是合格的人選。

(C) 以前的工作經驗。

27. 最晚要在週三當天進行預約。

(A) 這家飯店不錯。

(B) 不，我還沒讀完。

(C) 你怎麼知道的？

28. 你們開往莫斯科的列車上有一節餐車，不是嗎？

(A) 對，而且食物很好吃。

(B) 機場在附近。

(C) 停車位很好找。

29. 你有打算買你昨天去看過的車嗎？

(A) 不，我沒辦法去接你。

(B) 那台太貴了。

(C) 我們入住的時間是下午兩點。

30. 本日班機上您要使用無線網路嗎？

(A) 請給我靠窗座位。

(B) 是免費的嗎？

(C) 兩小時後起飛。

31. 我該把會議議程印出來、還是用電郵寄給大家？

(A) 大家都會帶筆電。

(B) 報告的第一頁。

(C) 在會議室 B。

Questions 32-34 refer to the following conversation.

M： Hello, I'm Justin, the facilities supervisor. Thanks for coming. **This is our company cafeteria, which needs to be completely remodeled.** 32

32-34 會話

男：哈囉，我是設備經理賈斯汀，感謝您跑一趟。**這裡是我們公司餐廳，需要進行全面改造。** 32

W：Thank you for hiring my design firm. OK, it looks like we'll have to get rid of everything. After we replace the floors, we can put in new tables and seats.

M：All right, but **we're holding a celebration banquet for our R&D Division during the first week of February,** 33 and we're planning on using the cafeteria. Will you finish before then?

W：If my team begins right away, it's definitely possible. **If I email you an invoice this afternoon, will you be able to make a faster decision?** 34

M：**Yes.** 34 Our CEO should approve it immediately if it's within our budget.

女：感謝您聘請我們設計公司。好，看來我們需要全面除舊。我們將地板汰舊換新後，就能擺進新的桌子和座椅。

男：好的，但**我們將在二月的第一週為本公司研發部門舉辦慶祝餐會，** 33 預計就會使用到這間餐廳。您能在這之前完工嗎？

女：若我的團隊即刻動工，極有可能可行。**如果我今天下午用電子郵件將請款帳單寄給您，您能更快做出決定嗎？** 34

男：**可以。** 34 只要不超過我們的預算，我們的執行長應該會馬上批准。

32. What is the main topic of the conversation?
(A) Renovating a cafeteria
(B) Reviewing research findings
(C) Designing some furniture
(D) Finding an event venue

32. 對話的主題為何？
(A) 整修餐廳
(B) 檢查研究發現
(C) 設計家具
(D) 找活動場地

33. What will happen during the first week of February?
(A) A budget proposal will be presented.
(B) A business will extend its office hours.
(C) A new CEO will be appointed.
(D) A company gathering will take place.

33. 二月第一週將發生什麼事？
(A) 將發表預算提案。
(B) 企業將延長營業時間。
(C) 將任命新的執行長。
(D) 將舉行公司聚會。

34. What will the woman most likely send in the afternoon?
(A) A blueprint
(B) Some pictures
(C) An invoice
(D) Some equipment

34. 女子在下午最有可能寄發什麼？
(A) 藍圖
(B) 幾張照片
(C) 請款帳單
(D) 一些設備

Questions 35-37 refer to the following conversation.

35-37 會話

W：**The chef just informed me that he's used up a lot of the ingredients for our meatball dish—the special today. We should tell the servers to stop taking orders for it from customers.** 35

M：Good idea. As you know, **we have a large party arriving soon at 7 o'clock.** 36 I think a few of those customers pre-ordered the meatball special, so we should make sure to have enough for them.

女：**主廚剛剛告訴我，他用來製作今日特餐「招牌肉丸」的食材已經用掉很多。我們應該要叫服務員不要再讓客人繼續點那道菜。** 35

男：好辦法。妳也知道，**我們很快就要在七點接待一大群人來聚餐。** 36 我想其中有幾位客人已經預訂肉丸特餐，所以我們要確保留下足夠的份量給他們。

W：OK, but **it's still being advertised on our menu board. Shouldn't I take it off?** 37

女：好，但**那道菜還寫在我們的菜單板上做推銷。要不要我去把它刪掉？** 37

35. What is the main topic of the conversation?
(A) The recipes of a renowned chef
(B) Extending a store's business hours
(C) The availability of a special dish
(D) How to best advertise a restaurant

35. 對話的主題為何？
(A) 知名廚師的食譜
(B) 延長店家營業時間
(C) 特餐的供應情形
(D) 最有效的餐廳宣傳方式

36. What does the man say will happen soon?
(A) A delivery will be made.
(B) A group of customers will arrive.
(C) Some new employees will be hired.
(D) Some products will become available.

36. 男子說即將會發生什麼事？
(A) 將遞送貨物。
(B) 一群客人將抵達。
(C) 將僱用一些新員工。
(D) 一些產品將開賣。

37. What does the woman ask the man?
(A) How many customers are waiting
(B) Where a chef learned to cook
(C) What time he will be leaving
(D) If she should update the menu offerings

37. 女子詢問男子什麼事？
(A) 有多少客人在等候
(B) 廚師學習烹飪的地方
(C) 他將離開的時間
(D) 她是否需要更新菜單的品項

Questions 38-40 refer to the following conversation with three speakers.

M：OK, that's the end of the company building tour. Now, we'll walk over to the personnel office so that **you can fill out your new hire documents.** 38 Are there any questions?

W1：Do we need to submit a special form to use the leisure center and sauna?

M：No. **The center and sauna are open daily from 7 A.M. to 9 P.M. You can access them with your staff ID badge.** 39 Anything else?

W2：Yes. I was just curious when we'd be going to the sales team's office. **I'm eager to finally meet our colleagues.** 40

M：**Oh, we'll go right after lunch. I'm sure the department members are also looking forward to meeting you two.** 40

38-40 三人會話

男：好，公司大樓的參觀到此結束了。我們現在要走到人事辦公室，好讓**妳們填寫妳們的到職文件。** 38 有任何問題嗎？

女1：使用休閒中心和三溫暖室需要先提交專用的表單嗎？

男：不用。**休閒中心和三溫暖室每天早上七點到晚上九點開放。妳們可憑員工證進入使用。** 39 還有其他問題嗎？

女2：有。我只是好奇我們什麼時候要去業務組的辦公室。**總算要和我們同事見面了，我等不及了。** 40

男：**哦，我們午餐後馬上過去。我確信部門同仁也期待見到妳們兩位。** 40

38. Who most likely are the women?
(A) Corporate lawyers
(B) New workers
(C) Fitness trainers
(D) Construction managers

38. 女子們最有可能的身分是？
(A) 企業律師
(B) 新進員工
(C) 健身教練
(D) 施工經理

39. What does the man say about the leisure facilities?
(A) The sauna is being renovated.
(B) They close early on the weekends.
(C) The membership fee has recently increased.
(D) They require a company ID to enter.

40. What will the women do after lunch?
(A) Participate in another building tour
(B) Meet some department members
(C) Listen to a speech
(D) Complete a questionnaire

39. 關於休閒設施，男子說了什麼？
(A) 三溫暖室正在整修。
(B) 在週末較早關閉。
(C) 會費最近增加了。
(D) 需要公司識別證才能進入。

40. 午餐後女子們會做什麼？
(A) 參加另一個大樓參觀
(B) 和部門同事們見面
(C) 聽演講
(D) 完成問卷填寫

Questions 41-43 refer to the following conversation.

M: Hello, it's Gordon Stevens, Manager of the Accounting Department. **Water from the ceiling has been dripping onto my desk,** 41 so I had to move my computer to another area of the room. Do you know what the cause of the leak is?
W: One of the pipes on the floor above your office must be leaking. **I'll send someone from my team to check it out right away.** 42
M: Thank you. Do you think it will be possible for you to repair it before noon today? **I'm expecting an important client at 3 o'clock in my office today.** 43
W: Yes, it shouldn't take too long.

41-43 會話

男：妳好，我是會計部經理高登．史蒂文斯。**目前一直有天花板漏水滴到我的桌上，**41 我因此得要把電腦移到辦公室的其他地方。妳知道漏水的原因嗎？
女：想必是你的辦公室樓上有條水管漏水了。**我馬上派一位部門同仁去檢查。**42
男：謝謝妳。想請教妳，你們在今天中午前有可能修好嗎？**今天下午三點我有一位重要客戶會來我的辦公室。**43
女：可以，應該不會太久。

41. Why is the man calling?
(A) To recommend a new office
(B) To request assistance with a computer
(C) To report a leak
(D) To reserve a meeting room

42. What does the woman say she will do?
(A) Revise a client list
(B) Send an employee to help
(C) Install an accounting program
(D) Call a utility company

43. What does the man say he will be doing at 3 o'clock?
(A) Meeting with a client
(B) Examining some documents
(C) Interviewing job applicants
(D) Leaving for a business trip

41. 男子為何打電話？
(A) 以推薦新的辦公室
(B) 以請求電腦方面的協助
(C) 以回報漏水
(D) 以預約會議室

42. 女子說她會做什麼？
(A) 修改客戶名單
(B) 派員工前去協助
(C) 安裝會計程式
(D) 致電（水、電等）公用事業機構

43. 男子說他三點時會做什麼？
(A) 會見客戶
(B) 審查文件
(C) 面試應徵者
(D) 啟程出差

Questions 44-46 refer to the following conversation.

44-46 會話

W：Hey, Chris. I know you're taking this Friday off, but **we need additional workers for that day. We're providing catering services for a party at the Performing Arts Center,** 44 and I was just told that more guests would be attending.

M：**Hmm . . . I'm expecting an important package this Friday. It's supposed to be delivered around 6 P.M.** 45

W：**Oh, the party is a dinner banquet, so I don't think it'll be possible then.** 45

M：Yeah, I'm sorry about that. **You might want to talk to Corinna, though. She told me she wanted to work extra hours.** 46

女：嘿，克里斯。我知道你本週五休假，但**當天我們需要額外人力。我們要在表演藝術中心為一場聚會提供外燴服務，**44 而且我剛得知出席賓客人數有所追加。

男：**嗯……我這週五要等一個重要的包裹到貨。應該是下午六點左右會送到。**45

女：**噢，那場聚會是晚餐宴會，所以我想是沒辦法囉。**45

男：對，很不好意思。**不過或許你可以和科琳娜商量看看。她跟我說過她想額外加班。**46

44. What industry do the speakers most likely work in?
(A) Food service
(B) Architecture
(C) Fine arts
(D) Packaging

44. 說話者最有可能任職什麼產業？
(A) 餐飲服務
(B) 建築
(C) 藝術
(D) 包裝

45. What does the man mean when he says, "It's supposed to be delivered around 6 P.M."?
(A) He may not be available for a task.
(B) He will have to place a new order.
(C) He plans to request a refund.
(D) He is not satisfied with a service.

45. 男子說：「應該是下午六點左右會送到」，其意思為何？
(A) 他可能無法抽身工作。
(B) 他將需要下新的訂單。
(C) 他打算要求退款。
(D) 他對服務不滿意。

46. What does the man say about Corinna?
(A) She will enroll in a training workshop.
(B) She drives her car to the office.
(C) She is more experienced than him.
(D) She is interested in working more hours.

46. 關於科琳娜，男子說了什麼？
(A) 她將報名培訓研習。
(B) 她自己開車上班。
(C) 她比男子更具經驗。
(D) 她有意增加工作時數。

Questions 47-49 refer to the following conversation.

47-49 會話

W: Hello, my name is Irene Marquéz, and I'm calling from Mahal Engineering. **Our company will be hosting some investors** 47 from Seoul, and **we have some documents that need to be translated** 47 48 before they arrive. You do English to Korean translations, right?

女：您好，這裡是馬哈爾工程的來電，我叫做艾琳．馬奎茲。**我們公司將接待幾位投資者** 47 從首爾來訪，而他們到達前，**我們有一些文件需要翻譯。**47 48 您有從事英文翻韓文的翻譯，是嗎？

M：Yes, that's correct. But I'll be interpreting at a conference both days this weekend, so I won't be able to do your work until next week. Would that be OK with you?

W：Actually, our meeting is scheduled for next Monday, so we need our annual earnings report translated by this Saturday at the latest.

M：Ah, in that case, **I can recommend a colleague of mine.** 49 Her specialty is financial documents. Let me get your email address, and I'll ask her to contact you.

男：是的，沒錯。不過本週末兩天我都要到一場會議從事口譯，因此我得等到下週才能做您的案子。請問這樣您方便嗎？

女：其實我們預定下週一開會，所以我們最晚必須在本週六前拿到年度營收報告的翻譯。

男：啊，這樣的話，**我可以引薦我的一位同事。** 49 她的專長是財經文件。請給我您的電子郵件地址，我會請她與您聯繫。

47. What is the woman preparing for?

(A) A business trip to Seoul
(B) An engineering seminar
(C) A corporate merger
(D) A meeting with investors

48. What is the woman calling about?

(A) A travel itinerary
(B) Translation services
(C) A conference room
(D) Contract details

49. What does the man offer to do?

(A) Make a reservation
(B) Send an email
(C) Refer a colleague
(D) Explain a schedule

47. 女子正在準備什麼事？

(A) 到首爾出差
(B) 工程研討會
(C) 公司合併
(D) 與投資者的會議

48. 女子打電話洽詢何事？

(A) 旅遊行程
(B) 翻譯服務
(C) 會議室
(D) 合約細則

49. 男子提議幫忙做何事？

(A) 預約
(B) 寄電子郵件
(C) 轉介同事
(D) 解釋行程表

Questions 50-52 refer to the following conversation.

W：**How far have you gotten on your presentation for the Finance Committee tomorrow?** 50 This presentation is essential to getting enough funding for our investment. So it's crucial that we clearly describe our plans for investing in Gio-tech's eco project.

M：It's nearly complete, but **I'm missing the recording of Gio-tech's welcome message.** 51 I'm not sure who has the video file.

W：Oh, that's right. I was supposed to email that to you. I'll go to my desk right now and send it to you.

50-52 會話

女：**你明天要向財務委員會簡報的內容，現在進展得如何？** 50 這次簡報對於我們的投資案能否取得足夠資金至關重要。所以我們得要清楚說明我方針對「喬科技」環保專案的投資計畫。

男：快完成了，但**我現在還缺喬科技的歡迎詞錄影檔。** 51 我不確定影片檔案在誰手上。

女：喔，對了。我之前就該用電子郵件寄給你的。我馬上就去我辦公桌傳給你。

M：Thanks. Also, we should make sure the file is compatible with the software in our computer. **Do you mind going to the conference room after your lunch break today to make sure the computer plays the file?** 52

男：謝謝。我們也得確認該檔案能與我們電腦的軟體相容。**方便麻煩妳今天午休以後去趟會議室，確認電腦可順利播放檔案嗎？** 52

50. What are the speakers discussing?
(A) An inventory check
(B) A finance presentation
(C) A business merger
(D) A television advertisement

50. 說話者在討論什麼？
(A) 盤點存貨
(B) 財務簡報發表
(C) 企業合併
(D) 電視廣告

51. What does the man say he is missing?
(A) A video file
(B) A signature
(C) A desk key
(D) An account password

51. 男子說他找不到什麼？
(A) 影片檔案
(B) 簽名
(C) 辦公桌鑰匙
(D) 帳戶密碼

52. What does the man ask the woman to do after lunch?
(A) Attend a committee meeting
(B) Submit an investment proposal
(C) Check a computer
(D) Review a contract

52. 男子請女子午餐後做什麼？
(A) 出席委員會會議
(B) 繳交投資提案
(C) 檢查電腦
(D) 審查合約

Questions 53-55 refer to the following conversation with three speakers.

W：Hello. My name is Vivian Hurns. **I'm here to pick up a research paper Professor Chun edited. I need to review the edits before submitting it for publishing next week.** 53
M1：Sure. Let me check. **Which professor was it again?** 54
W：**Dr. Chun.** 54
M1：OK. **I believe my coworker, Drew, met with him this morning.** 54 Just a moment, please. Drew?
M2：Yes?
M1：Did Dr. Chun leave a paper with you this morning?
M2：Yes. Ms. Hurns, **I just need to see your student ID before I hand this over to you.** 55
W：Certainly. Here you are.

53-55 三人會話

女：您好。我是薇薇安．航斯。**我來拿俊教授修改過的研究論文。我需要在下週送交出版前檢查修改過的內容。** 53
男1：好的。讓我確認一下。**能複述一次是哪位教授嗎？** 54
女：**俊博士。** 54
男1：好的，**我記得在今天早上，我的同事祖魯和他見過面了。** 54 請稍等一下。祖魯你在嗎？
男2：是，什麼事？
男1：俊博士今天早上有留一份論文給你嗎？
男2：有。航斯女士，**我這邊須要看一下妳的學生證，之後就把論文交給妳。** 55
女：沒問題。在這邊。

53. What will the woman do next week?
(A) Submit a research paper
(B) Give a guest lecture
(C) Publish a book
(D) Take an exam

53. 女子下週會做什麼？
(A) 提交研究論文
(B) 進行客座演講
(C) 出版書籍
(D) 參加考試

54. What did Drew do in the morning?
(A) He edited a document.
(B) He met with a professor.
(C) He purchased office supplies.
(D) He delivered a package.

54. 祖魯今天早上做了什麼事？
(A) 他編修了一份文件。
(B) 他和教授見過面。
(C) 他買了辦公用品。
(D) 他遞送了一件包裹。

55. What does Drew ask the woman to do?
(A) Complete a form
(B) Come back later
(C) Present identification
(D) Visit another office

55. 祖魯請女子做什麼？
(A) 填寫表格
(B) 稍後再來
(C) 出示身分證件
(D) 前往另一處辦公室

TEST 5 PART 3

21

Questions 56-58 refer to the following conversation.

M：Crystal, I'm concerned that we didn't sell many winter vacation packages this month. **I don't think our travel agency is doing enough to attract more customers.** 56
W：Well, **we're going to launch a new marketing campaign next week. That should help increase our sales.** 57
M：Maybe, **but winter's nearly over.**
W：Yeah ... Last year, we had a lot more winter vacations reserved around this time.
M：Hmm ... Why don't we get in touch with our transportation companies and hotels, and discuss two- to three-day packages? This might draw more customers looking to go on a short break.
W：That's a good idea. **I'll give our vendors a call right now.** 58

56-58 會話

男：克麗斯爾，這個月我們冬季度假套裝行程銷量不多，這讓我很擔心。**我覺得我們旅行社在吸引更多客戶方面還有待加強。** 56
女：嗯，**我們下週會開始新一波行銷活動，應該能幫我們的業績有所起色。** 57
男：也許吧，**但冬季已近尾聲了。**
女：對……去年這個期間前後，我們冬季度假行程的預約量遠超過現在。
男：嗯……我們不妨聯絡我們的客運業者和飯店，討論一下兩至三天的套裝行程？這或許能吸引到更多有意短期度假的客人。
女：這主意不錯。**我馬上打電話給我們的合作廠商。** 58

56. Who most likely are the speakers?
(A) Hotel workers
(B) Broadcasting executives
(C) Travel agents
(D) Restaurant employees

56. 說話者最有可能的身份為何？
(A) 飯店員工
(B) 廣電事業高層
(C) 旅行社員工
(D) 餐廳職員

57. What does the man imply when he says, "but winter's nearly over"?
(A) The woman needs to finish an assignment quickly.
(B) A marketing campaign will be released too late.
(C) Some data in a sales report must be revised.
(D) He would like to take his vacation at a later time.

57. 男子說：「但冬季已近尾聲了」，其暗示為何？
(A) 女子須儘快完成交辦任務。
(B) 行銷活動起步太晚。
(C) 銷售報告裡有些數據必須修正。
(D) 他想過陣子再去度假。

58. What will the woman do next?
(A) Speak with a supervisor
(B) Distribute a questionnaire
(C) Contact some businesses
(D) Print out additional flyers

58. 女子接下來會做什麼？
(A) 與主管談
(B) 發放問卷
(C) 聯絡廠商
(D) 增印傳單

Questions 59-61 refer to the following conversation.

M：Hi, it's Jason from Grapper Industries. I'm calling to follow up on your inquiry about renting our Pro-X Gauge.
W：Thanks for the call. **I manage a small factory,** 59 and I know your gauge keeps track of a machine's internal pressure. I'm looking for a device that can provide reliable information for our new mixing tanks.
M：Then **the Pro-X Gauge is ideal for you. It will accurately measure the pressure levels of your tanks throughout the day** 60 so that you'll be able to make sure your machine is operating well.
W：Great. I'm a little worried about the cost, though.
M：It's just $95 a month.
W：OK. But **I'll have to check our budget, so why don't I call you back tomorrow?** 61

59-61 會話

男：您好，我是格拉帕工業的傑森。您先前有詢問本公司 Pro-X 儀器的租用事宜，我來電對此做後續了解。
女：感謝來電。**我負責管理一家小工廠，** 59 又得知貴公司該款儀器可以監測機器的內部壓力。本廠有幾座新的混合槽，為此我正在找能提供可靠資訊的裝置。
男：那麼 **Pro-X 儀器就是您理想的選擇。它能夠為您全天精準測量槽內的壓力值，** 60 讓您可以確保您的機器正常運作。
女：非常好。不過我有點擔心價錢。
男：只需月付 95 美元。
女：好的。但**我得查一下我們的預算，那不如我明天回電給您？** 61

59. Who most likely is the woman?
(A) A corporate accountant
(B) A delivery driver
(C) A sales representative
(D) A plant manager

59. 女子最有可能的職業是？
(A) 企業會計師
(B) 貨運司機
(C) 銷售員
(D) 工廠經理

60. What feature of the Pro-X Gauge does the man mention?
(A) It tracks packages.
(B) It monitors pressure levels.
(C) It records daily finances.
(D) It calculates shipping rates.

60. 男子提到 Pro-X 儀器有什麼功能？
(A) 追蹤包裹。
(B) 監控壓力值。
(C) 記錄每日財務狀況。
(D) 計算運費。

61. Why does the woman say she will call back tomorrow?
(A) She has to review a financial plan.
(B) She is late for a meeting.
(C) She requires her supervisor's authorization.
(D) She would like to check out other models.

61. 女子為什麼說她將在明天回電？
(A) 她須查看財務規畫。
(B) 她開會遲到。
(C) 她需要主管的授權。
(D) 她想查看其他機型。

Questions 62-64 refer to the following conversation and report.

62-64 會話和報告

M：**I've reviewed expenses for our computer manufacturing plant 62 and prepared a report. Do you mind reading it over? 63**
W：**Sure. Hmm . . . Most of our expenditures have increased this month. 63 I think we should focus on lowering costs on packaging materials. 64**
M：Well, the packaging design for our new office computers is a bit complex. We should try to simplify it.
W：I agree. I'll look into how much this can save us.

Monthly Report	
Equipment Expenses	$9,000
Packaging Materials	**$8,000 64**
Property Rent	$6,000
Utilities (gas and electricity)	$1,000

男：**我檢視了我們電腦製造工廠的開支狀況 62 並作成了一份報告。能麻煩妳幫我看過一遍嗎？63**
女：**沒問題。嗯……我們這個月大部分開銷都增加了。63 我覺得我們應該著重降低包裝材料的成本。64**
男：嗯，我們新款辦公用電腦的包裝設計有點繁瑣。我們應該設法化繁為簡。
女：我同意。我會檢討此方案可以幫我們省下多少錢。

月結報告	
設備開支	9,000 美元
包裝材料	**8,000 美元 64**
廠房租金	6,000 美元
公用事業費用（瓦斯、電力）	1,000 美元

62. What kind of product does the company most likely make?
(A) Office furniture
(B) Cleaning supplies
(C) Clothing
(D) Electronics

62. 這家公司製造的產品類型最有可能為何？
(A) 辦公家具
(B) 清潔用品
(C) 服裝
(D) 電子用品

63. What does the woman point out about the report?
(A) Some monthly objectives were achieved.
(B) Some figures were incorrect.
(C) Some expenditures have gone up.
(D) Some sections are blank.

64. Look at the graphic. Which amount does the woman say might change?
(A) $9,000
(B) $8,000
(C) $6,000
(D) $1,000

63. 關於報告，女子指出什麼？
(A) 已達成部分的每月目標。
(B) 有些數據有誤。
(C) 有些支出增加了。
(D) 有些欄位空著。

64. 請據圖表作答。女子提到哪項費用可能會更動？
(A) 9,000 美元
(B) 8,000 美元
(C) 6,000 美元
(D) 1,000 美元

Questions 65-67 refer to the following conversation and GPS application.

W：Larry, thank you for coming to get me today. **I really appreciate you driving me to work while my van is being fixed.** 65

M：No problem. We live in the same neighborhood, so it's easy! Oh, **I just remembered that today's the day of that race. The street that I usually take to the office is closed off for the cyclists.** 66

W：Ah, I forgot about that. Well, I'm looking at my smartphone's GPS app, and **there are three alternative routes you could use. I suggest taking this one because it will get us to work in just 25 minutes.** 67

M：**All right. Sounds good to me.** 67

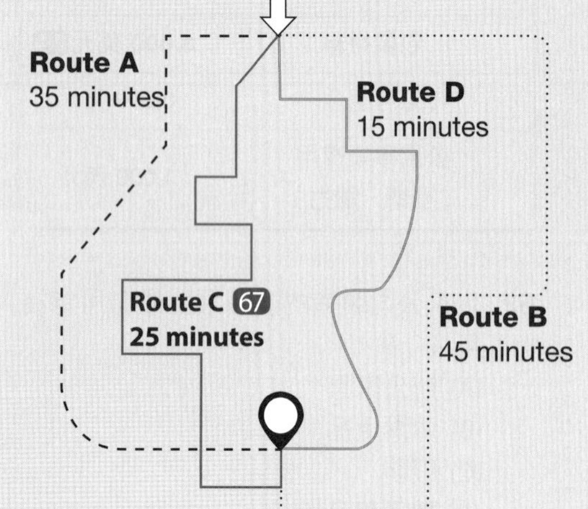

65-67 會話和定位應用程式

女：賴瑞，謝謝你今天來接我。**我的廂型車送修期間，真的很感謝你能載我上班。** 65

男：沒什麼啦。我們住同個社區，所以小事而已！噢，**我剛想起來今天有場比賽。我上班常走的那條街現在封鎖管制，給自行車賽的選手使用。** 66

女：啊，我忘了這件事。那麼，我現在查了一查智慧型手機的 GPS 應用程式，而**上面說可行的替代路線有三條。我建議選擇這條路，因為只要 25 分鐘就能到公司。** 67

男：**好的。聽起來不錯。** 67

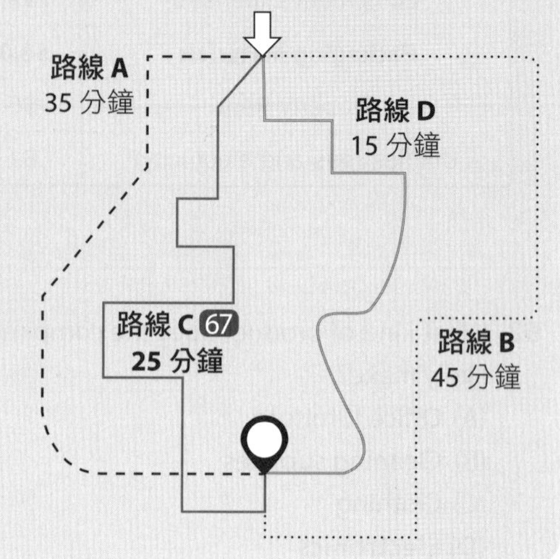

65. Why is the man driving the woman to work?
(A) Her public transit pass expired.
(B) She does not own a car.
(C) She recently moved to a new city.
(D) Her vehicle is being repaired.

66. What event does the man say is being held today?
(A) A retirement banquet
(B) A cycling competition
(C) An art exhibition
(D) A film festival

67. Look at the graphic. What route will the man probably take?
(A) Route A
(B) Route B
(C) Route C
(D) Route D

Questions 68-70 refer to the following conversation and schedule.

W：**I think the management meeting we just had with the executive board went well.** 68
M：Yeah. It won't be easy building additional manufacturing plants, but it's the right move.
W：Oh, by the way, before going into the meeting, I read your email regarding our new plants' completion dates. **We need to make one change. The work on the Westmark plant won't be finished on schedule.** 69
M：Got it. What's the reason?
W：**That region has been experiencing heavy snowfall, and the storm's been delaying the construction work.** 70 We need to move the completion date for the Westmark facility to sometime around mid-October.
M：Ah, I see. Well, at least this will give us additional time to find qualified factory workers.

To	Raya Shah
From	Brian McFadder

Plant Location	Completion Date
Newcrest	July 31
Westmark	**September 26** 69
Callington	October 27
Plateforth	November 30

65. 為什麼男子開車接送女子上班？
(A) 她的公共運輸票證已過期。
(B) 她未持有車子。
(C) 她最近搬到別的城市。
(D) 她的車正在修理。

66. 男子說今天有舉辦什麼活動？
(A) 退休宴會
(B) 自行車比賽
(C) 藝術展覽
(D) 電影節

67. 請據圖表作答。男子可能會走哪個路線？
(A) 路線 A
(B) 路線 B
(C) 路線 C
(D) 路線 D

68-70 會話和日程表

女：**我覺得剛才我們和執行董事會舉行的管理高層會議相當順利。** 68
男：對。增建製造工廠並不容易，但卻是正確的一步。
女：喔，順道一提，參加會議前，我讀了你有關新廠完工日期的電子郵件。**我們有個地方要更改。西馬克工廠的工程將無法如期完工。** 69
男：了解。原因是什麼？
女：**當地近來下了大雪，而暴風雪造成了建設工程延誤。** 70 我們得把西馬克工廠的完工日移到大概十月中。
男：噢，了解。嗯，至少如此一來，我們將得到更多時間物色符合資格的工廠員工。

收件人	拉雅．沙阿
寄件人	布萊恩．麥費德

廠房位置	完工日
新頂	7 月 31 日
西馬克	**9 月 26 日** 69
寇林頓	10 月 27 日
培特福斯	11 月 30 日

TEST 5
PART 3
21

68. What did the speakers just attend?

(A) An employee meeting

(B) A factory tour

(C) A career fair

(D) A product demonstration

68. 說話者剛參加完什麼？

(A) 職員會議

(B) 工廠參訪

(C) 職涯博覽會

(D) 產品展示會

69. Look at the graphic. What date has to be changed?

(A) July 31

(B) September 26

(C) October 27

(D) November 30

69. 請據圖表作答。哪個日期須更改？

(A) 7 月 31 日

(B) 9 月 26 日

(C) 10 月 27 日

(D) 11 月 30 日

70. What is causing a delay in construction?

(A) Some equipment is not working.

(B) Some materials have not been delivered.

(C) A building permit has been denied.

(D) An area has had inclement weather.

70. 何事導致建設工程延誤？

(A) 有些設備故障中。

(B) 有些材料沒有送到。

(C) 建築許可遭拒。

(D) 當地天候惡劣。

PART 4 P. 75–77

22

Questions 71-73 refer to the following broadcast.

M: You're tuning into 104.5 FM, Atlanta's number one radio station. It's time for your weekly community news. **It's been announced that the annual dance competition at Candler Park, scheduled for this weekend, has been postponed until further notice. 71 I know that many of you were looking forward to this, but some underground pipes burst, so technicians need to fix them. 72** You can check out our Web site for updates regarding the new date for the competition. **And now, here's Nancy Bates with a look at your local traffic report. 73**

71-73 廣播

男：您正在收聽 FM 104.5，亞特蘭大最棒的廣播電台。以下請聽每週社區新聞。**原定本週末在坎德公園舉行的年度舞蹈比賽已宣布延期，日期尚待後續通知。71 我知道很多聽眾對此引頸企盼，但因為部分地下管線破裂，需要技術人員維修。72** 關於比賽的新日期，您可至我們的網站查詢更新消息。**那麼現在，請南希・貝茨為您帶來本地交通報導。73**

71. According to the speaker, what event was postponed?

(A) A film festival

(B) A bicycle race

(C) A dance performance

(D) A cooking competition

71. 說話者提到何項活動延期了？

(A) 電影節

(B) 自行車比賽

(C) 舞蹈表演

(D) 烹飪比賽

72. Why was the event postponed?
(A) An application was rejected.
(B) A guest could not make it.
(C) Some funds were not secured.
(D) Some repair work needs to be done.

73. What will the listeners hear next?
(A) A new song
(B) A celebrity interview
(C) A traffic report
(D) A business advertisement

72. 活動為什麼延期？
(A) 申請遭拒。
(B) 嘉賓無法前來。
(C) 有資金沒有到位。
(D) 要進行維修工程。

73. 聽眾接下來會聽到什麼？
(A) 一首新歌
(B) 名人專訪
(C) 交通報導
(D) 企業廣告

Questions 74-76 refer to the following broadcast.

M: Thanks for tuning into Channel 8's evening news. **Earlier this afternoon, Bradbury Theater, the 125 year-old structure in downtown, was finally sold.** 74 It's one of the most recognizable buildings in our city, and plans are to have it converted into a shopping complex. **Wight and Company has been chosen for the job. With proven expertise in renovating old buildings, they were the ideal candidate for this difficult project.** 75 **City council members hope to generate more revenue for the town,** 76 and the new shopping complex will certainly contribute to the cause.

74-76 廣播

男：感謝收聽第 8 頻道的晚間新聞。**今天下午稍早，位於市中心、有著 125 年歷史的布瑞德貝里劇院終於售出。** 74 它是本市最具代表性的建築之一，目前規劃將其改建為複合式購物中心。**獲選承接該項工程的是懷特公司。該公司從事老屋新生的專業一向受到肯定，是託付這項艱鉅專案的理想選擇。** 75 **市議員希望為本市創造更多收入，** 76 而新的複合式購物中心勢必會為此願景有所貢獻。

TEST 5
PART 3 4

74. What happened in the afternoon?
(A) An old structure was sold.
(B) A movie premiere was held.
(C) A new product was released.
(D) An anniversary party took place.

75. According to the speaker, why was Wight and Company chosen?
(A) It knows how to do challenging renovations.
(B) It owns multiple shopping complexes.
(C) It will offer jobs to local residents.
(D) It has previously worked on government projects.

76. What do city council members hope to do?
(A) Increase revenue
(B) Hire better building designers
(C) Expand public transportation
(D) Construct more parks

74. 下午發生了什麼事？
(A) 舊建築售出了。
(B) 舉辦了電影首映會。
(C) 推出了新產品。
(D) 舉行了週年慶祝會。

75. 據說話者說法，懷特公司為何被選上？
(A) 它熟於從事棘手的整修工程。
(B) 它擁有多家複合式購物中心。
(C) 它將為當地居民提供工作機會。
(D) 它以前曾從事過政府專案。

76. 市議會議員希望做什麼？
(A) 增加收益
(B) 聘請更好的建築設計師
(C) 擴建公共運輸
(D) 建設更多公園

Questions 77-79 refer to the following speech.

W：I'm so happy to see you all here for the 9th annual Heartland Agricultural Management Convention. 77 This is actually the largest turnout we've ever had for the convention, and you'll get chances to meet various people in the field. 78 I hope everyone brought plenty of business cards. Now for me personally, this is kind of a sad moment. As I'm sure you're aware, I've been running this event for many years in hopes of creating a better future for our region and our industry. And I honestly believe that I have been making a difference. **So it was not an easy decision to leave my position as Convention Director.** 79 At the same time, however, I know that my replacement, Otto Hamilton, will keep up the good work.

77. What is the subject of the convention?

(A) Finance

(B) Agriculture

(C) Healthcare

(D) Travel

78. What does the speaker mean when she says, "I hope everyone brought plenty of business cards"?

(A) Identification cards are required for registration.

(B) Event organizers will be holding a raffle.

(C) There will be many networking opportunities.

(D) Some guests do not have name tags.

79. What does the speaker say is difficult?

(A) Preparing a presentation

(B) Managing a facility

(C) Securing a venue

(D) Quitting a role

77-79 演說

女：很高興看到各位齊聚第九屆的年度「心田農業管理大會」。77 其實本屆大會的與會人次已經創下史上新高，而各位有機會在現場與這個業界的各路人馬相逢。78 我希望各位都帶了很多名片。至於對我個人而言，此刻倒是有點感傷。想必各位知道，多年以來我持續籌辦本活動，希望為我們的地方和產業打造更美好的未來。平心而論，我相信自己不無貢獻。**因此要我卸下大會會長的職位，並不是個容易的決定。**79 然而同時我也知道，我的接班人奧托．漢密爾頓會持續做出好成績。

77. 大會主題為何？

(A) 財務金融

(B) 農業

(C) 醫療保健

(D) 旅行

78. 說話者說：「我希望各位都帶了很多名片」，其意思為何？

(A) 報名時需要身分識別證。

(B) 活動主辦方將舉辦抽獎。

(C) 將有很多機會交流人脈。

(D) 有些賓客沒有名牌。

79. 說話者提到何事很困難？

(A) 準備簡報

(B) 管理設施

(C) 取得活動場地

(D) 辭去職位

Questions 80-82 refer to the following telephone message.

M：Hello, this is Arthur Johnson from Office 881. **I'm supposed to have some carpets delivered to me this morning. I know that I have to notify the building manager to use the back entrance**

80-82 語音留言

男：您好，我是 881 辦公室的亞瑟．強森。**我有幾張地毯應該會在今天早上送到。我得知使用本大樓後門時，需要先告知大樓管理員，因此**

of the building, and that's why I'm calling you. The name of the company is Modern Office Furniture, and the people making the delivery should be here between 10 and 11 o'clock. 80 **Could you please let them into the building when they arrive?** 81 If you need to contact me, **I'll be in the office organizing files all morning until noon.** 82 Thank you very much.

現在致電給您。那間廠商的名字叫做「現代辦公家具」，而送貨員應該會在 10 點到 11 點之間抵達這邊。 80 **他們到的時候，能請您讓他們進入大樓嗎？** 81 如果您須要聯絡我，**我中午前的整個早上都會在辦公室整理文件。** 82 非常感謝。

80. What is the purpose of the message?

(A) To make changes to an order

(B) To request additional workers

(C) To inquire about office vacancies

(D) To explain details about a delivery

80. 留言的目的為何？

(A) 以更改訂單

(B) 以要求增添員工

(C) 以詢問辦公室職缺

(D) 以解釋送貨相關細節

81. What does the speaker want the listener to do?

(A) Contact a factory supervisor

(B) Send a package to an office

(C) Review a company policy

(D) Allow access to a building

81. 說話者希望聽者做什麼？

(A) 聯絡工廠主管

(B) 寄包裹到辦公室

(C) 審查公司政策

(D) 允許進入大樓

82. What does the speaker say he will be doing this morning?

(A) Training an employee

(B) Cleaning his apartment

(C) Working in his office

(D) Visiting a client

82. 說話者說他今早會做什麼？

(A) 訓練員工

(B) 打掃公寓

(C) 在他的辦公室工作

(D) 拜訪客戶

Questions 83-85 refer to the following announcement.

83-85 宣布

W： Attention, all travelers. **As there are a large number of people traveling through our airport today, there are significant delays at the check-in counters of all gates.** 83 To speed up the process, **make sure to have your passport and ticket ready for our agents** 84 when your flight is called. Also, **attendants with yellow badges will be coming around to identify those passengers who require special assistance and check their departure times** 85 to make sure that they get on their flights on time.

女： 各位旅客請注意。**由於今天本機場來往的旅客人數眾多，所有登機門的登機櫃檯皆有明顯的時間延誤情形。** 83 為加快作業流程，**請先確實準備好您的護照與機票**，以便在廣播登機時**出示給我們的工作人員** 84 另外，**佩戴黃色徽章的乘務員將會到場巡視，找到需要特殊協助的乘客，並確認他們的起飛時間** 85 以確保他們能準時搭上班機。

TEST 5 PART 4 22

83. What problem is being addressed?
(A) Inclement weather
(B) Passenger delays
(C) Technical difficulties
(D) Missing bags

84. What are listeners asked to do?
(A) Prepare to present documents
(B) Go to a different gate of the airport
(C) Complete a special request form
(D) Request a refund for a ticket

85. According to the speaker, what will attendants be doing?
(A) Checking departure times
(B) Issuing new tickets
(C) Offering shuttle service
(D) Distributing luggage tags

83. 說話者正在應對什麼問題？
(A) 天候惡劣
(B) 旅客延誤
(C) 技術障礙
(D) 包包遺失

84. 聽者被要求做什麼？
(A) 準備出示文件
(B) 到機場別的登機門
(C) 完成特殊申請表
(D) 要求機票退款

85. 據說話者說法，乘務員會做什麼？
(A) 確認起飛時間
(B) 發放新的票券
(C) 提供接駁服務
(D) 分發行李標籤

Questions 86-88 refer to the following notice.

M： Welcome to today's concert here at the Bach Auditorium. We apologize for the late start. **There was an unexpected turn of events. We seem to be having some difficulties with our speaker system.** 86 Our technicians are currently working on the problem, and we expect the concert to start momentarily. In the meantime, **we suggest you visit the front desk in the lobby where copies of the orchestra's new album are available for purchase.** 87 Also, don't forget to take a look at **the posters by the exit advertising future shows for this fall.** 88

86-88 通知

男： 歡迎來到巴哈演藝廳欣賞今天的音樂會。很抱歉開場時間耽擱了。**現場適才出現了意外狀況。我們的音響系統似乎發生了一點狀況。** 86 目前技術人員正在排除問題，我們預計音樂會很快可以開場。於此期間，**我們建議您可以移步至大廳前台，那裡備有這次管弦樂團的新專輯可供選購。** 87 另外，也別忘了看一下**出口處的海報，上面有宣傳未來在今年秋季的演出。** 88

86. Why does the speaker say, "There was an unexpected turn of events"?
(A) Some equipment is not working.
(B) Some instruments are missing.
(C) A musician is arriving late.
(D) The venue is being renovated.

87. According to the speaker, what can be purchased in the lobby?
(A) Snacks and drinks
(B) Performance tickets
(C) An orchestra's recordings
(D) Signed posters of musicians

86. 說話者為什麼說：「現場適才出現了意外狀況」？
(A) 有些設備運作失常。
(B) 有些樂器不見了。
(C) 有位樂手遲到了。
(D) 場地正在整修。

87. 根據說話者說法，在大廳能買到什麼？
(A) 零食和飲料
(B) 表演門票
(C) 管弦樂團的唱片
(D) 音樂家簽名海報

88. What is being advertised at the auditorium?
(A) Music lessons
(B) Upcoming performances
(C) Guided tours
(D) Famous restaurants

88. 演藝廳裡刊登著何種廣告？
(A) 音樂課程
(B) 近期將登場的演出
(C) 導覽參訪
(D) 著名餐廳

Questions 89-91 refer to the following announcement.

89-91 宣布

W：**Just one thing before we start our delivery routes for the day. I know that you all have a lot of deliveries to make and a tight schedule, but we need to follow protocol when delivering packages. 89 It's critical that you get a signature from each recipient before moving on to the next location. We have been hearing that many packages are simply left on doorsteps, and that cannot be tolerated. 90 All of this information is coming from our customers.** As Dispatch Manager, it's my responsibility to make sure that we are making deliveries quickly, but without sacrificing security. **Starting immediately, a new client relations manager will be contacting random recipients and checking if you are properly following this procedure. 91**

女：**開始跑今天的送貨行程前，我只有一件事想說。我知道你們都有很多貨物要送，而且行程緊迫，但交遞包裹時我們還是必須遵守規範。89 每次把貨送到時，都要取得收件人簽名，才能前往下個送貨點，這點至關重要。據我們得知，有很多次包裹是直接被丟在門口，這是無法容忍的。90 這些訊息都是客戶反映的。**我身為配送經理，有責任確保到貨迅速，但安全性也不打折。**此時此刻起，將有一位新的客戶關係經理會隨機聯絡收件人，來檢查大家是否妥善遵守這項程序。91**

89. Where do the listeners most likely work?
(A) At an electronics manufacturer
(B) At a courier company
(C) At a security firm
(D) At a grocery store

89. 聽者最有可能在哪裡工作？
(A) 在電子用品製造商
(B) 在快遞公司
(C) 在保全公司
(D) 在雜貨店

90. Why does the speaker say, "All of this information is coming from our customers"?
(A) To emphasize the importance of a process
(B) To express her disagreement with an opinion
(C) To recognize the listeners' efforts
(D) To ensure listeners report to their supervisors

90. 說話者為什麼說：「這些訊息都是客戶反映的」？
(A) 以強調流程的重要性
(B) 以對一項意見表示反對
(C) 以肯定聽者的努力
(D) 以確保聽者向主管回報

91. According to the speaker, what will a new manager start doing?
(A) Working on the weekends
(B) Visiting different branches
(C) Conducting inspections
(D) Purchasing replacement parts

91. 據說話者說法，新經理將會開始做什麼？
(A) 在週末工作
(B) 拜訪其他分部
(C) 執行檢查
(D) 採買替換零件

Questions 92-94 refer to the following announcement.

M： Last on the schedule today, **I'd like to discuss the matter of moving our patient records that are on paper to an electronic database.** 92 All of the records will now be stored electronically like many other health clinics in the city, and **there's one main benefit I'd like to mention. Removing all the paper files that are in our office will create a lot more space** 93 that we can use for other purposes. **I've asked the office manager to get in touch with a recycling company that specializes in document disposal** 94 to come next week and take away all of the paper records so that we can use the space.

92. What is the announcement mainly about?
(A) A revised safety policy
(B) A new office manager
(C) A conversion to an electronic database
(D) A directory of local health clinics

93. What is mentioned as an advantage of the change?
(A) There will be more free space.
(B) Information will be protected.
(C) There will be fewer accidents.
(D) Productivity will be increased.

94. What has the office manager been asked to do?
(A) Arrange for medical checkups
(B) Send patient records
(C) Contact a document-disposal company
(D) Create an employee evaluation form

92-94 宣布

男： 就本日的最後一項議程，**我想討論我們把患者病歷從紙本轉移到電子資料庫一事。** 92 現在所有病歷都會比照市內許多其他醫療診所，以電子方式儲存，**此舉有個主要的好處，我認為值得一提。清除掉辦公室裡的紙本文件後，會騰出更多空間，** 93 可作其他用途。**我已經請辦公室主任聯絡專門處理廢棄文件的回收公司，** 94 請他們下週來把紙本病歷全部收走，以方便我們使用這些空間。

92. 宣布的主要內容為何？
(A) 修正後的安全政策
(B) 新任辦公室主任
(C) 改採電子資料庫
(D) 當地醫療診所的名錄

93. 說話者提及改變後有何優點？
(A) 可用空間將增加。
(B) 資訊將受保障。
(C) 事故將減少。
(D) 產能將提高。

94. 辦公室主任受指示做什麼？
(A) 安排健康檢查
(B) 寄送病歷
(C) 聯絡廢棄文件處理公司
(D) 制定員工考核表

Questions 95-97 refer to the following excerpt from a meeting and schedule.

W： Good morning, everyone. As you know, the company will be holding several informational sessions for employees next week. **Although they are not mandatory, as members of the marketing team,** 95 **I would like to urge every one of you to attend the session on social**

95-97 會議摘錄和行程表

女： 大家早安。誠如各位所知，公司下週將為員工舉辦幾場資訊課程。**雖然並非強制參加，但作為行銷團隊的成員，** 95 **我想強烈鼓勵各位參加關於社群媒體的課程。** 96 我有信心該課程將有助你們更懂得我們消費

media. 96 I am confident that this class will help give you a better idea of the needs of our consumers. **Also, participants in each session will be provided with lunch, compliments of the company.** 97 If you're interested, please let me know by tomorrow afternoon.

Informational Sessions	
Monday	Advanced Computer Skills Course
Tuesday	Best Accounting Software Programs
Wednesday 96	**Popular Social Networking Sites**
Thursday	Effective Employee Motivation Techniques

者的需求。**另外，對於參與任一場課程的學員，公司都會免費供應午餐。** 97 如果各位有興趣，請在明天下午前告訴我。

資訊課程	
週一	進階電腦技能課程
週二	最佳會計軟體程式
週三 96	**熱門社群網站**
週四	有效激勵員工的技巧

95. Which department does the speaker most likely work in?
(A) Information Technology
(B) Marketing
(C) Accounting
(D) Human Resources

95. 說話者最有可能在哪個部門工作？
(A) 資訊技術
(B) 行銷
(C) 會計
(D) 人力資源

96. Look at the graphic. When are the listeners encouraged to attend a session?
(A) Monday
(B) Tuesday
(C) Wednesday
(D) Thursday

96. 請據圖表作答。聽者獲鼓勵參加哪一天的課程？
(A) 週一
(B) 週二
(C) 週三
(D) 週四

97. What will participants receive at every session?
(A) A free meal
(B) A certificate
(C) A bonus
(D) A survey form

97. 每堂課的參與者都將獲得什麼？
(A) 免費餐點
(B) 證書
(C) 獎金
(D) 調查表

Questions 98-100 refer to the following excerpt from a meeting and neighborhood map.

98-100 會議摘錄和社區地圖

W：**As you all know, we've been receiving more requests for our recycling pickup services, thanks to our community awareness program.** 98 We'll now be making more than one stop in several neighborhoods. **We'll start by changing our Monday route.** 99 Since this route has experienced the biggest increase in customers,

女：**如大家所知，多虧社區的觀念宣導計畫有成，我們接到更多載收資源回收物的要求。** 98 現在，我們要把幾個社區的停靠次數增加至超過一次。**我們首先要調整的就是週一的路線。** 99 有鑑該路線的顧客數量成長最多，我們將把服務分成為週

we're going to spread the work over two days—Monday and Tuesday. This is a good thing. **I hope that by gaining more customers, we'll finally be able to buy better machines that can process recyclables more quickly.** 100

一、週二兩天進行。這麼做有益無害。**我希望隨著顧客增加，我們終將能購置更優良的機器，加速處理資源回收物。** 100

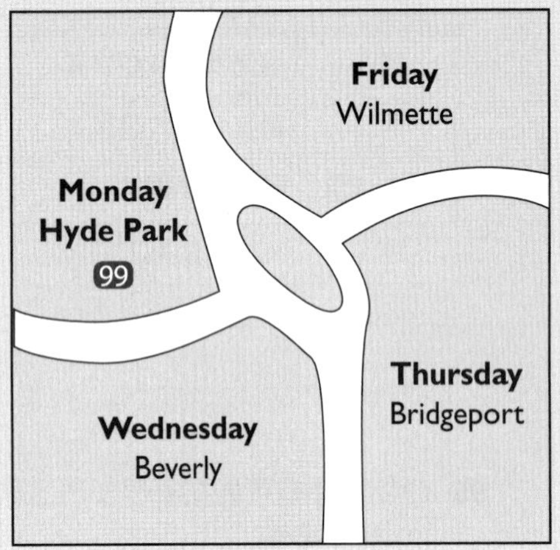

98. Where does the speaker most likely work?
(A) At a vehicle rental agency
(B) At a dental clinic
(C) At a recycling company
(D) At a public transportation service

99. Look at the graphic. Which neighborhood will be affected by a schedule change?
(A) Hyde Park
(B) Beverly
(C) Bridgeport
(D) Wilmette

100. What does the speaker hope to purchase?
(A) New machinery
(B) Packaging boxes
(C) A larger warehouse
(D) More advertising space

98. 說話者最有可能在哪裡工作？
(A) 在租車公司
(B) 在牙醫診所
(C) 在資源回收公司
(D) 在公共運輸服務單位

99. 請據圖表作答。哪一社區將受到時程變更的影響？
(A) 海德公園
(B) 比佛利
(C) 橋港
(D) 威爾梅特

100. 說話者希望採購什麼？
(A) 新的機具
(B) 包裝盒
(C) 更大的倉庫
(D) 更多廣告版面

ACTUAL TEST 

PART 1 P. 78–81

23

1. **(A) The woman is seated by a tree.**
   (B) The woman is organizing some folders on a table.
   (C) The woman is drinking from a water bottle.
   (D) The woman is closing a laptop computer.

2. (A) A woman is pouring a beverage.
   (B) A man is setting down a plate.
   (C) A customer is sipping from a glass.
   (D) A diner is reading a menu.

3. (A) She is arranging glass bottles on a shelf.
   (B) She is placing plastic containers on the floor.
   (C) She is wearing laboratory gloves.
   (D) She is setting up video equipment.

4. (A) Some shirts have been laid out on a shelf.
   (B) Some merchandise is on display outside a store.
   (C) Leaves are scattered on a walkway.
   (D) A sign is being taken down from an awning.

5. (A) A man is handing out some documents.
   (B) Some people are attending a meeting.
   (C) A woman is pointing at a screen.
   (D) Some people are taking their seats.

6. (A) A bicycle is being wheeled into a building.
   (B) Some women are jogging through a park.
   (C) There's a woman polishing a statue.
   (D) There are shadows on a path.

1. **(A) 女子坐在樹旁。**
   (B) 女子正在整理桌上的檔案夾。
   (C) 女子正在喝水壺的水。
   (D) 女子正在闔上筆電。

2. (A) 女子正在倒飲料。
   (B) 男子正放下盤子。
   (C) 客人正在舉杯啜飲。
   (D) 用餐者正在看菜單。

3. (A) 她正在整理架上的玻璃瓶。
   (B) 她正把塑膠容器放在地板。
   (C) 她正戴著實驗室手套。
   (D) 她正在設置影像設備。

4. (A) 架子上平鋪著幾件襯衫。
   (B) 有些商品在店外展示。
   (C) 葉子散落在人行道上。
   (D) 遮篷上的標示正在取下。

5. (A) 男子正在發放文件。
   (B) 一些人正在開會。
   (C) 女子手指著螢幕。
   (D) 一些人正在入座。

6. (A) 一輛腳踏車正要牽進大樓裡。
   (B) 有些女子正穿越公園慢跑。
   (C) 女子正在把雕像擦亮。
   (D) 有些陰影正落在道路上。

PART 2 P. 82

24

7. When's the new Greek restaurant opening in our town?
   (A) A renowned chef.
   (B) Ten job openings.
   (C) Sometime in May.

7. 我們鎮上新的希臘餐廳何時開幕？
   (A) 一位知名大廚。
   (B) 十個職缺。
   (C) 五月期間。

8. Pardon me. Is this seat taken?
(A) Yes, it's on my desk.
(B) Yes. Someone's sitting there.
(C) I'll take it down now.

8. 不好意思。這個位子有人坐嗎？
(A) 是，在我桌上。
(B) 是。這裡有人坐。
(C) 我現在就把它拿下來。

9. Why did you buy a compact car?
(A) Because it's easy to park.
(B) It's a new credit card.
(C) At the auto dealership.

9. 你為什麼要買小型車？
(A) 因為停車方便。
(B) 這張是新的信用卡。
(C) 在汽車經銷商。

10. Where do you get your hair cut?
(A) Yes, it was too long.
(B) At a salon near my work.
(C) About once a month.

10. 你在哪裡剪頭髮？
(A) 對，太長了。
(B) 在我公司附近的沙龍。
(C) 大約每個月一次。

11. Who's the new floor supervisor?
(A) They're on the 2nd floor.
(B) I didn't know that either.
(C) A former coworker of mine.

11. 新的樓層主管是誰？
(A) 他們在二樓。
(B) 我之前也不知道。
(C) 我以前的一位同事。

12. Should I ship this package to the head office?
(A) More delivery drivers.
(B) Bruce will drop it off later.
(C) I sent them by email.

12. 我該把這個包裹寄到總部嗎？
(A) 更多貨運司機。
(B) 布魯斯稍後會送過去。
(C) 我用電郵把它們寄出了。

13. These wrist watches are handmade, right?
(A) Actually, they're not.
(B) Here's the guest list.
(C) I'm not sure what time it is.

13. 這些腕錶是手工製作的，對嗎？
(A) 其實，並不是。
(B) 賓客名單在這裡。
(C) 我不確定現在幾點。

14. Can you help me load these boxes into my truck?
(A) In the storage room.
(B) I've already downloaded them.
(C) Sure. Where's your truck parked?

14. 你能幫我把這些箱子搬上我的卡車嗎？
(A) 在倉庫裡。
(B) 我已經把它們下載好了。
(C) 當然可以。你的卡車停在哪？

15. Why are you setting up a computer on that desk?
(A) A part-time employee is starting today.
(B) Yes. Put it on my desk, please.
(C) Every morning before work.

15. 你為什麼在那張桌子上裝設電腦？
(A) 今天會有兼職人員到職。
(B) 對。請把它放我桌上。
(C) 每天早上上班前。

16. When will the keynote speech begin?
(A) By the CEO.
(B) In Conference Room 3.
(C) Let me check the schedule.

16. 主題演講何時開始？
(A) 由執行長。
(B) 在三號會議室。
(C) 讓我查看時程表。

17. What material is this bag made of?
(A) A mix of different fabrics.
(B) It's a luxury brand.
(C) This is a smaller size.

17. 這個包包是用什麼材質做的？
(A) 不同布料混合而成。
(B) 這是奢侈品牌。
(C) 這是較小的尺碼。

18. How was the movie yesterday?
(A) It was very entertaining.
(B) About one and a half hours.
(C) Sorry, I'm busy.

18. 昨天看的電影怎麼樣？
(A) 很有趣。
(B) 大約一個半小時。
(C) 對不起，我很忙。

19. Didn't you attend the company party last night?
(A) Make a right at the next light.
(B) I had to finish an assignment.
(C) We'll be there by 8.

19. 你昨晚沒參加公司聚會嗎？
(A) 下個紅綠燈右轉。
(B) 當時我得完成交辦工作。
(C) 我們會八點前到。

20. I'm traveling to Amsterdam for my next business trip.
(A) When will you be leaving?
(B) Get off at the next stop.
(C) The flight has been delayed.

20. 我下次出差要去阿姆斯特丹。
(A) 你何時會出發？
(B) 下一站下車。
(C) 航班延誤了。

21. Where should we install this photocopier?
(A) All the software is included.
(B) We don't have room in this office.
(C) A well-known photographer.

21. 我們應該把這台影印機裝設在哪裡？
(A) 所有軟體都有內附。
(B) 我們這間辦公室沒有空間了。
(C) 一位知名攝影師。

22. The number of people taking your exercise class increased, didn't it?
(A) Group aerobics classes on weeknights.
(B) Yes, the online ad was effective.
(C) Contact the new fitness center.

22. 你的健身班參加人數增加了，不是嗎？
(A) 平日晚間的團體有氧課程。
(B) 對，網路廣告很有效。
(C) 聯絡新的健身中心。

23. Do you have time to review the budget report before noon?
(A) A decrease in spending.
(B) I'm in meetings all morning.
(C) On the accounting team.

23. 你中午前有時間審查預算報告嗎？
(A) 支出的減少。
(B) 我整個早上都要開會。
(C) 關於會計部門。

24. Should we drive or take the subway to the conference center?
(A) A business management seminar.
(B) I'm OK, thank you.
(C) It's right by the subway exit.

24. 我們是該開車還是搭地鐵前往會議中心呢？
(A) 企業管理研討會。
(B) 我這樣就好，謝謝。
(C) 它剛好在地鐵出口旁。

25. We will have to reschedule the meeting to June 23.
(A) When will you finish?
(B) It was delivered on the 21st.
(C) I'll mark it in my calendar.

25. 我們須將會議日期改到 6 月 23 日。
(A) 你何時結束？
(B) 它在 21 日遞交了。
(C) 我會記到行事曆上。

26. I can show the slides again from the beginning if you want.
(A) There's no time for that.
(B) Sign on the left side of the paper.
(C) We'll take some if you have extras.

26. 若你們想要，我可以從頭再放一次投影片。
(A) 沒有時間了。
(B) 請在文件左側簽名。
(C) 如果你有多的，我們就拿一些。

27. Are you enrolled in the marketing strategy course?
(A) I took it last year.
(B) I have a small role in the play.
(C) A local business school.

27. 你報名行銷策略課程了嗎？
(A) 我去年上過了。
(B) 我在劇中出演小角色。
(C) 當地商學院。

28. Who's picking up the buyers from the train station?
(A) Traveling to Los Angeles.
(B) A 2:50 arrival.
(C) It should say on their itinerary.

28. 誰會去車站接買主／採購員？
(A) 前往洛杉磯。
(B) 2:50 抵達。
(C) 他們的行程表上應該有寫。

29. Which store location has the best sales numbers so far?
(A) No, an in-store discount.
(B) The data will be released this afternoon.
(C) It's sold at all participating locations.

29. 到目前為止，哪一家門市的業績最好？
(A) 不，一項店內折扣。
(B) 今天下午會公布數據。
(C) 所有參與活動的門市都有販售。

30. You ordered the extra supplies, didn't you?
(A) Their food is delicious.
(B) Sure, I'll have a few more.
(C) The manager said we won't need them.

30. 你有訂購額外的用品，沒錯吧？
(A) 他們的食物很好吃。
(B) 當然好，請再給我一些。
(C) 經理說我們不需要。

31. How did the executive director like the project proposal?
(A) The annual sales projection.
(B) He talked to Lawrence about it.
(C) I hope to, in the future.

31. 執行董事對這項專案企劃書的看法如何？
(A) 年銷售額預估。
(B) 他和勞倫斯談過此事了。
(C) 我希望是，有朝一日。

PART 3 P. 83–86

25

Questions 32-34 refer to the following conversation.

M：**Welcome to Sansor's Law Office.** 32 What can I assist you with?
W：Hello, my name is Carrie Lin, and I'm here for my 2 P.M. meeting with Jeffrey Bowers.
M：Hmm . . . I can't find your name in the system.
W：Well, I set up the meeting over the phone yesterday morning.
M：Ah, **our server experienced some issues yesterday, so there's a good chance your reservation did not get entered into the schedule.** 33 I'm sorry for the inconvenience. If you're willing to wait, I can arrange a meeting for you within 30 minutes.

32-34 會話

男：**歡迎光臨桑索爾律師事務所。** 32 有什麼我可以為您服務的嗎？
女：您好，我叫林凱莉，我有約在下午兩點要和傑佛瑞·鮑爾斯會談。
男：唔……我在系統裡搜尋不到您的名字。
女：嗯，我是昨天早上用電話約好會談的。
男：噢，**昨天我們伺服器發生一點狀況，所以您的預約很可能沒有排進行程表裡。** 33 很抱歉造成不便。如果您願意等候的話，我可以在 30 分鐘內為您安排一場會談。

W：That should be fine.
M：Thank you for understanding. By the way, **feel free to visit our lounge area, and pick up some snacks and beverages.** 34

女：應該沒問題。
男：感謝您的體諒。順道一提，**歡迎自行前往我們的休息區，取用一些點心和飲料。** 34

32. Where does the conversation probably take place?
(A) At a health clinic
(B) At a hotel
(C) At a restaurant
(D) At a law firm

32. 這段對話可能是在哪裡發生的？
(A) 在醫療診所
(B) 在飯店
(C) 在餐廳
(D) 在律師事務所

33. Why does the man apologize?
(A) An invoice is incorrect.
(B) Some data was not saved.
(C) There are no more parking spaces.
(D) A product is defective.

33. 男子為何道歉？
(A) 帳單有誤。
(B) 部分資料未儲存。
(C) 停車位不足。
(D) 產品有缺陷。

34. What does the man encourage the woman to pick up?
(A) A parking permit
(B) A magazine
(C) Some forms
(D) Some refreshments

34. 男子建議女子取用什麼？
(A) 停車許可
(B) 雜誌
(C) 一些表格
(D) 一些茶點

Questions 35-37 refer to the following conversation.

35-37 會話

W：Hi, Will. I'm planning to open a consulting firm, and I was thinking of renting an office in the Telco Complex on Memphis Avenue. You have a shop there, right?
M：Yeah, and **it's right in the middle of the downtown area, so it should be easy for your clients to get to your office.** 35
W：That's exactly why I'm considering this location. I actually checked out an office there last week, but it was in the basement. **I set up another appointment to check out one on the 3rd floor.** 36
M：Ah, great. Actually, **the tenants and I are going to have a luncheon this Sunday at the complex's barbecue area. You should join us if you're interested.** 37

女：嗨，威爾。我正在籌劃成立一家顧問公司，而我想到了在孟菲斯大道上的特爾科綜合大樓裡租用辦公室。你有在那裡開店，對嗎？
男：對，而且**這一棟正好就位在市中心，所以妳的客戶要來洽公應該會很方便。** 35
女：我就是為此才考慮這個地點。其實，我上週有去那裡看了一間辦公室，但是那間位在地下室。**我又另外約了一次，打算要看在三樓的另一間。** 36
男：喔，這樣很好。其實**在這個週日，我和幾名租戶會在大樓的燒烤區舉辦午餐聚會。如果妳有興趣，就前來同樂吧。** 37

35. What does the man mention about the Telco Complex?
(A) It offers cheap rental rates.
(B) It is in a quiet neighborhood.
(C) It offers a free parking space.
(D) It is conveniently located.

35. 關於特爾科綜合大樓，男子提到什麼？
(A) 有提供便宜的租金。
(B) 位在安靜的社區。
(C) 有提供免費停車位。
(D) 地點交通便利。

36. What does the woman say she has done?
(A) She has purchased a vehicle.
(B) She has scheduled a meeting.
(C) She has quit her current job.
(D) She has contacted a relocation firm.

36. 女子說她做了什麼？
(A) 她買了車。
(B) 她安排了會面。
(C) 她辭掉了現職。
(D) 她聯絡了搬家公司。

37. What does the man invite the woman to?
(A) A store opening
(B) A cooking contest
(C) A building tour
(D) A lunch gathering

37. 男子邀請女子參加什麼？
(A) 店家開幕
(B) 烹飪比賽
(C) 大樓導覽
(D) 午餐聚會

Questions 38-40 refer to the following conversation with three speakers.

M：I'm sure you're all aware that our museum hasn't been getting many visitors recently. **I've called everyone to this meeting to brainstorm ways to solve this problem.** 38 Mara, you told me you had a suggestion to draw more visitors, right?

W1：Well, **we should consider replacing our current audio equipment with small mobile players.** 39 What are your thoughts, Tiffany?

W2：I agree with you. Our audio tours are still delivered at the exhibits' kiosks. Other museums in the city are using portable equipment.

W1：It'll be a little pricey to purchase these audio players, but we can start charging guests a rental fee.

M：That's a good idea. **I'll contact one of our vendors and arrange a consultation.** 40

38-40 三人會話

男　：想必妳們知道，我們博物館的參觀的人數最近不見起色。**我召集大家開會是想集思廣益，想出解決這個問題的辦法。** 38 瑪拉，妳跟我說過妳有項建議，可以吸引更多遊客，對嗎？

女 1：嗯，**我們應該要考慮替換現有的音響設備，改用小型行動播放裝置。** 39 蒂芬妮，妳覺得怎麼樣呢？

女 2：我同意妳的說法。我們還在用展覽台播放語音導覽。市內的其他博物館都已經在使用可攜式裝置了。

女 1：購買這些播放設備會有點小貴，但我們可以開始向遊客收租借費。

男　：這主意不錯。**我會聯絡我們其中一家供應商，安排諮詢會談。** 40

38. Why did the man call the meeting?
(A) To discuss a budget report
(B) To give a new employee orientation
(C) To come up with some solutions
(D) To go over a revised policy

38. 男子為何召開會議？
(A) 為討論預算報告
(B) 為新進員工進行培訓
(C) 為想出解決方案
(D) 為檢視修改後的規則

39. What will probably change at the business?
(A) A brochure
(B) A Web site
(C) Some operating hours
(D) Some devices

40. What will the man do next?
(A) Submit a payment
(B) Make an appointment
(C) Review some applications
(D) Install some equipment

39. 該業者的哪方面將有改變？
(A) 小冊子
(B) 網站
(C) 部分營業時間
(D) 部分裝置

40. 男子接下來會做什麼？
(A) 進行付款
(B) 預約會面
(C) 審查申請
(D) 安裝設備

Questions 41-43 refer to the following conversation.

M：Hey, Julia. **I need you to drop by a client's office on Nader Avenue.** It's Berman's Newspaper Company. **They want to replace the floor tiles in their lobby.** 41
W：Didn't the office manager say they didn't need new ones?
M：Well, he decided that the current tiles were too old. **Please go over to their office once you're done installing the wallpaper at Hearth Software, Inc.'s headquarters.** 42
W：Um . . . The work here will take me all day.
M：Ah, OK. Well, **I'll check what appointments Kenneth has today and see if he can make some time.** 43
W：All right. If not, I can stop by tomorrow.

41-43 會話

男：嘿，茱莉亞。**我需要妳去一趟一間客戶的辦公室，就在納德街上，**名叫「伯曼報社」。**他們想更換門廳的地磚。** 41
女：那邊的辦公室主任不是說他們不需要新的地磚嗎？
男：嗯，他認為目前的瓷磚太舊了。**麻煩妳在赫爾斯軟體公司總部完成壁紙鋪設後，前往報社那邊的辦公室。** 42
女：嗯……我在這裡的作業要花上一整天。
男：噢，好。那麼，**我再確認一下肯尼斯今天有什麼行程，然後看他有沒有辦法抽出時間。** 43
女：好的。如果他沒辦法，我明天可以跑一趟。

41. What most likely is the woman's profession?
(A) Journalist
(B) Interior designer
(C) Software technician
(D) Realtor

42. Why does the woman say, "The work here will take me all day"?
(A) To turn down a request
(B) To approve a plan
(C) To volunteer for an assignment
(D) To ask for an extension

41. 女子的職業最有可能為何？
(A) 記者
(B) 室內設計師
(C) 軟體技術員
(D) 房地產經紀人

42. 女子為何說：「我在這裡的作業要花上一整天」？
(A) 以拒絕請求
(B) 以批准計畫
(C) 以自願接受交辦任務
(D) 以要求延期

43. What does the man say he will do?
(A) Go to an office
(B) Purchase more supplies
(C) Check a colleague's schedule
(D) Contact a client

43. 男子說他會做什麼？
(A) 去一處辦公室
(B) 採買更多用品
(C) 確認同事的行程
(D) 聯絡客戶

Questions 44-46 refer to the following conversation.

44-46 會話

W：Hi, **I recently dropped a management course at the Wayne Institute of Business** 44 because of a scheduling conflict. I thought my registration fee would be refunded within one week. But it's been over three weeks, and I haven't received it yet.
M：**I'm sorry for the delay. There were some problems with the computer system,** 45 and some refunds weren't processed correctly. Can you please tell me your name?
W：My name is Mito Shizuma. When will I be able to receive my refund then?
M：Well, according to our records, we processed your refund today, so **you should get it by Thursday. You can track your refund status online at www.wayneib.com.** 46

女：您好，**我最近**因為行程衝突，**取消了韋恩商學院的管理課程。** 44 我以為我的報名費會在一週內退還。但現在已經過了三個星期，而我還是沒收到。
男：**很抱歉發生延誤情形。之前電腦系統出了一點問題，** 45 而未能妥善處理部分退款。能請教您的大名嗎？
女：我的名字是靜間美登。那麼我何時將能收到退款呢？
男：嗯，根據我們的紀錄，您的退款今天已處理了，因此**您應該會在週四前收到款項。您可以上網到 www.wayneib.com 追蹤退款狀態。** 46

44. What did the woman recently do?
(A) Registered at a fitness center
(B) Exchanged a defective product
(C) Taught a business course
(D) Canceled enrollment in a class

45. What has caused a delay?
(A) A name was missing.
(B) A system malfunctioned.
(C) A form was incomplete.
(D) A payment was not made.

46. What does the man suggest?
(A) Signing up for another class
(B) Reading a manual
(C) Checking a Web site
(D) Coming back at a later time

44. 女子最近做了什麼？
(A) 報名使用健身房
(B) 更換瑕疵品
(C) 教授商務課程
(D) 取消課程報名

45. 造成延誤的原因為何？
(A) 姓名遺失。
(B) 系統故障。
(C) 表單不完整。
(D) 未付款。

46. 男子建議什麼？
(A) 報名另一堂課
(B) 閱讀說明手冊
(C) 前往網站查看
(D) 稍後再來

Questions 47-49 refer to the following conversation.

M：Hello, I wanted to tell you that **I really enjoyed listening to your lecture on publishing. I've been trying to publish a book based on my travels, but I didn't know where to begin. I never knew I could do it on my own** 47 online.

W：Thank you. I'm happy that it was useful to you. I know there was a lot of information. I hope I covered everything you wanted.

M：Yes, everything was explained well. **I did have an issue, though. You posted a list of Web sites that you recommended for self-publishing,** 48 49 **but there wasn't much time to write down every address while you went through your slides.** 48

W：Oh, I'm really sorry about that. That list is quite long. **I'm going to email the links to you and all the other attendees tomorrow.** 49

47. What was the topic of the woman's lecture?
(A) Web site designs
(B) Vacation spots
(C) Self-publishing
(D) Popular books

48. What problem did the man have during the lecture?
(A) He had trouble finding a seat.
(B) He did not understand some material.
(C) He could not ask any questions.
(D) He was not able to write down some information.

49. What does the woman say she will send to attendees?
(A) Links to some Web sites
(B) A survey form
(C) A list of future events
(D) A copy of some slides

47-49 會話

男：您好，我想告訴您，**您針對出版的演講真讓我聽得如沐春風。我一直想從我的旅行經驗中取材並出版成書，但此前都不知該從何處著手。過去我從來沒想過可以自行**在線上**完成。**47

女：謝謝。很高興對您有幫助。我知道資訊量蠻龐雜的。希望我有談及您想知道的所有內容。

男：有的，一切都講得條理分明。**不過我有個問題。您剛才有展示一份可供從事個人出版的推薦網站清單，**48 49 **但您播放投影片時，沒有太多的時間讓我記下每條網址。**48

女：噢，真的不好意思。那份清單很長。**我明天會用電子郵件把連結寄給您和其他所有到場的聽眾。**49

47. 女子的演講主題為何？
(A) 網站設計
(B) 度假勝地
(C) 個人出版
(D) 熱門書籍

48. 男子在演講中遇到什麼問題？
(A) 他找不到座位。
(B) 他無法理解部分資料。
(C) 他不能問任何問題。
(D) 他無法記下部分資訊。

49. 女子說她會寄送什麼給到場的聽眾？
(A) 幾個網站的連結
(B) 調查表單
(C) 未來活動清單
(D) 幾張投影片的副本

Questions 50-52 refer to the following conversation.

W：Hello. **I'm a delivery driver for Stadwell Kitchen Appliances,** 50 and I'm here to drop off the stoves you purchased.

M：Oh, they arrived sooner than expected! I'm looking forward to using them for a long time.

W：Well, **we're well-known for producing stoves that last longer than any other brand.** 51 Anyway, just sign this confirmation receipt, and we'll move these stoves into your kitchen.

M：OK. Wait a minute—**this invoice lists only two stainless steel stoves, but I'm certain that we ordered three. I'm pretty sure this isn't correct.** 52

W：Hmm . . . I'll have to contact the warehouse. Please give me a few minutes while I try to figure out what happened.

50-52 會話

女：您好。**我是「許塔德威廚房設備」的貨運司機，** 50 我現在到達了，幫您送來您之前採購的爐具。

男：哦，到貨速度比我預料的還要快！我很期待能夠長期使用它們。

女：嗯，**本公司製造的爐具是出了名的耐用，他牌很難相提並論。** 51 不說這個了，請在確認單上簽名，然後我們會把這些爐具搬進廚房。

男：好的。先等一下，**這張發貨單上只列了兩個不銹鋼爐，但我確定我們訂了三個。這肯定是弄錯了。** 52

女：嗯……我得跟倉庫聯絡。請給我幾分鐘，讓我釐清出了什麼狀況。

50. What kind of business does the woman work at?
(A) A utility company
(B) An appliance manufacturer
(C) An auto shop
(D) A catering business

50. 女子在什麼行業工作？
(A) 公用事業公司
(B) 設備製造商
(C) 汽車維修行
(D) 外燴業者

51. What does the woman say the business is known for?
(A) Its affordable pricing
(B) Its helpful employees
(C) Its wide collection
(D) Its durable products

51. 女子說該公司以什麼知名？
(A) 價格合理
(B) 員工樂於助人
(C) 類型多樣
(D) 耐用的產品

52. What problem does the man mention?
(A) Some merchandise is damaged.
(B) An item is missing.
(C) An extra fee has been charged.
(D) Some boxes are too heavy to transport.

52. 男子提到什麼問題？
(A) 有些商品已損壞。
(B) 有項產品遺漏。
(C) 收取了額外費用。
(D) 部分箱子過重以致運送困難。

Questions 53-55 refer to the following conversation.

W：Good afternoon. **This is the Barrel Lounge.** 53

M：Hello. I'm putting together a farewell party. **Someone referred me to your café,** 53 but I wanted to see if we could bring in some bottles of wine.

53-55 會話

女：午安。**這裡是酒桶酒吧。** 53

男：您好。我正在籌辦歡送會。**有人向我推薦你們這家咖啡酒吧，** 53 但我想問我們能不能自帶幾瓶酒到店。

W：Unfortunately, outside beverages are not permitted here. However, you can choose from our wide selection of wines.
M：Hmm . . . How much do you charge for a bottle of red wine?
W：**Our most affordable one costs $40.** 54
M：**Oh . . . Gallagher's Tavern's cheapest bottle is $25.**
W：I see. OK, **why don't I put you on hold so that I can talk to my supervisor and see if we can work something out?** 55
M：All right. Thank you.

女：很抱歉，我們店裡不允許自帶酒水。不過本店備有各式各樣的葡萄酒，可供您挑選。
男：嗯……請問你們一瓶紅酒多少錢？
女：**我們最便宜的一款是每瓶 40 美元。** 54
男：**喔……加拉格爾酒館裡最便宜的一瓶是 25 美元。**
女：了解。這樣的話，**何不讓我先保留您的通話，好讓我和主管討論，看我們能否找出可行的方案？** 55
男：可以。謝謝。

53. Where does the woman probably work?
(A) At a party decoration shop
(B) At a packaging plant
(C) At a café
(D) At a hotel

53. 女子可能在哪裡工作？
(A) 在派對裝飾品店
(B) 在包裝工廠
(C) 在咖啡酒吧
(D) 在飯店

54. Why does the man say, "Gallagher's Tavern's cheapest bottle is $25"?
(A) To correct a mistake
(B) To compliment a service
(C) To recommend an item
(D) To request a discount

54. 男子為什麼說：「加拉格爾酒館裡最便宜的一瓶是 25 美元」？
(A) 以糾正錯誤
(B) 以讚美服務
(C) 以推薦產品
(D) 以要求折扣

55. How does the woman offer to assist the man?
(A) By refunding his purchase
(B) By letting him sample a product
(C) By reserving some merchandise
(D) By talking to a supervisor

55. 女子提議如何協助男子呢？
(A) 為他購買的商品退款
(B) 讓他試用產品
(C) 預留某些商品
(D) 和主管交談

Questions 56-58 refer to the following conversation.

56-58 會話

M：Excuse me, Cecilia. Since you're our Department Manager, **I was hoping I could get your approval to use five of my vacation days at the start of May.** 56 And in case you're wondering, I've completed my portion of the Kaiser Flight project already.
W：That's good to hear. **But there are still a few more tasks that must be finished before the end of the month, and I'm worried that the project won't be completed on time without you.** 57

男：不好意思，賽西莉亞。因為妳是我們部門經理，**我希望能得到妳的批准，讓我在五月初使用我的五天休假。** 56 另外為防妳會掛心，針對凱澤航空專案，我已經完成我負責的部分了。
女：真是好消息。**但還有一些多的工作必須趕在該月底前完成，我擔心要是你不在，專案會無法準時完成。** 57

M：That won't be an issue. **I'm willing to take on extra work** 58 and finish it before I leave.
W：Great. That would be very helpful. I'll see to it that you receive the necessary assignments right away. Then there shouldn't be a problem if you're gone during that time.

男：這不礙事，**我願意承接額外的工作，** 58 並會在休假前就完成。
女：太好了，真是幫了大忙。我會安排讓你馬上收到必要的交辦事項。如此一來，你不在的那段時間應該就不會有問題了。

56. What is the man asking for?
(A) Some job descriptions
(B) An increase in his salary
(C) More funds for a project
(D) Some time off from work

56. 男子提出什麼要求？
(A) 工作說明
(B) 加薪
(C) 更多專案資金
(D) 一段休假

57. What is the woman concerned about?
(A) Achieving a sales target
(B) Impressing an important client
(C) Meeting a project deadline
(D) Recruiting skilled employees

57. 女子擔心什麼事？
(A) 達成銷售目標
(B) 讓重要客戶刮目相看
(C) 趕上專案期限
(D) 招聘技術工

58. What does the man say he can do?
(A) Accept additional assignments
(B) Train more staff members
(C) Post a vacation schedule
(D) Contact the Human Resources Manager

58. 男子說他能做什麼？
(A) 接受額外交辦任務
(B) 培訓更多員工
(C) 張貼休假時程表
(D) 聯絡人資經理

Questions 59-61 refer to the following conversation with three speakers.

W：Hello, Jeremy. Hello, Ernie. **I wanted to go over the magazine ad we're designing for Fergus Accessories.** 59
M1：Let's take a look. Hmm . . . **The background is so bright that the pictures of the jewelry aren't clearly visible.** 60
M2：**Jeremy's right.** 60 They just look like part of a background. We need to do something about this.
M1：Daisy, can you take care of this issue soon? We need to get this printed by next Thursday.
W：Yes, I can. **I'll use a darker color for the background so that jewelry stands out better. I'll make a new draft of the layout by the end of the day today.** 61
M1：Thanks.

59-61 三人會話

女：哈囉，傑瑞米。哈囉，厄尼。**我想仔細檢討我們為佛格斯飾品所設計的雜誌廣告。** 59
男 1：我們來看一下吧。嗯⋯⋯**這幅背景太亮了，導致珠寶的圖片都不太醒目。** 60
男 2：**傑瑞米說的對。** 60 它們（珠寶圖片）看起來跟背景合而為一了。我們需要想辦法處理。
男 1：黛西，妳能儘速解決這個問題嗎？我們需要在下週四之前送印。
女：是，我可以處理。**我會選用較深的顏色來做背景，這樣珠寶本身就能凸顯出來。我今天下班前會做出新的版面草圖。** 61
男 1：謝啦。

59. What industry do the speakers most likely work in?
(A) Jewelry
(B) Healthcare
(C) Journalism
(D) Marketing

60. What is the problem?
(A) Some descriptions are inaccurate.
(B) An image is missing.
(C) A design is not good.
(D) Some materials were damaged.

61. What does the woman promise to do by the end of today?
(A) Install a program
(B) Create a new draft
(C) Send an invoice
(D) Call a business

59. 說話者最有可能在哪個產業工作？
(A) 珠寶
(B) 醫療保健
(C) 新聞
(D) 行銷

60. 目前遇到什麼問題？
(A) 有些說明不精確。
(B) 缺少一張照片。
(C) 設計不盡理想。
(D) 有些素材受損。

61. 女子答應今天下班前會做什麼？
(A) 安裝程式
(B) 作好新草圖
(C) 寄送帳單
(D) 打電話給業者

Questions 62-64 refer to the following conversation and product list.

M：Good afternoon! **Is there anything you're looking for in particular?** 62
W：Oh, I'm glad you asked! **I'd like to buy a winter coat, but I'm not quite sure which one is best.** 62
M：Hmm . . . What exactly did you have in mind?
W：Well, I go skiing a lot, so I want to get something nice and warm. But it can't be too expensive.
M：I understand, and **we have some really reasonably-priced padded jackets at the moment.** 63 Check out this catalog.
W：**Ah, I like them a lot.** 63 Do you have that red one in a women's medium size?
M：**I'll search our computer database** 64 to find out if we have that color in that size. Give me a moment.

Winter Suits Manufacturer: Groenlandia Ltd.	p. 3
Sweater Vests Manufacturer: La Lluvia	p. 6
Padded Jackets **Manufacturer: Allons Co.** 63	p. 9
Long Coats Manufacturer: Cara Norte	p. 11

62-64 會話和產品清單

男：午安！**您有特別在找什麼嗎？** 62
女：噢，問得正是時候！**我想買件冬季外套，但我不太確定哪一件最好。** 62
男：嗯……您有什麼具體的需求嗎？
女：這個嘛，我經常去滑雪，所以想買一件又好又保暖的，但也不能太貴。
男：了解，那**我們目前有幾款價格非常實惠的襯墊夾克。** 63 請看看這個型錄。
女：**啊，這幾款我很喜歡。** 63 紅色的這一件你們有女性 M 號的嗎？
男：**我會在我們的電腦資料庫搜尋看看，** 64 看是否有該款顏色的尺寸。請稍等一下。

冬季套裝 製造商：格陵蘭迪亞有限公司	第 3 頁
毛織背心 製造商：拉雨	第 6 頁
襯墊夾克 **製造商：齊走企業** 63	第 9 頁
長板大衣外套 製造商：山之北面	第 11 頁

62. What most likely is the man's job?
(A) Computer programmer
(B) Fashion designer
(C) Sales representative
(D) Personal trainer

63. Look at the graphic. Which manufacturer does the woman say she likes?
(A) Groenlandia Ltd.
(B) La Lluvia
(C) Allons Co.
(D) Cara Norte

64. What does the man offer to do?
(A) Provide a coupon
(B) Print a catalog
(C) Call a different branch
(D) Search a system

62. 男子最有可能的職業為何？
(A) 電腦程式編制員
(B) 時裝設計師
(C) 銷售員
(D) 私人教練

63. 請據圖表作答。女子說喜歡哪家製造商？
(A) 格陵蘭迪亞有限公司
(B) 拉雨
(C) 齊走企業
(D) 山之北面

64. 男子提議幫忙做什麼？
(A) 提供優惠券
(B) 印出型錄
(C) 致電別間分店
(D) 搜尋系統資料

Questions 65-67 refer to the following conversation and price list.

M： Hey, Rebecca. **I know you wanted to order USB flash drives with your firm's name to distribute to everyone at your company's 30th anniversary dinner.** 65 Here are some samples and a price list of our products.

W： Thank you. **We don't have a big budget for the anniversary dinner, so I'll just go with the cheapest option.** 66

M： Of course. That's understandable.

W： But even this price is still more than we had expected. Do you think you could give us a discount?

M： **The prices listed here are for an order of at least 50 items. If you'd like to order more than 100 items, I can take 10 percent off the total.** 67 You could keep the remaining flash drives for a future occasion.

Custom USB Flash Drives	
1 GB Memory 66	**$5.25**
2 GB Memory	$5.75
4 GB Memory	$6.00
8 GB Memory	$6.50

65-67 會話和價目表

男： 瑞貝卡，您好。**我得知您想訂製印有貴公司大名的 USB 隨身碟，用來在公司 30 週年紀念晚宴上分送給大家。** 65 這邊提供您幾個樣品，以及我們產品的價目表。

女： 謝謝。**我們週年晚宴的預算不多，所以我就採用最便宜的選項。** 66

男： 當然行。這可以理解。

女： 但即便是這個價格，也還是超過我們的預期。您覺得可以給我們折扣嗎？

男： **這張清單上列的是訂購滿至少 50 件的價格。如果您欲訂購超過 100 件，我可以再提供總價 10% 的折扣。** 67 您可以將這次多餘的隨身碟留存，供之後其他場合使用。

訂製 USB 隨身碟	
1 GB 記憶體 66	**5.25 美元**
2 GB 記憶體	5.75 美元
4 GB 記憶體	6.00 美元
8 GB 記憶體	6.50 美元

65. What does the woman plan to do with the flash drives?
(A) Display them at a shop
(B) Send them to her friends
(C) Sell them to some clients
(D) Give them to event guests

65. 女子打算如何使用隨身碟？
(A) 在商店展示
(B) 寄送給朋友
(C) 賣給一些客戶
(D) 送給活動的賓客

66. Look at the graphic. Which memory capacity does the woman decide to choose?
(A) 1 GB
(B) 2 GB
(C) 4 GB
(D) 8 GB

66. 請據圖表作答。女子決定選擇哪個記憶體容量？
(A) 1 GB
(B) 2 GB
(C) 4 GB
(D) 8 GB

67. What does the man suggest?
(A) Calling another store
(B) Selecting a different product
(C) Adjusting the quantity of an order
(D) Revising a budget

67. 男子建議什麼？
(A) 致電另一家店
(B) 選擇別的產品
(C) 調整訂購數量
(D) 修改預算

Questions 68-70 refer to the following conversation and ferry schedule.

M：**According to the ferry schedule, Michelle Funakoshi is due to arrive about an hour late.** 68
W：I'm not surprised. The storm earlier caused several boats to slow down.
M：That means there's no rush to drive over to the port.
W：Actually, **Highway 702 is undergoing some emergency repairs. So we'll have to take side streets, meaning it will take longer to get to the port. Let's leave in the next five minutes.** 69
M：All right. **But there'll still be a bit of extra time before she arrives, so let's grab a coffee there.** 70

Arriving From	Time	Status
Dalian	2:30 P.M.	Arrived
Tianjin	2:55 P.M.	Arrived
Fukuoka	3:25 P.M.	On schedule
Vladivostok 68	**3:40 P.M.**	**Delayed**

68-70 會話和渡輪時間表

男：**根據渡輪班次時間表，「船越蜜雪號」預計會晚約一小時抵達。** 68
女：我並不意外。稍早的暴風雨讓很多船隻耽擱了。
男：也就是說，現在不用趕著開車去港口。
女：其實，**702 公路正在進行緊急維修。因此我們必須改走小路過去，這代表到港口的費時會更久。我們五分鐘後出發吧。** 69
男：好啊。**不過在她（渡輪）抵達前還會有一小段空檔，所以到時我們就在那裡喝杯咖啡吧。** 70

來自	時間	狀態
大連	下午 2:30	已抵達
天津	下午 2:55	已抵達
福岡	下午 3:25	準點
海參崴 68	**下午 3:40**	**誤點**

68. Look at the graphic. Which city is Michelle Funakoshi traveling from?
(A) Dalian
(B) Tianjin
(C) Fukuoka
(D) Vladivostok

68. 請據圖表作答。「船越蜜雪號」從哪座城市出發？
(A) 大連
(B) 天津
(C) 福岡
(D) 海參崴

69. According to the woman, why should the speakers leave soon?
(A) A highway is inaccessible.
(B) Tickets must be bought in advance.
(C) A store will be closing within the hour.
(D) The port is undergoing construction.

69. 據女子說法，說話者為何不久就應該要動身？
(A) 有條公路無法通行。
(B) 必須提前購買票券。
(C) 有家商店將在一小時內關閉。
(D) 港口目前有建設工程。

70. What does the man suggest doing while they wait?
(A) Going over a presentation
(B) Touring a facility
(C) Checking a map
(D) Getting a beverage

70. 男子建議等待時可以做什麼？
(A) 檢查簡報內容
(B) 參訪設施
(C) 查看地圖
(D) 喝杯飲料

PART 4 P. 87–89

Questions 71-73 refer to the following telephone message.

71-73 語音留言

M： Good morning, Hye-young. This is Adam Yardley from Marketing. **As you know, we're supposed to have a meeting tomorrow afternoon to discuss RXO Footwear's new advertising campaign. But unfortunately, we're going to have to move it to another day.** 71 **Some potential clients are visiting tomorrow, and management has asked me to give a presentation about our current projects.** 72 I understand that you had some interesting ideas, so **why don't you bring them up with Karen?** 73 She's involved in the campaign as much as I am.

男： 惠英早安。我是行銷部的亞當・雅德利。**如妳所知，我們應該要在明天下午開會討論 RXO 鞋廠的新廣告活動。但很不湊巧，我們得另外擇期開會了。** 71 **明天會有幾位潛在客戶來訪，而公司高層指派我針對我們目前的專案做個簡報。** 72 我了解妳有些有趣的點子，那麼**妳何不向凱倫提出來看看呢？** 73 她對這次廣告活動的參與度並不下於我。

71. Why is the speaker contacting the listener?
(A) To arrange a transportation service
(B) To check a client's schedule
(C) To postpone an appointment
(D) To discuss a job advertisement

71. 說話者為何聯絡聽者？
(A) 以安排交通服務
(B) 以查看客戶行程表
(C) 以延後約定行程
(D) 以討論徵才廣告

72. What is the speaker doing tomorrow afternoon?
(A) Filming a commercial
(B) Going on a business trip
(C) Holding a training session for new employees
(D) Sharing information about some projects

73. What does the speaker recommend that the listener do?
(A) Contact a business
(B) Book a larger conference room
(C) Speak to another coworker
(D) Register for a marketing class

Questions 74-76 refer to the following introduction.

W: As chairman of the Global Health Association, I would like to introduce Mr. Sawada. **Mr. Sawada has been a medical professional for over four decades.** 74 **He recently received an award for the creation of a software program** 75 that automatically arranges patient health records by category. This allows doctors and nurses to easily locate their patient's files at any time and helps to facilitate faster service. And **now, Mr. Sawada will give a demonstration** 76 on how the software works and go over its key features.

74. What industry does Mr. Sawada work in?
(A) Information Technology
(B) Healthcare
(C) Engineering
(D) Finance

75. What main accomplishment is Mr. Sawada recognized for?
(A) Making financial donations
(B) Improving work conditions
(C) Revising a national curriculum
(D) Developing a computer program

76. According to the speaker, what will Mr. Sawada do next?
(A) Provide a demonstration
(B) Tour a building
(C) Present an award
(D) Attend a book signing

72. 說話者明天下午會做什麼？
(A) 拍攝廣告
(B) 動身出差
(C) 舉辦新人培訓課程
(D) 分享幾項專案的資訊

73. 說話者建議聽者做什麼？
(A) 聯絡業者
(B) 預約較大的會議室
(C) 和另一個同事談談
(D) 報名行銷課程

74-76 開場白

女：作為全球衛生協會主席，我想向各位介紹澤田先生。**澤田先生是位執業超過 40 年的醫療專業人士。** 74 **最近他因打造出一款**能自動將病患病歷分門別類的**軟體程式而獲獎** 75 這程式能讓醫護人員輕易地隨時找到患者檔案，也加快了服務速度。那麼，**現在將由澤田先生示範** 76 這項軟體的用法，並介紹幾項主要功能。

74. 澤田先生在何種產業工作？
(A) 資訊科技
(B) 醫療保健
(C) 工程
(D) 財務金融

75. 澤田先生備受肯定的主要成就為何？
(A) 捐款
(B) 改善工作條件
(C) 修改國定課程
(D) 開發電腦程式

76. 據說話者說法。澤田先生接著會做什麼？
(A) 進行示範
(B) 導覽建築
(C) 頒獎
(D) 出席簽書會

Questions 77-79 refer to the following telephone message.

M： Hey, this is Chris. **I'm driving in for our meeting, but there seems to be a lot of construction on the highway. 77 I've forgotten whether or not I gave you the final copy of the proposal, but let me send it to you now so that you can begin the budget meeting. 78** And **we'll need Jeanell to draft the post-meeting summary.** 79 I'll let her know. **She's prepared that report before.** 79 OK, talk to you soon.

77. What does the speaker imply when he says, "there seems to be a lot of construction on the highway"?

(A) He is going to take public transportation.
(B) He wants to change a project location.
(C) He will arrive late to a meeting.
(D) He is unable to hear the listener's message.

78. What will the speaker send to the listener?

(A) A list of participants
(B) A proposal
(C) An invoice
(D) Directions to an office

79. What does the speaker want Jeanell to do?

(A) Prepare a report
(B) Contact a client
(C) Conduct some training
(D) Transfer some money

77-79 語音留言

男：嗨，我是克里斯。**我正開車趕往我們的會議，但看樣子公路上有很多路段在施工。77 我忘了我是不是有把最終版的提案書給你，不過我現在會寄給你，以便你們開始預算會議。78** 另外，**我們要請珍妮爾草擬會議紀要。**79 我會交代她。**她之前作過這類報告。**79 就這樣，待會見囉。

77. 說話者說：「看樣子公路上有很多路段在施工」，其暗示什麼？

(A) 他想搭公共運輸。
(B) 他想更換專案地點。
(C) 他會晚到會議。
(D) 他聽不見聽者的留言。

78. 說話者會寄給聽者什麼？

(A) 參與者名單
(B) 提案書
(C) 帳單
(D) 到辦公室的路線

79. 說話者要珍妮爾做什麼？

(A) 作成報告
(B) 聯絡客戶
(C) 執行訓練
(D) 轉出款項

Questions 80-82 refer to the following advertisement.

W： Do you record a lot of videos but don't know how to make them look professional? Then **what you need is Expert Movie Designer, the best software program** 80 for video editing and special effects. **Expert Movie Designer is the only video editing software that includes online tutorials, which allow users to easily learn how to edit their own videos.** 81 By following these step-by-step tutorials, you will be creating amazing material in no time.

80-82 廣告

女：您是不是錄了很多影片，卻不知如何賦予這些影片專業感呢？那麼**您需要的就是「專家影片設計師」，這款軟體程式** 80 是用來編輯影片、製成特效的**最佳首選。「專家影片設計師」是唯一內附線上教學的影片編輯軟體，讓使用者可以輕鬆學會編輯自己影片的方式。**81 跟著教學內容循序漸進，您很快就會創作出超棒的素材。還是對本

Still not convinced about our product? Then **check out what all of our satisfied customers have to say about our product at www.expertmoviedesigner.co.uk.** 82

產品半信半疑嗎？那就**請到 www.expertmoviedesigner.co.uk 查看本產品所有愛用消費者的心得評價。** 82

80. What product is being advertised?
(A) A software program
(B) A video recorder
(C) A mobile phone
(D) A laptop computer

81. What does the speaker say is special about the product?
(A) It has an extended warranty.
(B) It supports any language.
(C) It includes instructional material.
(D) It can be custom-made.

82. Why should listeners visit a Web site?
(A) To order a product
(B) To sign up for a lesson
(C) To download a user guide
(D) To read customer testimonials

80. 這是什麼產品的廣告？
(A) 軟體程式
(B) 錄影機
(C) 手機
(D) 筆電

81. 關於產品，說話者提到什麼特色？
(A) 有延長保固。
(B) 支援任何語言。
(C) 附有教學內容。
(D) 可以客製化。

82. 聽者為什麼要前往網站？
(A) 訂購產品
(B) 報名課程
(C) 下載使用指南
(D) 查看顧客評論

Questions 83-85 refer to the following excerpt from a meeting.

W：Everyone, please take a seat, so we can start. **I want to pick up from our last discussion regarding the plans for June's technology expo.** 83 It's been over three months since we started accepting requests for booth space, but we've received fewer than 100 applications. **I'm a little worried because we need to have a lot of booths to attract more attendees.** 84 **But just remember that the application deadline is at the end of the month.** OK, moving on . . . **I'm putting together a group** 85 to create a satisfaction questionnaire that will be sent to participants after the expo is over. **If you're interested in being a part of this team, please come see me once the meeting ends.** 85

83-85 會議摘錄

女：各位請就座，以便我們可以開始。**我想接續我們上一次有關六月科技展籌辦的討論。** 83 我們開始接受展場攤位申請後已經三個多月了，收到的申請件數卻不到 100 件。**我有點擔心，因為我們需要有很多展位以便吸引更多人到場。** 84 **但也請記得，申請截止日是在這個月底。** 好，接著是……**我正在籌組一個團隊** 85 來製作滿意度問卷調查表，要在展覽結束後寄發給參與者。**如果你有興趣加入這支團隊，請在會後就過來找我。** 85

83. Who most likely are the listeners?
(A) Job recruiters
(B) Event coordinators
(C) Financial advisors
(D) Local reporters

84. What does the speaker imply when she says, "the application deadline is at the end of the month"?
(A) She is planning to extend a deadline.
(B) She does not want the listeners to worry.
(C) Some guidelines need to be revised.
(D) Some fees have not been received.

85. Why should the listeners talk to the speaker after the meeting?
(A) To borrow some materials
(B) To submit a payment
(C) To join a project group
(D) To decide on some menu items

83. 聽者最有可能是什麼職業的人？
(A) 招聘人員
(B) 活動籌劃人員
(C) 理財顧問
(D) 地方記者

84. 說話者說：「申請截止日是在這個月底」，其用意為何？
(A) 她打算延長截止日。
(B) 她不想要聽者擔心。
(C) 有些準則需要修改。
(D) 有些費用尚未收到。

85. 會議結束後，聽者為何要和說話者交談？
(A) 以借用材料
(B) 以繳交費用
(C) 以加入專案小組
(D) 以選定菜單品項

Questions 86-88 refer to the following talk.

M: Good afternoon. I hope all of you are enjoying your first day at work. My name is Clay Bernard, and **I'm the trainer for all new IT personnel here at Rossmore Corporation.** 86 This afternoon, I will teach you how to use our company's database. I had planned on starting by showing you a video that gives an overview of the database, but **the projector seems to be out of order,** 87 so we'll have to wait until someone brings us a new one. **Meanwhile, since all of you need ID badges, I'll take you to the administration office now to get that taken care of.** 88 Hopefully, when we get back, we can get on with the training.

86-88 談話

男：午安。我希望大家進公司上班的第一天都過得很愉快。我的名字叫克萊．伯納德，**是羅斯莫爾企業所有新進資訊技術員的培訓講師。** 86 這個下午，我將教你們使用本公司的資料庫。我本來打算播放一段影片來大略介紹該資料庫，但**投影機似乎壞了，** 87 所以我們得等人拿台新的過來。**同時，由於各位都需要有識別證，我現在會帶你們到行政部門把此事辦理妥當。** 88 但願我們回來時，就可以繼續進行培訓。

86. Where most likely is the talk being given?
(A) At a training session
(B) At a company dinner
(C) At a job fair
(D) At a sales meeting

87. What does the speaker say is broken?
(A) A phone
(B) A speaker
(C) A camera
(D) A projector

86. 這談話最有可能是在哪裡進行的？
(A) 在培訓課程上
(B) 在公司晚宴上
(C) 在就業博覽會上
(D) 在業務會議上

87. 說話者說何物故障了？
(A) 電話
(B) 喇叭
(C) 相機
(D) 投影機

88. What will the listeners do next?
(A) Give a presentation
(B) Obtain identification badges
(C) Report to their managers
(D) Enter some data

88. 聽者接下來會做什麼？
(A) 做簡報
(B) 領取識別證件
(C) 向主管報告
(D) 輸入資料

Questions 89-91 refer to the following excerpt from a meeting.

89-91 會議摘錄

M：Welcome to the monthly branch managers meeting. I want to talk about our existing accounts. **Our acquisition of Dos Mundos will bring in a lot of new clients, but we won't have access to their information until all the details of the purchase are set.** 89 **Who can say how long that will take?** Meanwhile, **we need to generate more revenue by talking to current clients.** 90 I want each of you to create a plan for contacting your top customers and increasing the amount they are investing with us by at least 30 percent. Over the next few weeks, **I'll be making some time to discuss the plans with each branch manager individually.** 91

男：歡迎來到各分公司經理的每月例會，在此我想談談我們現有的客戶事宜。**我們收購「雙世界」後將會引進許多新客戶，但我們得等到所有收購細節談妥後，才能得到對方的資訊。**89 **誰知道這要多久時間？**與此同時，**我們必須和現有客戶持續接洽，以期提升收益。**90 我想要請各位都制定一項計劃，藉此聯絡你們的頂級客戶群，並讓他們給我們的投資額增加至少三成。在接下來的幾個星期裡，**我會抽出一些時間和每一位分公司經理個別討論計畫。**91

89. What does the man imply when he says, "Who can say how long that will take"?
(A) He wants the exact completion date of a project.
(B) He is requesting suggestions from the listeners.
(C) He would like staff members to work more hours.
(D) He does not know when a merger will be finalized.

89. 男子說：「誰知道這要多久時間」，言下之意為何？
(A) 他想知道專案完成的確切日期。
(B) 他正在徵詢聽者的建議。
(C) 他想要員工增加工作時數。
(D) 他不知道併購案何時落定。

90. What is the subject of the meeting?
(A) Expanding a product line
(B) Opening a new store
(C) Increasing profits
(D) Finding a different supplier

90. 會議的主題為何？
(A) 擴大產品線
(B) 開設新店面
(C) 增加利潤
(D) 尋找別的供應商

91. What does the man say he will make some time to do?
(A) Visit various branches
(B) Conduct individual meetings
(C) Revise some legal documents
(D) Contact a Dos Mundos employee

91. 男子說他會抽出時間做什麼？
(A) 訪視各分公司
(B) 舉行個別會議
(C) 修改部分法律文件
(D) 聯絡「雙世界」的員工

Questions 92-94 refer to the following news report.

W：Let's move on to the local news. **Yesterday, Kaufman County Board members authorized the construction of new apartment buildings on Peakview Road.** 92 The project will start this March and is scheduled to be completed by next fall. **The location's biggest advantage is that it is right across the street from the community recreation center. Tenants who wish to exercise at the center need only walk a few minutes.** 93 **Listeners are encouraged to check the Kaufman County's Web site to download floor plans of the buildings.** 94 Units will be available for rent or to buy.

92-94 新聞報導

女：接著關心地方新聞。**考夫曼郡議會的議員們昨日批准了巔景路上的一項新公寓大樓建設案。** 92 該建案將於今年三月動工，預計明年秋天完工。**該地點的最大優點就是坐落於社區休閒中心的正對面。想要到中心做運動的住戶，只需走短短幾分鐘路程。** 93 **歡迎各位聽眾前往考夫曼郡官網查看，以便下載公寓大樓的樓層平面圖。** 94 公寓物件將可供租用或購買。

92. What was recently authorized?
(A) The construction of some residential buildings
(B) The opening of a community library
(C) The extension of some subway lines
(D) The restoration of a historic museum

92. 最近批准了什麼項目？
(A) 幾棟住宅大樓的建案
(B) 社區圖書館的啟用
(C) 幾條地鐵路線的擴建
(D) 歷史悠久的博物館修復作業

93. According to the speaker, what is an advantage of a location?
(A) The area is quiet.
(B) A fitness facility is nearby.
(C) There are many parking spaces.
(D) The scenery is beautiful.

93. 據說話者說法，地點的優勢為何？
(A) 該區很安靜。
(B) 附近有運動設施。
(C) 有很多停車位。
(D) 風景很美。

94. Why are listeners encouraged to visit a Web site?
(A) To sign up for a membership
(B) To watch a video
(C) To fill out a survey
(D) To download some files

94. 為什麼鼓勵聽者訪問官網？
(A) 以註冊會員
(B) 以觀看影片
(C) 以填寫問卷
(D) 以下載幾筆檔案

Questions 95-97 refer to the following telephone message and chart.

M：Hi, this is Steve from Roland's Baked Goods. **I'm calling about the revolving ovens you sold us a few months ago.** 95 This equipment is fantastic, and it's made a huge difference for our business. **Since we installed the machinery, the production of one of our baked goods**

95-97 語音留言和長條圖

男：您好，我是「羅蘭烘焙食品鋪」的史蒂夫。**我這次來電是想洽詢幾個月前您賣給我們的旋轉式烤箱。** 95 這項設備非常好用，讓本店的生意發生巨大的改變。**自從設置該款機器以來，我們其中一項烘焙產品的**

has gone up by 40 percent. 96 As a result, I was hoping we could purchase ovens for other branches. **I'd like to start with the one in Sussex, since at the end of the month it will be getting remodeled.** 97 Please call me back when you get a chance.

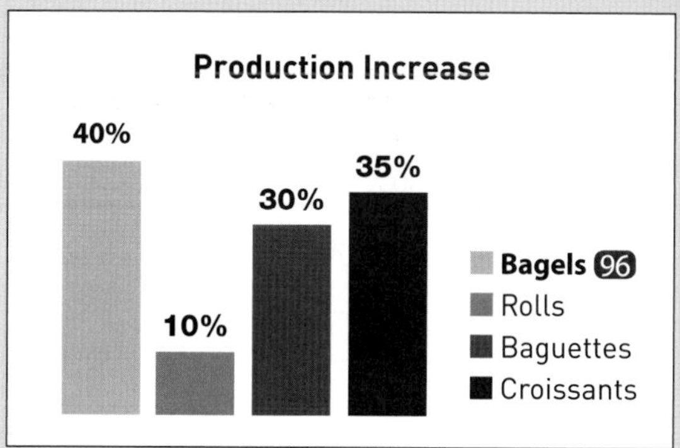

95. Who is the message for?
(A) A bakery manager
(B) A warehouse supervisor
(C) A machinery salesperson
(D) A food importer

96. Look at the graphic. Which product's production does the speaker mention?
(A) Bagels
(B) Rolls
(C) Baguettes
(D) Croissants

97. What will happen at the end of the month?
(A) A building renovation will start.
(B) New products will be offered.
(C) A special offer will expire.
(D) A demonstration will be given.

Questions 98-100 refer to the following excerpt from a meeting and label.

W: Hello, **I called all of you here because I wanted to go over the first month's sales figures for our new Powercharge energy bar.** 98 Unfortunately, we were not able to meet our sales goal due to many customer complaints. **According to Wally Cruz, the owner of**

產量成長了 40%。 96 因此，我希望能採購烤箱供其他分店使用。**我想先從薩克斯郡的分店開始，因為該店在本月底將進行整修。** 97 您方便時，麻煩回電給我。

產量增幅
40%
10%
30%
35%
焙果 96
蛋糕捲
長棍麵包
可頌

95. 這則語音留言的對象是誰？
(A) 麵包店經理
(B) 倉庫主管
(C) 機器設備銷售員
(D) 食品進口商

96. 請據圖表作答。說話者提及何項產品的生產情形？
(A) 焙果
(B) 蛋糕捲
(C) 長棍麵包
(D) 可頌

97. 本月底將會發生什麼事？
(A) 有間建物將開始整修。
(B) 新產品將開賣。
(C) 特價將截止。
(D) 有場展示會將舉行。

98-100 會議摘錄和標示

女：哈囉，**我召集大家前來的原因，是想要仔細檢討我們的新產品「動力補給能量棒」首月的銷售數據。** 98 遺憾的是，由於許多消費者投訴，我們無法達成銷售目標。**根據「鮮好貨」老闆瓦利．克魯茲的說法，**

Fresh and Good, many of his supermarket's customers have expressed concern with the first ingredient—there are more than 200 milligrams, and that's quite a lot. 99 100 So I'll talk to the operations manager in charge of our manufacturing plant to see if they can adjust the bar's ingredients for the next batch. 100

在他的超市有不少顧客對於第一項成分表達擔憂：該項含量超過 200 毫克，實在是相當多。99 100 因此，我會和負責製造廠的營運主管討論，看看他們能否調整下一批能量棒的成分。100

Nutrition Facts

Serving size - 1 Bar	
Calories 180	
Sodium 100 - 210mg	
Fiber - 8g	
Sugar - 25g	
Potassium - 150mg	

營養標示

份量：一條	
熱量：180大卡	
鈉 100 —210毫克	
纖維質—8克	
糖—25克	
鉀—150毫克	

98. What is the main purpose of the meeting?
(A) To introduce a new employee
(B) To discuss the sales of a product
(C) To announce the building of a new plant
(D) To describe a manufacturing process

98. 該會議的主要目的為何？
(A) 以介紹新員工
(B) 以討論一項產品的銷售
(C) 以宣布興建新工廠
(D) 以述說製造過程

99. What type of business is Fresh and Good?
(A) A grocery store
(B) A restaurant
(C) A local farm
(D) A food manufacturer

99. 「鮮好貨」是什麼類型的企業？
(A) 雜貨店
(B) 餐廳
(C) 當地農場
(D) 食品製造商

100. Look at the graphic. Which of the ingredients does the speaker say needs to be reduced?
(A) Sodium
(B) Fiber
(C) Sugar
(D) Potassium

100. 請據圖表作答。說話者說需要減少哪種成分？
(A) 鈉
(B) 纖維質
(C) 糖
(D) 鉀

ACTUAL TEST 7

PART 1 P. 90–93

1. (A) He's shutting a garage door.
(B) He's mowing the lawn.
(C) He's handling a ladder.
(D) He's entering an office building.

1. (A) 他正把車庫門關上。
(B) 他正在修剪草坪。
(C) 他正在搬運梯子。
(D) 他正進入辦公大樓。

2. (A) She's looking into a display case.
(B) She's paying for an item.
(C) She's opening a jar.
(D) She's examining a product.

2. (A) 她正看向展示櫃。
(B) 她正為商品付款。
(C) 她正在打開罐子。
(D) 她正在查看產品。

3. (A) Some papers are laid on the floor.
(B) Some workers are painting a table.
(C) A man is pointing at a laptop.
(D) A woman is holding a drinking glass.

3. (A) 一些文件攤放在地板上。
(B) 有些員工正在粉刷桌子。
(C) 男子指著筆記型電腦。
(D) 女子正拿著飲料杯。

4. (A) A passenger is getting out of a car.
(B) A tree is being planted.
(C) A vehicle is being sprayed with water.
(D) A man is rolling up a hose.

4. (A) 有位乘客正在下車。
(B) 有人正在種植樹木。
(C) 有人正在向車輛噴水。
(D) 男子正把水管捲起。

5. (A) A truck is being towed away.
(B) A bike is mounted on the bus.
(C) People are entering a store.
(D) Some signs are being installed on a wall.

5. (A) 卡車正遭到拖吊。
(B) 腳踏車固定在公車上。
(C) 人們正走進商店。
(D) 牆上正在裝設幾個標誌。

6. (A) A customer is putting produce into a basket.
(B) Cartons of fruit are being delivered to a warehouse.
(C) Shopkeepers are setting up a canopy.
(D) An awning is shading some merchandise.

6. (A) 客人正將農產品放進籃子。
(B) 幾箱水果正被送往倉庫。
(C) 店主們正在架設遮陽篷。
(D) 篷子的陰影遮住一些商品。

PART 2 P. 94

28

7. Where should I store these tablecloths for the charity banquet?
(A) Not everyone can make it.
(B) In the supply closet over there.
(C) Some grilled chicken and vegetables.

7. 我該把這些慈善餐會用的桌布收到哪裡？
(A) 不是每個人都辦得到／能準時到。
(B) 那邊的用品儲藏室裡。
(C) 一些烤雞和蔬菜。

8. When should I drop off my car?
(A) You dropped it on the floor.
(B) Sometime after 3 P.M.
(C) At the car park.

9. Who has been chosen to give the opening speech at the workshop?
(A) They'll announce that today.
(B) In Conference Room 1A.
(C) It starts at 11.

10. Why don't we try to call Ms. Cruz again in about an hour?
(A) Around this time last month.
(B) Because it wasn't there.
(C) Yes, she should be back by then.

11. Won't you be at the merger negotiation next Monday?
(A) An important decision.
(B) No, I'll be away on business all week.
(C) My major was in Psychology.

12. Why isn't my laptop starting?
(A) Is the battery charged?
(B) In a few seconds.
(C) Through the Web site.

13. How did you assemble this cabinet?
(A) Much longer than I thought.
(B) To organize our files.
(C) I just followed the instructions.

14. This tape dispenser is Alice's, isn't it?
(A) Yes, you should give it back to her.
(B) In the supply cabinet.
(C) Would you be able to do that?

15. Could you update this employee list?
(A) Kim, Sun-Hee, and Mark.
(B) I'll find some time today.
(C) The software update.

16. When will the production of the new model be finished?
(A) Fashion models in magazines.
(B) Let's see the final product.
(C) Not before November.

8. 我應該何時交還車輛？
(A) 你放地板上就好。
(B) 下午三點以後。
(C) 在停車場。

9. 誰獲選在這次研習上做開幕致詞？
(A) 他們今天會宣布。
(B) 在 1A 會議室。
(C) 11 點開始。

10. 我們何不約一小時後再打給克魯茲女士呢？
(A) 上個月的大概這個時間。
(B) 因為它不在那邊。
(C) 好，到時她應該回來了。

11. 下週一的合併協商你不會到場嗎？
(A) 一項重要決定。
(B) 不會，我一整週都要出差。
(C) 我主修心理學。

12. 為什麼我的筆電無法啟動？
(A) 電池有充電嗎？
(B) 幾秒鐘後。
(C) 透過網站。

13. 你是如何組裝這個櫃子的？
(A) 比我預期的更久。
(B) 為了整理我們的文件。
(C) 我就是按照說明書。

14. 這個膠帶台是愛麗絲的，不是嗎？
(A) 是的，你應該要還給她。
(B) 在辦公用品櫃中。
(C) 你能做到嗎？

15. 你可以更新這份員工名單嗎？
(A) 金、善熙和馬克。
(B) 我今天會找時間。
(C) 軟體更新。

16. 新型號的產製何時會完成？
(A) 雜誌裡的時裝模特。
(B) 讓我們來看看最後的成品吧。
(C) 最快 11 月。

17. Where can I get a copy of the presentation?
(A) There's coffee in the break room.
(B) Did you check your email?
(C) Tomorrow morning at 11.

18. Can the packages be shipped now, or do they need to be labeled?
(A) I'm making the labels right now.
(B) I picked them up this morning.
(C) No, I am not taking my car.

19. How did you enjoy your dessert?
(A) Just a slice of chocolate cake.
(B) It was delicious. Thanks for recommending it.
(C) Yes, to share with my friend.

20. Did it seem like there were more attendees this year than before?
(A) This was my first time participating in the conference.
(B) It's going to be held this Friday.
(C) I already emailed you the guest list.

21. Where did Mr. Kim work when he first joined the firm?
(A) There is one across the street.
(B) In the Accounting Department.
(C) More than 10 years ago.

22. Isn't Nisha Rowshan the most qualified applicant?
(A) No, she's new to this field.
(B) Several openings on the sales team.
(C) An impressive résumé.

23. Should I send out the invitation to everyone or just the new employees?
(A) Business strategies for next year.
(B) Anytime before noon.
(C) We only have a few seats available.

24. Can I show you my report before the meeting starts?
(A) Your presentation was great.
(B) Sure, but we don't have much time.
(C) I'll meet you at 1 o'clock.

17. 我在哪裡可以拿到簡報副本？
(A) 休息室裡有咖啡。
(B) 你檢查過你的電子郵件信箱了嗎？
(C) 明天早上 11 點。

18. 包裏現在可以出貨嗎，還是須貼上標籤？
(A) 我正在製作標籤。
(B) 我今天早上去取的。
(C) 不，我不會開我的車。

19. 你的甜點口味如何？
(A) 就一片巧克力蛋糕。
(B) 好吃。謝謝推薦。
(C) 對，要和我朋友分享。

20. 今年的參加人數看起來有比以前的多嗎？
(A) 這是我第一次參加這個會議。
(B) 將會在本週五舉行。
(C) 我已把賓客名單電郵給你了。

21. 金先生剛進公司時在哪個部門工作？
(A) 馬路對面有一家／個。
(B) 在會計部。
(C) 十多年前。

22. 妮莎．羅珊不是最適合的應徵者嗎？
(A) 不，她不太熟悉這個領域。
(B) 業務團隊的幾個職缺。
(C) 令人印象深刻的履歷。

23. 我應該寄邀請函給所有人，還是只給新進員工？
(A) 明年的經營策略。
(B) 中午前的時間都行。
(C) 我們只剩幾個座位了。

24. 會議開始前，我能給你看一下我的報告嗎？
(A) 你的簡報很棒。
(B) 當然好，但我們時間不太多。
(C) 我一點會跟你見面。

25. Scott wants us to attend a meeting with the publishing team this afternoon.

(A) I have to visit a client today.

(B) I bought that book, too.

(C) Yes, it's a sample issue.

26. We have a guest performer at the anniversary event, don't we?

(A) I'd love to go to the concert.

(B) We were founded 30 years ago.

(C) Yes, she's right over there.

27. The technician said the new computers will be installed tomorrow.

(A) That's when our project is due.

(B) An increase in storage capacity.

(C) The computer lab is over here.

28. Did you read the email about the updated safety guidelines?

(A) I'll lead the meeting.

(B) No. When did we get it?

(C) It's a temporary password.

29. Will you send this invoice to Ms. Jensen?

(A) I'll do it right away.

(B) A shipping company.

(C) No, it didn't.

30. Have you read what the food critics said about that restaurant?

(A) Well, we could eat somewhere else.

(B) A reservation for four at noon.

(C) I'll read the menu to you.

31. Can you contact the marketing team and give them an update?

(A) Isn't that the newer model?

(B) It arrived a month late.

(C) I have a meeting with them at 1.

25. 史考特要我們今天下午和出版團隊開會。

(A) 我今天得去拜訪客戶。

(B) 我也買了那本書。

(C) 對，它是樣刊。

26. 週年紀念活動會有表演嘉賓，不是嗎？

(A) 我很想去聽音樂會。

(B) 我們（公司）是 30 年前成立的。

(C) 對，她就在那裡。

27. 技術人員說，新電腦明天會裝好。

(A) 那天是我們專案的截止日。

(B) 儲存容量增加。

(C) 電腦實驗室在這裡。

28. 你看了有關更新版安全準則的電子郵件了嗎？

(A) 我會主持會議。

(B) 沒有。我們何時收到的？

(C) 這是臨時密碼。

29. 你能把這份帳單寄給詹森女士嗎？

(A) 我馬上辦。

(B) 一家航運公司。

(C) 不，它不是。

30. 你有看過美食評論家對那家餐廳的評論嗎？

(A) 那我們可以去別處吃飯。

(B) 中午預約四位。

(C) 我把菜單念給你聽。

31. 你能聯絡行銷團隊，告訴他們最新的情況嗎？

(A) 那不是較新的型號嗎？

(B) 晚了一個月才到。

(C) 我一點要跟他們開會。

Questions 32-34 refer to the following conversation.

M：Hi, Giselle. **Some important packages are arriving at my home tomorrow morning, and I really have to be there to receive them. Do you think I could work from home?** 32

W：Sure, but how is the renovation budget you've been working on for the new recreation center coming along? The project's deadline is getting closer, and **I'm worried that we might be late sending in our work.** 33

M：I'm almost done with it. I can send you the final draft by tomorrow morning.

W：OK, as long as **the budget is finished by tomorrow, we should be fine. The proposal won't be presented to our clients until late next week.** 34

32-34 會話

男：嗨，吉賽爾。**明天早上會有幾個重要的包裹送到我家，到時我真的得在家收貨。妳覺得我可以在家工作嗎？** 32

女：當然可以，但你手邊進行中的新休閒中心整修預算案，不知進展得如何？專案截止日期步步逼近，而**我擔心我們可能無法如期交出我們的案子。** 33

男：我快完成了。我明早之前可以將最終版草案傳給妳。

女：好，只要**明天之前做完預算，我們應該就沒問題。這個提案要到下週後半才會提交給我們的客戶。** 34

32. What would the man like to do tomorrow?
(A) Leave the office early
(B) Speak to a client
(C) Work from home
(D) Make a presentation

32. 男子明天想做什麼？
(A) 早點下班
(B) 與客戶洽談
(C) 在家工作
(D) 進行簡報

33. What is the woman concerned about?
(A) Losing customers
(B) Submitting work late
(C) Holding a conference
(D) Finding some paperwork

33. 女子擔憂何事？
(A) 失去客戶
(B) 工作案遲交
(C) 舉辦會議
(D) 找尋文件

34. What does the woman say will happen next week?
(A) A business will open.
(B) A proposal will be given.
(C) A machine will be installed.
(D) A new employee will be hired.

34. 女子說下週會發生何事？
(A) 有業者將開業。
(B) 將交出提案。
(C) 將安裝機器。
(D) 將僱用新員工。

Questions 35-37 refer to the following conversation.

M：Excuse me. **Do you have any travel guides for tourists?** 35 You know, brochures that contain information about local attractions. **Most hotels usually have them.** 35

35-37 會話

男：不好意思。**你們有觀光客用的旅遊指南嗎？** 35 妳應該懂，就是寫有當地景點資訊的那種小手冊。**大多數的飯店通常都有提供。** 35

W：Oh yes. I know what you're talking about. There should be some in your room.
M：Are you sure? All I saw was a telephone directory. Anyway, **I'm looking for a bus tour company. I heard that there is one in the area. Can you tell me where it is? 36**
W：Sure. There's a business called Gem Sightseeing a few kilometers away from here. **I'll call their office and ask when their tours are scheduled for. 37**

女：喔，有的。我明白您的意思。您的房間裡應該有幾本。
男：妳確定嗎？我只有看到電話簿。算了，**我現在正在找一家觀光巴士公司。聽說這附近有一間。能請妳告訴我位置嗎？36**
女：當然可以。距離飯店幾公里處有一家名為「寶石觀光」的業者。**我會打電話到他們辦公室，詢問他們行程的時間安排。37**

35. What most likely is the woman's job?
(A) Travel agent
(B) Bus driver
(C) Telephone operator
(D) Hotel clerk

36. What does the man ask the woman to do?
(A) Direct him to a tour company
(B) Make a lunch reservation for him
(C) Take a message for him
(D) Move him to a larger room

37. What does the woman offer to do?
(A) Arrange transportation
(B) Ask for directions
(C) Purchase a ticket
(D) Inquire about a schedule

35. 女子的職業最有可能為何？
(A) 旅行社人員
(B) 巴士駕駛
(C) 接線生
(D) 飯店服務員

36. 男子要求女子做什麼？
(A) 指引他到旅遊公司
(B) 為他預訂午餐
(C) 幫他接收留言
(D) 將他換到更大的房間

37. 女子提議幫忙做什麼？
(A) 安排交通
(B) 問路
(C) 購票
(D) 詢問行程安排

Questions 38-40 refer to the following conversation.

M：Thank you for calling Wally's Computer Store. How may I assist you?
W：Hello, I own a small graphic design agency, and two of our printers broke down. **Are you able to repair printers? 38**
M：Yes, we'd be glad to fix them. Just come by today, and we'll have them ready for you by this Friday.
W：Hmm . . . **I'll be out of town meeting a client on Friday, 39** so I can't visit then. Is it OK if I drop by on Saturday to pick them up?
M：That's fine.
W：You're located at 1500 James Avenue, right?
M：Yes. **Just remember to come before 4 P.M. 40** We close early on weekends.

38-40 會話

男：感謝您來電「瓦力電腦行」。有什麼我能協助您的嗎？
女：你好，我經營一家小型平面設計公司，而我們有兩台印表機壞了。**你們有辦法修理印表機嗎？38**
男：可以，我們很樂意維修它們。只要您今天過來，我們本週五前就能為您把它們修好。
女：嗯……**我週五將到外地去會見客戶，39** 所以我到時沒辦法過去。我星期六再過去領回的話方便嗎？
男：沒問題的。
女：你們在詹姆斯大道 1500 號，對嗎？
男：對。**但請記得在下午四點前過來。40** 我們週末比較早關門。

38. What would the woman like the man to do?
(A) Give a demonstration
(B) Revise some designs
(C) Fix some machines
(D) Visit an office

38. 女子想要男子做什麼？
(A) 進行示範
(B) 修改設計
(C) 修理機器
(D) 造訪辦公室

39. Why is the woman unavailable on Friday?
(A) She will be meeting her parents.
(B) She will be on a business trip.
(C) She will be getting a medical check-up.
(D) She will be leaving on vacation.

39. 女子週五為何沒空？
(A) 她要和父母見面。
(B) 她將出差。
(C) 她要做健檢。
(D) 她將放假出遊。

40. What does the man remind the woman to do?
(A) Print out a map
(B) Review an invoice
(C) Arrive before a certain time
(D) Talk to a store manager

40. 男子提醒女子做什麼？
(A) 印出地圖
(B) 檢查帳單
(C) 在特定時間前抵達
(D) 和店經理談談

Questions 41-43 refer to the following conversation.

41-43 會話

M：Ms. Reynolds. All the tables are set up, and the restaurant is ready to open at 9 o'clock. Would you like me to take care of anything else?
W：Actually, yes. I got a call from the city's Maintenance Department yesterday, and they said **a crew will be coming today to repair the sidewalk** 41 right outside our restaurant. Customers might think we're closed because of the work, and **I'm worried that we may lose business.** 42
M：Well, **I'll put out a sign** 43 to let customers know we're open for business, and that they should use the side door to come in.

男：雷諾茲女士。座席都備妥了，餐廳已做好九點開門的準備。您還有其他事項需要我處理的嗎？
女：其實還有一事。我昨天接到市政府養護工程部的電話，他們說**今天會有工作人員來維修**我們餐廳外面的**人行道。** 41 因為施工的關係，客人可能會以為我們沒開店，**我擔心我們生意可能會流失。** 42
男：好，**我會擺出告示，** 43 讓客人知道我們有營業，而他們應該要從側門進入。

41. What does the woman say will happen today?
(A) Kitchen appliances will be installed.
(B) A corporate event will take place.
(C) Repair work will begin.
(D) A plant inspection will be performed.

41. 女子說今天會發生何事？
(A) 將安裝廚房電器。
(B) 將舉行企業活動。
(C) 維修工程將開始。
(D) 將進行工廠檢查。

42. What is the woman worried about?
(A) Losing customers
(B) Spending more money
(C) Delayed shipments
(D) Power outages

42. 女子擔心什麼？
(A) 流失顧客
(B) 花費增加
(C) 貨運延遲
(D) 停電

TEST 7
PART 3
29

43. What does the man offer to do?
(A) Contact some customers
(B) Work additional hours
(C) Order some supplies
(D) Display a sign

43. 男子提議幫忙做什麼？
(A) 聯絡客人
(B) 加班
(C) 訂購用品
(D) 擺出告示

Questions 44-46 refer to the following conversation with three speakers.

44-46 三人會話

W1：OK, I think we've covered everything about the 20-year anniversary party. I think it's going to be the best one yet.
M：I agree. **Donna, you really have done well planning the event so far. I'm excited about taking over for you.** 44
W1：Donna, can you think of anything else Jay should be aware of?
W2：Actually, yes. **Remember that we have very strict rules about entertainment expenses. So please be sure to watch spending and make sure that we don't go over budget.** 45
M：Understood. And Donna, congratulations again on your promotion!
W2：Thank you. **I can't wait to travel abroad and meet all of our foreign clients face-to-face!** 46

女 1：好，我覺得這次 20 週年派對的相關事項都準備得面面俱到了。我覺得這會是最精彩的一場。
男：我同意。**唐娜，妳這次活動籌劃到現在，真的辦得很出色。我很高興能接替妳的工作。** 44
女 1：唐娜，妳還能想到什麼要傑伊留意的嗎？
女 2：其實還有。**要記得，我們公司對娛樂開銷有非常嚴格的規定。所以請務必要注意支出，確保我們不會超出預算。** 45
男：了解。那麼，唐娜，再次恭喜妳晉升！
女 2：謝謝。**我等不及要出國出差，親身和我們所有的外國客戶相見！** 46

44. What is the main topic of the conversation?
(A) Arranging travel accommodations
(B) Changing an event coordinator
(C) Planning a musical performance
(D) Selecting a better venue

44. 對話的主題為何？
(A) 安排旅行住宿
(B) 變更活動統籌者
(C) 策劃音樂表演
(D) 選擇更好的場地

45. What does Donna instruct the man to do?
(A) Meet with some clients
(B) Conduct some research
(C) Monitor a budget
(D) Review a floor plan

45. 唐娜指示男子做什麼？
(A) 會見客戶
(B) 執行研究
(C) 控管預算
(D) 審查樓層平面圖

46. What does Donna say she looks forward to?
(A) Going on international business trips
(B) Managing a new team
(C) Working on a promotional campaign
(D) Receiving an award

46. 唐娜說她期待什麼？
(A) 出國出差
(B) 管理新團隊
(C) 辦理促銷活動
(D) 獲獎

Questions 47-49 refer to the following conversation.

M：**Welcome to Stanson Insurance. Do you have an appointment with one of our agents?** 47

W：Actually, **I'm with NCB Courier, and I have a package for Ms. Dorsett.** 48

M：OK. **You can just leave it with me, and I'll make sure it gets to her.** 47

W：Sorry, but **Ms. Dorsett has to be the one to receive this package directly.** 49

M：Well, **Ms. Dorsett has just stepped out for lunch.**

W：All right. I'll be back later in the afternoon then.

47-49 會話

男：**歡迎光臨斯坦森保險。您和我們的專員有約嗎？** 47

女：其實**我是 NCB 快遞的人，我有包裹要交給多塞特女士。** 48

男：好的。**您把它交給我就可以了，我會確實轉交給她的。** 47

女：抱歉，但**這個包裹必須要多塞特女士本人親自收取。** 49

男：這樣啊，**多塞特女士才剛離開去吃午餐。**

女：好的。那我下午晚點再來。

47. Who most likely is the man?
(A) An insurance agent
(B) A receptionist
(C) A cleaning worker
(D) A technician

48. Why did the woman visit the office?
(A) To make a delivery
(B) To complete an application
(C) To submit a payment
(D) To visit a colleague

49. What does the man mean when he says, "Ms. Dorsett has just stepped out for lunch"?
(A) He will order some lunch.
(B) Ms. Dorsett is unavailable.
(C) Ms. Dorsett forgot about an appointment.
(D) A meeting must be postponed.

47. 男子最有可能的職業為何？
(A) 保險專員
(B) 接待員
(C) 清潔工
(D) 技術員

48. 女子為什麼造訪該辦公室？
(A) 為了送貨
(B) 為了完成申請
(C) 為了繳交款項
(D) 為了拜訪同事

49. 男子說：「多塞特女士才剛離開去吃午餐」，其意思為何？
(A) 他會訂購午餐。
(B) 多塞特女士不在。
(C) 多塞特女士忘記有約了。
(D) 會議必須延後。

Questions 50-52 refer to the following conversation.

M：Good evening, Ms. Decker. **I'm sorry for not responding to the voicemail message you left me** 50 yesterday. I'm just getting ready to return from my business trip to Milan. You said that you wanted to discuss the marketing campaign for the Roscar Corporation.

50-52 會話

男：午安，德克女士。**我很抱歉沒能回覆妳昨天留給我的語音留言。** 50 我正準備要從米蘭出差回來。妳之前提到，妳想討論「羅斯卡企業」的行銷活動。

W：Yes. **Roscar will be sending their representatives to our company on Tuesday to talk about the campaign. And I have told Bomin to create a presentation for them.** 51 But she needs your video files.

M：Oh, I thought I had already given them to her. I'll send them to her once I get into the office tomorrow morning.

W：You know, **I think it might be better if the two of you worked together on the presentation.** 52 The Roscar Corporation is a very important client, so we must impress them on Tuesday.

女：是的。**週二羅斯卡方面會派代表到我們公司討論該項活動。我已經交代普閔要為他們製作簡報。** 51 但她需要你的影片檔。

男：噢，我以為已經給過她了。我明天早上一到辦公室就會把東西寄給她。

女：話說回來，**我認為如果你們兩位能一起製作簡報會比較妥當。** 52 羅斯卡企業是很重要的客戶，所以我們週二必須讓他們刮目相看。

50. Why does the man apologize to the woman?

(A) He did not respond to a telephone message.
(B) He is not able to complete a project on time.
(C) He will be late for a meeting.
(D) He submitted the wrong document.

50. 男子為何向女子道歉？

(A) 他沒有回覆語音留言。
(B) 他無法準時完成專案。
(C) 他開會將遲到。
(D) 他交了錯誤的文件。

51. What must be ready by Tuesday?

(A) An employee questionnaire
(B) An expense report
(C) A client presentation
(D) A flight itinerary

51. 週二前必須準備好什麼？

(A) 員工問卷
(B) 開支報告
(C) 給客戶的簡報
(D) 航班行程

52. What does the woman request that the man do?

(A) Pick up a customer
(B) Collaborate with a colleague
(C) Reserve a meeting room
(D) Hire a consultant

52. 女子要求男子做什麼？

(A) 接客戶
(B) 與同事合作
(C) 預約會議室
(D) 聘請顧問

Questions 53-55 refer to the following conversation.

M：Hi. I have a morning membership here at the swimming pool, but can I come in the evening sometimes?

W：May I ask why?

M：**I just changed jobs,** 53 so I won't have time to come to the pool in the morning on certain days.

W：Well, we normally don't allow that. But **I suppose we could make an exception depending on which days of the week they'll be.** 54

M：**They'll be Tuesdays and Thursdays. So it'll only be twice a week.** 54

53-55 會話

男：您好。我是這間游泳池的晨間會員，但我可以偶爾在晚上入場嗎？

女：方便請教原因嗎？

男：**我剛換工作，** 53 所以有幾天早上沒時間來游泳池。

女：嗯，我們一般來說不會許可。但**我想取決於您是要星期幾過來，我們可能可以例外處理。** 54

男：**會是星期二、四。所以一週只會有兩次。** 54

W：**I think that should be OK.** It doesn't get too crowded on those evenings.
M：Thank you. I appreciate it.
W：**If you give me your membership number, I'll make a note of it in your file.** 55

女：**那我想應該沒問題。**這兩天晚間不會太多人。
男：謝謝。非常感謝。
女：**麻煩給我您的會員號碼，我會在您的檔案資料上做個註記。**55

53. What did the man recently do?
(A) He returned from his vacation.
(B) He moved to a new city.
(C) He purchased swimming gear.
(D) He started working at a new company.

53. 男子最近做了什麼？
(A) 他度假完回來。
(B) 他搬到新的城市。
(C) 他買了游泳裝備。
(D) 他開始在新的公司上班。

54. What does the woman mean when she says, "I think that should be OK"?
(A) A membership fee will be discounted.
(B) A schedule can be adjusted.
(C) The man can pay by credit card.
(D) The man will be able to upgrade his service.

54. 女子說：「那我想應該沒問題」，其意思為何？
(A) 會員費將會打折。
(B) 時程可以調整。
(C) 男子可用信用卡付款。
(D) 男子的服務將能升級。

55. What will the man probably do next?
(A) Email the woman a file
(B) Sign up for some classes
(C) Provide some information
(D) Look around a facility

55. 男子接下來可能會做什麼？
(A) 把檔案用電郵寄給女子
(B) 報名幾堂課
(C) 提供一些資訊
(D) 參觀設施

Questions 56-58 refer to the following conversation with three speakers.

W ：**I called this meeting so that we can discuss where we're going to stay when we travel to Tokyo for the conference.** 56
M1：**What about the hotel in Shibuya we reserved last year?** 57
W ：**That place ended up putting us over the budget,** 57 so we have to find another location this year.
M1：Well, there's this inn called Jiro's House that provides affordable rates, even during the peak seasons. I've stayed there a few times, and they offer great amenities and spacious rooms.
W ：OK. Michael, as you're responsible for our team's finances, **can you please find out more about Jiro's House?** 58
M2：**Of course.** 58 I'll also check whether they offer any special discounts.

56-58 三人會話

女 ：**我召集這次會議是為了討論去東京參加大會時，我們要在哪裡住宿。**56
男 1：**我們去年在澀谷訂的那間飯店怎麼樣？**57
女 ：**那一間最後讓我們預算破表，**57 所以今年我們得找另一個地方。
男 1：那麼，有一家叫「次郎之家」的旅館，即使是在旺季，價格也很公道。我以前在那裡住過幾次，他們提供的設施很棒、房間也寬敞。
女 ：好。麥可，因為你負責我們團隊的財務，**可以請你去進一步了解次郎之家嗎？**58
男 2：**當然行。**58 我也會查看他們是否提供任何特別優惠。

56. What upcoming event are the speakers talking about?
(A) A business trip
(B) A retirement celebration
(C) A holiday party
(D) A board meeting

57. What problem occurred last year?
(A) Some documents were lost.
(B) Some equipment was damaged.
(C) A reservation was lost.
(D) A budget was exceeded.

58. What does Michael say he will do?
(A) Make a deposit
(B) Conduct some research
(C) Contact a manager
(D) Review some itineraries

56. 說話者正在討論哪一項即將進行的活動？
(A) 出差
(B) 退休慶祝會
(C) 假日聚會
(D) 董事會會議

57. 去年發生了什麼問題？
(A) 文件遺失。
(B) 設備損壞。
(C) 預約遺漏。
(D) 預算超支。

58. 麥可提到他將做什麼？
(A) 存入款項
(B) 做點調查
(C) 聯絡經理
(D) 看看旅遊行程

Questions 59-61 refer to the following conversation.

W：Mark, **I think I know a less expensive way to order our office supplies.** 59
M：Really?
W：Yes. **I came across this site on the Internet, and their prices are 30 percent lower than our current supplier.** 59
M：Hmm . . . But you have to keep in mind that even though online stores offer cheaper prices, they charge a lot for shipping.
W：Well, that's only on small orders. **This store doesn't charge for delivery on bulk purchases of over $300.** 60
M：But **that doesn't really apply to us since that's a lot more than we usually purchase at one time.** 60
W：I didn't think about that.
M：**If we're going to order that much at once, we'll have to get the staff to complete the request forms ahead of time.** 61

59-61 會話

女：馬克，**我想我找到方法，可以節省我們訂購辦公用品的開銷了。** 59
男：真的嗎？
女：沒錯。**我在網路上偶然找到了這個網站，而他們的售價比我們現在的供應商低了 30%。** 59
男：嗯……但妳要知道，即使網路商店提供更划算的商品價格，運費會很可觀的。
女：嗯，只有小筆訂單才會。**大量採購的金額超過 300 美元的話，這家店就會提供免運費。** 60
男：但**那對我們來說並不真的適用，因為那會遠超過我們平常一次購買的量。** 60
女：這我倒沒想到。
男：**如果要一次訂購那麼多，我們將必須請同仁提前寫好需求表。** 61

59. What change does the woman suggest?
(A) Renovating a Web site
(B) Ordering from another company
(C) Hiring additional workers
(D) Lowering some prices

59. 女子建議改變什麼？
(A) 整建網站
(B) 從另一家公司訂貨
(C) 僱用更多員工
(D) 調降某些價格

60. What does the man mean when he says, "that doesn't really apply to us"?
(A) A service fee cannot be waived.
(B) An item cannot be shipped.
(C) A coupon cannot be used.
(D) A policy cannot be changed.

61. What might staff be asked to do?
(A) Fill out forms in advance
(B) Purchase less than usual
(C) Make deliveries
(D) Train employees

Questions 62-64 refer to the following conversation and train timetable.

M： Good afternoon, passengers. Kindly be prepared to present your tickets as I walk by.
W： Hello, this is my ticket. **Did I get on the right train? I need to get to Faverton.** 62
M： **Unfortunately, no.** 62 **You're on the XB10 Train.** 63 It won't stop at that destination.
W： Oh, this is not good. What can I do?
M： Hmm . . . **We've already departed from Hemsforth Station, so you should transfer to the other train at our next stop.** 63
W： All right. Will it take long for the train to arrive? **I'm in a rush because I have to make a presentation at a conference at 3:40.** 64
M： Not really—about 15 minutes. I think you'll have enough time to get to your conference.

Train Timetable

	Hemsforth	**Bertiz** 63	Faverton	Poly
XB10 Train	2:20 P.M.	2:50 P.M.		3:40 P.M.
XB20 Train	2:50 P.M.	3:05 P.M.	3:20 P.M.	

62. What is the woman's problem?
(A) An express train has just departed.
(B) A train is experiencing mechanical issues.
(C) She brought an expired train ticket.
(D) She boarded the wrong train.

60. 男子說：「那對我們來說並不真的適用」，其意思為何？
(A) 有項服務費無法減免。
(B) 有項商品無法運送。
(C) 有張優惠券無法使用。
(D) 有項政策無法更改。

61. 員工可能會被要求做什麼？
(A) 提前填寫表單
(B) 比平常減少購買量
(C) 送貨
(D) 培訓員工

62-64 會話和列車時刻表

男：各位乘客午安。煩請準備好您的車票，在我經過時出示。
女：您好，這是我的票。**我搭對車了嗎？我要到法弗頓。**62
男：很抱歉，不對的。62 **您現在搭的是 XB10 列車。**63 本列車不會停靠那一站。
女：噢，這可不好。我可以怎麼辦？
男：嗯……**我們已經從亨斯佛斯站離開了，因此您應該在下一站改搭其他班次列車。**63
女：好的。列車還要很久才會到站嗎？**我得在 3 點 40 分到一場會議上做報告，所以在趕時間。**64
男：不用很久，大約 15 分鐘。我想您將有充足時間趕赴會議。

列車時刻表

	亨斯福斯	**貝爾蒂茲** 63	法弗頓	保利
XB10 列車	下午 2:20	下午 2:50		下午 3:40
XB20 列車	下午 2:50	下午 3:05	下午 3:20	

62. 女子遇到什麼問題？
(A) 一班直達車剛離站。
(B) 列車遇到機械問題。
(C) 她帶了過期車票。
(D) 她坐錯了火車。

63. Look at the graphic. At which station should the woman transfer?
(A) Hemsforth
(B) Bertiz
(C) Faverton
(D) Poly

64. Why is the woman in a hurry?
(A) She will be speaking at a conference.
(B) She is going to watch a performance.
(C) She needs to get on a train.
(D) She is interviewing for a job.

63. 請據圖表作答。女子應在哪一站轉乘？
(A) 亨斯福斯
(B) 貝爾蒂茲
(C) 法弗頓
(D) 保利

64. 女子為什麼很匆忙呢？
(A) 她將在會議上演講。
(B) 她要去看表演。
(C) 她須搭上火車。
(D) 她正要去面試工作。

Questions 65-67 refer to the following conversation and list.

M：Hello, Ms. Roberts. **My name is Brad Ford, and I'm the Vice President of the Reinheim Consulting Group.** 65 I'd like to congratulate you on winning the Investment Management Award tonight.
W：Thank you, sir. It's an honor to meet someone from such a famous firm.
M：Well, I've wanted to meet you for a while. Listen, **we're looking for someone to fill our senior analyst position, and we think you'd be a perfect fit for the job.** 66
W：I appreciate the offer. But I'm not interested in switching companies at the moment.
M：I understand. **I'll see if the winner of Corporate Finance Award is interested in the offer.** 67 Anyway, congratulations again.

Name	Award
1 Stacey Roberts	Investment Management
2 Brian Lee	Global Pension
3 Richard Kim 67	**Corporate Finance**
4 Jamie Brown	Real Estate

65-67 會話和名單

男：羅柏茲女士您好。**我叫布萊得・福德，是萊恩海姆顧問集團的副總裁。** 65 我想恭喜您今晚榮獲投資管理獎。
女：謝謝您，先生。貴公司很有名，能遇見其中一員真是我的榮幸。
男：這樣啊，我一直想和您見上一面。是這樣的，**我們公司正在徵求人才擔任高級分析師一職，我們認為您是完美的人選。** 66
女：多謝您的邀約。但我目前沒有興趣轉任其他公司。
男：我了解。**我會再看看企業財務獎的得主對此邀約有沒有興趣。** 67 無論如何，再次恭喜。

姓名	獎項
1 史黛西・羅柏茲	投資管理
2 布萊恩・李	全球退休基金
3 理查・金 67	**企業財務**
4 傑米・布朗	不動產

65. Who is the man?
(A) An event planner
(B) An executive officer
(C) An awards presenter
(D) A job applicant

65. 男子的身分為何？
(A) 活動策劃者
(B) 公司高層幹部
(C) 頒獎人
(D) 求職者

66. What is mentioned about the Reinheim Consulting Group?
(A) It is located overseas.
(B) It offers group sessions.
(C) It has a position open.
(D) It specializes in advertising.

67. Look at the graphic. Who most likely will the man talk to next?
(A) Stacey Roberts
(B) Brian Lee
(C) Richard Kim
(D) Jamie Brown

Questions 68-70 refer to the following conversation and coupon.

M: Hi, I'm Brad York from Florence Technologies. **I ordered for 300 business cards last week. I need 200 more, and I was wondering if I could get all of them by Friday.** 68 70

W: I'm afraid not. We're really busy, and **we won't be able to print the additional business cards until late next week.** 69

M: That's fine. I'll just place another order. But **you can still send the first 300 cards to me by Friday, right?** 69

W: Of course. Those are ready to go.

M: Thank you. By the way, **I forgot that I had this coupon. Could I use it for the new order?** 70

W: **Of course.** 70 I'll use the same credit card information as last time.

Discount Coupon

Order for 100 business cards → $5 OFF
Order for 200 business cards $10 OFF 70
Order for 300 business cards → $15 OFF
Order for 400 business cards → $20 OFF

66. 關於萊恩海姆顧問集團，對話中提到什麼？
(A) 位於海外。
(B) 提供團體課程。
(C) 有職位開缺。
(D) 專精廣告業。

67. 請據圖表作答。男子接著最有可能和誰說話？
(A) 史黛西・羅柏茲
(B) 布萊恩・李
(C) 理查・金
(D) 傑米・布朗

68-70 會話和折價券

男：您好，我是佛羅倫斯科技的布萊得・約克。**我上週訂了 300 張名片。我需要加訂 200 張，想知道我能否在週五以前全數一併收貨。** 68 70

女：恐怕沒辦法。我們真的很繁忙，而**我們要到下週後半才有辦法印製額外的名片。** 69

男：沒關係的。我會另外下一筆訂單。**但您還是能在週五前把首批 300 張名片寄給我，對嗎？** 69

女：當然。那些已準備好要出貨了。

男：謝謝。順便問一下，**我之前忘了我有這張優惠券。我可以將它用於新訂單嗎？** 70

女：**當然可以。** 70 我會使用和上一筆相同的信用卡資訊。

折價券

訂購 100 張名片 → 折扣 5 美元
訂購 200 張名片 → 折扣 10 美元 70
訂購 300 張名片 → 折扣 15 美元
訂購 400 張名片 → 折扣 20 美元

68. Why is the man calling?
(A) To reschedule a delivery
(B) To increase an order
(C) To apply for a membership card
(D) To inquire about an invoice

68. 男子為何撥打電話？
(A) 以更改交貨時間
(B) 以追加訂單
(C) 以申辦會員卡
(D) 以詢問帳單事宜

69. Where does the woman probably work?
(A) At a printing company
(B) At a flower shop
(C) At a bookstore
(D) At a bank

69. 女子可能在哪裡工作？
(A) 在印刷公司
(B) 在花店
(C) 在書店
(D) 在銀行

70. Look at the graphic. What discount will the man most likely receive?
(A) $5
(B) $10
(C) $15
(D) $20

70. 請據圖表作答。男子將最有可能得到多少折扣？
(A) 5 美元
(B) 10 美元
(C) 15 美元
(D) 20 美元

PART 4 P. 99–101

30

Questions 71-73 refer to the following broadcast.

W： This is PABC Radio with your local morning update. We have some wonderful news for those planning to go to **the concert in Braxton Stadium this afternoon.** 71 The current rain should stop by the morning, leaving clear skies for OB Rock Band's performance at 3:00 P.M. But right now, **the rain is causing more traffic, especially towards the city center. Make sure you allow more time if you're driving into that area.** 72 And now onto the show, *Money Matters*. Here with us today is **renowned financial expert Michael Robinson,** 73 author of *Spend Smart*. He'll be answering questions from our listeners on money issues, so stay tuned.

71-73 廣播

女： 這裡是 PABC 電台，給您帶來在地晨間快報。我們有一些好消息，要分享給打算**今天下午去貝克斯頓體育館**參加**演唱會**的聽眾。71 目前的降雨可望在早上停歇，因此下午三點 OB 搖滾樂隊演出時，將有晴朗的好天氣。不過現在**由於雨勢關係，交通較為壅塞，尤其是往市中心的方向。如果您正要開車進入該區域，請務必多加預留時間。**72 接著進行的節目是《資金有關係》。今天我們請到**知名財經專家麥可．羅賓森，**73 他是《開銷有智慧》一書的作者。他將為本節目的聽眾回答財務相關的問題，請持續鎖定。

71. According to the speaker, what is scheduled for the afternoon?
(A) A store opening
(B) A road closure
(C) A sports event
(D) A musical performance

71. 據說話者說法，下午預定有什麼事？
(A) 店家開幕
(B) 道路封鎖
(C) 體育活動
(D) 音樂表演

72. What does the speaker suggest for the people traveling to the city center?
(A) Sharing cars
(B) Allowing extra time
(C) Taking a detour
(D) Bringing an umbrella

73. Who is Michael Robinson?
(A) A news reporter
(B) A rock musician
(C) A financial expert
(D) A city official

Questions 74-76 refer to the following telephone message.

M: Iris, this is Martin calling. **I wanted to thank you again for opening up the store this morning** 74 while I'm out attending a conference. However, I just passed by the store, and **I saw that there's still some trash by the entrance. I'm driving to the convention center now. Do you think you could clean it up before customers start coming in?** 75 By the way, **a technician will be stopping by later in the afternoon. He'll be setting up the new security cameras we ordered last week.** 76 Keep me updated on how things go. Thank you.

74. Why does the speaker thank the listener?
(A) For attending a convention
(B) For opening up a business
(C) For submitting a payment
(D) For preparing a presentation

75. What does the speaker imply when he says, "I'm driving to the convention center now"?
(A) He does not know where to park.
(B) He cannot make it to a meeting on time.
(C) He is unable to take care of an issue.
(D) He needs to take an alternate route.

76. According to the speaker, what will happen in the afternoon?
(A) An order will be placed.
(B) A sale will start.
(C) Some devices will be installed.
(D) Some documents will be mailed.

72. 說話者對前往市中心的人有何建議？
(A) 共乘汽車
(B) 留有額外時間
(C) 繞路
(D) 攜帶雨傘

73. 誰是麥可・羅賓森？
(A) 新聞記者
(B) 搖滾樂手
(C) 財經專家
(D) 市府官員

74-76 語音留言

男：艾莉絲，我是馬丁。**我想再次感謝妳，在今天早上**我出差去開會時**幫忙開店。** 74 不過我剛剛行經店門口，然後**發現入口附近還有些垃圾。我現在正開車前往會議中心。妳覺得妳有辦法在客人開始來店前清理乾淨嗎？** 75 順道一提，**有位技術人員下午晚點會來。他要來安裝我們上週訂購的幾台新監視器。** 76 有新的狀況再請讓我知道。謝謝妳。

74. 說話者為什麼要感謝聽者？
(A) 幫忙參加大會
(B) 幫忙開店
(C) 幫忙付款
(D) 幫忙準備簡報

75. 說話者說：「我現在正開車前往會議中心」，言下之意為何？
(A) 他不知道停車位置。
(B) 他無法準時赴會。
(C) 他無法處理問題。
(D) 他須走替代路線。

76. 據說話者說法，下午會發生何事？
(A) 將會下訂單。
(B) 特賣將開始。
(C) 將安裝幾個裝置。
(D) 將郵寄幾份文件。

Questions 77-79 refer to the following excerpt from a meeting.

77-79 會議摘錄

W：Before we bring this meeting to an end, **I'd like to give everyone a heads-up about some upcoming changes to our current menu.** 77 Our restaurant's corporate office notified me that **they plan on adding several low calorie choices to our menu. And our head chef, Harold, will lead the team that will develop the recipes for the new dishes.** 78 Once the recipes are set, we will offer the new dishes at our restaurant. **By doing so, we hope to attract more health-conscious diners and increase our business** 79 by 20 percent next year.

女：本次會議結束前，**我想提醒大家我們現有的菜單即將進行一些更動。** 77 我們餐廳的公司辦公室通知我，**他們計劃在我們的菜單新增幾道低卡菜色。我們的主廚哈洛將率領團隊，開發新菜色的食譜。** 78 只要食譜大功告成，新的菜品就將在我們的餐廳推出。**藉此，我們希望吸引到更多注重健康的顧客，並**在明年**讓我們的業績增幅** 79 達到 20%。

77. What is the speaker discussing?
(A) Hiring a head chef
(B) Relocating a corporate office
(C) Changing a menu
(D) Renovating a diner

78. What does the speaker say Harold will help do?
(A) Train some kitchen workers
(B) Create some healthy recipes
(C) Manage a new restaurant location
(D) Find a different food supplier

79. According to the speaker, what is the purpose of the change?
(A) To retain current personnel
(B) To lower business expenses
(C) To improve employee morale
(D) To bring in more customers

77. 說話者正在討論什麼？
(A) 聘請主廚
(B) 搬遷公司辦公室
(C) 變更菜單
(D) 整修餐廳

78. 說話者說哈洛會協助什麼？
(A) 訓練廚房員工
(B) 制定健康食譜
(C) 管理新餐廳分店
(D) 找別的食品供應商

79. 據說話者說法，此一變動的目的為何？
(A) 以保留現有員工
(B) 以減少營業開銷
(C) 以提振員工士氣
(D) 以吸引更多顧客

Questions 80-82 refer to the following excerpt from a talk.

80-82 談話摘錄

M：Now, **I'd like to discuss a problem with how we record our working hours here at the accounting firm. We have recently found out that the project codes we've been using are outdated.** 80 It's very important that we use the correct codes when entering our hours because these codes are used to calculate the time spent on a client's account. **To resolve this issue,**

男：現在，**我想討論我們這間會計事務所裡記錄工時的問題。我們最近發現目前所使用的專案代碼已經過期了。** 80 這些代碼是用來計算花在各個客戶帳戶上的時間，所以我們要使用正確的代碼來輸入時數，這一點非常重要。**為解決這項問題，我想請各位重新輸入上個月的工時。**

I want all of you to re-enter your working hours for the last month. I'll pass around new timesheets 81 with the revised project codes. **If you are unable to find your project code, please see Perry Kay, and she'll look it up for you.** 82

我會傳閱新的時數表， 81 上面有修正後的專案代碼。**如果找不到你的專案代碼，請找派瑞．凱，她會幫你查詢。** 82

80. What problem is the speaker addressing?
(A) Some project deadlines will not be met.
(B) A contract has not been finalized.
(C) Some time-recording information is out of date.
(D) A client account has been terminated.

80. 說話者指出什麼問題？
(A) 有些專案期限無法遵守。
(B) 合約尚未敲定。
(C) 有些時間記錄資訊已過期。
(D) 客戶的帳戶已遭終止。

81. What are listeners instructed to do?
(A) Correct their timesheets
(B) Meet their clients
(C) Remove current software
(D) Use new passwords

81. 聽者被指示做什麼？
(A) 修正時數表
(B) 會見客戶
(C) 移除現有軟體
(D) 使用新密碼

82. Why should listeners contact Perry Kay?
(A) To resolve customer complaints
(B) To update contact information
(C) To request a code
(D) To submit a proposal

82. 聽者為何應要洽詢派瑞．凱？
(A) 以解決客戶投訴
(B) 以更新聯絡資訊
(C) 以索取代碼
(D) 以繳交提案

Questions 83-85 refer to the following introduction.

83-85 開場白

W：Hello everyone, and **welcome to the 3rd annual National Professional Engineers Conference.** 83 Our first guest speaker today is **Charlene Young, who is one of the foremost environmental engineers in the world.** 84 She is renowned for her innovative designs in the development of water distribution systems, recycling methods, sewage treatment plants, and other pollution prevention and control systems. She has won several awards in recognition of her continued efforts to seek new ways to reduce pollution. There'll be a small break outside the lobby after her presentation, and **juice will be provided,** 85 **<u>compliments of Barry's Corner.</u>** Now, please welcome Charlene Young.

女：大家好，在此**歡迎蒞臨第三屆全國專業工程師年會。** 83 我們今天第一位演講嘉賓是**夏琳．楊，她是全球頂尖的環境工程師。** 84 她以其創新設計聞名，開發項目涵蓋配水系統、回收措施、污水處理廠以及其他污染防治和控制系統。夏琳至今已獲獎多次，以表彰她努力不懈地探尋減少污染的新方法。在她演講過後，大廳外將舉行簡短茶敘，**並將供應<u>由「拜瑞角落」致贈的</u>果汁。** 85 現在，請一起歡迎夏琳．楊。

83. Where is the introduction taking place?
(A) At a fundraising banquet
(B) At a professional conference
(C) At a training seminar
(D) At an awards ceremony

84. Who is Charlene Young?
(A) A human resources manager
(B) A chief executive officer
(C) An environmental engineer
(D) An event organizer

85. What does the speaker mean when she says, "compliments of Barry's Corner"?
(A) Beverages were supplied by a business.
(B) A company has received positive feedback.
(C) Food was catered by a restaurant.
(D) A demonstration was given by an organization.

83. 這段開場白在哪裡進行？
(A) 在募款餐會
(B) 在專業會議
(C) 在培訓研討會
(D) 在頒獎典禮

84. 夏琳．楊的職業為何？
(A) 人力資源經理
(B) 執行長
(C) 環境工程師
(D) 活動策劃者

85. 說話者說：「由『拜瑞角落』致贈的」，其意思為何？
(A) 飲品由某商家提供。
(B) 公司收到了正面回饋。
(C) 食物由某餐廳供應。
(D) 一個團體做了示範。

Questions 86-88 refer to the following excerpt from a meeting.

W：OK, **let's talk about the final item on the agenda: customer responses to the feedback forms that were sent out this month.** 86 **We had a lot of positive reviews and several surprises as well. There were many customers who were disappointed by our universal notebook chargers and made negative comments about them.** 87 Most of them said that the charger gets too hot, while others have mentioned that the plug bends too easily. So **Brian, I want you to take the lead and put together a team to find solutions to these problems and report back to me in three days.** 88

86-88 會議摘錄

女：好，**我們來討論議程的最後一個項目：針對本月寄出的回饋意見單，已有不少顧客回覆。** 86 **我們收到了很多正面評論，但也有幾份令人感到詫異。許多顧客對我們的通用筆電充電器不甚滿意，並給予負面評價。** 87 其中大多說到充電器過熱，有些則提及插頭太過容易彎掉。因此，**布萊恩，我想要你帶頭籌組一個團隊，找出這些問題的解決方案，並在三天後向我報告。** 88

86. What has the company recently done?
(A) Bought new equipment
(B) Received customer feedback
(C) Recruited more employees
(D) Updated a computer system

86. 該公司最近做了什麼？
(A) 買新設備
(B) 收到顧客意見回饋
(C) 僱用更多員工
(D) 更新電腦系統

87. What does the speaker say was surprising?
(A) Complaints about a product
(B) Costs of delivery
(C) Forecasts of sales
(D) Advancements in technology

88. What does the speaker ask Brian to do?
(A) Complete a questionnaire
(B) Lead a group
(C) Try out a product
(D) Visit a store

87. 說話者說什麼事讓人感到意外？
(A) 產品相關投訴
(B) 貨運費用
(C) 銷售預測
(D) 科技進展

88. 說話者要求布萊恩做什麼？
(A) 填寫問卷
(B) 帶領團隊
(C) 試用產品
(D) 到訪商店

TEST 7 PART 4

30

Questions 89-91 refer to the following advertisement.

M：**Do you want a comfortable fitness watch?** 89 **Englewood Tech recently released one that is durable as well.** 90 The Y4 tracks every step during activities, such as running or hiking, and due to its shock resistant feature, you don't have to worry about dropping it! This product is perfect for those who enjoy outdoor sports in all kinds of conditions. **Head over to our Web site where you can read some user testimonials.** 91

89-91 廣告

男：**您想要舒適的健身手錶嗎？** 89 **鷹木科技最近推出一款同時兼具耐用性的產品。** 90 進行諸如跑步或健行等活動時，這款「Y4」將記錄下踏過的每一步，而且因為具備抗震功能，您不必擔心摔著了它！本產品非常適合喜歡在各種環境從事戶外運動的人。**歡迎前往我們的網站，查看使用者的一些推薦心得。** 91

89. What is being advertised?
(A) A digital camera
(B) A fitness watch
(C) A computer
(D) A television

90. What does the speaker emphasize about the product?
(A) It is colorful.
(B) It is affordable.
(C) It is lightweight.
(D) It is durable.

91. Why should the listeners visit a Web site?
(A) To check out user reviews
(B) To reserve an item
(C) To find a store location
(D) To obtain a discount voucher

89. 廣告推銷的是什麼？
(A) 數位相機
(B) 健身手錶
(C) 電腦
(D) 電視

90. 關於產品，說話者強調了什麼？
(A) 色彩繽紛。
(B) 價格合理。
(C) 重量輕巧。
(D) 很耐用。

91. 聽者為何要訪問網站？
(A) 以查看使用者評論
(B) 以預訂產品
(C) 以尋找店舖位置
(D) 以獲得折扣券

Questions 92-94 refer to the following news report.

W： Welcome, and thanks for tuning into Channel 2's *Your City*, where we update you on community events and activities. **We've got a story for you today about the city's new agriculture project,** 92 which will provide vegetables, meat, and dairy products to local restaurants. The lead farmer, Marissa Gomez, is confident that **the project will provide many benefits, but the most important one will be having less expensive produce.** 93 Because all goods will be coming from farms in this area, there will be significant cost savings. **Ms. Gomez says she still isn't sure when the project will be completed.** 94 **After all, this is an enormous task.**

92. What industry is the speaker reporting on?
(A) Hospitality
(B) Construction
(C) Finance
(D) Agriculture

93. According to the speaker, what benefit will the project provide to the public?
(A) Access to cheaper products
(B) Better financing options
(C) More job openings
(D) Improvement of public health

94. What does the speaker imply when she says, "this is an enormous task"?
(A) A budget should be adjusted.
(B) More workers should be hired.
(C) Extra time may be needed.
(D) A larger venue may be required.

Questions 95-97 refer to the following telephone message and coupon.

M： Hello, this is Roberto. **I wanted to give you an update about the dinner we're planning for the new employees.** 95 **Now, the date of the event is still October 22, and I've just**

92-94 新聞報導

女：歡迎，感謝各位鎖定第二頻道的《你的城市》，我們將帶給您社區大小事的最新快報。**我們今天的報導要帶您關注本市的一項農業新專案，**92 計劃要為在地餐廳提供蔬菜、肉類和乳製品。農民代表瑪麗莎．戈麥茲確信，**該專案將提供多項好處，但其中首要的是就能取得更便宜的農產品。**93 由於產品全都將由本地農家供應，未來可望大幅降低成本。**戈麥茲女士表示，她還不確定專案何時會達成。**94 **畢竟，這可是大工程。**

92. 説話者報導關注的產業為何？
(A) 餐旅業
(B) 營建業
(C) 財務金融業
(D) 農業

93. 據説話者説法，該專案能為大眾帶來什麼好處？
(A) 取得更便宜的產品
(B) 更好的融資選擇
(C) 更多的工作機會
(D) 改善公共衛生

94. 説話者説：「這可是大工程」，其意思為何？
(A) 預算須調整。
(B) 應僱用更多工人。
(C) 可能需要更多時間。
(D) 可能需要更大場地。

95-97 語音留言和折價券

男：你好，我是羅伯托。**關於我們為新進員工籌辦的晚宴，我想告知你最新進度。**95 **目前，活動日期仍是 10 月 22 日，而我剛剛確認過將會**

confirmed that 35 people will be attending. However, I'm afraid we won't be able to use that coupon from Sushi Heaven as planned. 96 I'm going to look into a couple of different locations. Oh, also, Bill is going to host a talent show after everyone's eaten. **Could you put together a list of people who are interested in participating?** 97

Sushi Heaven
Private parties welcome! Book a banquet hall for 5 hours! 20% discount for groups of 20 or more! **Offer valid at all Sushi Heaven locations until October 21.** 96

有 35 人參加。不過，恐怕我們無法按計畫使用「壽司天堂」的折價券。96 我會再研究看看幾個不同地點。喔，還有，等大家吃飽後，比爾會主持一場才藝表演。**能請你彙整有興趣參加者的名單嗎？** 97

壽司天堂
歡迎私人聚會！ 預訂宴會廳 5 個小時！ 20 人或以上的團體可享 20%的折扣！ **任一壽司天堂門市皆可使用 有效期限至 10 月 21 日。** 96

95. Why is the event being held?
(A) To reward some employees
(B) To mark a company's anniversary
(C) To welcome new staff
(D) To celebrate an office relocation

96. Look at the graphic. Why is the speaker unable to use the coupon for the event?
(A) The coupon does not apply to large groups.
(B) The coupon will expire before the event takes place.
(C) The event will run longer than anticipated.
(D) The event will be held on the weekend.

97. What does the speaker want the listener to do?
(A) Decide on a venue
(B) Provide a meal preference
(C) Make a deposit
(D) Create a list

95. 為何要舉辦活動？
(A) 以獎勵幾位員工
(B) 以慶祝公司週年慶
(C) 以歡迎新進同仁
(D) 以慶祝公司喬遷

96. 請據圖表作答。説話者辦這次活動為何不能使用折價券？
(A) 折價券不適用大型團體。
(B) 折價券將在活動日前過期。
(C) 活動用時會超出預期。
(D) 活動辦在週末。

97. 説話者想要聽者做什麼？
(A) 決定場地
(B) 提供餐飲偏好
(C) 存入款項
(D) 列出名單

Questions 98-100 refer to the following telephone message and timetable.

M：**Hello, it's Nicolas Damira calling from Oakwood Avenue Realtors.** 98 **Don't forget that you still need to sign one more form before I can give you the keys to your apartment.** 99 **You also said that you plan on**

98-100 語音留言和時刻表

男：**您好，我這裡是「橡木林大道房地產」的尼可拉斯．達米拉來電。** 98 **請別忘記您還須要簽署一份文件，我才能將公寓鑰匙交給您。** 99 **您也提到過，您下午稍早打算搭乘公共**

TEST 7
PART 4
30

using public transportation to get to work on Orchard Road early in the afternoon. The Market Lane bus stop is just a three-minute walk from your apartment complex, and you'll want to take bus 909. 100 I'll have a copy of the afternoon timetable waiting for you when you drop by to complete the remaining paperwork. Talk to you soon.

Bus 909 Timetable	
Union Drive	12:10 P.M.
Market Lane	**12:25 P.M.** 100
Oakwood Avenue	12:40 P.M.
Orchard Road	12:55 P.M.

運輸前往果園路上班。只要從您的公寓綜合大樓走三分鐘，就能到達市場巷的公車站，而您可搭乘 909 號公車。 100 我會先印一份下午班車時刻表，等您過來簽署完剩餘文件時拿取。待會兒見。

909 公車時刻表	
聯合大道	下午 12:10
市場巷	**下午 12:25** 100
橡木林大道	下午 12:40
果樹路	下午 12:55

98. Who most likely is the speaker?
(A) A career advisor
(B) A construction manager
(C) A public transportation official
(D) A real estate agent

99. What does the speaker remind the listener to do?
(A) Sign a document
(B) Retrieve an item
(C) Review a reservation
(D) Make a deposit

100. Look at the graphic. When would the listener board the bus?
(A) 12:10 P.M.
(B) 12:25 P.M.
(C) 12:40 P.M.
(D) 12:55 P.M.

98. 說話者最有可能是什麼人？
(A) 職涯顧問
(B) 工程經理
(C) 公共運輸官員
(D) 房地產經紀人

99. 說話者提醒聽者做什麼？
(A) 簽署文件
(B) 取回物品
(C) 查看預訂
(D) 存入款項

100. 請據圖表作答。聽者會於何時搭公車？
(A) 下午 12:10
(B) 下午 12:25
(C) 下午 12:40
(D) 下午 12:55

ACTUAL TEST 8

PART 1 P. 102–105

1. **(A) He is adjusting a shelf.**
   (B) He is replacing a light.
   (C) He is cleaning a countertop.
   (D) He is hammering a nail.

2. (A) Some workers are repairing a road.
   (B) A man is kneeling to check the tire of a car.
   (C) A driver is getting out of a vehicle.
   (D) Some men are securing a car for towing.

3. **(A) Some people are enjoying a performance.**
   (B) Some musicians are putting away their instruments.
   (C) A guitar is being placed on a stand.
   (D) A group is exiting a stage.

4. (A) The woman is looking through a drawer.
   (B) They are exchanging a document.
   (C) The woman is reaching for a keyboard on the desk.
   (D) They are seated near an entrance.

5. (A) A bridge leads to a platform.
   (B) A train is stopped at a station.
   (C) Some commuters are waiting in line.
   (D) Some lampposts are being repaired.

6. (A) A sign is hanging from an awning.
   (B) There are potted plants along a wall.
   (C) Some paint is being applied to the building.
   (D) There are curtains over the windows.

1. **(A) 他正在調整架子。**
   (B) 他正在更換電燈。
   (C) 他正在清理料理檯。
   (D) 他正在用鎚子釘釘子。

2. (A) 幾名工人正在修路。
   (B) 一名男子跪著檢查汽車輪胎。
   (C) 駕駛正在下車。
   (D) 幾名男子正在固定車輛以便拖吊。

3. **(A) 幾個人正在享受表演。**
   (B) 幾名音樂家正在收拾他們的樂器。
   (C) 吉他正被放到架子上。
   (D) 團體正從舞台退場。

4. (A) 女子在查看抽屜。
   (B) 他們正在傳遞文件。
   (C) 女子正伸手拿桌上的鍵盤。
   (D) 他們坐在入口附近。

5. (A) 橋梁通往月台。
   (B) 列車被停在車站內。
   (C) 幾名通勤者正在排隊。
   (D) 幾盞燈柱正在維修中。

6. (A) 遮陽篷上掛著標誌。
   (B) 盆栽沿著牆邊擺放。
   (C) 建築物正在上漆中。
   (D) 窗戶上掛著窗簾。

PART 2 P. 106

7. Do you know where the nearest café is?
   (A) Yes, it's across the street.
   (B) Two cups of tea.
   (C) She's on her way.

7. 你知道最近的咖啡廳在哪嗎？
   (A) 知道，是在對街。
   (B) 兩杯茶。
   (C) 她在路上了。

8. When is Mr. Cho's last day at work?
(A) Next Friday.
(B) With the finance team.
(C) He drives his car.

8. 曹先生的離職日是什麼時候？
(A) 下週五。
(B) 和財務團隊一起。
(C) 他自己開車。

9. How much do you pay monthly for your home Internet?
(A) Around 45 euros.
(B) Sure, I'll sign up for it.
(C) Only once or twice.

9. 你每個月要付多少家用網路費？
(A) 約 45 歐元。
(B) 當然，我會報名參加。
(C) 僅一次或兩次。

10. Would you like something to drink?
(A) Yes, I like it.
(B) No, thanks. I'm not thirsty.
(C) The menu on the Web site.

10. 您想喝點什麼嗎？
(A) 對，我喜歡。
(B) 不，謝謝。我不渴。
(C) 網站上的菜單。

11. Weren't the auto parts sent out last week?
(A) A new car dealership.
(B) We had to delay the delivery.
(C) Mr. Banner is.

11. 上週沒有寄出汽車零件嗎？
(A) 新的汽車經銷商。
(B) 我們必須延後交貨。
(C) 是班納先生。

12. Has the museum picked out the artifacts for the exhibit?
(A) That's a beautiful sculpture.
(B) It opens on the 15th.
(C) I'm going to call them now.

12. 博物館選好展覽要用的文物了嗎？
(A) 那是座美麗的雕像。
(B) 它在 15 日開放參觀。
(C) 我現在打電話給他們。

13. Is our assembly line working again?
(A) Not yet, but it should be soon.
(B) Yes, it was.
(C) It's a tight deadline.

13. 我們的生產線恢復運作了嗎？
(A) 還沒有，但應該快了。
(B) 對，它之前是。
(C) 期限很趕。

14. Where will the jewelry convention take place next month?
(A) At the end of the month.
(B) In Atlanta, like last time.
(C) She's the keynote speaker.

14. 下個月珠寶展將在哪裡舉行？
(A) 在月底。
(B) 在亞特蘭大，和上次一樣。
(C) 她是主題演講者。

15. Why don't we hand in the budget report?
(A) No, we don't.
(B) Sure. I'll submit it now.
(C) Yesterday morning.

15. 我們為何不交出預算報告？
(A) 不，我們沒有。
(B) 當然行。我現在就將它交出。
(C) 昨天早上。

16. Mr. Anderson landed at 6 this morning, didn't he?
(A) All flights were canceled.
(B) No, at the landscaping company.
(C) Well, there's a two-year warranty.

16. 安德森先生的班機今早六點著陸了，不是嗎？
(A) 全部航班都取消了。
(B) 不，在景觀美化公司。
(C) 嗯，有兩年保固。

17. Why are the guests arriving so late?
(A) The delivery already arrived.
(B) No. The earlier train.
(C) Let's go ask Mr. Rogers.

18. Who's leading the McAllister project?
(A) It hasn't been decided yet.
(B) She'll lead you to the building.
(C) On the 1st of May.

19. Hasn't this month's workshop been canceled?
(A) No, it's been postponed.
(B) I had no problems with it.
(C) An employee training session.

20. When is the payment due?
(A) I have one too.
(B) 500 dollars a month.
(C) It needs to be sent by Thursday.

21. The air conditioner should be fixed by tomorrow, right?
(A) OK, I'll take a few.
(B) Actually, it was done this morning.
(C) Poor weather conditions.

22. Are you printing this on one side only, or do you want it double-sided?
(A) No, the printer is out of ink.
(B) Load the paper in this tray.
(C) Double-sided, please.

23. I'd better keep my jacket on in here.
(A) I can turn on the heater.
(B) We'll keep your bag for you.
(C) At a department store.

24. Who'll be the interpreter at the International Economics Forum?
(A) I heard it's being held in March.
(B) You bought an electronic dictionary?
(C) Ms. Allen from the RMK Agency.

25. How many times have you visited Korea?
(A) I've never been there.
(B) Round-trip tickets, please.
(C) I moved last month.

17. 賓客為何這麼晚到達？
(A) 貨物已經送達。
(B) 沒有。較早的火車。
(C) 我們去問羅傑斯先生。

18. 「麥卡利斯特」專案是誰在主導？
(A) 還沒有決定。
(B) 她會帶你到大樓。
(C) 在 5 月 1 日。

19. 這個月的研習沒有取消嗎？
(A) 沒有，是延後了。
(B) 我對此沒有問題。
(C) 員工培訓課程。

20. 什麼時候付款到期？
(A) 我也有一個。
(B) 每月 500 美元。
(C) 要在週四之前繳款。

21. 空調應該明天之前會修好，對嗎？
(A) 好，我拿一點。
(B) 其實，今天早上就完成了。
(C) 天氣狀況不佳。

22. 你是只要印單面，還是想印雙面？
(A) 不，印表機沒墨水了。
(B) 在這個紙匣填裝紙張。
(C) 雙面，麻煩了。

23. 我在這裡還是穿著夾克比較好。
(A) 我可以開暖氣。
(B) 我們會顧好你的包包。
(C) 在百貨公司。

24. 誰會擔任國際經濟論壇的口譯？
(A) 我聽說是三月舉行。
(B) 你買了電子辭典嗎？
(C) RMK 代理的艾倫女士。

25. 你去過韓國幾次？
(A) 我從沒去過那裡。
(B) 麻煩給我來回票。
(C) 我上個月搬家了。

26. Do any of you have time to help me move the bookshelves?
(A) Up on the 12th floor.
(B) I finished reading that yesterday.
(C) The part-time worker should be here soon.

26. 你們誰有時間幫我搬書架嗎？
(A) 搬到樓上 12 樓。
(B) 我昨天讀完了。
(C) 兼職員工應該快來了。

27. I'm not sure how to send documents with this new fax machine.
(A) To an important client.
(B) I haven't used it yet either.
(C) Thank you for helping me.

27. 我不確定要怎麼用這台新的傳真機發送文件。
(A) 給重要客戶。
(B) 我也沒用過。
(C) 謝謝你幫我。

28. Are you available for a meeting this Wednesday?
(A) All the department managers.
(B) OK. I'm not busy this weekend.
(C) I should be free later in the day.

28. 你這個週三有空開會嗎？
(A) 全體部門經理。
(B) 好。我這個週末不忙。
(C) 我當天稍晚應該有時間。

29. How do I install this software?
(A) Of course you can upgrade it.
(B) I have enough, thanks.
(C) Have you asked Mr. Walker?

29.. 我該如何安裝這款軟體？
(A) 你當然可以將它升級。
(B) 我這邊夠了，謝謝。
(C) 你問過沃克先生嗎？

30. The moving van just arrived in front of our office building.
(A) I'll go get the manager.
(B) Who moved the chairs?
(C) To the new headquarters.

30. 搬運車輛剛到我們的辦公大樓前。
(A) 我去找經理。
(B) 誰搬了椅子？
(C) 搬到新總部。

31. You saw the notice for the management workshop, didn't you?
(A) It's a new shop.
(B) He was just promoted.
(C) Yes, I already signed up.

31. 你看到管理研習的通知了，對嗎？
(A) 這家店是新開的。
(B) 他剛剛升職。
(C) 對，我已經報名了。

PART 3 P. 107–110

33

Questions 32-34 refer to the following conversation with three speakers.

32-34 三人會話

W：Mr. Wong, Mr. Hoover, **I know I haven't been doing a good job keeping the museum neat recently. But it's because I've been so busy sorting through the new historical documents** 32 **that I don't have much time to clean.** 33

女：黃先生、胡佛先生，**我知道我最近沒有維護好博物館的整潔。但這是因為我一直忙著分類、整理新的歷史文獻，** 32 **以致我沒多少時間可以打掃。** 33

M1：No worries! **We've all been busy lately, so it's getting more difficult to find the time to wipe the display glass.** 33
M2：We should consider hiring a cleaning company.
W：Yeah. **I can get in touch with several local companies if you'd like.** 34
M2：Oh yes, that would be very helpful. Thank you.

男 1：別擔心！**我們大家最近都很忙，所以越來越難抽空來擦拭展示櫃的玻璃。** 33
男 2：我們應該考慮僱用清潔公司。
女：是啊。**如果你們想要，我可以聯絡幾家本地的業者。** 34
男 2：喔，好的，那就幫了大忙了。謝謝。

32. What kind of business do the speakers most likely work for?
(A) A public library
(B) An architecture firm
(C) A printing shop
(D) A history museum

33. What problem is being discussed?
(A) Some supplies are running low.
(B) Some paperwork is missing.
(C) Some glass is dirty.
(D) Some expenses are too high.

34. What will the woman probably do next?
(A) Install some equipment
(B) Contact some businesses
(C) Review a budget
(D) Make a deposit

32. 說話者最有可能在哪類業者上班？
(A) 公共圖書館
(B) 建築公司
(C) 印刷店
(D) 歷史博物館

33. 他們正在討論什麼問題？
(A) 某些用品快用完了。
(B) 缺少某些文件。
(C) 有些玻璃髒了。
(D) 有些費用太高。

34. 女子接著可能會做什麼？
(A) 安裝一些設備
(B) 聯絡幾家公司
(C) 審查預算
(D) 存入款項

Questions 35-37 refer to the following conversation.

35-37 會話

W：Good morning. Thank you for calling Gellar Gas Company. May I please have your name and account number?
M：My name is Scott Prentice. I just moved here, so **I don't have an account with your company yet. Can you help me set one up now?** 35
W：**Actually, another department handles new customers. I can transfer your call to that department,** 36 **or you can do it yourself on our Web site.** 37 Do you have the address?
M：Yes, I do. I didn't know an account could be set up online. **I'll go ahead and do that then.** 37 Thanks.

女：早安。感謝您來電蓋勒瓦斯公司。能請教您的大名和帳號嗎？
男：我的名字是史考特．普朗提斯。我剛搬來這邊，因此**還沒有在貴公司開立帳號。可以請你現在幫我開一個嗎？** 35
女：**其實，新客戶是由另一個部門負責辦理的。我可以將您的來電轉到該部門，** 36 **或者您也可以到我們的網站自行進行。** 37 您知道網址嗎？
男：是，我知道。我之前不知道可以在線上開立帳號。**那麼我就自己去辦理。** 37 謝謝。

33

35. Why is the man calling?
(A) To inquire about a bill
(B) To report a gas leak
(C) To open an account
(D) To cancel a service

35. 男子為何撥打電話？
(A) 以詢問帳單事宜
(B) 以回報瓦斯外洩
(C) 以設立帳號
(D) 以取消服務

36. Why is the woman unable to help the man?
(A) He lost his password.
(B) He called the wrong department.
(C) The company's office is not open.
(D) A Web site is down.

36. 女子為何無法幫助男子？
(A) 他忘記密碼。
(B) 他打電話找錯部門。
(C) 公司的營業處還未營業。
(D) 網站當機。

37. What will the man probably do next?
(A) Visit a Web site
(B) Provide a confirmation number
(C) Call another company
(D) Complete an application

37. 男子接下來會做什麼？
(A) 訪問網站
(B) 提供確認碼
(C) 致電另一家公司
(D) 填寫申請表

Questions 38-40 refer to the following conversation.

W：Hello, I want to book a ticket for the train that departs to Chicago at 4 o'clock this afternoon.

M：Let me look in the computer system. **The blizzard has forced many people to make sudden changes to their travel arrangements.** 38 There aren't many seats left today.

W：Yeah, I figured. **I was just told this morning that I have to inspect our Chicago factory tomorrow.** 39 That's the reason I'm in such a rush.

M：**I'm checking for available seats for the 4 P.M. train.** 40 **Ah, there's a train that leaves at 8 o'clock.**

W：Hmm . . . OK. I'll get a ticket for that one. I just need to get there today.

38-40 會話

女：您好，我想訂一張今天下午四點開往芝加哥的車票。

男：讓我查詢一下電腦系統。**這次的暴風雪迫使很多人突然變更他們的行程安排。** 38 今天剩下的座位不多了。

女：是啊，我想也是。**我今天早上才接獲通知，我明天得去視察我們在芝加哥的工廠。** 39 所以我才會這麼急。

男：**我正在查詢下午四點該班列車的空位。** 40 **噢，有一班八點出發的列車。**

女：嗯……好。我就買那班車的車票。我只要今天抵達當地即可。

38. What does the man say has caused a problem?
(A) Some damaged machines
(B) Inclement weather
(C) Heavy traffic
(D) An old booking system

38. 男子說問題的起因為何？
(A) 有些毀損的機器
(B) 天候惡劣
(C) 交通壅塞
(D) 舊的訂票系統

39. What is the woman planning to do tomorrow?
(A) Get a medical check-up
(B) Attend a seminar
(C) Fix a computer
(D) Visit a factory

40. Why does the man say, "there's a train that leaves at 8 o'clock"?
(A) To recommend an alternative choice
(B) To provide a seat upgrade
(C) To offer an explanation for a delay
(D) To point out an error

39. 女子明天計劃做什麼？
(A) 接受健檢
(B) 參加研討會
(C) 維修電腦
(D) 訪視工廠

40. 男子為什麼說：「有一班八點出發的列車」？
(A) 以推薦替代方案
(B) 以提供座艙升級
(C) 以解釋延誤
(D) 以指出錯誤

TEST 8 PART 3

33

Questions 41-43 refer to the following conversation.

M：Hi, **it's Eric Shuuman from the apartment management office.** 41 You left a message about a problem in your bedroom.
W：Oh yes. Thank you for calling me back right away. **I just discovered a large water stain on my bedroom's ceiling. I think there might be a leak** 42 coming from the apartment right above me.
M：Actually, there is a dripping water pipe in that apartment, so our maintenance crew is up there fixing the problem right now.
W：I see. Do you think you could send the workers over to my place when they're finished? **I'd like them to check my ceiling to see how bad the damage is.** 43

41-43 會話

男：您好，**我是公寓管理室的艾瑞克．舒曼。** 41 您先前有留言提到您的臥室有點問題。
女：哦，是的。感謝您馬上就回電給我。**我剛剛發現我的臥室天花板上出現一塊大水漬。我想**在我正上方的公寓房間**可能漏水了。** 42
男：那一戶公寓的確有一條水管正在滴水，所以我們的維修團隊正在樓上那邊處理問題。
女：了解。等到工作人員處理完後，能請您再派他們到我家嗎？**我想請他們檢查我這裡天花板的毀損嚴重程度。** 43

41. Where is the man calling from?
(A) An apartment management office
(B) A hotel front desk
(C) A furniture store
(D) A construction company

42. What problem are the speakers discussing?
(A) A water leak
(B) A reservation error
(C) Some missing orders
(D) Some defective cables

43. What does the woman request?
(A) An exchange for a product
(B) A discount on a service
(C) A list of replacement parts
(D) An inspection for damage

41. 男子從哪裡撥打電話？
(A) 公寓管理室
(B) 飯店櫃檯
(C) 家具行
(D) 建設公司

42. 說話者正在討論什麼問題？
(A) 漏水
(B) 預約出錯
(C) 遺失的訂單
(D) 損壞的電纜

43. 女子提出什麼要求？
(A) 更換產品
(B) 服務收費折扣
(C) 備用零件清單
(D) 檢查毀損情形

Questions 44-46 refer to the following conversation.

M: Hello, I'm calling from the Cedar Fitness Club. I saw your ad online, and **we'd like to have some T-shirts made to advertise our business.** 44 Could I get some information about the prices?

W: Of course. They're 6 dollars each. However, **if you order them in bulk, we will give you up to 20 percent off** 45 the total price depending on the quantity.

M: That sounds reasonable. We also want to have our gym's logo printed on the front of the shirts. Is that possible?

W: Sure. **All you have to do is visit our Web site** 46 and upload an image of the logo when placing your order.

44-46 會話

男：您好，我這裡是「雪松健身中心」來電。我在網路上看到你們的廣告，然後**我們想要訂製一些 T 恤，用來宣傳我們的業務。** 44 能否讓我了解一些價格相關資訊呢？

女：當然可以。每件 6 美元。然而，**如果您是大量訂購，我們**會再根據數量，**最高將給您**總價 **20%的折扣。** 45

男：聽起來很合理。我們也想要在 T 恤正面印上我們健身房的標誌。這有辦法做到嗎？

女：當然行。**您只需前往我們的網站，** 46 並在下訂單時上傳標誌圖檔即可。

44. What does the man want to purchase?
(A) Gym equipment
(B) Office supplies
(C) Advertising space
(D) Promotional clothing

44. 男子想購買什麼？
(A) 健身器材
(B) 辦公用品
(C) 廣告版面
(D) 宣傳用服飾

45. How can the man receive a discount?
(A) By subscribing to a magazine
(B) By placing a large order
(C) By signing up for a membership
(D) By paying in cash

45. 男子該如何取得折扣？
(A) 經由訂閱雜誌
(B) 經由下大筆訂單
(C) 經由註冊成為會員
(D) 以現金支付

46. What does the woman tell the man to do?
(A) Visit another location
(B) Speak to a supervisor
(C) Go to a Web site
(D) Check out a sample

46. 女子指示男子怎麼做？
(A) 去另一個店面
(B) 和主管談談
(C) 前往網站
(D) 查看樣品

Questions 47-49 refer to the following conversation.

W: Dustin, **have you heard that the company is going to try to make our offices more energy-efficient?** 47 They recently set up a Strategy Committee and are asking employees to participate.

M: Yes, I received an email about it last week. It sounds quite promising. **Are you planning on getting involved with the committee?** 48

47-49 會話

女：達斯汀，**現在公司有意設法讓我們辦公室變得更加節能，這你聽說了嗎？** 47 公司最近成立了策略委員會，而且正在徵詢員工參加。

男：有，我上週有收到相關電子郵件。聽起來大有可為。**妳有打算去加入委員會嗎？** 48

W：Well, **I'll attend the first meeting this Thursday to get further details before I decide to join.** 48 Since I'm currently between projects, I have some free time. How about you?

M：**I want to go, but I'll be busy that day. I'll be doing the marketing presentation** 49 at the Tourette Corporation, so I probably won't have any time. But please let me know what you learn at the meeting.

女：嗯，**我會出席本週四的第一場會議，了解更多資訊後，再決定加入與否。** 48 我目前手上沒有專案要進行，所以還算有空。那你呢？

男：**我是想去，但我那天會很忙。我到時要**到圖雷特企業**進行行銷簡報，** 49 所以可能沒時間。不過，還請妳再告訴我妳在會議上得知的內容。

47. What is the company's plan?
(A) To increase energy efficiency
(B) To reduce travel expenses
(C) To open an overseas branch
(D) To elect new board members

47. 該公司有何規劃？
(A) 想提高能源效率
(B) 想減少差旅開銷
(C) 想開設海外分支
(D) 想遴選新的董事會成員

48. What is the woman considering?
(A) Submitting a proposal
(B) Contacting an organizer
(C) Joining a committee
(D) Performing a survey

48. 女子正在考慮什麼？
(A) 繳交提案
(B) 聯絡策劃人
(C) 加入委員會
(D) 進行調查

49. Why is the man unable to attend the meeting?
(A) He is picking up a client.
(B) He is giving a presentation.
(C) He is training an employee.
(D) He is going on a vacation.

49. 男子為何不能出席會議？
(A) 他將要接客戶。
(B) 他將進行簡報。
(C) 他將培訓員工。
(D) 他將要去度假。

Questions 50-52 refer to the following conversation.

50-52 會話

M：Hi, Chung-Hee. **Someone told me you wanted to speak to me about our upcoming staff party.** 50 How are the preparations coming along?

W：Well, we're not going to have live musical performances this time. Instead, we are buying new audio equipment so that we can have recorded music playing at the party. **Do you mind picking up the equipment on Sunday morning and bringing it to the reception hall?** 51

M：I'm afraid I can't. **My son has a baseball game that Sunday morning, and I promised him that I would be there.** 52 So I won't have time before the party.

男：嗨，鄭熙。**有人告訴我，你想和我討論即將登場的員工聚會。** 50 準備工作進行得怎麼樣了？

女：嗯，我們這次不會安排現場音樂表演。作為替代，我們會採買新的音響設備，以便我們能在聚會上播放錄製的音樂。**能麻煩你在週日早上去載設備，之後送到接待大廳嗎？** 51

男：我恐怕無法幫忙。**那個星期天早上我兒子有棒球比賽，我已經答應他我會到場了。** 52 所以我在聚會前不會有時間。

50. What type of event are the speakers discussing?
(A) A music festival
(B) A gallery opening
(C) A business seminar
(D) A company party

51. What does the woman ask the man to do?
(A) Transport some equipment
(B) Reserve a reception hall
(C) Set up some tables
(D) Contact a band

52. What does the man say he has to do Sunday morning?
(A) Practice a musical instrument
(B) Attend a sporting event
(C) Work extra hours
(D) Get his car repaired

50. 說話者正在討論哪種活動？
(A) 音樂節
(B) 藝廊開幕
(C) 企業研討會
(D) 公司聚會

51. 女子要求男子做什麼？
(A) 運送一些設備
(B) 預約接待大廳
(C) 擺設幾張桌子
(D) 聯絡樂團

52. 男子說他週日早上必須做什麼？
(A) 練習樂器
(B) 出席體育活動
(C) 加班
(D) 將車送修

Questions 53-55 refer to the following conversation with three speakers.

W1：Good afternoon, Mr. Anderson, Ms. Walsh. I'm pleased you've decided to take another look at this commercial space. Like I said over the phone, the price has been lowered again.
M：Well, **it's perfect for our store,** 53 **but we have one major concern.** 54
W2：**We don't have the budget to pay for any serious repair work.** 54 This floor for example... How long has it been since it was replaced?
W1：It's only been three years. And the building underwent extensive remodeling last year.
W2：That's good to hear. I'm surprised that the landlord is selling this place at such a low price.
W1：Well, **he's moving to another country, so he needs to sell the place as soon as possible.** 55

53-55 三人會話

女 1：安德森先生、沃爾什女士，午安。很高興兩位決定再次參觀這個商用店面。正如我在電話裡報告的，價格又再度調降了。
男：嗯，**這是我們開店的完美地點，** 53 **但我們有個主要的顧慮。** 54
女 2：**我們沒有預算可以支應任何重大的維修。** 54 以這地板來說……有多久沒換了？
女 1：只有三年。而且這棟建築才在去年進行過大規模翻修。
女 2：那真是好消息。我很驚訝屋主會以這麼低的價格出售這個地方。
女 1：這個嘛，**他即將移居國外，所以得要儘快把這個地方脫手。** 55

53. Who most likely are Mr. Anderson and Ms. Walsh?
(A) Real estate agents
(B) Business owners
(C) Construction workers
(D) City officials

53. 安德森先生和沃爾什女士最有可能的身分是？
(A) 房地產經紀人
(B) 商家老闆
(C) 建築工人
(D) 市府官員

54. What are Mr. Anderson and Ms. Walsh concerned about?
(A) Paying for major renovations
(B) Attracting more clients
(C) The size of an office space
(D) The date of a move

55. What is mentioned about the landlord?
(A) He will meet the speakers tomorrow.
(B) He will negotiate a price.
(C) He is currently on a business trip.
(D) He is relocating overseas.

54. 安德森先生和沃爾什女士擔心什麼？
(A) 支付重大裝修的費用
(B) 吸引更多客戶
(C) 辦公空間的大小
(D) 搬遷日期

55. 關於屋主，對話中提到什麼？
(A) 他明天將和說話者見面。
(B) 他將議價。
(C) 他目前正在出差。
(D) 他正要移居海外。

TEST 8 PART 3

33

Questions 56-58 refer to the following conversation.

M : Olga, **I just came back from the mixing room, and there seems to be something wrong with the ingredients for our ice cream.** 56 The texture is too thick.
W : That's not good. **I also noticed yesterday that our ice cream wasn't as creamy as it normally is.** 57 I wonder what's causing the problem. Do you think it might be the mixer?
M : Hmm . . . **That machine is very old, and it's been repaired quite a few times. Maybe it's finally time to buy a new one.** 58

56-58 會話

男：奧爾加，**我剛去了一趟攪拌室回來，而我們冰淇淋的材料似乎出了點問題。** 56 口感太黏稠了。
女：那可不行。**我昨天也注意到，我們的冰淇淋不像平常一樣細緻滑順。** 57 我想知道問題出在哪。你覺得可能是攪拌機的關係嗎？
男：嗯……**那台機器真的很舊，而且已經一修再修。也許終於是時候買一台新的了。** 58

56. What industry do the speakers most likely work in?
(A) Clothing manufacturing
(B) Event organizing
(C) Equipment sales
(D) Food production

57. What problem are the speakers discussing?
(A) A customer complaint was received.
(B) The quality of a product is poor.
(C) Some tools have not been cleaned.
(D) More workers are needed.

58. What does the man suggest?
(A) Lowering prices
(B) Informing a manager
(C) Discarding some materials
(D) Replacing a machine

56. 說話者最有可能在什麼產業工作？
(A) 服裝製造
(B) 活動策劃
(C) 設備銷售
(D) 食品生產

57. 說話者正在討論哪項問題？
(A) 收到一名客戶投訴。
(B) 產品品質不佳。
(C) 部分工具未經清潔。
(D) 需要更多人手。

58. 男子有什麼建議？
(A) 調降價格
(B) 通知經理
(C) 丟棄材料
(D) 更換機器

Questions 59-61 refer to the following conversation.

W：**Hey, Francesco, an important client is visiting from Thailand later this week. 59 Do you think you could show them around our headquarters on Friday afternoon? 60**

M：Actually, **I'm leading a workshop all day on Friday.**

W：Oh, that's right. Do you know if Leslie's available?

M：Maybe . . . I can talk to her about it if you want.

W：That'd be great. Just keep me updated.

M：Sure. It seems like we've been getting a lot more business in Southeast Asia these days. That's exciting!

W：Yeah. **And if we keep getting more business like this, it might be possible for us to construct a new plant in the region by the end of this year. 61**

59-61 會話

女：**嘿，汎切斯科，本週過幾天會有一名重要客戶從泰國來訪。59 你覺得你有辦法在週五下午帶他們參觀公司總部嗎？60**

男：其實，**我週五整天都得主持一場研習。**

女：噢，這倒也是。你知道萊斯利有沒有空嗎？

男：可能有……如果妳想要話，我可以跟她談談。

女：這樣就太好了。請隨時向我報告最新情況。

男：當然。看來我們近來正大幅擴展在東南亞的業務。很讓人振奮！

女：對啊。**而且如果我們能持續接獲更多類似的業務，今年年底前公司就有可能在當地建設新的工廠。61**

59. Who is visiting the company?

(A) A property manager
(B) A local journalist
(C) A government employee
(D) An overseas client

60. Why does the man say, "I'm leading a workshop all day on Friday"?

(A) He is unable to take on a task.
(B) He would like some help with an event.
(C) He would like an updated guest list.
(D) He is concerned about giving a presentation.

61. According to the woman, what does the company hope to do by the end of the year?

(A) Transfer some workers
(B) Launch a product line
(C) Build another facility
(D) Appoint a new CEO

59. 誰會前來公司造訪？

(A) 物業管理人員
(B) 地方記者
(C) 政府職員
(D) 海外客戶

60. 男子說：「我週五整天都得主持一場研習」，其意思為何？

(A) 他不能接下任務。
(B) 他需要活動相關協助。
(C) 他想要更新版的賓客名單。
(D) 他對進行簡報感到擔憂。

61. 根據女子說法，公司在年底前希望做到什麼？

(A) 調動幾名員工
(B) 推出新系列產品
(C) 建造另一座工廠
(D) 任命新任執行長

Questions 62-64 refer to the following conversation and voucher.

W：Good morning, Ken. **You heard about Shirley's transfer, right?** 62 She'll be taking over the branch manager position in Washington next week.

M：This is the first time I've heard about it. That sounds like an exciting opportunity!

W：I agree. Anyway, a few of us are planning to treat her to lunch this Friday at Mallie's Place. You should join us.

M：Sure, thanks for inviting me. As a matter of fact, I have a voucher for that café. Here, you'll see that they have some nice dessert deals this month.

W：Oh, let's see. **Shirley really likes strawberry pie. We can get a pie to share after the meal.** 63

M：Great! By the way, we should make sure they'll have space that day. **Why don't I book a table for us?** 64

Mallie's Place

Dessert Deals for May

Strawberry Pie – 10% OFF 63
Vanilla Ice Cream – 20% OFF
Chocolate Cake – 30% OFF
Banana Pudding – 40% OFF

62-64 會話和優待券

女：肯，早安。**你聽說了雪莉的調動，對吧？** 62 她下週就將接任華盛頓分公司經理一職了。

男：我現在才第一次聽說。聽起來是很讓人心動的機會！

女：我同意。總之，我們幾個人打算這週五到麥利小舖請她吃午餐。你也該來共襄盛舉。

男：當然好，感謝妳邀請我。其實我有那家咖啡廳的優待券。在這裡，妳會看到他們這個月有些不錯的甜點優惠。

女：哦，我看一下。**雪莉真的很喜歡吃草莓派。我們飯後可以點個派，大家一起吃。** 63

男：太棒了！順道一提，我們該要確認當天會有空位。**不如我來幫大家預訂一桌？** 64

麥利小舖

五月甜點優惠

草莓派—折扣 10% 63
香草冰淇淋—折扣 20%
巧克力蛋糕—折扣 30%
香蕉布丁—折扣 40%

TEST 8 PART 3 33

62. What information does the woman share with the man?
(A) A product will be launched early.
(B) A managers' meeting will be held.
(C) A contract will be awarded soon.
(D) A colleague will be transferred.

63. Look at the graphic. Which discount will the speakers most likely receive?
(A) 10%
(B) 20%
(C) 30%
(D) 40%

62. 女子與男子分享了什麼消息？
(A) 有項產品將提前上市。
(B) 將舉行經理會議。
(C) 即將批出合約。
(D) 一位同事將調任。

63. 請據圖表作答。說話者將最有可能獲得何項折扣？
(A) 10%
(B) 20%
(C) 30%
(D) 40%

64. What does the man offer to do?
(A) Update a calendar
(B) Contact a different café
(C) Make a reservation
(D) Rent a vehicle

64. 男子提議幫忙做什麼？
(A) 更新行事曆
(B) 接洽別的咖啡廳
(C) 訂位
(D) 租車

Questions 65-67 refer to the following conversation and graphic design.

M：Hey, Violet. I'm finally done with the initial design for the new Max Energy Bar, and I'd like your opinion on it.
W：Let's see . . . Oh, it looks nice. But I'm not sure the bar's name is being displayed effectively. As you know, **we're marketing Max Energy Bar as a helpful fitness supplement.** 65
M：OK, how do you think I should change it then?
W：Well, **you could place the firm's logo at the bottom next to the price, and then, move up the name of the bar.** 66 By doing that, you should grab the attention of those who are looking for something to improve their fitness workouts.
M：Ah, thank you for the suggestion!
W：No problem. **The clients aren't coming in until next Friday,** 67 so you still have time.

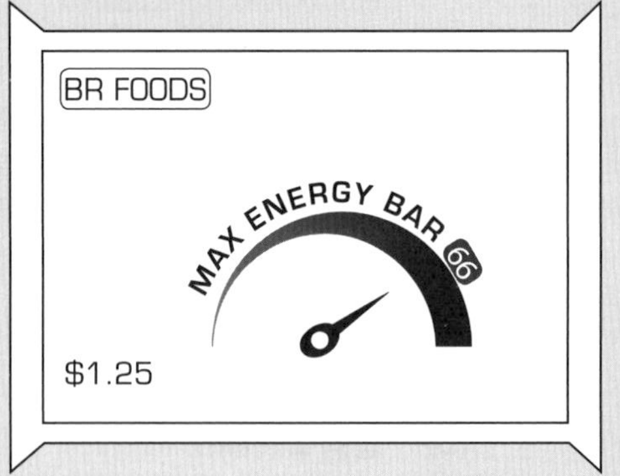

65-67 會話和平面設計

男：嘿，維奧莉特。我終於完成了新品「全滿能量棒」的設計初稿，想聽聽妳的意見。
女：我看一下……哦，看起來不錯。但我不確定能量棒的商品名稱呈現的效果如何。你也知道，**現在我們宣傳全滿能量棒時，就是主打作為有用的健身補給品。** 65
男：好的，那妳覺得我應該怎麼修改呢？
女：嗯，**你可以把公司標誌移到底部，置於售價旁邊，接著，再把能量棒的商品名稱移上去。** 66 這樣一來，你應該可以吸引那些正在尋覓能改善健身運動狀態的產品的人。
男：啊，謝謝妳的建議！
女：不客氣。**客戶要下週五才會來，** 67 因此你還有時間。

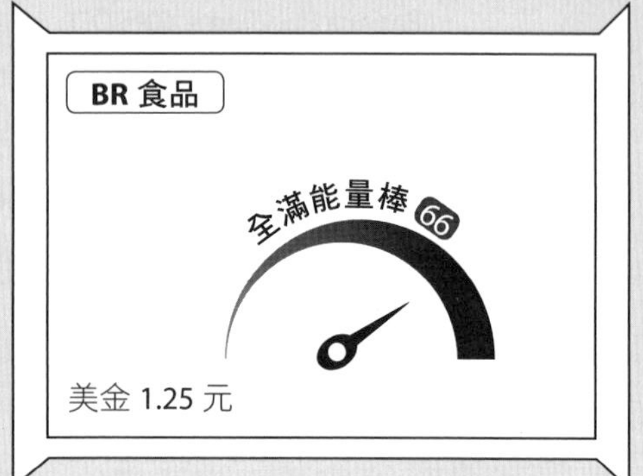

65. What does the woman say is the target market for Max Energy Bar?
(A) Food experts
(B) Traveling workers
(C) Fitness enthusiasts
(D) Senior citizens

65. 女子說「全滿能量棒」的目標市場為何者？
(A) 食品專家
(B) 旅行工作者
(C) 健身愛好者
(D) 高齡人士

66. Look at the graphic. What will be displayed at the top of the bar wrapper after a change?
(A) The firm's logo
(B) The product's name
(C) The energy meter
(D) The price

67. What is scheduled for next week?
(A) An industry convention
(B) A store opening
(C) A client visit
(D) A sales event

66. 請據圖表作答。更改設計後，能量棒包裝的最上方會標出什麼？
(A) 公司標誌
(B) 產品名稱
(C) 電表
(D) 價格

67. 下週有何預定事項？
(A) 產業博覽會
(B) 店家開幕
(C) 客戶來訪
(D) 促銷活動

33

Questions 68-70 refer to the following conversation and flyer.

M： Hello, Mandy. I'm in charge of our firm's upcoming Health Awareness Week. Here's a flyer.
W： Thank you. **I'm excited that everyone is getting multi-vitamin bottles this year.** 68 They are manufactured by a well-known company. **There were no presents last year.** 68
M： I'm looking forward to that. Which event are you planning to go to?
W： Hmm . . . I do want to learn more about nutrition, but I'll be visiting a client that day. Oh, **Wednesday's event sounds really fun! My schedule should be open that day.** 69
M： I see. By the way, **can you take some more flyers and give them to your employees in Publishing?** 70 That way, we can hand them out faster.

HEALTH AWARENESS WEEK

Only open to LCO Employees
Free Admission!

Mon	Tue	**Wed**	Thu	Fri
Medical Consultations	Nutrition Seminar	**Cooking Class** 69	Farm Visit	Well-being Lunch

68-70 會話和傳單

男： 哈囉，曼蒂。我負責我們公司即將舉行的「健康宣導週」。給妳一張傳單。
女： 謝謝。**我很高興今年每個人都會收到瓶裝綜合維生素。** 68 送的是知名公司生產的產品。**去年可沒有禮物。** 68
男： 這我也很期待。妳打算參加哪一場活動？
女： 嗯……我想更了解營養議題，但那天我要去訪問客戶。哦，**週三的活動聽起來真有趣！我當天的行程應該有空檔。** 69
男： 了解。順道一提，**能請妳多拿幾張傳單，並分發給妳在出版部的職員嗎？** 70 這樣我們可以更快把傳單發完。

健康宣導週

僅開放給 LCO 員工
免費進場！

週一	週二	**週三**	週四	週五
醫療諮詢	營養講座	**烹飪課** 69	農場參訪	幸福午餐

68. What does the woman say is new about the Health Awareness Week this year?
(A) A contest will be held.
(B) A movie will be shown to staff.
(C) Presents will be provided to staff.
(D) Celebrities will be signing autographs.

69. Look at the graphic. Which event will the woman probably attend?
(A) The medical consultations
(B) The nutrition seminar
(C) The cooking class
(D) The farm visit

70. What does the man ask the woman to do?
(A) Contact some department managers
(B) Review an order form
(C) Complete a questionnaire
(D) Distribute some materials

68. 關於健康宣導週，女子說今年有何不同？
(A) 將舉行比賽。
(B) 將向員工放映電影。
(C) 將有贈品給員工。
(D) 將舉行名人簽名會。

69. 請據圖表作答。女子可能會參加什麼活動？
(A) 醫療諮詢
(B) 營養講座
(C) 烹飪課
(D) 農場參訪

70. 男子請女子做什麼？
(A) 聯絡幾名部門經理
(B) 檢查訂購單
(C) 填寫問卷
(D) 發放資料

34

PART 4 P. 111–113

Questions 71-73 refer to the following talk.

W：**I've asked all of you to gather here this morning to tell you about the new packaging machines. They are a lot faster than the previous model that we were using here at our factory.** 71 72 They can package items at twice the speed of the old machines. **Now, please look at the checklist that I've just handed out and follow along while I show you how to operate the machines.** 73

71-73 談話

女：**我請各位今天早上集合，是為了向你們介紹新的包裝機器。它們比我們工廠以前使用的機型要快上許多。** 71 72 它們包貨的速度是舊型機器的兩倍之多。**現在，在我示範機台操作方式的同時，請一邊跟著參閱我剛剛發下的檢查表。** 73

71. Who is the intended audience for the talk?
(A) Sales staff members
(B) Delivery drivers
(C) Factory employees
(D) Security guards

72. What is mentioned as an advantage of the new machines?
(A) They work faster.
(B) They seldom malfunction.
(C) They are reasonably priced.
(D) They are energy-efficient.

71. 這段談話的對象聽眾是誰？
(A) 銷售人員
(B) 貨運司機
(C) 工廠員工
(D) 保全人員

72. 談話提到何項新款機器的優點？
(A) 作業更快速。
(B) 很少故障。
(C) 價格合理。
(D) 節省能源。

73. What is the speaker about to do?
(A) Give a demonstration
(B) Place an order
(C) Attend a meeting
(D) Call a supplier

73. 說話者即將做什麼？
(A) 進行示範
(B) 下訂單
(C) 參加會議
(D) 致電供應商

Questions 74-76 refer to the following recorded message.

74-76 答錄訊息

M：**You've reached the Culliver Hills Department of Parks and Recreation.** 74 Please be aware that we have changed the application procedure for booking community picnic areas. **Because of the recent high volume of applications, reservations will now take at least seven business days to process.** 75 **Make sure to submit a complete description of your event along with the reservation form.** 76 A department spokesperson will be with you in just a moment. Thank you for your patience.

男：**這裡是格列佛丘的公園遊憩部。** 74 請注意，我們已經更改了預約社區野餐區的申請程序。**由於最近的申請件數繁多，現在將需要至少七個工作天處理預約。** 75 **繳交預約單時，請務必同時附上您的活動的完整說明。** 76 稍後將有部門發言人與您通話。感謝您的耐心等候。

TEST 8

PART 3 4

34

74. Which department in Culliver Hills recorded the message?
(A) Health
(B) Transportation
(C) Parks and Recreation
(D) Planning and Development

74. 格列佛丘的哪個部門錄了這則訊息？
(A) 衛生
(B) 交通
(C) 公園遊憩
(D) 規劃開發

75. According to the message, why is a procedure taking longer to complete?
(A) More applications are being received.
(B) A community center is being renovated.
(C) There has been a shortage of workers.
(D) There has been inclement weather.

75. 據這段訊息內容，為何作業程序得花更久時間完成？
(A) 收到的申請件數增加。
(B) 社區活動中心正在整修。
(C) 人力不足。
(D) 天候惡劣。

76. What does the speaker ask the listeners to do?
(A) Meet with a city official
(B) Submit a payment
(C) Present a photo ID
(D) Include a detailed description

76. 說話者要求聽者做什麼？
(A) 與市府官員會面
(B) 繳交款項
(C) 出示附相片的身分證件
(D) 附上詳細說明

Questions 77-79 refer to the following excerpt from a meeting.

W：**I called today's meeting because I have some news to share. I know all of you are busy with your training sessions at our gym.** 77 **But don't worry, you won't be late for any of your appointments.** If you remember, **we had an expert come in on Monday, Jeffrey Polumbus, to evaluate our fitness center.** 78 Although a lot of members are satisfied with our personal trainers, Jeffrey pointed out that we could still do better. He said we could generate more money if we sell more vitamin products to gym members. **I know that selling vitamin supplements isn't your area of expertise. That's why Jeffrey is back today to hold a brief activity to practice some useful sales tactics.** 79

77. What does the speaker imply when she says, "you won't be late for any of your appointments"?
(A) Appointments must be canceled in advance.
(B) Some members have complained.
(C) Workers should come to work on time.
(D) A meeting will be short.

78. What does the speaker say happened on Monday?
(A) An expert examined a business.
(B) A fitness center closed early.
(C) A promotional event was held.
(D) A new policy was announced.

79. According to the speaker, what will the listeners practice?
(A) Building customer relationships
(B) Selling some products
(C) Cooking healthy meals
(D) Installing exercise machines

77-79 會議摘錄

女：**我今天召開會議，是因為有些訊息要分享。我知道各位在我們健身房裡，都為了你們的健身教程忙碌不已。** 77 **但別擔心，不會來不及去你們約好的任何行程。**如果大家記得，**週一我們請來一位叫傑佛瑞·波倫布斯的專家到本健身中心進行評鑑。** 78 儘管許多會員都很滿意我們的個人教練，但傑佛瑞指出我們還有進步空間。他說到，如果我們賣出更多維生素商品給健身房的會員，就能創造更多收益。**我知道兜售維生素補充劑並非各位擅長的領域。正因如此，今天傑佛瑞又到場舉辦一場簡短活動，來教練一些有用的銷售策略。** 79

77. 說話者說：「不會來不及去你們約好的任何行程」，其暗示為何？
(A) 必須提前取消約定行程。
(B) 幾名會員提出投訴。
(C) 員工應準時到班。
(D) 會議會很簡短。

78. 說話者說週一發生了什麼事？
(A) 有專家檢視了業者。
(B) 健身房提前關門。
(C) 舉辦了促銷活動。
(D) 公布了新政策。

79. 據說話者說法，聽者會做何項練習？
(A) 建立客戶關係
(B) 銷售一些產品
(C) 烹煮健康餐點
(D) 安裝健身器材

Questions 80-82 refer to the following talk.

80-82 談話

M：OK, let's begin today's team meeting. **I'm going to go over a new procedure that will be implemented at our post office.** 80 Right now, **all packages that come in are given a label with the name and address of the recipient. However, beginning next Monday, all packages will also include barcodes.** 81 We will scan the barcodes every time we receive a piece of mail. **This will help us record the exact date and time a package comes in and goes out.** 81 All right, to get you all familiar with this process, **I'll pass out scanners to everyone so that you can try scanning some packages yourself.** 82

男：好，我們開始今天的團隊會議。**我將要說明我們郵局將要實施的一項新程序。**80 目前，**所有收進來的包裹都會貼上有收件人姓名和地址的標籤。但從下週一開始，所有包裹都還須附加條碼。**81 之後每次我們收取郵件時，都要掃描條碼。**這能幫我們記錄包裹收發的確切日期和時間。**81 好，為了讓你們都熟悉這項流程，**我會把掃描機傳下去給各位，以便你們可以自行試著掃描幾份包裹。**82

80. What type of business do the listeners work for?
(A) A post office
(B) A stationery store
(C) A printing center
(D) A health clinic

80. 聽者在什麼類型的企業服務？
(A) 郵局
(B) 文具店
(C) 影印店
(D) 醫療診所

81. According to the speaker, what is being changed?
(A) How work schedules are created
(B) How payments are processed
(C) How information is recorded
(D) How facilities are inspected

81. 據說話者說法，有什麼事項將異動？
(A) 建立排班表的方式
(B) 處理付款的方式
(C) 記錄資訊的方式
(D) 檢查設施的方式

82. What will the listeners do next?
(A) Fill out some forms
(B) Use some devices
(C) Watch a demonstration
(D) Read a user guide

82. 聽者接著會做什麼？
(A) 填寫表格
(B) 使用裝置
(C) 觀看示範
(D) 閱讀使用說明書

Questions 83-85 refer to the following introduction.

83-85 開場白

W：**Thank you all for coming to today's digital advertising presentation:** 83 *Making your Product Stand Out Above Others*. I'm Ashna Faraj, the content manager at JCB. **I'm sorry that we weren't able to begin on time. I missed my train and had to wait for the next one.** 84 We've got a lot to cover, so let's begin. **Oh, it looks as though not everyone has gotten the handout.** 85 **I have extras here in the front.**

女：**感謝各位蒞臨今天的數位廣告簡報：**83「讓你的產品脫穎而出」。我是阿許納．法拉吉，擔任 JCB 公司的內容經理。**我很抱歉我們未能準時開始。我沒有趕上我要搭的列車，只好等下一班車。**84 我們要談的內容很多，所以我們開始吧。**噢，好像不是每個人都有拿到講義。**85 **我前面這邊還有多幾份。**

83. What type of event is taking place?
(A) A business opening
(B) A product launch
(C) A marketing presentation
(D) A retirement party

84. Why was the event delayed?
(A) Some devices were not working.
(B) A speaker arrived late.
(C) A facility was being cleaned.
(D) Some bad weather was approaching.

85. What does the speaker imply when she says, "I have extras here in the front"?
(A) Some listeners should pick up a document.
(B) Complimentary beverages are available.
(C) Tickets will be given away.
(D) Attendees should return some merchandise.

83. 正在舉辦什麼類型的活動？
(A) 公司開業
(B) 產品發布
(C) 行銷簡報
(D) 退休慶祝會

84. 活動為什麼延誤了？
(A) 部分裝置故障。
(B) 講者遲到
(C) 設施正在打掃中。
(D) 惡劣天候將至。

85. 說話者說：「我前面這邊還有多幾份」，其暗示為何？
(A) 部分聽者應領取一份文件。
(B) 提供免費飲料。
(C) 將會分送票券。
(D) 參加者須退還部分商品。

Questions 86-88 refer to the following announcement.

W：**I'm pleased to announce that Retro-Fit Designs has just purchased a new printer.** 86 We can now offer our clients the highest quality design images while maintaining our commitment to being environmentally friendly. This latest model uses vegetable oil-based inks, so **it doesn't pollute the environment. Also, the inks are completely recyclable.** 87 On Wednesday, we will be providing training on how to properly maintain and use the new printer. And **to make sure that all workers can attend, we'll be offering two training sessions,** 88 one at 9:00 A.M. and one at 4:00 P.M.

86-88 宣布

女：**我很高興宣布，「復古翻新設計」剛採購了一台新印表機。** 86 我們現在不僅能向客戶提供最高品質的設計圖，也同時恪守我們對環保的承諾。這台最新型的機器使用植物性油墨，因此**不會污染環境。此外，油墨可完全回收。** 87 我們將在週三提供正確保養、使用新印表機的訓練教程。而**為了確保全體員工都能參加，我們將提供兩場培訓課程，** 88 上午九點一場以及下午四點一場。

86. What is the purpose of the announcement?
(A) To describe a new printer
(B) To outline safety regulations
(C) To announce an upcoming inspection
(D) To share some sales figures

87. What benefit does the speaker mention?
(A) Less maintenance work
(B) Increased sales
(C) Reduced damage to the environment
(D) Greater morale among employees

86. 這項宣布的目的為何？
(A) 以說明新款印表機
(B) 以概述安全規則
(C) 以公告即將進行的檢查
(D) 以分享一些銷售數據

87. 說話者提到什麼好處？
(A) 減輕維修作業
(B) 增加銷量
(C) 減少對環境的破壞
(D) 提振員工士氣

88. According to the speaker, why have two training sessions been scheduled?
(A) To ensure sufficient practice time
(B) To accommodate all employees
(C) To meet a project deadline
(D) To comply with company policy

Questions 89-91 refer to the following introduction.

M：Hello, everyone, and welcome to the convention. I hope you didn't have too much trouble finding this room. **I'm sorry for any confusion. The program should have included the new location of the event, but I guess it didn't.** 89 Anyway, I'm excited to introduce today's speaker: Hunter Griffin. **Mr. Griffin is a senior consultant at Midway Bank.** 90 His job is to help his clients create smart savings and investment plans. He has a lot of experience in teaching people how to be more organized with their money. **I'm sure you all agree that careful planning is crucial to maintaining financial stability. To learn more, let's welcome Mr. Griffin.** 91

89. Why does the speaker apologize?
(A) A machine is not working.
(B) A presentation was canceled.
(C) A program was inaccurate.
(D) A registration procedure was confusing.

90. Who most likely is Mr. Griffin?
(A) An event organizer
(B) A financial advisor
(C) A building manager
(D) A newspaper journalist

91. What will Mr. Griffin discuss?
(A) Team management tips
(B) Public speaking skills
(C) Marketing trends
(D) Careful planning

88. 根據說話者說法，為什麼安排了兩場培訓課程？
(A) 以確保練習時間充足
(B) 以配合全體員工
(C) 以趕上專案截止日期
(D) 以遵守公司政策

89-91 開場白

男：哈囉，大家好，歡迎蒞臨本次大會。我希望這次的會場沒有讓各位太難找路。**若造成困擾，我深感抱歉。議程表上應該要寫上新的會場位置的，但我想是漏掉了。** 89 無論如何，我很高興介紹今天的講者：航特．葛里芬。**葛里芬先生是「中道銀行」資深顧問。** 90 他的工作是幫助客戶制定明智的儲蓄和投資計畫。他在教導如何更有條理的理財上有著豐富的經驗。**我確信各位都同意要維持財務穩定，謹慎規劃是至關重要的。就讓我們歡迎葛里芬先生帶來更多內容。** 91

89. 說話者為何致歉？
(A) 機器故障。
(B) 簡報取消。
(C) 議程表不正確。
(D) 報名流程令人困惑。

90. 葛里芬先生最有可能的身分是？
(A) 活動策劃人員
(B) 理財顧問
(C) 大樓管理員
(D) 報社記者

91. 葛里芬先生將討論何事？
(A) 團隊管理訣竅
(B) 公開演講技巧
(C) 行銷趨勢
(D) 謹慎規劃

Questions 92-94 refer to the following talk.

W：**Thanks again for letting me visit your construction company to explain the Mundial Videoconferencing Software.** 92 Since you all are involved in major global design projects, I have no doubt that you need to coordinate with engineers around the world. **With this program, you can cut back on the number of face-to-face meetings required, which should bring travel expenses down.** 93 Suppose you are working with an engineer in India on a project there. **You can conduct a meeting online to complete your initial planning instead of traveling to India.** 93 **Now, I'm sure you'd like to know how to use the program.** 94 **Did everybody turn on their laptops?**

92. Where do the listeners work?
(A) At a software company
(B) At a graphic design studio
(C) At a construction firm
(D) At a travel agency

93. According to the speaker, how can the listeners save money?
(A) By selecting an affordable distributor
(B) By hiring a foreign business partner
(C) By using fuel-efficient vehicles
(D) By holding online meetings

94. What does the speaker imply when she says, "Did everybody turn on their laptops"?
(A) She will update a system.
(B) She will demonstrate a product.
(C) Her laptop is not working.
(D) Her password is incorrect.

92-94 談話

女：**再次感謝各位讓我到訪貴建設公司，說明這款「環球視訊會議軟體」。** 92 由於各位都有經手全球性的重大設計專案，我確信在座各位都須與世界各地的工程師協作。**有了這套程式，您們可以減少得要親身赴會的次數，這可望能減少差旅支出。** 93 假設您正在和一名印度工程師合作當地專案。**您可以透過線上會議完成您的初期規劃，而不用出差到印度。** 93 **現在，我確信大家會想了解本程式的使用方法。** 94 **各位都打開筆電了嗎？**

92. 聽者在哪裡工作？
(A) 在軟體公司
(B) 在平面設計工作室
(C) 在建設公司
(D) 在旅行社

93. 據說話者說法，聽者能如何省錢？
(A) 透過選擇價格合理的經銷商
(B) 透過僱用國外商業夥伴
(C) 透過使用省油車輛
(D) 透過舉行線上會議

94. 說話者說：「各位都打開筆電了嗎？」，其暗示為何？
(A) 她將更新系統。
(B) 她將示範使用產品。
(C) 她的筆電故障了。
(D) 她的密碼錯誤。

Questions 95-97 refer to the following excerpt from a meeting and product information page.

M：Thank you for attending this morning's meeting. **We're going to begin by going over some comments regarding our custom dress shirts.** 95 Our shop allows people to design dress shirts

95-97 會議摘錄和產品資訊頁

男：感謝各位參加今早的會議。**我們首先要檢討的是有關我們客製西裝襯衫的一些評論。** 95 我們的店裡能讓顧客從顏色、布料、衣領、袖長等

by choosing an option from each of the four style components: color, fabric, collar, and sleeve length. **A large number of customers have mentioned that they would like more fabrics to choose from, so beginning in February, we'll be adding two additional fabrics options. 96 Now this next part really worries me. Some customers have complained that their shirts have had small tears.** 97 This issue needs to be fixed immediately.

Dress Shirt Styling	
Color: 6 choices	**Fabric: 3 choices** 96
Blue Indigo Red Yellow Green Purple	**Polyester Cotton Flannel**
Collar: 4 choices	Sleeves: 2 choices
Classic Mandarin Spread Pinned	Long Short

四種組合樣式中，各擇其一來設計出西服襯衫。**許多客戶提到，想要能有更多種布料可以選擇，因此從二月開始，我們將新增兩種布料選項。96 那麼，接下來的部分是真的讓我擔心的。一些顧客投訴說，他們的襯衫上有幾處小裂口。**97 這項問題必須立刻解決。

西裝襯衫樣式	
顏色：六種選擇	**布料：三種選擇** 96
藍 靛 紅 黃 綠 紫	**聚酯纖維 綿 法蘭絨**
衣領：四種選擇	袖長：兩種選擇
標準領 立領 寬角領 帶針領	長 短

95. What is the speaker mainly discussing?
(A) Customer comments
(B) A delivery method
(C) A marketing strategy
(D) Sales figures

96. Look at the graphic. Which option quantity will increase in February?
(A) 6
(B) 3
(C) 4
(D) 2

97. What is the speaker concerned about?
(A) A Web site needs to be updated.
(B) Some employees have wrong information.
(C) Some items are getting damaged.
(D) A rival has launched a similar product.

95. 說話者主要在討論什麼？
(A) 客戶評論
(B) 送貨方式
(C) 行銷策略
(D) 銷售數據

96. 請據圖表作答。哪一種選擇的數量會在二月增加？
(A) 六
(B) 三
(C) 四
(D) 二

97. 說話者擔心什麼？
(A) 網站須更新。
(B) 員工掌握錯誤的資訊。
(C) 有些產品損壞。
(D) 同業已推出類似產品。

Questions 98-100 refer to the following telephone message and order form.

M：Hello, it's Jun from BSA, Inc. **I'm calling in regards to the catering order request for the Innovative Leader's Conference.** 98 **One of our employees found a lot of unused utensils in our storage room. So we won't need any for this event.** 99 **Please take out this item from the order and adjust the total amount accordingly.** 100 Once you've done so, **please email the revised invoice to me.** 100 Thank you.

Customer Order: BSA

Order Item	Total Number
Hamburgers	20
Chicken soup	24
Bottled water	20
Forks and spoons 99	**24**

98. What kind of event is being held?
    (A) A business conference
    (B) An awards ceremony
    (C) A graduation party
    (D) A cooking demonstration

99. Look at the graphic. Which item on the order form will be removed?
    (A) Hamburgers
    (B) Chicken soup
    (C) Bottled water
    (D) Forks and spoons

100. What does the speaker ask the listener to do?
    (A) Pick up a package
    (B) Make a payment
    (C) Update an invoice
    (D) Give a speech

98-100 語音留言和訂單

男：您好，我是 BSA 公司的俊。**我這次來電是關於「創新領導會議」外燴訂單需求的事宜。** 98 **我們有位員工在倉庫找到大量未使用的餐具，所以活動上這部分我們就都不需要了。** 99 **請從訂單中移除這個項目，並依此調整總額。** 100 處理好後，**請將修改後的帳單以電子郵件寄給我。**謝謝。

訂購客戶：BSA

訂購項目	總數
漢堡	20
雞湯	24
瓶裝水	20
叉子和湯匙 99	**24**

98. 將舉行什麼類型的活動？
    (A) 商務會議
    (B) 頒獎典禮
    (C) 畢業宴會
    (D) 烹飪示範

99. 請據圖表作答。訂單中的哪個項目應刪除？
    (A) 漢堡
    (B) 雞湯
    (C) 瓶裝水
    (D) 叉子和湯匙

100. 說話者要求聽者做什麼？
    (A) 領取包裹
    (B) 付款
    (C) 更新帳單
    (D) 發表演說

ACTUAL TEST 9

PART 1 P. 114–117

35

1. (A) A woman is hammering a nail.
   (B) A woman is setting down some tools.
   (C) A woman is wiping a wall.
   (D) A woman is using a power tool.

2. (A) One of the people is putting down his bag.
   (B) One of the people is cleaning a window.
   (C) Some people are grasping a railing.
   (D) Some people are descending some steps.

3. (A) Some chairs are stacked on top of each other.
   (B) A table has been set for a meal.
   (C) A curtain is being drawn.
   (D) Some plates are drying on a rack.

4. (A) A man is drinking from his cup.
   (B) A woman is talking on her mobile phone.
   (C) People are seated in separate booths.
   (D) People are looking out the windows.

5. (A) She's washing some dishes.
   (B) She's pouring liquid into a pot.
   (C) She's reaching for a cupboard.
   (D) She's cleaning the kitchen.

6. **(A) A stairway is divided by a handrail.**
   (B) A man is holding onto a pole.
   (C) The people are climbing up the staircase.
   (D) Some banners are being removed from the ceiling.

1. (A) 女子正用鎚子釘釘子。
   (B) 女子正放下工具。
   (C) 女子正在擦洗牆壁。
   (D) 女子正在使用電動工具。

2. (A) 其中一人正放下他的包包。
   (B) 其中一人正在清潔窗戶。
   (C) 幾個人正抓著欄杆。
   (D) 幾個人正走下階梯。

3. (A) 幾張椅子上下堆疊著。
   (B) 用餐桌席已擺設好。
   (C) 窗簾正在拉動。
   (D) 幾張盤子正在架上晾乾。

4. (A) 男子正在喝他杯裡的水。
   (B) 女子正在用手機通話。
   (C) 人們坐在分隔的座位區。
   (D) 人們正看向窗外。

5. (A) 她正在清洗碗盤。
   (B) 她正將液體倒入壺中。
   (C) 她正在伸手開櫥櫃。
   (D) 她正在打掃廚房。

6. **(A) 樓梯被扶手從中隔開。**
   (B) 男子正握著柱子。
   (C) 人們正在爬樓梯。
   (D) 正從天花板卸下幾面布條。

PART 2 P. 118

36

7. When will the project be completed?
   (A) Will you have time around then?
   (B) By the end of May.
   (C) For an overseas client.

7. 專案何時會完成？
   (A) 那個時間前後你會有空嗎？
   (B) 五月底前。
   (C) 給一位海外客戶。

8. Do you have a spare pen I can borrow?
(A) Is a blue one OK?
(B) The pen wasn't that expensive.
(C) I borrowed this book from Kevin.

8. 你有多的筆可以借我嗎？
(A) 藍色的筆可以嗎？
(B) 那支筆沒那麼貴。
(C) 我向凱文借這本書。

9. Why is Marcia not at her desk today?
(A) I left it on your desk.
(B) No, it was yesterday.
(C) Because she's visiting the Seattle office.

9. 為什麼瑪西亞今天不在位子上？
(A) 我把它放在你桌上。
(B) 不，是昨天。
(C) 因為她正出訪西雅圖辦事處。

10. We need to prepare more copies of our presentation handouts.
(A) A training session.
(B) How many people will be attending?
(C) It's in room 2A.

10. 我們需要準備更多份簡報的資料。
(A) 培訓課程。
(B) 有多少人會參加？
(C) 在 2A 室。

11. Would you like to try a bowl of our new salad?
(A) I'll try to be there.
(B) It was very informative.
(C) Does it have any nuts?

11. 您想來碗我們的新品沙拉嗎？
(A) 我會試著到那裡。
(B) 資訊非常豐富。
(C) 裡面有含堅果嗎？

12. Was it Nadia or Harry who updated the presentation slides?
(A) A multimedia projector.
(B) Sorry, I'm not quite sure.
(C) Let me confirm the date.

12. 更新簡報投影片的人是娜迪亞還是哈利？
(A) 多媒體投影機。
(B) 抱歉，我不是很確定。
(C) 讓我確認日期。

13. Who's working the night shift tonight?
(A) He's a good worker.
(B) By tomorrow morning.
(C) It's my turn.

13. 誰今晚要輪值夜班？
(A) 他是好員工。
(B) 明天早上之前。
(C) 輪到我了。

14. Has the air conditioner been repaired yet?
(A) About 25 degrees.
(B) Yes, I'll accept the conditions.
(C) The technician's still here.

14. 空調已經修好了嗎？
(A) 大約 25 度。
(B) 對，我會接受這些條款。
(C) 技術人員還在這裡。

15. I'm here to see Dr. Baker for an examination.
(A) Yes, 3 o'clock is OK.
(B) He's not available at the moment.
(C) I'm afraid we don't accept cash.

15. 我來找貝克醫生進行檢查。
(A) 對，三點可以。
(B) 他目前不在。
(C) 抱歉，我們不收現金。

16. When are you going to return the library books?
(A) She's the librarian at the local university.
(B) The rooms were already booked.
(C) They're due early next week.

16. 你什麼時候要歸還圖書館的書？
(A) 她是當地一所大學的圖書館員。
(B) 房間已經預訂好了。
(C) 書是下週初到期。

17. Where can I receive my authorization card?
(A) The security desk has them.
(B) By 8 o'clock.
(C) After the training orientation.

18. You're being moved to the HR Department, right?
(A) No, they changed their mind.
(B) Some revisions to my résumé.
(C) A new apartment.

19. Why don't I add pictures to the menu?
(A) Here is the revenue report.
(B) I'm not very hungry.
(C) That's a really good idea.

20. Who's opening the store this Saturday?
(A) A special sales event.
(B) I'll display the sign.
(C) I'll take a look at the calendar.

21. Isn't the press conference with the CEO today?
(A) Over 20 reporters.
(B) A public statement.
(C) It's been rescheduled.

22. Would you like some dessert, or should I get you the check?
(A) What kind of cakes do you have?
(B) They liked it, too.
(C) Thank you for checking.

23. I need the quarterly sales report as soon as possible.
(A) A new product promotion.
(B) I'll email it to you in a minute.
(C) It wasn't for sale.

24. What's the cost of this box of whiteboard markers?
(A) It might be on sale.
(B) A marketing firm.
(C) A board of directors.

25. There's no fee for parking at the company building, right?
(A) For almost five years now.
(B) I take public transportation.
(C) Would you like the receipt?

17. 我在哪裡可以獲得我的授權卡？
(A) 它們是在保全櫃台。
(B) 八點之前。
(C) 新進人員培訓會之後。

18. 你要調任到人力資源部門，對吧？
(A) 不，他們改變想法了。
(B) 對我的履歷的幾項修改。
(C) 一間新公寓。

19. 何不我來在菜單上附加照片？
(A) 收益報告在這裡。
(B) 我不太餓。
(C) 這個想法真的很好。

20. 本週六誰會開店？
(A) 特賣活動。
(B) 我會展示出標示。
(C) 我會去查看班表。

21. 今天不是要和執行長開記者會嗎？
(A) 超過 20 名記者。
(B) 公開聲明。
(C) 已經改期了。

22. 您要來些甜點嗎，還是我來給您結帳呢？
(A) 你們有哪種蛋糕？
(B) 他們也喜歡。
(C) 感謝您幫忙檢查。

23. 我需要儘快拿到季度業績報表。
(A) 新品促銷。
(B) 我馬上用電子郵件寄給你。
(C) 它是非賣品。

24. 這盒白板筆的價格是多少？
(A) 它可能正在特價。
(B) 一家行銷公司。
(C) 董事會。

25. 公司大樓裡停車免費，對嗎？
(A) 現在已經快五年了。
(B) 我是搭公共運輸。
(C) 您需要收據嗎？

26. Which songs should I play for the ceremony?
(A) She's ordered two cakes.
(B) It's up to you.
(C) I just listened to them.

26. 我應該在典禮上播放哪些歌曲？
(A) 她點了兩份蛋糕。
(B) 你決定就好。
(C) 我剛才聽他們說話。

27. I'm really disappointed with the quality of Mr. Lee's report.
(A) I had an appointment with the director.
(B) Yes, it contains too many mistakes.
(C) Please repaint it this week.

27. 我對李先生的報告品質非常失望。
(A) 我和主管有約。
(B) 對，裡面有太多錯誤。
(C) 請在本週重新粉刷。

28. Should we buy more vegetables at the Sunday farmers' market?
(A) I agree. It wasn't easy.
(B) OK, let's drop by the pharmacy.
(C) We still have some left from last week.

28. 我們該在週日的農民市集上多買點蔬菜嗎？
(A) 我同意。這不容易。
(B) 好，我們去一趟藥局。
(C) 我們還有一些上週剩下來的。

29. Where are the expense reimbursement forms?
(A) You should ask Mr. Chan.
(B) On a business trip.
(C) A dinner with a client.

29. 開銷報支單放在哪裡？
(A) 你應該問陳先生。
(B) 在出差。
(C) 和客戶的晚餐。

30. Will you be driving to the sports stadium?
(A) It's the last game of the year.
(B) The subway is more convenient.
(C) I joined the company baseball team.

30. 你會開車去體育館嗎？
(A) 這是今年最後一場比賽。
(B) 地鐵更方便。
(C) 我加入了公司的棒球隊。

31. Why is the marketing proposal taking so long?
(A) By the marketing team.
(B) Hasn't Jamie sent it to you?
(C) I'd like to propose a toast to the presenter.

31. 為什麼行銷提案用時這麼久？
(A) 由行銷團隊。
(B) 傑米還沒把它寄給你嗎？
(C) 我想敬主持人一杯。

PART 3 P. 119–122

37

Questions 32-34 refer to the following conversation.

M：Excuse me. **I saw an ad posted on the notice board in your gallery for art classes. I was wondering if it's possible to sign up for the oil painting class** 32 on Monday nights.
W：**Unfortunately, the classroom is quite small, so it can't accommodate more than 10 people,** 33 and the class has already been filled.
M：Oh, that's too bad. Do you think you'll be offering a second class?

32-34 會話

男：不好意思。**我看到你們藝廊的布告欄上有張貼美術課的廣告。我想知道能不能報名參加**週一晚上的**油畫課。** 32
女：**很遺憾，那間教室很小，所以無法容納超過十人，** 33 而上課人數已經額滿了。
男：喔，真不巧。妳覺得你們會開第二個班嗎？

W: Actually, we're considering having another one on Thursday nights. **I can put your name on the waiting list if you'd like.** 34

女：我們其實正在考慮於每週四晚上另外開班。**如果您有意願，我可以把您的名字加入候補名單。** 34

32. What does the man want to do at the art gallery?
(A) Register for a class
(B) Display a painting
(C) Meet an artist
(D) Volunteer for an event

32. 男子想在藝廊做什麼？
(A) 報名課程
(B) 展出畫作
(C) 會見藝術家
(D) 志願參與活動

33. What problem does the woman mention?
(A) A board is broken.
(B) A document is missing.
(C) A curator is not available.
(D) A room is not big enough.

33. 女子提到什麼問題？
(A) 看板損壞。
(B) 文件遺失。
(C) 策展人沒空。
(D) 空間不夠大。

34. What does the woman offer to do for the man?
(A) Refund a payment
(B) Order materials from a store
(C) Post a schedule
(D) Add his name to a list

34. 女子提議為男子做什麼？
(A) 退款
(B) 從商店訂材料
(C) 公布時間表
(D) 把他的名字加進名單

36

Questions 35-37 refer to the following conversation.

35-37 會話

W：Hi. **I found a note on my apartment door, and it says that there is a package for me here at the security office.** 35 My name is Rena. R-E-N-A.

M：Hmm, are you a resident of the building? **Your name is not on the list of tenants in our database.** 36

W：Oh, **that's probably because I just moved here last weekend.** 36 I'm in Apartment 445.

M：OK, but I would have to see some form of verification that you live there before giving you the package. **Do you mind showing me your lease agreement?** 37

女：嗨。**我在我公寓的門上看到一張通知，上面說警衛室這裡有寄給我的包裹。** 35 我的名字是瑞娜，拼法是 R-E-N-A。

男：唔，您是這棟大樓的住戶嗎？**我們資料庫的住戶名單上沒有您的名字。** 36

女：哦，**那可能是因為我上週末才剛搬來。** 36 我住在 445 室。

男：好的，但給您包裹之前，我得要查看能證明您住在該處的相關文件。**方便請您出示您的租約給我看嗎？** 37

35. What does the woman want to do?
(A) Use a computer
(B) Claim a package
(C) Book a room
(D) See a friend

35. 女子想做什麼？
(A) 使用電腦
(B) 領取包裹
(C) 預訂房間
(D) 和朋友見面

36. Why most likely is the woman's name missing from the list?
(A) Her name was spelled incorrectly.
(B) Her subscription was canceled.
(C) She is a past employee.
(D) She is a new resident.

37. What does the man ask for?
(A) A contract
(B) An account number
(C) A photo identification
(D) A mailing address

36. 名單上缺少女子的名字，最有可能的原因為何？
(A) 她的名字被拼錯了。
(B) 她的訂閱已取消。
(C) 她是前員工。
(D) 她是新來的住戶。

37. 男子要求何項事物？
(A) 合約
(B) 帳號
(C) 附相片的身分證件
(D) 郵寄地址

Questions 38-40 refer to the following conversation.

M：Excuse me, **I'll be opening up my own café next month, and I'm looking for some outdoor furniture to buy for the patio area** 38 at my shop. The only issue is that I have a very limited budget.
W：Oh, I see. **Why don't you apply for our installment plan then?** 39 That way, you only have to pay a portion of the total amount each month. All you have to do is complete this application form.
M：That sounds good. But **how long does it take for the application to be processed?** 40 Will it be approved right away, or do I have to wait a while?
W：It should only take about 20 to 25 minutes. Once you're approved, you can take your purchase home today.

38-40 會話

男：不好意思，**我下個月就要開自己的咖啡廳了，而我正在物色一些**我的店裡**露台區要用的戶外家具。**38 唯一的問題是，我的預算很有限。
女：噢，我了解。**您何不申請我們的分期付款方案呢？**39 如此一來，您僅須按月支付一部分的總金額。您只要填寫這張申請表就可以了。
男：聽起來不錯。但是**申請要花多久時間處理？**40 這是會馬上通過，還是我得要等上一段時間？
女：應該只需約 20 到 25 分鐘。一旦核准，您今天就能將您採購的商品帶回家。

38. What would the man like to purchase?
(A) Bathroom supplies
(B) Patio furniture
(C) A carpet
(D) A beverage machine

39. What does the woman suggest the man do?
(A) Select a different model
(B) Come back later
(C) Check some measurements
(D) Sign up for a payment plan

38. 男子想買什麼？
(A) 浴廁用品
(B) 露台家具
(C) 地毯
(D) 飲料機

39. 女子建議男子做什麼？
(A) 選擇不同型號
(B) 稍後再來
(C) 確認尺寸
(D) 申請一項付款方案

40. What does the man ask the woman about?
(A) The operation hours of a business
(B) The location of a store
(C) The length of an application process
(D) The details of a warranty

40. 男子詢問女子何項事宜？
(A) 店家營業時間
(B) 商店地點
(C) 處理申請的用時長度
(D) 保固服務細節

Questions 41-43 refer to the following conversation with three speakers.

W1：**Welcome to the Annual Electronics Expo.** 41 Did you register beforehand?
M：Yes, I received my registration packet in the mail, but **I lost my visitor's badge.** 42
W1：Ah, well, if you show me another valid form of ID, I can let you into the event.
M：Here you go.
W1：OK, Mr. James Won. You're on the list. You can go in.
M：Thanks! But could I get a new badge?
W1：Yes, let me talk to my manager about that. Ms. Park, Mr. Won here needs a new visitor's badge.
W2：Hello, Mr. Won. I can take care of that for you, but I'll need some time. **Why don't you visit our desk again in about one hour?** 43 I should have your badge ready by then.

41-43 三人會話

女 1：**歡迎蒞臨年度電子展。** 41 您有事先報名嗎？
男：有的，我有收到郵寄來的報名資料包，但**我把訪客證弄丟了。** 42
女 1：啊，那麼，如果您出示其他有效身分證件給我看，我可以讓您進入活動現場。
男：在這裡。
女 1：好的，詹姆斯．元先生。您有在名單上，您可以入場了。
男：謝謝！但我可以領一張新的名牌嗎？
女 1：可以，讓我和經理說明一下情形。朴女士，這位元先生需要新的訪客證。
女 2：您好，元先生。我能負責為您處理這件事，不過我需要一點時間。**您何不約一小時後再回來我們的櫃台？** 43 到時我應該就能幫您把名牌準備妥當。

41. Where are the speakers?
(A) At an athletic competition
(B) At a technology convention
(C) At a music festival
(D) At a gallery opening

42. What is the man's problem?
(A) He missed an important event.
(B) He brought an expired credit card.
(C) He is unable to reach a manager.
(D) He misplaced a badge.

43. What does the manager ask the man to do?
(A) Submit an extra fee
(B) Refer to a map
(C) Sign some paperwork
(D) Return at another time

41. 說話者人在何處？
(A) 在運動競賽
(B) 在科技會展
(C) 在音樂節
(D) 在藝廊開幕會

42. 男子遇到什麼問題？
(A) 他錯過了重要活動。
(B) 他帶了過期的信用卡。
(C) 他無法聯絡上經理。
(D) 他弄丟了名牌。

43. 經理請男子做什麼？
(A) 繳交額外費用
(B) 參閱地圖
(C) 簽署文件
(D) 其他時間再來

Questions 44-46 refer to the following conversation.

M：Hi, Colleen. Do you happen to know anyone who's fluent in Japanese? I started doing business with a new client in Japan. I know some Japanese, but **I'd still like someone to check the translation for a sales presentation I'll be giving there.** 44

W：Actually, I do. Her name is Yuriko Sugimoto, and she works at a publishing company, but **she's on vacation now** 45 and won't return until next Thursday.

M：That's OK. My presentation is in three weeks, so I have time. I just need my slides proofread before I depart for Japan. By the way, **has Ms. Sugimoto done this kind of work before?** 46

W：I think so, but I'll talk to her when she comes back and have her contact you directly.

44. What does the man require assistance with?

(A) Finding a language course

(B) Scheduling a business trip

(C) Preparing for a presentation

(D) Submitting a job application

45. Why is Yuriko Sugimoto unable to help immediately?

(A) She is working on another project.

(B) She is away on vacation.

(C) She has not received training.

(D) She is meeting a client.

46. What does the man want to know about Yuriko Sugimoto?

(A) The contact information of her references

(B) The arrival time of her flight

(C) Her hourly fee

(D) Details about her work experience

44-46 會話

男：嗨，柯琳。妳有沒有剛好認識日語流利的人？我開始和日本的一個新客戶做生意。我懂一點日語，但**我將要到日本進行業務簡報，還是希望有人能幫我檢查翻譯。** 44

女：我倒真有認識一位。她名叫杉本百合子，在一家出版社工作，但**她目前正在休假，** 45 要等到下週四才會回來。

男：沒關係。我的簡報是在三週後進行，因此我還有時間。我只要在出發赴日之前，讓我的投影片校對過即可。順道一問，**杉本女士以前做過這類工作嗎？** 46

女：我想是有的，但等她回來我會再告知她，並請她直接與你聯絡。

44. 男子需要哪方面的協助？

(A) 找尋語言課程

(B) 商務旅行排程

(C) 準備簡報

(D) 繳交應徵表

45. 杉本百合子為何無法立刻幫忙？

(A) 她正在忙另一項專案。

(B) 她正休假不在。

(C) 她還沒受過培訓。

(D) 她正在會見客戶。

46. 關於杉本百合子，男子想知道什麼？

(A) 她推薦人的聯絡資訊

(B) 她的班機的抵達時間

(C) 她每小時的收費

(D) 她工作經歷的細節

Questions 47-49 refer to the following conversation.

W：Hi, George. It's Helen. **I sent an email to you yesterday regarding the construction budget for the new Westvale Shopping Center, but I'm not sure whether you got it or not.** 47 I hope I sent it to the correct email address.

M：Hi, Helen. You sent it to the right address, and I got your message. **I'm sorry I didn't reply to you yesterday.** 48 I'll answer your questions and email you back by noon today.

W：I appreciate it. I have a meeting with the shopping center project supervisors at 3 P.M., and **I'd like to report the approximate budget to them at the meeting.** 49

47-49 會話

女：嗨，喬治。我是海倫。**我昨天有寄給你一封電子郵件，內容是關於新的西維爾購物中心的建設預算，但是我不確定你有沒有收到。** 47 希望我有寄到正確的電子郵件地址。

男：嗨，海倫。妳寄的地址是對的，我也有收到妳的訊息。**很抱歉昨天我沒有回覆妳。** 48 我今天中午前會回信給妳，回答妳的問題。

女：謝謝。我下午三點將和負責購物中心建案的管理高層開會，而**我想在會議上向他們報告粗估的預算。** 49

47. What does the woman say she is unsure about?
(A) Whether a message was received
(B) Whether a facility is available
(C) The arrangements for a meeting
(D) The length of a project

48. Why does the man apologize?
(A) He sent the woman incorrect information.
(B) He missed an important meeting.
(C) He did not contact the woman yesterday.
(D) He will not be able to meet a deadline.

49. What does the woman want to have for a meeting?
(A) A list of attendees
(B) A budget estimate
(C) A blueprint of a building
(D) An updated agenda

47. 女子說她不確定什麼？
(A) 訊息是否傳達到
(B) 設施能否使用
(C) 會議的安排
(D) 專案的時長

48. 男子為何道歉？
(A) 他寄了錯誤資訊給女子。
(B) 他錯過了一場重要的會議。
(C) 他昨天沒有聯絡女子。
(D) 他將無法趕上期限。

49. 女子希望備妥何物，以便開會？
(A) 與會者名單
(B) 預算估算
(C) 建築藍圖
(D) 更新版議程

Questions 50-52 refer to the following conversation with three speakers.

M1：Hello, my name is Jay Collins. **I had a 3 P.M. legal consultation with Mr. Workman, but I couldn't make it because I was stuck in heavy traffic.** 50 Is it still possible to see him today?

W：I'm not sure . . . His schedule is a lot tighter this week. His partner, **Laura Feinstein, is traveling for the holidays,** 51 so he's been meeting

50-52 三人會話

男 1：妳好，我的名字是杰・柯林斯。**我下午三點和沃克曼先生約好了要進行法律諮詢，但我因為塞車沒能趕上。** 50 今天還有辦法見到他嗎？

女：我不確定……他這週的行程緊湊許多。他的合夥人**蘿拉・費因斯坦正休假出遊，** 51 所以他近期都在和她的其中幾位客戶開會。不過其

TEST 9
PART 3
37

with some of her clients. But actually, here he comes right now. Hello, Mr. Workman.

M2：Hi, Linda.

W：Mr. Collins missed his scheduled consultation earlier, but would you be able to meet with him now?

M2：Sure. **Just give me a couple minutes to fax these documents.** 52

實，沃克曼先生現在來了。哈囉，沃克曼先生。

男 2：嗨，琳達。

女：柯林斯先生錯過了他稍早預約的諮詢，不過您現在可以見他嗎？

男 2：當然可以。**再給我幾分鐘來傳真這些文件就好。** 52

50. Why did Mr. Collins miss his consultation?
(A) He forgot to check a schedule.
(B) He woke up too late.
(C) He experienced some traffic.
(D) He had to finish an assignment.

50. 柯林斯先生為什麼錯過諮詢？
(A) 他忘了確認行程表。
(B) 他太晚起床。
(C) 他碰上塞車。
(D) 他須做完交辦事項。

51. What is mentioned about Ms. Feinstein?
(A) She went on vacation.
(B) She is a well-known lawyer.
(C) She will retire soon.
(D) She received a prize.

51. 關於費因斯坦女士，對話中提到了什麼？
(A) 她去度假了。
(B) 她是著名律師。
(C) 她即將退休。
(D) 她獲頒獎項。

52. What will Mr. Workman do next?
(A) Review an agreement
(B) Fax some papers
(C) Give a tour
(D) Call some clients

52. 沃克曼先生接下來會做什麼？
(A) 審查合約
(B) 傳真文件
(C) 導覽參觀
(D) 致電客戶

Questions 53-55 refer to the following conversation.

M：Cindy, this is Reggie Hemsley from the production team. **I'm calling because one of the lights in our studio went out.** 53

W：I'm sorry to hear that. **I'll send Jimmy down right away to fix that for you.** 54

M：Um . . . **Actually, we'll be conducting an interview here in 10 minutes. I think we're fine for now, but if you can send him later on . . .** 54

W：**Of course. Once you're done, just send me a text message.** 54 Should he check for anything else while he's there?

M：No, I don't think so. Anyway, **this is the first time I'll be interviewing someone through our video conference system, so it should be interesting.** 55

53-55 會話

男：辛蒂，我是製作組的雷吉．赫姆斯利。**我們攝影棚有盞燈熄掉了，所以打電話知會。** 53

女：很遺憾會這樣。**我馬上請吉米下樓幫你修理。** 54

男：嗯……**其實，十分鐘後我們會在這裡進行採訪。我想我們現在狀況還好，要不然妳讓他晚點再來……** 54

女：**當然可以。等你那邊結束再傳簡訊給我就好。** 54 他過去那邊時，還有其他需要讓他檢查的地方嗎？

男：不，我想是沒有。無論如何，**等會兒將是我第一次透過我們的視訊會議系統採訪他人，因此應該會很有趣。** 55

53. Why is Mr. Hemsley calling?
(A) To arrange a recording session
(B) To ask for a document
(C) To reschedule an appointment
(D) To report an issue

53. 赫姆斯利先生為何打電話？
(A) 以安排錄音時間
(B) 以索取文件
(C) 以更改約定時間
(D) 以告知問題

54. What does Mr. Hemsley mean when he says, "we'll be conducting an interview here in 10 minutes"?
(A) He will be temporarily unavailable.
(B) He requires assistance immediately.
(C) He is going to leave the office soon.
(D) He wants to reserve a conference room.

54. 赫姆斯利先生說：「十分鐘後我們會在這裡進行採訪」，其意思為何？
(A) 他暫時不會有空。
(B) 他立即需要幫助。
(C) 他即將離開辦公室。
(D) 他想預約會議室。

55. What does Mr. Hemsley say is unique about the interview?
(A) It will include a meeting with the CEO.
(B) It will be a group interview.
(C) It will include a luncheon.
(D) It will be done remotely.

55. 關於採訪，赫姆斯利先生提到何項特點？
(A) 將包括和執行長的會談。
(B) 將為團體訪談。
(C) 將包含午餐會。
(D) 將遠距進行。

Questions 56-58 refer to the following conversation.

M：Hello. My name is Shamus Emory. **I have an appointment to check out a rental unit at this office building for my art classes.** 56

W：Welcome, Mr. Emory. Thank you for coming. I'm Wendy Kim, and I'm the complex's property manager.

M：Pleased to meet you. **I'd like to get some space on the top floor. That way, my students can look out at the wonderful scenery around here while doing their work.** 57

W：Of course. We'll look there first. **Also, did I tell you that there is a large cafeteria on the first floor? It can only be used by tenants and employees of this complex.** 58 Your students would have access to it as well.

56-58 會話

男：哈囉。我的名字是夏慕斯·埃默里。**我有約好要看這棟辦公大樓裡出租的單位，用途是開設藝術課程。** 56

女：歡迎，埃默里先生。感謝您前來。我是溫蒂·金，擔任這棟複合式大樓的物業經理。

男：很高興和您見面。**我想要找位在頂樓的空間。這樣一來，我的學生在創作還能一邊眺望周邊美景。** 57

女：沒問題。我們會先到那裡看看。另外，**我有跟您提過，一樓設有很寬敞的自助式餐廳嗎？那裡只有本大樓的承租戶和員工能使用。** 58 您的學生到時也可以前往使用。

56. What most likely is the man's job?
(A) Instructor
(B) Lawyer
(C) Architect
(D) Realtor

56. 男子的職業最有可能為何？
(A) 講師
(B) 律師
(C) 建築師
(D) 房仲

57. Why does the man want an office on the top floor?
(A) It is reasonably priced.
(B) It is quiet.
(C) It has the most space.
(D) It has a good view.

57. 為什麼男子想要頂樓的辦公室？
(A) 價格合理。
(B) 安靜清幽。
(C) 空間最大。
(D) 視野很好。

58. What benefit is mentioned?
(A) An office has been expanded recently.
(B) A complex has its own dining area.
(C) An office is fully furnished.
(D) A complex is in a convenient location.

58. 對話中提到何項好處？
(A) 辦公室最近剛擴建。
(B) 複合大樓有自己的用餐區。
(C) 辦公室家具配置齊全。
(D) 複合大樓的地點交通便利。

Questions 59-61 refer to the following conversation.

W1：Hello, Giselle. **I looked over our manufacturing schedule.** 59 Aren't we supposed to begin making the uniforms for Tarco Bistro this week?
W2：Actually, I wanted to discuss that with you . . .
W1：We guaranteed that the uniforms would be completed by the 25th of this month, right?
W2：We did. But the thing is, we still haven't gotten the nylon fabric. **I contacted our supplier to see what is causing the delay.** 60
W1：**Oh, what happened?** 60
W2：Well, **I'm meeting with them in our office in 20 minutes.**
W1：All right. Keep me informed. **If the shipment is delayed any longer, we'll most likely have to use another company to supply the fabric.** 61

59-61 會話

女 1：吉賽爾妳好。**我看了我們的生產排程表。** 59 本週我們不是應該開始製作塔爾可餐酒館的制服嗎？
女 2：其實之前我有想和妳討論這件事……
女 1：我們承諾過制服會在這個月的 25 日完成，對吧？
女 2：對的。但問題是，我們還是沒收到尼龍布料。**我已經聯絡我們的供應商，問他們延誤的原因。** 60
女 1：**哦，是什麼狀況？** 60
女 2：這個嘛，**我 20 分鐘後會在我們辦公室和他們開會。**
女 1：了解。請告訴我後續消息。**如果這批貨繼續延誤下去，我們極有可能會需要找另一家公司來供應布料。** 61

59. Where is the conversation most likely taking place?
(A) At a factory
(B) At a restaurant
(C) At a clothing store
(D) At an advertising agency

59. 這段對話最有可能在哪裡發生？
(A) 在工廠
(B) 在餐廳
(C) 在服飾店
(D) 在廣告公司

60. What does Giselle imply when she says, "I'm meeting with them in our office in 20 minutes"?
(A) She has to print some documents.
(B) She is unable to participate in an event.
(C) She needs a larger meeting room.
(D) She will have an answer soon.

60. 吉賽爾說：「我 20 分鐘後會在我們辦公室和他們開會」，其暗示為何？
(A) 她須印出一些文件。
(B) 她無法參加活動。
(C) 她需要更大的會議室。
(D) 她很快會得到答案。

61. What may happen due to a delay?
(A) Some overtime could be required.
(B) Some training sessions could be held.
(C) A deadline could be extended.
(D) A new supplier could be hired.

61. 延誤可能造成何事發生？
(A) 可能需要加班。
(B) 可能舉辦培訓課程。
(C) 截止期限可能延後。
(D) 可能採用新的供應商。

Questions 62-64 refer to the following conversation and sign.

M：Good morning. What is the reason for your visit to the Terreston Department of Transportation?
W：Hello. I'd like to register for the driver's license exam.
M：**It'll be $45 to sign up.** 62
W：**Oh, that's more than I expected.** 62 OK, when is the earliest date I can take it?
M：Give me a moment to check the system. All right, it looks like there is an available slot on May 27.
W：Hmm . . . **I'll be out of town for a business trip during the last week of May.** 63
M：Then, how about June 4?
W：That'll work!
M：Great. Just fill out this form so that I can make a reservation for you. **Afterward, go to the next window to submit your payment.** 64

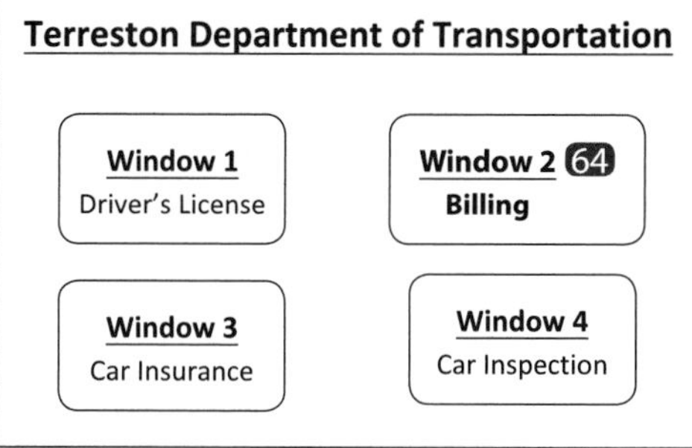

62-64 會話和標示圖

男：早安。請問您來特赫斯頓交通局是要辦什麼事嗎？
女：您好。我想報名駕照考試。
男：**報名費為 45 美元。** 62
女：**噢，比我預期的還要貴。** 62 好吧，請問我最快什麼時候可以考試？
男：請稍等一會，讓我查一下系統。好的，看起來 5 月 27 日有個名額。
女：嗯⋯⋯**我在五月最後一個星期會到外地出差。** 63
男：那麼，6 月 4 日如何？
女：那天可以！
男：好極了。那就請填寫這份表單，以便我幫您做預約。**之後，請去您旁邊的窗口繳交費用。** 64

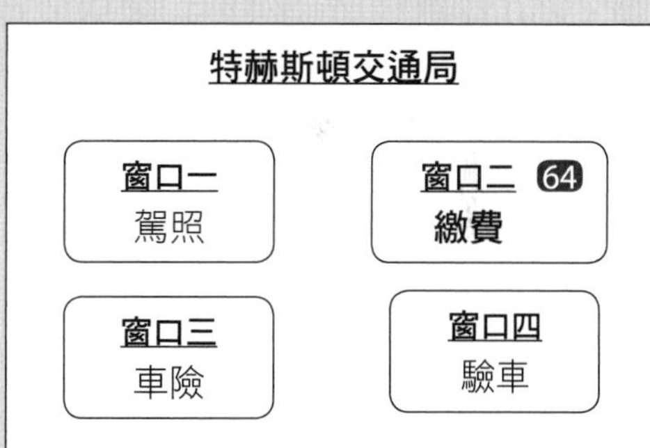

62. What is the woman surprised about?
(A) A wait time
(B) A sign-up fee
(C) Results of a car inspection
(D) The speed of a service

62. 女子對何事感到驚訝？
(A) 等候時間
(B) 報名費
(C) 驗車結果
(D) 服務速度

63. According to the woman, what will she do during the last week of May?
(A) Order some parts
(B) Enroll in a class
(C) Rent a vehicle
(D) Go on a business trip

63. 據女子說法，她在五月最後一週會做什麼？
(A) 訂購零件
(B) 報名課程
(C) 租車
(D) 出差

64. Look at the graphic. Which window will the woman most likely go to next?

(A) Window 1

(B) Window 2

(C) Window 3

(D) Window 4

64. 請據圖表作答。女子接下來最有可能前往幾號窗口？

(A) 窗口一

(B) 窗口二

(C) 窗口三

(D) 窗口四

Questions 65-67 refer to the following conversation and floor plans.

M：Hello, **I'm planning to move to Cerksville during the first week of July. My firm is transferring me to our branch there,** 65 and the HR manager referred me to your agency. I'm looking for an apartment with two rooms.

W：All right. Let me show you some of our available listings.

M：Thank you. Oh, it looks like there are three-room places, too.

W：Yes, both of them are actually located downtown and are very roomy.

M：Hmm, but I'd like to keep it under $800 a month.

W：Well, **how about this two-bedroom apartment? It's $750, so it should be within your budget.** 66

M：**OK, I want to check it out.** 66 **Can I make an appointment to do that next week?** 67

W：**Let me look at my schedule.** 67

65-67 會話和樓層平面圖

男：哈囉，**我計劃在七月第一週會搬到瑟克維爾。我被公司轉調到那裡的分公司，** 65 而公司人資經理向我介紹你們這家業者。我正在找兩房公寓。

女：好。讓我給您看我們一些現有公寓的清單。

男：謝謝。哦，好像也有看到三房的公寓。

女：對，那兩間其實都位於市區中心，而且非常寬敞。

男：嗯，但我想控制在每月 800 美元以下。

女：嗯，**那麼這間兩房公寓怎麼樣？750 美元，因此應該在您預算之內。** 66

男：**好，我想去這間看看。** 66 **我可以預約下週去看房嗎？** 67

女：**讓我看一下我的行程。** 67

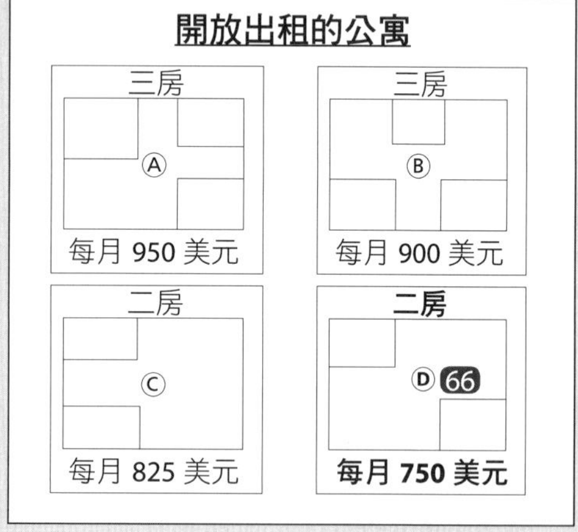

65. Why does the man say he is moving to Cerksville?

(A) He is opening his own store.

(B) He is being transferred to another office.

(C) He would like a more convenient commute.

(D) He wants to live closer to his family.

65. 男子提到他為什麼將搬到瑟克維爾？

(A) 他將要自己開店。

(B) 他受調任到另一處辦公地點。

(C) 他想要通勤更方便。

(D) 他想和家人住得更近。

66. Look at the graphic. Which apartment is the man most interested in?
(A) Apartment A
(B) Apartment B
(C) Apartment C
(D) Apartment D

67. What will the speakers probably do next?
(A) Look over a rental contract
(B) Discuss parking options
(C) Set up an appointment
(D) Edit some blueprints

Questions 68-70 refer to the following conversation and Web page.

M：Hey, Daniela, it's great to see you. Are you still working at the same place?
W：Yes, for the moment. **I like the job because it pays pretty well. 68 But I really want my work to involve visiting different cities around the world. My current company hasn't expanded abroad yet, so I'm hoping to find something new. 69**
M：Well, you should visit the job advertising Web site: employnet.com. You can narrow the search parameters by the type of travel that the position requires.
W：Oh, nice. I'll check that out later. What about you? How's your job treating you?
M：**Well, my last day of work is actually next Thursday. I'm planning to go into business for myself next month. I'm looking forward to being a boss! 70**

www.employnet.com

Open Positions

▪ Brand Manager	Some in-state travel
▪ Marketing Manager 69	**Overseas business trips**
▪ Advertising Director	Work at headquarters
▪ Publicity Director	Visit local regions

66. 請據圖表作答。男子最感興趣的是哪間公寓？
(A) 公寓 A
(B) 公寓 B
(C) 公寓 C
(D) 公寓 D

67. 說話者接著可能會做什麼？
(A) 檢視租約
(B) 討論停車選擇
(C) 安排預約時間
(D) 修改幾張藍圖

68-70 會話和網頁

男：嘿，丹尼拉，很高興看到妳。妳還在同一個地方工作嗎？
女：對，目前還是。**我喜歡這份工作，因為薪水很不錯。68 但我真的想要我的工作內容可以包括造訪世界各地不同城市。我目前待的公司還沒有擴展到海外，所以我希望能找份新工作。69**
男：嗯，妳應該上 employnet.com 這個求職網站看看。妳可以依據職位要求的出差類型，來縮小搜尋範圍。
女：哦，真好用。我待會就瞧瞧。你呢？你的工作還好嗎？
男：**嗯，其實下週四就會是我最後一天上班。我打算下個月自己創業。我很期待當老闆！70**

www.employnet.com

職缺

▪ 品牌經理	有時須國內出差
▪ 行銷經理 69	**海外出差**
▪ 廣告主任	在總部上班
▪ 公關主任	造訪當地地區

68. What does the woman like about her current job?
(A) The hours are flexible.
(B) Her boss is kind.
(C) It offers a good salary.
(D) It is in a convenient location.

68. 關於目前的工作，女子喜歡什麼？
(A) 工作時間很彈性。
(B) 她的老闆很友善。
(C) 提供的薪水不錯。
(D) 公司地點交通便利。

69. Look at the graphic. Which position will the woman probably apply for?
(A) Brand Manager
(B) Marketing Manager
(C) Advertising Director
(D) Publicity Director

69. 請據圖表作答。女子可能將應徵哪個職位？
(A) 品牌經理
(B) 行銷經理
(C) 廣告主任
(D) 公關主任

70. What does the man say he will do soon?
(A) Go on a trip
(B) Relocate to another team
(C) Accept a promotion
(D) Start his own company

70. 男子說他很快將會做什麼？
(A) 去旅行
(B) 調到另一個團隊
(C) 接受晉升
(D) 自行創業

PART 4 P. 123–125

38

Questions 71-73 refer to the following announcement.

M：I'd like to move on to the last item on our agenda today. **Our company is committed to helping staff members maintain a healthy lifestyle, so we're going to be providing complimentary exercise classes.** 71 A fitness trainer will be holding a session once a week in our event room. **Participating employees will get complimentary healthy snacks and drinks after every session.** 72 **If you're interested, visit the company's Web site to download a registration form. Once you've completed it, just hand it in to me by next Friday.** 73

71-73 宣布

男：接下來我想討論今天議程的最後一個項目。**我們公司致力協助全體同仁維持健康的生活型態，所以我們將提供免費的運動課程。** 71 在我們的活動室，會有健身教練主持每週一次的課程。**參加的員工在每堂課後，將收到贈送的健康零食和飲料。** 72 **如果你們感興趣，請上公司網站下載報名表。填好之後，下週五之前交給我即可。** 73

71. What does the speaker say is available to staff?
(A) A fitness program
(B) A company loan
(C) A volunteer opportunity
(D) A medical checkup

71. 說話者說員工可使用什麼？
(A) 健身課程
(B) 公司貸款
(C) 志工機會
(D) 健康檢查

72. According to the speaker, what will employees receive for their participation?
(A) Complimentary parking
(B) Extra vacation days
(C) A cash bonus
(D) Free refreshments

73. What must employees do to register?
(A) Submit a form
(B) Contact a business
(C) Attend a workshop
(D) Pay a fee

Questions 74-76 refer to the following telephone message.

W：This message is for Greg. **My name is Pam, coach of the Fairview Bruins soccer team.** 74 I just received the schedule for the use of the soccer field next month. **My team has the field from 7 to 8 P.M. But here's the thing: most of my players live on the other side of town, which means some won't get home until after 9.** 75 **Your team has the field from 6 to 7. Do you mind giving me a call when you have some time?** 76 My number is 555-9284.

74. What kind of team does the speaker coach?
(A) Baseball
(B) Soccer
(C) Hockey
(D) Golf

75. What does the speaker mention about her players?
(A) Many of them live far away.
(B) Most of them work late.
(C) They are going to participate in a tournament.
(D) They need to practice more often.

76. Why does the speaker say, "Your team has the field from 6 to 7"?
(A) To request a switch
(B) To extend a game time
(C) To praise a team member
(D) To verify an appointment

72. 據說話者說法，參加的員工可以獲得什麼？
(A) 免費停車
(B) 額外休假
(C) 現金獎勵
(D) 免費點心飲料

73. 員工必須做什麼才能報名？
(A) 提交表單
(B) 聯絡業者
(C) 參加研習
(D) 付費

74-76 語音留言

女：這則留言是要給格雷葛的。**我名叫帕姆，是美景棕熊足球隊的教練。** 74 我剛收到下個月足球場的使用時間表。**我的隊伍能在晚上七點到八點使用球場。但有個問題：本隊大多數的球員都住在鎮上的另一頭，這意味部分球員將在九點以後才能回到家。** 75 **您的隊伍是六點到七點能使用球場。方便請您有空時打通電話給我嗎？** 76 我的電話是 555-9284。

74. 說話者指導哪一類隊伍？
(A) 棒球
(B) 足球
(C) 曲棍球
(D) 高爾夫球

75. 關於她的球員，說話者提到什麼事？
(A) 許多球員住得很遠。
(B) 多數球員工作到很晚。
(C) 他們將參加比賽。
(D) 他們須更常練習

76. 為何說話者要說：「您的隊伍是六點到七點能使用球場」？
(A) 以要求交換
(B) 以延長比賽時間
(C) 以稱讚一名隊員
(D) 以確認預約

37
38

Questions 77-79 refer to the following announcement.

W：**We still need more volunteers to help clean up the front of the library on Saturday, May 12. 77 78 This is a great chance to do your part to support the community. 77** If you would like to lend a hand, come to the main entrance of the library by 10 A.M. This year, we're going to focus on the large planters outside the building. **We'll be pulling out weeds and ivy, and trimming overgrown shrubs and bushes. 78** Bring yard tools if you have any, and make sure to wear gloves. I think we could make the library look nice and neat in a few hours. Obviously, the more workers we have, the faster we will finish. And just like last year, **sandwiches will be provided by Dom's Deli and will be given out 79** to all volunteers at noon.

77-79 宣布

女：**我們在 5 月 12 日週六當天，還需要更多志工來幫忙打掃圖書館前的衛生。77 78 這是您為社區付出自己一份心力的大好機會。78** 若您願意貢獻一臂之力，請在上午十點前到圖書館大門集合。今年，我們會著重清理大樓外的大型盆栽。**我們會拔除雜草和常春藤，並且修剪叢生的矮樹和灌木叢。78** 若您有任何園藝工具，都請帶過來，並務必戴上手套。我想我們幾個小時內就能將圖書館清得漂亮整潔。顯然，越多人手來幫忙，我們就會越快完成。另外和去年一樣，**「多姆熟食」將供應三明治**，會在中午時**發放 79** 給所有志工。

77. What is the purpose of the announcement?
(A) To describe a new menu
(B) To explain a parking policy
(C) To promote a volunteer opportunity
(D) To introduce a keynote speaker

78. What will happen on May 12?
(A) Some equipment will be installed.
(B) Some gardening work will be done.
(C) An art exhibition will be held.
(D) A parking area will be closed.

79. What does the speaker say will be distributed?
(A) A book
(B) A tool
(C) Some food
(D) Some plants

77. 這段宣布目的為何？
(A) 以說明新菜單
(B) 以解釋停車規定
(C) 以推廣志工服務機會
(D) 以介紹主題演講者

78. 何事將在 5 月 12 日發生？
(A) 將安裝一些設備。
(B) 將做些園藝工作。
(C) 將舉辦藝術展。
(D) 停車場將關閉。

79. 說話者說到時會發放什麼？
(A) 書本
(B) 工具
(C) 食物
(D) 植物

Questions 80-82 refer to the following news report.

M：**Now for today's community news. This Saturday, the yearly Harvest Festival will take place at downtown Riverton's outdoor market from 7 A.M. to 11 P.M. 80** There will be live performances, refreshments, and a variety

80-82 新聞報導

男：**現在請聽今天的社區新聞。這個週六，一年一度的豐收節將從上午七點到晚上十一點於市中心的河頓露天市場舉行。80** 到時將有現場演出、茶點和各式競賽與抽獎活動。

of contests and drawings for prizes. **To find out more about the list of events, please go to www.KC102.com.** 81 **We anticipate heavy traffic all weekend, so driving and parking will be more difficult than usual. If you're heading to the downtown area,** 82 **there are a few subway lines.**

欲知活動一覽表的更多資訊，請上 www.KC102.com 查閱。81 我們預期整個週末都將湧現車潮，因此行車和停車會比平時更加困難。如果您到時要前往市中心，82 有幾條地鐵路線可以搭乘。

80. What is the report mainly about?
(A) A town festival
(B) A community fundraiser
(C) An art exhibition
(D) A renovation project

80. 報導主要是關於什麼事？
(A) 市鎮節慶
(B) 社區募款活動
(C) 藝術展覽
(D) 整修工程

81. What does the speaker say is available on a Web site?
(A) Job descriptions
(B) A price chart
(C) A list of events
(D) Traffic updates

81. 説話者説網站有提供什麼？
(A) 工作説明
(B) 價格表
(C) 活動一覽表
(D) 交通資訊更新

82. Why does the speaker say, "there are a few subway lines"?
(A) The subway system is complex.
(B) He takes the subway to the office daily.
(C) Visitors should ride the subway to an event.
(D) Additional subway lines must be built.

82. 説話者為什麼要説：「有幾條地鐵路線可以搭乘」？
(A) 地鐵系統很複雜。
(B) 他每天搭地鐵上班。
(C) 遊客應搭地鐵來參加活動。
(D) 必須增建地鐵路線。

Questions 83-85 refer to the following excerpt from a meeting.

83-85 會議摘錄

W：Thank you for joining today's meeting. As you all know, **Balk Automotive has chosen our agency to create an ad series** 83 for their new line of sports cars. These vehicles will be out in March, so we'll need to finalize the designs soon. **For the rest of the meeting today, I want to brainstorm some ideas.** 84 We'll split into groups of four. **But before we do that, here's a brochure that provides some information about each of the cars that will come out.** 85

女：感謝各位今日到場開會。如大家所知，**鮑克汽車已選定本公司來操刀一系列的廣告**，83 以宣傳他們的新系列跑車。該系列車款將在三月上市，所以我們須儘快將設計拍板。**本日會議接下來的時間，我想請各位集思廣益提出一些想法。**84 我們將分成四人一組。**不過開始之前，這裡有本小冊子，裡面針對每款將上市的車提供了一些資訊。**85

TEST 9 PART 4

38

83. What industry does the speaker most likely work in?
(A) Automobile
(B) Publishing
(C) Sports
(D) Advertising

84. What would the speaker like the listeners to do at today's meeting?
(A) Watch a video
(B) Test some products
(C) Discuss some ideas
(D) Sign a document

85. What will the speaker do next?
(A) Take a group picture
(B) Provide details about some vehicles
(C) Meet some new staff members
(D) Print out a catalog

83. 說話者最有可能任職何種行業？
(A) 汽車
(B) 出版
(C) 運動
(D) 廣告

84. 說話者想要聽者在今天會議上做什麼？
(A) 觀看影片
(B) 測試幾項產品
(C) 討論一些想法
(D) 簽署文件

85. 說話者接下來會做什麼？
(A) 拍攝團體照
(B) 提供幾款車的詳情
(C) 和新進同仁見面
(D) 印出型錄

Questions 86-88 refer to the following excerpt from a speech.

M：**I am very pleased to see that such a large crowd has gathered here today for the retirement celebration of our dear colleague, Randy Milton.** 86 It's not really surprising that so many people want to honor Randy for his achievements with the company. Though he is multi-talented, **what I appreciate most is Randy's ability to lead others.** 87 When he was promoted to Chief Marketing Officer, we were just a small agency advertising for local businesses. But thanks to his leadership, **we are now one of the most renowned advertising agencies in the country.** 88 On behalf of everyone here, I would like to say thank you Randy, and best of luck in your retirement!

86-88 演說摘錄

男：**我很高興看到今天有這麼多人齊聚一堂，共同參加我們親愛的同事蘭迪・米爾頓的退休慶祝會。** 86 會有這麼多人想來向蘭迪為其在公司的成就而致敬，真的不令人意外。雖然他在各方面都具備才能，**我最為欣賞的則是蘭迪領導眾人的能力。** 87 他升任行銷長之際，我們還只是一家為本地商家做廣告的小公司。但多虧他領導有方，**如今我們已躋身國內最知名的廣告公司之列。** 88 謹代表在場所有人，我要向蘭迪致謝，並祝您退休後一切順利！

86. What is the purpose of the speech?
(A) To announce an award recipient
(B) To honor a retiring employee
(C) To explain organizational changes
(D) To promote a marketing campaign

86. 演說的目的為何？
(A) 以宣布得獎者
(B) 以表揚退休員工
(C) 以解釋組織異動
(D) 以宣傳行銷活動

87. What does the speaker say he appreciates about Randy Milton?
(A) His leadership ability
(B) His technical knowledge
(C) His design skills
(D) His financial expertise

88. What does the speaker say about the company?
(A) It will have a new headquarters.
(B) It was featured in a magazine.
(C) It is well-known throughout the country.
(D) It plans on hiring more workers.

87. 關於蘭迪・米爾頓，說話者表示欣賞他的什麼？
(A) 他的領導能力
(B) 他的技術知識
(C) 他的設計技巧
(D) 他的財經專業

88. 關於該公司，說話者說了什麼？
(A) 將有新總部。
(B) 受到雜誌專題介紹。
(C) 全國聞名。
(D) 計畫僱用更多員工。

Questions 89-91 refer to the following excerpt from a meeting.

W：**I'd like to thank all the executives for joining me today.** 89 As Vice President of Operations, it is my job to make sure that everything here runs smoothly and efficiently. As you recall, several departments transferred to our headquarters to make communication easier. However, **the engineering team is saying that there is too much noise in the office now. The facility manager offered to set up bigger partitions to help block out the sound, but I think it would be better to rent another small office in the building for them. It would cost more, but it's definitely worth considering.** 90 **We can't afford for Engineering to lose focus. They would be much more efficient if they didn't have to worry about other people distracting them.** 91

89-91 會議摘錄

女：**感謝各位公司幹部今天前來和我開會。** 89 我身為營運副總，確保公司一切都順利、有效地運作是我的職責。各位都記得，為了方便溝通，有幾個部門調配到了公司總部。然而，**工程部說現在辦公室太吵雜了。設備經理提議安裝更厚的隔板來隔音，但我認為倒不如在這棟大樓內另租一間小辦公室供他們使用。此舉會增加開銷，但絕對值得考慮。** 90 **我們承擔不起工程部精神渙散的後果。他們如果不用擔心受到他人干擾，工作效率會大增。** 91

89. Who are the listeners?
(A) Property managers
(B) Interior designers
(C) Company executives
(D) Mechanical engineers

90. Why is the speaker discussing a change?
(A) A budget is being reduced.
(B) A work area is too noisy.
(C) A department is understaffed.
(D) A manager is retiring.

89. 聽者的身分是？
(A) 物業經理人
(B) 室內設計師
(C) 公司高層幹部
(D) 機械工程師

90. 說話者為什麼在討論一項異動？
(A) 預算正要縮減。
(B) 工作場所太吵雜。
(C) 有個部門人力短缺。
(D) 有位經理將退休。

91. Why does the speaker say, "We can't afford for Engineering to lose focus"?
(A) To approve a revised process
(B) To criticize another team
(C) To justify the reason for a proposal
(D) To complain about a new product

91. 說話者為什麼要說：「我們承擔不起工程部精神渙散的後果」？
(A) 為批准修改後的程序
(B) 為批評其他團隊
(C) 為提案提出合理原因
(D) 為抱怨一項新品

Questions 92-94 refer to the following excerpt from a meeting.

W：And now, for our last order of business: our unlimited vacation policy. 92 **As you know, under this program, you are allowed to take as many personal days away from the office as you'd like. We understand that a well-rested employee is happier in the workplace, and as a result, performs much better. So, to motivate our staff to get out of the office more, we're willing to pay for a round-trip ticket for two to a destination of your choice.** 93 Now, you might ask yourself, "How do I take advantage of this opportunity?" Well, **I have here a brochure that outlines the rules and process. I'll pass it out after this meeting.** 94

92-94 會議摘要

女：那麼現在，輪到我們會議事項最後一項：不受限制的休假規則。 92 **你們都知道，在這項制度下，你們可以根據自身意願，要請多少事假都行。我們深知獲得充分休息的員工在職場當中會更快樂，也因此表現更出色。所以，為了鼓勵同仁增加休假，公司願意招待一組雙人的來回機票，目的地則由你們來選。** 93 現在，你們可能想問：「我該怎麼利用這個機會？」那麼，**我這裡有本小冊子，裡頭有規則和程序的簡介。開完會後我會把它傳閱下去。** 94

92. What is the speaker mainly discussing?
(A) A corporate policy
(B) A visiting client
(C) An annual budget
(D) An evaluation process

92. 說話者主要在討論什麼？
(A) 公司規定
(B) 來訪的客戶
(C) 年度預算
(D) 評鑑程序

93. What are the listeners encouraged to do?
(A) Participate in a survey
(B) Join a social gathering
(C) Take some time off
(D) Visit some clients

93. 聽者被鼓勵做什麼？
(A) 參與調查
(B) 參加社交聚會
(C) 休假一段時間
(D) 拜訪幾名客戶

94. What will the speaker do after the meeting?
(A) Distribute a brochure
(B) Order some tickets
(C) Interview some candidates
(D) Send out a survey

94. 會後說話者將做什麼？
(A) 傳發小冊子
(B) 訂幾張票
(C) 面試幾名求職者
(D) 發放調查問卷

Questions 95-97 refer to the following telephone message and list.

M : Ms. Menks, this is Roger calling from Mecho Auto. I'd like to inform you that we've finished checking your van. You can pick it up any time tomorrow. But **make sure you come before 5 P.M. because we are closing early tomorrow to remodel our shop.** 95 Also, while we were performing the maintenance, we found several issues that you may want to consider fixing. **Since we can't make the repairs without your approval, we made a list of the problems and sent it to your email address that you gave us yesterday.** 96 Please look it over and let us know if you'd like us to take care of any of the items on the list. And just so you know, for a limited time, **we're offering a special reduced price on seat replacements.** 97

Suggested Items to Repair	
1 97	**Damaged passenger seat**
2	Worn-out tires
3	Broken glove compartment
4	Loose rearview mirror

95-97 語音留言和清單

男： 孟克斯女士，這裡是「梅丘汽車」來電給您，我是羅杰。我想通知您，我們已檢查完您的廂型車，您明天可以隨時過來取車。但**因為本店將進行整修，明日會提早關門，請您務必在下午五點前過來。** 95 另外，我們在保養過程中發現了幾項您可能會想考慮修理的問題。**由於未經您的同意我們無法進行維修，我們把問題列成了清單，並寄到您昨天留給我們的電子郵件地址。** 96 請您查閱並告知我們您是否有意讓我們處理清單上的任何項目。另外也告知您，**針對座椅更換，我們目前提供**期間限定的**特別折扣價**。97

建議維修項目	
1 97	**受損的乘客座椅**
2	磨損的輪胎
3	毀壞的前座置物箱
4	鬆脫的後照鏡

TEST 9 PART 4

38

95. What does the speaker mention about Mecho Auto?
(A) It offers a pick-up service.
(B) It has extended its operating hours.
(C) It will undergo renovations.
(D) It is moving to another location.

96. According to the speaker, what did Ms. Menks do yesterday?
(A) Provided an email address
(B) Approved a request
(C) Made a payment
(D) Ordered additional supplies

97. Look at the graphic. Which item number can Ms. Menks receive a discount on?
(A) 1
(B) 2
(C) 3
(D) 4

95. 關於梅丘汽車，說話者提到什麼？
(A) 提供接送服務。
(B) 延長了營業時間。
(C) 將進行整修。
(D) 將搬遷到另一個地點。

96. 據說話者說法，孟克斯女士昨天做了什麼？
(A) 提供電子郵件地址
(B) 批准一項請求
(C) 支付款項
(D) 訂購更多用品

97. 請據圖表作答。孟克斯女士在哪個項目可以獲得折扣？
(A) 1
(B) 2
(C) 3
(D) 4

Questions 98-100 refer to the following telephone message and map.

M：Hello, **this is Hafiz from Allentown Realtors. I've got an excellent spot for your new hair salon.** 98 **It's on the west side of town, directly across the street from Hooper's Supermarket.** 99 This area should give you a lot of visibility, especially now that the coffee shop is open 24 hours a day, and there are always people coming and going. I went ahead and called the owner, and he said that they've already gotten a few offers on the place. **I know that this location is pricey, and it costs a bit more than what you initially had in mind. But it is an ideal spot, so I really think the higher price is worth it.** 100 Give me a call, and let's discuss it.

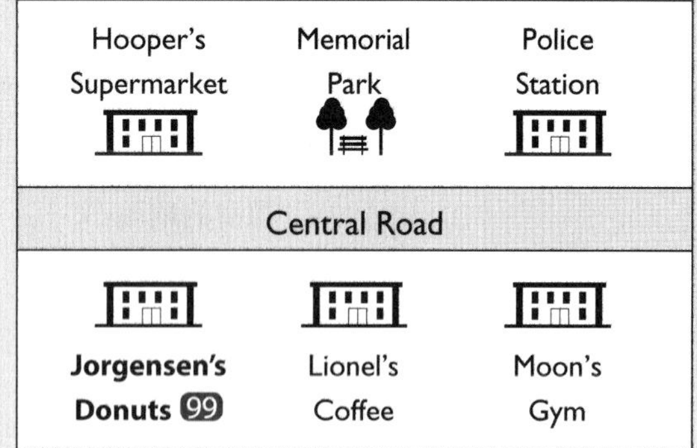

98. What most likely is the speaker's job?
(A) Hair stylist
(B) Supermarket manager
(C) Coffee shop owner
(D) Real estate agent

99. Look at the graphic. Which location is the speaker describing?
(A) Hooper's Supermarket
(B) Lionel's Coffee
(C) Jorgensen's Donuts
(D) Moon's Gym

100. What plan does the speaker recommend changing?
(A) A building design
(B) A budget
(C) An advertisement
(D) A project timetable

98-100 語音留言和地圖

男：您好，**我是「亞倫鎮房地產」的哈菲茲。我為您的新美髮沙龍找到一處絕佳的地點。** 98 **該店面就坐落在城鎮西側、胡伯超市的正對面。** 99 那個地段應該能讓您的店面獲得高度的能見度，特別是那間咖啡廳現在 24 小時營業，附近總是人來人往。我先打過電話給房東了，他說他們已經收到幾份該間的報價。**我明白這個地點要價不菲，且比您原先所想的略高一籌。但該位置很理想，因此我真心認為價格較高也值得。** 100 請打給我，讓我們討論一下。

胡伯超市
紀念公園
警察局
中央路
約根森甜甜圈 99
萊昂內爾咖啡
月亮健身房

98. 說話者的職業最有可能為何？
(A) 髮型設計師
(B) 超市經理
(C) 咖啡廳老闆
(D) 房仲人員

99. 請據圖表作答。說話者描述的是哪個地點？
(A) 胡伯超市
(B) 萊昂內爾咖啡
(C) 約根森甜甜圈
(D) 月亮健身房

100. 說話者建議變更何項規畫？
(A) 建築設計
(B) 預算
(C) 廣告
(D) 專案時程表

ACTUAL TEST 10

PART 1 P. 126–129

1. **(A) She's carrying a basket.**
   (B) She's washing some clothes.
   (C) She's folding a towel.
   (D) She's organizing some boxes.

2. **(A) A server is standing by a table.**
   (B) Some people are waiting to be seated.
   (C) Some customers are paying for their meal.
   (D) A woman is pouring a beverage into a glass.

3. (A) A fan is being installed in a room.
   (B) A photo is being removed from a frame.
   (C) Some furniture is being delivered to a home.
   (D) Some artwork has been hung on the walls.

4. (A) Some construction tools are being unloaded from a truck.
   (B) Some shelves are being disassembled.
   (C) A worker is taking measurements of a wooden board.
   (D) A man is operating machinery.

5. (A) Some books are being shelved by the door.
   (B) Some cords have been extended on the desk.
   (C) A man is connecting a keyboard to a computer.
   (D) A man is sliding a cart under a workstation.

6. **(A) There's a parking area near the beach.**
   (B) People are getting on a boat from a pier.
   (C) Yachts are floating under a bridge.
   (D) Some tables are being set up outside a restaurant.

1. **(A) 她正拿著籃子。**
   (B) 她正洗著幾件衣服。
   (C) 她正在折一條毛巾。
   (D) 她正在整理幾個箱子。

2. **(A) 服務生正站在桌邊。**
   (B) 幾個人正在等待入座。
   (C) 幾名顧客正在為他們的餐點付帳。
   (D) 女子正把飲料倒進玻璃杯中。

3. (A) 房間裡正在安裝風扇。
   (B) 照片正從相框裡移出。
   (C) 家具正送往一處房子。
   (D) 藝術品掛在牆上。

4. (A) 幾件建築工具正從卡車上卸下來。
   (B) 幾座架子正在拆卸中。
   (C) 工人正在測量木板。
   (D) 男子正在操作機械。

5. (A) 門邊有幾本書正在歸架。
   (B) 幾條電線在桌上延伸著。
   (C) 男子正把鍵盤接上電腦。
   (D) 男子正把推車推到工作區桌下。

6. **(A) 海灘附近有停車場。**
   (B) 人們正從碼頭登船。
   (C) 遊艇漂浮在橋下。
   (D) 餐廳外正在擺設幾張桌子。

TEST 10 PART 1 2

PART 2 P. 130

7. Who's the event coordinator for the car trade show?
   (A) In the display booth.
   (B) That'd be Brian Johnson.
   (C) Check the back of the truck.

7. 汽車貿易展的活動統籌者是誰？
   (A) 在該展覽攤位。
   (B) 是布萊恩・強森。
   (C) 查看卡車後側。

8. Mr. Keith has completed the management training course, hasn't he?
(A) No, the accounting manager.
(B) Yes, last month.
(C) Fifty people per session.

9. Pardon me. Why hasn't the performance started yet?
(A) Two tickets for the 7 P.M. show.
(B) At the Silverton Auditorium.
(C) One of the musicians is running late.

10. Where can I find information on upcoming local events?
(A) At the community center.
(B) Throughout the summer.
(C) She's a local artist.

11. How can we complete the project before the deadline?
(A) To be honest, I don't know, either.
(B) By 5 P.M. on Wednesday.
(C) Yes, the report has already been finished.

12. When will the company directory be completed?
(A) I'm on my last page.
(B) On the 4th floor.
(C) A list of names.

13. Is there a phone charger I can borrow?
(A) My battery is full.
(B) I paid back my loan.
(C) There's one by that wall.

14. Didn't you buy a jacket here last week?
(A) I brought a coat, too.
(B) It's supposed to be cold today.
(C) Yes, a leather one.

15. Could you help the diners at that table?
(A) They won't attend the conference.
(B) I reserved a table for two.
(C) Sure, no problem.

16. I'll get coffee for everyone before this morning's meeting.
(A) No, to discuss the budget.
(B) That's very nice of you.
(C) A very popular café.

8. 基思先生完成了管理培訓課程，不是嗎？
(A) 不，會計經理。
(B) 對，上個月。
(C) 每堂課 50 人。

9. 不好意思。表演為什麼還沒開始呢？
(A) 晚上七點的演出，兩張票。
(B) 在銀頓禮堂。
(C) 其中一位音樂家遲到了。

10. 我可以在哪裡找到本地近期活動的消息？
(A) 在社區活動中心。
(B) 整個夏天。
(C) 她是本地藝術家。

11. 我們如何能在截止日前完成專案？
(A) 老實說，我也不知道。
(B) 週三下午五點之前。
(C) 是，報告已經完成了。

12. 工商名錄何時會完成？
(A) 我在處理最後一頁了。
(B) 在四樓。
(C) 一張名單。

13. 有手機充電器可借我用嗎？
(A) 我的電池充滿電了。
(B) 我還清了貸款。
(C) 那邊的牆上有一個。

14. 你上週不是在這邊買了夾克嗎？
(A) 我也帶了件大衣。
(B) 今天應該會很冷。
(C) 對，一件皮革製的。

15. 你能協助在那一桌用餐的人嗎？
(A) 他們不會去參加會議。
(B) 我預訂了一桌兩位。
(C) 當然，沒問題。

16. 今早開會前，我會幫大家帶咖啡。
(A) 不，為了討論預算。
(B) 你人真好。
(C) 一家很熱門的咖啡廳。

17. Doesn't the restaurant stay open until 10 P.M.?
(A) It just opened this week.
(B) That sounds like a great idea.
(C) Not on weeknights.

18. When will the job interview in the meeting room finish?
(A) She's a qualified candidate.
(B) It's almost over.
(C) I'll see you there.

19. It's OK to contact him on the weekend, isn't it?
(A) The number of employees.
(B) Next Sunday at noon.
(C) It shouldn't be a problem.

20. Would you mind printing a report for me?
(A) Yes, put it next to the printer.
(B) In color, please.
(C) No, I don't mind at all.

21. Why did you modify the settings on the camera?
(A) Three camera operators.
(B) A new software.
(C) The studio was too dark.

22. The home appliance convention was held in Berlin last year, right?
(A) Yes, we unveiled our new products there.
(B) No, I bought a TV.
(C) Which speakers?

23. Should we order new monitors for the design team or not?
(A) Their current ones are too old.
(B) The sign was purchased yesterday.
(C) They offer free installation.

24. How will we recruit five new employees?
(A) They're at an orientation.
(B) The date for the interviews.
(C) By listing the openings on our Web site.

25. Your new car will be ready to be picked up at noon tomorrow.
(A) Great. I'll come by then.
(B) Change the tires.
(C) I can give you a ride.

17. 那家餐廳不是營業到晚上十點嗎？
(A) 它本週剛開幕。
(B) 那聽起來是個好主意。
(C) 平日晚上沒有。

18. 會議室的求職面試何時會結束？
(A) 她是符合條件的人選。
(B) 差不多快結束了。
(C) 我們那裡見。

19. 週末可以聯絡他，不是嗎？
(A) 員工的數量。
(B) 下個週日的正午。
(C) 這應該沒問題。

20. 想請您幫我印出報告，會麻煩嗎？
(A) 對，把它放到印表機旁邊。
(B) 用彩色，謝謝。
(C) 不，一點都不麻煩。

21. 你為什麼更改了相機設定？
(A) 三名相機操作員。
(B) 一款新軟體。
(C) 工作室太暗了。

22. 家電展去年在柏林舉行，對嗎？
(A) 對，我們在那裡首度發表自家新品。
(B) 不，我買了電視。
(C) 哪幾名講者？

23. 我們該幫設計團隊訂購新的螢幕嗎，還是不用？
(A) 他們現在用的太舊了。
(B) 招牌是昨天買的。
(C) 他們提供免費安裝服務。

24. 我們要怎麼招聘五名新員工？
(A) 他們正在新人說明會上。
(B) 幾場面試的日期。
(C) 藉由在我們網站上列出職缺。

25. 您的新車明天中午就將準備好取車了。
(A) 很好。我到時會過來。
(B) 更換輪胎。
(C) 我可以載你一程。

26. Didn't you put in a request for a vacation leave?
(A) Yes, but it got declined.
(B) A trip to New Zealand.
(C) I requested a window seat.

26. 你不是申請休假了嗎？
(A) 是，但被拒絕了。
(B) 紐西蘭之旅。
(C) 我要求了靠窗座位。

27. How long did the marketing presentation last?
(A) Yes, for the advertising campaign.
(B) It's on the 1st floor.
(C) There was only one slide.

27. 行銷簡報進行了多久時間？
(A) 對，用於廣告活動。
(B) 它在一樓。
(C) 只有一張投影片。

28. Why were so many train tickets sold this month?
(A) There's a long holiday coming up.
(B) Our monthly meeting is this afternoon.
(C) I like traveling by plane.

28. 為什麼這個月賣了那麼多張火車票？
(A) 長假即將到來。
(B) 我們的每月例會是在今天下午。
(C) 我喜歡搭飛機旅行。

29. Is it going to snow during our charity event on Tuesday?
(A) Preparations are going really slow.
(B) Raising money for the arts program.
(C) Yes, make sure to dress warm.

29. 我們週二的慈善活動時會下雪嗎？
(A) 準備進度相當緩慢。
(B) 為藝術計畫募款。
(C) 對，務必要穿暖一點。

30. Remember to pick up your personal belongings from the security desk.
(A) Of course. I won't forget.
(B) A jacket and a bag.
(C) It belongs to my coworker.

30. 記得到保全櫃台領走你的個人物品。
(A) 當然。我不會忘記的。
(B) 外套和袋子。
(C) 它屬於我的同事。

31. When are we going to update the computer software?
(A) Probably on the Web site.
(B) Hiro already took care of it.
(C) Faster than the current one.

31. 我們何時要更新電腦軟體？
(A) 可能在網站上。
(B) 希洛已經處理好了。
(C) 比目前這一款更快。

PART 3 P. 131–134

41

Questions 32-34 refer to the following conversation.

32-34 會話

W：Hi, Clark. **I attended the workshop yesterday on our company's new accounting software, but I'm having a hard time entering my expense report with it.** 32 Have you tried using it yet?
M：No. **I wasn't at the workshop,** 33 but **I'm on my way to see Alice in the IT Department.** 34 She's going to teach me how the program works.

女：克拉克你好。**我昨天參加了我們公司新款會計軟體的研習，但我現在要輸入開支報告時遇到了困難。** 32 你試著用過它了嗎？
男：還沒有。**我之前沒有去參加研習，** 33 **但我正要去資訊技術部找愛麗絲。** 34 她會教我那款程式的操作方式。

W：Oh, I didn't know you weren't there yesterday. **Is it OK if I go with you and ask for Alice's help as well?** 34

女：哦，我不知道你昨天沒來。**我可以和你一起過去找愛麗絲幫忙嗎？** 34

32. What does the woman need help with?
(A) Organizing a workshop
(B) Using a computer program
(C) Making a presentation
(D) Finding a report

32. 女子有何事需要幫助？
(A) 籌辦研習
(B) 使用電腦程式
(C) 發表簡報
(D) 找出報告

33. Why is the man unable to help?
(A) He is leaving work soon.
(B) He lost some documents.
(C) He missed a training session.
(D) He has to meet a client.

33. 男子為什麼無法幫忙？
(A) 他快下班了。
(B) 他遺失了一些文件。
(C) 他沒參加到培訓課程。
(D) 他得要見客戶。

34. What will the speakers probably do next?
(A) Speak with a coworker
(B) Complete a project
(C) Prepare some forms
(D) Send out some emails

34. 說話者接下來可能會做什麼？
(A) 與同事交談
(B) 完成專案
(C) 準備表單
(D) 發送電子郵件

Questions 35-37 refer to the following conversation with three speakers.

W1：**Welcome to Falcor Public Library.** 35
M：Hello, I'm Jeremy Kim, and I want to pick up a book that I reserved in advance.
W1：Of course, Mr. Kim.
M：Also, I was wondering if I would be able to keep this book for one month instead of two weeks. **I'll be going on a business trip next week** 36 and won't be returning until the end of the month.
W1：Hmm . . . I'm not sure if that's possible. I'll talk to the head librarian. **Ms. Chin, what is our rule about allowing patrons to extend their rental period for another two weeks?** 37
W2：We can allow it, Tammy. Mr. Kim just needs to fill out a form acknowledging he'll return the book at the end of the month.

35-37 三人會話

女 1：**歡迎來到佛可公共圖書館。** 35
男：哈囉，我是傑瑞米．金，我想領取我先前預約的書。
女 1：好的，金先生。
男：另外我想要知道，我借用這本書的期限能否從兩個星期變更為一個月。**我下週要出差，** 36 要到這個月底才會回來。
女 1：嗯……我不確定可不可行。我來和圖書館館長討論一下。**秦女士，關於開放讀者延長借閱期限兩週，我們的規定是什麼？** 37
女 2：這部份我們能開放，譚美。金先生只須填寫表格，確認他將在這個月底還書即可。

35. Where are the speakers?
(A) At a car rental business
(B) At a travel agency
(C) At a public library
(D) At an electronics repair shop

36. What will the man do next week?
(A) Attend an autograph signing session
(B) Participate in a tour
(C) Renew a membership contract
(D) Depart for a business trip

37. Why does Tammy talk to Ms. Chin?
(A) To refer her to a service
(B) To get approval for a purchase
(C) To inquire about a rule
(D) To check on the status of a delivery

35. 說話者人在何地？
(A) 在租車公司
(B) 在旅行社
(C) 在公共圖書館
(D) 在電子用品維修行

36. 男子下週將做什麼？
(A) 參加簽名會活動
(B) 參加旅遊行程
(C) 會員合約續約
(D) 動身出差

37. 譚美為何找秦女士交談？
(A) 以向她引介一項服務
(B) 以取得採購核可
(C) 以詢問一項規定
(D) 以確認貨運狀態

Questions 38-40 refer to the following conversation.

W： Mike, do you know if the new family restaurant by the natural history museum is any good? **I'm in charge of organizing the monthly department luncheon, and I'm looking for a new place to have it this month.** 38

M： Well, I went there with a friend last week, and they had a lot of menu choices. But it took too long to get our food. And **it looked like they were understaffed. They should hire more employees.** 39

W： Oh, that's too bad. Well, all of the other restaurants I've called in the area are already fully booked. So **I guess we have no choice but to have our gathering in our company's banquet hall again.** 40

38-40 會話

女： 麥克，自然歷史博物館旁邊有新開一間家庭餐館，你知道那家好不好吃嗎？**我負責舉辦每月例行的部門午餐會，目前我在尋找新的地點，來辦理本月的聚餐。** 38

男： 這個嘛，我上週和一個朋友去過那裡，他們有蠻多的菜色可以選擇。但我們等餐送來的時間太久了。而**他們人手似乎不足。他們應該要僱用更多員工。** 39

女： 哦，太糟糕了。好吧，這附近我打電話問過的所有其他餐廳，每家的預約都額滿。所以**我想我們別無選擇，只能又在公司的宴會廳辦聚餐了。** 40

38. What event are the speakers discussing?
(A) A guided tour
(B) A luncheon
(C) A training session
(D) A client meeting

39. What problem does the man mention?
(A) Some items are unavailable.
(B) There are not enough seats.
(C) Reservations have not been made.
(D) More staff is needed.

38. 說話者正在討論哪項活動？
(A) 導覽行程
(B) 午餐會
(C) 培訓課程
(D) 客戶會議

39. 男子提到什麼問題？
(A) 有些品項無法供應。
(B) 座位不夠。
(C) 未曾預約。
(D) 需要更多員工。

40. What does the woman decide to do?
(A) Send an email
(B) Postpone a gathering
(C) Use a company facility
(D) Hire a new employee

40. 女子決定要做什麼？
(A) 寄送電子郵件
(B) 延後聚會
(C) 使用公司場地
(D) 僱用新員工

Questions 41-43 refer to the following conversation.

41-43 會話

W：Hi, Ted. You work at Gerry's House Furniture, right? **I heard on the radio that a new factory is going to be built** 41 in the city. Do you have any more information about it?
M：Well, the company is expanding, and **the owner plans on generating more jobs in this area.** 42 We expect to start production on the new site next month, and **we will need to hire a lot of workers.** 42
W：That's great. This will really boost the local economy. Also, my son's been looking for a job, and he's a skilled furniture designer.
M：Oh, **why don't you send his résumé to my company email address?** 43 I'll personally review it and see if there is a suitable position for him at Gerry's.

女：嗨，泰德。你是在「蓋瑞家庭家具」上班，對嗎？**我聽廣播提到，本市會有一間新工廠開設。** 41 對此你有掌握什麼詳情嗎？
男：嗯，公司正在擴張，而**老闆計劃在本地創造更多工作機會。** 42 我們預計下個月讓新廠開工生產，到時**我們將需要僱用大量員工。** 42
女：太好了。這確實將會促進本地經濟。而且，我的兒子正在找工作，他還是技術純熟的家具設計師。
男：哦，**妳何不把他的履歷表寄到我公司的電子郵件信箱呢？** 43 我會親自審查他的履歷，並看一下蓋瑞家具有沒有適合他的職位。

TEST 10
PART 3
41

41. What does the woman say she has heard about?
(A) The renovation of a building
(B) The acquisition of a company
(C) The construction of a new facility
(D) The launch of a new product

41. 女子說她聽說了什麼？
(A) 大樓整修
(B) 公司收購
(C) 新廠建設
(D) 新品上市

42. What benefit is expected?
(A) Lower rental rates
(B) More employment opportunities
(C) Increased tourism
(D) Clearer company guidelines

42. 預期帶來的效益為何者？
(A) 降低租金
(B) 更多就業機會
(C) 促進觀光
(D) 更明確的公司準則

43. What does the man suggest the woman do?
(A) Tell her son to call him directly
(B) Forward a résumé
(C) Visit a company's Web site
(D) Speak with a manager

43. 男子建議女子做什麼？
(A) 叫她兒子直接打電話給他
(B) 轉寄一份履歷
(C) 造訪公司網站
(D) 和經理交談

Questions 44-46 refer to the following conversation.

W：Hello, **the executive card holders in your store look great. I'd like to purchase some, but I want to know if it's possible for you to put our company logo on them.** 44

M：Sure, we can do that for you. But since **customizing the card holders is a special order,** 46 **you'd have to go to our store's Web site to order them.** 45

W：Oh, I see. I'll need to order about 100 card holders for an upcoming seminar, so do you think you can give me a discount on my order?

M：I'm sorry, but **we don't offer discounts on any special orders.** 46

44-46 會話

女：您好，**貴店的名片卡夾看起來很棒。我想購買幾件，但我想知道你們能不能在上面放上我們公司的標誌。** 44

男：當然，我們可以幫您做到。但因為**訂製卡夾算是特殊訂單，** 46 **您要到本店的網站上訂購。** 45

女：喔，了解。我須為即將舉行的研討會訂購約 100 個卡夾，那麼你覺得你能給我的訂單一點折扣嗎？

男：很抱歉，但是**針對任何特殊訂單，我們沒有提供折扣。** 46

44. What special feature does the woman request for the card holders?

(A) Water-resistant material
(B) A company logo
(C) Specific colors
(D) An extra large size

44. 女子要求卡夾要有什麼特殊元素？

(A) 防水材質
(B) 公司標誌
(C) 特定顏色
(D) 特大尺寸

45. What does the man say she must do?

(A) Order from a Web site
(B) Make a deposit
(C) Provide a sample
(D) Speak to a craftsperson

45. 男子說她必須做什麼？

(A) 從網站上訂購
(B) 存入款項
(C) 提供樣品
(D) 和工匠談談

46. What does the man say about discounts?

(A) They must be approved by a supervisor.
(B) They require a membership card.
(C) They are not available for customized items.
(D) They are only offered for online orders.

46. 關於折扣，男子說了什麼？

(A) 它們（折扣）須主管批准。
(B) 需有會員卡才能享有折扣。
(C) 折扣不適用訂製產品。
(D) 折扣僅適用於網路訂單。

Questions 47-49 refer to the following conversation.

W：Hi, my name is Cambria Price. I'm glad to see Weiman Global Associates at this year's career fair. **I'm looking for employment at a law firm.** 47

M：Thank you for coming by, Ms. Price. We have several openings, but **all candidates must have experience working with international clients.** 48

47-49 會話

女：您好，我的名字是坎布里亞．普萊斯。我很高興能在今年的就業博覽會上，和威曼全球聯合企業相見。**我正在尋找律師事務所的工作。** 47

男：普萊斯女士，感謝您前來。我們有幾個職缺，不過**所有應徵者都必須具備和國際客戶共事過的經驗。** 48

W：Well, I interned at a law office that offered its services to many international clients, and I'm also fluent in Mandarin and Russian. More details are listed in my résumé. Let me give you a copy.

M：Thank you. **We're going to be conducting interviews after lunch. Could you come back then?** 49 We'd like to hear more about your skills and experience.

女：嗯，我之前實習時待的律師事務所有對很多國際客戶提供服務，而且我的華語和俄語都很流利。我的履歷表上列有更多詳細資訊。讓我給您一份。

男：謝謝您。**我們會在午餐時間過後舉行面試。您到時能再過來嗎？** 49 我們想更深入了解您的技能和經驗。

47. What type of business does the woman want to work for?
(A) A translation firm
(B) A law firm
(C) A marketing agency
(D) A publishing agency

47. 女子想在哪種公司任職？
(A) 翻譯公司
(B) 律師事務所
(C) 行銷公司
(D) 出版社

48. What job requirement is mentioned?
(A) A degree in business
(B) Knowledge of a specific product
(C) Event organizing skills
(D) International experience

48. 對話中提到哪項職位需求？
(A) 商學位
(B) 特定產品的知識
(C) 活動策劃的技能
(D) 國際經驗

49. What does the man ask the woman to do?
(A) Prepare a presentation
(B) Fill out a questionnaire
(C) Return at a later time
(D) Submit a reference letter

49. 男子要求女子做何事？
(A) 準備簡報
(B) 填寫問卷
(C) 稍後再來
(D) 繳交推薦信

Questions 50-52 refer to the following conversation with three speakers.

50-52 三人會話

W1：**Hey, Kathy. I've got a caller from a law firm on the line.** 50 He may be interested in our services.

W2：Thank you for calling Eco Recyclers, this is Kathy. How may I be of assistance?

M：Hello, **I'm an attorney** 50 in this area, and **I'd like to dispose of some old computers and printers in a safe manner.** 51 Would your company be able to get rid of these items?

W2：Of course, I'll explain the process. Once you schedule an appointment, one of our workers will come by to pick up your equipment.

M：How much do you charge for that?

女 1：**嘿，凱西。我接到一通律師事務所打來的電話。** 50 他可能對我們的服務有興趣。

女 2：這裡是「生態回收公司」，感謝您的來電，我叫凱西。有什麼我能協助您的嗎？

男：您好，**我是在本地從業的律師，** 50 **而我想以安全的方式，來處理掉幾台舊電腦和印表機。** 51 貴公司有辦法來清理這些東西嗎？

女 2：當然可以。我來說明一下作業流程。待您預約好時間後，我們一名同仁就會過去收取您的設備。

男：這樣收費是多少呢？

TEST 10
PART 3
41

W2：That depends. **If you'd like, I can stop by your office any time next week to go over the exact details.** 52
M：**Sure,** 52 I'm free next Wednesday.

女 2：視情況而定。**如果您願意，我可以在下週的任一時間，前往您的辦公室詳細說明具體細節。** 52
男　：**當然好，** 52 我下週三有空。

50. Where does the man work?
(A) At a law firm
(B) At a printing center
(C) At a recycling plant
(D) At an advertising agency

50. 男子的工作地點為何？
(A) 在律師事務所
(B) 在印刷中心
(C) 在回收工廠
(D) 在廣告公司

51. What would the man like to do?
(A) Register for a training session
(B) Purchase new equipment
(C) Store some merchandise
(D) Get rid of old electronics

51. 男子想做什麼？
(A) 報名培訓課程
(B) 購買新設備
(C) 儲放一些商品
(D) 丟棄舊電子設備

52. What will Kathy probably do next week?
(A) Deliver a package
(B) Give the man a tour
(C) Participate in a workshop
(D) Visit the man's office

52. 凱西下週可能會做什麼？
(A) 運送包裹
(B) 帶男子參觀
(C) 參加研習
(D) 造訪男子的辦公室

Questions 53-55 refer to the following conversation.

M：Suzie, **I talked to Michael in HR** 55 this morning, and he said that **our new intern, Burt, is going to start work on November 21.** 53
W：Oh, that means we won't be here to train him.
M：**Right. We'll be at the technology conference in Tokyo that week.** 53
W：Well, **why don't we just have him start in December instead?** 54 After all, there will only be about a week left in November.
M：Yeah. **That's a good idea. I'll call Michael and see what he says about it.** 55

53-55 會話

男：蘇西，**我今早和人資部的麥可談過，** 55 而他說**我們的新實習生博特將在 11 月 21 日開始上班。** 53
女：哦，那就意味到時我們不在公司，無法訓練他。
男：**沒錯。我們那週會出席東京的科技會議。** 53
女：那麼，**我們何不就改成讓他 12 月開始上班呢？** 54 畢竟，到時候 11 月也只剩下一週而已。
男：對啊。**這個主意不錯。我會打給麥可，徵詢一下他的意見。** 55

53. Where will the speakers be on November 21?
(A) At a job fair
(B) At a store opening
(C) At a technology conference
(D) At an anniversary celebration

53. 說話者 11 月 21 日將在哪裡？
(A) 在就業博覽會
(B) 在店家開幕會
(C) 在科技會議
(D) 在週年慶祝會

54. What does the man mean when he says, "That's a good idea"?
(A) The location of an event should be changed.
(B) The start date of an internship should be moved.
(C) The length of a training session should be shortened.
(D) The order of speakers should be switched.

54. 男子說:「這個主意不錯」,其意思為何?
(A) 應更改活動地點。
(B) 應變更實習開始日期。
(C) 應縮短培訓課程長度。
(D) 須調整講者順序。

55. What will the man probably do next?
(A) Talk to an HR employee
(B) Make a reservation
(C) Prepare a contract
(D) Look for a piece of equipment

55. 男子接著可能做什麼?
(A) 與人資部職員交談
(B) 做好預約
(C) 準備合約
(D) 尋找一件設備

Questions 56-58 refer to the following conversation.

56-58 會話

TEST 10 PART 3

41

M: Excuse me. **I'm looking for a door knob for my house. The original one broke recently.** 56 A friend of mine suggested that I come to this hardware store when I told her I was doing some repair work in my house. Here. I brought the door knob to show you.

W: Well, we carry quite a lot of replacement parts for homes, and **we have the same type of knob you need, just not in that color,** 57 though. But let me show you what we have anyways.

M: Hmm, I was really hoping that I could find one in the same color so that it will match the other ones in the house.

W: I can probably order one for you from the manufacturer. But **it's going to take quite a while for the item to arrive.** 58 Five to seven weeks at least. Would that be OK with you?

男: 不好意思。**我正在找我家要用的門把。原本的那個最近壞掉了。** 56 我跟一個朋友說我在家裡修理一些東西,她就建議我來這家五金行。我把門把帶過來給妳看了,在這邊。

女: 嗯,我們有賣很多住家用的替換配件,而且**我們備有您所需要的同款門把,只是顏色並不相符。** 57 不過,還是讓我拿給您看我們現有的貨。

男: 唔,我真的很希望能找到相同顏色的門把,才能和家裡的其他門把相配。

女: 或許我可以幫您向製造商訂購一件。但**得等上好一段時間才會到貨。** 58 至少五到七週時間。這樣您同意嗎?

56. What does the man want to do?
(A) Buy some furniture
(B) Return some supplies
(C) Replace a broken item
(D) Organize a warehouse

56. 男子想做什麼?
(A) 購買幾件家具
(B) 退還幾件用品
(C) 更換毀損的物件
(D) 整理倉庫

57. What does the woman say about some merchandise?
(A) A color is not in stock.
(B) A size is not available.
(C) The prices have been reduced.
(D) The products are handmade.

57. 針對某項商品,女子說了什麼?
(A) 有款顏色缺貨。
(B) 有個尺碼目前沒有賣。
(C) 價格已調降。
(D) 產品為手工製作。

58. What does the woman caution the man about?
(A) Complicated installation procedures
(B) Costly shipping charges
(C) An easily damaged item
(D) A long waiting period

58. 女子提醒男子何事？
(A) 安裝過程複雜
(B) 運費昂貴
(C) 商品容易損壞
(D) 等待時間很長

Questions 59-61 refer to the following conversation.

M：You've reached Bruno's. What can I assist you with?
W：Hello. **I accidentally dropped my smartphone in my swimming pool. And I wanted to bring it into your store today to get it repaired.** 59
M：I'm afraid all of our technicians are busy today. **You should open the phone up and let it dry for a few hours.** 60
W：**I've tried that.** Is there really no way you can help me? I'm going on vacation tomorrow, and I really need this device.
M：Well, I have some time before my next consultation, but **you'll have to come in within the next 30 minutes.** 61
W：Great. **I'll be there in 15 minutes.** 61

59-61 會話

男：這裡是「布魯諾商行」。有什麼我能協助您的嗎？
女：您好。**我不小心把我的智慧型手機掉到我家泳池裡了。我想要今天帶過去您店裡修理。**59
男：今天的話，恐怕我們所有的技術人員都很忙。**您應該把手機拆開，將它晾個幾小時。**60
女：**我試過了。**您真的完全沒辦法幫我嗎？我明天要去度假，我真的很需要這支手機。
男：嗯，在我開始下一場的諮詢前，我還有一些時間，但**您要在 30 分鐘內來到這邊。**61
女：太好了。**我 15 分鐘後會到。**61

59. What is the woman calling about?
(A) A damaged phone
(B) A pool service
(C) A travel itinerary
(D) A promotional deal

59. 女子的來電與何事有關？
(A) 手機損壞
(B) 泳池服務
(C) 旅遊行程
(D) 優惠促銷

60. What does the woman imply when she says, "I've tried that"?
(A) She spoke with a technician earlier.
(B) She is pleased with some results.
(C) A coupon code was applied.
(D) An idea was not effective.

60. 女子說：「我試過了」，其暗示為何？
(A) 她稍早和一名技術人員談過。
(B) 有些結果讓她感到滿意。
(C) 優惠代碼已使用。
(D) 有個主意沒有效果。

61. What does the woman decide to do?
(A) Place another order
(B) Visit a business
(C) Talk to the man's supervisor
(D) Cancel a trip

61. 女子決定做什麼？
(A) 另下一筆訂單
(B) 前往商家
(C) 與男子的主管交談
(D) 取消旅行

Questions 62-64 refer to the following conversation and order form.

W：Rodney, the catering company just called me.
M：Oh, regarding the holiday party?
W：Yeah. We need to send them the finalized order by the end of the week. I'm going over the form, and **I realized we'll need additional fruit bowls.** 62
M：Ah, yes. We forgot to account for the two vegetarians in R&D. Can you get in touch with the caterer again to let them know about this? By the way, **did you talk to Gary Burke about what he needs for his live guitar show?** 63
W：I did. **He actually emailed me a list earlier. I'll go ahead and forward that to you right now so that you can look over it.** 64

Order Form	
Menu Item	**Quantity**
Cheeseburger	5
Fruit Bowl	**7** 62
Shrimp Pasta	9
Chicken Sandwich	15
Beverages	36

62-64 會話和訂購單

女：羅德尼，外燴公司剛剛來電給我。
男：哦，有關假日派對的事嗎？
女：對。我們須在本週結束前把定案的訂單寄給他們。我正在檢查訂購單，然後**我想到我們得要加訂水果拼盤。** 62
男：噢，對啊。我們忘記算上研發部兩位吃素的同仁。妳可以再聯絡外燴業者，告知他們此事嗎？順道一提，**妳和蓋瑞．柏克討論過他的現場吉他演奏需要哪些物品了嗎？** 63
女：有的。**其實他不久前才用電子郵件寄給我一份清單。我馬上就把信轉寄給你，以便讓你過目。** 64

訂購單	
菜單品項	數量
起司漢堡	5
水果拼盤	**7** 62
鮮蝦義大利麵	9
雞肉三明治	15
飲料	36

62. Look at the graphic. Which quantity on the order form must be revised?
(A) 5
(B) 7
(C) 9
(D) 15

63. Who most likely is Mr. Burke?
(A) A custodian
(B) A researcher
(C) A chef
(D) A musician

64. What will the woman probably do next?
(A) Mail a package
(B) Forward a file
(C) Contact a store
(D) Update a schedule

62. 請根據圖表作答。訂單上的哪個數量必須修改？
(A) 5
(B) 7
(C) 9
(D) 15

63. 柏克先生最有可能的職業為何？
(A) 看守員
(B) 研究人員
(C) 廚師
(D) 音樂家

64. 女子接著可能會做什麼？
(A) 郵寄包裹
(B) 轉寄檔案
(C) 聯絡店家
(D) 更新行程

Questions 65-67 refer to the following conversation and voucher.

65-67 會話和優惠券

W: Hello, **I'd like to purchase tickets for *Marvelous Fiction* for this Friday at 8 P.M.** 65

M: **I'm afraid all of the show times for that day are sold out because it's the opening night of the movie.** 65

W: Hmm . . . **What about the next day? Are there any available times?** 66

M: Yes, **but only in the evening.** 66

W: That's fine. OK, **I'd like two middle row seats for the 9 P.M. show then.** 66 Here's my credit card. Oh! And I also have this voucher.

M: Thank you. Let's see . . . This voucher can only be applied to one ticket.

W: I understand.

M: OK. Here's your receipt. Also, **if you're planning to have dinner around here that day, you should try the Organic Planter.** 67 It just opened last week.

女：您好，**我想買本週五晚上八點《奇妙小說》的票。** 65

男：**恐怕當天所有放映場次的票都已熱賣一空了，畢竟那是該電影首映日當晚。** 65

女：嗯……**那隔天呢？有還有空位的場次嗎？** 66

男：有的，**但只有在晚場時段。** 66

女：沒關係。好的，**那麼我要晚上九點那場，中間排的座位兩張。** 66 這邊是我的信用卡。噢！我還有這張優惠券。

男：謝謝。我看一下……這張優惠券只能適用一張票。

女：我了解。

男：好的。這是您的收據。另外，**如果您當天打算在這附近用晚餐，可以試著到「有機園園長」看看。** 67 它上週才剛開幕。

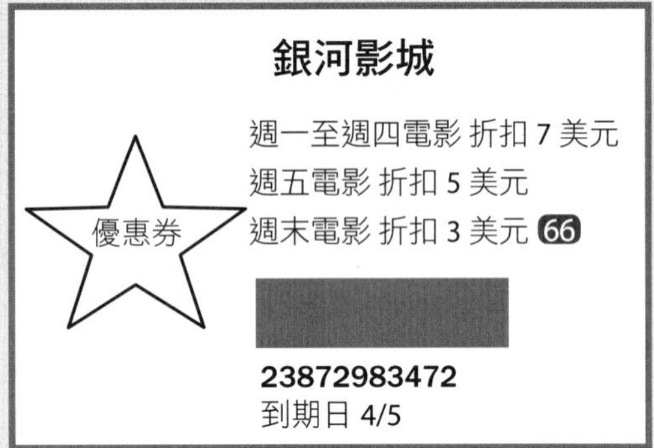

65. What does the man mention about *Marvelous Fiction*?

(A) Its actors are all famous.

(B) It is sold out for the weekend.

(C) Its first screening is on Friday.

(D) It has received positive reviews.

65. 關於《奇妙小說》，男子提到什麼？

(A) 演員全都很有名。

(B) 週末的票都賣光了。

(C) 首映日在週五。

(D) 獲得正面評價。

66. Look at the graphic. Which discount did the woman receive?

(A) $3

(B) $5

(C) $7

(D) $9

66. 請根據圖表作答。女子得到哪個折扣？

(A) 3 美元

(B) 5 美元

(C) 7 美元

(D) 9 美元

67. What does the man recommend?
(A) Bringing a receipt
(B) Checking out a restaurant
(C) Arriving early to a theater
(D) Using a credit card

67. 男子有何建議？
(A) 帶上收據
(B) 去一家餐廳看看
(C) 提早到電影院
(D) 使用信用卡

Questions 68-70 refer to the following conversation and warranty information.

M： Darho Electronics. What can I help you with?
W： Hello, **the sports watch I ordered from you last month broke.** 68 I have a one-year warranty, so I want to exchange the item.
M： I see. While we do offer warranties on all of our merchandise, there are some restrictions. Not all issues are covered, so depending on the situation, you might not be able to exchange your device.
W： Oh, well . . . **I accidentally dropped something on it, which cracked the screen.** 69
M： Hmm . . . Regrettably, **our warranty does not offer coverage for that kind of case.** 69
W： Really?
M： I'm afraid so. You should just look into replacing the screen.
W： OK. **I'll call different stores to see which place offers the cheapest repair rate.** 70

Warranty Restrictions

The following are not covered under warranty:
1. Products owned for more than one year
2. **Products damaged by an accident** 69
3. Products that get lost
4. Products with parts from different manufacturers

68-70 會話和保固資訊

男： 這裡是「達羅電子」。有什麼我能協助您的嗎？
女： 您好，**我上個月向你們訂購的運動手錶壞了。** 68 我這裡有一年保固，所以我想換貨。
男： 了解。雖然我們所有的商品都有提供保固，但有一些限制。並非所有問題都在保固範圍內，因此取決於個別情況，您可能會無法換貨。
女： 哦，那麼……**我不小心掉了東西、撞到手錶上，把螢幕撞裂了。** 69
男： 嗯……很遺憾，**這類情況並不在我們提供的保固範圍內。** 69
女： 真的嗎？
男： 恐怕是的。您應該考慮的是更換螢幕。
女： 好的。**我會打給幾間不同店家，看哪一間提供的維修費最便宜。** 70

保固限制

以下情形不在保固範圍內：
1. 產品持有超過一年
2. 意外損壞產品 69
3. 產品遺失
4. 使用不同製造商零件的產品

68. What kind of product is being discussed?
(A) A phone
(B) A television
(C) A computer
(D) A watch

68. 正在討論的產品為何？
(A) 電話
(B) 電視
(C) 電腦
(D) 手錶

TEST 10 PART 3 41

69. Look at the graphic. Which restriction does the man refer to?
(A) Restriction 1
(B) Restriction 2
(C) Restriction 3
(D) Restriction 4

70. What does the woman say she will do?
(A) Check a user guide
(B) Speak to a manager
(C) Test some other items
(D) Compare some costs

69. 請根據圖表作答。男子參照的是哪項限制？
(A) 限制 1
(B) 限制 2
(C) 限制 3
(D) 限制 4

70. 女子說她之後會做什麼？
(A) 查閱使用指南
(B) 和經理交談
(C) 測試其他產品
(D) 比較幾筆費用

PART 4 P. 135–137

42

Questions 71-73 refer to the following instructions.

M：On behalf of Blumenthal Associates, I'd like to welcome you all to our firm. **Let's get started with some forms. Please look at the first one, as it is the most important. The accounting team must receive this to enter you into the payroll system. 71 If you do not turn it in by this Wednesday, you may not be able to receive your first month's salary on time. 72** Take some time to carefully go over the rest of the paperwork. **If you have any inquiries regarding the forms, feel free to direct them to me. 73**

71-73 說明

男：我謹代表「布魯門索聯合企業」歡迎大家進入我們公司。**我們首先要處理一些表格。請先看第一份，因為那份是最重要的。這份必須要交給會計部收取，以便幫各位加入薪資系統。71 如果你們沒有在本週三以前把它交出，可能就無法準時收到你們的首筆月薪。72** 請花點時間，仔細看過其餘文件。**如果你們對表單有任何疑問，就拿來問我，別客氣。73**

71. What is the speaker giving instructions about?
(A) Updating a system
(B) Completing some documents
(C) Entering some work hours
(D) Ordering office supplies

72. According to the speaker, what could happen if a deadline is missed?
(A) A delivery could be delayed.
(B) A vacation request could be denied.
(C) A payment could be postponed.
(D) A budget proposal could be rejected.

71. 說話者說明的內容與何事有關？
(A) 更新系統
(B) 填寫幾份文件
(C) 輸入工作時數
(D) 訂購辦公用品

72. 據說話者說法，如果錯過某個截止日期可能會怎樣？
(A) 可能延誤交貨。
(B) 休假申請可能遭到拒絕。
(C) 款項可能會延後支付。
(D) 預算案可能遭到否決。

73. What does the speaker say he can do?
(A) Address some inquiries
(B) Contact a department
(C) Check some equipment
(D) Provide a tour

73. 說話者說他能做什麼？
(A) 解決一些問題
(B) 聯絡一個部門
(C) 檢查一些設備
(D) 提供導覽

Questions 74-76 refer to the following excerpt from a workshop.

74-76 研習節錄

M：OK, **that's the end of this class on sales techniques** 74 here at Cooper Solutions. I saw significant progress from some of you during our role-play activities. **Don't forget, this session was recorded and will be available on our Web site for free. We recommend that you have a look at it from home, so you can review the key points you've learned today.** 75 **And for those of you looking for a more personalized session,** 76 **Francine has more than 25 years of experience.**

男：好的，「庫柏顧問」這裡教授的**銷售技巧課程到此迎來尾聲。** 74 在我們進行角色扮演活動時，我看到有幾位有很顯著的進步。**別忘了，這次課程有錄影且將在我們網站上免費開放瀏覽。我建議各位在家觀看一下，以便可以複習您今天學到的關鍵要點。** 75 **而對於想要上更加個人化的課程的人，** 76 **法蘭馨有超過 25 年的經驗。**

74. What is the focus of the workshop?
(A) Management skills
(B) Investment tips
(C) Advertising solutions
(D) Sales strategies

74. 研習的重點內容為何？
(A) 管理技能
(B) 投資訣竅
(C) 廣告方案
(D) 銷售策略

75. What are the listeners encouraged to do at home?
(A) Design a cover letter
(B) View a video
(C) Make a daily schedule
(D) Write a review

75. 聽者被鼓勵在家做什麼？
(A) 設計求職信
(B) 觀看影片
(C) 規劃每日行程表
(D) 撰寫評論

76. Why does the speaker say, "Francine has more than 25 years of experience"?
(A) To recommend Francine's services
(B) To announce Francine's promotion
(C) To discuss Francine's retirement
(D) To support Francine's decision

76. 說話者為什麼要說：「法蘭馨有超過 25 年的經驗」？
(A) 以推薦法蘭馨的服務
(B) 以宣布法蘭馨的晉升
(C) 以討論法蘭馨的退休
(D) 以支持法蘭馨的決定

Questions 77-79 refer to the following broadcast.

W：Today, Baleville **transportation officials announced that some changes will be implemented to the city's subway service. On the nights of baseball games, trains will run every five minutes so that people can get to the stadium and go back home more quickly.** 77 **The changes were made in response to the constant complaints** 78 about the lack of subway trains when a major event is held in the city. In addition, more express trains will be operating for people who live far from the stadium. So if you decide to take the subway on game nights, **be sure to check out the route map** 79 to locate the station closest to you.

77. What is the broadcast about?
    (A) A public holiday
    (B) A new stadium
    (C) Results of a sports competition
    (D) Improvements to public transportation

78. According to the speaker, why has a change been made?
    (A) To promote local shops
    (B) To attract more tourists
    (C) To respond to complaints
    (D) To comply with new laws

79. What does the speaker encourage listeners to do?
    (A) Buy tickets in advance
    (B) Consult a map
    (C) Volunteer at an event
    (D) Vote in an election

77-79 廣播

女：貝爾維爾**交通局官員**於今天**宣布，本市的地鐵服務將會實施幾項異動。往後在有棒球比賽舉行的晚間時段，每五分鐘就會行駛一班列車，以便可以加快民眾前往體育館和返家的速度。** 77 本市舉辦大型活動的時候，地鐵班次都不盡充足，**對此一向投訴不斷，所以做出這次異動來因應。** 78 另外也將會加開直達車，以服務住家距離體育館很遠的民眾。因此若您決定在舉辦球賽的晚間搭乘地鐵，**請務必查看路線圖，** 79 來尋找離您最近的車站。

77. 廣播的內容和什麼有關？
    (A) 國定假日
    (B) 新的體育館
    (C) 體育競賽的結果
    (D) 公共運輸的改進

78. 據說話者說法，做出異動的原因為何？
    (A) 以推廣當地店家
    (B) 以吸引更多遊客
    (C) 以回應投訴
    (D) 以符合新法規

79. 說話者鼓勵聽者做什麼？
    (A) 提前購票
    (B) 參照地圖
    (C) 當活動志工
    (D) 在選舉中投票

Questions 80-82 refer to the following talk.

M：I'm happy to see everyone here this morning. **Today is the first day of the technology expo, and we want to make sure everything goes as planned.** 80 It's sure to be an exciting event. Jackie, I've noticed that you've set out the information pamphlets on the desks. Thanks for doing that. **Martin will be bringing in some boxes of water bottles soon. They have our**

80-82 談話

男：我很高興今天早上在這裡見到大家。**今天是科技博覽會的首日，我們想要確保一切按計畫進行。** 80 這一定會是場令人興奮的活動。傑基，我注意到你已把摺頁文宣擺在桌上了。感謝你這麼做。**馬丁很快就會將幾箱瓶裝水送到。瓶裝水上面有我們公司的標誌。請把它們發**

company logo on them. Please hand them out to people who stop by our booth. 81 All right, I see some hands up. But before I answer your questions, **let's go over our schedule one more time.** 82

放給到訪我們展位的人。 81 好，我看到有些人舉手。不過回答你們的問題之前，**讓我們再次確認時間表。** 82

80. What is the topic of the talk?
(A) An industry convention
(B) An advertising proposal
(C) A worksite regulation
(D) A revised brochure

81. What are the listeners asked to do?
(A) Examine some paperwork
(B) Work additional hours
(C) Clean an area
(D) Distribute some beverages

82. What will the speaker do next?
(A) Review a schedule
(B) Conduct an interview
(C) Test some products
(D) Meet some clients

80. 談話的主題為何？
(A) 產業會展
(B) 廣告提案
(C) 工作場所規定
(D) 修訂版手冊

81. 聽者被要求做什麼？
(A) 檢查一些文件
(B) 加班
(C) 清潔一個區域
(D) 發放一些飲品

82. 說話者接著會做什麼？
(A) 複查時間表
(B) 進行面試
(C) 測試一些產品
(D) 見幾名客戶

Questions 83-85 refer to the following instructions.

83-85 說明

W：Pay attention, everyone. **Your job is to make sure that the laboratory is ready to be used by the technicians before they arrive here every day.** 83 First of all, make sure all the supplies are in stock. **You do this by looking at the list on this wall and checking to see if all of the items are on that shelf. If something from the list is not there, look in the large cabinet in the corner of the room,** 84 **or talk to Heather. OK, now, I'll show you how to put on the safety equipment.** 85

女：各位請注意。**你們的工作是確保實驗室預備就緒，以便每天技術人員到達後可以使用。** 83 首先，要確保所有用品都有存量。**為此你們要查看牆上的清單，並檢查架子上是否備齊所有的物品。如果有清單中的物品不在架子上，就到實驗室角落的大櫃子查看，** 84 **或是跟希瑟說。好，現在，我會向你們展示安全裝備的穿戴方式。** 85

83. Where does the speaker most likely work?
(A) At a bookstore
(B) At a laboratory
(C) At a museum
(D) At a café

83. 說話者最有可能在哪裡工作？
(A) 在書店
(B) 在實驗室
(C) 在博物館
(D) 在咖啡廳

TEST 10 PART 4 42

84. Why does the speaker say, "talk to Heather"?
(A) To check the availability of an item
(B) To check the number of visitors
(C) To check the choices on a menu
(D) To check the payment of an invoice

85. What will the listeners do next?
(A) Fill out a form
(B) Go to lunch
(C) Tour an office building
(D) Watch a demonstration

84. 說話者為什麼說：「跟希瑟說」？
(A) 以確認物品供給情形
(B) 以確認訪客人數
(C) 以確認菜單上的選項
(D) 以確認帳單的支付情況

85. 聽者接著會做什麼？
(A) 填寫表格
(B) 去吃午餐
(C) 參觀辦公大樓
(D) 觀看示範

Questions 86-88 refer to the following introduction.

M：Hello, everyone. **Welcome to a special dinner to benefit the senior citizens of our community. It is our hope that we will raise enough money tonight** 86 to renovate the local park in order that we can provide a safe outdoor public space for the elderly. **Arnold Vans, a civil engineer, will be leading this project,** 87 and he will talk about the renovation plans tonight. Arnold is an active member of our city, and we are pleased to have him oversee this effort. Also, before I forget, **Sawyer's Department Store has prepared a gift set for everyone attending tonight's event, so make sure to pick one up on your way out.** 88

86-88 開場白

男：大家好。**歡迎蒞臨特別晚宴，來造福我們的社區長者。我們希望今晚能夠籌措充足資金** 86 來整修地方公園，以便我們能提供年長者一個安全的戶外公共場所。**這個專案將由土木工程師阿諾．范斯帶領，** 87 而他今晚將談談這次整建的計畫。阿諾是本市很積極的一份子，我們樂見讓他來監督這項工程。另外，我先説一下以免忘記：**索亞百貨準備了禮物盒，要送給每位出席今晚活動的人，所以請您離開時務必領取一份。** 88

86. What type of event is taking place?
(A) A retirement dinner
(B) A community fundraiser
(C) A business opening
(D) An awards ceremony

87. What will Arnold Vans be in charge of?
(A) Renovating a public property
(B) Designing new products
(C) Managing a branch office
(D) Improving marketing strategies

88. What are the attendees asked to do at the end of the evening?
(A) Take a group picture
(B) Register for membership
(C) Submit comments
(D) Pick up a gift

86. 正在舉辦哪一類型的活動？
(A) 退休晚宴
(B) 社區募款活動
(C) 店家開幕會
(D) 頒獎典禮

87. 阿諾．范斯將負責什麼？
(A) 整修公有設施
(B) 設計新產品
(C) 管理分支機構
(D) 改善行銷策略

88. 晚上活動結束時，出席者被要求做什麼？
(A) 拍團體照
(B) 註冊會員
(C) 提交意見
(D) 領取禮物

Questions 89-91 refer to the following announcement.

W：Good morning. **As I'm sure you're all aware, we heard from a lot of clients yesterday who were unhappy about being unable to access our online banking site. 89 The site is working just fine now, 90 but we're still getting lots of calls.** In response, we've decided to offer account holders free access to our Premium services. **I just emailed you all a file containing the terms and conditions of this offer. So I'd like all of you to read it now, and then, I'll take any questions. 91**

89-91 宣布

女：早安。**正如我確信各位都有注意到的，我們昨天獲悉很多客戶對於連不上我們網路銀行的網站很不滿。89 網站現在已正常運作，90 但我們仍持續接到很多電話。**為因應此事，我們決定為本行儲蓄免費提供我們的進階升級版服務。**我剛已用電子郵件把檔案寄給各位，內含這項優惠的合約條款。所以我想要各位現在馬上查看，而若有任何問題，我會再回答。91**

89. Where does the speaker most likely work?
(A) At a bank
(B) At a factory
(C) At a software developer
(D) At a telephone service provider

90. What does the speaker mean when she says, "but we're still getting a lot of calls"?
(A) More employees are required.
(B) Complaints are still being received.
(C) A marketing strategy was successful.
(D) Some orders have not been fulfilled.

91. What will the listeners probably do next?
(A) Review a file
(B) Sign a contract
(C) Contact some clients
(D) Upgrade a program

89. 說話者最有可能在哪裡工作？
(A) 在銀行
(B) 在工廠
(C) 在軟體開發商
(D) 在電信服務供應商

90. 當說話者說：「但我們仍持續接到很多電話」，其意思為何？
(A) 需要更多員工。
(B) 仍持續收到投訴。
(C) 行銷策略很成功。
(D) 幾筆訂單未履行。

91. 聽者接著可能會做什麼？
(A) 檢視一份檔案
(B) 簽訂合約
(C) 聯絡幾名客戶
(D) 更新程式

Questions 92-94 refer to the following talk.

M：Welcome to our booth here at the Global Manufacturers Convention. Do you need a better tool for tracking and managing inventory at your warehouses? **If so, I'd like to introduce you to our inventory barcode scanner. 92 Think back to the times when you physically counted your items, only to realize that the numbers don't match the ones in your system. Well, you won't have to worry about that anymore. With**

92-94 談話

男：歡迎來到我們在全球製造商博覽會所設的展位。您需要有更好用的工具，來追蹤、管理您的倉庫庫存嗎？**若是如此，我想向您介紹我們的庫存條碼掃描器。92 回想一下吧，有好幾次您親自盤點貨品後，卻發現到其數量和您系統上的數字有所出入。哎，您不必再為此擔心了。有了我們的條碼掃描器，您隨**

our barcode scanner, you'll always have the accurate figures. 93 **OK, now, let me teach you how to use the scanner. I'll begin by scanning this item.** 94

時都能得到正確的數字。 93 **好，現在讓我教您掃描器的使用方式。我首先會掃描這個產品。** 94

92. What product is the speaker discussing?
(A) A finance software program
(B) An assembly machine
(C) A storage container
(D) An inventory barcode scanner

92. 說話者正在討論什麼產品？
(A) 財務軟體程式
(B) 裝配機
(C) 儲藏容器
(D) 庫存條碼掃描器

93. What does the speaker say the product will help avoid?
(A) Having incorrect data
(B) Causing product defects
(C) Experiencing system failures
(D) Losing important documents

93. 說話者說到，該產品將協助避免什麼事？
(A) 拿到不正確的數據
(B) 造成產品缺陷
(C) 遇上系統故障
(D) 遺失重要文件

94. What will the speaker do next?
(A) Distribute some brochures
(B) Print a document
(C) Answer some questions
(D) Give a tutorial

94. 說話者接著會做什麼？
(A) 發放幾本小冊子
(B) 列印文件
(C) 回答一些問題
(D) 進行教學

Questions 95-97 refer to the following telephone message and schedule.

95-97 語音留言和行程表

W：Hi, Eric. This is Rita from Kansai Productions. **I wanted to confirm that I looked over your proposal for a new live television series in Osaka.** 95 I'd like you to come by our studio on Friday to talk about it in more detail. **My 11 o'clock appointment got postponed, so it'd be good to meet at that time.** 96 Oh, by the way, **it would be helpful if you could send me a list of expected costs for the project.** 97 Talk to you soon.

Rita Matsumoto's Friday Appointments

10:00 A.M.	Management meeting
11:00 A.M.	**Budget review** 96
12:00 P.M.	Client consultation
1:00 P.M.	HR presentation

女：嗨，艾瑞克。我是「關西製作」的梨多。**我想向您確認，我看了您要在大阪製播新的電視現場直播系列節目的提案。** 95 我想請您週五到我們工作室詳談內容。**我在 11 點的約定行程延後了，所以可以在這個時段見面。** 96 噢，順道一提，**如果您能把專案預估花費的清單寄給我，將會有所幫助。** 97 到時再聊。

松本梨多週五行程

早上 10:00	管理會議
早上 11:00	**預算審查** 96
中午 12:00	客戶諮詢
下午 1:00	人資簡報

95. What does the speaker want to talk about?
(A) A production deadline
(B) A new TV series
(C) A job opening in Osaka
(D) A construction proposal

96. Look at the graphic. Which of the speaker's appointments was postponed?
(A) Management meeting
(B) Budget review
(C) Client consultation
(D) HR presentation

97. What does the speaker ask the listener to send?
(A) An application form
(B) A travel itinerary
(C) A guest list
(D) A price estimate

Questions 98-100 refer to the following excerpt from a meeting and sales chart.

M：**Welcome to our quarterly sales meeting. Today, we'll be looking at our best-selling television model.** 98 Since its release in the summer, the Clarity Pro has been very popular with consumers. **Unfortunately, after our biggest rival unveiled their new model, there was a sharp decrease in sales for the Clarity Pro.** 99 In response, we temporarily reduced the price of the Clarity Pro. **During this promotional period, we broke our record for most units sold in a month.** 100 This was a great idea from our marketing team to help boost sales.

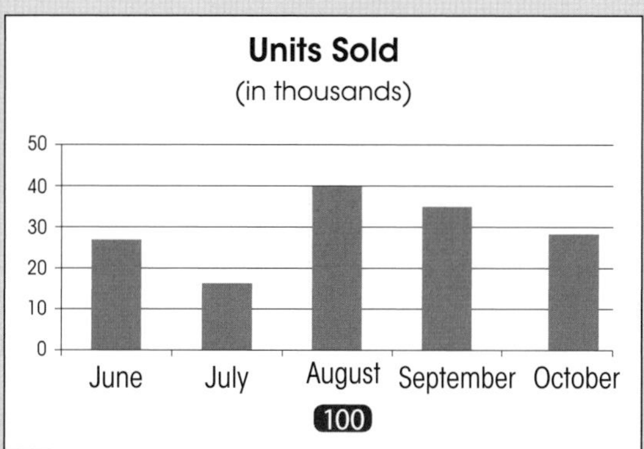

95. 說話者想要討論何事？
(A) 製作截止期限
(B) 新系列的電視節目
(C) 大阪的職缺
(D) 施工提案

96. 請據圖表作答。說話者哪項約定行程延後了？
(A) 管理會議
(B) 預算審查
(C) 客戶諮詢
(D) 人資簡報

97. 說話者要求聽者寄送什麼？
(A) 申請表單
(B) 旅遊行程
(C) 來賓名單
(D) 估價單

98-100 會議摘要和銷量長條圖

男：**歡迎參加我們的季度銷售會議。今天我們要關注的是本公司最暢銷的電視型號。** 98 從今年夏天「清晰專家」推出以來，就持續受到消費者歡迎。**遺憾的是，我們的最大的同行業者推出他們的新型號後，清晰專家的銷量就急劇減少。** 99 作為因應，我們曾暫時調降清晰專家的售價。**該次促銷期間，我們的單月銷量創下新高紀錄。** 100 這是我們行銷團隊的好點子，有助於刺激銷量。

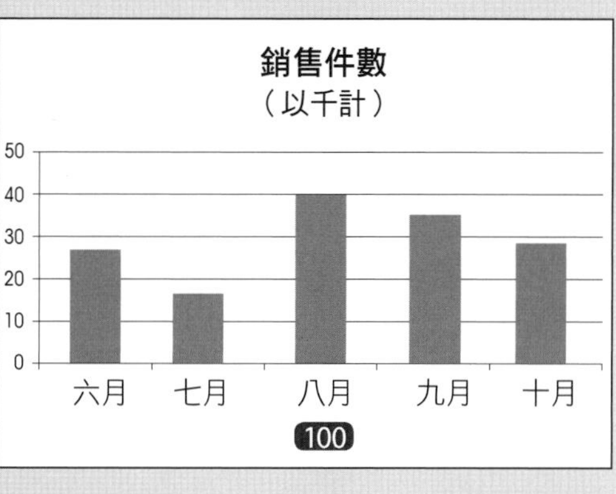

TEST 10
PART 4
42

98. Where does the speaker most likely work?
(A) At a sporting goods store
(B) At an electronics maker
(C) At an accounting firm
(D) At a broadcasting station

99. According to the speaker, what caused a decrease in sales?
(A) A consumer gave a poor rating.
(B) A manufacturer raised its prices.
(C) A factory closed down.
(D) A competitor released a new product.

100. Look at the graphic. When did the company discount a product?
(A) In June
(B) In July
(C) In August
(D) In September

98. 說話者最有可能在哪裡工作？
(A) 在體育用品店
(B) 在電子用品製造商
(C) 在會計事務所
(D) 在廣播電台

99. 根據說話者說法，何事造成銷量下滑？
(A) 有消費者給了負面評價。
(B) 製造商提高了價格。
(C) 工廠關閉。
(D) 同業推出了新產品。

100. 請根據圖表作答。公司何時給予產品折價？
(A) 在六月
(B) 在七月
(C) 在八月
(D) 在九月

Answer Sheet

ACTUAL TEST 01

LISTENING SECTION																				
	1	Ⓐ Ⓑ Ⓒ Ⓓ	11	Ⓐ Ⓑ Ⓒ Ⓓ	21	Ⓐ Ⓑ Ⓒ Ⓓ	31	Ⓐ Ⓑ Ⓒ Ⓓ	41	Ⓐ Ⓑ Ⓒ Ⓓ	51	Ⓐ Ⓑ Ⓒ Ⓓ	61	Ⓐ Ⓑ Ⓒ Ⓓ	71	Ⓐ Ⓑ Ⓒ Ⓓ	81	Ⓐ Ⓑ Ⓒ Ⓓ	91	Ⓐ Ⓑ Ⓒ Ⓓ
	2	Ⓐ Ⓑ Ⓒ Ⓓ	12	Ⓐ Ⓑ Ⓒ Ⓓ	22	Ⓐ Ⓑ Ⓒ Ⓓ	32	Ⓐ Ⓑ Ⓒ Ⓓ	42	Ⓐ Ⓑ Ⓒ Ⓓ	52	Ⓐ Ⓑ Ⓒ Ⓓ	62	Ⓐ Ⓑ Ⓒ Ⓓ	72	Ⓐ Ⓑ Ⓒ Ⓓ	82	Ⓐ Ⓑ Ⓒ Ⓓ	92	Ⓐ Ⓑ Ⓒ Ⓓ
	3	Ⓐ Ⓑ Ⓒ Ⓓ	13	Ⓐ Ⓑ Ⓒ Ⓓ	23	Ⓐ Ⓑ Ⓒ Ⓓ	33	Ⓐ Ⓑ Ⓒ Ⓓ	43	Ⓐ Ⓑ Ⓒ Ⓓ	53	Ⓐ Ⓑ Ⓒ Ⓓ	63	Ⓐ Ⓑ Ⓒ Ⓓ	73	Ⓐ Ⓑ Ⓒ Ⓓ	83	Ⓐ Ⓑ Ⓒ Ⓓ	93	Ⓐ Ⓑ Ⓒ Ⓓ
	4	Ⓐ Ⓑ Ⓒ Ⓓ	14	Ⓐ Ⓑ Ⓒ Ⓓ	24	Ⓐ Ⓑ Ⓒ Ⓓ	34	Ⓐ Ⓑ Ⓒ Ⓓ	44	Ⓐ Ⓑ Ⓒ Ⓓ	54	Ⓐ Ⓑ Ⓒ Ⓓ	64	Ⓐ Ⓑ Ⓒ Ⓓ	74	Ⓐ Ⓑ Ⓒ Ⓓ	84	Ⓐ Ⓑ Ⓒ Ⓓ	94	Ⓐ Ⓑ Ⓒ Ⓓ
	5	Ⓐ Ⓑ Ⓒ Ⓓ	15	Ⓐ Ⓑ Ⓒ Ⓓ	25	Ⓐ Ⓑ Ⓒ Ⓓ	35	Ⓐ Ⓑ Ⓒ Ⓓ	45	Ⓐ Ⓑ Ⓒ Ⓓ	55	Ⓐ Ⓑ Ⓒ Ⓓ	65	Ⓐ Ⓑ Ⓒ Ⓓ	75	Ⓐ Ⓑ Ⓒ Ⓓ	85	Ⓐ Ⓑ Ⓒ Ⓓ	95	Ⓐ Ⓑ Ⓒ Ⓓ
	6	Ⓐ Ⓑ Ⓒ Ⓓ	16	Ⓐ Ⓑ Ⓒ Ⓓ	26	Ⓐ Ⓑ Ⓒ Ⓓ	36	Ⓐ Ⓑ Ⓒ Ⓓ	46	Ⓐ Ⓑ Ⓒ Ⓓ	56	Ⓐ Ⓑ Ⓒ Ⓓ	66	Ⓐ Ⓑ Ⓒ Ⓓ	76	Ⓐ Ⓑ Ⓒ Ⓓ	86	Ⓐ Ⓑ Ⓒ Ⓓ	96	Ⓐ Ⓑ Ⓒ Ⓓ
	7	Ⓐ Ⓑ Ⓒ Ⓓ	17	Ⓐ Ⓑ Ⓒ Ⓓ	27	Ⓐ Ⓑ Ⓒ Ⓓ	37	Ⓐ Ⓑ Ⓒ Ⓓ	47	Ⓐ Ⓑ Ⓒ Ⓓ	57	Ⓐ Ⓑ Ⓒ Ⓓ	67	Ⓐ Ⓑ Ⓒ Ⓓ	77	Ⓐ Ⓑ Ⓒ Ⓓ	87	Ⓐ Ⓑ Ⓒ Ⓓ	97	Ⓐ Ⓑ Ⓒ Ⓓ
	8	Ⓐ Ⓑ Ⓒ Ⓓ	18	Ⓐ Ⓑ Ⓒ Ⓓ	28	Ⓐ Ⓑ Ⓒ Ⓓ	38	Ⓐ Ⓑ Ⓒ Ⓓ	48	Ⓐ Ⓑ Ⓒ Ⓓ	58	Ⓐ Ⓑ Ⓒ Ⓓ	68	Ⓐ Ⓑ Ⓒ Ⓓ	78	Ⓐ Ⓑ Ⓒ Ⓓ	88	Ⓐ Ⓑ Ⓒ Ⓓ	98	Ⓐ Ⓑ Ⓒ Ⓓ
	9	Ⓐ Ⓑ Ⓒ Ⓓ	19	Ⓐ Ⓑ Ⓒ Ⓓ	29	Ⓐ Ⓑ Ⓒ Ⓓ	39	Ⓐ Ⓑ Ⓒ Ⓓ	49	Ⓐ Ⓑ Ⓒ Ⓓ	59	Ⓐ Ⓑ Ⓒ Ⓓ	69	Ⓐ Ⓑ Ⓒ Ⓓ	79	Ⓐ Ⓑ Ⓒ Ⓓ	89	Ⓐ Ⓑ Ⓒ Ⓓ	99	Ⓐ Ⓑ Ⓒ Ⓓ
	10	Ⓐ Ⓑ Ⓒ Ⓓ	20	Ⓐ Ⓑ Ⓒ Ⓓ	30	Ⓐ Ⓑ Ⓒ Ⓓ	40	Ⓐ Ⓑ Ⓒ Ⓓ	50	Ⓐ Ⓑ Ⓒ Ⓓ	60	Ⓐ Ⓑ Ⓒ Ⓓ	70	Ⓐ Ⓑ Ⓒ Ⓓ	80	Ⓐ Ⓑ Ⓒ Ⓓ	90	Ⓐ Ⓑ Ⓒ Ⓓ	100	Ⓐ Ⓑ Ⓒ Ⓓ

ACTUAL TEST 02

LISTENING SECTION																				
	1	Ⓐ Ⓑ Ⓒ Ⓓ	11	Ⓐ Ⓑ Ⓒ Ⓓ	21	Ⓐ Ⓑ Ⓒ Ⓓ	31	Ⓐ Ⓑ Ⓒ Ⓓ	41	Ⓐ Ⓑ Ⓒ Ⓓ	51	Ⓐ Ⓑ Ⓒ Ⓓ	61	Ⓐ Ⓑ Ⓒ Ⓓ	71	Ⓐ Ⓑ Ⓒ Ⓓ	81	Ⓐ Ⓑ Ⓒ Ⓓ	91	Ⓐ Ⓑ Ⓒ Ⓓ
	2	Ⓐ Ⓑ Ⓒ Ⓓ	12	Ⓐ Ⓑ Ⓒ Ⓓ	22	Ⓐ Ⓑ Ⓒ Ⓓ	32	Ⓐ Ⓑ Ⓒ Ⓓ	42	Ⓐ Ⓑ Ⓒ Ⓓ	52	Ⓐ Ⓑ Ⓒ Ⓓ	62	Ⓐ Ⓑ Ⓒ Ⓓ	72	Ⓐ Ⓑ Ⓒ Ⓓ	82	Ⓐ Ⓑ Ⓒ Ⓓ	92	Ⓐ Ⓑ Ⓒ Ⓓ
	3	Ⓐ Ⓑ Ⓒ Ⓓ	13	Ⓐ Ⓑ Ⓒ Ⓓ	23	Ⓐ Ⓑ Ⓒ Ⓓ	33	Ⓐ Ⓑ Ⓒ Ⓓ	43	Ⓐ Ⓑ Ⓒ Ⓓ	53	Ⓐ Ⓑ Ⓒ Ⓓ	63	Ⓐ Ⓑ Ⓒ Ⓓ	73	Ⓐ Ⓑ Ⓒ Ⓓ	83	Ⓐ Ⓑ Ⓒ Ⓓ	93	Ⓐ Ⓑ Ⓒ Ⓓ
	4	Ⓐ Ⓑ Ⓒ Ⓓ	14	Ⓐ Ⓑ Ⓒ Ⓓ	24	Ⓐ Ⓑ Ⓒ Ⓓ	34	Ⓐ Ⓑ Ⓒ Ⓓ	44	Ⓐ Ⓑ Ⓒ Ⓓ	54	Ⓐ Ⓑ Ⓒ Ⓓ	64	Ⓐ Ⓑ Ⓒ Ⓓ	74	Ⓐ Ⓑ Ⓒ Ⓓ	84	Ⓐ Ⓑ Ⓒ Ⓓ	94	Ⓐ Ⓑ Ⓒ Ⓓ
	5	Ⓐ Ⓑ Ⓒ Ⓓ	15	Ⓐ Ⓑ Ⓒ Ⓓ	25	Ⓐ Ⓑ Ⓒ Ⓓ	35	Ⓐ Ⓑ Ⓒ Ⓓ	45	Ⓐ Ⓑ Ⓒ Ⓓ	55	Ⓐ Ⓑ Ⓒ Ⓓ	65	Ⓐ Ⓑ Ⓒ Ⓓ	75	Ⓐ Ⓑ Ⓒ Ⓓ	85	Ⓐ Ⓑ Ⓒ Ⓓ	95	Ⓐ Ⓑ Ⓒ Ⓓ
	6	Ⓐ Ⓑ Ⓒ Ⓓ	16	Ⓐ Ⓑ Ⓒ Ⓓ	26	Ⓐ Ⓑ Ⓒ Ⓓ	36	Ⓐ Ⓑ Ⓒ Ⓓ	46	Ⓐ Ⓑ Ⓒ Ⓓ	56	Ⓐ Ⓑ Ⓒ Ⓓ	66	Ⓐ Ⓑ Ⓒ Ⓓ	76	Ⓐ Ⓑ Ⓒ Ⓓ	86	Ⓐ Ⓑ Ⓒ Ⓓ	96	Ⓐ Ⓑ Ⓒ Ⓓ
	7	Ⓐ Ⓑ Ⓒ Ⓓ	17	Ⓐ Ⓑ Ⓒ Ⓓ	27	Ⓐ Ⓑ Ⓒ Ⓓ	37	Ⓐ Ⓑ Ⓒ Ⓓ	47	Ⓐ Ⓑ Ⓒ Ⓓ	57	Ⓐ Ⓑ Ⓒ Ⓓ	67	Ⓐ Ⓑ Ⓒ Ⓓ	77	Ⓐ Ⓑ Ⓒ Ⓓ	87	Ⓐ Ⓑ Ⓒ Ⓓ	97	Ⓐ Ⓑ Ⓒ Ⓓ
	8	Ⓐ Ⓑ Ⓒ Ⓓ	18	Ⓐ Ⓑ Ⓒ Ⓓ	28	Ⓐ Ⓑ Ⓒ Ⓓ	38	Ⓐ Ⓑ Ⓒ Ⓓ	48	Ⓐ Ⓑ Ⓒ Ⓓ	58	Ⓐ Ⓑ Ⓒ Ⓓ	68	Ⓐ Ⓑ Ⓒ Ⓓ	78	Ⓐ Ⓑ Ⓒ Ⓓ	88	Ⓐ Ⓑ Ⓒ Ⓓ	98	Ⓐ Ⓑ Ⓒ Ⓓ
	9	Ⓐ Ⓑ Ⓒ Ⓓ	19	Ⓐ Ⓑ Ⓒ Ⓓ	29	Ⓐ Ⓑ Ⓒ Ⓓ	39	Ⓐ Ⓑ Ⓒ Ⓓ	49	Ⓐ Ⓑ Ⓒ Ⓓ	59	Ⓐ Ⓑ Ⓒ Ⓓ	69	Ⓐ Ⓑ Ⓒ Ⓓ	79	Ⓐ Ⓑ Ⓒ Ⓓ	89	Ⓐ Ⓑ Ⓒ Ⓓ	99	Ⓐ Ⓑ Ⓒ Ⓓ
	10	Ⓐ Ⓑ Ⓒ Ⓓ	20	Ⓐ Ⓑ Ⓒ Ⓓ	30	Ⓐ Ⓑ Ⓒ Ⓓ	40	Ⓐ Ⓑ Ⓒ Ⓓ	50	Ⓐ Ⓑ Ⓒ Ⓓ	60	Ⓐ Ⓑ Ⓒ Ⓓ	70	Ⓐ Ⓑ Ⓒ Ⓓ	80	Ⓐ Ⓑ Ⓒ Ⓓ	90	Ⓐ Ⓑ Ⓒ Ⓓ	100	Ⓐ Ⓑ Ⓒ Ⓓ

Answer Sheet

ACTUAL TEST 03

LISTENING SECTION																				
	1	Ⓐ Ⓑ Ⓒ Ⓓ	11	Ⓐ Ⓑ Ⓒ Ⓓ	21	Ⓐ Ⓑ Ⓒ Ⓓ	31	Ⓐ Ⓑ Ⓒ Ⓓ	41	Ⓐ Ⓑ Ⓒ Ⓓ	51	Ⓐ Ⓑ Ⓒ Ⓓ	61	Ⓐ Ⓑ Ⓒ Ⓓ	71	Ⓐ Ⓑ Ⓒ Ⓓ	81	Ⓐ Ⓑ Ⓒ Ⓓ	91	Ⓐ Ⓑ Ⓒ Ⓓ
	2	Ⓐ Ⓑ Ⓒ Ⓓ	12	Ⓐ Ⓑ Ⓒ Ⓓ	22	Ⓐ Ⓑ Ⓒ Ⓓ	32	Ⓐ Ⓑ Ⓒ Ⓓ	42	Ⓐ Ⓑ Ⓒ Ⓓ	52	Ⓐ Ⓑ Ⓒ Ⓓ	62	Ⓐ Ⓑ Ⓒ Ⓓ	72	Ⓐ Ⓑ Ⓒ Ⓓ	82	Ⓐ Ⓑ Ⓒ Ⓓ	92	Ⓐ Ⓑ Ⓒ Ⓓ
	3	Ⓐ Ⓑ Ⓒ Ⓓ	13	Ⓐ Ⓑ Ⓒ Ⓓ	23	Ⓐ Ⓑ Ⓒ Ⓓ	33	Ⓐ Ⓑ Ⓒ Ⓓ	43	Ⓐ Ⓑ Ⓒ Ⓓ	53	Ⓐ Ⓑ Ⓒ Ⓓ	63	Ⓐ Ⓑ Ⓒ Ⓓ	73	Ⓐ Ⓑ Ⓒ Ⓓ	83	Ⓐ Ⓑ Ⓒ Ⓓ	93	Ⓐ Ⓑ Ⓒ Ⓓ
	4	Ⓐ Ⓑ Ⓒ Ⓓ	14	Ⓐ Ⓑ Ⓒ Ⓓ	24	Ⓐ Ⓑ Ⓒ Ⓓ	34	Ⓐ Ⓑ Ⓒ Ⓓ	44	Ⓐ Ⓑ Ⓒ Ⓓ	54	Ⓐ Ⓑ Ⓒ Ⓓ	64	Ⓐ Ⓑ Ⓒ Ⓓ	74	Ⓐ Ⓑ Ⓒ Ⓓ	84	Ⓐ Ⓑ Ⓒ Ⓓ	94	Ⓐ Ⓑ Ⓒ Ⓓ
	5	Ⓐ Ⓑ Ⓒ Ⓓ	15	Ⓐ Ⓑ Ⓒ Ⓓ	25	Ⓐ Ⓑ Ⓒ Ⓓ	35	Ⓐ Ⓑ Ⓒ Ⓓ	45	Ⓐ Ⓑ Ⓒ Ⓓ	55	Ⓐ Ⓑ Ⓒ Ⓓ	65	Ⓐ Ⓑ Ⓒ Ⓓ	75	Ⓐ Ⓑ Ⓒ Ⓓ	85	Ⓐ Ⓑ Ⓒ Ⓓ	95	Ⓐ Ⓑ Ⓒ Ⓓ
	6	Ⓐ Ⓑ Ⓒ Ⓓ	16	Ⓐ Ⓑ Ⓒ Ⓓ	26	Ⓐ Ⓑ Ⓒ Ⓓ	36	Ⓐ Ⓑ Ⓒ Ⓓ	46	Ⓐ Ⓑ Ⓒ Ⓓ	56	Ⓐ Ⓑ Ⓒ Ⓓ	66	Ⓐ Ⓑ Ⓒ Ⓓ	76	Ⓐ Ⓑ Ⓒ Ⓓ	86	Ⓐ Ⓑ Ⓒ Ⓓ	96	Ⓐ Ⓑ Ⓒ Ⓓ
	7	Ⓐ Ⓑ Ⓒ Ⓓ	17	Ⓐ Ⓑ Ⓒ Ⓓ	27	Ⓐ Ⓑ Ⓒ Ⓓ	37	Ⓐ Ⓑ Ⓒ Ⓓ	47	Ⓐ Ⓑ Ⓒ Ⓓ	57	Ⓐ Ⓑ Ⓒ Ⓓ	67	Ⓐ Ⓑ Ⓒ Ⓓ	77	Ⓐ Ⓑ Ⓒ Ⓓ	87	Ⓐ Ⓑ Ⓒ Ⓓ	97	Ⓐ Ⓑ Ⓒ Ⓓ
	8	Ⓐ Ⓑ Ⓒ Ⓓ	18	Ⓐ Ⓑ Ⓒ Ⓓ	28	Ⓐ Ⓑ Ⓒ Ⓓ	38	Ⓐ Ⓑ Ⓒ Ⓓ	48	Ⓐ Ⓑ Ⓒ Ⓓ	58	Ⓐ Ⓑ Ⓒ Ⓓ	68	Ⓐ Ⓑ Ⓒ Ⓓ	78	Ⓐ Ⓑ Ⓒ Ⓓ	88	Ⓐ Ⓑ Ⓒ Ⓓ	98	Ⓐ Ⓑ Ⓒ Ⓓ
	9	Ⓐ Ⓑ Ⓒ Ⓓ	19	Ⓐ Ⓑ Ⓒ Ⓓ	29	Ⓐ Ⓑ Ⓒ Ⓓ	39	Ⓐ Ⓑ Ⓒ Ⓓ	49	Ⓐ Ⓑ Ⓒ Ⓓ	59	Ⓐ Ⓑ Ⓒ Ⓓ	69	Ⓐ Ⓑ Ⓒ Ⓓ	79	Ⓐ Ⓑ Ⓒ Ⓓ	89	Ⓐ Ⓑ Ⓒ Ⓓ	99	Ⓐ Ⓑ Ⓒ Ⓓ
	10	Ⓐ Ⓑ Ⓒ Ⓓ	20	Ⓐ Ⓑ Ⓒ Ⓓ	30	Ⓐ Ⓑ Ⓒ Ⓓ	40	Ⓐ Ⓑ Ⓒ Ⓓ	50	Ⓐ Ⓑ Ⓒ Ⓓ	60	Ⓐ Ⓑ Ⓒ Ⓓ	70	Ⓐ Ⓑ Ⓒ Ⓓ	80	Ⓐ Ⓑ Ⓒ Ⓓ	90	Ⓐ Ⓑ Ⓒ Ⓓ	100	Ⓐ Ⓑ Ⓒ Ⓓ

ACTUAL TEST 04

LISTENING SECTION																				
	1	Ⓐ Ⓑ Ⓒ Ⓓ	11	Ⓐ Ⓑ Ⓒ Ⓓ	21	Ⓐ Ⓑ Ⓒ Ⓓ	31	Ⓐ Ⓑ Ⓒ Ⓓ	41	Ⓐ Ⓑ Ⓒ Ⓓ	51	Ⓐ Ⓑ Ⓒ Ⓓ	61	Ⓐ Ⓑ Ⓒ Ⓓ	71	Ⓐ Ⓑ Ⓒ Ⓓ	81	Ⓐ Ⓑ Ⓒ Ⓓ	91	Ⓐ Ⓑ Ⓒ Ⓓ
	2	Ⓐ Ⓑ Ⓒ Ⓓ	12	Ⓐ Ⓑ Ⓒ Ⓓ	22	Ⓐ Ⓑ Ⓒ Ⓓ	32	Ⓐ Ⓑ Ⓒ Ⓓ	42	Ⓐ Ⓑ Ⓒ Ⓓ	52	Ⓐ Ⓑ Ⓒ Ⓓ	62	Ⓐ Ⓑ Ⓒ Ⓓ	72	Ⓐ Ⓑ Ⓒ Ⓓ	82	Ⓐ Ⓑ Ⓒ Ⓓ	92	Ⓐ Ⓑ Ⓒ Ⓓ
	3	Ⓐ Ⓑ Ⓒ Ⓓ	13	Ⓐ Ⓑ Ⓒ Ⓓ	23	Ⓐ Ⓑ Ⓒ Ⓓ	33	Ⓐ Ⓑ Ⓒ Ⓓ	43	Ⓐ Ⓑ Ⓒ Ⓓ	53	Ⓐ Ⓑ Ⓒ Ⓓ	63	Ⓐ Ⓑ Ⓒ Ⓓ	73	Ⓐ Ⓑ Ⓒ Ⓓ	83	Ⓐ Ⓑ Ⓒ Ⓓ	93	Ⓐ Ⓑ Ⓒ Ⓓ
	4	Ⓐ Ⓑ Ⓒ Ⓓ	14	Ⓐ Ⓑ Ⓒ Ⓓ	24	Ⓐ Ⓑ Ⓒ Ⓓ	34	Ⓐ Ⓑ Ⓒ Ⓓ	44	Ⓐ Ⓑ Ⓒ Ⓓ	54	Ⓐ Ⓑ Ⓒ Ⓓ	64	Ⓐ Ⓑ Ⓒ Ⓓ	74	Ⓐ Ⓑ Ⓒ Ⓓ	84	Ⓐ Ⓑ Ⓒ Ⓓ	94	Ⓐ Ⓑ Ⓒ Ⓓ
	5	Ⓐ Ⓑ Ⓒ Ⓓ	15	Ⓐ Ⓑ Ⓒ Ⓓ	25	Ⓐ Ⓑ Ⓒ Ⓓ	35	Ⓐ Ⓑ Ⓒ Ⓓ	45	Ⓐ Ⓑ Ⓒ Ⓓ	55	Ⓐ Ⓑ Ⓒ Ⓓ	65	Ⓐ Ⓑ Ⓒ Ⓓ	75	Ⓐ Ⓑ Ⓒ Ⓓ	85	Ⓐ Ⓑ Ⓒ Ⓓ	95	Ⓐ Ⓑ Ⓒ Ⓓ
	6	Ⓐ Ⓑ Ⓒ Ⓓ	16	Ⓐ Ⓑ Ⓒ Ⓓ	26	Ⓐ Ⓑ Ⓒ Ⓓ	36	Ⓐ Ⓑ Ⓒ Ⓓ	46	Ⓐ Ⓑ Ⓒ Ⓓ	56	Ⓐ Ⓑ Ⓒ Ⓓ	66	Ⓐ Ⓑ Ⓒ Ⓓ	76	Ⓐ Ⓑ Ⓒ Ⓓ	86	Ⓐ Ⓑ Ⓒ Ⓓ	96	Ⓐ Ⓑ Ⓒ Ⓓ
	7	Ⓐ Ⓑ Ⓒ Ⓓ	17	Ⓐ Ⓑ Ⓒ Ⓓ	27	Ⓐ Ⓑ Ⓒ Ⓓ	37	Ⓐ Ⓑ Ⓒ Ⓓ	47	Ⓐ Ⓑ Ⓒ Ⓓ	57	Ⓐ Ⓑ Ⓒ Ⓓ	67	Ⓐ Ⓑ Ⓒ Ⓓ	77	Ⓐ Ⓑ Ⓒ Ⓓ	87	Ⓐ Ⓑ Ⓒ Ⓓ	97	Ⓐ Ⓑ Ⓒ Ⓓ
	8	Ⓐ Ⓑ Ⓒ Ⓓ	18	Ⓐ Ⓑ Ⓒ Ⓓ	28	Ⓐ Ⓑ Ⓒ Ⓓ	38	Ⓐ Ⓑ Ⓒ Ⓓ	48	Ⓐ Ⓑ Ⓒ Ⓓ	58	Ⓐ Ⓑ Ⓒ Ⓓ	68	Ⓐ Ⓑ Ⓒ Ⓓ	78	Ⓐ Ⓑ Ⓒ Ⓓ	88	Ⓐ Ⓑ Ⓒ Ⓓ	98	Ⓐ Ⓑ Ⓒ Ⓓ
	9	Ⓐ Ⓑ Ⓒ Ⓓ	19	Ⓐ Ⓑ Ⓒ Ⓓ	29	Ⓐ Ⓑ Ⓒ Ⓓ	39	Ⓐ Ⓑ Ⓒ Ⓓ	49	Ⓐ Ⓑ Ⓒ Ⓓ	59	Ⓐ Ⓑ Ⓒ Ⓓ	69	Ⓐ Ⓑ Ⓒ Ⓓ	79	Ⓐ Ⓑ Ⓒ Ⓓ	89	Ⓐ Ⓑ Ⓒ Ⓓ	99	Ⓐ Ⓑ Ⓒ Ⓓ
	10	Ⓐ Ⓑ Ⓒ Ⓓ	20	Ⓐ Ⓑ Ⓒ Ⓓ	30	Ⓐ Ⓑ Ⓒ Ⓓ	40	Ⓐ Ⓑ Ⓒ Ⓓ	50	Ⓐ Ⓑ Ⓒ Ⓓ	60	Ⓐ Ⓑ Ⓒ Ⓓ	70	Ⓐ Ⓑ Ⓒ Ⓓ	80	Ⓐ Ⓑ Ⓒ Ⓓ	90	Ⓐ Ⓑ Ⓒ Ⓓ	100	Ⓐ Ⓑ Ⓒ Ⓓ

Answer Sheet

ACTUAL TEST 05

LISTENING SECTION	No.	Answer	No.	Answer	No.	Answer	No.	Answer	No.	Answer	No.	Answer	No.	Answer	No.	Answer	No.	Answer	No.	Answer
	1	Ⓐ Ⓑ Ⓒ Ⓓ	11	Ⓐ Ⓑ Ⓒ Ⓓ	21	Ⓐ Ⓑ Ⓒ Ⓓ	31	Ⓐ Ⓑ Ⓒ Ⓓ	41	Ⓐ Ⓑ Ⓒ Ⓓ	51	Ⓐ Ⓑ Ⓒ Ⓓ	61	Ⓐ Ⓑ Ⓒ Ⓓ	71	Ⓐ Ⓑ Ⓒ Ⓓ	81	Ⓐ Ⓑ Ⓒ Ⓓ	91	Ⓐ Ⓑ Ⓒ Ⓓ
	2	Ⓐ Ⓑ Ⓒ Ⓓ	12	Ⓐ Ⓑ Ⓒ Ⓓ	22	Ⓐ Ⓑ Ⓒ Ⓓ	32	Ⓐ Ⓑ Ⓒ Ⓓ	42	Ⓐ Ⓑ Ⓒ Ⓓ	52	Ⓐ Ⓑ Ⓒ Ⓓ	62	Ⓐ Ⓑ Ⓒ Ⓓ	72	Ⓐ Ⓑ Ⓒ Ⓓ	82	Ⓐ Ⓑ Ⓒ Ⓓ	92	Ⓐ Ⓑ Ⓒ Ⓓ
	3	Ⓐ Ⓑ Ⓒ Ⓓ	13	Ⓐ Ⓑ Ⓒ Ⓓ	23	Ⓐ Ⓑ Ⓒ Ⓓ	33	Ⓐ Ⓑ Ⓒ Ⓓ	43	Ⓐ Ⓑ Ⓒ Ⓓ	53	Ⓐ Ⓑ Ⓒ Ⓓ	63	Ⓐ Ⓑ Ⓒ Ⓓ	73	Ⓐ Ⓑ Ⓒ Ⓓ	83	Ⓐ Ⓑ Ⓒ Ⓓ	93	Ⓐ Ⓑ Ⓒ Ⓓ
	4	Ⓐ Ⓑ Ⓒ Ⓓ	14	Ⓐ Ⓑ Ⓒ Ⓓ	24	Ⓐ Ⓑ Ⓒ Ⓓ	34	Ⓐ Ⓑ Ⓒ Ⓓ	44	Ⓐ Ⓑ Ⓒ Ⓓ	54	Ⓐ Ⓑ Ⓒ Ⓓ	64	Ⓐ Ⓑ Ⓒ Ⓓ	74	Ⓐ Ⓑ Ⓒ Ⓓ	84	Ⓐ Ⓑ Ⓒ Ⓓ	94	Ⓐ Ⓑ Ⓒ Ⓓ
	5	Ⓐ Ⓑ Ⓒ Ⓓ	15	Ⓐ Ⓑ Ⓒ Ⓓ	25	Ⓐ Ⓑ Ⓒ Ⓓ	35	Ⓐ Ⓑ Ⓒ Ⓓ	45	Ⓐ Ⓑ Ⓒ Ⓓ	55	Ⓐ Ⓑ Ⓒ Ⓓ	65	Ⓐ Ⓑ Ⓒ Ⓓ	75	Ⓐ Ⓑ Ⓒ Ⓓ	85	Ⓐ Ⓑ Ⓒ Ⓓ	95	Ⓐ Ⓑ Ⓒ Ⓓ
	6	Ⓐ Ⓑ Ⓒ Ⓓ	16	Ⓐ Ⓑ Ⓒ Ⓓ	26	Ⓐ Ⓑ Ⓒ Ⓓ	36	Ⓐ Ⓑ Ⓒ Ⓓ	46	Ⓐ Ⓑ Ⓒ Ⓓ	56	Ⓐ Ⓑ Ⓒ Ⓓ	66	Ⓐ Ⓑ Ⓒ Ⓓ	76	Ⓐ Ⓑ Ⓒ Ⓓ	86	Ⓐ Ⓑ Ⓒ Ⓓ	96	Ⓐ Ⓑ Ⓒ Ⓓ
	7	Ⓐ Ⓑ Ⓒ Ⓓ	17	Ⓐ Ⓑ Ⓒ Ⓓ	27	Ⓐ Ⓑ Ⓒ Ⓓ	37	Ⓐ Ⓑ Ⓒ Ⓓ	47	Ⓐ Ⓑ Ⓒ Ⓓ	57	Ⓐ Ⓑ Ⓒ Ⓓ	67	Ⓐ Ⓑ Ⓒ Ⓓ	77	Ⓐ Ⓑ Ⓒ Ⓓ	87	Ⓐ Ⓑ Ⓒ Ⓓ	97	Ⓐ Ⓑ Ⓒ Ⓓ
	8	Ⓐ Ⓑ Ⓒ Ⓓ	18	Ⓐ Ⓑ Ⓒ Ⓓ	28	Ⓐ Ⓑ Ⓒ Ⓓ	38	Ⓐ Ⓑ Ⓒ Ⓓ	48	Ⓐ Ⓑ Ⓒ Ⓓ	58	Ⓐ Ⓑ Ⓒ Ⓓ	68	Ⓐ Ⓑ Ⓒ Ⓓ	78	Ⓐ Ⓑ Ⓒ Ⓓ	88	Ⓐ Ⓑ Ⓒ Ⓓ	98	Ⓐ Ⓑ Ⓒ Ⓓ
	9	Ⓐ Ⓑ Ⓒ Ⓓ	19	Ⓐ Ⓑ Ⓒ Ⓓ	29	Ⓐ Ⓑ Ⓒ Ⓓ	39	Ⓐ Ⓑ Ⓒ Ⓓ	49	Ⓐ Ⓑ Ⓒ Ⓓ	59	Ⓐ Ⓑ Ⓒ Ⓓ	69	Ⓐ Ⓑ Ⓒ Ⓓ	79	Ⓐ Ⓑ Ⓒ Ⓓ	89	Ⓐ Ⓑ Ⓒ Ⓓ	99	Ⓐ Ⓑ Ⓒ Ⓓ
	10	Ⓐ Ⓑ Ⓒ Ⓓ	20	Ⓐ Ⓑ Ⓒ Ⓓ	30	Ⓐ Ⓑ Ⓒ Ⓓ	40	Ⓐ Ⓑ Ⓒ Ⓓ	50	Ⓐ Ⓑ Ⓒ Ⓓ	60	Ⓐ Ⓑ Ⓒ Ⓓ	70	Ⓐ Ⓑ Ⓒ Ⓓ	80	Ⓐ Ⓑ Ⓒ Ⓓ	90	Ⓐ Ⓑ Ⓒ Ⓓ	100	Ⓐ Ⓑ Ⓒ Ⓓ

ACTUAL TEST 06

LISTENING SECTION	No.	Answer	No.	Answer	No.	Answer	No.	Answer	No.	Answer	No.	Answer	No.	Answer	No.	Answer	No.	Answer	No.	Answer
	1	Ⓐ Ⓑ Ⓒ Ⓓ	11	Ⓐ Ⓑ Ⓒ Ⓓ	21	Ⓐ Ⓑ Ⓒ Ⓓ	31	Ⓐ Ⓑ Ⓒ Ⓓ	41	Ⓐ Ⓑ Ⓒ Ⓓ	51	Ⓐ Ⓑ Ⓒ Ⓓ	61	Ⓐ Ⓑ Ⓒ Ⓓ	71	Ⓐ Ⓑ Ⓒ Ⓓ	81	Ⓐ Ⓑ Ⓒ Ⓓ	91	Ⓐ Ⓑ Ⓒ Ⓓ
	2	Ⓐ Ⓑ Ⓒ Ⓓ	12	Ⓐ Ⓑ Ⓒ Ⓓ	22	Ⓐ Ⓑ Ⓒ Ⓓ	32	Ⓐ Ⓑ Ⓒ Ⓓ	42	Ⓐ Ⓑ Ⓒ Ⓓ	52	Ⓐ Ⓑ Ⓒ Ⓓ	62	Ⓐ Ⓑ Ⓒ Ⓓ	72	Ⓐ Ⓑ Ⓒ Ⓓ	82	Ⓐ Ⓑ Ⓒ Ⓓ	92	Ⓐ Ⓑ Ⓒ Ⓓ
	3	Ⓐ Ⓑ Ⓒ Ⓓ	13	Ⓐ Ⓑ Ⓒ Ⓓ	23	Ⓐ Ⓑ Ⓒ Ⓓ	33	Ⓐ Ⓑ Ⓒ Ⓓ	43	Ⓐ Ⓑ Ⓒ Ⓓ	53	Ⓐ Ⓑ Ⓒ Ⓓ	63	Ⓐ Ⓑ Ⓒ Ⓓ	73	Ⓐ Ⓑ Ⓒ Ⓓ	83	Ⓐ Ⓑ Ⓒ Ⓓ	93	Ⓐ Ⓑ Ⓒ Ⓓ
	4	Ⓐ Ⓑ Ⓒ Ⓓ	14	Ⓐ Ⓑ Ⓒ Ⓓ	24	Ⓐ Ⓑ Ⓒ Ⓓ	34	Ⓐ Ⓑ Ⓒ Ⓓ	44	Ⓐ Ⓑ Ⓒ Ⓓ	54	Ⓐ Ⓑ Ⓒ Ⓓ	64	Ⓐ Ⓑ Ⓒ Ⓓ	74	Ⓐ Ⓑ Ⓒ Ⓓ	84	Ⓐ Ⓑ Ⓒ Ⓓ	94	Ⓐ Ⓑ Ⓒ Ⓓ
	5	Ⓐ Ⓑ Ⓒ Ⓓ	15	Ⓐ Ⓑ Ⓒ Ⓓ	25	Ⓐ Ⓑ Ⓒ Ⓓ	35	Ⓐ Ⓑ Ⓒ Ⓓ	45	Ⓐ Ⓑ Ⓒ Ⓓ	55	Ⓐ Ⓑ Ⓒ Ⓓ	65	Ⓐ Ⓑ Ⓒ Ⓓ	75	Ⓐ Ⓑ Ⓒ Ⓓ	85	Ⓐ Ⓑ Ⓒ Ⓓ	95	Ⓐ Ⓑ Ⓒ Ⓓ
	6	Ⓐ Ⓑ Ⓒ Ⓓ	16	Ⓐ Ⓑ Ⓒ Ⓓ	26	Ⓐ Ⓑ Ⓒ Ⓓ	36	Ⓐ Ⓑ Ⓒ Ⓓ	46	Ⓐ Ⓑ Ⓒ Ⓓ	56	Ⓐ Ⓑ Ⓒ Ⓓ	66	Ⓐ Ⓑ Ⓒ Ⓓ	76	Ⓐ Ⓑ Ⓒ Ⓓ	86	Ⓐ Ⓑ Ⓒ Ⓓ	96	Ⓐ Ⓑ Ⓒ Ⓓ
	7	Ⓐ Ⓑ Ⓒ Ⓓ	17	Ⓐ Ⓑ Ⓒ Ⓓ	27	Ⓐ Ⓑ Ⓒ Ⓓ	37	Ⓐ Ⓑ Ⓒ Ⓓ	47	Ⓐ Ⓑ Ⓒ Ⓓ	57	Ⓐ Ⓑ Ⓒ Ⓓ	67	Ⓐ Ⓑ Ⓒ Ⓓ	77	Ⓐ Ⓑ Ⓒ Ⓓ	87	Ⓐ Ⓑ Ⓒ Ⓓ	97	Ⓐ Ⓑ Ⓒ Ⓓ
	8	Ⓐ Ⓑ Ⓒ Ⓓ	18	Ⓐ Ⓑ Ⓒ Ⓓ	28	Ⓐ Ⓑ Ⓒ Ⓓ	38	Ⓐ Ⓑ Ⓒ Ⓓ	48	Ⓐ Ⓑ Ⓒ Ⓓ	58	Ⓐ Ⓑ Ⓒ Ⓓ	68	Ⓐ Ⓑ Ⓒ Ⓓ	78	Ⓐ Ⓑ Ⓒ Ⓓ	88	Ⓐ Ⓑ Ⓒ Ⓓ	98	Ⓐ Ⓑ Ⓒ Ⓓ
	9	Ⓐ Ⓑ Ⓒ Ⓓ	19	Ⓐ Ⓑ Ⓒ Ⓓ	29	Ⓐ Ⓑ Ⓒ Ⓓ	39	Ⓐ Ⓑ Ⓒ Ⓓ	49	Ⓐ Ⓑ Ⓒ Ⓓ	59	Ⓐ Ⓑ Ⓒ Ⓓ	69	Ⓐ Ⓑ Ⓒ Ⓓ	79	Ⓐ Ⓑ Ⓒ Ⓓ	89	Ⓐ Ⓑ Ⓒ Ⓓ	99	Ⓐ Ⓑ Ⓒ Ⓓ
	10	Ⓐ Ⓑ Ⓒ Ⓓ	20	Ⓐ Ⓑ Ⓒ Ⓓ	30	Ⓐ Ⓑ Ⓒ Ⓓ	40	Ⓐ Ⓑ Ⓒ Ⓓ	50	Ⓐ Ⓑ Ⓒ Ⓓ	60	Ⓐ Ⓑ Ⓒ Ⓓ	70	Ⓐ Ⓑ Ⓒ Ⓓ	80	Ⓐ Ⓑ Ⓒ Ⓓ	90	Ⓐ Ⓑ Ⓒ Ⓓ	100	Ⓐ Ⓑ Ⓒ Ⓓ

Answer Sheet

ACTUAL TEST 07

LISTENING SECTION																			
1	Ⓐ Ⓑ Ⓒ Ⓓ	11	Ⓐ Ⓑ Ⓒ Ⓓ	21	Ⓐ Ⓑ Ⓒ Ⓓ	31	Ⓐ Ⓑ Ⓒ Ⓓ	41	Ⓐ Ⓑ Ⓒ Ⓓ	51	Ⓐ Ⓑ Ⓒ Ⓓ	61	Ⓐ Ⓑ Ⓒ Ⓓ	71	Ⓐ Ⓑ Ⓒ Ⓓ	81	Ⓐ Ⓑ Ⓒ Ⓓ	91	Ⓐ Ⓑ Ⓒ Ⓓ
2	Ⓐ Ⓑ Ⓒ Ⓓ	12	Ⓐ Ⓑ Ⓒ Ⓓ	22	Ⓐ Ⓑ Ⓒ Ⓓ	32	Ⓐ Ⓑ Ⓒ Ⓓ	42	Ⓐ Ⓑ Ⓒ Ⓓ	52	Ⓐ Ⓑ Ⓒ Ⓓ	62	Ⓐ Ⓑ Ⓒ Ⓓ	72	Ⓐ Ⓑ Ⓒ Ⓓ	82	Ⓐ Ⓑ Ⓒ Ⓓ	92	Ⓐ Ⓑ Ⓒ Ⓓ
3	Ⓐ Ⓑ Ⓒ Ⓓ	13	Ⓐ Ⓑ Ⓒ Ⓓ	23	Ⓐ Ⓑ Ⓒ Ⓓ	33	Ⓐ Ⓑ Ⓒ Ⓓ	43	Ⓐ Ⓑ Ⓒ Ⓓ	53	Ⓐ Ⓑ Ⓒ Ⓓ	63	Ⓐ Ⓑ Ⓒ Ⓓ	73	Ⓐ Ⓑ Ⓒ Ⓓ	83	Ⓐ Ⓑ Ⓒ Ⓓ	93	Ⓐ Ⓑ Ⓒ Ⓓ
4	Ⓐ Ⓑ Ⓒ Ⓓ	14	Ⓐ Ⓑ Ⓒ Ⓓ	24	Ⓐ Ⓑ Ⓒ Ⓓ	34	Ⓐ Ⓑ Ⓒ Ⓓ	44	Ⓐ Ⓑ Ⓒ Ⓓ	54	Ⓐ Ⓑ Ⓒ Ⓓ	64	Ⓐ Ⓑ Ⓒ Ⓓ	74	Ⓐ Ⓑ Ⓒ Ⓓ	84	Ⓐ Ⓑ Ⓒ Ⓓ	94	Ⓐ Ⓑ Ⓒ Ⓓ
5	Ⓐ Ⓑ Ⓒ Ⓓ	15	Ⓐ Ⓑ Ⓒ Ⓓ	25	Ⓐ Ⓑ Ⓒ Ⓓ	35	Ⓐ Ⓑ Ⓒ Ⓓ	45	Ⓐ Ⓑ Ⓒ Ⓓ	55	Ⓐ Ⓑ Ⓒ Ⓓ	65	Ⓐ Ⓑ Ⓒ Ⓓ	75	Ⓐ Ⓑ Ⓒ Ⓓ	85	Ⓐ Ⓑ Ⓒ Ⓓ	95	Ⓐ Ⓑ Ⓒ Ⓓ
6	Ⓐ Ⓑ Ⓒ Ⓓ	16	Ⓐ Ⓑ Ⓒ Ⓓ	26	Ⓐ Ⓑ Ⓒ Ⓓ	36	Ⓐ Ⓑ Ⓒ Ⓓ	46	Ⓐ Ⓑ Ⓒ Ⓓ	56	Ⓐ Ⓑ Ⓒ Ⓓ	66	Ⓐ Ⓑ Ⓒ Ⓓ	76	Ⓐ Ⓑ Ⓒ Ⓓ	86	Ⓐ Ⓑ Ⓒ Ⓓ	96	Ⓐ Ⓑ Ⓒ Ⓓ
7	Ⓐ Ⓑ Ⓒ Ⓓ	17	Ⓐ Ⓑ Ⓒ Ⓓ	27	Ⓐ Ⓑ Ⓒ Ⓓ	37	Ⓐ Ⓑ Ⓒ Ⓓ	47	Ⓐ Ⓑ Ⓒ Ⓓ	57	Ⓐ Ⓑ Ⓒ Ⓓ	67	Ⓐ Ⓑ Ⓒ Ⓓ	77	Ⓐ Ⓑ Ⓒ Ⓓ	87	Ⓐ Ⓑ Ⓒ Ⓓ	97	Ⓐ Ⓑ Ⓒ Ⓓ
8	Ⓐ Ⓑ Ⓒ Ⓓ	18	Ⓐ Ⓑ Ⓒ Ⓓ	28	Ⓐ Ⓑ Ⓒ Ⓓ	38	Ⓐ Ⓑ Ⓒ Ⓓ	48	Ⓐ Ⓑ Ⓒ Ⓓ	58	Ⓐ Ⓑ Ⓒ Ⓓ	68	Ⓐ Ⓑ Ⓒ Ⓓ	78	Ⓐ Ⓑ Ⓒ Ⓓ	88	Ⓐ Ⓑ Ⓒ Ⓓ	98	Ⓐ Ⓑ Ⓒ Ⓓ
9	Ⓐ Ⓑ Ⓒ Ⓓ	19	Ⓐ Ⓑ Ⓒ Ⓓ	29	Ⓐ Ⓑ Ⓒ Ⓓ	39	Ⓐ Ⓑ Ⓒ Ⓓ	49	Ⓐ Ⓑ Ⓒ Ⓓ	59	Ⓐ Ⓑ Ⓒ Ⓓ	69	Ⓐ Ⓑ Ⓒ Ⓓ	79	Ⓐ Ⓑ Ⓒ Ⓓ	89	Ⓐ Ⓑ Ⓒ Ⓓ	99	Ⓐ Ⓑ Ⓒ Ⓓ
10	Ⓐ Ⓑ Ⓒ Ⓓ	20	Ⓐ Ⓑ Ⓒ Ⓓ	30	Ⓐ Ⓑ Ⓒ Ⓓ	40	Ⓐ Ⓑ Ⓒ Ⓓ	50	Ⓐ Ⓑ Ⓒ Ⓓ	60	Ⓐ Ⓑ Ⓒ Ⓓ	70	Ⓐ Ⓑ Ⓒ Ⓓ	80	Ⓐ Ⓑ Ⓒ Ⓓ	90	Ⓐ Ⓑ Ⓒ Ⓓ	100	Ⓐ Ⓑ Ⓒ Ⓓ

ACTUAL TEST 08

LISTENING SECTION																			
1	Ⓐ Ⓑ Ⓒ Ⓓ	11	Ⓐ Ⓑ Ⓒ Ⓓ	21	Ⓐ Ⓑ Ⓒ Ⓓ	31	Ⓐ Ⓑ Ⓒ Ⓓ	41	Ⓐ Ⓑ Ⓒ Ⓓ	51	Ⓐ Ⓑ Ⓒ Ⓓ	61	Ⓐ Ⓑ Ⓒ Ⓓ	71	Ⓐ Ⓑ Ⓒ Ⓓ	81	Ⓐ Ⓑ Ⓒ Ⓓ	91	Ⓐ Ⓑ Ⓒ Ⓓ
2	Ⓐ Ⓑ Ⓒ Ⓓ	12	Ⓐ Ⓑ Ⓒ Ⓓ	22	Ⓐ Ⓑ Ⓒ Ⓓ	32	Ⓐ Ⓑ Ⓒ Ⓓ	42	Ⓐ Ⓑ Ⓒ Ⓓ	52	Ⓐ Ⓑ Ⓒ Ⓓ	62	Ⓐ Ⓑ Ⓒ Ⓓ	72	Ⓐ Ⓑ Ⓒ Ⓓ	82	Ⓐ Ⓑ Ⓒ Ⓓ	92	Ⓐ Ⓑ Ⓒ Ⓓ
3	Ⓐ Ⓑ Ⓒ Ⓓ	13	Ⓐ Ⓑ Ⓒ Ⓓ	23	Ⓐ Ⓑ Ⓒ Ⓓ	33	Ⓐ Ⓑ Ⓒ Ⓓ	43	Ⓐ Ⓑ Ⓒ Ⓓ	53	Ⓐ Ⓑ Ⓒ Ⓓ	63	Ⓐ Ⓑ Ⓒ Ⓓ	73	Ⓐ Ⓑ Ⓒ Ⓓ	83	Ⓐ Ⓑ Ⓒ Ⓓ	93	Ⓐ Ⓑ Ⓒ Ⓓ
4	Ⓐ Ⓑ Ⓒ Ⓓ	14	Ⓐ Ⓑ Ⓒ Ⓓ	24	Ⓐ Ⓑ Ⓒ Ⓓ	34	Ⓐ Ⓑ Ⓒ Ⓓ	44	Ⓐ Ⓑ Ⓒ Ⓓ	54	Ⓐ Ⓑ Ⓒ Ⓓ	64	Ⓐ Ⓑ Ⓒ Ⓓ	74	Ⓐ Ⓑ Ⓒ Ⓓ	84	Ⓐ Ⓑ Ⓒ Ⓓ	94	Ⓐ Ⓑ Ⓒ Ⓓ
5	Ⓐ Ⓑ Ⓒ Ⓓ	15	Ⓐ Ⓑ Ⓒ Ⓓ	25	Ⓐ Ⓑ Ⓒ Ⓓ	35	Ⓐ Ⓑ Ⓒ Ⓓ	45	Ⓐ Ⓑ Ⓒ Ⓓ	55	Ⓐ Ⓑ Ⓒ Ⓓ	65	Ⓐ Ⓑ Ⓒ Ⓓ	75	Ⓐ Ⓑ Ⓒ Ⓓ	85	Ⓐ Ⓑ Ⓒ Ⓓ	95	Ⓐ Ⓑ Ⓒ Ⓓ
6	Ⓐ Ⓑ Ⓒ Ⓓ	16	Ⓐ Ⓑ Ⓒ Ⓓ	26	Ⓐ Ⓑ Ⓒ Ⓓ	36	Ⓐ Ⓑ Ⓒ Ⓓ	46	Ⓐ Ⓑ Ⓒ Ⓓ	56	Ⓐ Ⓑ Ⓒ Ⓓ	66	Ⓐ Ⓑ Ⓒ Ⓓ	76	Ⓐ Ⓑ Ⓒ Ⓓ	86	Ⓐ Ⓑ Ⓒ Ⓓ	96	Ⓐ Ⓑ Ⓒ Ⓓ
7	Ⓐ Ⓑ Ⓒ Ⓓ	17	Ⓐ Ⓑ Ⓒ Ⓓ	27	Ⓐ Ⓑ Ⓒ Ⓓ	37	Ⓐ Ⓑ Ⓒ Ⓓ	47	Ⓐ Ⓑ Ⓒ Ⓓ	57	Ⓐ Ⓑ Ⓒ Ⓓ	67	Ⓐ Ⓑ Ⓒ Ⓓ	77	Ⓐ Ⓑ Ⓒ Ⓓ	87	Ⓐ Ⓑ Ⓒ Ⓓ	97	Ⓐ Ⓑ Ⓒ Ⓓ
8	Ⓐ Ⓑ Ⓒ Ⓓ	18	Ⓐ Ⓑ Ⓒ Ⓓ	28	Ⓐ Ⓑ Ⓒ Ⓓ	38	Ⓐ Ⓑ Ⓒ Ⓓ	48	Ⓐ Ⓑ Ⓒ Ⓓ	58	Ⓐ Ⓑ Ⓒ Ⓓ	68	Ⓐ Ⓑ Ⓒ Ⓓ	78	Ⓐ Ⓑ Ⓒ Ⓓ	88	Ⓐ Ⓑ Ⓒ Ⓓ	98	Ⓐ Ⓑ Ⓒ Ⓓ
9	Ⓐ Ⓑ Ⓒ Ⓓ	19	Ⓐ Ⓑ Ⓒ Ⓓ	29	Ⓐ Ⓑ Ⓒ Ⓓ	39	Ⓐ Ⓑ Ⓒ Ⓓ	49	Ⓐ Ⓑ Ⓒ Ⓓ	59	Ⓐ Ⓑ Ⓒ Ⓓ	69	Ⓐ Ⓑ Ⓒ Ⓓ	79	Ⓐ Ⓑ Ⓒ Ⓓ	89	Ⓐ Ⓑ Ⓒ Ⓓ	99	Ⓐ Ⓑ Ⓒ Ⓓ
10	Ⓐ Ⓑ Ⓒ Ⓓ	20	Ⓐ Ⓑ Ⓒ Ⓓ	30	Ⓐ Ⓑ Ⓒ Ⓓ	40	Ⓐ Ⓑ Ⓒ Ⓓ	50	Ⓐ Ⓑ Ⓒ Ⓓ	60	Ⓐ Ⓑ Ⓒ Ⓓ	70	Ⓐ Ⓑ Ⓒ Ⓓ	80	Ⓐ Ⓑ Ⓒ Ⓓ	90	Ⓐ Ⓑ Ⓒ Ⓓ	100	Ⓐ Ⓑ Ⓒ Ⓓ

Answer Sheet

ACTUAL TEST 09

LISTENING SECTION																				
	1	Ⓐ Ⓑ Ⓒ Ⓓ	11	Ⓐ Ⓑ Ⓒ Ⓓ	21	Ⓐ Ⓑ Ⓒ Ⓓ	31	Ⓐ Ⓑ Ⓒ Ⓓ	41	Ⓐ Ⓑ Ⓒ Ⓓ	51	Ⓐ Ⓑ Ⓒ Ⓓ	61	Ⓐ Ⓑ Ⓒ Ⓓ	71	Ⓐ Ⓑ Ⓒ Ⓓ	81	Ⓐ Ⓑ Ⓒ Ⓓ	91	Ⓐ Ⓑ Ⓒ Ⓓ
	2	Ⓐ Ⓑ Ⓒ Ⓓ	12	Ⓐ Ⓑ Ⓒ Ⓓ	22	Ⓐ Ⓑ Ⓒ Ⓓ	32	Ⓐ Ⓑ Ⓒ Ⓓ	42	Ⓐ Ⓑ Ⓒ Ⓓ	52	Ⓐ Ⓑ Ⓒ Ⓓ	62	Ⓐ Ⓑ Ⓒ Ⓓ	72	Ⓐ Ⓑ Ⓒ Ⓓ	82	Ⓐ Ⓑ Ⓒ Ⓓ	92	Ⓐ Ⓑ Ⓒ Ⓓ
	3	Ⓐ Ⓑ Ⓒ Ⓓ	13	Ⓐ Ⓑ Ⓒ Ⓓ	23	Ⓐ Ⓑ Ⓒ Ⓓ	33	Ⓐ Ⓑ Ⓒ Ⓓ	43	Ⓐ Ⓑ Ⓒ Ⓓ	53	Ⓐ Ⓑ Ⓒ Ⓓ	63	Ⓐ Ⓑ Ⓒ Ⓓ	73	Ⓐ Ⓑ Ⓒ Ⓓ	83	Ⓐ Ⓑ Ⓒ Ⓓ	93	Ⓐ Ⓑ Ⓒ Ⓓ
	4	Ⓐ Ⓑ Ⓒ Ⓓ	14	Ⓐ Ⓑ Ⓒ Ⓓ	24	Ⓐ Ⓑ Ⓒ Ⓓ	34	Ⓐ Ⓑ Ⓒ Ⓓ	44	Ⓐ Ⓑ Ⓒ Ⓓ	54	Ⓐ Ⓑ Ⓒ Ⓓ	64	Ⓐ Ⓑ Ⓒ Ⓓ	74	Ⓐ Ⓑ Ⓒ Ⓓ	84	Ⓐ Ⓑ Ⓒ Ⓓ	94	Ⓐ Ⓑ Ⓒ Ⓓ
	5	Ⓐ Ⓑ Ⓒ Ⓓ	15	Ⓐ Ⓑ Ⓒ Ⓓ	25	Ⓐ Ⓑ Ⓒ Ⓓ	35	Ⓐ Ⓑ Ⓒ Ⓓ	45	Ⓐ Ⓑ Ⓒ Ⓓ	55	Ⓐ Ⓑ Ⓒ Ⓓ	65	Ⓐ Ⓑ Ⓒ Ⓓ	75	Ⓐ Ⓑ Ⓒ Ⓓ	85	Ⓐ Ⓑ Ⓒ Ⓓ	95	Ⓐ Ⓑ Ⓒ Ⓓ
	6	Ⓐ Ⓑ Ⓒ Ⓓ	16	Ⓐ Ⓑ Ⓒ Ⓓ	26	Ⓐ Ⓑ Ⓒ Ⓓ	36	Ⓐ Ⓑ Ⓒ Ⓓ	46	Ⓐ Ⓑ Ⓒ Ⓓ	56	Ⓐ Ⓑ Ⓒ Ⓓ	66	Ⓐ Ⓑ Ⓒ Ⓓ	76	Ⓐ Ⓑ Ⓒ Ⓓ	86	Ⓐ Ⓑ Ⓒ Ⓓ	96	Ⓐ Ⓑ Ⓒ Ⓓ
	7	Ⓐ Ⓑ Ⓒ Ⓓ	17	Ⓐ Ⓑ Ⓒ Ⓓ	27	Ⓐ Ⓑ Ⓒ Ⓓ	37	Ⓐ Ⓑ Ⓒ Ⓓ	47	Ⓐ Ⓑ Ⓒ Ⓓ	57	Ⓐ Ⓑ Ⓒ Ⓓ	67	Ⓐ Ⓑ Ⓒ Ⓓ	77	Ⓐ Ⓑ Ⓒ Ⓓ	87	Ⓐ Ⓑ Ⓒ Ⓓ	97	Ⓐ Ⓑ Ⓒ Ⓓ
	8	Ⓐ Ⓑ Ⓒ Ⓓ	18	Ⓐ Ⓑ Ⓒ Ⓓ	28	Ⓐ Ⓑ Ⓒ Ⓓ	38	Ⓐ Ⓑ Ⓒ Ⓓ	48	Ⓐ Ⓑ Ⓒ Ⓓ	58	Ⓐ Ⓑ Ⓒ Ⓓ	68	Ⓐ Ⓑ Ⓒ Ⓓ	78	Ⓐ Ⓑ Ⓒ Ⓓ	88	Ⓐ Ⓑ Ⓒ Ⓓ	98	Ⓐ Ⓑ Ⓒ Ⓓ
	9	Ⓐ Ⓑ Ⓒ Ⓓ	19	Ⓐ Ⓑ Ⓒ Ⓓ	29	Ⓐ Ⓑ Ⓒ Ⓓ	39	Ⓐ Ⓑ Ⓒ Ⓓ	49	Ⓐ Ⓑ Ⓒ Ⓓ	59	Ⓐ Ⓑ Ⓒ Ⓓ	69	Ⓐ Ⓑ Ⓒ Ⓓ	79	Ⓐ Ⓑ Ⓒ Ⓓ	89	Ⓐ Ⓑ Ⓒ Ⓓ	99	Ⓐ Ⓑ Ⓒ Ⓓ
	10	Ⓐ Ⓑ Ⓒ Ⓓ	20	Ⓐ Ⓑ Ⓒ Ⓓ	30	Ⓐ Ⓑ Ⓒ Ⓓ	40	Ⓐ Ⓑ Ⓒ Ⓓ	50	Ⓐ Ⓑ Ⓒ Ⓓ	60	Ⓐ Ⓑ Ⓒ Ⓓ	70	Ⓐ Ⓑ Ⓒ Ⓓ	80	Ⓐ Ⓑ Ⓒ Ⓓ	90	Ⓐ Ⓑ Ⓒ Ⓓ	100	Ⓐ Ⓑ Ⓒ Ⓓ

ACTUAL TEST 10

LISTENING SECTION																				
	1	Ⓐ Ⓑ Ⓒ Ⓓ	11	Ⓐ Ⓑ Ⓒ Ⓓ	21	Ⓐ Ⓑ Ⓒ Ⓓ	31	Ⓐ Ⓑ Ⓒ Ⓓ	41	Ⓐ Ⓑ Ⓒ Ⓓ	51	Ⓐ Ⓑ Ⓒ Ⓓ	61	Ⓐ Ⓑ Ⓒ Ⓓ	71	Ⓐ Ⓑ Ⓒ Ⓓ	81	Ⓐ Ⓑ Ⓒ Ⓓ	91	Ⓐ Ⓑ Ⓒ Ⓓ
	2	Ⓐ Ⓑ Ⓒ Ⓓ	12	Ⓐ Ⓑ Ⓒ Ⓓ	22	Ⓐ Ⓑ Ⓒ Ⓓ	32	Ⓐ Ⓑ Ⓒ Ⓓ	42	Ⓐ Ⓑ Ⓒ Ⓓ	52	Ⓐ Ⓑ Ⓒ Ⓓ	62	Ⓐ Ⓑ Ⓒ Ⓓ	72	Ⓐ Ⓑ Ⓒ Ⓓ	82	Ⓐ Ⓑ Ⓒ Ⓓ	92	Ⓐ Ⓑ Ⓒ Ⓓ
	3	Ⓐ Ⓑ Ⓒ Ⓓ	13	Ⓐ Ⓑ Ⓒ Ⓓ	23	Ⓐ Ⓑ Ⓒ Ⓓ	33	Ⓐ Ⓑ Ⓒ Ⓓ	43	Ⓐ Ⓑ Ⓒ Ⓓ	53	Ⓐ Ⓑ Ⓒ Ⓓ	63	Ⓐ Ⓑ Ⓒ Ⓓ	73	Ⓐ Ⓑ Ⓒ Ⓓ	83	Ⓐ Ⓑ Ⓒ Ⓓ	93	Ⓐ Ⓑ Ⓒ Ⓓ
	4	Ⓐ Ⓑ Ⓒ Ⓓ	14	Ⓐ Ⓑ Ⓒ Ⓓ	24	Ⓐ Ⓑ Ⓒ Ⓓ	34	Ⓐ Ⓑ Ⓒ Ⓓ	44	Ⓐ Ⓑ Ⓒ Ⓓ	54	Ⓐ Ⓑ Ⓒ Ⓓ	64	Ⓐ Ⓑ Ⓒ Ⓓ	74	Ⓐ Ⓑ Ⓒ Ⓓ	84	Ⓐ Ⓑ Ⓒ Ⓓ	94	Ⓐ Ⓑ Ⓒ Ⓓ
	5	Ⓐ Ⓑ Ⓒ Ⓓ	15	Ⓐ Ⓑ Ⓒ Ⓓ	25	Ⓐ Ⓑ Ⓒ Ⓓ	35	Ⓐ Ⓑ Ⓒ Ⓓ	45	Ⓐ Ⓑ Ⓒ Ⓓ	55	Ⓐ Ⓑ Ⓒ Ⓓ	65	Ⓐ Ⓑ Ⓒ Ⓓ	75	Ⓐ Ⓑ Ⓒ Ⓓ	85	Ⓐ Ⓑ Ⓒ Ⓓ	95	Ⓐ Ⓑ Ⓒ Ⓓ
	6	Ⓐ Ⓑ Ⓒ Ⓓ	16	Ⓐ Ⓑ Ⓒ Ⓓ	26	Ⓐ Ⓑ Ⓒ Ⓓ	36	Ⓐ Ⓑ Ⓒ Ⓓ	46	Ⓐ Ⓑ Ⓒ Ⓓ	56	Ⓐ Ⓑ Ⓒ Ⓓ	66	Ⓐ Ⓑ Ⓒ Ⓓ	76	Ⓐ Ⓑ Ⓒ Ⓓ	86	Ⓐ Ⓑ Ⓒ Ⓓ	96	Ⓐ Ⓑ Ⓒ Ⓓ
	7	Ⓐ Ⓑ Ⓒ Ⓓ	17	Ⓐ Ⓑ Ⓒ Ⓓ	27	Ⓐ Ⓑ Ⓒ Ⓓ	37	Ⓐ Ⓑ Ⓒ Ⓓ	47	Ⓐ Ⓑ Ⓒ Ⓓ	57	Ⓐ Ⓑ Ⓒ Ⓓ	67	Ⓐ Ⓑ Ⓒ Ⓓ	77	Ⓐ Ⓑ Ⓒ Ⓓ	87	Ⓐ Ⓑ Ⓒ Ⓓ	97	Ⓐ Ⓑ Ⓒ Ⓓ
	8	Ⓐ Ⓑ Ⓒ Ⓓ	18	Ⓐ Ⓑ Ⓒ Ⓓ	28	Ⓐ Ⓑ Ⓒ Ⓓ	38	Ⓐ Ⓑ Ⓒ Ⓓ	48	Ⓐ Ⓑ Ⓒ Ⓓ	58	Ⓐ Ⓑ Ⓒ Ⓓ	68	Ⓐ Ⓑ Ⓒ Ⓓ	78	Ⓐ Ⓑ Ⓒ Ⓓ	88	Ⓐ Ⓑ Ⓒ Ⓓ	98	Ⓐ Ⓑ Ⓒ Ⓓ
	9	Ⓐ Ⓑ Ⓒ Ⓓ	19	Ⓐ Ⓑ Ⓒ Ⓓ	29	Ⓐ Ⓑ Ⓒ Ⓓ	39	Ⓐ Ⓑ Ⓒ Ⓓ	49	Ⓐ Ⓑ Ⓒ Ⓓ	59	Ⓐ Ⓑ Ⓒ Ⓓ	69	Ⓐ Ⓑ Ⓒ Ⓓ	79	Ⓐ Ⓑ Ⓒ Ⓓ	89	Ⓐ Ⓑ Ⓒ Ⓓ	99	Ⓐ Ⓑ Ⓒ Ⓓ
	10	Ⓐ Ⓑ Ⓒ Ⓓ	20	Ⓐ Ⓑ Ⓒ Ⓓ	30	Ⓐ Ⓑ Ⓒ Ⓓ	40	Ⓐ Ⓑ Ⓒ Ⓓ	50	Ⓐ Ⓑ Ⓒ Ⓓ	60	Ⓐ Ⓑ Ⓒ Ⓓ	70	Ⓐ Ⓑ Ⓒ Ⓓ	80	Ⓐ Ⓑ Ⓒ Ⓓ	90	Ⓐ Ⓑ Ⓒ Ⓓ	100	Ⓐ Ⓑ Ⓒ Ⓓ

Answers

Actual Test 01

1 (A)	21 (B)	41 (A)	61 (A)	81 (D)
2 (B)	22 (C)	42 (D)	62 (B)	82 (B)
3 (A)	23 (C)	43 (A)	63 (D)	83 (B)
4 (D)	24 (B)	44 (B)	64 (C)	84 (B)
5 (A)	25 (A)	45 (C)	65 (A)	85 (D)
6 (D)	26 (C)	46 (A)	66 (D)	86 (C)
7 (A)	27 (A)	47 (A)	67 (D)	87 (A)
8 (C)	28 (B)	48 (D)	68 (B)	88 (A)
9 (A)	29 (C)	49 (B)	69 (A)	89 (C)
10 (C)	30 (A)	50 (D)	70 (D)	90 (C)
11 (B)	31 (C)	51 (C)	71 (C)	91 (D)
12 (A)	32 (D)	52 (A)	72 (A)	92 (A)
13 (B)	33 (C)	53 (A)	73 (D)	93 (A)
14 (A)	34 (B)	54 (C)	74 (D)	94 (D)
15 (C)	35 (D)	55 (B)	75 (B)	95 (C)
16 (A)	36 (A)	56 (D)	76 (C)	96 (D)
17 (A)	37 (A)	57 (C)	77 (B)	97 (A)
18 (C)	38 (C)	58 (B)	78 (D)	98 (A)
19 (A)	39 (A)	59 (B)	79 (C)	99 (C)
20 (C)	40 (D)	60 (D)	80 (D)	100 (D)

Actual Test 02

1 (C)	21 (B)	41 (D)	61 (C)	81 (A)
2 (B)	22 (A)	42 (B)	62 (A)	82 (C)
3 (C)	23 (A)	43 (D)	63 (B)	83 (A)
4 (D)	24 (C)	44 (B)	64 (D)	84 (D)
5 (B)	25 (A)	45 (D)	65 (A)	85 (A)
6 (B)	26 (A)	46 (A)	66 (B)	86 (C)
7 (A)	27 (B)	47 (B)	67 (D)	87 (D)
8 (A)	28 (C)	48 (D)	68 (A)	88 (A)
9 (B)	29 (C)	49 (B)	69 (D)	89 (B)
10 (C)	30 (A)	50 (B)	70 (D)	90 (A)
11 (B)	31 (B)	51 (C)	71 (B)	91 (D)
12 (C)	32 (B)	52 (C)	72 (D)	92 (B)
13 (C)	33 (A)	53 (A)	73 (A)	93 (A)
14 (A)	34 (D)	54 (D)	74 (D)	94 (B)
15 (A)	35 (A)	55 (B)	75 (A)	95 (C)
16 (C)	36 (D)	56 (D)	76 (D)	96 (A)
17 (B)	37 (C)	57 (B)	77 (D)	97 (A)
18 (B)	38 (B)	58 (A)	78 (C)	98 (B)
19 (B)	39 (D)	59 (C)	79 (B)	99 (B)
20 (C)	40 (C)	60 (B)	80 (D)	100 (A)

Actual Test 03

1 (D)	21 (C)	41 (D)	61 (D)	81 (B)
2 (A)	22 (A)	42 (B)	62 (B)	82 (A)
3 (B)	23 (A)	43 (A)	63 (A)	83 (A)
4 (A)	24 (B)	44 (C)	64 (B)	84 (C)
5 (D)	25 (A)	45 (D)	65 (A)	85 (C)
6 (A)	26 (A)	46 (C)	66 (C)	86 (A)
7 (C)	27 (B)	47 (D)	67 (C)	87 (B)
8 (B)	28 (C)	48 (B)	68 (B)	88 (D)
9 (A)	29 (A)	49 (A)	69 (A)	89 (B)
10 (A)	30 (B)	50 (D)	70 (A)	90 (A)
11 (B)	31 (A)	51 (B)	71 (B)	91 (C)
12 (A)	32 (D)	52 (A)	72 (D)	92 (D)
13 (C)	33 (B)	53 (B)	73 (C)	93 (D)
14 (A)	34 (A)	54 (C)	74 (A)	94 (B)
15 (A)	35 (A)	55 (D)	75 (A)	95 (C)
16 (A)	36 (A)	56 (B)	76 (A)	96 (D)
17 (C)	37 (D)	57 (A)	77 (C)	97 (A)
18 (C)	38 (D)	58 (B)	78 (D)	98 (A)
19 (A)	39 (C)	59 (A)	79 (D)	99 (C)
20 (A)	40 (A)	60 (B)	80 (B)	100 (A)

Actual Test 04

1 (D)	21 (C)	41 (D)	61 (A)	81 (C)
2 (C)	22 (B)	42 (A)	62 (B)	82 (D)
3 (C)	23 (A)	43 (D)	63 (A)	83 (A)
4 (B)	24 (A)	44 (D)	64 (C)	84 (C)
5 (B)	25 (C)	45 (D)	65 (C)	85 (A)
6 (D)	26 (C)	46 (C)	66 (A)	86 (D)
7 (B)	27 (A)	47 (C)	67 (C)	87 (C)
8 (B)	28 (A)	48 (D)	68 (A)	88 (C)
9 (A)	29 (B)	49 (A)	69 (C)	89 (D)
10 (B)	30 (B)	50 (D)	70 (C)	90 (D)
11 (C)	31 (C)	51 (B)	71 (D)	91 (A)
12 (C)	32 (A)	52 (D)	72 (C)	92 (B)
13 (A)	33 (A)	53 (B)	73 (A)	93 (D)
14 (B)	34 (D)	54 (A)	74 (B)	94 (D)
15 (A)	35 (C)	55 (D)	75 (C)	95 (C)
16 (A)	36 (D)	56 (A)	76 (D)	96 (B)
17 (C)	37 (C)	57 (D)	77 (D)	97 (C)
18 (C)	38 (C)	58 (B)	78 (D)	98 (A)
19 (A)	39 (D)	59 (B)	79 (A)	99 (C)
20 (A)	40 (A)	60 (C)	80 (A)	100 (A)

Actual Test 05

1 (C)	21 (B)	41 (C)	61 (A)	81 (D)
2 (C)	22 (A)	42 (B)	62 (D)	82 (C)
3 (A)	23 (A)	43 (A)	63 (C)	83 (B)
4 (B)	24 (B)	44 (A)	64 (B)	84 (A)
5 (C)	25 (C)	45 (A)	65 (D)	85 (A)
6 (C)	26 (A)	46 (D)	66 (B)	86 (A)
7 (C)	27 (C)	47 (D)	67 (C)	87 (C)
8 (B)	28 (A)	48 (B)	68 (A)	88 (B)
9 (C)	29 (B)	49 (C)	69 (B)	89 (B)
10 (B)	30 (B)	50 (B)	70 (D)	90 (A)
11 (C)	31 (A)	51 (A)	71 (C)	91 (C)
12 (C)	32 (A)	52 (C)	72 (D)	92 (C)
13 (A)	33 (D)	53 (A)	73 (C)	93 (A)
14 (B)	34 (C)	54 (B)	74 (A)	94 (C)
15 (C)	35 (C)	55 (C)	75 (A)	95 (B)
16 (C)	36 (B)	56 (C)	76 (A)	96 (C)
17 (C)	37 (D)	57 (B)	77 (B)	97 (A)
18 (B)	38 (B)	58 (C)	78 (C)	98 (C)
19 (C)	39 (D)	59 (D)	79 (D)	99 (A)
20 (A)	40 (B)	60 (B)	80 (D)	100(A)

Actual Test 06

1 (A)	21 (B)	41 (B)	61 (B)	81 (C)
2 (B)	22 (B)	42 (A)	62 (C)	82 (D)
3 (C)	23 (B)	43 (C)	63 (C)	83 (B)
4 (B)	24 (C)	44 (D)	64 (D)	84 (B)
5 (B)	25 (C)	45 (B)	65 (D)	85 (C)
6 (D)	26 (A)	46 (C)	66 (A)	86 (A)
7 (C)	27 (A)	47 (C)	67 (C)	87 (D)
8 (B)	28 (C)	48 (D)	68 (D)	88 (B)
9 (A)	29 (B)	49 (A)	69 (A)	89 (D)
10 (B)	30 (C)	50 (B)	70 (D)	90 (C)
11 (C)	31 (B)	51 (D)	71 (C)	91 (B)
12 (B)	32 (D)	52 (B)	72 (D)	92 (A)
13 (A)	33 (B)	53 (C)	73 (C)	93 (B)
14 (C)	34 (D)	54 (D)	74 (B)	94 (D)
15 (A)	35 (D)	55 (D)	75 (D)	95 (C)
16 (C)	36 (B)	56 (D)	76 (A)	96 (A)
17 (A)	37 (D)	57 (C)	77 (C)	97 (A)
18 (A)	38 (C)	58 (A)	78 (B)	98 (B)
19 (B)	39 (D)	59 (D)	79 (A)	99 (A)
20 (A)	40 (B)	60 (C)	80 (A)	100(A)

Actual Test 07

1 (C)	21 (B)	41 (C)	61 (A)	81 (A)
2 (D)	22 (A)	42 (A)	62 (D)	82 (C)
3 (C)	23 (C)	43 (D)	63 (B)	83 (B)
4 (C)	24 (B)	44 (B)	64 (A)	84 (C)
5 (B)	25 (A)	45 (C)	65 (B)	85 (A)
6 (D)	26 (C)	46 (A)	66 (C)	86 (B)
7 (B)	27 (A)	47 (B)	67 (C)	87 (A)
8 (B)	28 (B)	48 (A)	68 (B)	88 (B)
9 (A)	29 (A)	49 (B)	69 (A)	89 (B)
10 (C)	30 (A)	50 (A)	70 (B)	90 (D)
11 (B)	31 (C)	51 (C)	71 (D)	91 (A)
12 (A)	32 (C)	52 (B)	72 (B)	92 (D)
13 (C)	33 (B)	53 (D)	73 (C)	93 (A)
14 (A)	34 (B)	54 (B)	74 (B)	94 (C)
15 (B)	35 (D)	55 (C)	75 (C)	95 (C)
16 (C)	36 (A)	56 (A)	76 (C)	96 (B)
17 (B)	37 (D)	57 (D)	77 (C)	97 (D)
18 (A)	38 (C)	58 (B)	78 (B)	98 (D)
19 (B)	39 (B)	59 (B)	79 (D)	99 (A)
20 (A)	40 (C)	60 (A)	80 (C)	100(B)

Actual Test 08

1 (A)	21 (B)	41 (A)	61 (C)	81 (C)
2 (D)	22 (C)	42 (A)	62 (D)	82 (B)
3 (A)	23 (A)	43 (D)	63 (A)	83 (C)
4 (B)	24 (C)	44 (D)	64 (C)	84 (B)
5 (B)	25 (A)	45 (B)	65 (C)	85 (A)
6 (B)	26 (C)	46 (C)	66 (B)	86 (A)
7 (A)	27 (B)	47 (A)	67 (C)	87 (C)
8 (A)	28 (C)	48 (C)	68 (C)	88 (B)
9 (A)	29 (C)	49 (B)	69 (C)	89 (C)
10 (B)	30 (A)	50 (D)	70 (D)	90 (B)
11 (B)	31 (C)	51 (A)	71 (C)	91 (D)
12 (C)	32 (D)	52 (B)	72 (A)	92 (C)
13 (A)	33 (C)	53 (B)	73 (A)	93 (D)
14 (B)	34 (B)	54 (A)	74 (C)	94 (B)
15 (B)	35 (C)	55 (D)	75 (A)	95 (A)
16 (A)	36 (B)	56 (D)	76 (D)	96 (B)
17 (C)	37 (A)	57 (B)	77 (D)	97 (C)
18 (A)	38 (B)	58 (D)	78 (A)	98 (A)
19 (A)	39 (D)	59 (D)	79 (B)	99 (D)
20 (C)	40 (A)	60 (A)	80 (A)	100(C)

Actual Test 09

1 (D)	**21** (C)	**41** (B)	**61** (D)	**81** (C)
2 (D)	**22** (A)	**42** (D)	**62** (B)	**82** (C)
3 (B)	**23** (B)	**43** (D)	**63** (D)	**83** (D)
4 (C)	**24** (A)	**44** (C)	**64** (B)	**84** (C)
5 (B)	**25** (B)	**45** (B)	**65** (B)	**85** (B)
6 (A)	**26** (B)	**46** (D)	**66** (D)	**86** (B)
7 (B)	**27** (B)	**47** (A)	**67** (C)	**87** (A)
8 (A)	**28** (C)	**48** (C)	**68** (C)	**88** (C)
9 (C)	**29** (A)	**49** (B)	**69** (B)	**89** (C)
10 (B)	**30** (B)	**50** (C)	**70** (D)	**90** (B)
11 (C)	**31** (B)	**51** (A)	**71** (A)	**91** (C)
12 (B)	**32** (A)	**52** (B)	**72** (D)	**92** (A)
13 (C)	**33** (D)	**53** (D)	**73** (A)	**93** (C)
14 (C)	**34** (D)	**54** (A)	**74** (B)	**94** (A)
15 (B)	**35** (B)	**55** (D)	**75** (A)	**95** (C)
16 (C)	**36** (D)	**56** (A)	**76** (A)	**96** (A)
17 (A)	**37** (A)	**57** (D)	**77** (C)	**97** (A)
18 (A)	**38** (B)	**58** (B)	**78** (B)	**98** (D)
19 (C)	**39** (D)	**59** (A)	**79** (C)	**99** (C)
20 (C)	**40** (C)	**60** (D)	**80** (A)	**100** (B)

Actual Test 10

1 (A)	**21** (C)	**41** (C)	**61** (B)	**81** (D)
2 (A)	**22** (A)	**42** (B)	**62** (B)	**82** (A)
3 (D)	**23** (A)	**43** (B)	**63** (D)	**83** (B)
4 (C)	**24** (C)	**44** (B)	**64** (B)	**84** (A)
5 (B)	**25** (A)	**45** (A)	**65** (C)	**85** (D)
6 (A)	**26** (A)	**46** (C)	**66** (A)	**86** (B)
7 (B)	**27** (C)	**47** (B)	**67** (B)	**87** (A)
8 (B)	**28** (A)	**48** (D)	**68** (D)	**88** (D)
9 (C)	**29** (C)	**49** (C)	**69** (B)	**89** (A)
10 (A)	**30** (A)	**50** (A)	**70** (D)	**90** (B)
11 (A)	**31** (B)	**51** (D)	**71** (B)	**91** (A)
12 (A)	**32** (B)	**52** (D)	**72** (C)	**92** (D)
13 (C)	**33** (C)	**53** (C)	**73** (A)	**93** (A)
14 (C)	**34** (A)	**54** (B)	**74** (D)	**94** (D)
15 (C)	**35** (C)	**55** (A)	**75** (B)	**95** (B)
16 (B)	**36** (D)	**56** (C)	**76** (A)	**96** (B)
17 (C)	**37** (C)	**57** (A)	**77** (D)	**97** (D)
18 (B)	**38** (B)	**58** (D)	**78** (C)	**98** (B)
19 (C)	**39** (D)	**59** (A)	**79** (B)	**99** (D)
20 (C)	**40** (C)	**60** (D)	**80** (A)	**100** (C)

多益分數換算表

聽力測驗		閱讀測驗	
答對題數	分數	答對題數	分數
96 ~ 100	480 ~ 495	96 ~ 100	450 ~ 495
91 ~ 95	470 ~ 495	91 ~ 95	420 ~ 465
86 ~ 90	440 ~ 490	86 ~ 90	400 ~ 435
81 ~ 85	410 ~ 460	81 ~ 85	370 ~ 410
76 ~ 80	390 ~ 430	76 ~ 80	340 ~ 380
71 ~ 75	360 ~ 400	71 ~ 75	310 ~ 355
66 ~ 70	330 ~ 370	66 ~ 70	280 ~ 325
61 ~ 65	300 ~ 345	61 ~ 65	260 ~ 300
56 ~ 60	270 ~ 315	56 ~ 60	230 ~ 270
51 ~ 55	240 ~ 285	51 ~ 55	200 ~ 245
46 ~ 50	210 ~ 255	46 ~ 50	170 ~ 215
41 ~ 45	180 ~ 225	41 ~ 45	140 ~ 185
36 ~ 40	150 ~ 195	36 ~ 40	120 ~ 160
31 ~ 35	120 ~ 165	31 ~ 35	90 ~ 130
26 ~ 30	90 ~ 135	26 ~ 30	60 ~ 105
21 ~ 25	60 ~ 105	21 ~ 25	30 ~ 75
16 ~ 20	40 ~ 75	16 ~ 20	10 ~ 50
11 ~ 15	10 ~ 45	11 ~ 15	5 ~ 20
6 ~ 10	5 ~ 20	6 ~ 10	5
1 ~ 5	5	1 ~ 5	5
0	0	0	0

註：上述表格僅供參考，實際計分以官方分數為準。

新制多益聽力滿分奪金演練

1000 題練出黃金應試力

作　　者　PAGODA Academy
譯　　者　蘇裕承／關亭薇
編　　輯　高詣軒
主　　編　丁宥暄
校　　對　黃詩韻
內文排版　林書玉
封面設計　林書玉
製程管理　洪巧玲
出 版 者　寂天文化事業股份有限公司
發 行 人　周均亮
電　　話　+886-(0)2-2365-9739
傳　　真　+886-(0)2-2365-9835
網　　址　www.icosmos.com.tw
讀者服務　onlineservice@icosmos.com.tw
出版日期　2021 年 5 月 初版一刷

郵撥帳號 1998620-0 寂天文化事業股份有限公司
劃撥金額 600 元（含）以上者，郵資免費。
訂購金額 600 元以下者，請外加郵資 65 元。
〔若有破損，請寄回更換，謝謝。〕

國家圖書館出版品預行編目 (CIP) 資料

新制多益聽力滿分奪金演練：1000 題練出黃金應試力 (寂天雲隨身聽 APP 版)/ PAGODA Academy 著；蘇裕承，關亭薇譯 . -- 初版 . -- 臺北市：寂天文化事業股份有限公司，2021.05
　面；　公分
ISBN 978-626-300-005-6(16K 平裝)

1. 多益測驗

805.1895　　110004787